EDITH WHARTON

EDITH WHARTON

COLLECTED STORIES
1911–1937

THE LIBRARY OF AMERICA

The paper used in this publication meets the
minimum requirements of the American National Standard for
Information Sciences—Permanence of Paper for Printed
Library Materials, ANSI z39.48—1984.

Distributed to the trade in the United States
by Penguin Putnam, Inc.
and in Canada by Penguin Books Canada Ltd.

Library of Congress Catalog Number: 00–057595
For cataloging information, see end of Notes.
ISBN 1–883011–94–9

First Printing
The Library of America—122

Manufactured in the United States of America

Contents

COLLECTED STORIES 1911–1937

Xingu

M<small>RS</small>. B<small>ALLINGER</small> is one of the ladies who pursue Culture in bands, as though it were dangerous to meet alone. To this end she had founded the Lunch Club, an association composed of herself and several other indomitable huntresses of erudition. The Lunch Club, after three or four winters of lunching and debate, had acquired such local distinction that the entertainment of distinguished strangers became one of its accepted functions; in recognition of which it duly extended to the celebrated "Osric Dane," on the day of her arrival in Hillbridge, an invitation to be present at the next meeting.

The club was to meet at Mrs. Ballinger's. The other members, behind her back, were of one voice in deploring her unwillingness to cede her rights in favor of Mrs. Plinth, whose house made a more impressive setting for the entertainment of celebrities; while, as Mrs. Leveret observed, there was always the picture-gallery to fall back on.

Mrs. Plinth made no secret of sharing this view. She had always regarded it as one of her obligations to entertain the Lunch Club's distinguished guests. Mrs. Plinth was almost as proud of her obligations as she was of her picture-gallery; she was in fact fond of implying that the one possession implied the other, and that only a woman of her wealth could afford to live up to a standard as high as that which she had set herself. An all-round sense of duty, roughly adaptable to various ends, was, in her opinion, all that Providence exacted of the more humbly stationed; but the power which had predestined Mrs. Plinth to keep a footman clearly intended her to maintain an equally specialized staff of responsibilities. It was the more to be regretted that Mrs. Ballinger, whose obligations to society were bounded by the narrow scope of two parlour-maids, should have been so tenacious of the right to entertain Osric Dane.

The question of that lady's reception had for a month past profoundly moved the members of the Lunch Club. It was not that they felt themselves unequal to the task, but that their sense of the opportunity plunged them into the agreeable uncertainty of the lady who weighs the alternatives of a well-stocked wardrobe. If such subsidiary members as Mrs. Leveret were fluttered by the thought of exchanging ideas with the author of "The Wings of Death," no forebodings disturbed the conscious adequacy of Mrs. Plinth, Mrs. Ballinger and Miss Van Vluyck. "The Wings of Death" had, in fact, at Miss Van Vluyck's suggestion, been chosen as the subject of discussion at the last club meeting, and each member had thus been enabled to express her own opinion or to appropriate whatever sounded well in the comments of the others.

Mrs. Roby alone had abstained from profiting by the opportunity; but it was now openly recognised that, as a member of the Lunch Club, Mrs. Roby was a failure. "It all comes," as Miss Van Vluyck put it, "of accepting a woman on a man's estimation." Mrs. Roby, returning to Hillbridge from a prolonged sojourn in exotic lands—the other ladies no longer took the trouble to remember where—had been heralded by the distinguished biologist, Professor Foreland, as the most agreeable woman he had ever met; and the members of the Lunch Club, impressed by an encomium that carried the weight of a diploma, and rashly assuming that the Professor's social sympathies would follow the line of his professional bent, had seized the chance of annexing a biological member. Their disillusionment was complete. At Miss Van Vluyck's first off-hand mention of the pterodactyl Mrs. Roby had confusedly murmured: "I know so little about metres—" and after that painful betrayal of incompetence she had prudently withdrawn from farther participation in the mental gymnastics of the club.

"I suppose she flattered him," Miss Van Vluyck summed up—"or else it's the way she does her hair."

The dimensions of Miss Van Vluyck's dining-room having restricted the membership of the club to six, the non-conductiveness of one member was a serious obstacle to the exchange of ideas, and some wonder had already been expressed that Mrs. Roby should care to live, as it were, on the intellectual bounty of the others. This feeling was increased by the discovery that she had not yet read "The Wings of Death."

She owned to having heard the name of Osric Dane; but that—incredible as it appeared—was the extent of her acquaintance with the celebrated novelist. The ladies could not conceal their surprise; but Mrs. Ballinger, whose pride in the club made her wish to put even Mrs. Roby in the best possible light, gently insinuated that, though she had not had time to acquaint herself with "The Wings of Death," she must at least be familiar with its equally remarkable predecessor, "The Supreme Instant."

Mrs. Roby wrinkled her sunny brows in a conscientious effort of memory, as a result of which she recalled that, oh, yes, she *had* seen the book at her brother's, when she was staying with him in Brazil, and had even carried it off to read one day on a boating party; but they had all got to shying things at each other in the boat, and the book had gone overboard, so she had never had the chance—

The picture evoked by this anecdote did not increase Mrs. Roby's credit with the club, and there was a painful pause, which was broken by Mrs. Plinth's remarking: "I can understand that, with all your other pursuits, you should not find much time for reading; but I should have thought you might at least have *got up* 'The Wings of Death' before Osric Dane's arrival."

Mrs. Roby took this rebuke good-humouredly. She had meant, she owned, to glance through the book; but she had been so absorbed in a novel of Trollope's that—

"No one reads Trollope now," Mrs. Ballinger interrupted.

Mrs. Roby looked pained. "I'm only just beginning," she confessed.

"And does he interest you?" Mrs. Plinth enquired.

"He amuses me."

"Amusement," said Mrs. Plinth, "is hardly what I look for in my choice of books."

"Oh, certainly, 'The Wings of Death' is not amusing," ventured Mrs. Leveret, whose manner of putting forth an opinion was like that of an obliging salesman with a variety of other styles to submit if his first selection does not suit.

"Was it *meant* to be?" enquired Mrs. Plinth, who was fond of asking questions that she permitted no one but herself to answer. "Assuredly not."

"Assuredly not—that is what I was going to say," assented Mrs. Leveret, hastily rolling up her opinion and reaching for another. "It was meant to—to elevate."

Miss Van Vluyck adjusted her spectacles as though they were the black cap of condemnation. "I hardly see," she interposed, "how a book steeped in the bitterest pessimism can be said to elevate, however much it may instruct."

"I meant, of course, to instruct," said Mrs. Leveret, flurried by the unexpected distinction between two terms which she had supposed to be synonymous. Mrs. Leveret's enjoyment of the Lunch Club was frequently marred by such surprises; and not knowing her own value to the other ladies as a mirror for their mental complacency she was sometimes troubled by a doubt of her worthiness to join in their debates. It was only the fact of having a dull sister who thought her clever that saved her from a sense of hopeless inferiority.

"Do they get married in the end?" Mrs. Roby interposed.

"They—who?" the Lunch Club collectively exclaimed.

"Why, the girl and man. It's a novel, isn't it? I always think that's the one thing that matters. If they're parted it spoils my dinner."

Mrs. Plinth and Mrs. Ballinger exchanged scandalised glances, and the latter said: "I should hardly advise you to read 'The Wings of Death' in that spirit. For my part, when there are so many books one *has* to read, I wonder how any one can find time for those that are merely amusing."

"The beautiful part of it," Laura Glyde murmured, "is surely just this—that no one can tell *how* 'The Wings of Death' ends. Osric Dane, overcome by the awful significance of her own meaning, has mercifully veiled it—perhaps even from herself—as Apelles, in representing the sacrifice of Iphigenia, veiled the face of Agamemnon."

"What's that? Is it poetry?" whispered Mrs. Leveret to Mrs. Plinth, who, disdaining a definite reply, said coldly: "You should look it up. I always make it a point to look things up." Her tone added—"though I might easily have it done for me by the footman."

"I was about to say," Miss Van Vluyck resumed, "that it must always be a question whether a book *can* instruct unless it elevates."

"Oh—" murmured Mrs. Leveret, now feeling herself hopelessly astray.

"I don't know," said Mrs. Ballinger, scenting in Miss Van Vluyck's tone a tendency to depreciate the coveted distinction of entertaining Osric Dane; "I don't know that such a question can seriously be raised as to a book which has attracted more attention among thoughtful people than any novel since 'Robert Elsmere.' "

"Oh, but don't you see," exclaimed Laura Glyde, "that it's just the dark hopelessness of it all—the wonderful tone-scheme of black on black—that makes it such an artistic achievement? It reminded me when I read it of Prince Rupert's *manière noire* . . . the book is etched, not painted, yet one feels the colour-values so intensely. . . ."

"Who is *he?*" Mrs. Leveret whispered to her neighbour. "Some one she's met abroad?"

"The wonderful part of the book," Mrs. Ballinger conceded, "is that it may be looked at from so many points of view. I hear that as a study of determinism Professor Lupton ranks it with 'The Data of Ethics.' "

"I'm told that Osric Dane spent ten years in preparatory studies before beginning to write it," said Mrs. Plinth. "She looks up everything—verifies everything. It has always been my principle, as you know. Nothing would induce me, now, to put aside a book before I'd finished it, just because I can buy as many more as I want."

"And what do *you* think of 'The Wings of Death'?" Mrs. Roby abruptly asked her.

It was the kind of question that might be termed out of order, and the ladies glanced at each other as though disclaiming any share in such a breach of discipline. They all knew there was nothing Mrs. Plinth so much disliked as being asked her opinion of a book. Books were written to read; if one read them what more could be expected? To be questioned in detail regarding the contents of a volume seemed to her as great an outrage as being searched for smuggled laces at the Custom House. The club had always respected this idiosyncrasy of Mrs. Plinth's. Such opinions as she had were imposing and substantial: her mind, like her house, was furnished with monumental "pieces" that were not meant to be disarranged; and it was one of the unwritten rules of the Lunch Club that, within her own province, each member's habits of thought should be respected. The meeting therefore closed with an increased sense, on the part of the other ladies, of Mrs. Roby's hopeless unfitness to be one of them.

II

Mrs. Leveret, on the eventful day, arrived early at Mrs. Ballinger's, her volume of Appropriate Allusions in her pocket.

It always flustered Mrs. Leveret to be late at the Lunch Club: she liked to collect her thoughts and gather a hint, as the others assembled, of the turn the conversation was likely to take. To-day, however, she felt herself completely at a loss; and even the familiar contact of Appropriate Allusions, which stuck into her as she sat down, failed to give her any reassurance. It was an admirable little volume, compiled to meet all the social emergencies; so that, whether on the occasion of Anniversaries, joyful or melancholy (as the classification ran), of Banquets, social or municipal, or of Baptisms, Church of England or sectarian, its student need never be at a loss for a pertinent reference. Mrs. Leveret, though she had for years devoutly conned its pages, valued it, however, rather for its moral support than for its practical services; for though in the privacy of her own room she commanded an army of quotations, these invariably deserted her at the critical moment, and the only phrase she retained—*Canst thou draw out leviathan with a hook?*—was one she had never yet found occasion to apply.

To-day she felt that even the complete mastery of the volume would hardly have insured her self-possession; for she thought it probable that, even if she *did*, in some miraculous way, remember an Allusion, it would be only to find that Osric Dane used a different volume (Mrs. Leveret was convinced that literary people always carried them), and would consequently not recognise her quotations.

Mrs. Leveret's sense of being adrift was intensified by the appearance of Mrs. Ballinger's drawing-room. To a careless eye its aspect was unchanged; but those acquainted with Mrs.

Ballinger's way of arranging her books would instantly have detected the marks of recent perturbation. Mrs. Ballinger's province, as a member of the Lunch Club, was the Book of the Day. On that, whatever it was, from a novel to a treatise on experimental psychology, she was confidently, authoritatively "up." What became of last year's books, or last week's even; what she did with the "subjects" she had previously professed with equal authority; no one had ever yet discovered. Her mind was an hotel where facts came and went like transient lodgers, without leaving their address behind, and frequently without paying for their board. It was Mrs. Ballinger's boast that she was "abreast with the Thought of the Day," and her pride that this advanced position should be expressed by the books on her table. These volumes, frequently renewed, and almost always damp from the press, bore names generally unfamiliar to Mrs. Leveret, and giving her, as she furtively scanned them, a disheartening glimpse of new fields of knowledge to be breathlessly traversed in Mrs. Ballinger's wake. But to-day a number of maturer-looking volumes were adroitly mingled with the *primeurs* of the press—Karl Marx jostled Professor Bergson, and the "Confessions of St. Augustine" lay beside the last work on "Mendelism"; so that even to Mrs. Leveret's fluttered perceptions it was clear that Mrs. Ballinger didn't in the least know what Osric Dane was likely to talk about, and had taken measures to be prepared for anything. Mrs. Leveret felt like a passenger on an ocean steamer who is told that there is no immediate danger, but that she had better put on her life-belt.

It was a relief to be roused from these forebodings by Miss Van Vluyck's arrival.

"Well, my dear," the new-comer briskly asked her hostess, "what subjects are we to discuss to-day?"

Mrs. Ballinger was furtively replacing a volume of Wordsworth by a copy of Verlaine. "I hardly know," she said, somewhat nervously. "Perhaps we had better leave that to circumstances."

"Circumstances?" said Miss Van Vluyck drily. "That means, I suppose, that Laura Glyde will take the floor as usual, and we shall be deluged with literature."

Philanthropy and statistics were Miss Van Vluyck's province, and she resented any tendency to divert their guest's attention from these topics.

Mrs. Plinth at this moment appeared.

"Literature?" she protested in a tone of remonstrance. "But this is perfectly unexpected. I understood we were to talk of Osric Dane's novel."

Mrs. Ballinger winced at the discrimination, but let it pass. "We can hardly make that our chief subject—at least not *too* intentionally," she suggested. "Of course we can let our talk *drift* in that direction; but we ought to have some other topic as an introduction, and that is what I wanted to consult you about. The fact is, we know so little of Osric Dane's tastes and interests that it is difficult to make any special preparation."

"It may be difficult," said Mrs. Plinth with decision, "but it is necessary. I know what that happy-go-lucky principle leads to. As I told one of my nieces the other day, there are certain emergencies for which a lady should always be prepared. It's in shocking taste to wear colours when one pays a visit of condolence, or a last year's dress when there are reports that one's husband is on the wrong side of the market; and so it is with conversation. All I ask is that I should know beforehand what is to be talked about; then I feel sure of being able to say the proper thing."

"I quite agree with you," Mrs. Ballinger assented; "but—"

And at that instant, heralded by the fluttered parlour-maid, Osric Dane appeared upon the threshold.

Mrs. Leveret told her sister afterward that she had known at a glance what was coming. She saw that Osric Dane was not going to meet them half way. That distinguished personage had indeed entered with an air of compulsion not calculated to promote the easy exercise of hospitality. She looked as though she were about to be photographed for a new edition of her books.

The desire to propitiate a divinity is generally in inverse ratio to its responsiveness, and the sense of discouragement produced by Osric Dane's entrance visibly increased the Lunch Club's eagerness to please her. Any lingering idea that she might consider herself under an obligation to her entertainers was at once dispelled by her manner: as Mrs. Leveret said afterward to her sister, she had a way of looking at you that made you feel as if there was something wrong with your hat. This evidence of greatness produced such an immediate impression on the ladies that a shudder of awe ran through them when Mrs. Roby, as their hostess led the great personage into the dining-room, turned back to whisper to the others: "What a brute she is!"

The hour about the table did not tend to revise this verdict. It was passed by Osric Dane in the silent deglutition of Mrs. Ballinger's menu, and by the members of the club in the emission of tentative platitudes which their guest seemed to swallow as perfunctorily as the successive courses of the luncheon.

Mrs. Ballinger's reluctance to fix a topic had thrown the club into a mental disarray which increased with the return to the drawing-room, where the actual business of discussion was to open. Each lady waited for the other to speak; and there was a general shock of disappointment when their hostess opened the conversation by the painfully commonplace enquiry: "Is this your first visit to Hillbridge?"

Even Mrs. Leveret was conscious that this was a bad beginning; and a vague impulse of deprecation made Miss Glyde interject: "It is a very small place indeed."

Mrs. Plinth bristled. "We have a great many representative people," she said, in the tone of one who speaks for her order.

Osric Dane turned to her. "What do they represent?" she asked.

Mrs. Plinth's constitutional dislike to being questioned was intensified by her sense of unpreparedness; and her reproachful glance passed the question on to Mrs. Ballinger.

"Why," said that lady, glancing in turn at the other members, "as a community I hope it is not too much to say that we stand for culture."

"For art—" Miss Glyde interjected.

"For art and literature," Mrs. Ballinger emended.

"And for sociology, I trust," snapped Miss Van Vluyck.

"We have a standard," said Mrs. Plinth, feeling herself suddenly secure on the vast expanse of a generalisation; and Mrs. Leveret, thinking there must be room for more than one on so broad a statement, took courage to murmur: "Oh, certainly; we have a standard."

"The object of our little club," Mrs. Ballinger continued, "is to concentrate the highest tendencies of Hillbridge—to centralise and focus its intellectual effort."

This was felt to be so happy that the ladies drew an almost audible breath of relief.

"We aspire," the President went on, "to be in touch with whatever is highest in art, literature and ethics."

Osric Dane again turned to her. "What ethics?" she asked.

A tremor of apprehension encircled the room. None of the ladies required any preparation to pronounce on a question of morals; but when they were called ethics it was different. The club, when fresh from the "Encyclopædia Britannica," the "Reader's Handbook" or Smith's "Classical Dictionary," could deal confidently with any subject; but when taken unawares it had been known to define agnosticism as a heresy of the Early Church and Professor Froude as a distinguished histologist; and such minor members as Mrs. Leveret still secretly regarded ethics as something vaguely pagan.

Even to Mrs. Ballinger, Osric Dane's question was unsettling, and there was a general sense of gratitude when Laura Glyde leaned forward to say, with her most sympathetic accent: "You must excuse us, Mrs. Dane, for not being able, just at present, to talk of anything but 'The Wings of Death.'"

"Yes," said Miss Van Vluyck, with a sudden resolve to carry the war into the enemy's camp. "We are so anxious to know the exact purpose you had in mind in writing your wonderful book."

"You will find," Mrs. Plinth interposed, "that we are not superficial readers."

"We are eager to hear from you," Miss Van Vluyck continued, "if the pessimistic tendency of the book is an expression of your own convictions or—"

"Or merely," Miss Glyde thrust in, "a sombre background brushed in to throw your figures into more vivid relief. *Are* you not primarily plastic?"

"*I* have always maintained," Mrs. Ballinger interposed, "that you represent the purely objective method—"

Osric Dane helped herself critically to coffee. "How do you define objective?" she then enquired.

There was a flurried pause before Laura Glyde intensely murmured: "In reading *you* we don't define, we feel."

Osric Dane smiled. "The cerebellum," she remarked, "is not infrequently the seat of the literary emotions." And she took a second lump of sugar.

The sting that this remark was vaguely felt to conceal was almost neutralised by the satisfaction of being addressed in such technical language.

"Ah, the cerebellum," said Miss Van Vluyck complacently. "The club took a course in psychology last winter."

"Which psychology?" asked Osric Dane.

There was an agonising pause, during which each member of the club secretly deplored the distressing inefficiency of the others. Only Mrs. Roby went on placidly sipping her chartreuse. At last Mrs. Ballinger said, with an attempt at a high tone: "Well, really, you know, it was last year that we took psychology, and this winter we have been so absorbed in—"

She broke off, nervously trying to recall some of the club's discussions; but her faculties seemed to be paralysed by the petrifying stare of Osric Dane. What *had* the club been absorbed in? Mrs. Ballinger, with a vague purpose of gaining time, repeated slowly: "We've been so intensely absorbed in—"

Mrs. Roby put down her liqueur glass and drew near the group with a smile.

"In Xingu?" she gently prompted.

A thrill ran through the other members. They exchanged confused glances, and then, with one accord, turned a gaze of mingled relief and interrogation on their rescuer. The expression of each denoted a different phase of the same emotion. Mrs. Plinth was the first to compose her features to an air of reassurance: after a moment's hasty adjustment her look almost implied that it was she who had given the word to Mrs. Ballinger.

"Xingu, of course!" exclaimed the latter with her accustomed promptness, while Miss Van Vluyck and Laura Glyde seemed to be plumbing the depths of memory, and Mrs. Leveret, feeling apprehensively for Appropriate Allusions, was somehow reassured by the uncomfortable pressure of its bulk against her person.

Osric Dane's change of countenance was no less striking than that of her entertainers. She too put down her coffee-cup, but with a look of distinct annoyance; she too wore, for a brief moment, what Mrs. Roby afterward described as the look of feeling for something in the back of her head; and before she could dissemble these momentary signs of weakness, Mrs. Roby, turning to her with a deferential smile, had said: "And we've been so hoping that to-day you would tell us just what you think of it."

Osric Dane received the homage of the smile as a matter of course; but the accompanying question obviously embarrassed her, and it became clear to her observers that she was not quick at shifting her facial scenery. It was as though her countenance had so long been set in an expression of unchallenged superiority that the muscles had stiffened, and refused to obey her orders.

"Xingu—" she said, as if seeking in her turn to gain time.

Mrs. Roby continued to press her. "Knowing how engrossing the subject is, you will understand how it happens that the club has let everything else go to the wall for the moment. Since we took up Xingu I might almost say—were it not for your books—that nothing else seems to us worth remembering."

Osric Dane's stern features were darkened rather than lit up by an uneasy smile. "I am glad to hear that you make one exception," she gave out between narrowed lips.

"Oh, of course," Mrs. Roby said prettily; "but as you have shown us that—so very naturally!—you don't care to talk of your own things, we really can't let you off from telling us exactly what you think about Xingu; especially," she added, with a still more persuasive smile, "as some people say that one of your last books was saturated with it."

It was an *it*, then—the assurance sped like fire through the parched minds of the other members. In their eagerness to gain the least little clue to Xingu they almost forgot the joy of assisting at the discomfiture of Mrs. Dane.

The latter reddened nervously under her antagonist's challenge. "May I ask," she faltered out, "to which of my books you refer?"

Mrs. Roby did not falter. "That's just what I want you to tell us; because, though I was present, I didn't actually take part."

"Present at what?" Mrs. Dane took her up; and for an instant the trembling members of the Lunch Club thought that the champion Providence had raised up for them had lost a point. But Mrs. Roby explained herself gaily: "At the discussion, of course. And so we're dreadfully anxious to know just how it was that you went into the Xingu."

There was a portentous pause, a silence so big with incalculable dangers that the members with one accord checked the words on their lips, like soldiers dropping their arms to watch a single combat between their leaders. Then Mrs. Dane gave expression to their inmost dread by saying sharply: "Ah—you say *the* Xingu, do you?"

Mrs. Roby smiled undauntedly. "It *is* a shade pedantic, isn't it? Personally, I always drop the article; but I don't know how the other members feel about it."

The other members looked as though they would willingly have dispensed with this appeal to their opinion, and Mrs. Roby, after a bright glance about the group, went on: "They probably think, as I do, that nothing really matters except the thing itself—except Xingu."

No immediate reply seemed to occur to Mrs. Dane, and Mrs. Ballinger gathered courage to say: "Surely every one must feel that about Xingu."

Mrs. Plinth came to her support with a heavy murmur of assent, and Laura Glyde sighed out emotionally: "I have known cases where it has changed a whole life."

"It has done me worlds of good," Mrs. Leveret interjected, seeming to herself to remember that she had either taken it or read it the winter before.

"Of course," Mrs. Roby admitted, "the difficulty is that one must give up so much time to it. It's very long."

"I can't imagine," said Miss Van Vluyck, "grudging the time given to such a subject."

"And deep in places," Mrs. Roby pursued; (so then it was a book!) "And it isn't easy to skip."

"I never skip," said Mrs. Plinth dogmatically.

"Ah, it's dangerous to, in Xingu. Even at the start there are places where one can't. One must just wade through."

"I should hardly call it *wading*," said Mrs. Ballinger sarcastically.

Mrs. Roby sent her a look of interest. "Ah—you always found it went swimmingly?"

Mrs. Ballinger hesitated. "Of course there are difficult passages," she conceded.

"Yes; some are not at all clear—even," Mrs. Roby added, "if one is familiar with the original."

"As I suppose you are?" Osric Dane interposed, suddenly fixing her with a look of challenge.

Mrs. Roby met it by a deprecating gesture. "Oh, it's really not difficult up to a certain point; though some of the branches are very little known, and it's almost impossible to get at the source."

"Have you ever tried?" Mrs. Plinth enquired, still distrustful of Mrs. Roby's thoroughness.

Mrs. Roby was silent for a moment; then she replied with lowered lids: "No—but a friend of mine did; a very brilliant man; and he told me it was best for women—not to. . . ."

A shudder ran around the room. Mrs. Leveret coughed so that the parlour-maid, who was handing the cigarettes, should not hear; Miss Van Vluyck's face took on a nauseated expression, and Mrs. Plinth looked as if she were passing some one she did not care to bow to. But the most remarkable result of Mrs. Roby's words was the effect they produced on the Lunch Club's distinguished guest. Osric Dane's impassive features suddenly softened to an expression of the warmest human sympathy, and edging her chair toward Mrs. Roby's she asked: "Did he really? And—did you find he was right?"

Mrs. Ballinger, in whom annoyance at Mrs. Roby's unwonted assumption of prominence was beginning to displace gratitude for the aid she had rendered, could not consent to her being allowed, by such dubious means, to monopolise the attention of their guest. If Osric Dane had not enough self-respect to resent Mrs. Roby's flippancy, at least the Lunch Club would do so in the person of its President.

Mrs. Ballinger laid her hand on Mrs. Roby's arm. "We must not forget," she said with a frigid amiability, "that absorbing as Xingu is to *us*, it may be less interesting to—"

"Oh, no, on the contrary, I assure you," Osric Dane intervened.

"—to others," Mrs. Ballinger finished firmly; "and we must not allow our little meeting to end without persuading Mrs. Dane to say a few words to us on a subject which, to-day, is much more present in all our thoughts. I refer, of course, to 'The Wings of Death.'"

The other members, animated by various degrees of the same sentiment, and encouraged by the humanised mien of their redoubtable guest, repeated after Mrs. Ballinger: "Oh, yes, you really *must* talk to us a little about your book."

Osric Dane's expression became as bored, though not as haughty, as when her work had been previously mentioned. But before she could respond to Mrs. Ballinger's request, Mrs. Roby had risen from her seat, and was pulling down her veil over her frivolous nose.

"I'm so sorry," she said, advancing toward her hostess with outstretched hand, "but before Mrs. Dane begins I think I'd better run away. Unluckily, as you know, I haven't read her books, so I should be at a terrible disadvantage among you all, and besides, I've an engagement to play bridge."

If Mrs. Roby had simply pleaded her ignorance of Osric Dane's works as a reason for withdrawing, the Lunch Club, in view of her recent prowess, might have approved such evidence of discretion; but to couple this excuse with the brazen announcement that she was foregoing the privilege for the purpose of joining a bridge-party was only one more instance of her deplorable lack of discrimination.

The ladies were disposed, however, to feel that her departure—now that she had performed the sole service she was ever likely to render them—would probably make for greater order and dignity in the impending discussion, besides relieving them of the sense of self-distrust which her presence always mysteriously produced. Mrs. Ballinger therefore restricted herself to a formal murmur of regret, and the other members were just grouping themselves comfortably about Osric Dane when the latter, to their dismay, started up from the sofa on which she had been seated.

"Oh wait—do wait, and I'll go with you!" she called out to Mrs. Roby; and, seizing the hands of the disconcerted members, she administered a series of farewell pressures with the mechanical haste of a railway-conductor punching tickets.

"I'm so sorry—I'd quite forgotten—" she flung back at them from the threshold; and as she joined Mrs. Roby, who had turned in surprise at her appeal, the other ladies had the mortification of hearing her say, in a voice which she did not take the pains to lower: "If you'll let me walk a little way with you, I should so like to ask you a few more questions about Xingu . . ."

III

The incident had been so rapid that the door closed on the departing pair before the other members had time to understand what was happening. Then a sense of the indignity put upon them by Osric Dane's unceremonious desertion began to contend with the confused feeling that they had been cheated out of their due without exactly knowing how or why.

There was a silence, during which Mrs. Ballinger, with a perfunctory hand, rearranged the skilfully grouped literature at which her distinguished guest had not so much as glanced; then Miss Van Vluyck tartly pronounced: "Well, I can't say that I consider Osric Dane's departure a great loss."

This confession crystallised the resentment of the other members, and Mrs. Leveret exclaimed: "I do believe she came on purpose to be nasty!"

It was Mrs. Plinth's private opinion that Osric Dane's attitude toward the Lunch Club might have been very different had it welcomed her in the majestic setting of the Plinth drawing-rooms; but not liking to reflect on the inadequacy of Mrs. Ballinger's establishment she sought a roundabout satisfaction in depreciating her lack of foresight.

"I said from the first that we ought to have had a subject ready. It's what always happens when you're unprepared. Now if we'd only got up Xingu—"

The slowness of Mrs. Plinth's mental processes was always allowed for by the club; but this instance of it was too much for Mrs. Ballinger's equanimity.

"Xingu!" she scoffed. "Why, it was the fact of our knowing so much more about it than she did—unprepared though we were—that made Osric Dane so furious. I should have thought that was plain enough to everybody!"

This retort impressed even Mrs. Plinth, and Laura Glyde, moved by an impulse of generosity, said: "Yes, we really ought to be grateful to Mrs. Roby for introducing the topic. It may have made Osric Dane furious, but at least it made her civil."

"I am glad we were able to show her," added Miss Van Vluyck, "that a broad and up-to-date culture is not confined to the great intellectual centres."

This increased the satisfaction of the other members, and they began to forget their wrath against Osric Dane in the pleasure of having contributed to her discomfiture.

Miss Van Vluyck thoughtfully rubbed her spectacles. "What surprised me most," she continued, "was that Fanny Roby should be so up on Xingu."

This remark threw a slight chill on the company, but Mrs. Ballinger said with an air of indulgent irony: "Mrs. Roby always has the knack of making a little go a long way; still, we certainly owe her a debt for happening to remember that she'd heard of Xingu." And this was felt by the other members to be graceful way of cancelling once for all the club's obligation to Mrs. Roby.

Even Mrs. Leveret took courage to speed a timid shaft of irony. "I fancy Osric Dane hardly expected to take a lesson in Xingu at Hillbridge!"

Mrs. Ballinger smiled. "When she asked me what we represented—do you remember?—I wish I'd simply said we represented Xingu!"

All the ladies laughed appreciatively at this sally, except Mrs. Plinth, who said, after a moment's deliberation: "I'm not sure it would have been wise to do so."

Mrs. Ballinger, who was already beginning to feel as if she had launched at Osric Dane the retort which had just occurred to her, turned ironically on Mrs. Plinth. "May I ask why?" she enquired.

Mrs. Plinth looked grave. "Surely," she said, "I understood from Mrs. Roby herself that the subject was one it was as well not to go into too deeply?"

Miss Van Vluyck rejoined with precision: "I think that applied only to an investigation of the origin of the—of the—";

and suddenly she found that her usually accurate memory had failed her. "It's a part of the subject I never studied myself," she concluded.

"Nor I," said Mrs. Ballinger.

Laura Glyde bent toward them with widened eyes. "And yet it seems—doesn't it?—the part that is fullest of an esoteric fascination?"

"I don't know on what you base that," said Miss Van Vluyck argumentatively.

"Well, didn't you notice how intensely interested Osric Dane became as soon as she heard what the brilliant foreigner—he *was* a foreigner, wasn't he?—had told Mrs. Roby about the origin—the origin of the rite—or whatever you call it?"

Mrs. Plinth looked disapproving, and Mrs. Ballinger visibly wavered. Then she said: "It may not be desirable to touch on the—on that part of the subject in general conversation; but, from the importance it evidently has to a woman of Osric Dane's distinction, I feel as if we ought not to be afraid to discuss it among ourselves—without gloves—though with closed doors, if necessary."

"I'm quite of your opinion," Miss Van Vluyck came briskly to her support; "on condition, that is, that all grossness of language is avoided."

"Oh, I'm sure we shall understand without that," Mrs. Leveret tittered; and Laura Glyde added significantly: "I fancy we can read between the lines," while Mrs. Ballinger rose to assure herself that the doors were really closed.

Mrs. Plinth had not yet given her adhesion. "I hardly see," she began, "what benefit is to be derived from investigating such peculiar customs—"

But Mrs. Ballinger's patience had reached the extreme limit of tension. "This at least," she returned; "that we shall not be placed again in the humiliating position of finding ourselves less up on our own subjects than Fanny Roby!"

Even to Mrs. Plinth this argument was conclusive. She peered furtively about the room and lowered her commanding tones to ask: "Have you got a copy?"

"A—a copy?" stammered Mrs. Ballinger. She was aware that the other members were looking at her expectantly, and that this answer was inadequate, so she supported it by asking another question. "A copy of what?"

Her companions bent their expectant gaze on Mrs. Plinth, who, in turn, appeared less sure of herself than usual. "Why, of—of—the book," she explained.

"What book?" snapped Miss Van Vluyck, almost as sharply as Osric Dane.

Mrs. Ballinger looked at Laura Glyde, whose eyes were interrogatively fixed on Mrs. Leveret. The fact of being deferred to was so new to the latter that it filled her with an insane temerity. "Why, Xingu, of course!" she exclaimed.

A profound silence followed this challenge to the resources of Mrs. Ballinger's library, and the latter, after glancing nervously toward the Books of the Day, returned with dignity: "It's not a thing one cares to leave about."

"I should think *not!*" exclaimed Mrs. Plinth.

"It *is* a book, then?" said Miss Van Vluyck.

This again threw the company into disarray, and Mrs. Ballinger, with an impatient sigh, rejoined: "Why—there *is* a book—naturally. . . ."

"Then why did Miss Glyde call it a religion?"

Laura Glyde started up. "A religion? I never—"

"Yes, you did," Miss Van Vluyck insisted; "you spoke of rites; and Mrs. Plinth said it was a custom."

Miss Glyde was evidently making a desperate effort to recall her statement; but accuracy of detail was not her strongest point. At length she began in a deep murmur: "Surely they used to do something of the kind at the Eleusinian mysteries—"

"Oh—" said Miss Van Vluyck, on the verge of disapproval; and Mrs. Plinth protested: "I understood there was to be no indelicacy!"

Mrs. Ballinger could not control her irritation. "Really, it is too bad that we should not be able to talk the matter over quietly among ourselves. Personally, I think that if one goes into Xingu at all—"

"Oh, so do I!" cried Miss Glyde.

"And I don't see how one can avoid doing so, if one wishes to keep up with the Thought of the Day—"

Mrs. Leveret uttered an exclamation of relief. "There—that's it!" she interposed.

"What's it?" the President took her up.

"Why—it's a—a Thought: I mean a philosophy."

This seemed to bring a certain relief to Mrs. Ballinger and Laura Glyde, but Miss Van Vluyck said: "Excuse me if I tell you that you're all mistaken. Xingu happens to be a language."

"A language!" the Lunch Club cried.

"Certainly. Don't you remember Fanny Roby's saying that there were several branches, and that some were hard to trace? What could that apply to but dialects?"

Mrs. Ballinger could no longer restrain a contemptuous laugh. "Really, if the Lunch Club has reached such a pass that it has to go to Fanny Roby for instruction on a subject like Xingu, it had almost better cease to exist!"

"It's really her fault for not being clearer," Laura Glyde put in.

"Oh, clearness and Fanny Roby!" Mrs. Ballinger shrugged. "I daresay we shall find she was mistaken on almost every point."

"Why not look it up?" said Mrs. Plinth.

As a rule this recurrent suggestion of Mrs. Plinth's was ignored in the heat of discussion, and only resorted to afterward in the privacy of each member's home. But on the present occasion the desire to ascribe their own confusion of thought to the vague and contradictory nature of Mrs. Roby's statements caused the members of the Lunch Club to utter a collective demand for a book of reference.

At this point the production of her treasured volume gave Mrs. Leveret, for a moment, the unusual experience of occupying the centre front; but she was not able to hold it long, for Appropriate Allusions contained no mention of Xingu.

"Oh, that's not the kind of thing we want!" exclaimed Miss Van Vluyck. She cast a disparaging glance over Mrs. Ballinger's assortment of literature, and added impatiently: "Haven't you any useful books?"

"Of course I have," replied Mrs. Ballinger indignantly; "I keep them in my husband's dressing-room."

From this region, after some difficulty and delay, the parlour-maid produced the W–Z volume of an Encyclopædia and, in deference to the fact that the demand for it had come from Miss Van Vluyck, laid the ponderous tome before her.

There was a moment of painful suspense while Miss Van Vluyck rubbed her spectacles, adjusted them, and turned to Z; and a murmur of surprise when she said: "It isn't here."

"I suppose," said Mrs. Plinth, "it's not fit to be put in a book of reference."

"Oh, nonsense!" exclaimed Mrs. Ballinger. "Try X."

Miss Van Vluyck turned back through the volume, peering short-sightedly up and down the pages, till she came to a stop and remained motionless, like a dog on a point.

"Well, have you found it?" Mrs. Ballinger enquired after a considerable delay.

"Yes. I've found it," said Miss Van Vluyck in a queer voice.

Mrs. Plinth hastily interposed: "I beg you won't read it aloud if there's anything offensive."

Miss Van Vluyck, without answering, continued her silent scrutiny.

"Well, what *is* it?" exclaimed Laura Glyde excitedly.

"*Do* tell us!" urged Mrs. Leveret, feeling that she would have something awful to tell her sister.

Miss Van Vluyck pushed the volume aside and turned slowly toward the expectant group.

"It's a river."

"A *river*?"

"Yes: in Brazil. Isn't that where she's been living?"

"Who? Fanny Roby? Oh, but you must be mistaken. You've been reading the wrong thing," Mrs. Ballinger exclaimed, leaning over her to seize the volume.

"It's the only *Xingu* in the Encyclopædia; and she *has* been living in Brazil," Miss Van Vluyck persisted.

"Yes: her brother has a consulship there," Mrs. Leveret interposed.

"But it's too ridiculous! I—we—why we *all* remember studying Xingu last year—or the year before last," Mrs. Ballinger stammered.

"I thought I did when *you* said so," Laura Glyde avowed.

"*I* said so?" cried Mrs. Ballinger.

"Yes. You said it had crowded everything else out of your mind."

"Well *you* said it had changed your whole life!"

"For that matter, Miss Van Vluyck said she had never grudged the time she'd given it."

Mrs. Plinth interposed: "I made it clear that I knew nothing whatever of the original."

Mrs. Ballinger broke off the dispute with a groan. "Oh, what does it all matter if she's been making fools of us? I believe Miss Van Vluyck's right—she was talking of the river all the while!"

"How could she? It's too preposterous," Miss Glyde exclaimed.

"Listen." Miss Van Vluyck had repossessed herself of the Encyclopædia, and restored her spectacles to a nose reddened by excitement. " 'The Xingu, one of the principal rivers of Brazil, rises on the plateau of Mato Grosso, and flows in a northerly direction for a length of no less than one thousand one hundred and eighteen miles, entering the Amazon near the mouth of the latter river. The upper course of the Xingu is auriferous and fed by numerous branches. Its source was first discovered in 1884 by the German explorer von den Steinen, after a difficult and dangerous expedition through a region inhabited by tribes still in the Stone Age of culture.' "

The ladies received this communication in a state of stupefied silence from which Mrs. Leveret was the first to rally. "She certainly *did* speak of its having branches."

The word seemed to snap the last thread of their incredulity. "And of its great length," gasped Mrs. Ballinger.

"She said it was awfully deep, and you couldn't skip—you just had to wade through," Miss Glyde added.

The idea worked its way more slowly through Mrs. Plinth's compact resistances. "How could there be anything improper about a river?" she enquired.

"Improper?"

"Why, what she said about the source—that it was corrupt?"

"Not corrupt, but hard to get at," Laura Glyde corrected. "Some one who'd been there had told her so. I daresay it was the explorer himself—doesn't it say the expedition was dangerous?"

" 'Difficult and dangerous,' " read Miss Van Vluyck.

Mrs. Ballinger pressed her hands to her throbbing temples.

"There's nothing she said that wouldn't apply to a river—to this river!" She swung about excitedly to the other members. "Why, do you remember her telling us that she hadn't read 'The Supreme Instant' because she'd taken it on a boating party while she was staying with her brother, and some one had 'shied' it overboard—'shied' of course was her own expression."

The ladies breathlessly signified that the expression had not escaped them.

"Well—and then didn't she tell Osric Dane that one of her books was simply saturated with Xingu? Of course it was, if one of Mrs. Roby's rowdy friends had thrown it into the river!"

This surprising reconstruction of the scene in which they had just participated left the members of the Lunch Club inarticulate. At length, Mrs. Plinth, after visibly labouring with the problem, said in a heavy tone: "Osric Dane was taken in too."

Mrs. Leveret took courage at this. "Perhaps that's what Mrs. Roby did it for. She said Osric Dane was a brute, and she may have wanted to give her a lesson."

Miss Van Vluyck frowned. "It was hardly worth while to do it at our expense."

"At least," said Miss Glyde with a touch of bitterness, "she succeeded in interesting her, which was more than we did."

"What chance had we?" rejoined Mrs. Ballinger. "Mrs. Roby monopolised her from the first. And *that*, I've no doubt, was her purpose—to give Osric Dane a false impression of her own standing in the club. She would hesitate at nothing to attract attention: we all know how she took in poor Professor Foreland."

"She actually makes him give bridge-teas every Thursday," Mrs. Leveret piped up.

Laura Glyde struck her hands together. "Why, this is Thursday, and it's *there* she's gone, of course; and taken Osric with her!"

"And they're shrieking over us at this moment," said Mrs. Ballinger between her teeth.

This possibility seemed too preposterous to be admitted. "She would hardly dare," said Miss Van Vluyck, "confess the imposture to Osric Dane."

"I'm not so sure: I thought I saw her make a sign as she left. If she hadn't made a sign, why should Osric Dane have rushed out after her?"

"Well, you know, we'd all been telling her how wonderful Xingu was, and she said she wanted to find out more about it," Mrs. Leveret said, with a tardy impulse of justice to the absent.

This reminder, far from mitigating the wrath of the other members, gave it a stronger impetus.

"Yes—and that's exactly what they're both laughing over now," said Laura Glyde ironically.

Mrs. Plinth stood up and gathered her expensive furs about her monumental form. "I have no wish to criticise," she said; "but unless the Lunch Club can protect its members against the recurrence of such—such unbecoming scenes, I for one—"

"Oh, so do I!" agreed Miss Glyde, rising also.

Miss Van Vluyck closed the Encyclopædia and proceeded to button herself into her jacket. "My time is really too valuable—" she began.

"I fancy we are all of one mind," said Mrs. Ballinger, looking searchingly at Mrs. Leveret, who looked at the others.

"I always deprecate anything like a scandal—" Mrs. Plinth continued.

"She has been the cause of one to-day!" exclaimed Miss Glyde.

Mrs. Leveret moaned: "I don't see how she *could*!" and Miss Van Vluyck said, picking up her note-book: "Some women stop at nothing."

"—but if," Mrs. Plinth took up her argument impressively, "anything of the kind had happened in *my* house" (it never would have, her tone implied), "I should have felt that I owed it to myself either to ask for Mrs. Roby's resignation—or to offer mine."

"Oh, Mrs. Plinth—" gasped the Lunch Club.

"Fortunately for me," Mrs. Plinth continued with an awful magnanimity, "the matter was taken out of my hands by our President's decision that the right to entertain distinguished guests was a privilege vested in her office; and I think the other members will agree that, as she was alone in this opinion, she ought to be alone in deciding on the best way of effacing its—its really deplorable consequences."

A deep silence followed this outbreak of Mrs. Plinth's long-stored resentment.

"I don't see why *I* should be expected to ask her to resign—" Mrs. Ballinger at length began; but Laura Glyde turned back to remind her: "You know she made you say that you'd got on swimmingly in Xingu."

An ill-timed giggle escaped from Mrs. Leveret, and Mrs. Ballinger energetically continued "—but you needn't think for a moment that I'm afraid to!"

The door of the drawing-room closed on the retreating backs of the Lunch Club, and the President of that distinguished association, seating herself at her writing-table, and pushing away a copy of "The Wings of Death" to make room for her elbow, drew forth a sheet of the club's note-paper, on which she began to write: "My dear Mrs. Roby—"

Coming Home

THE young men of our American Relief Corps are beginning to come back from the front with stories.

There was no time to pick them up during the first months—the whole business was too wild and grim. The horror has not decreased, but nerves and sight are beginning to be disciplined to it. In the earlier days, moreover, such fragments of experience as one got were torn from their setting like bits of flesh scattered by shrapnel. Now things that seemed disjointed are beginning to link themselves together, and the broken bones of history are rising from the battle-fields.

I can't say that, in this respect, all the members of the Relief Corps have made the most of their opportunity. Some are unobservant, or perhaps simply inarticulate; others, when going beyond the bald statistics of their job, tend to drop into sentiment and cinema scenes; and none but H. Macy Greer has the gift of making the thing told seem as true as if one had seen it. So it is on H. Macy Greer that I depend, and when his motor dashes him back to Paris for supplies I never fail to hunt him down and coax him to my rooms for dinner and a long cigar.

Greer is a small hard-muscled youth, with pleasant manners, a sallow face, straight hemp-coloured hair and grey eyes of unexpected inwardness. He has a voice like thick soup, and speaks with the slovenly drawl of the new generation of Americans, dragging his words along like reluctant dogs on a string, and depriving his narrative of every shade of expression that intelligent intonation gives. But his eyes see so much that they make one see even what his foggy voice obscures.

Some of his tales are dark and dreadful, some are unutterably sad, and some end in a huge laugh of irony. I am not sure how I ought to classify the one I have written down here.

II

On my first dash to the Northern fighting line—Greer told me the other night—I carried supplies to an ambulance where

26

the surgeon asked me to have a talk with an officer who was badly wounded and fretting for news of his people in the east of France.

He was a young Frenchman, a cavalry lieutenant, trim and slim, with a pleasant smile and obstinate blue eyes that I liked. He looked as if he could hold on tight when it was worth his while. He had had a leg smashed, poor devil, in the first fighting in Flanders, and had been dragging on for weeks in the squalid camp-hospital where I found him. He didn't waste any words on himself, but began at once about his family. They were living, when the war broke out, at their country-place in the Vosges; his father and mother, his sister, just eighteen, and his brother Alain, two years younger. His father, the Comte de Réchamp, had married late in life, and was over seventy: his mother, a good deal younger, was crippled with rheumatism; and there was, besides—to round off the group—a helpless but intensely alive and domineering old grandmother about whom all the others revolved. You know how French families hang together, and throw out branches that make new roots but keep hold of the central trunk, like that tree—what's it called?—that they give pictures of in books about the East.

Jean de Réchamp—that was my lieutenant's name—told me his family was a typical case. "We're very *province*," he said. "My people live at Réchamp all the year. We have a house at Nancy—rather a fine old hôtel—but my parents go there only once in two or three years, for a few weeks. That's our 'season.' . . . Imagine the point of view! Or rather don't, because you couldn't. . . ." (He had been about the world a good deal, and known something of other angles of vision.)

Well, of this helpless exposed little knot of people he had had no word—simply nothing—since the first of August. He was at home, staying with them at Réchamp, when war broke out. He was mobilised the first day, and had only time to throw his traps into a cart and dash to the station. His depot was on the other side of France, and communications with the East by mail and telegraph were completely interrupted during the first weeks. His regiment was sent at once to the fighting line, and the first news he got came to him in October, from a communiqué in a Paris paper a month old, saying: "The enemy yesterday retook Réchamp." After that, dead silence: and the poor devil left in the trenches to digest that "*retook*"!

There are thousands and thousands of just such cases; and men bearing them, and cracking jokes, and hitting out as hard as they can. Jean de Réchamp knew this, and tried to crack jokes too—but he got his leg smashed just afterward, and ever since he'd been lying on a straw pallet under a horse-blanket, saying to himself: "*Réchamp retaken.*"

"Of course," he explained with a weary smile, "as long as you can tot up your daily bag in the trenches it's a sort of satisfaction—though I don't quite know why; anyhow, you're so dead-beat at night that no dreams come. But lying here staring at the ceiling one goes through the whole business once an hour, at the least: the attack, the slaughter, the ruins . . . and worse. . . . Haven't I seen and heard things enough on *this* side to know what's been happening on the other? Don't try to sugar the dose. I *like* it bitter."

I was three days in the neighbourhood, and I went back every day to see him. He liked to talk to me because he had a faint hope of my getting news of his family when I returned to Paris. I hadn't much myself, but there was no use telling him so. Besides, things change from day to day, and when we parted I promised to get word to him as soon as I could find out anything. We both knew, of course, that that would not be till Réchamp was taken a third time—by his own troops; and perhaps soon after that, I should be able to get there, or near there, and make enquiries myself. To make sure that I should forget nothing, he drew the family photographs from under his pillow, and handed them over: the little witch-grandmother, with a face like a withered walnut, the father, a fine broken-looking old boy with a Roman nose and a weak chin, the mother, in crape, simple, serious and provincial, the little sister ditto, and Alain, the young brother—just the age the brutes have been carrying off to German prisons—an over-grown thread-paper boy with too much forehead and eyes, and not a muscle in his body. A charming-looking family, distinguished and amiable; but all, except the grandmother, rather usual. The kind of people who come in sets.

As I pocketed the photographs I noticed that another lay face down by his pillow. "Is that for me too?" I asked.

He coloured and shook his head, and I felt I had blundered. But after a moment he turned the photograph over and held it out.

"It's the young girl I am engaged to. She was at Réchamp visiting my parents when war was declared; but she was to leave the day after I did. . . ." He hesitated. "There may have been some difficulty about her going. . . . I should like to be sure she got away. . . . Her name is Yvonne Malo."

He did not offer me the photograph, and I did not need it. That girl had a face of her own! Dark and keen and splendid: a type so different from the others that I found myself staring. If he had not said *"ma fiancée"* I should have understood better. After another pause he went on: "I will give you her address in Paris. She has no family: she lives alone—she is a musician. Perhaps you may find her there." His colour deepened again as he added: "But I know nothing—I have had no news of her either."

To ease the silence that followed I suggested: "But if she has no family, wouldn't she have been likely to stay with your people, and wouldn't that be the reason of your not hearing from her?"

"Oh, no—I don't think she stayed." He seemed about to add: "If she could help it," but shut his lips and slid the picture out of sight.

As soon as I got back to Paris I made enquiries, but without result. The Germans had been pushed back from that particular spot after a fortnight's intermittent occupation; but their lines were close by, across the valley, and Réchamp was still in a net of trenches. No one could get to it, and apparently no news could come from it. For the moment, at any rate, I found it impossible to get in touch with the place.

My enquiries about Mlle. Malo were equally unfruitful. I went to the address Réchamp had given me, somewhere off in Passy, among gardens, in what they call a "Square," no doubt because it's oblong: a kind of long narrow court with æsthetic-looking studio buildings round it. Mlle. Malo lived in one of them, on the top floor, the concierge said, and I looked up and saw a big studio window, and a roof-terrace with dead gourds dangling from a pergola. But she wasn't there, she hadn't been there, and they had no news of her. I wrote to Réchamp of my double failure, he sent me back a line of thanks; and after that for a long while I heard no more of him.

By the beginning of November the enemy's hold had begun to loosen in the Argonne and along the Vosges, and one day we were sent off to the East with a couple of ambulances. Of course we had to have military chauffeurs, and the one attached to my ambulance happened to be a fellow I knew. The day before we started, in talking over our route with him, I said: "I suppose we can manage to get to Réchamp now?" He looked puzzled—it was such a little place that he'd forgotten the name. "Why do you want to get there?" he wondered. I told him, and he gave an exclamation. "Good God! Of course—but how extraordinary! Jean de Réchamp's here now, in Paris, too lame for the front, and driving a motor." We stared at each other, and he went on: "He must take my place—he must go with you. I don't know how it can be done; but done it shall be."

Done it was, and the next morning at daylight I found Jean de Réchamp at the wheel of my car. He looked another fellow from the wreck I had left in the Flemish hospital; all made over, and burning with activity, but older, and with lines about his eyes. He had had news from his people in the interval, and had learned that they were still at Réchamp, and well. What was more surprising was that Mlle. Malo was with them—had never left. Alain had been got away to England, where he remained; but none of the others had budged. They had fitted up an ambulance in the château, and Mlle. Malo and the little sister were nursing the wounded. There were not many details in the letters, and they had been a long time on the way; but their tone was so reassuring that Jean could give himself up to unclouded anticipation. You may fancy if he was grateful for the chance I was giving him; for of course he couldn't have seen his people in any other way.

Our permits, as you know, don't as a rule let us into the firing-line: we only take supplies to second-line ambulances, and carry back the badly wounded in need of delicate operations. So I wasn't in the least sure we should be allowed to go to Réchamp—though I had made up my mind to get there, anyhow.

We were about a fortnight on the way, coming and going in Champagne and the Argonne, and that gave us time to get to know each other. It was bitter cold, and after our long runs over the lonely frozen hills we used to crawl into the café of the inn—if there was one—and talk and talk. We put up in fairly rough places, generally in a farm house or a cottage packed with soldiers; for the villages have all remained empty since the autumn, except when troops are quartered in them. Usually, to keep warm, we had to go up after supper to the room we shared, and get under the blankets with our clothes on. Once some jolly Sisters of Charity took us in at their Hospice, and we slept two nights in an ice-cold whitewashed cell—but what tales we heard around their kitchen-fire! The Sisters had stayed alone to face the Germans, had seen the town burn, and had made the Teutons turn the hose on the singed roof of their Hospice and beat the fire back from it. It's a pity those Sisters of Charity can't marry. . . .

Réchamp told me a lot in those days. I don't believe he was talkative before the war, but his long weeks in hospital, starving for news, had unstrung him. And then he was mad with excitement at getting back to his own place. In the interval he'd heard how other people caught in their country-houses had fared—you know the stories we all refused to believe at first, and that we now prefer not to think about. . . . Well, he'd been thinking about those stories pretty steadily for some months; and he kept repeating: "My people say they're all right—but they give no details."

"You see," he explained, "there never were such helpless beings. Even if there had been time to leave, they couldn't have done it. My mother had been having one of her worst attacks of rheumatism—she was in bed, helpless, when I left. And my grandmother, who is a demon of activity in the house, won't stir out of it. We haven't been able to coax her into the garden for years. She says it's draughty; and you know how we all feel about draughts! As for my father, he hasn't had to decide anything since the Comte de Chambord refused to adopt the tricolour. My father decided that he was right, and since then there has been nothing particular for him to take a stand about. But I know how he behaved just as well as if I'd been there—he kept saying: 'One must act—one must act!' and sitting in his chair and doing nothing. Oh, I'm not disrespectful: they were *like* that in his generation! Besides—it's better to laugh at things, isn't it?" And suddenly his face would darken. . . .

On the whole, however, his spirits were good till we began to traverse the line of ruined towns between Sainte Menehould and Bar-le-Duc. "This is the way the devils came," he kept saying to me; and I saw he was hard at work picturing the work they must have done in his own neighbourhood.

"But since your sister writes that your people are safe!"

"They may have made her write that to reassure me. They'd heard I was badly wounded. And, mind you, there's never been a line from my mother."

"But you say your mother's hands are so lame that she can't hold a pen. And wouldn't Mlle. Malo have written you the truth?"

At that his frown would lift. "Oh, yes. She would despise any attempt at concealment."

"Well, then—what the deuce is the matter?"

"It's when I see these devils' traces—" he could only mutter.

One day, when we had passed through a particularly devastated little place, and had got from the curé some more than usually abominable details of things done there, Réchamp broke out to me over the kitchen-fire of our night's lodging. "When I hear things like that I don't believe anybody who tells me my people are all right!"

"But you know well enough," I insisted, "that the Germans are not all alike—that it all depends on the particular officer. . . ."

"Yes, yes, I know," he assented, with a visible effort at impartiality. "Only, you see—as one gets nearer. . . ." He went on to say that, when he had been sent from the ambulance at the front to a hospital at Moulins, he had been for a day or two in a ward next to some wounded German soldiers—bad cases, they were—and had heard them talking. They didn't know he knew German, and he had heard things. . . . There was one name always coming back in their talk, von

Scharlach, Oberst von Scharlach. One of them, a young fellow, said: "I wish now I'd cut my hand off rather than do what he told us to that night. . . . Every time the fever comes I see it all again. I wish I'd been struck dead first." They all said "Scharlach" with a kind of terror in their voices, as if he might hear them even there, and come down on them horribly. Réchamp had asked where their regiment came from, and had been told: From the Vosges. That had set his brain working, and whenever he saw a ruined village, or heard a tale of savagery, the Scharlach nerve began to quiver. At such times it was no use reminding him that the Germans had had at least three hundred thousand men in the East in August. He simply didn't listen. . . .

III

The day before we started for Réchamp his spirits flew up again, and that night he became confidential. "You've been such a friend to me that there are certain things—seeing what's ahead of us—that I should like to explain"; and, noticing my surprise, he went on: "I mean about my people. The state of mind in my *milieu* must be so remote from anything you're used to in your happy country. . . . But perhaps I can make you understand. . . ."

I saw that what he wanted was to talk to me of the girl he was engaged to. Mlle. Malo, left an orphan at ten, had been the ward of a neighbour of the Réchamps', a chap with an old name and a starred château, who had lost almost everything else at baccarat before he was forty, and had repented, had the gout and studied agriculture for the rest of his life. The girl's father was a rather brilliant painter, who died young, and her mother, who followed him in a year or two, was a Pole: you may fancy that, with such antecedents, the girl was just the mixture to shake down quietly into French country life with a gouty and repentant guardian. The Marquis de Corvenaire— that was his name—brought her down to his place, got an old maid sister to come and stay, and really, as far as one knows, brought his ward up rather decently. Now and then she used to be driven over to play with the young Réchamps, and Jean remembered her as an ugly little girl in a plaid frock, who

used to invent wonderful games and get tired of playing them
just as the other children were beginning to learn how. But
her domineering ways and searching questions did not meet
with his mother's approval, and her visits were not encouraged. When she was seventeen her guardian died and left her
a little money. The maiden sister had gone dotty, there was
nobody to look after Yvonne, and she went to Paris, to an
aunt, broke loose from the aunt when she came of age, set up
her studio, travelled, painted, played the violin, knew lots of
people; and never laid eyes on Jean de Réchamp till about a
year before the war, when her guardian's place was sold, and
she had to go down there to see about her interest in the
property.

The old Réchamps heard she was coming, but didn't ask
her to stay. Jean drove over to the shut-up château, however,
and found Mlle. Malo lunching on a corner of the kitchen
table. She exclaimed: "My little Jean!" flew to him with a kiss
for each cheek, and made him sit down and share her omelet.
. . . The ugly little girl had shed her chrysalis—and you may
fancy if he went back once or twice!

Mlle. Malo was staying at the château all alone, with the
farmer's wife to come in and cook her dinner: not a soul in
the house at night but herself and her brindled sheep dog.
She had to be there a week, and Jean suggested to his people
to ask her to Réchamp. But at Réchamp they hesitated,
coughed, looked away, said the spare-rooms were all upside
down, and the valet-de-chambre laid up with the mumps, and
the cook short-handed—till finally the irrepressible grandmother broke out: "A young girl who chooses to live alone—
probably prefers to live alone!"

There was a deadly silence, and Jean did not raise the question again; but I can imagine his blue eyes getting obstinate.

Soon after Mlle. Malo's return to Paris he followed her and
began to frequent the Passy studio. The life there was unlike
anything he had ever seen—or conceived as possible, short of
the prairies. He had sampled the usual varieties of French
womankind, and explored most of the social layers; but he
had missed the newest, that of the artistic-emancipated. I
don't know much about that set myself, but from his descrip-
tions I should say they were a good deal like intelligent

Americans, except that they don't seem to keep art and life in such water-tight compartments. But his great discovery was the new girl. Apparently he had never before known any but the traditional type, which predominates in the provinces, and still persists, he tells me, in the last fastnesses of the Faubourg St. Germain. The girl who comes and goes as she pleases, reads what she likes, has opinions about what she reads, who talks, looks, behaves with the independence of a married woman—and yet has kept the Diana-freshness—think how she must have shaken up such a man's inherited view of things! Mlle. Malo did far more than make Réchamp fall in love with her: she turned his world topsy-turvey, and prevented his ever again squeezing himself into his little old pigeon-hole of prejudices.

Before long they confessed their love—just like any young couple of Anglo-Saxons—and Jean went down to Réchamp to ask permission to marry her. Neither you nor I can quite enter into the state of mind of a young man of twenty-seven who has knocked about all over the globe, and been in and out of the usual sentimental coils—and who has to ask his parents' leave to get married! Don't let us try: it's no use. We should only end by picturing him as an incorrigible ninny. But there isn't a man in France who wouldn't feel it his duty to take that step, as Jean de Réchamp did. All we can do is to accept the premise and pass on.

Well—Jean went down and asked his father and his mother and his old grandmother if they would permit him to marry Mlle. Malo; and they all with one voice said they wouldn't. There was an uproar, in fact; and the old grandmother contributed the most piercing note to the concert. Marry Mlle. Malo! A young girl who lived alone! Travelled! Spent her time with foreigners—with musicians and painters! *A young girl!* Of course, if she had been a married woman—that is, a widow—much as they would have preferred a young girl for Jean, or even, if widow it had to be, a widow of another type—still, it was conceivable that, out of affection for him, they might have resigned themselves to his choice. But a young girl—bring such a young girl to Réchamp! Ask them to receive her under the same roof with their little Simone, their innocent Alain. . . .

He had a bad hour of it; but he held his own, keeping silent while they screamed, and stiffening as they began to wobble from exhaustion. Finally he took his mother apart, and tried to reason with her. His arguments were not much use, but his resolution impressed her, and he saw it. As for his father, nobody was afraid of Monsieur de Réchamp. When he said: "Never—never while I live, and there is a roof on Réchamp!" they all knew he had collapsed inside. But the grandmother was terrible. She was terrible because she was so old, and so clever at taking advantage of it. She could bring on a valvular heart-attack by just sitting still and holding her breath, as Jean and his mother had long since found out; and she always treated them to one when things weren't going as she liked. Madame de Réchamp promised Jean that she would intercede with her mother-in-law; but she hadn't much faith in the result, and when she came out of the old lady's room she whispered: "She's just sitting there holding her breath."

The next day Jean himself advanced to the attack. His grandmother was the most intelligent member of the family, and she knew he knew it, and liked him for having found it out; so when he had her alone she listened to him without resorting to any valvular tricks. "Of course," he explained, "you're much too clever not to understand that the times have changed, and manners with them, and that what a woman was criticised for doing yesterday she is ridiculed for not doing to-day. Nearly all the old social thou-shalt-nots have gone: intelligent people nowadays don't give a fig for them, and that simple fact has abolished them. They only existed as long as there was some one left for them to scare." His grandmother listened with a sparkle of admiration in her ancient eyes. "And of course," Jean pursued, "that can't be the real reason for your opposing my marriage—a marriage with a young girl you've always known, who has been received here—"

"Ah, that's it—we've always known her!" the old lady snapped him up.

"What of that? I don't see—"

"Of course you don't. You're here so little: you don't hear things. . . ."

"What things?"

"Things in the air . . . that blow about. . . . You were doing your military service at the time. . . ."

"At what time?"

She leaned forward and laid a warning hand on his arm. "Why did Corvenaire leave her all that money—*why*?"

"But why not—why shouldn't he?" Jean stammered, indignant. Then she unpacked her bag—a heap of vague insinuations, baseless conjectures, village tattle, all, at the last analysis, based, as he succeeded in proving, and making her own, on a word launched at random by a discharged maid-servant who had retailed her grievance to the curé's housekeeper. "Oh, she does what she likes with Monsieur le Marquis, the young miss! *She* knows how. . . ." On that single phrase the neighbourhood had raised a slander built of adamant.

Well, I'll give you an idea of what a determined fellow Réchamp is, when I tell you he pulled it down—or thought he did. He kept his temper, hunted up the servant's record, proved her a liar and dishonest, cast grave doubts on the discretion of the curé's housekeeper, and poured such a flood of ridicule over the whole flimsy fable, and those who had believed in it, that in sheer shame-facedness at having based her objection on such grounds, his grandmother gave way, and brought his parents toppling down with her.

All this happened a few weeks before the war, and soon afterward Mlle. Malo came down to Réchamp. Jean had insisted on her coming: he wanted her presence there, as his betrothed, to be known to the neighbourhood. As for her, she seemed delighted to come. I could see from Réchamp's tone, when he reached this part of his story, that he rather thought I should expect its heroine to have shown a becoming reluctance—to have stood on her dignity. He was distinctly relieved when he found I expected no such thing.

"She's simplicity itself—it's her great quality. Vain complications don't exist for her, because she doesn't see them . . . that's what my people can't be made to understand. . . ."

I gathered from the last phrase that the visit had not been a complete success, and this explained his having let out, when he first told me of his fears for his family, that he was sure Mlle. Malo would not have remained at Réchamp if she could help it. Oh, no, decidedly, the visit was not a success. . . .

"You see," he explained with a half-embarrassed smile, "it was partly her fault. Other girls as clever, but less—how shall I say?—less proud, would have adapted themselves, arranged things, avoided startling allusions. She wouldn't stoop to that; she talked to my family as naturally as she did to me. You can imagine for instance, the effect of her saying: 'One night, after a supper at Montmartre, I was walking home with two or three pals'—. It was her way of affirming her convictions, and I adored her for it—but I wished she wouldn't!"

And he depicted, to my joy, the neighbours rumbling over to call in heraldic barouches (the mothers alone—with embarrassed excuses for not bringing their daughters), and the agony of not knowing, till they were in the room, if Yvonne would receive them with lowered lids and folded hands, sitting by in a *pose de fiancée* while the elders talked; or if she would take the opportunity to air her views on the separation of Church and State, or the necessity of making divorce easier. "It's not," he explained, "that she really takes much interest in such questions: she's much more absorbed in her music and painting. But anything her eye lights on sets her mind dancing—as she said to me once: 'It's your mother's friends' bonnets that make me stand up for divorce!' " He broke off abruptly to add: "Good God, how far off all that nonsense seems!"

IV

The next day we started for Réchamp, not sure if we could get through, but bound to, anyhow! It was the coldest day we'd had, the sky steel, the earth iron, and a snow-wind howling down on us from the north. The Vosges are splendid in winter. In summer they are just plump puddingy hills; when the wind strips them they turn to mountains. And we seemed to have the whole country to ourselves—the black firs, the blue shadows, the beech-woods cracking and groaning like rigging, the bursts of snowy sunlight from cold clouds. Not a soul in sight except the sentinels guarding the railways, muffled to the eyes, or peering out of their huts of pine-boughs at the cross-roads. Every now and then we passed a long string of seventy-fives, or a train of supply waggons or army ambulances, and at intervals a cavalryman cantered by, his cloak bellied out by the gale; but of ordinary people about the common jobs of life, not a sign.

The sense of loneliness and remoteness that the absence of the civil population produces everywhere in eastern France is increased by the fact that all the names and distances on the mile-stones have been scratched out and the sign-posts at the cross-roads thrown down. It was done, presumably, to throw the enemy off the track in September: and the signs have never been put back. The result is that one is forever losing one's way, for the soldiers quartered in the district know only the names of their particular villages, and those on the march can tell you nothing about the places they are passing through. We had got badly off our road several times during the trip, but on the last day's run Réchamp was in his own country, and knew every yard of the way—or thought he did. We had turned off the main road, and were running along between rather featureless fields and woods, crossed by a good many wood-roads with nothing to distinguish them; but he continued to push ahead, saying: "We don't turn till we get to a manor-house on a stream, with a big paper-mill across the road." He went on to tell me that the mill-owners lived in the manor, and were old friends of his people: good old local stock, who had lived there for generations and done a lot for the neighbourhood.

"It's queer I don't see their village-steeple from this rise. The village is just beyond the house. How the devil could I have missed the turn?" We ran on a little farther, and suddenly he stopped the motor with a jerk. We were at a cross-road, with a stream running under the bank on our right. The place looked like an abandoned stoneyard. I never saw completer ruin. To the left, a fortified gate gaped on emptiness; to the right, a mill-wheel hung in the stream. Everything else was as flat as your dinner-table.

"Was this what you were trying to see from that rise?" I asked; and I saw a tear or two running down his face.

"They were the kindest people: their only son got himself shot the first month in Champagne—"

He had jumped out of the car and was standing staring at the level waste. "The house was there—there was a splendid lime in the court. I used to sit under it and have a glass of *vin gris de Lorraine* with the old people. . . . Over there, where that cinder-heap is, all their children are buried." He walked across to the grave-yard under a blackened wall—a bit of the apse of the vanished church—and sat down on a grave-stone. "If the devils have done this *here*—so close to us," he burst out, and covered his face.

An old woman walked toward us down the road. Réchamp jumped up and ran to meet her. "Why, Marie-Jeanne, what are you doing in these ruins?" The old woman looked at him with unastonished eyes. She seemed incapable of any surprise. "They left my house standing. I'm glad to see Monsieur," she simply said. We followed her to the one house left in the waste of stones. It was a two-roomed cottage, propped against a cow-stable, but fairly decent, with a curtain in the window and a cat on the sill. Réchamp caught me by the arm and pointed to the door-panel. "Oberst von Scharlach" was scrawled on it. He turned as white as your table-cloth, and hung on to me a minute; then he spoke to the old woman. "The officers were quartered here: that was the reason they spared your house?"

She nodded. "Yes: I was lucky. But the gentlemen must come in and have a mouthful."

Réchamp's finger was on the name. "And this one—this was their commanding officer?"

"I suppose so. Is it somebody's name?" She had evidently never speculated on the meaning of the scrawl that had saved her.

"You remember him—their captain? Was his name Scharlach?" Réchamp persisted.

Under its rich weathering the old woman's face grew as pale as his. "Yes, that was his name—I heard it often enough."

"Describe him, then. What was he like? Tall and fair? They're all that—but what else? What in particular?"

She hesitated, and then said: "This one wasn't fair. He was dark, and had a scar that drew up the left corner of his mouth."

Réchamp turned to me. "It's the same. I heard the men describing him at Moulins."

We followed the old woman into the house, and while she gave us some bread and wine she told us about the wrecking of the village and the factory. It was one of the most damnable stories I've heard yet. Put together the worst of the typical horrors and you'll have a fair idea of it. Murder, outrage, torture: Scharlach's programme seemed to be fairly comprehensive. She ended off by saying: "His orderly showed me a silver-mounted flute he always travelled with, and a beautiful paint-box mounted in silver too. Before he left he sat down on my door-step and made a painting of the ruins. . . ."

Soon after leaving this place of death we got to the second lines and our troubles began. We had to do a lot of talking to get through the lines, but what Réchamp had just seen had made him eloquent. Luckily, too, the ambulance doctor, a charming fellow, was short of tetanus-serum, and I had some left; and while I went over with him to the pine-branch hut where he hid his wounded I explained Réchamp's case, and implored him to get us through. Finally it was settled that we should leave the ambulance there—for in the lines the ban against motors is absolute—and drive the remaining twelve miles. A sergeant fished out of a farmhouse a toothless old woman with a furry horse harnessed to a two-wheeled trap, and we started off by round-about wood-tracks. The horse was in no hurry, nor the old lady either; for there were bits of road that were pretty steadily currycombed by shell, and it was to everybody's interest not to cross them before twilight. Jean de Réchamp's excitement seemed to have dropped: he sat beside me dumb as a fish, staring straight ahead of him. I didn't feel talkative either, for a word the doctor had let drop had left me thinking. "That poor old granny mind the shells? Not she!" he had said when our crazy chariot drove up. "She doesn't know them from snow-flakes any more. Nothing matters to her now, except trying to outwit a German. They're all like that where Scharlach's been—you've heard of him? She had only one boy—half-witted: he cocked a broom-handle at them, and they burnt him. Oh, she'll take you to Réchamp safe enough."

"Where Scharlach's been"—so he had been as close as this to Réchamp! I was wondering if Jean knew it, and if that had sealed his lips and given him that flinty profile. The old horse's woolly flanks jogged on under the bare branches and the old woman's bent back jogged in time with it. She never once spoke or looked around at us. "It isn't the noise we make that'll give us away," I said at last; and just then the old woman turned her head and pointed silently with the osier-twig she used as a whip. Just ahead of us lay a heap of ruins: the wreck, apparently, of a great château and its dependencies. "Lermont!" Réchamp exclaimed, turning white. He made a motion to jump out and then dropped back into the seat. "What's the use?" he muttered. He leaned forward and touched the old woman's shoulder.

"I hadn't heard of this—when did it happen?"

"In September."

"*They* did it?"

"Yes. Our wounded were there. It's like this everywhere in our country."

I saw Jean stiffening himself for the next question. "At Réchamp, too?"

She relapsed into indifference. "I haven't been as far as Réchamp."

"But you must have seen people who'd been there—you must have heard."

"I've heard the masters were still there—so there must be something standing. Maybe though," she reflected, "they're in the cellars. . . ."

We continued to jog on through the dusk.

V

"There's the steeple!" Réchamp burst out.

Through the dimness I couldn't tell which way to look; but I suppose in the thickest midnight he would have known where he was. He jumped from the trap and took the old horse by the bridle. I made out that he was guiding us into a long village street edged by houses in which every light was extinguished. The snow on the ground sent up a pale reflection, and I began to see the gabled outline of the houses and the steeple at the head of the street. The place seemed as calm and unchanged as if the sound of war had never reached it. In the open space at the end of the village Réchamp checked the horse.

"The elm—there's the old elm in front of the church!" he shouted in a voice like a boy's. He ran back and caught me by both hands. "It was true, then—nothing's touched!" The old woman asked: "Is this Réchamp?" and he went back to the horse's head and turned the trap toward a tall gate between park walls. The gate was barred and padlocked, and not a gleam showed through the shutters of the porter's lodge; but Réchamp, after listening a minute or two, gave a low call twice repeated, and presently the lodge door opened, and an old man peered out. Well—I leave you to brush in the rest. Old family servant, tears and hugs and so on. I know you affect to scorn the cinema, and this was it, tremolo and all. Hang it! This war's going to teach us not to be afraid of the obvious.

We piled into the trap and drove down a long avenue to the house. Black as the grave, of course; but in another minute the door opened, and there, in the hall, was another servant, screening a light—and then more doors opened on another cinema-scene: fine old drawing-room with family portraits, shaded lamp, domestic group about the fire. They evidently thought it was the servant coming to announce dinner, and not a head turned at our approach. I could see them all over Jean's shoulder: a grey-haired lady knitting with stiff fingers, an old gentleman with a high nose and a weak chin sitting in a big carved armchair and looking more like a portrait than the portraits; a pretty girl at his feet, with a dog's head in her lap, and another girl, who had a Red Cross on her sleeve, at the table with a book. She had been reading aloud in a rich veiled voice, and broke off her last phrase to say: "Dinner. . . ." Then she looked up and saw Jean. Her dark face remained perfectly calm, but she lifted her hand in a just perceptible gesture of warning, and instantly understanding he drew back and pushed the servant forward in his place.

"Madame la Comtesse—it is some one outside asking for Mademoiselle."

The dark girl jumped up and ran out into the hall. I remember wondering: "Is it because she wants to have him to herself first—or because she's afraid of their being startled?" I wished myself out of the way, but she took no notice of me, and going straight to Jean flung her arms about him. I was behind him and could see her hands about his neck, and her brown fingers tightly locked. There wasn't much doubt about those two. . . .

The next minute she caught sight of me, and I was being rapidly tested by a pair of the finest eyes I ever saw—I don't apply the term to their setting, though that was fine too, but to the look itself, a look at once warm and resolute, all-promising and all-penetrating. I really can't do with fewer adjectives. . . .

Réchamp explained me, and she was full of thanks and welcome; not excessive, but—well, I don't know—eloquent! She gave every intonation all it could carry, and without the least emphasis: that's the wonder.

She went back to "prepare" the parents, as they say in melodrama; and in a minute or two we followed. What struck me first was that these insignificant and inadequate people had the command of the grand gesture—had *la ligne*. The mother had laid aside her knitting—*not* dropped it—and stood waiting with open arms. But even in clasping her son she seemed to include me in her welcome. I don't know how to describe it; but they never let me feel I was in the way. I suppose that's part of what you call distinction; knowing instinctively how to deal with unusual moments.

All the while, I was looking about me at the fine secure old room, in which nothing seemed altered or disturbed, the portraits smiling from the walls, the servants beaming in the doorway—and wondering how such things could have survived in the trail of death and havoc we had been following.

The same thought had evidently struck Jean, for he dropped his sister's hand and turned to gaze about him too.

"Then nothing's touched—*nothing*? I don't understand," he stammered.

Monsieur de Réchamp raised himself majestically from his chair, crossed the room and lifted Yvonne Malo's hand to his lips. "Nothing is touched—thanks to this hand and this brain."

Madame de Réchamp was shining on her son through tears. "Ah, yes—we owe it all to Yvonne."

"All, all! Grandmamma will tell you!" Simone chimed in; and Yvonne, brushing aside their praise with a half-impatient laugh, said to her betrothed: "But your grandmother! You must go up to her at once."

A wonderful specimen, that grandmother: I was taken to see her after dinner. She sat by the fire in a bare panelled bed-room, bolt upright in an armchair with ears, a knitting-table at her elbow with a shaded candle on it. She was even more withered and ancient than she looked in her photograph, and I judge she'd never been pretty; but she somehow made me feel as if I'd got through with prettiness. I don't know exactly what she reminded me of: a dried bouquet, or something rich and clovy that had turned brittle through long keeping in a sandal-wood box. I suppose her sandal-wood box had been Good Society. Well, I had a rare evening with her. Jean and his parents were called down to see the curé, who had hurried over to the château when he heard of the young man's arrival; and the old lady asked me to stay on and chat with her. She related their experiences with uncanny detachment, seeming chiefly to resent the indignity of having been made to descend into the cellar—"to avoid French shells, if you'll believe it: the Germans had the decency not to bombard us," she observed impartially. I was so struck by the absence of rancour in her tone that finally, out of sheer curiosity, I made an allusion to the horror of having the enemy under one's roof. "Oh, I might almost say I didn't see them," she returned. "I never go downstairs any longer; and they didn't do me the honour of coming beyond my door. A glance sufficed them—an old woman like me!" she added with a phosphorescent gleam of coquetry.

"But they searched the château, surely?"

"Oh, a mere form; they were very decent—very decent," she almost snapped at me. "There was a first moment, of course, when we feared it might be hard to get Monsieur de Réchamp away with my young grandson; but Mlle. Malo managed that very cleverly. They slipped off while the officers were dining." She looked at me with the smile of some arch old lady in a Louis XV pastel. "My grandson Jean's fiancée is a very clever young woman: in my time no young girl would have been so sure of herself, so cool and quick. After all, there is something to be said for the new way of bringing up girls. My poor daughter-in-law, at Yvonne's age, was a bleating baby: she is so still, at times. The convent doesn't develop character. I'm glad Yvonne was not brought up in a convent." And this champion of tradition smiled on me more intensely.

Little by little I got from her the story of the German approach: the distracted fugitives pouring in from the villages north of Réchamp, the sound of distant cannonading, and suddenly, the next afternoon, after a reassuring lull, the sight of a single spiked helmet at the end of the drive. In a few minutes a dozen followed: mostly officers; then all at once the place hummed with them. There were supply waggons and motors in the court, bundles of hay, stacks of rifles, artillerymen unharnessing and rubbing down their horses. The crowd was hot and thirsty, and in a moment the old lady, to her amazement, saw wine and cider being handed about by the Réchamp servants. "Or so at least I was told," she added, correcting herself, "for it's not my habit to look out of the window. I simply sat here and waited." Her seat, as she spoke, might have been a curule chair.

Downstairs, it appeared, Mlle. Malo had instantly taken her measures. *She* didn't sit and wait. Surprised in the garden with Simone, she had made the girl walk quietly back to the house and receive the officers with her on the doorstep. The officer in command—captain, or whatever he was—had arrived in a bad temper, cursing and swearing, and growling out menaces about spies. The day was intensely hot, and possibly he had had too much wine. At any rate Mlle. Malo had known how to "put him in his place"; and when he and the other officers entered they found the dining-table set out with refreshing drinks and cigars, melons, strawberries and iced coffee. "The clever creature! She even remembered that they liked whipped cream with their coffee!"

The effect had been miraculous. The captain—what was his name? Yes, Charlot, Charlot—Captain Charlot had been specially complimentary on the subject of the whipped cream and the cigars. Then he asked to see the other members of the family, and Mlle. Malo told him there were only two— two old women! "He made a face at that, and said all the same he should like to meet them; and she answered: 'One is

your hostess, the Comtesse de Réchamp, who is ill in bed'—
for my poor daughter-in-law was lying in bed paralyzed with
rheumatism—'and the other her mother-in-law, a very old
lady who never leaves her room.' "

"But aren't there any men in the family?" he had then
asked; and she had said: "Oh yes—two. The Comte de
Réchamp and his son."

"And where are they?"

"In England. Monsieur de Réchamp went a month ago to
take his son on a trip."

The officer said: "I was told they were here to-day"; and
Mlle. Malo replied: "You had better have the house searched
and satisfy yourself."

He laughed and said: "The idea *had* occurred to me." She
laughed also, and sitting down at the piano struck a few
chords. Captain Charlot, who had his foot on the threshold,
turned back—Simone had described the scene to her grandmother afterward. "Some of the brutes, it seems, are musical," the old lady explained; "and this was one of them. While
he was listening, some soldiers appeared in the court carrying
another who seemed to be wounded. It turned out afterward
that he'd been climbing a garden wall after fruit, and cut himself on the broken glass at the top; but the blood was
enough—they raised the usual dreadful outcry about an am-
bush, and a lieutenant clattered into the room where Mlle.
Malo sat playing Stravinsky." The old lady paused for her effect, and I was conscious of giving her all she wanted.

"Well—?"

"Will you believe it? It seems she looked at her watch-
bracelet and said: 'Do you gentlemen dress for dinner? *I* do—
but we've still time for a little Moussorgsky'—or whatever
wild names they call themselves—'if you'll make those people
outside hold their tongues.' Our captain looked at her again,
laughed, gave an order that sent the lieutenant right about,
and sat down beside her at the piano. Imagine my stupour,
dear sir: the drawing-room is directly under this room, and in
a moment I heard two voices coming up to me. Well, I won't
conceal from you that his was the finest. But then I always
adored a barytone." She folded her shrivelled hands among
their laces. "After that, the Germans were *très bien—très bien*.

They stayed two days, and there was nothing to complain of. Indeed, when the second detachment came, a week later, they never even entered the gates. Orders had been left that they should be quartered elsewhere. Of course we were lucky in happening on a man of the world like Captain Charlot."

"Yes, very lucky. It's odd, though, his having a French name."

"Very. It probably accounts for his breeding," she answered placidly; and left me marvelling at the happy remoteness of old age.

VI

The next morning early Jean de Réchamp came to my room. I was struck at once by the change in him: he had lost his first glow, and seemed nervous and hesitating. I knew what he had come for: to ask me to postpone our departure for another twenty-four hours. By rights we should have been off that morning; but there had been a sharp brush a few kilometres away, and a couple of poor devils had been brought to the château whom it would have been death to carry farther that day and criminal not to hurry to a base hospital the next morning. "We've simply *got* to stay till to-morrow: you're in luck," I said laughing.

He laughed back, but with a frown that made me feel I had been a brute to speak in that way of a respite due to such a cause.

"The men will pull through, you know—trust Mlle. Malo for that!" I said.

His frown did not lift. He went to the window and drummed on the pane.

"Do you see that breach in the wall, down there behind the trees? It's the only scratch the place has got. And think of Lermont! It's incredible—simply incredible!"

"But it's like that everywhere, isn't it? Everything depends on the officer in command."

"Yes: that's it, I suppose. I haven't had time to get a consecutive account of what happened: they're all too excited. Mlle. Malo is the only person who can tell me exactly how things went." He swung about on me. "Look here, it sounds absurd, what I'm asking; but try to get me an hour alone with her, will you?"

I stared at the request, and he went on, still half-laughing: "You see, they all hang on me; my father and mother, Simone, the curé, the servants. The whole village is coming up presently: they want to stuff their eyes full of me. It's natural enough, after living here all these long months cut off from everything. But the result is I haven't said two words to her yet."

"Well, you shall," I declared; and with an easier smile he turned to hurry down to a mass of thanksgiving which the curé was to celebrate in the private chapel. "My parents wanted it," he explained; "and after that the whole village will be upon us. But later—"

"Later I'll effect a diversion; I swear I will," I assured him.

By daylight, decidedly, Mlle. Malo was less handsome than in the evening. It was my first thought as she came toward me, that afternoon, under the limes. Jean was still indoors, with his people, receiving the village; I rather wondered she hadn't stayed there with him. Theoretically, her place was at his side; but I knew she was a young woman who didn't live by rule, and she had already struck me as having a distaste for superfluous expenditures of feeling.

Yes, she was less effective by day. She looked older for one thing; her face was pinched, and a little sallow and for the first time I noticed that her cheek-bones were too high. Her eyes, too, had lost their velvet depth: fine eyes still, but not unfathomable. But the smile with which she greeted me was charming: it ran over her tired face like a lamp-lighter kindling flames as he runs.

"I was looking for you," she said. "Shall we have a little talk? The reception is sure to last another hour: every one of the villagers is going to tell just what happened to him or her when the Germans came."

"And you've run away from the ceremony?"

"I'm a trifle tired of hearing the same adventures retold," she said, still smiling.

"But I thought there *were* no adventures—that that was the wonder of it?"

She shrugged. "It makes their stories a little dull, at any rate; we've not a hero or a martyr to show." She had strolled farther from the house as we talked, leading me in the direction of a bare horse-chestnut walk that led toward the park.

"Of course Jean's got to listen to it all, poor boy; but *I* needn't," she explained.

I didn't know exactly what to answer and we walked on a little way in silence; then she said: "If you'd carried him off this morning he would have escaped all this fuss." After a pause she added slowly: "On the whole, it might have been as well."

"To carry him off?"

"Yes." She stopped and looked at me. "I wish you *would*."

"Would?—Now?"

"Yes, now: as soon as you can. He's really not strong yet— he's drawn and nervous." ("So are you," I thought.) "And the excitement is greater than you can perhaps imagine—"

I gave her back her look. "Why, I think I *can* imagine. . . ."

She coloured up through her sallow skin and then laughed away her blush. "Oh, I don't mean the excitement of seeing *me*! But his parents, his grandmother, the curé, all the old associations—"

I considered for a moment; then I said: "As a matter of fact, you're about the only person he *hasn't* seen."

She checked a quick answer on her lips, and for a moment or two we faced each other silently. A sudden sense of intimacy, of complicity almost, came over me. What was it that the girl's silence was crying out to me?

"If I take him away now he won't have seen you at all," I continued.

She stood under the bare trees, keeping her eyes on me. "Then take him away now!" she retorted; and as she spoke I saw her face change, decompose into deadly apprehension and as quickly regain its usual calm. From where she stood she faced the courtyard, and glancing in the same direction I saw the throng of villagers coming out of the châteu. "Take him away—take him away at once!" she passionately commanded; and the next minute Jean de Réchamp detached himself from the group and began to limp down the walk in our direction.

What was I to do? I can't exaggerate the sense of urgency Mlle. Malo's appeal gave me, or my faith in her sincerity. No one who had seen her meeting with Réchamp the night before could have doubted her feeling for him: if she wanted him away it was not because she did not delight in his presence. Even now, as he approached, I saw her face veiled by a faint mist of emotion: it was like watching a fruit ripen under a midsummer sun. But she turned sharply from the house and began to walk on.

"Can't you give me a hint of your reason?" I suggested as I followed.

"My reason? I've given it!" I suppose I looked incredulous, for she added in a lower voice: "I don't want him to hear—yet—about all the horrors."

"The horrors? I thought there had been none here."

"All around us—" Her voice became a whisper. "Our friends . . . our neighbours . . . every one. . . ."

"He can hardly avoid hearing of that, can he? And besides, since you're all safe and happy. . . . Look here," I broke off, "he's coming after us. Don't we look as if we were running away?"

She turned around, suddenly paler; and in a stride or two Réchamp was at our side. He was pale too; and before I could find a pretext for slipping away he had begun to speak. But I saw at once that he didn't know or care if I was there.

"What was the name of the officer in command who was quartered here?" he asked, looking straight at the girl.

She raised her eye-brows slightly. "Do you mean to say that after listening for three hours to every inhabitant of Réchamp you haven't found that out?"

"They all call him something different. My grandmother says he had a French name: she calls him Charlot."

"Your grandmother was never taught German: his name was the Oberst von Scharlach." She did not remember my presence either: the two were still looking straight in each other's eyes.

Réchamp had grown white to the lips: he was rigid with the effort to control himself.

"Why didn't you tell me it was Scharlach who was here?" he brought out at last in a low voice.

She turned her eyes in my direction. "I was just explaining to Mr. Greer—"

"To Mr. Greer?" He looked at me too, half-angrily.

"I know the stories that are about," she continued quietly; "and I was saying to your friend that, since we had been so happy as to be spared, it seemed useless to dwell on what has happened elsewhere."

"Damn what happened elsewhere! I don't yet know what happened here."

I put a hand on his arm. Mlle. Malo was looking hard at me, but I wouldn't let her see I knew it. "I'm going to leave you to hear the whole story now," I said to Réchamp.

"But there isn't any story for him to hear!" she broke in. She pointed at the serene front of the château, looking out across its gardens to the unscarred fields. "We're safe; the place is untouched. Why brood on other horrors—horrors we were powerless to help?"

Réchamp held his ground doggedly. "But the man's name is a curse and an abomination. Wherever he went he spread ruin."

"So they say. Mayn't there be a mistake? Legends grow up so quickly in these dreadful times. Here—" she looked about her again at the peaceful scene—"here he behaved as you see. For heaven's sake be content with that!"

"Content?" He passed his hand across his forehead. "I'm blind with joy . . . or should be, if only . . ."

She looked at me entreatingly, almost desperately, and I took hold of Réchamp's arm with a warning pressure. "My dear fellow, don't you see that Mlle. Malo has been under a great strain? *La joie fait peur*—that's the trouble with both of you!"

He lowered his head. "Yes, I suppose it is." He took her hand and kissed it. "I beg your pardon. Greer's right: we're both on edge."

"Yes: I'll leave you for a little while, if you and Mr. Greer will excuse me." She included us both in a quiet look that seemed to me extremely noble, and walked slowly away toward the château. Réchamp stood gazing after her for a moment; then he dropped down on one of the benches at the edge of the path. He covered his face with his hands. "Scharlach—Scharlach!" I heard him repeat.

We sat there side by side for ten minutes or more without speaking. Finally I said: "Look here, Réchamp—she's right and you're wrong. I shall be sorry I brought you here if you don't see it before it's too late."

His face was still hidden; but presently he dropped his hands and answered me. "I do see. She's saved everything for me—my people and my house, and the ground we're standing on. And I worship it because she walks on it!"

"And so do your people: the war's done that for you, anyhow," I reminded him.

VII

The morning after we were off before dawn. Our time allowance was up, and it was thought advisable, on account of our wounded, to slip across the exposed bit of road in the dark.

Mlle. Malo was downstairs when we started, pale in her white dress, but calm and active. We had borrowed a farmer's cart in which our two men could be laid on a mattress, and she had stocked our trap with food and remedies. Nothing seemed to have been forgotten. While I was settling the men I suppose Réchamp turned back into the hall to bid her good-bye; anyhow, when she followed him out a moment later he looked quieter and less strained. He had taken leave of his parents and his sister upstairs, and Yvonne Malo stood alone in the dark doorway, watching us as we drove away.

There was not much talk between us during our slow drive back to the lines. We had to go at a snail's pace, for the roads were rough; and there was time for meditation. I knew well enough what my companion was thinking about and my own thoughts ran on the same lines. Though the story of the German occupation of Réchamp had been retold to us a dozen times the main facts did not vary. There were little discrepancies of detail, and gaps in the narrative here and there; but all the household, from the astute ancestress to the last bewildered pantry-boy, were at one in saying that Mlle. Malo's coolness and courage had saved the château and the village. The officer in command had arrived full of threats and insolence: Mlle. Malo had placated and disarmed him, turned

his suspicions to ridicule, entertained him and his comrades at
dinner, and contrived during that time—or rather while they
were making music afterward (which they did for half the
night, it seemed)—that Monsieur de Réchamp and Alain
should slip out of the cellar in which they had been hidden,
gain the end of the gardens through an old hidden passage,
and get off in the darkness. Meanwhile Simone had been safe
upstairs with her mother and grandmother, and none of the
officers lodged in the château had—after a first hasty inspection—set foot in any part of the house but the wing assigned
to them. On the third morning they had left, and Scharlach,
before going, had put in Mlle. Malo's hands a letter requesting whatever officer should follow him to show every consideration to the family of the Comte de Réchamp, and if
possible—owing to the grave illness of the Countess—avoid
taking up quarters in the château: a request which had been
scrupulously observed.

Such were the amazing but undisputed facts over which
Réchamp and I, in our different ways, were now pondering.
He hardly spoke, and when he did it was only to make some
casual reference to the road or to our wounded soldiers; but
all the while I sat at his side I kept hearing the echo of the
question he was inwardly asking himself, and hoping to God
he wouldn't put it to me. . . .

It was nearly noon when we finally reached the lines, and
the men had to have a rest before we could start again; but a
couple of hours later we landed them safely at the base hospital. From there we had intended to go back to Paris; but as
we were starting there came an unexpected summons to another point of the front, where there had been a successful
night-attack, and a lot of Germans taken in a blown-up
trench. The place was fifty miles away, and off my beat, but
the number of wounded on both sides was exceptionally
heavy, and all the available ambulances had already started. An
urgent call had come for more, and there was nothing for it
but to go; so we went.

We found things in a bad mess at the second line shanty-
hospital where they were dumping the wounded as fast as
they could bring them in. At first we were told that none
were fit to be carried farther that night; and after we had

done what we could we went off to hunt up a shake-down in the village. But a few minutes later an orderly overtook us with a message from the surgeon. There was a German with an abdominal wound who was in a bad way, but might be saved by an operation if he could be got back to the base before midnight. Would we take him at once and then come back for others?

There is only one answer to such requests, and a few minutes later we were back at the hospital, and the wounded man was being carried out on a stretcher. In the shaky lantern gleam I caught a glimpse of a livid face and a torn uniform, and saw that he was an officer, and nearly done for. Réchamp had climbed to the box, and seemed not to be noticing what was going on at the back of the motor. I understood that he loathed the job, and wanted not to see the face of the man we were carrying; so when we had got him settled I jumped into the ambulance beside him and called out to Réchamp that we were ready. A second later an *infirmier* ran up with a little packet and pushed it into my hand. "His papers," he explained. I pocketed them and pulled the door shut, and we were off.

The man lay motionless on his back, conscious, but desperately weak. Once I turned my pocket-lamp on him and saw that he was young—about thirty—with damp dark hair and a thin face. He had received a flesh-wound above the eyes, and his forehead was bandaged, but the rest of the face uncovered. As the light fell on him he lifted his eyelids and looked at me: his look was inscrutable.

For half an hour or so I sat there in the dark, the sense of that face pressing close on me. It was a damnable face— meanly handsome, basely proud. In my one glimpse of it I had seen that the man was suffering atrociously, but as we slid along through the night he made no sound. At length the motor stopped with a violent jerk that drew a single moan from him. I turned the light on him, but he lay perfectly still, lips and lids shut, making no sign; and I jumped out and ran round to the front to see what had happened.

The motor had stopped for lack of gasolene and was stock still in the deep mud. Réchamp muttered something about a leak in his tank. As he bent over it, the lantern flame struck up into his face, which was set and business-like. It struck me vaguely that he showed no particular surprise.

"What's to be done?" I asked.

"I think I can tinker it up; but we've got to have more essence to go on with."

I stared at him in despair: it was a good hour's walk back to the lines, and we weren't so sure of getting any gasolene when we got there! But there was no help for it; and as Réchamp was dead lame, no alternative but for me to go.

I opened the ambulance door, gave another look at the motionless man inside and took out a remedy which I handed over to Réchamp with a word of explanation. "You know how to give a hypo? Keep a close eye on him and pop this in if you see a change—not otherwise."

He nodded. "Do you suppose he'll die?" he asked below his breath.

"No, I don't. If we get him to the hospital before morning I think he'll pull through."

"Oh, all right." He unhooked one of the motor lanterns and handed it over to me. "I'll do my best," he said as I turned away.

Getting back to the lines through that pitch-black forest, and finding somebody to bring the gasolene back for me was about the weariest job I ever tackled. I couldn't imagine why it wasn't daylight when we finally got to the place where I had left the motor. It seemed to me as if I had been gone twelve hours when I finally caught sight of the grey bulk of the car through the thinning darkness.

Réchamp came forward to meet us, and took hold of my arm as I was opening the door of the car. "The man's dead," he said.

I had lifted up my pocket-lamp, and its light fell on Réchamp's face, which was perfectly composed, and seemed less gaunt and drawn than at any time since we had started on our trip.

"Dead? Why—how? What happened? Did you give him the hypodermic?" I stammered, taken aback.

"No time to. He died in a minute."

"How do you know he did? Were you with him?"

"Of course I was with him," Réchamp retorted, with a sudden harshness which made me aware that I had grown harsh myself. But I had been almost sure the man wasn't anywhere near death when I left him. I opened the door of the ambulance and climbed in with my lantern. He didn't appear to have moved, but he was dead sure enough—had been for two or three hours, by the feel of him. It must have happened not long after I left. . . . Well, I'm not a doctor, anyhow. . . .

I don't think Réchamp and I exchanged a word during the rest of that run. But it was my fault and not his if we didn't. By the mere rub of his sleeve against mine as we sat side by side on the motor I knew he was conscious of no bar between us: he had somehow got back, in the night's interval, to a state of wholesome stolidity, while I, on the contrary, was tingling all over with exposed nerves.

I was glad enough when we got back to the base at last, and the grim load we carried was lifted out and taken into the hospital. Réchamp waited in the courtyard beside his car, lighting a cigarette in the cold early sunlight; but I followed the bearers and the surgeon into the whitewashed room where the dead man was laid out to be undressed. I had a burning spot at the pit of my stomach while his clothes were ripped off him and the bandages undone: I couldn't take my eyes from the surgeon's face. But the surgeon, with a big batch of wounded on his hands, was probably thinking more of the living than the dead; and besides, we were near the front, and the body before him was an enemy's.

He finished his examination and scribbled something in a note-book. "Death must have taken place nearly five hours ago," he merely remarked: it was the conclusion I had already come to myself.

"And how about the papers?" the surgeon continued. "You have them, I suppose? This way, please."

We left the half-stripped body on the blood-stained oil-cloth, and he led me into an office where a functionary sat behind a littered desk.

"The papers? Thank you. You haven't examined them? Let us see, then."

I handed over the leather note-case I had thrust into my pocket the evening before, and saw for the first time its silver-edged corners and the coronet in one of them. The official took out the papers and spread them on the desk between us. I watched him absently while he did so.

Suddenly he uttered an exclamation. "Ah—that's a haul!" he said, and pushed a bit of paper toward me. On it was engraved the name: Oberst Graf Benno von Scharlach. . . .

"A good riddance," said the surgeon over my shoulder.

I went back to the courtyard and saw Réchamp still smoking his cigarette in the cold sunlight. I don't suppose I'd been in the hospital ten minutes; but I felt as old as Methuselah.

My friend greeted me with a smile. "Ready for breakfast?" he said, and a little chill ran down my spine. . . . But I said: "Oh, all right—come along. . . ."

For, after all, I *knew* there wasn't a paper of any sort on that man when he was lifted into my ambulance the night before: the French officials attend to their business too carefully for me not to have been sure of that. And there wasn't the least shred of evidence to prove that he hadn't died of his wounds during the unlucky delay in the forest; or that Réchamp had known his tank was leaking when we started out from the lines.

"I could do with a *café complet*, couldn't you?" Réchamp suggested, looking straight at me with his good blue eyes; and arm in arm we started off to hunt for the inn. . . .

Autres Temps . . .

M RS. LIDCOTE, as the huge menacing mass of New York defined itself far off across the waters, shrank back into her corner of the deck and sat listening with a kind of unreasoning terror to the steady onward drive of the screws.

She had set out on the voyage quietly enough,—in what she called her "reasonable" mood,—but the week at sea had given her too much time to think of things and had left her too long alone with the past.

When she was alone, it was always the past that occupied her. She couldn't get away from it, and she didn't any longer care to. During her long years of exile she had made her terms with it, had learned to accept the fact that it would always be there, huge, obstructing, encumbering, bigger and more dominant than anything the future could ever conjure up. And, at any rate, she was sure of it, she understood it, knew how to reckon with it; she had learned to screen and manage and protect it as one does an afflicted member of one's family.

There had never been any danger of her being allowed to forget the past. It looked out at her from the face of every acquaintance, it appeared suddenly in the eyes of strangers when a word enlightened them: "Yes, *the* Mrs. Lidcote, don't you know?" It had sprung at her the first day out, when, across the dining-room, from the captain's table, she had seen Mrs. Lorin Boulger's revolving eye-glass pause and the eye behind it grow as blank as a dropped blind. The next day, of course, the captain had asked: "You know your ambassadress, Mrs. Boulger?" and she had replied that, No, she seldom left Florence, and hadn't been to Rome for more than a day since the Boulgers had been sent to Italy. She was so used to these phrases that it cost her no effort to repeat them. And the captain had promptly changed the subject.

No, she didn't, as a rule, mind the past, because she was used to it and understood it. It was a great concrete fact in her path that she had to walk around every time she moved in any direction. But now, in the light of the unhappy event that had summoned her from Italy,—the sudden unanticipated news of her daughter's divorce from Horace Pursh and remarriage with Wilbour Barkley—the past, her own poor miserable past, started up at her with eyes of accusation, became, to her disordered fancy, like the afflicted relative suddenly breaking away from nurses and keepers and publicly parading the horror and misery she had, all the long years, so patiently screened and secluded.

Yes, there it had stood before her through the agitated weeks since the news had come—during her interminable journey from India, where Leila's letter had overtaken her, and the feverish halt in her apartment in Florence, where she had had to stop and gather up her possessions for a fresh start—there it had stood grinning at her with a new balefulness which seemed to say: "Oh, but you've got to look at me *now*, because I'm not only your own past but Leila's present."

Certainly it was a master-stroke of those arch-ironists of the shears and spindle to duplicate her own story in her daughter's. Mrs. Lidcote had always somewhat grimly fancied that, having so signally failed to be of use to Leila in other ways, she would at least serve her as a warning. She had even abstained from defending herself, from making the best of her case, had stoically refused to plead extenuating circumstances, lest Leila's impulsive sympathy should lead to deductions that might react disastrously on her own life. And now that very thing had happened, and Mrs. Lidcote could hear the whole of New York saying with one voice: "Yes, Leila's done just what her mother did. With such an example what could you expect?"

Yet if she had been an example, poor woman, she had been an awful one; she had been, she would have supposed, of more use as a deterrent than a hundred blameless mothers as incentives. For how could any one who had seen anything of her life in the last eighteen years have had the courage to repeat so disastrous an experiment?

Well, logic in such cases didn't count, example didn't count, nothing probably counted but having the same impulses in the blood; and that was the dark inheritance she had bestowed upon her daughter. Leila hadn't consciously copied her; she had simply "taken after" her, had been a projection of her own long-past rebellion.

Mrs. Lidcote had deplored, when she started, that the *Utopia* was a slow steamer, and would take eight full days to bring her to her unhappy daughter; but now, as the moment of reunion approached, she would willingly have turned the boat about and fled back to the high seas. It was not only because she felt still so unprepared to face what New York had in store for her, but because she needed more time to dispose of what the *Utopia* had already given her. The past was bad enough, but the present and future were worse, because they were less comprehensible, and because, as she grew older, surprises and inconsequences troubled her more than the worst certainties.

There was Mrs. Boulger, for instance. In the light, or rather the darkness, of new developments, it might really be that Mrs. Boulger had not meant to cut her, but had simply failed to recognize her. Mrs. Lidcote had arrived at this hypothesis simply by listening to the conversation of the persons sitting next to her on deck—two lively young women with the latest Paris hats on their heads and the latest New York ideas in them. These ladies, as to whom it would have been impossible for a person with Mrs. Lidcote's old-fashioned categories to determine whether they were married or unmarried, "nice" or "horrid," or any one or other of the definite things which young women, in her youth and her society, were conveniently assumed to be, had revealed a familiarity with the world of New York that, again according to Mrs. Lidcote's traditions, should have implied a recognized place in it. But in the present fluid state of manners what did anything imply except what their hats implied—that no one could tell what was coming next?

They seemed, at any rate, to frequent a group of idle and opulent people who executed the same gestures and revolved on the same pivots as Mrs. Lidcote's daughter and her friends: their Coras, Matties and Mabels seemed at any moment likely to reveal familiar patronymics, and once one of the speakers, summing up a discussion of which Mrs. Lidcote had missed the beginning, had affirmed with headlong confidence: "Leila? Oh, *Leila's* all right."

Could it be *her* Leila, the mother had wondered, with a sharp thrill of apprehension? If only they would mention surnames! But their talk leaped elliptically from allusion to allusion, their unfinished sentences dangled over bottomless pits of conjecture, and they gave their bewildered hearer the impression not so much of talking only of their intimates, as of being intimate with every one alive.

Her old friend Franklin Ide could have told her, perhaps; but here was the last day of the voyage, and she hadn't yet found courage to ask him. Great as had been the joy of discovering his name on the passenger-list and seeing his friendly bearded face in the throng against the taffrail at Cherbourg, she had as yet said nothing to him except, when they had met: "Of course I'm going out to Leila."

She had said nothing to Franklin Ide because she had always instinctively shrunk from taking him into her confidence. She was sure he felt sorry for her, sorrier perhaps than any one had ever felt; but he had always paid her the supreme tribute of not showing it. His attitude allowed her to imagine that compassion was not the basis of his feeling for her, and it was part of her joy in his friendship that it was the one relation seemingly unconditioned by her state, the only one in which she could think and feel and behave like any other woman.

Now, however, as the problem of New York loomed nearer, she began to regret that she had not spoken, had not at least questioned him about the hints she had gathered on the way. He did not know the two ladies next to her, he did not even, as it chanced, know Mrs. Lorin Boulger; but he knew New York, and New York was the sphinx whose riddle she must read or perish.

Almost as the thought passed through her mind his stooping shoulders and grizzled head detached themselves against the blaze of light in the west, and he sauntered down the empty deck and dropped into the chair at her side.

"You're expecting the Barkleys to meet you, I suppose?" he asked.

It was the first time she had heard any one pronounce her daughter's new name, and it occurred to her that her friend, who was shy and inarticulate, had been trying to say it all the way over and had at last shot it out at her only because he felt it must be now or never.

"I don't know. I cabled, of course. But I believe she's at— they're at—*his* place somewhere."

"Oh, Barkley's; yes, near Lenox, isn't it? But she's sure to come to town to meet you."

He said it so easily and naturally that her own constraint was relieved, and suddenly, before she knew what she meant to do, she had burst out: "She may dislike the idea of seeing people."

Ide, whose absent short-sighted gaze had been fixed on the slowly gliding water, turned in his seat to stare at his companion.

"Who? Leila?" he said with an incredulous laugh.

Mrs. Lidcote flushed to her faded hair and grew pale again. "It took *me* a long time—to get used to it," she said.

His look grew gently commiserating. "I think you'll find—" he paused for a word—"that things are different now—altogether easier."

"That's what I've been wondering—ever since we started." She was determined now to speak. She moved nearer, so that their arms touched, and she could drop her voice to a murmur. "You see, it all came on me in a flash. My going off to India and Siam on that long trip kept me away from letters for weeks at a time; and she didn't want to tell me beforehand—oh, I understand *that*, poor child! You know how good she's always been to me; how she's tried to spare me. And she knew, of course, what a state of horror I'd be in. She knew I'd rush off to her at once and try to stop it. So she never gave me a hint of anything, and she even managed to muzzle Susy Suffern—you know Susy is the one of the family who keeps me informed about things at home. I don't yet see how she prevented Susy's telling me; but she did. And her first letter, the one I got up at Bangkok, simply said the thing was over—the divorce, I mean—and that the very next day she'd—well, I suppose there was no use waiting; and *he* seems to have behaved as well as possible, to have wanted to marry her as much as—"

"Who? Barkley?" he helped her out. "I should say so! Why what do you suppose—" He interrupted himself. "He'll be devoted to her, I assure you."

"Oh, of course; I'm sure he will. He's written me—really beautifully. But it's a terrible strain on a man's devotion. I'm not sure that Leila realizes—"

Ide sounded again his little reassuring laugh. "I'm not sure that you realize. *They're* all right."

It was the very phrase that the young lady in the next seat had applied to the unknown "Leila," and its recurrence on Ide's lips flushed Mrs. Lidcote with fresh courage.

"I wish I knew just what you mean. The two young women next to me—the ones with the wonderful hats—have been talking in the same way."

"What? About Leila?"

"About *a* Leila; I fancied it might be mine. And about society in general. All their friends seem to be divorced; some of them seem to announce their engagements before they get their decree. One of them—*her* name was Mabel—as far as I could make out, her husband found out that she meant to divorce him by noticing that she wore a new engagement-ring."

"Well, you see Leila did everything 'regularly,' as the French say," Ide rejoined.

"Yes; but are these people in society? The people my neighbours talk about?"

He shrugged his shoulders. "It would take an arbitration commission a good many sittings to define the boundaries of society nowadays. But at any rate they're in New York; and I assure you you're *not*; you're farther and farther from it."

"But I've been back there several times to see Leila." She hesitated and looked away from him. Then she brought out slowly: "And I've never noticed—the least change—in—in my own case—"

"Oh," he sounded deprecatingly, and she trembled with the fear of having gone too far. But the hour was past when such scruples could restrain her. She must know where she was and where Leila was. "Mrs. Boulger still cuts me," she brought out with an embarrassed laugh.

"Are you sure? You've probably cut *her*; if not now, at least in the past. And in a cut if you're not first you're nowhere. That's what keeps up so many quarrels."

The word roused Mrs. Lidcote to a renewed sense of realities. "But the Purshes," she said—"the Purshes are so strong! There are so many of them, and they all back each other up, just as my husband's family did. I know what it means to have a clan against one. They're stronger than any number of separate friends. The Purshes will *never* forgive Leila for leaving Horace. Why, his mother opposed his marrying her because of—of me. She tried to get Leila to promise that she wouldn't see me when they went to Europe on their honeymoon. And now she'll say it was my example."

Her companion, vaguely stroking his beard, mused a moment upon this; then he asked, with seeming irrelevance, "What did Leila say when you wrote that you were coming?"

"She said it wasn't the least necessary, but that I'd better come, because it was the only way to convince me that it wasn't."

"Well, then, that proves she's not afraid of the Purshes."

She breathed a long sigh of remembrance. "Oh, just at first, you know—one never is."

He laid his hand on hers with a gesture of intelligence and pity. "You'll see, you'll see," he said.

A shadow lengthened down the deck before them, and a steward stood there, proffering a Marconigram.

"Oh, now I shall know!" she exclaimed.

She tore the message open, and then let it fall on her knees, dropping her hands on it in silence.

Ide's enquiry roused her: "It's all right?"

"Oh, quite right. Perfectly. She can't come; but she's sending Susy Suffern. She says Susy will explain." After another silence she added, with a sudden gush of bitterness: "As if I needed any explanation!"

She felt Ide's hesitating glance upon her. "She's in the country?"

"Yes. 'Prevented last moment. Longing for you, expecting you. Love from both.' Don't you *see*, the poor darling, that she couldn't face it?"

"No, I don't." He waited. "Do you mean to go to her immediately?"

"It will be too late to catch a train this evening; but I shall take the first to-morrow morning." She considered a moment. "Perhaps it's better. I need a talk with Susy first. She's to meet me at the dock, and I'll take her straight back to the hotel with me."

As she developed this plan, she had the sense that Ide was still thoughtfully, even gravely, considering her. When she ceased, he remained silent a moment; then he said almost ceremoniously: "If your talk with Miss Suffern doesn't last too late, may I come and see you when it's over? I shall be dining at my club, and I'll call you up at about ten, if I may. I'm off to Chicago on business to-morrow morning, and it would be a satisfaction to know, before I start, that your cousin's been able to reassure you, as I know she will."

He spoke with a shy deliberateness that, even to Mrs. Lidcote's troubled perceptions, sounded a long-silenced note of feeling. Perhaps the breaking down of the barrier of reticence between them had released unsuspected emotions in both. The tone of his appeal moved her curiously and loosened the tight strain of her fears.

"Oh, yes, come—do come," she said, rising. The huge threat of New York was imminent now, dwarfing, under long reaches of embattled masonry, the great deck she stood on and all the little specks of life it carried. One of them, drifting nearer, took the shape of her maid, followed by luggage-laden stewards, and signing to her that it was time to go below. As they descended to the main deck, the throng swept her against Mrs. Lorin Boulger's shoulder, and she heard the ambassadress call out to some one, over the vexed sea of hats: "So sorry! I should have been delighted, but I've promised to spend Sunday with some friends at Lenox."

II

Susy Suffern's explanation did not end till after ten o'clock, and she had just gone when Franklin Ide, who, complying with an old New York tradition, had caused himself to be preceded by a long white box of roses, was shown into Mrs. Lidcote's sitting-room.

He came forward with his shy half-humorous smile and, taking her hand, looked at her for a moment without speaking.

"It's all right," he then pronounced.

Mrs. Lidcote returned his smile. "It's extraordinary. Everything's changed. Even Susy has changed; and you know the extent to which Susy used to represent the old New York. There's no old New York left, it seems. She talked in the most amazing way. She snaps her fingers at the Purshes. She told me—*me*, that every woman had a right to happiness and that self-expression was the highest duty. She accused me of misunderstanding Leila; she said my point of view was conventional! She was bursting with pride at having been in the secret, and wearing a brooch that Wilbour Barkley'd given her!"

Franklin Ide had seated himself in the arm-chair she had pushed forward for him under the electric chandelier. He threw back his head and laughed. "What did I tell you?"

"Yes; but I can't believe that Susy's not mistaken. Poor dear, she has the habit of lost causes; and she may feel that, having stuck to me, she can do no less than stick to Leila."

"But she didn't—did she?—openly defy the world for you? She didn't snap her fingers at the Lidcotes?"

Mrs. Lidcote shook her head, still smiling. "No. It was enough to defy *my* family. It was doubtful at one time if they would tolerate her seeing me, and she almost had to disinfect herself after each visit. I believe that at first my sister-in-law wouldn't let the girls come down when Susy dined with her."

"Well, isn't your cousin's present attitude the best possible proof that times have changed?"

"Yes, yes; I know." She leaned forward from her sofa-corner, fixing her eyes on his thin kindly face, which gleamed on her indistinctly through her tears. "If it's true, it's—it's dazzling. She says Leila's perfectly happy. It's as if an angel had gone about lifting gravestones, and the buried people walked again, and the living didn't shrink from them."

"That's about it," he assented.

She drew a deep breath, and sat looking away from him down the long perspective of lamp-fringed streets over which her windows hung.

"I can understand how happy you must be," he began at length.

She turned to him impetuously. "Yes, yes; I'm happy. But I'm lonely, too—lonelier than ever. I didn't take up much room in the world before; but now—where is there a corner for me? Oh, since I've begun to confess myself, why shouldn't I go on? Telling you this lifts a gravestone from *me*! You see, before this, Leila needed me. She was unhappy, and I knew it, and though we hardly ever talked of it I felt that, in a way, the thought that I'd been through the same thing, and down to the dregs of it, helped her. And her needing me helped *me*. And when the news of her marriage came my first thought

was that now she'd need me more than ever, that she'd have
no one but me to turn to. Yes, under all my distress there was
a fierce joy in that. It was so new and wonderful to feel again
that there was one person who wouldn't be able to get on
without me! And now what you and Susy tell me seems to
have taken my child from me; and just at first that's all I can
feel."

"Of course it's all you feel." He looked at her musingly.
"Why didn't Leila come to meet you?"

"That was really my fault. You see, I'd cabled that I was not
sure of being able to get off on the *Utopia*, and apparently
my second cable was delayed, and when she received it she'd
already asked some people over Sunday—one or two of her
old friends, Susy says. I'm so glad they should have wanted
to go to her at once; but naturally I'd rather have been
alone with her."

"You still mean to go, then?"

"Oh, I must. Susy wanted to drag me off to Ridgefield with
her over Sunday, and Leila sent me word that of course I
might go if I wanted to, and that I was not to think of her;
but I know how disappointed she would be. Susy said she was
afraid I might be upset at her having people to stay, and that,
if I minded, she wouldn't urge me to come. But if *they* don't
mind, why should I? And of course, if they're willing to go to
Leila it must mean—"

"Of course. I'm glad you recognize that," Franklin Ide exclaimed abruptly. He stood up and went over to her, taking
her hand with one of his quick gestures. "There's something
I want to say to you," he began—

The next morning, in the train, through all the other con-
tending thoughts in Mrs. Lidcote's mind there ran the warm
undercurrent of what Franklin Ide had wanted to say to her.

He had wanted, she knew, to say it once before, when,
nearly eight years earlier, the hazard of meeting at the end of
a rainy autumn in a deserted Swiss hotel had thrown them for
a fortnight into unwonted propinquity. They had walked and
talked together, borrowed each other's books and newspapers, spent the long chill evenings over the fire in the dim
lamplight of her little pitch-pine sitting-room; and she had

been wonderfully comforted by his presence, and hard frozen places in her had melted, and she had known that she would be desperately sorry when he went. And then, just at the end, in his odd indirect way, he had let her see that it rested with her to have him stay. She could still relive the sleepless night she had given to that discovery. It was preposterous, of course, to think of repaying his devotion by accepting such a sacrifice; but how find reasons to convince him? She could not bear to let him think her less touched, less inclined to him than she was: the generosity of his love deserved that she should repay it with the truth. Yet how let him see what she felt, and yet refuse what he offered? How confess to him what had been on her lips when he made the offer: "I've seen what it did to one man; and there must never, never be another"? The tacit ignoring of her past had been the element in which their friendship lived, and she could not suddenly, to him of all men, begin to talk of herself like a guilty woman in a play. Somehow, in the end, she had managed it, had averted a direct explanation, had made him understand that her life was over, that she existed only for her daughter, and that a more definite word from him would have been almost a breach of delicacy. She was so used to behaving as if her life were over! And, at any rate, he had taken her hint, and she had been able to spare her sensitiveness and his. The next year, when he came to Florence to see her, they met again in the old friendly way; and that till now had continued to be the tenor of their intimacy.

And now, suddenly and unexpectedly, he had brought up the question again, directly this time, and in such a form that she could not evade it: putting the renewal of his plea, after so long an interval, on the ground that, on her own showing, her chief argument against it no longer existed.

"You tell me Leila's happy. If she's happy, she doesn't need you—need you, that is, in the same way as before. You wanted, I know, to be always in reach, always free and available if she should suddenly call you to her or take refuge with you. I understood that—I respected it. I didn't urge my case because I saw it was useless. You couldn't, I understood well enough, have felt free to take such happiness as life with me might give you while she was unhappy, and, as you imagined, with no hope of release. Even then I didn't feel as you did about it; I understood better the trend of things here. But ten years ago the change hadn't really come; and I had no way of convincing you that it was coming. Still, I always fancied that Leila might not think her case was closed, and so I chose to think that ours wasn't either. Let me go on thinking so, at any rate, till you've seen her, and confirmed with your own eyes what Susy Suffern tells you."

III

All through what Susy Suffern told and retold her during their four-hours' flight to the hills this plea of Ide's kept coming back to Mrs. Lidcote. She did not yet know what she felt as to its bearing on her own fate, but it was something on which her confused thoughts could stay themselves amid the welter of new impressions, and she was inexpressibly glad that he had said what he had, and said it at that particular moment. It helped her to hold fast to her identity in the rush of strange names and new categories that her cousin's talk poured out on her.

With the progress of the journey Miss Suffern's communications grew more and more amazing. She was like a cicerone preparing the mind of an inexperienced traveller for the marvels about to burst on it.

"You won't know Leila. She's had her pearls reset. Sargent's to paint her. Oh, and I was to tell you that she hopes you won't mind being the least bit squeezed over Sunday. The house was built by Wilbour's father, you know, and it's rather old-fashioned—only ten spare bedrooms. Of course that's small for what they mean to do, and she'll show you the new plans they've had made. Their idea is to keep the present house as a wing. She told me to explain—she's so dreadfully sorry not to be able to give you a sitting-room just at first. They're thinking of Egypt for next winter, unless, of course, Wilbour gets his appointment. Oh, didn't she write you about that? Why, he wants Rome, you know—the second secretaryship. Or, rather, he wanted England; but Leila insisted that if they went abroad she must be near you. And of course what she says is law. Oh, they quite hope they'll get it.

You see Horace's uncle is in the Cabinet,—one of the assistant secretaries,—and I believe he has a good deal of pull—"

"Horace's uncle? You mean Wilbour's, I suppose," Mrs. Lidcote interjected, with a gasp of which a fraction was given to Miss Suffern's flippant use of the language.

"Wilbour's? No, I don't. I mean Horace's. There's no bad feeling between them, I assure you. Since Horace's engagement was announced—you didn't know Horace was engaged? Why, he's marrying one of Bishop Thorbury's girls: the red-haired one who wrote the novel that every one's talking about, 'This Flesh of Mine.' They're to be married in the cathedral. Of course Horace *can*, because it was Leila who—but, as I say, there's not the *least* feeling, and Horace wrote himself to his uncle about Wilbour."

Mrs. Lidcote's thoughts fled back to what she had said to Ide the day before on the deck of the *Utopia*. "I didn't take up much room before, but now where is there a corner for me?" Where indeed in this crowded, topsy-turvy world, with its headlong changes and helter-skelter readjustments, its new tolerances and indifferences and accommodations, was there room for a character fashioned by slower sterner processes and a life broken under their inexorable pressure? And then, in a flash, she viewed the chaos from a new angle, and order seemed to move upon the void. If the old processes were changed, her case was changed with them; she, too, was a part of the general readjustment, a tiny fragment of the new pattern worked out in bolder freer harmonies. Since her daughter had no penalty to pay, was not she herself released by the same stroke? The rich arrears of youth and joy were gone; but was there not time enough left to accumulate new stores of happiness? That, of course, was what Franklin Ide had felt and had meant her to feel. He had seen at once what the change in her daughter's situation would make in her view of her own. It was almost—wondrously enough!—as if Leila's folly had been the means of vindicating hers.

Everything else for the moment faded for Mrs. Lidcote in the glow of her daughter's embrace. It was unnatural, it was almost terrifying, to find herself standing on a strange threshold, under an unknown roof, in a big hall full of pictures, flowers, firelight, and hurrying servants, and in this spacious unfamiliar confusion to discover Leila, bareheaded, laughing, authoritative, with a strange young man jovially echoing her welcome and transmitting her orders; but once Mrs. Lidcote had her child on her breast, and her child's "It's all right, you old darling!" in her ears, every other feeling was lost in the deep sense of well-being that only Leila's hug could give.

The sense was still with her, warming her veins and pleasantly fluttering her heart, as she went up to her room after luncheon. A little constrained by the presence of visitors, and not altogether sorry to defer for a few hours the "long talk" with her daughter for which she somehow felt herself tremulously unready, she had withdrawn, on the plea of fatigue, to the bright luxurious bedroom into which Leila had again and again apologized for having been obliged to squeeze her. The room was bigger and finer than any in her small apartment in Florence; but it was not the standard of affluence implied in her daughter's tone about it that chiefly struck her, nor yet the finish and complexity of its appointments. It was the look it shared with the rest of the house, and with the perspective of the gardens beneath its windows, of being part of an "establishment"—of something solid, avowed, founded on sacraments and precedents and principles. There was nothing about the place, or about Leila and Wilbour, that suggested either passion or peril: their relation seemed as comfortable as their furniture and as respectable as their balance at the bank.

This was, in the whole confusing experience, the thing that confused Mrs. Lidcote most, that gave her at once the deepest feeling of security for Leila and the strongest sense of apprehension for herself. Yes, there was something oppressive in the completeness and compactness of Leila's well-being. Ide had been right: her daughter did not need her. Leila, with her first embrace, had unconsciously attested the fact in the same phrase as Ide himself and as the two young women with the hats. "It's all right, you old darling!" she had said; and her mother sat alone, trying to fit herself into the new scheme of things which such a certainty betokened.

Her first distinct feeling was one of irrational resentment. If such a change was to come, why had it not come sooner? Here was she, a woman not yet old, who had paid with the

best years of her life for the theft of the happiness that her
daughter's contemporaries were taking as their due. There
was no sense, no sequence, in it. She had had what she
wanted, but she had had to pay too much for it. She had had
to pay the last bitterest price of learning that love has a price:
that it is worth so much and no more. She had known the anguish of watching the man she loved discover this first, and of
reading the discovery in his eyes. It was a part of her history
that she had not trusted herself to think of for a long time
past: she always took a big turn about that haunted corner.
But now, at the sight of the young man downstairs, so openly
and jovially Leila's, she was overwhelmed at the senseless
waste of her own adventure, and wrung with the irony of perceiving that the success or failure of the deepest human experiences may hang on a matter of chronology.

Then gradually the thought of Ide returned to her. "I
chose to think that our case wasn't closed," he had said. She
had been deeply touched by that. To every one else her case
had been closed so long! *Finis* was scrawled all over her. But
here was one man who had believed and waited, and what if
what he believed in and waited for were coming true? If
Leila's "all right" should really foreshadow hers?

As yet, of course, it was impossible to tell. She had fancied,
indeed, when she entered the drawing-room before luncheon,
that a too-sudden hush had fallen on the assembled group of
Leila's friends, on the slender vociferous young women and
the lounging golf-stockinged young men. They had all received her politely, with the kind of petrified politeness that
may be either a tribute to age or a protest at laxity; but to
them, of course, she must be an old woman because she was
Leila's mother, and in a society so dominated by youth the
mere presence of maturity was a constraint.

One of the young girls, however, had presently emerged
from the group, and, attaching herself to Mrs. Lidcote, had
listened to her with a blue gaze of admiration which gave the
older woman a sudden happy consciousness of her long-for-
gotten social graces. It was agreeable to find herself attracting
this young Charlotte Wynn, whose mother had been among
her closest friends, and in whom something of the soberness and softness of the earlier manners had survived. But the

little colloquy, broken up by the announcement of luncheon, could of course result in nothing more definite than this reminiscent emotion.

No, she could not yet tell how her own case was to be fitted into the new order of things; but there were more people —"older people" Leila had put it—arriving by the afternoon train, and that evening at dinner she would doubtless be able to judge. She began to wonder nervously who the new-comers might be. Probably she would be spared the embarrassment of finding old acquaintances among them; but it was odd that her daughter had mentioned no names.

Leila had proposed that, later in the afternoon, Wilbour should take her mother for a drive: she said she wanted them to have a "nice, quiet talk." But Mrs. Lidcote wished her talk with Leila to come first, and had, moreover, at luncheon, caught stray allusions to an impending tennis-match in which her son-in-law was engaged. Her fatigue had been a sufficient pretext for declining the drive, and she had begged Leila to think of her as peacefully resting in her room till such time as they could snatch their quiet moment.

"Before tea, then, you duck!" Leila with a last kiss had decided; and presently Mrs. Lidcote, through her open window, had heard the fresh loud voices of her daughter's visitors chiming across the gardens from the tennis-court.

IV

Leila had come and gone, and they had had their talk. It had not lasted as long as Mrs. Lidcote wished, for in the middle of it Leila had been summoned to the telephone to receive an important message from town, and had sent word to her mother that she couldn't come back just then, as one of the young ladies had been called away unexpectedly and arrangements had to be made for her departure. But the mother and daughter had had almost an hour together, and Mrs. Lidcote was happy. She had never seen Leila so tender, so solicitous. The only thing that troubled her was the very excess of this solicitude, the exaggerated expression of her daughter's annoyance that their first moments together should have been marred by the presence of strangers.

"Not strangers to me, darling, since they're friends of yours," her mother had assured her.

"Yes; but I know your feeling, you queer wild mother. I know how you've always hated people." (*Hated people!* Had Leila forgotten why?) "And that's why I told Susy that if you preferred to go with her to Ridgefield on Sunday I should perfectly understand, and patiently wait for our good hug. But you didn't really mind them at luncheon, did you, dearest?"

Mrs. Lidcote, at that, had suddenly thrown a startled look at her daughter. "I don't mind things of that kind any longer," she had simply answered.

"But that doesn't console me for having exposed you to the bother of it, for having let you come here when I ought to have *ordered* you off to Ridgefield with Susy. If Susy hadn't been stupid she'd have made you go there with her. I hate to think of you up here all alone."

Again Mrs. Lidcote tried to read something more than a rather obtuse devotion in her daughter's radiant gaze. "I'm glad to have had a rest this afternoon, dear; and later—"

"Oh, yes, later, when all this fuss is over, we'll more than make up for it, sha'n't we, you precious darling?" And at this point Leila had been summoned to the telephone, leaving Mrs. Lidcote to her conjectures.

These were still floating before her in cloudy uncertainty when Miss Suffern tapped at the door.

"You've come to take me down to tea? I'd forgotten how late it was," Mrs. Lidcote exclaimed.

Miss Suffern, a plump peering little woman, with prim hair and a conciliatory smile, nervously adjusted the pendent bugles of her elaborate black dress. Miss Suffern was always in mourning, and always commemorating the demise of distant relatives by wearing the discarded wardrobe of their next of kin. "It isn't *exactly* mourning," she would say; "but it's the only stitch of black poor Julia had—and of course George was only my mother's step-cousin."

As she came forward Mrs. Lidcote found herself humorously wondering whether she were mourning Horace Pursh's divorce in one of his mother's old black satins.

"Oh, *did* you mean to go down for tea?" Susy Suffern peered at her, a little fluttered. "Leila sent me up to keep you company. She thought it would be cozier for you to stay here. She was afraid you were feeling rather tired."

"I was; but I've had the whole afternoon to rest in. And this wonderful sofa to help me."

"Leila told me to tell you that she'd rush up for a minute before dinner, after everybody had arrived; but the train is always dreadfully late. She's in despair at not giving you a sitting-room; she wanted to know if I thought you really minded."

"Of course I don't mind. It's not like Leila to think I should." Mrs. Lidcote drew aside to make way for the house-maid, who appeared in the doorway bearing a table spread with a bewildering variety of tea-cakes.

"Leila saw to it herself," Miss Suffern murmured as the door closed. "Her one idea is that you should feel happy here."

It struck Mrs. Lidcote as one more mark of the subverted state of things that her daughter's solicitude should find ex-pression in the multiplicity of sandwiches and the piping-hot-ness of muffins; but then everything that had happened since her arrival seemed to increase her confusion.

The note of a motor-horn down the drive gave another turn to her thoughts. "Are those the new arrivals already?" she asked.

"Oh, dear, no; they won't be here till after seven." Miss Suffern craned her head from the window to catch a glimpse of the motor. "It must be Charlotte leaving."

"Was it the little Wynn girl who was called away in a hurry? I hope it's not on account of illness."

"Oh, no; I believe there was some mistake about dates. Her mother telephoned her that she was expected at the Stepleys, at Fishkill, and she had to be rushed over to Albany to catch a train."

Mrs. Lidcote meditated. "I'm sorry. She's a charming young thing. I hoped I should have another talk with her this evening after dinner."

"Yes; it's too bad." Miss Suffern's gaze grew vague. "You *do* look tired, you know," she continued, seating herself at the tea-table and preparing to dispense its delicacies. "You must go straight back to your sofa and let me wait on you. The ex-

citement has told on you more than you think, and you mustn't
fight against it any longer. Just stay quietly up here and let
yourself go. You'll have Leila to yourself on Monday."

Mrs. Lidcote received the tea-cup which her cousin proffered, but showed no other disposition to obey her injunc-
tions. For a moment she stirred her tea in silence; then she
asked: "Is it your idea that I should stay quietly up here till
Monday?"

Miss Suffern set down her cup with a gesture so sudden
that it endangered an adjacent plate of scones. When she had
assured herself of the safety of the scones she looked up with
a fluttered laugh. "Perhaps, dear, by to-morrow you'll be feeling differently. The air here, you know—"

"Yes, I know." Mrs. Lidcote bent forward to help herself to
a scone. "Who's arriving this evening?" she asked.

Miss Suffern frowned and peered. "You know my wretched
head for names. Leila told me—but there are so many—"

"So many? She didn't tell me she expected a big party."

"Oh, not big: but rather outside of her little group. And of
course, as it's the first time, she's a little excited at having the
older set."

"The older set? Our contemporaries, you mean?"

"Why—yes." Miss Suffern paused as if to gather herself up
for a leap. "The Ashton Gileses," she brought out.

"The Ashton Gileses? Really? I shall be glad to see Mary
Giles again. It must be eighteen years," said Mrs. Lidcote
steadily.

"Yes," Miss Suffern gasped, precipitately refilling her cup.

"The Ashton Gileses; and who else?"

"Well, the Sam Fresbies. But the most important person, of
course, is Mrs. Lorin Boulger."

"Mrs. Boulger? Leila didn't tell me she was coming."

"Didn't she? I suppose she forgot everything when she saw
you. But the party was got up for Mrs. Boulger. You see, it's
very important that she should—well, take a fancy to Leila
and Wilbour; his being appointed to Rome virtually depends
on it. And you know Leila insists on Rome in order to be near
you. So she asked Mary Giles, who's intimate with the
Boulgers, if the visit couldn't possibly be arranged; and
Mary's cable caught Mrs. Boulger at Cherbourg. She's to be

only a fortnight in America; and getting her to come directly here was rather a triumph."

"Yes; I see it was," said Mrs. Lidcote.

"You know, she's rather—rather fussy; and Mary was a little doubtful if—"

"If she would, on account of Leila?" Mrs. Lidcote murmured.

"Well, yes. In her official position. But luckily she's a friend of the Barkleys. And finding the Gileses and Fresbies here will make it all right. The times have changed!" Susy Suffern indulgently summed up.

Mrs. Lidcote smiled. "Yes; a few years ago it would have seemed improbable that I should ever again be dining with Mary Giles and Harriet Fresbie and Mrs. Lorin Boulger."

Miss Suffern did not at the moment seem disposed to enlarge upon this theme; and after an interval of silence Mrs. Lidcote suddenly resumed: "Do they know I'm here, by the way?"

The effect of her question was to produce in Miss Suffern an exaggerated access of peering and frowning. She twitched the tea-things about, fingered her bugles, and, looking at the clock, exclaimed amazedly: "Mercy! Is it seven already?"

"Not that it can make any difference, I suppose," Mrs. Lidcote continued. "But did Leila tell them I was coming?"

Miss Suffern looked at her with pain. "Why, you don't suppose, dearest, that Leila would do anything—"

Mrs. Lidcote went on: "For, of course, it's of the first importance, as you say, that Mrs. Lorin Boulger should be favorably impressed, in order that Wilbour may have the best possible chance of getting Rome."

"I *told* Leila you'd feel that, dear. You see, it's actually on *your* account—so that they may get a post near you—that Leila invited Mrs. Boulger."

"Yes, I see that." Mrs. Lidcote, abruptly rising from her seat, turned her eyes to the clock. "But, as you say, it's getting late. Oughtn't we to dress for dinner?"

Miss Suffern, at the suggestion, stood up also, an agitated hand among her bugles. "I do wish I could persuade you to stay up here this evening. I'm sure Leila'd be happier if you would. Really, you're much too tired to come down."

"What nonsense, Susy!" Mrs. Lidcote spoke with a sudden sharpness, her hand stretched to the bell. "When do we dine? At half-past eight? Then I must really send you packing. At my age it takes time to dress."

Miss Suffern, thus projected toward the threshold, lingered there to repeat: "Leila'll never forgive herself if you make an effort you're not up to." But Mrs. Lidcote smiled on her without answering, and the icy light-wave propelled her through the door.

V

Mrs. Lidcote, though she had made the gesture of ringing for her maid, had not done so.

When the door closed, she continued to stand motionless in the middle of her soft spacious room. The fire which had been kindled at twilight danced on the brightness of silver and mirrors and sober gilding; and the sofa toward which she had been urged by Miss Suffern heaped up its cushions in inviting proximity to a table laden with new books and papers. She could not recall having ever been more luxuriously housed, or having ever had so strange a sense of being out alone, under the night, in a wind-beaten plain. She sat down by the fire and thought.

A knock on the door made her lift her head, and she saw her daughter on the threshold. The intricate ordering of Leila's fair hair and the flying folds of her dressing-gown showed that she had interrupted her dressing to hasten to her mother; but once in the room she paused a moment, smiling uncertainly, as though she had forgotten the object of her haste.

Mrs. Lidcote rose to her feet. "Time to dress, dearest? Don't scold! I sha'n't be late."

"To dress?" Leila stood before her with a puzzled look. "Why, I thought, dear—I mean, I hoped you'd decided just to stay here quietly and rest."

Her mother smiled. "But I've been resting all the afternoon!"

"Yes, but—you know you *do* look tired. And when Susy told me just now that you meant to make the effort—"

"You came to stop me?"

"I came to tell you that you needn't feel in the least obliged—"

"Of course. I understand that."

There was a pause during which Leila, vaguely averting herself from her mother's scrutiny, drifted toward the dressing-table and began to disturb the symmetry of the brushes and bottles laid out on it.

"Do your visitors know that I'm here?" Mrs. Lidcote suddenly went on.

"Do they— Of course—why, naturally," Leila rejoined, absorbed in trying to turn the stopper of a salts-bottle.

"Then won't they think it odd if I don't appear?"

"Oh, not in the least, dearest. I assure you they'll *all* understand." Leila laid down the bottle and turned back to her mother, her face alight with reassurance.

Mrs. Lidcote stood motionless, her head erect, her smiling eyes on her daughter's. "Will they think it odd if I *do*?"

Leila stopped short, her lips half parted to reply. As she paused, the colour stole over her bare neck, swept up to her throat, and burst into flame in her cheeks. Thence it sent its devastating crimson up to her very temples, to the lobes of her ears, to the edges of her eyelids, beating all over her in fiery waves, as if fanned by some imperceptible wind.

Mrs. Lidcote silently watched the conflagration; then she turned away her eyes with a slight laugh. "I only meant that I was afraid it might upset the arrangement of your dinner-table if I didn't come down. If you can assure me that it won't, I believe I'll take you at your word and go back to this irresistible sofa." She paused, as if waiting for her daughter to speak; then she held out her arms. "Run off and dress, dearest; and don't have me on your mind." She clasped Leila close, pressing a long kiss on the last afterglow of her subsiding blush. "I do feel the least bit overdone, and if it won't inconvenience you to have me drop out of things, I believe I'll basely take to my bed and stay there till your party scatters. And now run off, or you'll be late; and make my excuses to them all."

VI

The Barkleys' visitors had dispersed, and Mrs. Lidcote, completely restored by her two days' rest, found herself, on the following Monday alone with her children and Miss Suffern.

There was a note of jubilation in the air, for the party had "gone off" so extraordinarily well, and so completely, as it appeared, to the satisfaction of Mrs. Lorin Boulger, that Wilbour's early appointment to Rome was almost to be counted on. So certain did this seem that the prospect of a prompt reunion mitigated the distress with which Leila learned of her mother's decision to return almost immediately to Italy. No one understood this decision; it seemed to Leila absolutely unintelligible that Mrs. Lidcote should not stay on with them till their own fate was fixed, and Wilbour echoed her astonishment.

"Why shouldn't you, as Leila says, wait here till we can all pack up and go together?"

Mrs. Lidcote smiled her gratitude with her refusal. "After all, it's not yet sure that you'll be packing up."

"Oh, you ought to have seen Wilbour with Mrs. Boulger," Leila triumphed.

"No, you ought to have seen Leila with her," Leila's husband exulted.

Miss Suffern enthusiastically appended: "I *do* think inviting Harriet Fresbie was a stroke of genius!"

"Oh, we'll be with you soon," Leila laughed. "So soon that it's really foolish to separate."

But Mrs. Lidcote held out with the quiet firmness which her daughter knew it was useless to oppose. After her long months in India, it was really imperative, she declared, that she should get back to Florence and see what was happening to her little place there; and she had been so comfortable on the *Utopia* that she had a fancy to return by the same ship. There was nothing for it, therefore, but to acquiesce in her decision and keep her with them till the afternoon before the day of the *Utopia's* sailing. This arrangement fitted in with certain projects which, during her two days' seclusion, Mrs. Lidcote had silently matured. It had become to her of the first importance to get away as soon as she could, and the little place in Florence, which held her past in every fold of its curtains and between every page of its books, seemed now to her the one spot where that past would be endurable to look upon.

She was not unhappy during the intervening days. The sight of Leila's well-being, the sense of Leila's tenderness, were, after all, what she had come for; and of these she had had full measure. Leila had never been happier or more tender; and the contemplation of her bliss, and the enjoyment of her affection, were an absorbing occupation for her mother. But they were also a sharp strain on certain overtightened chords, and Mrs. Lidcote, when at last she found herself alone in the New York hotel to which she had returned the night before embarking, had the feeling that she had just escaped with her life from the clutch of a giant hand.

She had refused to let her daughter come to town with her; she had even rejected Susy Suffern's company. She wanted no viaticum but that of her own thoughts; and she let these come to her without shrinking from them as she sat in the same high-hung sitting-room in which, just a week before, she and Franklin Ide had had their memorable talk.

She had promised her friend to let him hear from her, but she had not kept her promise. She knew that he had probably come back from Chicago, and that if he learned of her sudden decision to return to Italy it would be impossible for her not to see him before sailing; and as she wished above all things not to see him she had kept silent, intending to send him a letter from the steamer.

There was no reason why she should wait till then to write it. The actual moment was more favorable, and the task, though not agreeable, would at least bridge over an hour of her lonely evening. She went up to the writing-table, drew out a sheet of paper and began to write his name. And as she did so, the door opened and he came in.

The words she met him with were the last she could have imagined herself saying when they had parted. "How in the world did you know that I was here?"

He caught her meaning in a flash. "You didn't want me to, then?" He stood looking at her. "I suppose I ought to have taken your silence as meaning that. But I happened to meet

Mrs. Wynn, who is stopping here, and she asked me to dine with her and Charlotte, and Charlotte's young man. They told me they'd seen you arriving this afternoon, and I couldn't help coming up."

There was a pause between them, which Mrs. Lidcote at last surprisingly broke with the exclamation: "Ah, she *did* recognize me, then!"

"Recognize you?" He stared. "Why—"

"Oh, I saw she did, though she never moved an eyelid. I saw it by Charlotte's blush. The child has the prettiest blush. I saw that her mother wouldn't let her speak to me."

Ide put down his hat with an impatient laugh. "Hasn't Leila cured you of your delusions?"

She looked at him intently. "Then you don't think Margaret Wynn meant to cut me?"

"I think your ideas are absurd."

She paused for a perceptible moment without taking this up; then she said, at a tangent: "I'm sailing to-morrow early. I meant to write to you—there's the letter I'd begun."

Ide followed her gesture, and then turned his eyes back to her face. "You didn't mean to see me, then, or even to let me know that you were going till you'd left?"

"I felt it would be easier to explain to you in a letter—"

"What in God's name is there to explain?" She made no reply, and he pressed on: "It can't be that you're worried about Leila, for Charlotte Wynn told me she'd been there last week, and there was a big party arriving when she left: Fresbies and Gileses, and Mrs. Lorin Boulger—all the board of examiners! If Leila has passed *that*, she's got her degree."

Mrs. Lidcote had dropped down into a corner of the sofa where she had sat during their talk of the week before. "I was stupid," she began abruptly. "I ought to have gone to Ridgefield with Susy. I didn't see till afterward that I was expected to."

"You were expected to?"

"Yes. Oh, it wasn't Leila's fault. She suffered—poor darling; she was distracted. But she'd asked her party before she knew I was arriving."

"Oh, as to that—" Ide drew a deep breath of relief. "I can understand that it must have been a disappointment not to

have you to herself just at first. But, after all, you were among
old friends or their children: the Gileses and Fresbies—and
little Charlotte Wynn." He paused a moment before the last
name, and scrutinized her hesitatingly. "Even if they came at
the wrong time, you must have been glad to see them all at
Leila's."

She gave him back his look with a faint smile. "I didn't see
them."

"You didn't see them?"

"No. That is, excepting little Charlotte Wynn. That child is
exquisite. We had a talk before luncheon the day I arrived.
But when her mother found out that I was staying in the
house she telephoned her to leave immediately, and so I
didn't see her again."

The colour rushed to Ide's sallow face. "I don't know
where you get such ideas!"

She pursued, as if she had not heard him: "Oh, and I saw
Mary Giles for a minute too. Susy Suffern brought her up to
my room the last evening, after dinner, when all the others
were at bridge. She meant it kindly—but it wasn't much use."

"But what were you doing in your room in the evening
after dinner?"

"Why, you see, when I found out my mistake in coming,—
how embarrassing it was for Leila, I mean—I simply told her
I was very tired, and preferred to stay upstairs till the party
was over."

Ide, with a groan, struck his hand against the arm of his
chair. "I wonder how much of all this you simply imagined!"

"I didn't imagine the fact of Harriet Fresbie's not even asking if she might see me when she knew I was in the house.
Nor of Mary Giles's getting Susy, at the eleventh hour, to
smuggle her up to my room when the others wouldn't know
where she'd gone; nor poor Leila's ghastly fear lest Mrs.
Lorin Boulger, for whom the party was given, should guess I
was in the house, and prevent her husband's giving Wilbour
the second secretaryship because she'd been obliged to spend
a night under the same roof with his mother-in-law!"

Ide continued to drum on his chair-arm with exasperated
fingers. "You don't *know* that any of the acts you describe are
due to the causes you suppose."

Mrs. Lidcote paused before replying, as if honestly trying to measure the weight of this argument. Then she said in a low tone: "I know that Leila was in an agony lest I should come down to dinner the first night. And it was for me she was afraid, not for herself. Leila is never afraid for herself."

"But the conclusions you draw are simply preposterous. There are narrow-minded women everywhere, but the women who were at Leila's knew perfectly well that their going there would give her a sort of social sanction, and if they were willing that she should have it, why on earth should they want to withhold it from you?"

"That's what I told myself a week ago, in this very room, after my first talk with Susy Suffern." She lifted a misty smile to his anxious eyes. "That's why I listened to what you said to me the same evening, and why your arguments half convinced me, and made me think that what had been possible for Leila might not be impossible for me. If the new dispensation had come, why not for me as well as for the others? I can't tell you the flight my imagination took!"

Franklin Ide rose from his seat and crossed the room to a chair near her sofa-corner. "All I cared about was that it seemed—for the moment—to be carrying you toward me," he said.

"I cared about that, too. That's why I meant to go away without seeing you." They gave each other grave look for look. "Because, you see, I was mistaken," she went on. "We were both mistaken. You say it's preposterous that the women who didn't object to accepting Leila's hospitality should have objected to meeting me under her roof. And so it is; but I begin to understand why. It's simply that society is much too busy to revise its own judgments. Probably no one in the house with me stopped to consider that my case and Leila's were identical. They only remembered that I'd done something which, at the time I did it, was condemned by society. My case has been passed on and classified: I'm the woman who has been cut for nearly twenty years. The older people have half forgotten why, and the younger ones have never really known: it's simply become a tradition to cut me. And traditions that have lost their meaning are the hardest of all to destroy."

Ide sat motionless while she spoke. As she ended, he stood up with a short laugh and walked across the room to the window. Outside, the immense black prospect of New York, strung with its myriad lines of light, stretched away into the smoky edges of the night. He showed it to her with a gesture.

"What do you suppose such words as you've been using— 'society,' 'tradition,' and the rest—mean to all the life out there?"

She came and stood by him in the window. "Less than nothing, of course. But you and I are not out there. We're shut up in a little tight round of habit and association, just as we're shut up in this room. Remember, I thought I'd got out of it once; but what really happened was that the other people went out, and left me in the same little room. The only difference was that I was there alone. Oh, I've made it habitable now, I'm used to it; but I've lost any illusions I may have had as to an angel's opening the door."

Ide again laughed impatiently. "Well, if the door won't open, why not let another prisoner in? At least it would be less of a solitude—"

She turned from the dark window back into the vividly lighted room.

"It would be more of a prison. You forget that I know all about that. We're all imprisoned, of course—all of us middling people, who don't carry our freedom in our brains. But we've accommodated ourselves to our different cells, and if we're moved suddenly into new ones we're likely to find a stone wall where we thought there was thin air, and to knock ourselves senseless against it. I saw a man do that once."

Ide, leaning with folded arms against the window-frame, watched her in silence as she moved restlessly about the room, gathering together some scattered books and tossing a handful of torn letters into the paper-basket. When she ceased, he rejoined: "All you say is based on preconceived theories. Why didn't you put them to the test by coming down to meet your old friends? Don't you see the inference they would naturally draw from your hiding yourself when they arrived? It looked as though you were afraid of them— or as though you hadn't forgiven them. Either way, you put them in the wrong instead of waiting to let them put you in

the right. If Leila had buried herself in a desert do you suppose society would have gone to fetch her out? You say you
were afraid for Leila and that she was afraid for you. Don't
you see what all these complications of feeling mean? Simply
that you were too nervous at the moment to let things happen naturally, just as you're too nervous now to judge them
rationally." He paused and turned his eyes to her face. "Don't
try to just yet. Give yourself a little more time. Give *me* a
little more time. I've always known it would take time."

He moved nearer, and she let him have her hand. With the
grave kindness of his face so close above her she felt like a
child roused out of frightened dreams and finding a light in
the room.

"Perhaps you're right—" she heard herself begin; then
something within her clutched her back, and her hand fell
away from him.

"I know I'm right: trust me," he urged. "We'll talk of this
in Florence soon."

She stood before him, feeling with despair his kindness, his
patience and his unreality. Everything he said seemed like a
painted gauze let down between herself and the real facts of
life; and a sudden desire seized her to tear the gauze into
shreds.

She drew back and looked at him with a smile of superficial
reassurance. "You *are* right—about not talking any longer
now. I'm nervous and tired, and it would do no good. I
brood over things too much. As you say, I must try not to
shrink from people." She turned away and glanced at the
clock. "Why, it's only ten! If I send you off I shall begin to
brood again; and if you stay we shall go on talking about the
same thing. Why shouldn't we go down and see Margaret
Wynn for half an hour?"

She spoke lightly and rapidly, her brilliant eyes on his face.
As she watched him, she saw it change, as if her smile had
thrown a too vivid light upon it.

"Oh, no—not to-night!" he exclaimed.

"Not to-night? Why, what other night have I, when I'm off
at dawn? Besides, I want to show you at once that I mean to
be more sensible—that I'm not going to be afraid of people
any more. And I should really like another glimpse of little

Charlotte." He stood before her, his hand in his beard, with the gesture he had in moments of perplexity. "Come!" she ordered him gaily, turning to the door.

He followed her and laid his hand on her arm. "Don't you think—hadn't you better let me go first and see? They told me they'd had a tiring day at the dressmaker's. I daresay they have gone to bed."

"But you said they'd a young man of Charlotte's dining with them. Surely he wouldn't have left by ten? At any rate, I'll go down with you and see. It takes so long if one sends a servant first." She put him gently aside, and then paused as a new thought struck her. "Or wait; my maid's in the next room. I'll tell her to go and ask if Margaret will receive me. Yes, that's much the best way."

She turned back and went toward the door that led to her bedroom; but before she could open it she felt Ide's quick touch again.

"I believe—I remember now—Charlotte's young man was suggesting that they should all go out—to a music-hall or something of the sort. I'm sure—I'm positively sure that you won't find them."

Her hand dropped from the door, his dropped from her arm, and as they drew back and faced each other she saw the blood rise slowly through his sallow skin, redden his neck and ears, encroach upon the edges of his beard, and settle in dull patches under his kind troubled eyes. She had seen the same blush on another face, and the same impulse of compassion she had then felt made her turn her gaze away again.

A knock on the door broke the silence, and a porter put his head into the room.

"It's only just to know how many pieces there'll be to go down to the steamer in the morning."

With the words she felt that the veil of painted gauze was torn in tatters, and that she was moving again among the grim edges of reality.

"Oh, dear," she exclaimed, "I never *can* remember! Wait a minute; I shall have to ask my maid."

She opened her bedroom door and called out: "Annette!"

Kerfol

"Y OU ought to buy it," said my host; "it's just the place for a solitary-minded devil like you. And it would be rather worth while to own the most romantic house in Brittany. The present people are dead broke, and it's going for a song—you ought to buy it."

It was not with the least idea of living up to the character my friend Lanrivain ascribed to me (as a matter of fact, under my unsociable exterior I have always had secret yearnings for domesticity) that I took his hint one autumn afternoon and went to Kerfol. My friend was motoring over to Quimper on business: he dropped me on the way, at a cross-road on a heath, and said: "First turn to the right and second to the left. Then straight ahead till you see an avenue. If you meet any peasants, don't ask your way. They don't understand French, and they would pretend they did and mix you up. I'll be back for you here by sunset—and don't forget the tombs in the chapel."

I followed Lanrivain's directions with the hesitation occasioned by the usual difficulty of remembering whether he had said the first turn to the right and second to the left, or the contrary. If I had met a peasant I should certainly have asked, and probably been sent astray; but I had the desert landscape to myself, and so stumbled on the right turn and walked across the heath till I came to an avenue. It was so unlike any other avenue I have ever seen that I instantly knew it must be *the* avenue. The grey-trunked trees sprang up straight to a great height and then interwove their pale-grey branches in a long tunnel through which the autumn light fell faintly. I know most trees by name, but I haven't to this day been able to decide what those trees were. They had the tall curve of elms, the tenuity of poplars, the ashen colour of olives under a rainy sky; and they stretched ahead of me for half a mile or more without a break in their arch. If ever I saw an avenue that unmistakably led to something, it was the avenue at Kerfol. My heart beat a little as I began to walk down it.

Presently the trees ended and I came to a fortified gate in a long wall. Between me and the wall was an open space of grass, with other grey avenues radiating from it. Behind the wall were tall slate roofs mossed with silver, a chapel belfry, the top of a keep. A moat filled with wild shrubs and brambles surrounded the place; the drawbridge had been replaced by a stone arch, and the portcullis by an iron gate. I stood for a long time on the hither side of the moat, gazing about me, and letting the influence of the place sink in. I said to myself: "If I wait long enough, the guardian will turn up and show me the tombs—" and I rather hoped he wouldn't turn up too soon.

I sat down on a stone and lit a cigarette. As soon as I had done it, it struck me as a puerile and portentous thing to do, with that great blind house looking down at me, and all the empty avenues converging on me. It may have been the depth of the silence that made me so conscious of my gesture. The squeak of my match sounded as loud as the scraping of a brake, and I almost fancied I heard it fall when I tossed it onto the grass. But there was more than that: a sense of irrelevance, of littleness, of futile bravado, in sitting there puffing my cigarette-smoke into the face of such a past.

I knew nothing of the history of Kerfol—I was new to Brittany, and Lanrivain had never mentioned the name to me till the day before—but one couldn't as much as glance at that pile without feeling in it a long accumulation of history. What kind of history I was not prepared to guess: perhaps only that sheer weight of many associated lives and deaths which gives a majesty to all old houses. But the aspect of Kerfol suggested something more—a perspective of stern and cruel memories stretching away, like its own grey avenues, into a blur of darkness.

Certainly no house had ever more completely and finally broken with the present. As it stood there, lifting its proud roofs and gables to the sky, it might have been its own funeral monument. "Tombs in the chapel? The whole place is a tomb!" I reflected. I hoped more and more that the guardian would not come. The details of the place, however striking, would seem trivial compared with its collective impressiveness; and I wanted only to sit there and be penetrated by the weight of its silence.

"It's the very place for you!" Lanrivain had said; and I was overcome by the almost blasphemous frivolity of suggesting to any living being that Kerfol was the place for him. "Is it possible that any one could *not* see—?" I wondered. I did not finish the thought: what I meant was undefinable. I stood up and wandered toward the gate. I was beginning to want to know more; not to *see* more—I was by now so sure it was not a question of seeing—but to feel more: feel all the place had to communicate. "But to get in one will have to rout out the keeper," I thought reluctantly, and hesitated. Finally I crossed the bridge and tried the iron gate. It yielded, and I walked through the tunnel formed by the thickness of the *chemin de ronde.* At the farther end, a wooden barricade had been laid across the entrance, and beyond it was a court enclosed in noble architecture. The main building faced me; and I now saw that one half was a mere ruined front, with gaping windows through which the wild growths of the moat and the trees of the park were visible. The rest of the house was still in its robust beauty. One end abutted on the round tower, the other on the small traceried chapel, and in an angle of the building stood a graceful well-head crowned with mossy urns. A few roses grew against the walls, and on an upper window-sill I remember noticing a pot of fuchsias.

My sense of the pressure of the invisible began to yield to my architectural interest. The building was so fine that I felt a desire to explore it for its own sake. I looked about the court, wondering in which corner the guardian lodged. Then I pushed open the barrier and went in. As I did so, a dog barred my way. He was such a remarkably beautiful little dog that for a moment he made me forget the splendid place he was defending. I was not sure of his breed at the time, but have since learned that it was Chinese, and that he was of a rare variety called the "Sleeve-dog." He was very small and golden brown, with large brown eyes and a ruffled throat: he looked like a large tawny chrysanthemum. I said to myself: "These little beasts always snap and scream, and somebody will be out in a minute."

The little animal stood before me, forbidding, almost menacing: there was anger in his large brown eyes. But he made no sound, he came no nearer. Instead, as I advanced, he gradually fell back, and I noticed that another dog, a vague rough brindled thing, had limped up on a lame leg. "There'll be a hubbub now," I thought; for at the same moment a third dog, a long-haired white mongrel, slipped out of a doorway and joined the others. All three stood looking at me with grave eyes; but not a sound came from them. As I advanced they continued to fall back on muffled paws, still watching me. "At a given point, they'll all charge at my ankles: it's one of the jokes that dogs who live together put up on one," I thought. I was not alarmed, for they were neither large nor formidable. But they let me wander about the court as I pleased, following me at a little distance—always the same distance—and always keeping their eyes on me. Presently I looked across at the ruined façade, and saw that in one of its empty window-frames another dog stood: a white pointer with one brown ear. He was an old grave dog, much more experienced than the others; and he seemed to be observing me with a deeper intentness.

"I'll hear from *him*," I said to myself; but he stood in the window-frame, against the trees of the park, and continued to watch me without moving. I stared back at him for a time, to see if the sense that he was being watched would not rouse him. Half the width of the court lay between us, and we gazed at each other silently across it. But he did not stir, and at last I turned away. Behind me I found the rest of the pack, with a newcomer added: a small black greyhound with pale agate-coloured eyes. He was shivering a little, and his expression was more timid than that of the others. I noticed that he kept a little behind them. And still there was not a sound.

I stood there for fully five minutes, the circle about me—waiting, as they seemed to be waiting. At last I went up to the little golden-brown dog and stooped to pat him. As I did so, I heard myself give a nervous laugh. The little dog did not start, or growl, or take his eyes from me—he simply slipped back about a yard, and then paused and continued to look at me. "Oh, hang it!" I exclaimed, and walked across the court toward the well.

As I advanced, the dogs separated and slid away into different corners of the court. I examined the urns on the well, tried a locked door or two, and looked up and down the dumb façade; then I faced about toward the chapel. When I turned I perceived that all the dogs had disappeared except the old pointer, who still watched me from the window. It was rather a relief to be rid of that cloud of witnesses; and I began to look about me for a way to the back of the house. "Perhaps there'll be somebody in the garden," I thought. I found a way across the moat, scrambled over a wall smothered in brambles, and got into the garden. A few lean hydrangeas and geraniums pined in the flower-beds, and the ancient house looked down on them indifferently. Its garden side was plainer and severer than the other: the long granite front, with its few windows and steep roof, looked like a fortress-prison. I walked around the farther wing, went up some disjointed steps, and entered the deep twilight of a narrow and incredibly old box-walk. The walk was just wide enough for one person to slip through, and its branches met overhead. It was like the ghost of a box-walk, its lustrous green all turning to the shadowy greyness of the avenues. I walked on and on, the branches hitting me in the face and springing back with a dry rattle; and at length I came out on the grassy top of the *chemin de ronde*. I walked along it to the gate-tower, looking down into the court, which was just below me. Not a human being was in sight; and neither were the dogs. I found a flight of steps in the thickness of the wall and went down them; and when I emerged again into the court, there stood the circle of dogs, the golden-brown one a little ahead of the others, the black greyhound shivering in the rear.

"Oh, hang it—you uncomfortable beasts, you!" I exclaimed, my voice startling me with a sudden echo. The dogs stood motionless, watching me. I knew by this time that they would not try to prevent my approaching the house, and the knowledge left me free to examine them. I had a feeling that they must be horribly cowed to be so silent and inert. Yet they did not look hungry or ill-treated. Their coats were smooth and they were not thin, except the shivering greyhound. It was more as if they had lived a long time with people who never spoke to them or looked at them: as though the silence of the place had gradually benumbed their busy inquisitive natures. And this strange passivity, this almost human lassitude, seemed to me sadder than the misery of starved and beaten animals. I should have liked to rouse them for a minute, to coax them into a game or a scamper; but the longer I looked into their fixed and weary eyes the more preposterous the idea became. With the windows of that house looking down on us, how could I have imagined such a thing? The dogs knew better: *they* knew what the house would tolerate and what it would not. I even fancied that they knew what was passing through my mind, and pitied me for my frivolity. But even that feeling probably reached them through a thick fog of listlessness. I had an idea that their distance from me was as nothing to my remoteness from them. The impression they produced was that of having in common one memory so deep and dark that nothing that had happened since was worth either a growl or a wag.

"I say," I broke out abruptly, addressing myself to the dumb circle, "do you know what you look like, the whole lot of you? You look as if you'd seen a ghost—that's how you look! I wonder if there *is* a ghost here, and nobody but you left for it to appear to?" The dogs continued to gaze at me without moving. . . .

It was dark when I saw Lanrivain's motor lamps at the crossroads—and I wasn't exactly sorry to see them. I had the sense of having escaped from the loneliest place in the whole world, and of not liking loneliness—to that degree—as much as I had imagined I should. My friend had brought his solicitor back from Quimper for the night, and seated beside a fat and affable stranger I felt no inclination to talk of Kerfol. . . .

But that evening, when Lanrivain and the solicitor were closeted in the study, Madame de Lanrivain began to question me in the drawing-room.

"Well—are you going to buy Kerfol?" she asked, tilting up her gay chin from her embroidery.

"I haven't decided yet. The fact is, I couldn't get into the house," I said, as if I had simply postponed my decision, and meant to go back for another look.

"You couldn't get in? Why, what happened? The family are mad to sell the place, and the old guardian has orders—"

"Very likely. But the old guardian wasn't there."

"What a pity! He must have gone to market. But his daughter—?"

"There was nobody about. At least I saw no one."

"How extraordinary! Literally nobody?"

"Nobody but a lot of dogs—a whole pack of them—who seemed to have the place to themselves."

Madame de Lanrivain let the embroidery slip to her knee and folded her hands on it. For several minutes she looked at me thoughtfully.

"A pack of dogs—you *saw* them?"

"Saw them? I saw nothing else!"

"How many?" She dropped her voice a little. "I've always wondered—"

I looked at her with surprise: I had supposed the place to be familiar to her. "Have you never been to Kerfol?" I asked.

"Oh, yes: often. But never on that day."

"What day?"

"I'd quite forgotten—and so had Hervé, I'm sure. If we'd remembered, we never should have sent you to-day—but then, after all, one doesn't half believe that sort of thing, does one?"

"What sort of thing?" I asked, involuntarily sinking my voice to the level of hers. Inwardly I was thinking: "I *knew* there was something. . . ."

Madame de Lanrivain cleared her throat and produced a re-assuring smile. "Didn't Hervé tell you the story of Kerfol? An ancestor of his was mixed up in it. You know every Breton house has its ghost-story; and some of them are rather unpleasant."

"Yes—but those dogs?"

"Well, those dogs are the ghosts of Kerfol. At least, the peasants say there's one day in the year when a lot of dogs appear there; and that day the keeper and his daughter go off to Morlaix and get drunk. The women in Brittany drink dreadfully." She stooped to match a silk; then she lifted her charming inquisitive Parisian face. "Did you *really* see a lot of dogs? There isn't one at Kerfol," she said.

II

Lanrivain, the next day, hunted out a shabby calf volume from the back of an upper shelf of his library.

"Yes—here it is. What does it call itself? *A History of the Assizes of the Duchy of Brittany. Quimper, 1702.* The book was written about a hundred years later than the Kerfol affair; but I believe the account is transcribed pretty literally from the judicial records. Anyhow, it's queer reading. And there's a Hervé de Lanrivain mixed up in it—not exactly *my* style, as you'll see. But then he's only a collateral. Here, take the book up to bed with you. I don't exactly remember the details; but after you've read it I'll bet anything you'll leave your light burning all night!"

I left my light burning all night, as he had predicted; but it was chiefly because, till near dawn, I was absorbed in my reading. The account of the trial of Anne de Cornault, wife of the lord of Kerfol, was long and closely printed. It was, as my friend had said, probably an almost literal transcription of what took place in the court-room; and the trial lasted nearly a month. Besides, the type of the book was very bad. . . .

At first I thought of translating the old record. But it is full of wearisome repetitions, and the main lines of the story are forever straying off into side issues. So I have tried to disentangle it, and give it here in a simpler form. At times, however, I have reverted to the text because no other words could have conveyed so exactly the sense of what I felt at Kerfol; and nowhere have I added anything of my own.

III

It was in the year 16— that Yves de Cornault, lord of the domain of Kerfol, went to the *pardon* of Locronan to perform his religious duties. He was a rich and powerful noble, then in his sixty-second year, but hale and sturdy, a great horseman and hunter and a pious man. So all his neighbours attested. In appearance he was short and broad, with a swarthy face, legs slightly bowed from the saddle, a hanging nose and broad hands with black hairs on them. He had married young and lost his wife and son soon after, and since then had lived alone at Kerfol. Twice a year he went to Morlaix, where he had a handsome house by the river, and spent a week or ten days there; and occasionally he rode to Rennes on business. Witnesses were found to declare that during these absences he led a life different from the one he was known to lead at Kerfol, where he busied himself with his estate, attended mass daily, and found his only amusement in hunting the wild boar and water-fowl. But these rumours are not particularly relevant, and it is certain that among people of his own class in the neighbourhood he passed for a stern and even austere man, observant of his religious obligations, and keeping strictly to himself. There was no talk of any familiarity with the women on his estate, though at that time the nobility were very free with their peasants. Some people said he had never looked at a woman since his wife's death; but such things are hard to prove, and the evidence on this point was not worth much.

Well, in his sixty-second year, Yves de Cornault went to the *pardon* at Locronan, and saw there a young lady of Douarnenez, who had ridden over pillion behind her father to do her duty to the saint. Her name was Anne de Barrigan, and she came of good old Breton stock, but much less great and powerful than that of Yves de Cornault; and her father had squandered his fortune at cards, and lived almost like a peasant in his little granite manor on the moors. . . . I have said I would add nothing of my own to this bald statement of a strange case; but I must interrupt myself here to describe the young lady who rode up to the lych-gate of Locronan at the very moment when the Baron de Cornault was also dismounting there. I take my description from a faded drawing in red crayon, sober and truthful enough to be by a late pupil of the Clouets, which hangs in Lanrivain's study, and is said to be a portrait of Anne de Barrigan. It is unsigned and has no mark of identity but the initials A. B., and the date 16—, the year after her marriage. It represents a young woman with a small oval face, almost pointed, yet wide enough for a full mouth with a tender depression at the corners. The nose is small, and the eyebrows are set rather high, far apart, and as lightly pencilled as the eyebrows in a Chinese painting. The forehead is high and serious, and the hair, which one feels to be fine and thick and fair, is drawn off it and lies close like a cap. The eyes are neither large nor small, hazel probably, with a look at once shy and steady. A pair of beautiful long hands are crossed below the lady's breast. . . .

The chaplain of Kerfol, and other witnesses, averred that
when the Baron came back from Locronan he jumped from
his horse, ordered another to be instantly saddled, called to a
young page to come with him, and rode away that same
evening to the south. His steward followed the next morning
with coffers laden on a pair of pack mules. The following
week Yves de Cornault rode back to Kerfol, sent for his vas-
sals and tenants, and told them he was to be married at All
Saints to Anne de Barrigan of Douarnenez. And on All Saints'
Day the marriage took place.

As to the next few years, the evidence on both sides seems
to show that they passed happily for the couple. No one was
found to say that Yves de Cornault had been unkind to his
wife, and it was plain to all that he was content with his bargain. Indeed, it was admitted by the chaplain and other witnesses for the prosecution that the young lady had a softening
influence on her husband, and that he became less exacting
with his tenants, less harsh to peasants and dependents, and
less subject to the fits of gloomy silence which had darkened
his widowhood. As to his wife, the only grievance her cham-
pions could call up in her behalf was that Kerfol was a lonely
place, and that when her husband was away on business at
Rennes or Morlaix—whither she was never taken—she was
not allowed so much as to walk in the park unaccompanied.
But no one asserted that she was unhappy, though one ser-
vant-woman said she had surprised her crying, and had heard
her say that she was a woman accursed to have no child, and
nothing in life to call her own. But that was a natural enough
feeling in a wife attached to her husband; and certainly it
must have been a great grief to Yves de Cornault that she
bore no son. Yet he never made her feel her childlessness as a
reproach—she admits this in her evidence—but seemed to try
to make her forget it by showering gifts and favours on her.
Rich though he was, he had never been open-handed; but
nothing was too fine for his wife, in the way of silks or gems
or linen, or whatever else she fancied. Every wandering merchant was welcome at Kerfol, and when the master was called
away he never came back without bringing his wife a handsome present—something curious and particular—from
Morlaix or Rennes or Quimper. One of the waiting-women

gave, in cross-examination, an interesting list of one year's gifts, which I copy. From Morlaix, a carved ivory junk, with Chinamen at the oars, that a strange sailor had brought back as a votive offering for Notre Dame de la Clarté, above Ploumanac'h; from Quimper, an embroidered gown, worked by the nuns of the Assumption; from Rennes, a silver rose that opened and showed an amber Virgin with a crown of garnets; from Morlaix, again, a length of Damascus velvet shot with gold, bought of a Jew from Syria; and for Michaelmas that same year, from Rennes, a necklet or bracelet of round stones—emeralds and pearls and rubies—strung like beads on a fine gold chain. This was the present that pleased the lady best, the woman said. Later on, as it happened, it was produced at the trial, and appears to have struck the Judges and the public as a curious and valuable jewel.

The very same winter, the Baron absented himself again, this time as far as Bordeaux, and on his return he brought his wife something even odder and prettier than the bracelet. It was a winter evening when he rode up to Kerfol and, walking into the hall, found her sitting by the hearth, her chin on her hand, looking into the fire. He carried a velvet box in his hand and, setting it down, lifted the lid and let out a little golden-brown dog.

Anne de Cornault exclaimed with pleasure as the little creature bounded toward her. "Oh, it looks like a bird or a butterfly!" she cried as she picked it up; and the dog put its paws on her shoulders and looked at her with eyes "like a Christian's." After that she would never have it out of her sight, and petted and talked to it as if it had been a child—as indeed it was the nearest thing to a child she was to know. Yves de Cornault was much pleased with his purchase. The dog had been brought to him by a sailor from an East India merchantman, and the sailor had bought it of a pilgrim in a bazaar at Jaffa, who had stolen it from a nobleman's wife in China: a perfectly permissible thing to do, since the pilgrim was a Christian and the nobleman a heathen doomed to hellfire. Yves de Cornault had paid a long price for the dog, for they were beginning to be in demand at the French court, and the sailor knew he had got hold of a good thing; but Anne's pleasure was so great that, to see her laugh and play with the little animal, her husband would doubtless have given twice the sum.

So far, all the evidence is at one, and the narrative plain sailing; but now the steering becomes difficult. I will try to keep as nearly as possible to Anne's own statements; though toward the end, poor thing. . . .

Well, to go back. The very year after the little brown dog was brought to Kerfol, Yves de Cornault, one winter night, was found dead at the head of a narrow flight of stairs leading down from his wife's rooms to a door opening on the court. It was his wife who found him and gave the alarm, so distracted, poor wretch, with fear and horror—for his blood was all over her—that at first the roused household could not make out what she was saying, and thought she had suddenly gone mad. But there, sure enough, at the top of the stairs lay her husband, stone dead, and head foremost, the blood from his wounds dripping down to the steps below him. He had been dreadfully scratched and gashed about the face and throat, as if with curious pointed weapons; and one of his legs had a deep tear in it which had cut an artery, and probably caused his death. But how did he come there, and who had murdered him?

His wife declared that she had been asleep in her bed, and hearing his cry had rushed out to find him lying on the stairs; but this was immediately questioned. In the first place, it was proved that from her room she could not have heard the struggle on the stairs, owing to the thickness of the walls and the length of the intervening passage; then it was evident that she had not been in bed and asleep, since she was dressed when she roused the house, and her bed had not been slept in. Moreover, the door at the bottom of the stairs was ajar, and it was noticed by the chaplain (an observant man) that the dress she wore was stained with blood about the knees, and that there were traces of small blood-stained hands low down on the staircase walls, so that it was conjectured that she had really been at the postern-door when her husband fell and, feeling her way up to him in the darkness on her hands and knees, had been stained by his blood dripping down on her. Of course it was argued on the other side that the blood-marks on her dress might have been caused by her kneeling down by her husband when she rushed out of her room; but there was the open door below, and the fact that the finger-marks in the staircase all pointed upward.

The accused held to her statement for the first two days, in spite of its improbability; but on the third day word was brought to her that Hervé de Lanrivain, a young nobleman of the neighbourhood, had been arrested for complicity in the crime. Two or three witnesses thereupon came forward to say that it was known throughout the country that Lanrivain had formerly been on good terms with the lady of Cornault; but that he had been absent from Brittany for over a year, and people had ceased to associate their names. The witnesses who made this statement were not of a very reputable sort. One was an old herb-gatherer suspected of witchcraft, an-other a drunken clerk from a neighbouring parish, the third a half-witted shepherd who could be made to say anything; and it was clear that the prosecution was not satisfied with its case, and would have liked to find more definite proof of Lan-rivain's complicity than the statement of the herb-gatherer, who swore to having seen him climbing the wall of the park on the night of the murder. One way of patching out incom-plete proofs in those days was to put some sort of pressure, moral or physical, on the accused person. It is not clear what pressure was put on Anne de Cornault; but on the third day, when she was brought in court, she "appeared weak and wan-dering," and after being encouraged to collect herself and speak the truth, on her honour and the wounds of her Blessed Redeemer, she confessed that she had in fact gone down the stairs to speak with Hervé de Lanrivain (who denied every-thing), and had been surprised there by the sound of her hus-band's fall. That was better; and the prosecution rubbed its hands with satisfaction. The satisfaction increased when vari-ous dependents living at Kerfol were induced to say—with ap-parent sincerity—that during the year or two preceding his death their master had once more grown uncertain and iras-cible, and subject to the fits of brooding silence which his household had learned to dread before his second marriage. This seemed to show that things had not been going well at Kerfol; though no one could be found to say that there had been any signs of open disagreement between husband and wife.

Anne de Cornault, when questioned as to her reason for going down at night to open the door to Hervé de Lanrivain, made an answer which must have sent a smile around the court. She said it was because she was lonely and wanted to talk with the young man. Was this the only reason? she was asked; and replied: "Yes, by the Cross over your Lordships' heads." "But why at midnight?" the court asked. "Because I could see him in no other way." I can see the exchange of glances across the ermine collars under the Crucifix.

Anne de Cornault, further questioned, said that her married life had been extremely lonely: "desolate" was the word she used. It was true that her husband seldom spoke harshly to her; but there were days when he did not speak at all. It was true that he had never struck or threatened her; but he kept her like a prisoner at Kerfol, and when he rode away to Morlaix or Quimper or Rennes he set so close a watch on her that she could not pick a flower in the garden without having a waiting-woman at her heels. "I am no Queen, to need such honours," she once said to him; and he had answered that a man who has a treasure does not leave the key in the lock when he goes out. "Then take me with you," she urged; but to this he said that towns were pernicious places, and young wives better off at their own firesides.

"But what did you want to say to Hervé de Lanrivain?" the court asked; and she answered: "To ask him to take me away."

"Ah—you confess that you went down to him with adulterous thoughts?"

"No."

"Then why did you want him to take you away?"

"Because I was afraid for my life."

"Of whom were you afraid?"

"Of my husband."

"Why were you afraid of your husband?"

"Because he had strangled my little dog."

Another smile must have passed around the court-room: in days when any nobleman had a right to hang his peasants— and most of them exercised it—pinching a pet animal's windpipe was nothing to make a fuss about.

At this point one of the Judges, who appears to have had a certain sympathy for the accused, suggested that she should be allowed to explain herself in her own way; and she thereupon made the following statement.

The first years of her marriage had been lonely; but her husband had not been unkind to her. If she had had a child she would not have been unhappy; but the days were long, and it rained too much.

It was true that her husband, whenever he went away and left her, brought her a handsome present on his return; but this did not make up for the loneliness. At least nothing had, till he brought her the little brown dog from the East: after that she was much less unhappy. Her husband seemed pleased that she was so fond of the dog; he gave her leave to put her jewelled bracelet around its neck, and to keep it always with her.

One day she had fallen asleep in her room, with the dog at her feet, as his habit was. Her feet were bare and resting on his back. Suddenly she was waked by her husband: he stood beside her, smiling not unkindly.

"You look like my great-grandmother, Juliane de Cornault, lying in the chapel with her feet on a little dog," he said.

The analogy sent a chill through her, but she laughed and answered: "Well, when I am dead you must put me beside her, carved in marble, with my dog at my feet."

"Oho—we'll wait and see," he said, laughing also, but with his black brows close together. "The dog is the emblem of fidelity."

"And do you doubt my right to lie with mine at my feet?"

"When I'm in doubt I find out," he answered. "I am an old man," he added, "and people say I make you lead a lonely life. But I swear you shall have your monument if you earn it."

"And I swear to be faithful," she returned, "if only for the sake of having my little dog at my feet."

Not long afterward he went on business to the Quimper Assizes; and while he was away his aunt, the widow of a great nobleman of the duchy, came to spend a night at Kerfol on her way to the *pardon* of Ste. Barbe. She was a woman of piety and consequence, and much respected by Yves de Cornault, and when she proposed to Anne to go with her to

Ste. Barbe no one could object, and even the chaplain declared himself in favour of the pilgrimage. So Anne set out for Ste. Barbe, and there for the first time she talked with Hervé de Lanrivain. He had come once or twice to Kerfol with his father, but she had never before exchanged a dozen words with him. They did not talk for more than five minutes now: it was under the chestnuts, as the procession was coming out of the chapel. He said: "I pity you," and she was surprised, for she had not supposed that any one thought her an object of pity. He added: "Call for me when you need me," and she smiled a little, but was glad afterward, and thought often of the meeting.

She confessed to having seen him three times afterward: not more. How or where she would not say—one had the impression that she feared to implicate some one. Their meetings had been rare and brief; and at the last he had told her that he was starting the next day for a foreign country, on a mission which was not without peril and might keep him for many months absent. He asked her for a remembrance, and she had none to give him but the collar about the little dog's neck. She was sorry afterward that she had given it, but he was so unhappy at going that she had not had the courage to refuse.

Her husband was away at the time. When he returned a few days later he picked up the animal to pet it, and noticed that its collar was missing. His wife told him that the dog had lost it in the undergrowth of the park, and that she and her maids had hunted a whole day for it. It was true, she explained to the court, that she had made the maids search for the necklet—they all believed the dog had lost it in the park. . . .

Her husband made no comment, and that evening at supper he was in his usual mood, between good and bad: you could never tell which. He talked a good deal, describing what he had seen and done at Rennes; but now and then he stopped and looked hard at her, and when she went to bed she found her little dog strangled on her pillow. The little thing was dead, but still warm; she stooped to lift it, and her distress turned to horror when she discovered that it had been strangled by twisting twice round its throat the necklet she had given to Lanrivain.

The next morning at dawn she buried the dog in the garden, and hid the necklet in her breast. She said nothing to her husband, then or later, and he said nothing to her; but that day he had a peasant hanged for stealing a faggot in the park, and the next day he nearly beat to death a young horse he was breaking.

Winter set in, and the short days passed, and the long nights, one by one; and she heard nothing of Hervé de Lanrivain. It might be that her husband had killed him; or merely that he had been robbed of the necklet. Day after day by the hearth among the spinning maids, night after night alone on her bed, she wondered and trembled. Sometimes at table her husband looked across at her and smiled; and then she felt sure that Lanrivain was dead. She dared not try to get news of him, for she was sure her husband would find out if she did: she had an idea that he could find out anything. Even when a witchwoman who was a noted seer, and could show you the whole world in her crystal, came to the castle for a night's shelter, and the maids flocked to her, Anne held back.

The winter was long and black and rainy. One day, in Yves de Cornault's absence, some gypsies came to Kerfol with a troop of performing dogs. Anne bought the smallest and cleverest, a white dog with a feathery coat and one blue and one brown eye. It seemed to have been ill-treated by the gypsies, and clung to her plaintively when she took it from them. That evening her husband came back, and when she went to bed she found the dog strangled on her pillow.

After that she said to herself that she would never have another dog; but one bitter cold evening a poor lean greyhound was found whining at the castle-gate, and she took him in and forbade the maids to speak of him to her husband. She hid him in a room that no one went to, smuggled food to him from her own plate, made him a warm bed to lie on and petted him like a child.

Yves de Cornault came home, and the next day she found the greyhound strangled on her pillow. She wept in secret, but said nothing, and resolved that even if she met a dog dying of hunger she would never bring him into the castle; but one day she found a young sheepdog, a brindled puppy with good blue eyes, lying with a broken leg in the snow of the park. Yves de Cornault was at Rennes, and she brought the dog in, warmed and fed it, tied up its leg and hid it in the castle till her husband's return. The day before, she gave it to a peasant woman who lived a long way off, and paid her handsomely to care for it and say nothing; but that night she heard a whining and scratching at her door, and when she opened it the lame puppy, drenched and shivering, jumped up on her with little sobbing barks. She hid him in her bed, and the next morning was about to have him taken back to the peasant woman when she heard her husband ride into the court. She shut the dog in a chest, and went down to receive him. An hour or two later, when she returned to her room, the puppy lay strangled on her pillow. . . .

After that she dared not make a pet of any other dog; and her loneliness became almost unendurable. Sometimes, when she crossed the court of the castle, and thought no one was looking, she stopped to pat the old pointer at the gate. But one day as she was caressing him her husband came out of the chapel; and the next day the old dog was gone. . . .

This curious narrative was not told in one sitting of the court, or received without impatience and incredulous comment. It was plain that the Judges were surprised by its puerility, and that it did not help the accused in the eyes of the public. It was an odd tale, certainly; but what did it prove? That Yves de Cornault disliked dogs, and that his wife, to gratify her own fancy, persistently ignored this dislike. As for pleading this trivial disagreement as an excuse for her relations—whatever their nature—with her supposed accomplice, the argument was so absurd that her own lawyer manifestly regretted having let her make use of it, and tried several times to cut short her story. But she went on to the end, with a kind of hypnotized insistence, as though the scenes she evoked were so real to her that she had forgotten where she was and imagined herself to be re-living them.

At length the Judge who had previously shown a certain kindness to her said (leaning forward a little, one may suppose, from his row of dozing colleagues): "Then you would have us believe that you murdered your husband because he would not let you keep a pet dog?"

"I did not murder my husband."

"Who did, then? Hervé de Lanrivain?"

"No."

"Who then? Can you tell us?"

"Yes, I can tell you. The dogs—" At that point she was carried out of the court in a swoon.

It was evident that her lawyer tried to get her to abandon this line of defense. Possibly her explanation, whatever it was, had seemed convincing when she poured it out to him in the heat of their first private colloquy; but now that it was exposed to the cold daylight of judicial scrutiny, and the banter of the town, he was thoroughly ashamed of it, and would have sacrificed her without a scruple to save his professional reputation. But the obstinate Judge—who perhaps, after all, was more inquisitive than kindly—evidently wanted to hear the story out, and she was ordered, the next day, to continue her deposition.

She said that after the disappearance of the old watchdog nothing particular happened for a month or two. Her husband was much as usual: she did not remember any special incident. But one evening a pedlar woman came to the castle and was selling trinkets to the maids. She had no heart for trinkets, but she stood looking on while the women made their choice. And then, she did not know how, but the pedlar coaxed her into buying for herself a pear-shaped pomander with a strong scent in it—she had once seen something of the kind on a gypsy woman. She had no desire for the pomander, and did not know why she had bought it. The pedlar said that whoever wore it had the power to read the future; but she did not really believe that, or care much either. However, she bought the thing and took it up to her room, where she sat turning it about in her hand. Then the strange scent attracted her and she began to wonder what kind of spice was in the box. She opened it and found a grey bean rolled in a strip of paper; and on the paper she saw a sign she knew, and a message from Hervé de Lanrivain, saying that he was at home again and would be at the door in the court that night after the moon had set. . . .

She burned the paper and sat down to think. It was nightfall, and her husband was at home. . . . She had no way of warning Lanrivain, and there was nothing to do but to wait. . . .

At this point I fancy the drowsy court-room beginning to wake up. Even to the oldest hand on the bench there must have been a certain relish in picturing the feelings of a woman on receiving such a message at nightfall from a man living twenty miles away, to whom she had no means of sending a warning. . . .

She was not a clever woman, I imagine; and as the first result of her cogitation she appears to have made the mistake of being, that evening, too kind to her husband. She could not ply him with wine, according to the traditional expedient, for though he drank heavily at times he had a strong head; and when he drank beyond its strength it was because he chose to, and not because a woman coaxed him. Not his wife, at any rate—she was an old story by now. As I read the case, I fancy there was no feeling for her left in him but the hatred occasioned by his supposed dishonour.

At any rate, she tried to call up her old graces; but early in the evening he complained of pains and fever, and left the hall to go up to the closet where he sometimes slept. His servant carried him a cup of hot wine, and brought back word that he was sleeping and not to be disturbed; and an hour later, when Anne lifted the tapestry and listened at his door, she heard his loud regular breathing. She thought it might be a feint, and stayed a long time barefooted in the passage, her ear to the crack; but the breathing went on too steadily and naturally to be other than that of a man in a sound sleep. She crept back to her room reassured, and stood in the window watching the moon set through the trees of the park. The sky was misty and starless, and after the moon went down the night was black as pitch. She knew the time had come, and stole along the passage, past her husband's door—where she stopped again to listen to his breathing—to the top of the stairs. There she paused a moment, and assured herself that no one was following her; then she began to go down the stairs in the darkness. They were so steep and winding that she had to go very slowly, for fear of stumbling. Her one thought was to get the door unbolted, tell Lanrivain to make his escape, and hasten back to her room. She had tried the bolt earlier in the evening, and managed to put a little grease on it; but never-theless, when she drew it, it gave a squeak . . . not loud, but it made her heart stop; and the next minute, overhead, she heard a noise. . . .

"What noise?" the prosecution interposed.

"My husband's voice calling out my name and cursing me."

"What did you hear after that?"

"A terrible scream and a fall."

"Where was Hervé de Lanrivain at this time?"

"He was standing outside in the court. I just made him out in the darkness. I told him for God's sake to go, and then I pushed the door shut."

"What did you do next?"

"I stood at the foot of the stairs and listened."

"What did you hear?"

"I heard dogs snarling and panting." (Visible discourage-ment of the bench, boredom of the public, and exasperation of the lawyer for the defense. Dogs again—! But the inquisi-tive Judge insisted.)

"What dogs?"

She bent her head and spoke so low that she had to be told to repeat her answer: "I don't know."

"How do you mean—you don't know?"

"I don't know what dogs. . . ."

The Judge again intervened: "Try to tell us exactly what happened. How long did you remain at the foot of the stairs?"

"Only a few minutes."

"And what was going on meanwhile overhead?"

"The dogs kept on snarling and panting. Once or twice he cried out. I think he moaned once. Then he was quiet."

"Then what happened?"

"Then I heard a sound like the noise of a pack when the wolf is thrown to them—gulping and lapping."

(There was a groan of disgust and repulsion through the court, and another attempted intervention by the distracted lawyer. But the inquisitive Judge was still inquisitive.)

"And all the while you did not go up?"

"Yes—I went up then—to drive them off."

"The dogs?"

"Yes."

"Well—?"

"When I got there it was quite dark. I found my husband's flint and steel and struck a spark. I saw him lying there. He was dead."

"And the dogs?"

"The dogs were gone."

"Gone—where to?"

"I don't know. There was no way out—and there were no dogs at Kerfol."

She straightened herself to her full height, threw her arms above her head, and fell down on the stone floor with a long scream. There was a moment of confusion in the court-room. Some one on the bench was heard to say: "This is clearly a case for the ecclesiastical authorities"—and the prisoner's lawyer doubtless jumped at the suggestion.

After this, the trial loses itself in a maze of cross-questioning and squabbling. Every witness who was called corroborated Anne de Cornault's statement that there were no dogs at Kerfol: had been none for several months. The master of the house had taken a dislike to dogs, there was no denying it. But, on the other hand, at the inquest, there had been long and bitter discussions as to the nature of the dead man's wounds. One of the surgeons called in had spoken of marks that looked like bites. The suggestion of witchcraft was revived, and the opposing lawyers hurled tomes of necromancy at each other.

At last Anne de Cornault was brought back into court—at the instance of the same Judge—and asked if she knew where the dogs she spoke of could have come from. On the body of her Redeemer she swore that she did not. Then the Judge put his final question: "If the dogs you think you heard had been known to you, do you think you would have recognized them by their barking?"

"Yes."

"Did you recognize them?"

"Yes."

"What dogs do you take them to have been?"

"My dead dogs," she said in a whisper. . . . She was taken out of court, not to reappear there again. There was some kind of ecclesiastical investigation, and the end of the business was that the Judges disagreed with each other, and with the ecclesiastical committee, and that Anne de Cornault was finally handed over to the keeping of her husband's family, who shut her up in the keep of Kerfol, where she is said to have died many years later, a harmless mad-woman.

So ends her story. As for that of Hervé de Lanrivain, I had only to apply to his collateral descendant for its subsequent details. The evidence against the young man being insufficient, and his family influence in the duchy considerable, he was set free, and left soon afterward for Paris. He was probably in no mood for a worldly life, and he appears to have come almost immediately under the influence of the famous M. Arnauld d'Andilly and the gentlemen of Port Royal. A year or two later he was received into their Order, and without achieving any particular distinction he followed its good and evil fortunes till his death some twenty years later. Lanrivain showed me a portrait of him by a pupil of Philippe de Champaigne: sad eyes, an impulsive mouth and a narrow brow. Poor Hervé de Lanrivain: it was a grey ending. Yet as I looked at his stiff and sallow effigy, in the dark dress of the Jansenists, I almost found myself envying his fate. After all, in the course of his life two great things had happened to him: he had loved romantically, and he must have talked with Pascal. . . .

The Long Run

The shade of those our days that had no tongue.

IT WAS last winter, after a twelve years' absence from New
York, that I saw again, at one of the Jim Cumnors' dinners, my old friend Halston Merrick.

The Cumnors' house is one of the few where, even after
such a lapse of time, one can be sure of finding familiar faces
and picking up old threads; where for a moment one can
abandon one's self to the illusion that New York humanity is
a shade less unstable than its bricks and mortar. And that
evening in particular I remember feeling that there could be
no pleasanter way of re-entering the confused and careless
world to which I was returning than through the quiet softly-
lit dining-room in which Mrs. Cumnor, with a characteristic
sense of my needing to be broken in gradually, had contrived
to assemble so many friendly faces.

I was glad to see them all, including the three or four I did
not know, or failed to recognize, but had no difficulty in passing as in the tradition and of the group; but I was most of all
glad—as I rather wonderingly found—to set eyes again on
Halston Merrick.

He and I had been at Harvard together, for one thing, and
had shared there curiosities and ardours a little outside the
current tendencies: had, on the whole, been more critical
than our comrades, and less amenable to the accepted. Then,
for the next following years, Merrick had been a vivid and
promising figure in young American life. Handsome, careless,
and free, he had wandered and tasted and compared. After
leaving Harvard he had spent two years at Oxford; then he
had accepted a private secretaryship to our Ambassador in
England, and had come back from this adventure with a fresh
curiosity about public affairs at home, and the conviction that
men of his kind should play a larger part in them. This led,
first, to his running for a State Senatorship which he failed to
get, and ultimately to a few months of intelligent activity in a
municipal office. Soon after being deprived of this post by a
change of party he had published a small volume of delicate

verse, and, a year later, an odd uneven brilliant book on Municipal Government. After that one hardly knew where to look for his next appearance; but chance rather disappointingly solved the problem by killing off his father and placing Halston at the head of the Merrick Iron Foundry at Yonkers.

His friends had gathered that, whenever this regrettable contingency should occur, he meant to dispose of the business and continue his life of free experiment. As often happens in just such cases, however, it was not the moment for a sale, and Merrick had to take over the management of the foundry. Some two years later he had a chance to free himself; but when it came he did not choose to take it. This tame sequel to an inspiriting start was disappointing to some of us, and I was among those disposed to regret Merrick's drop to the level of the prosperous. Then I went away to a big engineering job in China, and from there to Africa, and spent the next twelve years out of sight and sound of New York doings.

During that long interval I heard of no new phase in Merrick's evolution, but this did not surprise me, as I had never expected from him actions resonant enough to cross the globe. All I knew—and this did surprise me—was that he had not married, and that he was still in the iron business. All through those years, however, I never ceased to wish, in certain situations and at certain turns of thought, that Merrick were in reach, that I could tell this or that to Merrick. I had never, in the interval, found any one with just his quickness of perception and just his sureness of response.

After dinner, therefore, we irresistibly drew together. In Mrs. Cumnor's big easy drawing-room cigars were allowed, and there was no break in the communion of the sexes; and, this being the case, I ought to have sought a seat beside one of the ladies among whom we were allowed to remain. But, as had generally happened of old when Merrick was in sight, I found myself steering straight for him past all minor ports of call.

There had been no time, before dinner, for more than the barest expression of satisfaction at meeting, and our seats had been at opposite ends of the longish table, so that we got our first real look at each other in the secluded corner to which Mrs. Cumnor's vigilance now directed us.

Merrick was still handsome in his stooping tawny way: handsomer perhaps, with thinnish hair and more lines in his face, than in the young excess of his good looks. He was very glad to see me and conveyed his gladness by the same charming smile; but as soon as we began to talk I felt a change. It was not merely the change that years and experience and altered values bring. There was something more fundamental the matter with Merrick, something dreadful, unforeseen, unaccountable: Merrick had grown conventional and dull.

In the glow of his frank pleasure in seeing me I was ashamed to analyze the nature of the change; but presently our talk began to flag—fancy a talk with Merrick flagging!—and self-deception became impossible as I watched myself handing out platitudes with the gesture of the salesman offering something to a purchaser "equally good." The worst of it was that Merrick—Merrick, who had once felt everything!—didn't seem to feel the lack of spontaneity in my remarks, but hung on them with a harrowing faith in the resuscitating power of our past. It was as if he hugged the empty vessel of our friendship without perceiving that the last drop of its essence was dry.

But after all, I am exaggerating. Through my surprise and disappointment I felt a certain sense of well-being in the mere physical presence of my old friend. I liked looking at the way his dark hair waved away from the forehead, at the tautness of his dry brown cheek, the thoughtful backward tilt of his head, the way his brown eyes mused upon the scene through lowered lids. All the past was in his way of looking and sitting, and I wanted to stay near him, and felt that he wanted me to stay; but the devil of it was that neither of us knew what to talk about.

It was this difficulty which caused me, after a while, since I could not follow Merrick's talk, to follow his eyes in their roaming circuit of the room.

At the moment when our glances joined, his had paused on a lady seated at some distance from our corner. Immersed, at first, in the satisfaction of finding myself again with Merrick, I had been only half aware of this lady, as of one of the few persons present whom I did not know, or had failed to remember. There was nothing in her appearance to challenge my attention or to excite my curiosity, and I don't suppose I should have looked at her again if I had not noticed that my friend was doing so.

She was a woman of about forty-seven, with fair faded hair and a young figure. Her gray dress was handsome but ineffective, and her pale and rather serious face wore a small unvarying smile which might have been pinned on with her ornaments. She was one of the women in whom increasing years show rather what they have taken than what they have bestowed, and only on looking closely did one see that what they had taken must have been good of its kind.

Phil Cumnor and another man were talking to her, and the very intensity of the attention she bestowed on them betrayed the straining of rebellious thoughts. She never let her eyes stray or her smile drop; and at the proper moment I saw she was ready with the proper sentiment.

The party, like most of those that Mrs. Cumnor gathered about her, was not composed of exceptional beings. The people of the old vanished New York set were not exceptional: they were mostly cut on the same convenient and unobtrusive pattern; but they were often exceedingly "nice." And this obsolete quality marked every look and gesture of the lady I was scrutinizing.

While these reflections were passing through my mind I was aware that Merrick's eyes rested still on her. I took a cross-section of his look and found in it neither surprise nor absorption, but only a certain sober pleasure just about at the emotional level of the rest of the room. If he continued to look at her, his expression seemed to say, it was only because, all things considered, there were fewer reasons for looking at anybody else.

This made me wonder what were the reasons for looking at *her*; and as a first step toward enlightenment I said:—"I'm sure I've seen the lady over there in gray—"

Merrick detached his eyes and turned them on me with a wondering look.

"Seen her? You know her." He waited. "*Don't* you know her? It's Mrs. Reardon."

I wondered that he should wonder, for I could not re-member, in the Cumnor group or elsewhere, having known any one of the name he mentioned.

"But perhaps," he continued, "you hadn't heard of her marriage? You knew her as Mrs. Trant."

I gave him back his stare. "Not Mrs. Philip Trant?"

"Yes; Mrs. Philip Trant."

"Not Paulina?"

"Yes—Paulina," he said, with a just perceptible delay before the name.

In my surprise I continued to stare at him. He averted his eyes from mine after a moment, and I saw that they had strayed back to her. "You find her so changed?" he asked.

Something in his voice acted as a warning signal, and I tried to reduce my astonishment to less unbecoming propor-tions. "I don't find that she looks much older."

"No. Only different?" he suggested, as if there were noth-ing new to him in my perplexity.

"Yes—awfully different."

"I suppose we're all awfully different. To you, I mean—coming from so far?"

"I recognized all the rest of you," I said, hesitating. "And she used to be the one who stood out most."

There was a flash, a wave, a stir of something deep down in his eyes. "Yes," he said. "*That's* the difference."

"I see it is. She—she looks worn down. Soft but blurred, like the figures in that tapestry behind her."

He glanced at her again, as if to test the exactness of my analogy.

"Life wears everybody down," he said.

"Yes—except those it makes more distinct. They're the rare ones, of course; but she *was* rare."

He stood up suddenly, looking old and tired. "I believe I'll be off. I wish you'd come down to my place for Sunday. . . . No, don't shake hands—I want to slide away unawares."

He had backed away to the threshold and was turning the noiseless door-knob. Even Mrs. Cumnor's door-knobs had tact and didn't tell.

"Of course I'll come," I promised warmly. In the last ten minutes he had begun to interest me again.

"All right. Good-bye." Half through the door he paused to add:—"*She* remembers you. You ought to speak to her."

"I'm going to. But tell me a little more." I thought I saw a shade of constraint on his face, and did not add, as I had meant to: "Tell me—because she interests me—what wore her down?" Instead, I asked: "How soon after Trant's death did she remarry?"

He seemed to make an effort of memory. "It was seven years ago, I think."

"And is Reardon here to-night?"

"Yes; over there, talking to Mrs. Cumnor."

I looked across the broken groupings and saw a large glossy man with straw-coloured hair and a red face, whose shirt and shoes and complexion seemed all to have received a coat of the same expensive varnish.

As I looked there was a drop in the talk about us, and I heard Mr. Reardon pronounce in a big booming voice: "What I say is: what's the good of disturbing things? Thank the Lord, I'm content with what I've got!"

"Is *that* her husband? What's he like?"

"Oh, the best fellow in the world," said Merrick, going.

II

Merrick had a little place at Riverdale, where he went occasionally to be near the Iron Works, and where he hid his week-ends when the world was too much with him.

Here, on the following Saturday afternoon I found him awaiting me in a pleasant setting of books and prints and faded parental furniture.

We dined late, and smoked and talked afterward in his book-walled study till the terrier on the hearth-rug stood up and yawned for bed. When we took the hint and moved toward the staircase I felt, not that I had found the old Merrick again, but that I was on his track, had come across traces of his passage here and there in the thick jungle that had grown up between us. But I had a feeling that when I finally came on the man himself he might be dead. . . .

As we started upstairs he turned back with one of his abrupt shy movements, and walked into the study.

"Wait a bit!" he called to me.

I waited, and he came out in a moment carrying a limp folio.

"It's typewritten. Will you take a look at it? I've been trying to get to work again," he explained, thrusting the manuscript into my hand.

"What? Poetry, I hope?" I exclaimed.

He shook his head with a gleam of derision. "No—just general considerations. The fruit of fifty years of inexperience."

He showed me to my room and said good-night.

The following afternoon we took a long walk inland, across the hills, and I said to Merrick what I could of his book. Unluckily there wasn't much to say. The essays were judicious, polished and cultivated; but they lacked the freshness and audacity of his youthful work. I tried to conceal my opinion behind the usual generalisations, but he broke through these feints with a quick thrust to the heart of my meaning.

"It's worn down—blurred? Like the figures in the Cumnors' tapestry?"

I hesitated. "It's a little too damned resigned," I said.

"Ah," he exclaimed, "so am I. Resigned." He switched the bare brambles by the roadside. "A man can't serve two masters."

"You mean business and literature?"

"No; I mean theory and instinct. The gray tree and the green. You've got to choose which fruit you'll try; and you don't know till afterward which of the two has the dead core."

"How can anybody be sure that only one of them has?"

"I'm sure," said Merrick sharply.

We turned back to the subject of his essays, and I was astonished at the detachment with which he criticised and demolished them. Little by little, as we talked, his old perspective, his old standards came back to him; but with the difference that they no longer seemed like functions of his mind but merely like attitudes assumed or dropped at will. He could still, with an effort, put himself at the angle from which he had formerly seen things; but it was with the effort of a man climbing mountains after a sedentary life in the plain.

I tried to cut the talk short, but he kept coming back to it with nervous insistence, forcing me into the last retrenchments of hypocrisy, and anticipating the verdict I held back. I perceived that a great deal—immensely more than I could see a reason for—had hung for him on my opinion of his book.

Then, as suddenly, his insistence dropped and, as if ashamed of having forced himself so long on my attention, he began to talk rapidly and uninterestingly of other things.

We were alone again that evening, and after dinner, wishing to efface the impression of the afternoon, and above all to show that I wanted him to talk about himself, I reverted to his work. "You must need an outlet of that sort. When a man's once had it in him, as you have—and when other things begin to dwindle—"

He laughed. "Your theory is that a man ought to be able to return to the Muse as he comes back to his wife after he's ceased to interest other women?"

"No; as he comes back to his wife after the day's work is done." A new thought came to me as I looked at him. "You ought to have had one," I added.

He laughed again. "A wife, you mean? So that there'd have been some one waiting for me even if the Muse decamped?" He went on after a pause: "I've a notion that the kind of woman worth coming back to wouldn't be much more patient than the Muse. But as it happens I never tried—because, for fear they'd chuck me, I put them both out of doors together."

He turned his head and looked past me with a queer expression at the low panelled door at my back. "Out of that very door they went—the two of 'em, on a rainy night like this: and one stopped and looked back, to see if I wasn't going to call her—and I didn't—and so they both went. . . ."

III

"The Muse?" (said Merrick refilling my glass and stooping to pat the terrier as he went back to his chair)—"well, you've met the Muse in the little volume of sonnets you used to like; and you've met the woman too, and you used to like *her*; though you didn't know her when you saw her the other evening. . . .

"No, I won't ask you how she struck you when you talked to her: I know. She struck you like that stuff I gave you to read last night. She's conformed—I've conformed—the mills have caught us and ground us: ground us, oh, exceedingly small!

"But you remember what she was; and that's the reason why I'm telling you this now. . . .

"You may recall that after my father's death I tried to sell the Works. I was impatient to free myself from anything that would keep me tied to New York. I don't dislike my trade, and I've made, in the end, a fairly good thing of it; but industrialism was not, at that time, in the line of my tastes, and I know now that it wasn't what I was meant for. Above all, I wanted to get away, to see new places and rub up against different ideas. I had reached a time of life—the top of the first hill, so to speak—where the distance draws one, and everything in the foreground seems tame and stale. I was sick to death of the particular set of conformities I had grown up among; sick of being a pleasant popular young man with a long line of dinners on my list, and the dead certainty of meeting the same people, or their prototypes, at all of them.

"Well—I failed to sell the Works, and that increased my discontent. I went through moods of cold unsociability, alternating with sudden flushes of curiosity, when I gloated over stray scraps of talk overheard in railway stations and omnibuses, when strange faces that I passed in the street tantalized me with fugitive promises. I wanted to be among things that were unexpected and unknown; and it seemed to me that nobody about me understood in the least what I felt, but that somewhere just out of reach there was some one who *did*, and whom I must find or despair. . . .

"It was just then that, one evening, I saw Mrs. Trant for the first time.

"Yes: I know—you wonder what I mean. I'd known her, of course, as a girl; I'd met her several times after her marriage; and I'd lately been thrown with her, quite intimately and continuously, during a succession of country-house visits. But I had never, as it happened, really *seen* her. . . .

"It was at a dinner at the Cumnors'; and there she was, in front of the very tapestry we saw her against the other evening, with people about her, and her face turned from me, and nothing noticeable or different in her dress or manner; and suddenly she stood out for me against the familiar unimportant background, and for the first time I saw a meaning in the stale phrase of a picture's walking out of its frame. For, after all, most people *are* just that to us: pictures, furniture, the inanimate accessories of our little island-area of sensation. And then sometimes one of these graven images moves and throws out live filaments toward us, and the line they make draws us across the world as the moon-track seems to draw a boat across the water. . . .

"There she stood; and as this queer sensation came over me I felt that she was looking steadily at me, that her eyes were voluntarily, consciously resting on me with the weight of the very question I was asking.

"I went over and joined her, and she turned and walked with me into the music-room. Earlier in the evening some one had been singing, and there were low lights there, and a few couples still sitting in those confidential corners of which Mrs. Cumnor has the art; but we were under no illusion as to the nature of these presences. We knew that they were just painted in, and that the whole of life was in us two, flowing back and forward between us. We talked, of course; we had the attitudes, even the words, of the others: I remember her telling me her plans for the spring and asking me politely about mine! As if there were the least sense in plans, now that this thing had happened!

"When we went back into the drawing-room I had said nothing to her that I might not have said to any other woman of the party; but when we shook hands I knew we should meet the next day—and the next. . . .

"That's the way, I take it, that Nature has arranged the beginning of the great enduring loves; and likewise of the little epidermal flurries. And how is a man to know where he is going?

"From the first my feeling for Paulina Trant seemed to me a grave business; but then the Enemy is given to producing that illusion. Many a man—I'm talking of the kind with imagination—has thought he was seeking a soul when all he wanted was a closer view of its tenement. And I tried—honestly tried—

to make myself think I was in the latter case. Because, in the first place, I didn't, just then, want a big disturbing influence in my life; and because I didn't want to be a dupe; and because Paulina Trant was not, according to hearsay, the kind of woman for whom it was worth while to bring up the big batteries. . . .

"But my resistance was only half-hearted. What I really felt—*all* I really felt—was the flood of joy that comes of heightened emotion. She had given me that, and I wanted her to give it to me again. That's as near as I've ever come to analyzing my state in the beginning.

"I knew her story, as no doubt you know it: the current version, I mean. She had been poor and fond of enjoyment, and she had married that pompous stick Philip Trant because she needed a home, and perhaps also because she wanted a little luxury. Queer how we sneer at women for wanting the thing that gives them half their attraction!

"People shook their heads over the marriage, and divided, prematurely, into Philip's partisans and hers: for no one thought it would work. And they were almost disappointed when, after all, it did. She and her wooden consort seemed to get on well enough. There was a ripple, at one time, over her friendship with young Jim Dalham, who was always with her during a summer at Newport and an autumn in Italy; then the talk died out, and she and Trant were seen together, as before, on terms of apparent good-fellowship.

"This was the more surprising because, from the first, Paulina had never made the least attempt to change her tone or subdue her colours. In the gray Trant atmosphere she flashed with prismatic fires. She smoked, she talked subversively, she did as she liked and went where she chose, and danced over the Trant prejudices and the Trant principles as if they'd been a ball-room floor; and all without apparent offence to her solemn husband and his cloud of cousins. I believe her frankness and directness struck them dumb. She moved like a kind of primitive Una through the virtuous rout, and never got a finger-mark on her freshness.

"One of the finest things about her was the fact that she never, for an instant, used her situation as a means of enhancing her attraction. With a husband like Trant it would have been so easy! He was a man who always saw the small sides of big things. He thought most of life compressible into a set of by-laws and the rest unmentionable; and with his stiff frock-coated and tall-hatted mind, instinctively distrustful of intelligences in another dress, with his arbitrary classification of whatever he didn't understand into 'the kind of thing I don't approve of,' 'the kind of thing that isn't done,' and—deepest depth of all—'the kind of thing I'd rather not discuss,' he lived in bondage to a shadowy moral etiquette of which the complex rites and awful penalties had cast an abiding gloom upon his manner.

"A woman like his wife couldn't have asked a better foil; yet I'm sure she never consciously used his dullness to relieve her brilliancy. She may have felt that the case spoke for itself. But I believe her reserve was rather due to a lively sense of justice, and to the rare habit (you said she was rare) of looking at facts as they are, without any throwing of sentimental lime-lights. She knew Trant could no more help being Trant than she could help being herself—and there was an end of it. I've never known a woman who 'made up' so little mentally. . . .

"Perhaps her very reserve, the fierceness of her implicit rejection of sympathy, exposed her the more to—well, to what happened when we met. She said afterward that it was like having been shut up for months in the hold of a ship, and coming suddenly on deck on a day that was all flying blue and silver. . . .

"I won't try to tell you what she was. It's easier to tell you what her friendship made of me; and I can do that best by adopting her metaphor of the ship. Haven't you, sometimes, at the moment of starting on a journey, some glorious plunge into the unknown, been tripped up by the thought: 'If only one hadn't to come back'? Well, with her one had the sense that one would never have to come back; that the magic ship would always carry one farther. And what an air one breathed on it! And, oh, the wind, and the islands, and the sunsets!

"I said just now 'her friendship'; and I used the word advisedly. Love is deeper than friendship, but friendship is a good deal wider. The beauty of our relation was that it included both dimensions. Our thoughts met as naturally as our eyes: it was almost as if we loved each other because we liked each other. The quality of a love may be tested by the amount of friendship it contains, and in our case there was no dividing line between loving and liking, no disproportion between them, no barrier against which desire beat in vain or from which thought fell back unsatisfied. Ours was a robust passion that could give an open-eyed account of itself, and not a beautiful madness shrinking away from the proof. . . .

"For the first months friendship sufficed us, or rather gave us so much by the way that we were in no hurry to reach what we knew it was leading to. But we were moving there nevertheless, and one day we found ourselves on the borders. It came about through a sudden decision of Trant's to start on a long tour with his wife. We had never foreseen that: he seemed rooted in his New York habits and convinced that the whole social and financial machinery of the metropolis would cease to function if he did not keep an eye on it through the columns of his morning paper, and pronounce judgment on it in the afternoon at his club. But something new had happened to him: he caught a cold, which was followed by a touch of pleurisy, and instantly he perceived the intense interest and importance which ill-health may add to life. He took the fullest advantage of it. A discerning doctor recommended travel in a warm climate; and suddenly, the morning paper, the afternoon club, Fifth Avenue, Wall Street, all the complex phenomena of the metropolis, faded into insignificance, and the rest of the terrestrial globe, from being a mere geographical hypothesis, useful in enabling one to determine the latitude of New York, acquired reality and magnitude as a factor in the convalescence of Mr. Philip Trant.

"His wife was absorbed in preparations for the journey. To move him was like mobilizing an army, and weeks before the date set for their departure it was almost as if she were already gone.

"This foretaste of separation showed us what we were to each other. Yet I was letting her go—and there was no help for it, no way of preventing it. Resistance was as useless as the vain struggles in a nightmare. She was Trant's and not mine: part of his luggage when he travelled as she was part of his household furniture when he stayed at home. . . .

"The day she told me that their passages were taken—it was on a November afternoon, in her drawing-room in town—I turned away from her and, going to the window, stood looking out at the torrent of traffic interminably pouring down Fifth Avenue. I watched the senseless machinery of life revolving in the rain and mud, and tried to picture myself performing my small function in it after she had gone from me.

" 'It can't be—it can't be!' I exclaimed.

" 'What can't be?'

"I came back into the room and sat down by her. 'This—this—' I hadn't any words. 'Two weeks!' I said. 'What's two weeks?'

"She answered, vaguely, something about their thinking of Spain for the spring—

" 'Two weeks—two weeks!' I repeated. 'And the months we've lost—the days that belonged to us!'

" 'Yes,' she said, 'I'm thankful it's settled.'

"Our words seemed irrelevant, haphazard. It was as if each were answering a secret voice, and not what the other was saying.

" 'Don't you *feel* anything at all?' I remember bursting out at her. As I asked it the tears were streaming down her face. I felt angry with her, and was almost glad to note that her lids were red and that she didn't cry becomingly. I can't express my sensation to you except by saying that she seemed part of life's huge league against me. And suddenly I thought of an afternoon we had spent together in the country, on a ferny hill-side, when we had sat under a beech-tree, and her hand had lain palm upward in the moss, close to mine, and I had watched a little black-and-red beetle creeping over it. . . .

"The bell rang, and we heard the voice of a visitor and the click of an umbrella in the umbrella-stand.

"She rose to go into the inner drawing-room, and I caught her suddenly by the wrist. 'You understand,' I said, 'that we can't go on like this?'

" 'I understand,' she answered, and moved away to meet her visitor. As I went out I heard her saying in the other room: 'Yes, we're really off on the twelfth.'

IV

"I wrote her a long letter that night, and waited two days for a reply.

"On the third day I had a brief line saying that she was go-ing to spend Sunday with some friends who had a place near Riverdale, and that she would arrange to see me while she was there. That was all.

"It was on a Saturday that I received the note and I came out here the same night. The next morning was rainy, and I was in despair, for I had counted on her asking me to take her for a drive or a long walk. It was hopeless to try to say what I had to say to her in the drawing-room of a crowded coun-try-house. And only eleven days were left!

"I stayed indoors all the morning, fearing to go out lest she should telephone me. But no sign came, and I grew more and more restless and anxious. She was too free and frank for co-quetry, but her silence and evasiveness made me feel that, for some reason, she did not wish to hear what she knew I meant to say. Could it be that she was, after all, more conventional, less genuine, than I had thought? I went again and again over the whole maddening round of conjecture; but the only con-clusion I could rest in was that, if she loved me as I loved her, she would be as determined as I was to let no obstacle come between us during the days that were left.

"The luncheon-hour came and passed, and there was no word from her. I had ordered my trap to be ready, so that I might drive over as soon as she summoned me; but the hours dragged on, the early twilight came, and I sat here in this very chair, or measured up and down, up and down, the length of this very rug—and still there was no message and no letter.

"It had grown quite dark, and I had ordered away, impa-tiently, the servant who came in with the lamps: I couldn't *bear* any definite sign that the day was over! And I was stand-ing there on the rug, staring at the door, and noticing a bad crack in its panel, when I heard the sound of wheels on the gravel. A word at last, no doubt—a line to explain. . . . I didn't seem to care much for her reasons, and I stood where I was and continued to stare at the door. And suddenly it opened and she came in.

"The servant followed her with a light, and then went out and closed the door. Her face looked pale in the lamp-light, but her voice was as clear as a bell.

" 'Well,' she said, 'you see I've come.'

"I started toward her with hands outstretched. 'You've come—you've come!' I stammered.

"Yes; it was like her to come in that way—without dissimulation or explanation or excuse. It was like her, if she gave at all, to give not furtively or in haste, but openly, deliberately, without stinting the measure or counting the cost. But her quietness and serenity disconcerted me. She did not look like a woman who has yielded impetuously to an uncontrollable impulse. There was something almost solemn in her face.

"The effect of it stole over me as I looked at her, suddenly subduing the huge flush of gratified longing.

" 'You're here, here, here!' I kept repeating, like a child singing over a happy word.

" 'You said,' she continued, in her grave clear voice, 'that we couldn't go on as we were—'

" 'Ah, it's divine of you!' I held out my arms to her.

"She didn't draw back from them, but her faint smile said, 'Wait,' and lifting her hands she took the pins from her hat, and laid the hat on the table.

"As I saw her dear head bare in the lamp-light, with the thick hair waving away from the parting, I forgot everything but the bliss and wonder of her being here—here, in my house, on my hearth—that fourth rose from the corner of the rug is the exact spot where she was standing. . . .

"I drew her to the fire, and made her sit down in the chair you're in, and knelt down by her, and hid my face on her knees. She put her hand on my head, and I was happy to the depths of my soul.

" 'Oh, I forgot—' she exclaimed suddenly. I lifted my head and our eyes met. Hers were smiling.

"She reached out her hand, opened the little bag she had tossed down with her hat, and drew a small object from it. 'I left my trunk at the station. Here's the check. Can you send for it?' she asked.

"Her trunk—she wanted me to send for her trunk! Oh, yes—I see your smile, your 'lucky man!' Only, you see, I didn't love her in that way. I knew she couldn't come to my house without running a big risk of discovery, and my tenderness for her, my impulse to shield her, was stronger, even then, than vanity or desire. Judged from the point of view of those emotions I fell terribly short of my part. I hadn't any of the proper feelings. Such an act of romantic folly was so unlike her that it almost irritated me, and I found myself desperately wondering how I could get her to reconsider her plan without—well, without seeming to want her to.

"It's not the way a novel hero feels; it's probably not the way a man in real life ought to have felt. But it's the way I felt—and she saw it.

"She put her hands on my shoulders and looked at me with deep, deep eyes. 'Then you didn't expect me to stay?' she asked.

"I caught her hands and pressed them to me, stammering out that I hadn't dared to dream. . . .

" 'You thought I'd come—just for an hour?'

" 'How could I dare think more? I adore you, you know, for what you've done! But it would be known if you—if you stayed on. My servants—everybody about here knows you. I've no right to expose you to the risk.' She made no answer, and I went on tenderly: 'Give me, if you will, the next few hours: there's a train that will get you to town by midnight. And then we'll arrange something—in town—where it's safer for you—more easily managed. . . . It's beautiful, it's heavenly of you to have come; but I love you too much—I must take care of you and think for you—'

"I don't suppose it ever took me so long to say so few words, and though they were profoundly sincere they sounded unutterably shallow, irrelevant and grotesque. She made no effort to help me out, but sat silent, listening, with her meditative smile. 'It's my duty, dearest, as a man,' I rambled on. The more I love you the more I'm bound—'

" 'Yes; but you don't understand,' she interrupted.

"She rose as she spoke, and I got up also, and we stood and looked at each other.

" 'I haven't come for a night; if you want me I've come for always,' she said.

"Here again, if I give you an honest account of my feelings I shall write myself down as the poor-spirited creature I suppose I am. There wasn't, I swear, at the moment, a grain of selfishness, of personal reluctance, in my feeling. I worshipped every hair of her head—when we were together I was happy, when I was away from her something was gone from every good thing; but I had always looked on our love for each other, our possible relation to each other, as such situations are looked on in what is called society. I had supposed her, for all her freedom and originality, to be just as tacitly subservient to that view as I was: ready to take what she wanted on the terms on which society concedes such taking, and to pay for it by the usual restrictions, concealments and hypocrisies. In short, I supposed that she would 'play the game'—look out for her own safety, and expect me to look out for it. It sounds cheap enough, put that way—but it's the rule we live under, all of us. And the amazement of finding her suddenly outside of it, oblivious of it, unconscious of it, left me, for an awful minute, stammering at her like a graceless dolt. . . . Perhaps it wasn't even a minute; but in it she had gone the whole round of my thoughts.

" 'It's raining,' she said, very low. 'I suppose you can telephone for a trap?'

"There was no irony or resentment in her voice. She walked slowly across the room and paused before the Brangwyn etching over there. 'That's a good impression. *Will* you telephone, please?' she repeated.

"I found my voice again, and with it the power of movement. I followed her and dropped at her feet. 'You can't go like this!' I cried.

"She looked down on me from heights and heights. 'I can't stay like this,' she answered.

"I stood up and we faced each other like antagonists. 'You don't know,' I accused her passionately, 'in the least what you're asking me to ask of you!'

" 'Yes, I do: *everything*,' she breathed.

" 'And it's got to be that or nothing?'

" 'Oh, on both sides,' she reminded me.

" '*Not* on both sides. It's not fair. That's why—'

" 'Why you won't?'

" 'Why I cannot—may not!'

" 'Why you'll take a night and not a life?'

"The taunt, for a woman usually so sure of her aim, fell so short of the mark that its only effect was to increase my conviction of her helplessness. The very intensity of my longing for her made me tremble where she was fearless. I had to protect her first, and think of my own attitude afterward.

"She was too discerning not to see this too. Her face softened, grew inexpressibly appealing, and she dropped again into that chair you're in, leaned forward, and looked up with her grave smile.

" 'You think I'm beside myself—raving? (You're not thinking of yourself, I know.) I'm not: I never was saner. Since I've known you I've often thought this might happen. This thing between us isn't an ordinary thing. If it had been we shouldn't, all these months, have drifted. We should have wanted to skip to the last page—and then throw down the book. We shouldn't have felt we could *trust* the future as we did. We were in no hurry because we knew we shouldn't get tired; and when two people feel that about each other they must live together—or part. I don't see what else they can do. A little trip along the coast won't answer. It's the high seas—or else being tied up to Lethe wharf. And I'm for the high seas, my dear!'

"Think of sitting here—here, in this room, in this chair—and listening to that, and seeing the light on her hair, and hearing the sound of her voice! I don't suppose there ever was a scene just like it. . . .

"She was astounding—inexhaustible; through all my anguish of resistance I found a kind of fierce joy in following her. It was lucidity at white heat: the last sublimation of passion. She might have been an angel arguing a point in the empyrean if she hadn't been, so completely, a woman pleading for her life. . . .

"Her life: that was the thing at stake! She couldn't do with less of it than she was capable of; and a woman's life is inextricably part of the man's she cares for.

"That was why, she argued, she couldn't accept the usual solution: couldn't enter into the only relation that society tolerates between people situated like ourselves. Yes: she knew all the arguments on *that* side: didn't I suppose she'd been over them and over them? She knew (for hadn't she often said it of others?) what is said of the woman who, by throwing in her lot with her lover's, binds him to a lifelong duty which has the irksomeness without the dignity of marriage. Oh, she could talk on that side with the best of them: only she asked me to consider the other—the side of the man and woman who love each other deeply and completely enough to want their lives enlarged, and not diminished, by their love. What, in such a case—she reasoned—must be the inevitable effect of concealing, denying, disowning, the central fact, the motive power of one's existence? She asked me to picture the course of such a love: first working as a fever in the blood, distorting and deflecting everything, making all other interests insipid, all other duties irksome, and then, as the acknowledged claims of life regained their hold, gradually dying—the poor starved passion!—for want of the wholesome necessary food of common living and doing, yet leaving life impoverished by the loss of all it might have been.

" 'I'm not talking, dear—' I see her now, leaning toward me with shining eyes: 'I'm not talking of the people who haven't enough to fill their days, and to whom a little mystery, a little manœuvring, gives an illusion of importance that they can't afford to miss; I'm talking of you and me, with all our tastes and curiosities and activities; and I ask you what our love would become if we had to keep it apart from our lives, like a pretty useless animal that we went to peep at and feed with sweet-meats through its cage?'

"I won't, my dear fellow, go into the other side of our strange duel: the arguments I used were those that most men in my situation would have felt bound to use, and that most women in Paulina's accept instinctively, without even formulating them. The exceptionalness, the significance, of the case lay wholly in the fact that she had formulated them all and then rejected them. . . .

"There was one point I didn't, of course, touch on; and that was the popular conviction (which I confess I shared) that when a man and a woman agree to defy the world together the man really sacrifices much more than the woman. I was not even conscious of thinking of this at the time, though it may have lurked somewhere in the shadow of my scruples for her; but she dragged it out into the daylight and held me face to face with it.

" 'Remember, I'm not attempting to lay down any general rule,' she insisted; 'I'm not theorizing about Man and Woman, I'm talking about you and me. How do I know what's best for the woman in the next house? Very likely she'll bolt when it would have been better for her to stay at home. And it's the same with the man: he'll probably do the wrong thing. It's generally the weak heads that commit follies, when it's the strong ones that ought to: and my point is that you and I are both strong enough to behave like fools if we want to. . . .

" 'Take your own case first—because, in spite of the sentimentalists, it's the man who stands to lose most. You'll have to give up the Iron Works: which you don't much care about—because it won't be particularly agreeable for us to live in New York: which you don't care much about either. But you won't be sacrificing what is called "a career." You made up your mind long ago that your best chance of self-development, and consequently of general usefulness, lay in thinking rather than doing; and, when we first met, you were already planning to sell out your business, and travel and write. Well! Those ambitions are of a kind that won't be harmed by your dropping out of your social setting. On the contrary, such work as you want to do ought to gain by it, because you'll be brought nearer to life-as-it-is, in contrast to life-as-a-visiting-list. . . .'

"She threw back her head with a sudden laugh. 'And the joy of not having any more visits to make! I wonder if you've ever thought of *that*? Just at first, I mean; for society's getting so deplorably lax that, little by little, it will edge up to us—you'll see! I don't want to idealize the situation, dearest, and I won't conceal from you that in time we shall be called on. But, oh, the fun we shall have had in the interval! And then, for the first time we shall be able to dictate our own terms, one of which will be that no bores need apply. Think of being cured of all one's chronic bores! We shall feel as jolly as people do after a successful operation.'

"I don't know why this nonsense sticks in my mind when some of the graver things we said are less distinct. Perhaps it's because of a certain iridescent quality of feeling that made her gaiety seem like sunshine through a shower. . . .

" 'You ask me to think of myself?' she went on. 'But the beauty of our being together will be that, for the first time, I shall dare to! Now I have to think of all the tedious trifles I can pack the days with, because I'm afraid—I'm afraid—to hear the voice of the real me, down below, in the windowless underground hole where I keep her. . . .

" 'Remember again, please, it's not Woman, it's Paulina Trant, I'm talking of. The woman in the next house may have all sorts of reasons—honest reasons—for staying there. There may be some one there who needs her badly: for whom the light would go out if she went. Whereas to Philip I've been simply—well, what New York was before he decided to travel: the most important thing in life till he made up his mind to leave it; and now merely the starting-place of several lines of steamers. Oh, I didn't have to love you to know that! I only had to live with *him*. . . . If he lost his eye-glasses he'd think it was the fault of the eye-glasses; he'd really feel that the eye-glasses had been careless. And he'd be convinced that no others would suit him quite as well. But at the optician's he'd probably be told that he needed something a little different, and after that he'd feel that the old eye-glasses had never suited him at all, and that *that* was their fault too. . . .'

"At one moment—but I don't recall when—I remember she stood up with one of her quick movements, and came toward me, holding out her arms. 'Oh, my dear, I'm pleading for my life; do you suppose I shall ever want for arguments?' she cried. . . .

"After that, for a bit, nothing much remains with me except a sense of darkness and of conflict. The one spot of daylight in my whirling brain was the conviction that I couldn't—whatever happened—profit by the sudden impulse she had acted on, and allow her to take, in a moment of passion, a decision that was to shape her whole life. I couldn't so much as lift my little finger to keep her with me then, unless I were prepared to accept for her as well as for myself the full consequences of the future she had planned for us. . . .

"Well—there's the point: I wasn't. I felt in her—poor fatuous idiot that I was!—that lack of objective imagination which had always seemed to me to account, at least in part, for many of the so-called heroic qualities in women. When their feelings are involved they simply can't look ahead. Her unfaltering logic notwithstanding, I felt this about Paulina as I listened. She had a specious air of knowing where she was going, but she didn't. She seemed the genius of logic and understanding, but the demon of illusion spoke through her lips. . . .

"I said just now that I hadn't, at the outset, given my own side of the case a thought. It would have been truer to say that I hadn't given it a *separate* thought. But I couldn't think of her without seeing myself as a factor—the chief factor—in her problem, and without recognizing that whatever the experiment made of me, that it must fatally, in the end, make of her. If I couldn't carry the thing through she must break down with me: we should have to throw our separate selves into the melting-pot of this mad adventure, and be 'one' in a terrible indissoluble completeness of which marriage is only an imperfect counterpart. . . .

"There could be no better proof of her extraordinary power over me, and of the way she had managed to clear the air of sentimental illusion, than the fact that I presently found myself putting this before her with a merciless precision of touch.

" 'If we love each other enough to do a thing like this, we must love each other enough to see just what it is we're going to do.'

"So I invited her to the dissecting-table, and I see now the fearless eye with which she approached the cadaver. 'For that's what it is, you know,' she flashed out at me, at the end of my long demonstration. 'It's a dead body, like all the instances and examples and hypothetical cases that ever were! What do you expect to learn from *that*? The first great anatomist was the man who stuck his knife in a heart that was beating; and the only way to find out what doing a thing will be like is to do it!'

"She looked away from me suddenly, as if she were fixing her eyes on some vision on the outer rim of consciousness. 'No: there's one other way,' she exclaimed; 'and that is, *not* to do it! To abstain and refrain; and then see what we become, or what we don't become, in the long run, and to draw our inferences. That's the game that almost everybody about us is playing, I suppose; there's hardly one of the dull people one meets at dinner who hasn't had, just once, the chance of a berth on a ship that was off for the Happy Isles, and hasn't refused it for fear of sticking on a sand-bank!

" 'I'm doing my best, you know,' she continued, 'to see the sequel as you see it, as you believe it's your duty to me to see it. I know the instances you're thinking of: the listless couples wearing out their lives in shabby watering places, and hanging on the favour of hotel acquaintances; or the proud quarrelling wretches shut up alone in a fine house because they're too good for the only society they can get, and trying to cheat their boredom by squabbling with their tradesmen and spying on their servants. No doubt there are such cases; but I don't recognize either of us in those dismal figures. Why, to do it would be to admit that our life, yours and mine, is in the people about us and not in ourselves; that we're parasites and not self-sustaining creatures; and that the lives we're leading now are so brilliant, full and satisfying that what we should have to give up would surpass even the blessedness of being to-gether!'

"At that stage, I confess, the solid ground of my resistance began to give way under me. It was not that my convictions were shaken, but that she had swept me into a world whose laws were different, where one could reach out in directions that the slave of gravity hasn't pictured. But at the same time my opposition hardened from reason into instinct. I knew it was her voice, and not her logic, that was unsettling me. I knew that if she'd written out her thesis and sent it me by post I should have made short work of it; and again the part of me which I called by all the finest names: my chivalry, my unselfishness, my superior masculine experience, cried out with one voice: 'You can't let a woman use her graces to her own undoing—you can't, for her own sake, let her eyes convince you when her reasons don't!'

"And then, abruptly, and for the first time, a doubt entered me: a doubt of her perfect moral honesty. I don't know how else to describe my feeling that she wasn't playing fair, that in coming to my house, in throwing herself at my head (I called things by their names), she had perhaps not so much obeyed an irresistible impulse as deeply, deliberately reckoned on the dissolvent effect of her generosity, her rashness and her beauty. . . .

"From the moment that this mean doubt raised its head in me I was once more the creature of all the conventional scruples: I was repeating, before the looking-glass of my self-consciousness, all the stereotyped gestures of the 'man of honour.' . . . Oh, the sorry figure I must have cut! You'll understand my dropping the curtain on it as quickly as I can. . . .

"Yet I remember, as I made my point, being struck by its impressiveness. I was suffering and enjoying my own suffering. I told her that, whatever step we decided to take, I owed it to her to insist on its being taken soberly, deliberately—

"('No: it's "advisedly," isn't it? Oh, I was thinking of the Marriage Service,' she interposed with a faint laugh.)

"—that if I accepted, there, on the spot, her headlong beautiful gift of herself, I should feel I had taken an unfair advantage of her, an advantage which she would be justified in reproaching me with afterward; that I was not afraid to tell her this because she was intelligent enough to know that my scruples were the surest proof of the quality of my love; that I refused to owe my happiness to an unconsidered impulse; that we must see each other again, in her own house, in less agitating circumstances, when she had had time to reflect on my words, to study her heart and look into the future. . . .

"The factitious exhilaration produced by uttering these beautiful sentiments did not last very long, as you may imagine. It fell, little by little, under her quiet gaze, a gaze in which there was neither contempt nor irony nor wounded pride, but only a tender wistfulness of interrogation; and I think the acutest point in my suffering was reached when she said, as I ended: 'Oh; yes, of course I understand.'

" 'If only you hadn't come to me here!' I blurted out in the torture of my soul.

"She was on the threshold when I said it, and she turned and laid her hand gently on mine. 'There was no other way,' she said; and at the moment it seemed to me like some hackneyed phrase in a novel that she had used without any sense of its meaning.

"I don't remember what I answered or what more we either of us said. At the end a desperate longing to take her in my arms and keep her with me swept aside everything else, and I went up to her, pleading, stammering, urging I don't know what. . . . But she held me back with a quiet look, and went. I had ordered the carriage, as she asked me to; and my last definite recollection is of watching her drive off in the rain. . . .

"I had her promise that she would see me, two days later, at her house in town, and that we should then have what I called 'a decisive talk'; but I don't think that even at the moment I was the dupe of my phrase. I knew, and she knew, that the end had come. . . .

V

"It was about that time (Merrick went on after a long pause) that I definitely decided not to sell the Works, but to stick to my job and conform my life to it.

"I can't describe to you the rage of conformity that possessed me. Poetry, ideas—all the picture-making processes stopped. A kind of dull self-discipline seemed to me the only exercise worthy of a reflecting mind. I *had* to justify my great refusal, and I tried to do it by plunging myself up to the eyes into the very conditions I had been instinctively struggling to get away from. The only possible consolation would have been to find in a life of business routine and social submission such moral compensations as may reward the citizen if they fail the man; but to attain to these I should have had to accept the old delusion that the social and the individual man are two. Now, on the contrary, I found soon enough that I couldn't get one part of my machinery to work effectively while another wanted feeding: and that in rejecting what had seemed to me a negation of action I had made all my action negative.

"The best solution, of course, would have been to fall in love with another woman; but it was long before I could bring myself to wish that this might happen to me. . . . Then, at length, I suddenly and violently desired it; and as such impulses are seldom without some kind of imperfect issue I contrived, a year or two later, to work myself up into the wished-for state. . . . She was a woman in society, and with all the awe of that institution that Paulina lacked. Our relation was consequently one of those unavowed affairs in which triviality is the only alternative to tragedy. Luckily we had, on both sides, risked only as much as prudent people stake in a drawing-room game; and when the match was over I take it that we came out fairly even.

"My gain, at all events, was of an unexpected kind. The adventure had served only to make me understand Paulina's abhorrence of such experiments, and at every turn of the slight intrigue I had felt how exasperating and belittling such a relation was bound to be between two people who, had they been free, would have mated openly. And so from a brief phase of imperfect forgetting I was driven back to a deeper and more understanding remembrance. . . .

"This second incarnation of Paulina was one of the strangest episodes of the whole strange experience. Things she had said during our extraordinary talk, things I had hardly heard at the time, came back to me with singular vividness and a fuller meaning. I hadn't any longer the cold consolation of believing in my own perspicacity: I saw that her insight had been deeper and keener than mine.

"I remember, in particular, starting up in bed one sleepless night as there flashed into my head the meaning of her last words: 'There was no other way'; the phrase I had half-smiled at at the time, as a parrot-like echo of the novel-heroine's stock farewell. I had never, up to that moment, wholly understood why Paulina had come to my house that night. I had never been able to make that particular act—which could hardly, in the light of her subsequent conduct, be dismissed as a blind surge of passion—square with my conception of her character. She was at once the most spontaneous and the steadiest-minded woman I had ever known, and the last to wish to owe any advantage to surprise, to unpreparedness, to any play on the spring of sex. The better I came, retrospectively, to know her, the more sure I was of this, and the less intelligible her act appeared. And then, suddenly, after a night of hungry restless thinking, the flash of enlightenment came. She had come to my house, had brought her trunk with her, had thrown herself at my head with all possible violence and publicity, in order to give me a pretext, a loophole, an honourable excuse, for doing and saying—why, precisely what I had said and done!

"As the idea came to me it was as if some ironic hand had touched an electric button, and all my fatuous phrases had leapt out on me in fire.

"Of course she had known all along just the kind of thing I should say if I didn't at once open my arms to her; and to save my pride, my dignity, my conception of the figure I was cutting in her eyes, she had recklessly and magnificently provided me with the decentest pretext a man could have for doing a pusillanimous thing. . . .

"With that discovery the whole case took a different aspect. It hurt less to think of Paulina—and yet it hurt more. The tinge of bitterness, of doubt, in my thoughts of her had had a tonic quality. It was harder to go on persuading myself that I had done right as, bit by bit, my theories crumbled under the test of time. Yet, after all, as she herself had said, one could judge of results only in the long run. . . .

"The Trants stayed away for two years; and about a year after they got back, you may remember, Trant was killed in a railway accident. You know Fate's way of untying a knot after everybody has given up tugging at it!

"Well—there I was, completely justified: all my weaknesses turned into merits! I had 'saved' a weak woman from herself, I had kept her to the path of duty, I had spared her the humiliation of scandal and the misery of self-reproach; and now I had only to put out my hand and take my reward.

"I had avoided Paulina since her return, and she had made no effort to see me. But after Trant's death I wrote her a few lines, to which she sent a friendly answer; and when a decent interval had elapsed, and I asked if I might call on her, she answered at once that she would see me.

"I went to her house with the fixed intention of asking her to marry me—and I left it without having done so. Why? I don't know that I can tell you. Perhaps you would have had to sit there opposite her, knowing what I did and feeling as I did, to understand why. She was kind, she was compassionate—I could see she didn't want to make it hard for me. Perhaps she even wanted to make it easy. But there, between us, was the memory of the gesture I hadn't made, forever parodying the one I was attempting! There wasn't a word I could think of that hadn't an echo in it of words of hers I had been deaf to; there wasn't an appeal I could make that didn't mock the appeal I had rejected. I sat there and talked of her husband's death, of her plans, of my sympathy; and I knew she understood; and knowing that, in a way, made it harder. . . . The door-bell rang and the footman came in to ask if she would receive other visitors. She looked at me a moment and said 'Yes,' and I got up and shook hands and went away.

"A few days later she sailed for Europe, and the next time we met she had married Reardon. . . ."

VI

It was long past midnight, and the terrier's hints became imperious.

Merrick rose from his chair, pushed back a fallen log and put up the fender. He walked across the room and stared a moment at the Brangwyn etching before which Paulina Trant had paused at a memorable turn of their talk. Then he came back and laid his hand on my shoulder.

"She summed it all up, you know, when she said that one way of finding out whether a risk is worth taking is *not* to take it, and then to see what one becomes in the long run, and draw one's inferences. The long run—well, we've run it, she and I. I know what I've become, but that's nothing to the misery of knowing what she's become. She had to have some kind of life, and she married Reardon. Reardon's a very good fellow in his way; but the worst of it is that it's not her way. . . .

"No: the worst of it is that now she and I meet as friends. We dine at the same houses, we talk about the same people, we play bridge together, and I lend her books. And sometimes Reardon slaps me on the back and says: 'Come in and dine with us, old man! What you want is to be cheered up!' And I go and dine with them, and he tells me how jolly comfortable she makes him, and what an ass I am not to marry; and she presses on me a second helping of *poulet Maryland*, and I smoke one of Reardon's cigars, and at half-past ten I get into my overcoat, and walk back alone to my rooms. . . ."

The Triumph of Night

IT WAS clear that the sleigh from Weymore had not come; and the shivering young traveller from Boston, who had counted on jumping into it when he left the train at Northridge Junction, found himself standing alone on the open platform, exposed to the full assault of night-fall and winter.

The blast that swept him came off New Hampshire snow-fields and ice-hung forests. It seemed to have traversed interminable leagues of frozen silence, filling them with the same cold roar and sharpening its edge against the same bitter black-and-white landscape. Dark, searching and sword-like, it alternately muffled and harried its victim, like a bull-fighter now whirling his cloak and now planting his darts. This analogy brought home to the young man the fact that he himself had no cloak, and that the overcoat in which he had faced the relatively temperate air of Boston seemed no thicker than a sheet of paper on the bleak heights of Northridge. George Faxon said to himself that the place was uncommonly well-named. It clung to an exposed ledge over the valley from which the train had lifted him, and the wind combed it with teeth of steel that he seemed actually to hear scraping against the wooden sides of the station. Other building there was none: the village lay far down the road, and thither—since the Weymore sleigh had not come—Faxon saw himself under the necessity of plodding through several feet of snow.

He understood well enough what had happened: his hostess had forgotten that he was coming. Young as Faxon was, this sad lucidity of soul had been acquired as the result of long experience, and he knew that the visitors who can least afford to hire a carriage are almost always those whom their hosts forget to send for. Yet to say that Mrs. Culme had forgotten him was too crude a way of putting it. Similar incidents led him to think that she had probably told her maid to tell the butler to telephone the coachman to tell one of the grooms (if no one else needed him) to drive over to

Northridge to fetch the new secretary; but on a night like this, what groom who respected his rights would fail to forget the order?

Faxon's obvious course was to struggle through the drifts to the village, and there rout out a sleigh to convey him to Weymore; but what if, on his arrival at Mrs. Culme's, no one remembered to ask him what this devotion to duty had cost? That, again, was one of the contingencies he had expensively learned to look out for, and the perspicacity so acquired told him it would be cheaper to spend the night at the Northridge inn, and advise Mrs. Culme of his presence there by telephone. He had reached this decision, and was about to entrust his luggage to a vague man with a lantern, when his hopes were raised by the sound of bells.

Two sleighs were just dashing up to the station, and from the foremost there sprang a young man muffled in furs.

"Weymore?—No, these are not the Weymore sleighs."

The voice was that of the youth who had jumped to the platform—a voice so agreeable that, in spite of the words, it fell consolingly on Faxon's ears. At the same moment the wandering station-lantern, casting a transient light on the speaker, showed his features to be in the pleasantest harmony with his voice. He was very fair and very young—hardly in the twenties, Faxon thought—but his face, though full of a morning freshness, was a trifle too thin and fine-drawn, as though a vivid spirit contended in him with a strain of physical weakness. Faxon was perhaps the quicker to notice such delicacies of balance because his own temperament hung on lightly quivering nerves, which yet, as he believed, would never quite swing him beyond a normal sensibility.

"You expected a sleigh from Weymore?" the newcomer continued, standing beside Faxon like a slender column of fur.

Mrs. Culme's secretary explained his difficulty, and the other brushed it aside with a contemptuous "Oh, *Mrs. Culme*!" that carried both speakers a long way toward reciprocal understanding.

"But then you must be—" The youth broke off with a smile of interrogation.

"The new secretary? Yes. But apparently there are no notes to be answered this evening." Faxon's laugh deepened the sense of solidarity which had so promptly established itself between the two.

His friend laughed also. "Mrs. Culme," he explained, "was lunching at my uncle's to-day, and she said you were due this evening. But seven hours is a long time for Mrs. Culme to remember anything."

"Well," said Faxon philosophically, "I suppose that's one of the reasons why she needs a secretary. And I've always the inn at Northridge," he concluded.

"Oh, but you haven't, though! It burned down last week."

"The deuce it did!" said Faxon; but the humour of the situation struck him before its inconvenience. His life, for years past, had been mainly a succession of resigned adaptations, and he had learned, before dealing practically with his embarrassments, to extract from most of them a small tribute of amusement.

"Oh, well, there's sure to be somebody in the place who can put me up."

"No one *you* could put up with. Besides, Northridge is three miles off, and our place—in the opposite direction—is a little nearer." Through the darkness, Faxon saw his friend sketch a gesture of self-introduction. "My name's Frank Rainer, and I'm staying with my uncle at Overdale. I've driven over to meet two friends of his, who are due in a few minutes from New York. If you don't mind waiting till they arrive I'm sure Overdale can do you better than Northridge. We're only down from town for a few days, but the house is always ready for a lot of people."

"But your uncle—?" Faxon could only object, with the odd sense, through his embarrassment, that it would be magically dispelled by his invisible friend's next words.

"Oh, my uncle—you'll see! I answer for *him*! I daresay you've heard of him—John Lavington?"

John Lavington! There was a certain irony in asking if one had heard of John Lavington! Even from a post of observation as obscure as that of Mrs. Culme's secretary the rumour of John Lavington's money, of his pictures, his politics, his charities and his hospitality, was as difficult to escape as the roar of a cataract in a mountain solitude. It might almost have been said that the one place in which one would not have expected to come upon him was in just such a solitude as now surrounded the speakers—at least in this deepest hour of its desertedness. But it was just like Lavington's brilliant ubiquity to put one in the wrong even there.

"Oh, yes, I've heard of your uncle."

"Then you *will* come, won't you? We've only five minutes to wait," young Rainer urged, in the tone that dispels scruples by ignoring them; and Faxon found himself accepting the invitation as simply as it was offered.

A delay in the arrival of the New York train lengthened their five minutes to fifteen; and as they paced the icy platform Faxon began to see why it had seemed the most natural thing in the world to accede to his new acquaintance's suggestion. It was because Frank Rainer was one of the privileged beings who simplify human intercourse by the atmosphere of confidence and good humour they diffuse. He produced this effect, Faxon noted, by the exercise of no gift but his youth, and of no art but his sincerity; and these qualities were revealed in a smile of such sweetness that Faxon felt, as never before, what Nature can achieve when she deigns to match the face with the mind.

He learned that the young man was the ward, and the only nephew, of John Lavington, with whom he had made his home since the death of his mother, the great man's sister. Mr. Lavington, Rainer said, had been "a regular brick" to him—"But then he is to every one, you know"—and the young fellow's situation seemed in fact to be perfectly in keeping with his person. Apparently the only shade that had ever rested on him was cast by the physical weakness which Faxon had already detected. Young Rainer had been threatened with tuberculosis, and the disease was so far advanced that, according to the highest authorities, banishment to Arizona or New Mexico was inevitable. "But luckily my uncle didn't pack me off, as most people would have done, without getting another opinion. Whose? Oh, an awfully clever chap, a young doctor with a lot of new ideas, who simply laughed at my being sent away, and said I'd do perfectly well in New York if I didn't dine out too much, and if I dashed off occasionally to Northridge for a little fresh air. So it's really my uncle's doing that I'm not in exile—and I feel no end better since the new chap told me I needn't bother." Young Rainer went on to confess that he was extremely fond of dining out, dancing and similar distractions; and Faxon, listening to him, was inclined to think that the physician who had refused to cut him off altogether from these pleasures was probably a better psychologist than his seniors.

"All the same you ought to be careful, you know." The sense of elder-brotherly concern that forced the words from Faxon made him, as he spoke, slip his arm through Frank Rainer's.

The latter met the movement with a responsive pressure. "Oh, I *am*: awfully, awfully. And then my uncle has such an eye on me!"

"But if your uncle has such an eye on you, what does he say to your swallowing knives out here in this Siberian wild?"

Rainer raised his fur collar with a careless gesture. "It's not that that does it—the cold's good for me."

"And it's not the dinners and dances? What is it, then?" Faxon good-humouredly insisted; to which his companion answered with a laugh: "Well, my uncle says it's being bored; and I rather think he's right!"

His laugh ended in a spasm of coughing and a struggle for breath that made Faxon, still holding his arm, guide him hastily into the shelter of the fireless waiting-room.

Young Rainer had dropped down on the bench against the wall and pulled off one of his fur gloves to grope for a hand-kerchief. He tossed aside his cap and drew the handkerchief across his forehead, which was intensely white, and beaded with moisture, though his face retained a healthy glow. But Faxon's gaze remained fastened to the hand he had uncovered: it was so long, so colourless, so wasted, so much older than the brow he passed it over.

"It's queer—a healthy face but dying hands," the secretary mused: he somehow wished young Rainer had kept on his glove.

The whistle of the express drew the young men to their feet, and the next moment two heavily-furred gentlemen had descended to the platform and were breasting the rigour of the night. Frank Rainer introduced them as Mr. Grisben and Mr. Balch, and Faxon, while their luggage was being lifted into the second sleigh, discerned them, by the roving lantern-

gleam, to be an elderly grey-headed pair, of the average prosperous business cut.

They saluted their host's nephew with friendly familiarity,
and Mr. Grisben, who seemed the spokesman of the two,
ended his greeting with a genial—"and many many more of
them, dear boy!" which suggested to Faxon that their arrival
coincided with an anniversary. But he could not press the enquiry, for the seat allotted him was at the coachman's side,
while Frank Rainer joined his uncle's guests inside the sleigh.

A swift flight (behind such horses as one could be sure of
John Lavington's having) brought them to tall gate-posts, an
illuminated lodge, and an avenue on which the snow had
been levelled to the smoothness of marble. At the end of the
avenue the long house loomed up, its principal bulk dark, but
one wing sending out a ray of welcome; and the next moment
Faxon was receiving a violent impression of warmth and light,
of hot-house plants, hurrying servants, a vast spectacular oak
hall like a stage-setting, and, in its unreal middle distance, a
small figure, correctly dressed, conventionally featured, and
utterly unlike his rather florid conception of the great John
Lavington.

The surprise of the contrast remained with him through his
hurried dressing in the large luxurious bedroom to which he
had been shown. "I don't see where he comes in," was the
only way he could put it, so difficult was it to fit the exuberance of Lavington's public personality into his host's contracted frame and manner. Mr. Lavington, to whom Faxon's
case had been rapidly explained by young Rainer, had welcomed him with a sort of dry and stilted cordiality that exactly matched his narrow face, his stiff hand, and the whiff of
scent on his evening handkerchief. "Make yourself at home—
at home!" he had repeated, in a tone that suggested, on his
own part, a complete inability to perform the feat he urged
on his visitor. "Any friend of Frank's . . . delighted . . .
make yourself thoroughly at home!"

II

In spite of the balmy temperature and complicated conve-
niences of Faxon's bedroom, the injunction was not easy to

obey. It was wonderful luck to have found a night's shelter under the opulent roof of Overdale, and he tasted the physical satisfaction to the full. But the place, for all its ingenuities of comfort, was oddly cold and unwelcoming. He couldn't have said why, and could only suppose that Mr. Lavington's intense personality—intensely negative, but intense all the same—must, in some occult way, have penetrated every corner of his dwelling. Perhaps, though, it was merely that Faxon himself was tired and hungry, more deeply chilled than he had known till he came in from the cold, and unutterably sick of all strange houses, and of the prospect of perpetually treading other people's stairs.

"I hope you're not famished?" Rainer's slim figure was in the doorway. "My uncle has a little business to attend to with Mr. Grisben, and we don't dine for half an hour. Shall I fetch you, or can you find your way down? Come straight to the dining-room—the second door on the left of the long gallery."

He disappeared, leaving a ray of warmth behind him, and Faxon, relieved, lit a cigarette and sat down by the fire.

Looking about with less haste, he was struck by a detail that had escaped him. The room was full of flowers—a mere "bachelor's room," in the wing of a house opened only for a few days, in the dead middle of a New Hampshire winter! Flowers were everywhere, not in senseless profusion, but placed with the same conscious art that he had remarked in the grouping of the blossoming shrubs in the hall. A vase of arums stood on the writing-table, a cluster of strange-hued carnations on the stand at his elbow, and from bowls of glass and porcelain clumps of freesia-bulbs diffused their melting fragrance. The fact implied acres of glass—but that was the least interesting part of it. The flowers themselves, their quality, selection and arrangement, attested on some one's part—and on whose but John Lavington's?—a solicitous and sensitive passion for that particular form of beauty. Well, it simply made the man, as he had appeared to Faxon, all the harder to understand!

The half-hour elapsed, and Faxon, rejoicing at the prospect of food, set out to make his way to the dining-room. He had not noticed the direction he had followed in going to his room, and was puzzled, when he left it, to find that two stair-cases, of apparently equal importance, invited him. He chose the one to his right, and reached, at its foot, a long gallery such as Rainer had described. The gallery was empty, the doors down its length were closed; but Rainer had said: "The second to the left," and Faxon, after pausing for some chance enlightenment which did not come, laid his hand on the second knob to the left.

The room he entered was square, with dusky picture-hung walls. In its centre, about a table lit by veiled lamps, he fancied Mr. Lavington and his guests to be already seated at dinner; then he perceived that the table was covered not with viands but with papers, and that he had blundered into what seemed to be his host's study. As he paused Frank Rainer looked up.

"Oh, here's Mr. Faxon. Why not ask him—?"

Mr. Lavington, from the end of the table, reflected his nephew's smile in a glance of impartial benevolence.

"Certainly. Come in, Mr. Faxon. If you won't think it a liberty—"

Mr. Grisben, who sat opposite his host, turned his head toward the door. "Of course Mr. Faxon's an American citizen?"

Frank Rainer laughed. "That's all right! . . . Oh, no, not one of your pin-pointed pens, Uncle Jack! Haven't you got a quill somewhere?"

Mr. Balch, who spoke slowly and as if reluctantly, in a muffled voice of which there seemed to be very little left, raised his hand to say: "One moment: you acknowledge this to be—?"

"My last will and testament?" Rainer's laugh redoubled. "Well, I won't answer for the 'last.' It's the first, anyway."

"It's a mere formula," Mr. Balch explained.

"Well, here goes." Rainer dipped his quill in the ink-stand his uncle had pushed in his direction, and dashed a gallant signature across the document.

Faxon, understanding what was expected of him, and conjecturing that the young man was signing his will on the attainment of his majority, had placed himself behind Mr. Grisben, and stood awaiting his turn to affix his name to the instrument. Rainer, having signed, was about to push the

paper across the table to Mr. Balch; but the latter, again raising his hand, said in his sad imprisoned voice: "The seal—?"

"Oh, does there have to be a seal?"

Faxon, looking over Mr. Grisben at John Lavington, saw a
faint frown between his impassive eyes. "Really, Frank!" He
seemed, Faxon thought, slightly irritated by his nephew's
frivolity.

"Who's got a seal?" Frank Rainer continued, glancing
about the table. "There doesn't seem to be one here."

Mr. Grisben interposed. "A wafer will do. Lavington, you
have a wafer?"

Mr. Lavington had recovered his serenity. "There must be
some in one of the drawers. But I'm ashamed to say I don't
know where my secretary keeps these things. He ought to
have seen to it that a wafer was sent with the document."

"Oh, hang it—" Frank Rainer pushed the paper aside: "It's
the hand of God—and I'm as hungry as a wolf. Let's dine
first, Uncle Jack."

"I think I've a seal upstairs," said Faxon.

Mr. Lavington sent him a barely perceptible smile. "So
sorry to give you the trouble—"

"Oh, I say, don't send him after it now. Let's wait till after
dinner!"

Mr. Lavington continued to smile on his guest, and the latter, as if under the faint coercion of the smile, turned from
the room and ran upstairs. Having taken the seal from his
writing-case he came down again, and once more opened the
door of the study. No one was speaking when he entered—
they were evidently awaiting his return with the mute impatience of hunger, and he put the seal in Rainer's reach, and
stood watching while Mr. Grisben struck a match and held it
to one of the candles flanking the inkstand. As the wax descended on the paper Faxon remarked again the strange ema-
ciation, the premature physical weariness, of the hand that
held it: he wondered if Mr. Lavington had ever noticed his
nephew's hand, and if it were not poignantly visible to him
now.

With this thought in his mind, Faxon raised his eyes to look
at Mr. Lavington. The great man's gaze rested on Frank
Rainer with an expression of untroubled benevolence; and at

the same instant Faxon's attention was attracted by the presence in the room of another person, who must have joined
the group while he was upstairs searching for the seal. The
new-comer was a man of about Mr. Lavington's age and figure, who stood just behind his chair, and who, at the moment
when Faxon first saw him, was gazing at young Rainer with
an equal intensity of attention. The likeness between the two
men—perhaps increased by the fact that the hooded lamps on
the table left the figure behind the chair in shadow—struck
Faxon the more because of the contrast in their expression.
John Lavington, during his nephew's clumsy attempt to drop
the wax and apply the seal, continued to fasten on him a look
of half-amused affection; while the man behind the chair, so
oddly reduplicating the lines of his features and figure, turned
on the boy a face of pale hostility.

The impression was so startling that Faxon forgot what was
going on about him. He was just dimly aware of young
Rainer's exclaiming: "Your turn, Mr. Grisben!" of Mr.
Grisben's protesting: "No—no; Mr. Faxon first," and of the
pen's being thereupon transferred to his own hand. He received it with a deadly sense of being unable to move, or even
to understand what was expected of him, till he became conscious of Mr. Grisben's paternally pointing out the precise spot
on which he was to leave his autograph. The effort to fix his
attention and steady his hand prolonged the process of signing, and when he stood up—a strange weight of fatigue on all
his limbs—the figure behind Mr. Lavington's chair was gone.

Faxon felt an immediate sense of relief. It was puzzling that
the man's exit should have been so rapid and noiseless, but
the door behind Mr. Lavington was screened by a tapestry
hanging, and Faxon concluded that the unknown looker-on
had merely had to raise it to pass out. At any rate he was
gone, and with his withdrawal the strange weight was lifted.
Young Rainer was lighting a cigarette, Mr. Balch inscribing his
name at the foot of the document, Mr. Lavington—his eyes
no longer on his nephew—examining a strange white-winged
orchid in the vase at his elbow. Every thing suddenly seemed
to have grown natural and simple again, and Faxon found
himself responding with a smile to the affable gesture with
which his host declared: "And now, Mr. Faxon, we'll dine."

III

"I wonder how I blundered into the wrong room just now; I thought you told me to take the second door to the left," Faxon said to Frank Rainer as they followed the older men down the gallery.

"So I did; but I probably forgot to tell you which staircase to take. Coming from your bedroom, I ought to have said the fourth door to the right. It's a puzzling house, because my uncle keeps adding to it from year to year. He built this room last summer for his modern pictures."

Young Rainer, pausing to open another door, touched an electric button which sent a circle of light about the walls of a long room hung with canvases of the French impressionist school.

Faxon advanced, attracted by a shimmering Monet, but Rainer laid a hand on his arm.

"He bought that last week. But come along—I'll show you all this after dinner. Or *he* will, rather—he loves it."

"Does he really love things?"

Rainer stared, clearly perplexed at the question. "Rather! Flowers and pictures especially! Haven't you noticed the flowers? I suppose you think his manner's cold; it seems so at first; but he's really awfully keen about things."

Faxon looked quickly at the speaker. "Has your uncle a brother?"

"Brother? No—never had. He and my mother were the only ones."

"Or any relation who—who looks like him? Who might be mistaken for him?"

"Not that I ever heard of. Does he remind you of some one?"

"Yes."

"That's queer. We'll ask him if he's got a double. Come on!"

But another picture had arrested Faxon, and some minutes elapsed before he and his young host reached the dining-room. It was a large room, with the same conventionally handsome furniture and delicately grouped flowers; and Faxon's first glance showed him that only three men were seated about the dining-table. The man who had stood behind Mr. Lavington's chair was not present, and no seat awaited him.

When the young men entered, Mr. Grisben was speaking, and his host, who faced the door, sat looking down at his untouched soup-plate and turning the spoon about in his small dry hand.

"It's pretty late to call them rumours—they were devilish close to facts when we left town this morning," Mr. Grisben was saying, with an unexpected incisiveness of tone.

Mr. Lavington laid down his spoon and smiled interrogatively. "Oh, facts—what *are* facts? Just the way a thing happens to look at a given minute. . . ."

"You haven't heard anything from town?" Mr. Grisben persisted.

"Not a syllable. So you see. . . . Balch, a little more of that *petite marmite*. Mr. Faxon . . . between Frank and Mr. Grisben, please."

The dinner progressed through a series of complicated courses, ceremoniously dispensed by a prelatical butler attended by three tall footmen, and it was evident that Mr. Lavington took a certain satisfaction in the pageant. That, Faxon reflected, was probably the joint in his armour—that and the flowers. He had changed the subject—not abruptly but firmly—when the young men entered, but Faxon perceived that it still possessed the thoughts of the two elderly visitors, and Mr. Balch presently observed, in a voice that seemed to come from the last survivor down a mine-shaft: "If it *does* come, it will be the biggest crash since '93."

Mr. Lavington looked bored but polite. "Wall Street can stand crashes better than it could then. It's got a robuster constitution."

"Yes; but—"

"Speaking of constitutions," Mr. Grisben intervened: "Frank, are you taking care of yourself?"

A flush rose to young Rainer's cheeks.

"Why, of course! Isn't that what I'm here for?"

"You're here about three days in the month, aren't you? And the rest of the time it's crowded restaurants and hot ball-rooms in town. I thought you were to be shipped off to New Mexico?"

"Oh, I've got a new man who says that's rot."

"Well, you don't look as if your new man were right," said Mr. Grisben bluntly.

Faxon saw the lad's colour fade, and the rings of shadow deepen under his gay eyes. At the same moment his uncle turned to him with a renewed intensity of attention. There was such solicitude in Mr. Lavington's gaze that it seemed almost to fling a shield between his nephew and Mr. Grisben's tactless scrutiny.

"We think Frank's a good deal better," he began; "this new doctor—"

The butler, coming up, bent to whisper a word in his ear, and the communication caused a sudden change in Mr. Lavington's expression. His face was naturally so colourless that it seemed not so much to pale as to fade, to dwindle and recede into something blurred and blotted-out. He half rose, sat down again and sent a rigid smile about the table.

"Will you excuse me? The telephone. Peters, go on with the dinner." With small precise steps he walked out of the door which one of the footmen had thrown open.

A momentary silence fell on the group; then Mr. Grisben once more addressed himself to Rainer. "You ought to have gone, my boy; you ought to have gone."

The anxious look returned to the youth's eyes. "My uncle doesn't think so, really."

"You're not a baby, to be always governed by your uncle's opinion. You came of age to-day, didn't you? Your uncle spoils you . . . that's what's the matter. . . ."

The thrust evidently went home, for Rainer laughed and looked down with a slight accession of colour.

"But the doctor—"

"Use your common sense, Frank! You had to try twenty doctors to find one to tell you what you wanted to be told."

A look of apprehension overshadowed Rainer's gaiety. "Oh, come—I say! . . . What would *you* do?" he stammered.

"Pack up and jump on the first train." Mr. Grisben leaned forward and laid his hand kindly on the young man's arm. "Look here: my nephew Jim Grisben is out there ranching on a big scale. He'll take you in and be glad to have you. You say your new doctor thinks it won't do you any good; but he doesn't pretend to say it will do you harm, does he? Well, then—give it a trial. It'll take you out of hot theatres and night restaurants, anyhow. . . . And all the rest of it. . . . Eh, Balch?"

"Go!" said Mr. Balch hollowly. "Go *at once*," he added, as if a closer look at the youth's face had impressed on him the need of backing up his friend.

Young Rainer had turned ashy-pale. He tried to stiffen his mouth into a smile. "Do I look as bad as all that?"

Mr. Grisben was helping himself to terrapin. "You look like the day after an earthquake," he said.

The terrapin had encircled the table, and been deliberately enjoyed by Mr. Lavington's three visitors (Rainer, Faxon noticed, left his plate untouched) before the door was thrown open to re-admit their host.

Mr. Lavington advanced with an air of recovered composure. He seated himself, picked up his napkin and consulted the gold-monogrammed menu. "No, don't bring back the filet. . . . Some terrapin; yes. . . ." He looked affably about the table. "Sorry to have deserted you, but the storm has played the deuce with the wires, and I had to wait a long time before I could get a good connection. It must be blowing up for a blizzard."

"Uncle Jack," young Rainer broke out, "Mr. Grisben's been lecturing me."

Mr. Lavington was helping himself to terrapin. "Ah—what about?"

"He thinks I ought to have given New Mexico a show."

"I want him to go straight out to my nephew at Santa Paz and stay there till his next birthday." Mr. Lavington signed to the butler to hand the terrapin to Mr. Grisben, who, as he took a second helping, addressed himself again to Rainer. "Jim's in New York now, and going back the day after tomorrow in Olyphant's private car. I'll ask Olyphant to squeeze you in if you'll go. And when you've been out there a week or two, in the saddle all day and sleeping nine hours a night, I suspect you won't think much of the doctor who prescribed New York."

Faxon spoke up, he knew not why. "I was out there once: it's a splendid life. I saw a fellow—oh, a really *bad* case— who'd been simply made over by it."

"It *does* sound jolly," Rainer laughed, a sudden eagerness in his tone.

His uncle looked at him gently. "Perhaps Grisben's right. It's an opportunity—"

Faxon glanced up with a start: the figure dimly perceived in the study was now more visibly and tangibly planted behind Mr. Lavington's chair.

"That's right, Frank: you see your uncle approves. And the trip out there with Olyphant isn't a thing to be missed. So drop a few dozen dinners and be at the Grand Central the day after tomorrow at five."

Mr. Grisben's pleasant grey eye sought corroboration of his host, and Faxon, in a cold anguish of suspense, continued to watch him as he turned his glance on Mr. Lavington. One could not look at Lavington without seeing the presence at his back, and it was clear that, the next minute, some change in Mr. Grisben's expression must give his watcher a clue.

But Mr. Grisben's expression did not change: the gaze he fixed on his host remained unperturbed, and the clue he gave was the startling one of not seeming to see the other figure.

Faxon's first impulse was to look away, to look anywhere else, to resort again to the champagne glass the watchful butler had already brimmed; but some fatal attraction, at war in him with an overwhelming physical resistance, held his eyes upon the spot they feared.

The figure was still standing, more distinctly, and therefore more resemblingly, at Mr. Lavington's back; and while the latter continued to gaze affectionately at his nephew, his counterpart, as before, fixed young Rainer with eyes of deadly menace.

Faxon, with what felt like an actual wrench of the muscles, dragged his own eyes from the sight to scan the other countenances about the table; but not one revealed the least consciousness of what he saw, and a sense of mortal isolation sank upon him.

"It's worth considering, certainly—" he heard Mr. Lavington continue; and as Rainer's face lit up, the face behind his uncle's chair seemed to gather into its look all the fierce weariness of old unsatisfied hates. That was the thing that, as the minutes laboured by, Faxon was becoming most conscious of. The watcher behind the chair was no longer merely malevolent: he had grown suddenly, unutterably tired. His hatred seemed to well up out of the very depths of balked effort and thwarted hopes, and the fact made him more pitiable, and yet more dire.

Faxon's look reverted to Mr. Lavington, as if to surprise in him a corresponding change. At first none was visible: his pinched smile was screwed to his blank face like a gas-light to a white-washed wall. Then the fixity of the smile became ominous: Faxon saw that its wearer was afraid to let it go. It was evident that Mr. Lavington was unutterably tired too, and the discovery sent a colder current through Faxon's veins. Looking down at his untouched plate, he caught the soliciting twinkle of the champagne glass; but the sight of the wine turned him sick.

"Well, we'll go into the details presently," he heard Mr. Lavington say, still on the question of his nephew's future. "Let's have a cigar first. No—not here, Peters." He turned his smile on Faxon. "When we've had coffee I want to show you my pictures."

"Oh, by the way, Uncle Jack—Mr. Faxon wants to know if you've got a double?"

"A double?" Mr. Lavington, still smiling, continued to address himself to his guest. "Not that I know of. Have you seen one, Mr. Faxon?"

Faxon thought: "My God, if I look up now they'll *both* be looking at me!" To avoid raising his eyes he made as though to lift the glass to his lips; but his hand sank inert, and he looked up. Mr. Lavington's glance was politely bent on him, but with a loosening of the strain about his heart he saw that the figure behind the chair still kept its gaze on Rainer.

"Do you think you've seen my double, Mr. Faxon?"

Would the other face turn if he said yes? Faxon felt a dryness in his throat. "No," he answered.

"Ah? It's possible I've a dozen. I believe I'm extremely usual-looking," Mr. Lavington went on conversationally; and still the other face watched Rainer.

"It was . . . a mistake . . . a confusion of memory. . . ." Faxon heard himself stammer. Mr. Lavington pushed back his chair, and as he did so Mr. Grisben suddenly leaned forward.

"Lavington! What have we been thinking of? We haven't drunk Frank's health!"

Mr. Lavington reseated himself. "My dear boy! . . . Peters, another bottle. . . ." He turned to his nephew. "After such a sin of omission I don't presume to propose the toast myself . . . but Frank knows. . . . Go ahead, Grisben!"

The boy shone on his uncle. "No, no, Uncle Jack! Mr. Grisben won't mind. Nobody but *you*—today!"

The butler was replenishing the glasses. He filled Mr. Lavington's last, and Mr. Lavington put out his small hand to raise it. . . . As he did so, Faxon looked away.

"Well, then— All the good I've wished you in all the past years. . . . I put it into the prayer that the coming ones may be healthy and happy and many . . . and *many*, dear boy!"

Faxon saw the hands about him reach out for their glasses. Automatically, he reached for his. His eyes were still on the table, and he repeated to himself with a trembling vehemence: "I won't look up! I won't. . . . I won't. . . ."

His fingers clasped the glass and raised it to the level of his lips. He saw the other hands making the same motion. He heard Mr. Grisben's genial "Hear! Hear!" and Mr. Balch's hollow echo. He said to himself, as the rim of the glass touched his lips: "I won't look up! I swear I won't!—" and he looked.

The glass was so full that it required an extraordinary effort to hold it there, brimming and suspended, during the awful interval before he could trust his hand to lower it again, untouched, to the table. It was this merciful preoccupation which saved him, kept him from crying out, from losing his hold, from slipping down into the bottomless blackness that gaped for him. As long as the problem of the glass engaged him he felt able to keep his seat, manage his muscles, fit unnoticeably into the group; but as the glass touched the table his last link with safety snapped. He stood up and dashed out of the room.

IV

In the gallery, the instinct of self-preservation helped him to turn back and sign to young Rainer not to follow. He stammered out something about a touch of dizziness, and joining them presently; and the boy nodded sympathetically and drew back.

At the foot of the stairs Faxon ran against a servant. "I should like to telephone to Weymore," he said with dry lips.

"Sorry, sir; wires all down. We've been trying the last hour to get New York again for Mr. Lavington."

Faxon shot on to his room, burst into it, and bolted the door. The lamplight lay on furniture, flowers, books; in the ashes a log still glimmered. He dropped down on the sofa and hid his face. The room was profoundly silent, the whole house was still: nothing about him gave a hint of what was going on, darkly and dumbly, in the room he had flown from, and with the covering of his eyes oblivion and reassurance seemed to fall on him. But they fell for a moment only; then his lids opened again to the monstrous vision. There it was, stamped on his pupils, a part of him forever, an indelible horror burnt into his body and brain. But why into his—just his? Why had he alone been chosen to see what he had seen? What business was it of *his*, in God's name? Any one of the others, thus enlightened, might have exposed the horror and defeated it; but *he*, the one weaponless and defenceless spectator, the one whom none of the others would believe or understand if he attempted to reveal what he knew—*he* alone had been singled out as the victim of this dreadful initiation!

Suddenly he sat up, listening: he had heard a step on the stairs. Some one, no doubt, was coming to see how he was—to urge him, if he felt better, to go down and join the smokers. Cautiously he opened his door; yes, it was young Rainer's step. Faxon looked down the passage, remembered the other stairway and darted to it. All he wanted was to get out of the house. Not another instant would he breathe its abominable air! What business was it of *his*, in God's name?

He reached the opposite end of the lower gallery, and beyond it saw the hall by which he had entered. It was empty, and on a long table he recognized his coat and cap. He got into his coat, unbolted the door, and plunged into the purifying night.

The darkness was deep, and the cold so intense that for an instant it stopped his breathing. Then he perceived that only

a thin snow was falling, and resolutely he set his face for
flight. The trees along the avenue marked his way as he hastened with long strides over the beaten snow. Gradually, while
he walked, the tumult in his brain subsided. The impulse to
fly still drove him forward, but he began to feel that he was
flying from a terror of his own creating, and that the most urgent reason for escape was the need of hiding his state, of
shunning other eyes till he should regain his balance.

He had spent the long hours in the train in fruitless brood-
ings on a discouraging situation, and he remembered how his
bitterness had turned to exasperation when he found that the
Weymore sleigh was not awaiting him. It was absurd, of
course; but, though he had joked with Rainer over Mrs.
Culme's forgetfulness, to confess it had cost a pang. That was
what his rootless life had brought him to: for lack of a personal stake in things his sensibility was at the mercy of such
trifles. . . . Yes; that, and the cold and fatigue, the absence of
hope and the haunting sense of starved aptitudes, all these
had brought him to the perilous verge over which, once or
twice before, his terrified brain had hung.

Why else, in the name of any imaginable logic, human or
devilish, should he, a stranger, be singled out for this experience? What could it mean to him, how was he related to it,
what bearing had it on his case? . . . Unless, indeed, it was
just because he was a stranger—a stranger everywhere—
because he had no personal life, no warm screen of private
egotisms to shield him from exposure, that he had developed
this abnormal sensitiveness to the vicissitudes of others. The
thought pulled him up with a shudder. No! Such a fate was
too abominable; all that was strong and sound in him rejected
it. A thousand times better regard himself as ill, disorganized,
deluded, than as the predestined victim of such warnings!

He reached the gates and paused before the darkened
lodge. The wind had risen and was sweeping the snow into
his face. The cold had him in its grasp again, and he stood uncertain. Should he put his sanity to the test and go back? He
turned and looked down the dark drive to the house. A single ray shone through the trees, evoking a picture of the
lights, the flowers, the faces grouped about that fatal room.
He turned and plunged out into the road. . . .

He remembered that, about a mile from Overdale, the coachman had pointed out the road to Northridge; and he began to walk in that direction. Once in the road he had the gale in his face, and the wet snow on his moustache and eye-lashes instantly hardened to ice. The same ice seemed to be driving a million blades into his throat and lungs, but he pushed on, the vision of the warm room pursuing him.

The snow in the road was deep and uneven. He stumbled across ruts and sank into drifts, and the wind drove against him like a granite cliff. Now and then he stopped, gasping, as if an invisible hand had tightened an iron band about his body; then he started again, stiffening himself against the stealthy penetration of the cold. The snow continued to descend out of a pall of inscrutable darkness, and once or twice he paused, fearing he had missed the road to Northridge; but, seeing no sign of a turn, he ploughed on.

At last, feeling sure that he had walked for more than a mile, he halted and looked back. The act of turning brought immediate relief, first because it put his back to the wind, and then because, far down the road, it showed him the gleam of a lantern. A sleigh was coming—a sleigh that might perhaps give him a lift to the village! Fortified by the hope, he began to walk back toward the light. It came forward very slowly, with unaccountable zigzags and waverings; and even when he was within a few yards of it he could catch no sound of sleigh-bells. Then it paused and became stationary by the roadside, as though carried by a pedestrian who had stopped, exhausted by the cold. The thought made Faxon hasten on, and a moment later he was stooping over a motionless figure huddled against the snow-bank. The lantern had dropped from its bearer's hand, and Faxon, fearfully raising it, threw its light into the face of Frank Rainer.

"Rainer! What on earth are you doing here?"

The boy smiled back through his pallour. "What are *you*, I'd like to know?" he retorted; and, scrambling to his feet with a clutch on Faxon's arm, he added gaily: "Well, I've run you down!"

Faxon stood confounded, his heart sinking. The lad's face was grey.

"What madness—" he began.

"Yes, it *is*. What on earth did you do it for?"

"I? Do what? . . . Why I. . . . I was just taking a walk. . . . I often walk at night. . . ."

Frank Rainer burst into a laugh. "On such nights? Then you hadn't bolted?"

"Bolted?"

"Because I'd done something to offend you? My uncle thought you had."

Faxon grasped his arm. "Did your uncle send you after me?"

"Well, he gave me an awful rowing for not going up to your room with you when you said you were ill. And when we found you'd gone we were frightened—and he was awfully upset—so I said I'd catch you. . . . You're *not* ill, are you?"

"Ill? No. Never better." Faxon picked up the lantern. "Come; let's go back. It was awfully hot in that dining-room."

"Yes; I hoped it was only that."

They trudged on in silence for a few minutes; then Faxon questioned: "You're not too done up?"

"Oh, no. It's a lot easier with the wind behind us."

"All right. Don't talk any more."

They pushed ahead, walking, in spite of the light that guided them, more slowly than Faxon had walked alone into the gale. The fact of his companion's stumbling against a drift gave Faxon a pretext for saying: "Take hold of my arm," and Rainer obeying, gasped out: "I'm blown!"

"So am I. Who wouldn't be?"

"What a dance you led me! If it hadn't been for one of the servants happening to see you—"

"Yes; all right. And now, won't you kindly shut up?"

Rainer laughed and hung on him. "Oh, the cold doesn't hurt me. . . ."

For the first few minutes after Rainer had overtaken him, anxiety for the lad had been Faxon's only thought. But as each labouring step carried them nearer to the spot he had been fleeing, the reasons for his flight grew more ominous and more insistent. No, he was not ill, he was not distraught and deluded—he was the instrument singled out to warn and save; and here he was, irresistibly driven, dragging the victim back to his doom!

The intensity of the conviction had almost checked his steps. But what could he do or say? At all costs he must get Rainer out of the cold, into the house and into his bed. After that he would act.

The snow-fall was thickening, and as they reached a stretch of the road between open fields the wind took them at an angle, lashing their faces with barbed thongs. Rainer stopped to take breath, and Faxon felt the heavier pressure of his arm.

"When we get to the lodge, can't we telephone to the stable for a sleigh?"

"If they're not all asleep at the lodge."

"Oh, I'll manage. Don't talk!" Faxon ordered; and they plodded on. . .

At length the lantern ray showed ruts that curved away from the road under tree-darkness.

Faxon's spirits rose. "There's the gate! We'll be there in five minutes."

As he spoke he caught, above the boundary hedge, the gleam of a light at the farther end of the dark avenue. It was the same light that had shone on the scene of which every detail was burnt into his brain; and he felt again its overpowering reality. No—he couldn't let the boy go back!

They were at the lodge at last, and Faxon was hammering on the door. He said to himself: "I'll get him inside first, and make them give him a hot drink. Then I'll see—I'll find an argument. . . ."

There was no answer to his knocking, and after an interval Rainer said: "Look here—we'd better go on."

"No!"

"I can, perfectly—"

"You sha'n't go to the house, I say!" Faxon redoubled his blows, and at length steps sounded on the stairs. Rainer was leaning against the lintel, and as the door opened the light from the hall flashed on his pale face and fixed eyes. Faxon caught him by the arm and drew him in.

"It *was* cold out there," he sighed; and then, abruptly, as if invisible shears at a single stroke had cut every muscle in his body, he swerved, drooped on Faxon's arm, and seemed to sink into nothing at his feet.

The lodge-keeper and Faxon bent over him, and somehow, between them, lifted him into the kitchen and laid him on a sofa by the stove.

The lodge-keeper, stammering: "I'll ring up the house," dashed out of the room. But Faxon heard the words without heeding them: omens mattered nothing now, beside this woe fulfilled. He knelt down to undo the fur collar about Rainer's throat, and as he did so he felt a warm moisture on his hands. He held them up, and they were red. . . .

V

The palms threaded their endless line along the yellow river. The little steamer lay at the wharf, and George Faxon, sitting in the verandah of the wooden hotel, idly watched the coolies carrying the freight across the gang-plank.

He had been looking at such scenes for two months. Nearly five had elapsed since he had descended from the train at Northridge and strained his eyes for the sleigh that was to take him to Weymore: Weymore, which he was never to behold! . . . Part of the interval—the first part—was still a great grey blur. Even now he could not be quite sure how he had got back to Boston, reached the house of a cousin, and been thence transferred to a quiet room looking out on snow under bare trees. He looked out a long time at the same scene, and finally one day a man he had known at Harvard came to see him and invited him to go out on a business trip to the Malay Peninsula.

"You've had a bad shake-up, and it'll do you no end of good to get away from things."

When the doctor came the next day it turned out that he knew of the plan and approved it. "You ought to be quiet for a year. Just loaf and look at the landscape," he advised.

Faxon felt the first faint stirrings of curiosity.

"What's been the matter with me, anyway?"

"Well, over-work, I suppose. You must have been bottling up for a bad breakdown before you started for New Hampshire last December. And the shock of that poor boy's death did the rest."

Ah, yes—Rainer had died. He remembered. . . .

He started for the East, and gradually, by imperceptible degrees, life crept back into his weary bones and leaden brain. His friend was patient and considerate, and they travelled slowly and talked little. At first Faxon had felt a great shrinking from whatever touched on familiar things. He seldom looked at a newspaper and he never opened a letter without a contraction of the heart. It was not that he had any special cause for apprehension, but merely that a great trail of darkness lay on everything. He had looked too deep down into the abyss. . . . But little by little health and energy returned to him, and with them the common promptings of curiosity. He was beginning to wonder how the world was going, and when, presently, the hotel-keeper told him there were no letters for him in the steamer's mail-bag, he felt a distinct sense of disappointment. His friend had gone into the jungle on a long excursion, and he was lonely, unoccupied and wholesomely bored. He got up and strolled into the stuffy reading-room.

There he found a game of dominoes, a mutilated picture-puzzle, some copies of *Zion's Herald* and a pile of New York and London newspapers.

He began to glance through the papers, and was disappointed to find that they were less recent than he had hoped. Evidently the last numbers had been carried off by luckier travellers. He continued to turn them over, picking out the American ones first. These, as it happened, were the oldest: they dated back to December and January. To Faxon, however, they had all the flavour of novelty, since they covered the precise period during which he had virtually ceased to exist. It had never before occurred to him to wonder what had happened in the world during that interval of obliteration; but now he felt a sudden desire to know.

To prolong the pleasure, he began by sorting the papers chronologically, and as he found and spread out the earliest number, the date at the top of the page entered into his consciousness like a key slipping into a lock. It was the seventeenth of December: the date of the day after his arrival at Northridge. He glanced at the first page and read in blazing characters: "Reported Failure of Opal Cement Company.

Lavington's name involved. Gigantic Exposure of Corruption Shakes Wall Street to Its Foundations."

He read on, and when he had finished the first paper he turned to the next. There was a gap of three days, but the Opal Cement "Investigation" still held the centre of the stage. From its complex revelations of greed and ruin his eye wandered to the death notices, and he read: "Rainer. Suddenly, at Northridge, New Hampshire, Francis John, only son of the late . . ."

His eyes clouded, and he dropped the newspaper and sat for a long time with his face in his hands. When he looked up again he noticed that his gesture had pushed the other papers from the table and scattered them at his feet. The uppermost lay spread out before him, and heavily his eyes began their search again. "John Lavington comes forward with plan for reconstructing Company. Offers to put in ten millions of his own— The proposal under consideration by the District Attorney."

Ten millions . . . ten millions of his own. But if John Lavington was ruined? . . . Faxon stood up with a cry. That was it, then—that was what the warning meant! And if he had not fled from it, dashed wildly away from it into the night, he might have broken the spell of iniquity, the powers of darkness might not have prevailed! He caught up the pile of newspapers and began to glance through each in turn for the head-line: "Wills Admitted to Probate." In the last of all he found the paragraph he sought, and it stared up at him as if with Rainer's dying eyes.

That—*that* was what he had done! The powers of pity had singled him out to warn and save, and he had closed his ears to their call, and washed his hands of it, and fled. Washed his hands of it! That was the word. It caught him back to the dreadful moment in the lodge when, raising himself up from Rainer's side, he had looked at his hands and seen that they were red. . . .

Bunner Sisters

I N THE DAYS when New York's traffic moved at the pace of the drooping horse-car, when society applauded Christine Nilsson at the Academy of Music and basked in the sunsets of the Hudson River School on the walls of the National Academy of Design, an inconspicuous shop with a single show-window was intimately and favourably known to the feminine population of the quarter bordering on Stuyvesant Square.

It was a very small shop, in a shabby basement, in a side-street already doomed to decline; and from the miscellaneous display behind the window-pane, and the brevity of the sign surmounting it (merely "Bunner Sisters" in blotchy gold on a black ground) it would have been difficult for the uninitiated to guess the precise nature of the business carried on within. But that was of little consequence, since its fame was so purely local that the customers on whom its existence de-pended were almost congenitally aware of the exact range of "goods" to be found at Bunner Sisters'.

The house of which Bunner Sisters had annexed the base-ment was a private dwelling with a brick front, green shutters on weak hinges, and a dress-maker's sign in the window above the shop. On each side of its modest three stories stood higher buildings, with fronts of brown stone, cracked and blistered, cast-iron balconies and cat-haunted grass-patches behind twisted railings. These houses too had once been pri-vate, but now a cheap lunch-room filled the basement of one, while the other announced itself, above the knotty wistaria that clasped its central balcony, as the Mendoza Family Hotel. It was obvious from the chronic cluster of refuse-barrels at its area-gate and the blurred surface of its curtainless windows, that the families frequenting the Mendoza Hotel were not ex-acting in their tastes; though they doubtless indulged in as much fastidiousness as they could afford to pay for, and rather more than their landlord thought they had a right to express.

These three houses fairly exemplified the general character of the street, which, as it stretched eastward, rapidly fell from

shabbiness to squalor, with an increasing frequency of projecting sign-boards, and of swinging doors that softly shut or
opened at the touch of red-nosed men and pale little girls
with broken jugs. The middle of the street was full of irregular depressions, well adapted to retain the long swirls of dust
and straw and twisted paper that the wind drove up and down
its sad untended length; and toward the end of the day, when
traffic had been active, the fissured pavement formed a mosaic
of coloured hand-bills, lids of tomato-cans, old shoes, cigar-
stumps and banana skins, cemented together by a layer of
mud, or veiled in a powdering of dust, as the state of the
weather determined.

The sole refuge offered from the contemplation of this depressing waste was the sight of the Bunner Sisters' window.
Its panes were always well-washed, and though their display
of artificial flowers, bands of scalloped flannel, wire hat-
frames, and jars of home-made preserves, had the undefinable
greyish tinge of objects long preserved in the show-case of a
museum, the window revealed a background of orderly counters and white-washed walls in pleasant contrast to the adjoining dinginess.

The Bunner sisters were proud of the neatness of their shop
and content with its humble prosperity. It was not what they
had once imagined it would be, but though it presented but
a shrunken image of their earlier ambitions it enabled them to
pay their rent and keep themselves alive and out of debt; and
it was long since their hopes had soared higher.

Now and then, however, among their greyer hours there
came one not bright enough to be called sunny, but rather of
the silvery twilight hue which sometimes ends a day of storm.
It was such an hour that Ann Eliza, the elder of the firm, was
soberly enjoying as she sat one January evening in the back
room which served as bedroom, kitchen and parlour to herself and her sister Evelina. In the shop the blinds had been
drawn down, the counters cleared and the wares in the window lightly covered with an old sheet; but the shop-door remained unlocked till Evelina, who had taken a parcel to the
dyer's, should come back.

In the back room a kettle bubbled on the stove, and Ann
Eliza had laid a cloth over one end of the centre table, and

placed near the green-shaded sewing lamp two tea-cups, two
plates, a sugar-bowl and a piece of pie. The rest of the room
remained in a greenish shadow which discreetly veiled the
outline of an old-fashioned mahogany bedstead surmounted
by a chromo of a young lady in a night-gown who clung with
eloquently-rolling eyes to a crag described in illuminated letters as the Rock of Ages; and against the unshaded windows
two rocking-chairs and a sewing-machine were silhouetted on
the dusk.

Ann Eliza, her small and habitually anxious face smoothed
to unusual serenity, and the streaks of pale hair on her veined
temples shining glossily beneath the lamp, had seated herself
at the table, and was tying up, with her usual fumbling deliberation, a knotty object wrapped in paper. Now and then,
as she struggled with the string, which was too short, she
fancied she heard the click of the shop-door, and paused to
listen for her sister; then, as no one came, she straightened
her spectacles and entered into renewed conflict with the parcel. In honour of some event of obvious importance, she had
put on her double-dyed and triple-turned black silk. Age,
while bestowing on this garment a *patine* worthy of a
Renaissance bronze, had deprived it of whatever curves the
wearer's pre-Raphaelite figure had once been able to impress
on it; but this stiffness of outline gave it an air of sacerdotal
state which seemed to emphasize the importance of the
occasion.

Seen thus, in her sacramental black silk, a wisp of lace turned
over the collar and fastened by a mosaic brooch, and her face
smoothed into harmony with her apparel, Ann Eliza looked
ten years younger than behind the counter, in the heat and
burden of the day. It would have been as difficult to guess her
approximate age as that of the black silk, for she had the same
worn and glossy aspect as her dress; but a faint tinge of pink
still lingered on her cheek-bones, like the reflection of sunset
which sometimes colours the west long after the day is over.

When she had tied the parcel to her satisfaction, and laid it
with furtive accuracy just opposite her sister's plate, she sat
down, with an air of obviously-assumed indifference, in one
of the rocking-chairs near the window; and a moment later
the shop-door opened and Evelina entered.

The younger Bunner sister, who was a little taller than her elder, had a more pronounced nose, but a weaker slope of mouth and chin. She still permitted herself the frivolity of waving her pale hair, and its tight little ridges, stiff as the tresses of an Assyrian statue, were flattened under a dotted veil which ended at the tip of her cold-reddened nose. In her scant jacket and skirt of black cashmere she looked singularly nipped and faded; but it seemed possible that under happier conditions she might still warm into relative youth.

"Why, Ann Eliza," she exclaimed, in a thin voice pitched to chronic fretfulness, "what in the world you got your best silk on for?"

Ann Eliza had risen with a blush that made her steel-bowed spectacles incongruous.

"Why, Evelina, why shouldn't I, I sh'ld like to know? Ain't it your birthday, dear?" She put out her arms with the awkwardness of habitually repressed emotion.

Evelina, without seeming to notice the gesture, threw back the jacket from her narrow shoulders.

"Oh, pshaw," she said, less peevishly. "I guess we'd better give up birthdays. Much as we can do to keep Christmas nowadays."

"You hadn't oughter say that, Evelina. We ain't so badly off as all that. I guess you're cold and tired. Set down while I take the kettle off: it's right on the boil."

She pushed Evelina toward the table, keeping a sideward eye on her sister's listless movements, while her own hands were busy with the kettle. A moment later came the exclamation for which she waited.

"Why, Ann Eliza!" Evelina stood transfixed by the sight of the parcel beside her plate.

Ann Eliza, tremulously engaged in filling the teapot, lifted a look of hypocritical surprise.

"Sakes, Evelina! What's the matter?"

The younger sister had rapidly untied the string, and drawn from its wrappings a round nickel clock of the kind to be bought for a dollar-seventy-five.

"Oh, Ann Eliza, how could you?" She set the clock down, and the sisters exchanged agitated glances across the table.

"Well," the elder retorted, "*ain't* it your birthday?"

"Yes, but—"

"Well, and ain't you had to run round the corner to the Square every morning, rain or shine, to see what time it was, ever since we had to sell mother's watch last July? Ain't you, Evelina?"

"Yes, but—"

"There ain't any buts. We've always wanted a clock and now we've got one: that's all there is about it. Ain't she a beauty, Evelina?" Ann Eliza, putting back the kettle on the stove, leaned over her sister's shoulder to pass an approving hand over the circular rim of the clock. "Hear how loud she ticks. I was afraid you'd hear her soon as you come in."

"No. I wasn't thinking," murmured Evelina.

"Well, ain't you glad now?" Ann Eliza gently reproached her. The rebuke had no acerbity, for she knew that Evelina's seeming indifference was alive with unexpressed scruples.

"I'm real glad, sister; but you hadn't oughter. We could have got on well enough without."

"Evelina Bunner, just you sit down to your tea. I guess I know what I'd oughter and what I'd hadn't oughter just as well as you do—I'm old enough!"

"You're real good, Ann Eliza; but I know you've given up something you needed to get me this clock."

"What do I need, I'd like to know? Ain't I got a best black silk?" the elder sister said with a laugh full of nervous pleasure.

She poured out Evelina's tea, adding some condensed milk from the jug, and cutting for her the largest slice of pie; then she drew up her own chair to the table.

The two women ate in silence for a few moments before Evelina began to speak again. "The clock is perfectly lovely and I don't say it ain't a comfort to have it; but I hate to think what it must have cost you."

"No, it didn't, neither," Ann Eliza retorted. "I got it dirt cheap, if you want to know. And I paid for it out of a little extra work I did the other night on the machine for Mrs. Hawkins."

"The baby-waists?"

"Yes."

"There, I knew it! You swore to me you'd buy a new pair of shoes with that money."

"Well, and s'posin' I didn't want 'em—what then? I've patched up the old ones as good as new—and I do declare, Evelina Bunner, if you ask me another question you'll go and spoil all my pleasure."

"Very well, I won't," said the younger sister.

They continued to eat without farther words. Evelina yielded to her sister's entreaty that she should finish the pie, and poured out a second cup of tea, into which she put the last lump of sugar; and between them, on the table, the clock kept up its sociable tick.

"Where'd you get it, Ann Eliza?" asked Evelina, fascinated.

"Where'd you s'pose? Why, right round here, over acrost the Square, in the queerest little store you ever laid eyes on. I saw it in the window as I was passing, and I stepped right in and asked how much it was, and the store-keeper he was real pleasant about it. He was just the nicest man. I guess he's a German. I told him I couldn't give much, and he said, well, he knew what hard times was too. His name's Ramy— Herman Ramy: I saw it written up over the store. And he told me he used to work at Tiff'ny's, oh, for years, in the clock-department, and three years ago he took sick with some kinder fever, and lost his place, and when he got well they'd engaged somebody else and didn't want him, and so he started this little store by himself. I guess he's real smart, and he spoke quite like an educated man—but he looks sick."

Evelina was listening with absorbed attention. In the narrow lives of the two sisters such an episode was not to be under-rated.

"What you say his name was?" she asked as Ann Eliza paused.

"Herman Ramy."

"How old is he?"

"Well, I couldn't exactly tell you, he looked so sick—but I don't b'lieve he's much over forty."

By this time the plates had been cleared and the tea-pot emptied, and the two sisters rose from the table. Ann Eliza, tying an apron over her black silk, carefully removed all traces of the meal; then, after washing the cups and plates, and putting them away in a cupboard, she drew her rocking-chair to the lamp and sat down to a heap of mending. Evelina, meanwhile, had been roaming about the room in search of an abiding-place for the clock. A rosewood what-not with ornamental fret-work hung on the wall beside the devout young lady in dishabille, and after much weighing of alternatives the sisters decided to dethrone a broken china vase filled with dried grasses which had long stood on the top shelf, and to put the clock in its place; the vase, after farther consideration, being relegated to a small table covered with blue and white bead-work, which held a Bible and prayer-book, and an illustrated copy of Longfellow's poems given as a school-prize to their father.

This change having been made, and the effect studied from every angle of the room, Evelina languidly put her pinking-machine on the table, and sat down to the monotonous work of pinking a heap of black silk flounces. The strips of stuff slid slowly to the floor at her side, and the clock, from its commanding altitude, kept time with the dispiriting click of the instrument under her fingers.

II

The purchase of Evelina's clock had been a more important event in the life of Ann Eliza Bunner than her younger sister could divine. In the first place, there had been the demoralizing satisfaction of finding herself in possession of a sum of money which she need not put into the common fund, but could spend as she chose, without consulting Evelina, and then the excitement of her stealthy trips abroad, undertaken on the rare occasions when she could trump up a pretext for leaving the shop; since, as a rule, it was Evelina who took the bundles to the dyer's, and delivered the purchases of those among their customers who were too genteel to be seen carrying home a bonnet or a bundle of pinking—so that, had it not been for the excuse of having to see Mrs. Hawkins's teething baby, Ann Eliza would hardly have known what motive to allege for deserting her usual seat behind the counter.

The infrequency of her walks made them the chief events of her life. The mere act of going out from the monastic quiet of the shop into the tumult of the streets filled her with a subdued excitement which grew too intense for pleasure as she was swallowed by the engulfing roar of Broadway or Third Avenue, and began to do timid battle with their incessant cross-currents of humanity. After a glance or two into the great show-windows she usually allowed herself to be swept back into the shelter of a side-street, and finally regained her own roof in a state of breathless bewilderment and fatigue; but gradually, as her nerves were soothed by the familiar quiet of the little shop, and the click of Evelina's pinking-machine, certain sights and sounds would detach themselves from the torrent along which she had been swept, and she would devote the rest of the day to a mental reconstruction of the different episodes of her walk, till finally it took shape in her thought as a consecutive and highly-coloured experience, from which, for weeks afterwards, she would detach some fragmentary recollection in the course of her long dialogues with her sister.

But when, to the unwonted excitement of going out, was added the intenser interest of looking for a present for Evelina, Ann Eliza's agitation, sharpened by concealment, actually preyed upon her rest; and it was not till the present had been given, and she had unbosomed herself of the experiences connected with its purchase, that she could look back with anything like composure to that stirring moment of her life. From that day forward, however, she began to take a certain tranquil pleasure in thinking of Mr. Ramy's small shop, not unlike her own in its countrified obscurity, though the layer of dust which covered its counter and shelves made the comparison only superficially acceptable. Still, she did not judge the state of the shop severely, for Mr. Ramy had told her that he was alone in the world, and lone men, she was aware, did not know how to deal with dust. It gave her a good deal of occupation to wonder why he had never married, or if, on the other hand, he were a widower, and had lost all his dear little children; and she scarcely knew which alternative seemed to make him the more interesting. In either case, his life was assuredly a sad one; and she passed many hours in speculating on the manner in which he probably spent his evenings. She knew he lived at the back of his shop, for she had caught, on entering, a glimpse of a dingy room with a tumbled bed; and the pervading smell of cold fry suggested that he probably did his own cooking. She wondered if he did not often make his tea with water that had not boiled, and asked herself, almost jealously, who looked after the shop while he went to market. Then it occurred to her as likely that he bought his provisions at the same market as Evelina; and she was fascinated by the thought that he and her sister might constantly be meeting in total unconsciousness of the link between them. Whenever she reached this stage in her reflexions she lifted a furtive glance to the clock, whose loud staccato tick was becoming a part of her inmost being.

The seed sown by these long hours of meditation germinated at last in the secret wish to go to market some morning in Evelina's stead. As this purpose rose to the surface of Ann Eliza's thoughts she shrank back shyly from its contemplation. A plan so steeped in duplicity had never before taken shape in her crystalline soul. How was it possible for her to consider such a step? And, besides, (she did not possess sufficient logic to mark the downward trend of this "besides"), what excuse could she make that would not excite her sister's curiosity? From this second query it was an easy descent to the third: how soon could she manage to go?

It was Evelina herself, who furnished the necessary pretext by awaking with a sore throat on the day when she usually went to market. It was a Saturday, and as they always had their bit of steak on Sunday the expedition could not be postponed, and it seemed natural that Ann Eliza, as she tied an old stocking around Evelina's throat, should announce her intention of stepping round to the butcher's.

"Oh, Ann Eliza, they'll cheat you so," her sister wailed.

Ann Eliza brushed aside the imputation with a smile, and a few minutes later, having set the room to rights, and cast a last glance at the shop, she was tying on her bonnet with fumbling haste.

The morning was damp and cold, with a sky full of sulky clouds that would not make room for the sun, but as yet dropped only an occasional snow-flake. In the early light the street looked its meanest and most neglected; but to Ann Eliza, never greatly troubled by any untidiness for which she was not responsible, it seemed to wear a singularly friendly aspect.

A few minutes' walk brought her to the market where Evelina made her purchases, and where, if he had any sense of topographical fitness, Mr. Ramy must also deal.

Ann Eliza, making her way through the outskirts of potato-barrels and flabby fish, found no one in the shop but the gory-aproned butcher who stood in the background cutting chops.

As she approached him across the tessellation of fish-scales, blood and saw-dust, he laid aside his cleaver and not unsympathetically asked: "Sister sick?"

"Oh, not very—jest a cold," she answered, as guiltily as if Evelina's illness had been feigned. "We want a steak as usual, please—and my sister said you was to be sure to give me jest as good a cut as if it was her," she added with child-like candour.

"Oh, that's all right." The butcher picked up his weapon with a grin. "Your sister knows a cut as well as any of us," he remarked.

In another moment, Ann Eliza reflected, the steak would be cut and wrapped up, and no choice left her but to turn her disappointed steps toward home. She was too shy to try to delay the butcher by such conversational arts as she possessed, but the approach of a deaf old lady in an antiquated bonnet and mantle gave her her opportunity.

"Wait on her first, please," Ann Eliza whispered. "I ain't in any hurry."

The butcher advanced to his new customer, and Ann Eliza, palpitating in the back of the shop, saw that the old lady's hesitations between liver and pork chops were likely to be indefinitely prolonged. They were still unresolved when she was interrupted by the entrance of a blowsy Irish girl with a basket on her arm. The new-comer caused a momentary diversion, and when she had departed the old lady, who was evidently as intolerant of interruption as a professional story-teller, insisted on returning to the beginning of her complicated order, and weighing anew, with an anxious appeal to the butcher's arbitration, the relative advantages of pork and liver. But even her hesitations, and the intrusion on them of two or three other customers, were of no avail, for Mr. Ramy was not among those who entered the shop; and at last Ann

Eliza, ashamed of staying longer, reluctantly claimed her steak, and walked home through the thickening snow.

Even to her simple judgment the vanity of her hopes was plain, and in the clear light that disappointment turns upon our actions she wondered how she could have been foolish enough to suppose that, even if Mr. Ramy *did* go to that particular market, he would hit on the same day and hour as herself.

There followed a colourless week unmarked by farther incident. The old stocking cured Evelina's throat, and Mrs. Hawkins dropped in once or twice to talk of her baby's teeth; some new orders for pinking were received, and Evelina sold a bonnet to the lady with puffed sleeves. The lady with puffed sleeves—a resident of "the Square," whose name they had never learned, because she always carried her own parcels home—was the most distinguished and interesting figure on their horizon. She was youngish, she was elegant (as the title they had given her implied), and she had a sweet sad smile about which they had woven many histories; but even the news of her return to town—it was her first apparition that year—failed to arouse Ann Eliza's interest. All the small daily happenings which had once sufficed to fill the hours now appeared to her in their deadly insignificance; and for the first time in her long years of drudgery she rebelled at the dullness of her life. With Evelina such fits of discontent were habitual and openly proclaimed, and Ann Eliza still excused them as one of the prerogatives of youth. Besides, Evelina had not been intended by Providence to pine in such a narrow life: in the original plan of things, she had been meant to marry and have a baby, to wear silk on Sundays, and take a leading part in a Church circle. Hitherto opportunity had played her false; and for all her superior aspirations and carefully crimped hair she had remained as obscure and unsought as Ann Eliza. But the elder sister, who had long since accepted her own fate, had never accepted Evelina's. Once a pleasant young man who taught in Sunday-school had paid the younger Miss Bunner a few shy visits. That was years since, and he had speedily vanished from their view. Whether he had carried with him any of Evelina's illusions, Ann Eliza had never discovered; but his attentions had clad her sister in a halo of exquisite possibilities.

Ann Eliza, in those days, had never dreamed of allowing herself the luxury of self-pity; it seemed as much a personal right of Evelina's as her elaborately crinkled hair. But now she began to transfer to herself a portion of the sympathy she had so long bestowed on Evelina. She had at last recognized her right to set up some lost opportunities of her own; and once that dangerous precedent established, they began to crowd upon her memory.

It was at this stage of Ann Eliza's transformation that Evelina, looking up one evening from her work, said suddenly: "My! She's stopped."

Ann Eliza, raising her eyes from a brown merino seam, followed her sister's glance across the room. It was a Monday, and they always wound the clock on Sundays.

"Are you sure you wound her yesterday, Evelina?"

"Jest as sure as I live. She must be broke. I'll go and see."

Evelina laid down the hat she was trimming, and took the clock from its shelf.

"There—I knew it! She's wound jest as *tight*—what you suppose's happened to her, Ann Eliza?"

"I dunno, I'm sure," said the elder sister, wiping her spectacles before proceeding to a close examination of the clock.

With anxiously bent heads the two women shook and turned it, as though they were trying to revive a living thing, but it remained unresponsive to their touch, and at length Evelina laid it down with a sigh.

"Seems like somethin' *dead*, don't it, Ann Eliza? How still the room is!"

"Yes, ain't it?"

"Well, I'll put her back where she belongs," Evelina continued, in the tone of one about to perform the last offices for the departed. "And I guess," she added, "you'll have to step round to Mr. Ramy's to-morrow, and see if he can fix her."

Ann Eliza's face burned. "I—yes, I guess I'll have to," she stammered, stooping to pick up a spool of cotton which had rolled to the floor. A sudden heart-throb stretched the seams of her flat alpaca bosom, and a pulse leapt to life in each of her temples.

That night, long after Evelina slept, Ann Eliza lay awake in the unfamiliar silence, more acutely conscious of the nearness of the crippled clock than when it had volubly told out the minutes. The next morning she woke from a troubled dream of having carried it to Mr. Ramy's, and found that he and his shop had vanished; and all through the day's occupations the memory of this dream oppressed her.

It had been agreed that Ann Eliza should take the clock to be repaired as soon as they had dined; but while they were still at table a weak-eyed little girl in a black apron stabbed with innumerable pins burst in on them with the cry: "Oh, Miss Bunner, for mercy's sake! Miss Mellins has been took again."

Miss Mellins was the dress-maker upstairs, and the weak-eyed child one of her youthful apprentices.

Ann Eliza started from her seat. "I'll come at once. Quick, Evelina, the cordial!"

By this euphemistic name the sisters designated a bottle of cherry brandy, the last of a dozen inherited from their grandmother, which they kept locked in their cupboard against such emergencies. A moment later, cordial in hand, Ann Eliza was hurrying upstairs behind the weak-eyed child.

Miss Mellins's "turn" was sufficiently serious to detain Ann Eliza for nearly two hours, and dusk had fallen when she took up the depleted bottle of cordial and descended again to the shop. It was empty, as usual, and Evelina sat at her pinking-machine in the back room. Ann Eliza was still agitated by her efforts to restore the dress-maker, but in spite of her preoccupation she was struck, as soon as she entered, by the loud tick of the clock, which still stood on the shelf where she had left it.

"Why, she's going!" she gasped, before Evelina could question her about Miss Mellins. "Did she start up again by herself?"

"Oh, no; but I couldn't stand not knowing what time it was, I've got so accustomed to having her round; and just after you went upstairs Mrs. Hawkins dropped in, so I asked her to tend the store for a minute, and I clapped on my things and ran right round to Mr. Ramy's. It turned out there wasn't anything the matter with her—nothin' on'y a speck of dust in the works—and he fixed her for me in a minute and I brought her right back. Ain't it lovely to hear her going again? But tell me about Miss Mellins, quick!"

For a moment Ann Eliza found no words. Not till she learned that she had missed her chance did she understand how many hopes had hung upon it. Even now she did not know why she had wanted so much to see the clock-maker again.

"I s'pose it's because nothing's ever happened to me," she thought, with a twinge of envy for the fate which gave Evelina every opportunity that came their way. "She had the Sunday-school teacher too," Ann Eliza murmured to herself; but she was well-trained in the arts of renunciation, and after a scarcely perceptible pause she plunged into a detailed description of the dress-maker's "turn."

Evelina, when her curiosity was roused, was an insatiable questioner, and it was supper-time before she had come to the end of her enquiries about Miss Mellins; but when the two sisters had seated themselves at their evening meal Ann Eliza at last found a chance to say: "So she on'y had a speck of dust in her."

Evelina understood at once that the reference was not to Miss Mellins. "Yes—at least he thinks so," she answered, helping herself as a matter of course to the first cup of tea.

"On'y to think!" murmured Ann Eliza.

"But he isn't *sure*," Evelina continued, absently pushing the teapot toward her sister. "It may be something wrong with the—I forget what he called it. Anyhow, he said he'd call round and see, day after to-morrow, after supper."

"Who said?" gasped Ann Eliza.

"Why, Mr. Ramy, of course. I think he's real nice, Ann Eliza. And I don't believe he's forty; but he *does* look sick. I guess he's pretty lonesome, all by himself in that store. He as much as told me so, and somehow"—Evelina paused and bridled—"I kinder thought that maybe his saying he'd call round about the clock was on'y just an excuse. He said it just as I was going out of the store. What you think, Ann Eliza?"

"Oh, I don't har'ly know." To save herself, Ann Eliza could produce nothing warmer.

"Well, I don't pretend to be smarter than other folks," said Evelina, putting a conscious hand to her hair, "but I guess

Mr. Herman Ramy wouldn't be sorry to pass an evening here, 'stead of spending it all alone in that poky little place of his."

Her self-consciousness irritated Ann Eliza.

"I guess he's got plenty of friends of his own," she said, almost harshly.

"No, he ain't, either. He's got hardly any."

"Did he tell you that too?" Even to her own ears there was a faint sneer in the interrogation.

"Yes, he did," said Evelina, dropping her lids with a smile. "He seemed to be just crazy to talk to somebody—somebody agreeable, I mean. I think the man's unhappy, Ann Eliza."

"So do I," broke from the elder sister.

"He seems such an educated man, too. He was reading the paper when I went in. Ain't it sad to think of his being reduced to that little store, after being years at Tiff'ny's, and one of the head men in their clock-department?"

"He told you all that?"

"Why, yes. I think he'd a' told me everything ever happened to him if I'd had the time to stay and listen. I tell you he's dead lonely, Ann Eliza."

"Yes," said Ann Eliza.

III

Two days afterward, Ann Eliza noticed that Evelina, before they sat down to supper, pinned a crimson bow under her collar; and when the meal was finished the younger sister, who seldom concerned herself with the clearing of the table, set about with nervous haste to help Ann Eliza in the removal of the dishes.

"I hate to see food mussing about," she grumbled. "Ain't it hateful having to do everything in one room?"

"Oh, Evelina, I've always thought we was so comfortable," Ann Eliza protested.

"Well, so we are, comfortable enough; but I don't suppose there's any harm in my saying I wisht we had a parlour, is there? Anyway, we might manage to buy a screen to hide the bed."

Ann Eliza coloured. There was something vaguely embarrassing in Evelina's suggestion.

"I always think if we ask for more what we have may be taken from us," she ventured.

"Well, whoever took it wouldn't get much," Evelina retorted with a laugh as she swept up the table-cloth.

A few moments later the back room was in its usual flawless order and the two sisters had seated themselves near the lamp. Ann Eliza had taken up her sewing, and Evelina was preparing to make artificial flowers. The sisters usually relegated this more delicate business to the long leisure of the summer months; but to-night Evelina had brought out the box which lay all winter under the bed, and spread before her a bright array of muslin petals, yellow stamens and green corollas, and a tray of little implements curiously suggestive of the dental art. Ann Eliza made no remark on this unusual proceeding; perhaps she guessed why for that evening her sister had chosen a graceful task.

Presently a knock on the outer door made them look up; but Evelina, the first on her feet, said promptly: "Sit still. I'll see who it is."

Ann Eliza was glad to sit still: the baby's petticoat that she was stitching shook in her fingers.

"Sister, here's Mr. Ramy come to look at the clock," said Evelina, a moment later, in the high drawl she cultivated before strangers; and a shortish man with a pale bearded face and upturned coat-collar came stiffly into the room.

Ann Eliza let her work fall as she stood up. "You're very welcome, I'm sure, Mr. Ramy. It's real kind of you to call."

"Nod ad all, ma'am." A tendency to illustrate Grimm's law in the interchange of his consonants betrayed the clockmaker's nationality, but he was evidently used to speaking English, or at least the particular branch of the vernacular with which the Bunner sisters were familiar. "I don't like to led any clock go out of my store without being sure it gives satisfaction," he added.

"Oh,—but we were satisfied," Ann Eliza assured him.

"But I wasn't, you see, ma'am," said Mr. Ramy looking slowly about the room, "nor I won't be, not till I see that clock's going all right."

"May I assist you off with your coat, Mr. Ramy?" Evelina interposed. She could never trust Ann Eliza to remember these opening ceremonies.

"Thank you, ma'am," he replied, and taking his thread-bare over-coat and shabby hat she laid them on a chair with the gesture she imagined the lady with the puffed sleeves might make use of on similar occasions. Ann Eliza's social sense was roused, and she felt that the next act of hospitality must be hers. "Won't you suit yourself to a seat?" she suggested. "My sister will reach down the clock; but I'm sure she's all right again. She's went beautiful ever since you fixed her."

"Dat's good," said Mr. Ramy. His lips parted in a smile which showed a row of yellowish teeth with one or two gaps in it; but in spite of this disclosure Ann Eliza thought his smile extremely pleasant: there was something wistful and conciliating in it which agreed with the pathos of his sunken cheeks and prominent eyes. As he took the clock from Evelina and bent toward the lamp, the light fell on his bulging fore-head and wide skull thinly covered with grayish hair. His hands were pale and broad, with knotty joints and square finger-tips rimmed with grime; but his touch was as light as a woman's.

"Well, ladies, dat clock's all right," he pronounced.

"I'm sure we're very much obliged to you," said Evelina, throwing a glance at her sister.

"Oh," Ann Eliza murmured, involuntarily answering the admonition. She selected a key from the bunch that hung at her waist with her cutting-out scissors, and fitting it into the lock of the cupboard, brought out the cherry brandy and three old-fashioned glasses engraved with vine wreaths.

"It's a very cold night," she said, "and maybe you'd like a sip of this cordial. It was made a great while ago by our grandmother."

"It looks fine," said Mr. Ramy bowing, and Ann Eliza filled the glasses. In her own and Evelina's she poured only a few drops, but she filled their guest's to the brim. "My sister and I seldom take wine," she explained.

With another bow, which included both his hostesses, Mr. Ramy drank off the cherry brandy and pronounced it ex-cellent.

Evelina meanwhile, with an assumption of industry in-tended to put their guest at ease, had taken up her instru-ments and was twisting a rose-petal into shape.

"You make artificial flowers, I see, ma'am," said Mr. Ramy with interest. "It's very pretty work. I had a lady-vriend in Shermany dat used to make flowers." He put out a square finger-tip to touch the petal.

Evelina blushed a little. "You left Germany long ago, I suppose?"

"Dear me yes, a goot while ago. I was only ninedeen when I come to the States."

After this the conversation dragged on intermittently till Mr. Ramy, peering about the room with the short-sighted glance of his race, said with an air of interest: "You're pleasantly fixed here; it looks real cosy." The note of wistfulness in his voice was obscurely moving to Ann Eliza.

"Oh, we live very plainly," said Evelina, with an affectation of grandeur deeply impressive to her sister. "We have very simple tastes."

"You look real comfortable, anyhow," said Mr. Ramy. His bulging eyes seemed to muster the details of the scene with a gentle envy. "I wisht I had as good a store; but I guess no blace seems homelike when you're always alone in it."

For some minutes longer the conversation moved on at this desultory pace, and then Mr. Ramy, who had been obviously nerving himself for the difficult act of departure, took his leave with an abruptness which would have startled anyone used to the subtler gradations of intercourse. But to Ann Eliza and her sister there was nothing surprising in his abrupt retreat. The long-drawn agonies of preparing to leave, and the subsequent dumb plunge through the door, were so usual in their circle that they would have been as much embarrassed as Mr. Ramy if he had tried to put any fluency into his adieux.

After he had left both sisters remained silent for a while; then Evelina, laying aside her unfinished flower, said: "I'll go and lock up."

IV

Intolerably monotonous seemed now to the Bunner sisters the treadmill routine of the shop, colourless and long their evenings about the lamp, aimless their habitual interchange of

words to the weary accompaniment of the sewing and pinking machines.

It was perhaps with the idea of relieving the tension of their
mood that Evelina, the following Sunday, suggested inviting
Miss Mellins to supper. The Bunner sisters were not in a position to be lavish of the humblest hospitably, but two or three
times in the year they shared their evening meal with a friend;
and Miss Mellins, still flushed with the importance of her
"turn," seemed the most interesting guest they could invite.

As the three women seated themselves at the supper-table,
embellished by the unwonted addition of pound cake and
sweet pickles, the dress-maker's sharp swarthy person stood
out vividly between the neutral-tinted sisters. Miss Mellins
was a small woman with a glossy yellow face and a frizz of
black hair bristling with imitation tortoise-shell pins. Her
sleeves had a fashionable cut, and half a dozen metal bangles
rattled on her wrists. Her voice rattled like her bangles as she
poured forth a stream of anecdote and ejaculation; and her
round black eyes jumped with acrobatic velocity from one
face to another. Miss Mellins was always having or hearing of
amazing adventures. She had surprised a burglar in her room
at midnight (though how he got there, what he robbed her
of, and by what means he escaped had never been quite clear
to her auditors); she had been warned by anonymous letters
that her grocer (a rejected suitor) was putting poison in her
tea; she had a customer who was shadowed by detectives, and
another (a very wealthy lady) who had been arrested in a department store for kleptomania; she had been present at a
spiritualist seance where an old gentleman had died in a fit on
seeing a materialization of his mother-in-law; she had escaped
from two fires in her night-gown, and at the funeral of her
first cousin the horses attached to the hearse had run away
and smashed the coffin, precipitating her relative into an open
man-hole before the eyes of his distracted family.

A sceptical observer might have explained Miss Mellins's
proneness to adventure by the fact that she derived her chief
mental nourishment from the *Police Gazette* and the *Fireside
Weekly*; but her lot was cast in a circle where such insinuations
were not likely to be heard, and where the title-role in blood-
curdling drama had long been her recognized right.

"Yes," she was now saying, her emphatic eyes on Ann Eliza, "you may not believe it, Miss Bunner, and I don't know's I should myself if anybody else was to tell me, but over a year before ever I was born, my mother she went to see a gypsy fortune-teller that was exhibited in a tent on the Battery with the green-headed lady, though her father warned her not to—and what you s'pose she told her? Why, she told her these very words—says she: 'Your next child'll be a girl with jet-black curls, and she'll suffer from spasms.'"

"Mercy!" murmured Ann Eliza, a ripple of sympathy running down her spine.

"D'you ever have spasms before, Miss Mellins?" Evelina asked.

"Yes, ma'am," the dress-maker declared. "And where'd you suppose I had 'em? Why, at my cousin Emma McIntyre's wedding, her that married the apothecary over in Jersey City, though her mother appeared to her in a dream and told her she'd rue the day she done it, but as Emma said, she got more advice than she wanted from the living, and if she was to listen to spectres too she'd never be sure what she'd ought to do and what she'd oughtn't; but I will say her husband took to drink, and she never was the same woman after her fust baby—well, they had an elegant church wedding, and what you s'pose I saw as I was walkin' up the aisle with the wedding percession?"

"Well?" Ann Eliza whispered, forgetting to thread her needle.

"Why, a coffin, to be sure, right on the top step of the chancel—Emma's folks is 'piscopalians and she would have a church wedding, though *his* mother raised a terrible rumpus over it—well, there it set, right in front of where the minister stood that was going to marry 'em, a coffin, covered with a black velvet pall with a gold fringe, and a 'Gates Ajar' in white camelias atop of it."

"Goodness," said Evelina, starting, "there's a knock!"

"Who can it be?" shuddered Ann Eliza, still under the spell of Miss Mellins's hallucination.

Evelina rose and lit a candle to guide her through the shop. They heard her turn the key of the outer door, and a gust of night air stirred the close atmosphere of the back room; then

there was a sound of vivacious exclamations, and Evelina returned with Mr. Ramy.

Ann Eliza's heart rocked like a boat in a heavy sea, and the
dress-maker's eyes, distended with curiosity, sprang eagerly
from face to face.

"I just thought I'd call in again," said Mr. Ramy, evidently
somewhat disconcerted by the presence of Miss Mellins. "Just
to see how the clock's behaving," he added with his hollow-
cheeked smile.

"Oh, she's behaving beautiful," said Ann Eliza; "but we're
real glad to see you all the same. Miss Mellins, let me make
you acquainted with Mr. Ramy."

The dress-maker tossed back her head and dropped her
lids in condescending recognition of the stranger's presence;
and Mr. Ramy responded by an awkward bow. After the first
moment of constraint a renewed sense of satisfaction filled
the consciousness of the three women. The Bunner sisters
were not sorry to let Miss Mellins see that they received an
occasional evening visit, and Miss Mellins was clearly enchanted at the opportunity of pouring her latest tale into a
new ear. As for Mr. Ramy, he adjusted himself to the situation with greater ease than might have been expected, and
Evelina, who had been sorry that he should enter the room
while the remains of supper still lingered on the table,
blushed with pleasure at his good-humored offer to help her
"glear away."

The table cleared, Ann Eliza suggested a game of cards;
and it was after eleven o'clock when Mr. Ramy rose to take
leave. His adieux were so much less abrupt than on the occasion of his first visit that Evelina was able to satisfy her sense
of etiquette by escorting him, candle in hand, to the outer
door; and as the two disappeared into the shop Miss Mellins
playfully turned to Ann Eliza.

"Well, well, Miss Bunner," she murmured, jerking her chin
in the direction of the retreating figures, "I'd no idea your sister was keeping company. On'y to think!"

Ann Eliza, roused from a state of dreamy beatitude, turned
her timid eyes on the dress-maker.

"Oh, you're mistaken, Miss Mellins. We don't har'ly know
Mr. Ramy."

Miss Mellins smiled incredulously. "You go 'long, Miss Bunner. I guess there'll be a wedding somewheres round here before spring, and I'll be real offended if I ain't asked to make the dress. I've always seen her in a gored satin with rooshings."

Ann Eliza made no answer. She had grown very pale, and her eyes lingered searchingly on Evelina as the younger sister re-entered the room. Evelina's cheeks were pink, and her blue eyes glittered; but it seemed to Ann Eliza that the coquettish tilt of her head regrettably emphasized the weakness of her receding chin. It was the first time that Ann Eliza had ever seen a flaw in her sister's beauty, and her involuntary criticism startled her like a secret disloyalty.

That night, after the light had been put out, the elder sister knelt longer than usual at her prayers. In the silence of the darkened room she was offering up certain dreams and aspirations whose brief blossoming had lent a transient freshness to her days. She wondered now how she could ever have supposed that Mr. Ramy's visits had another cause than the one Miss Mellins suggested. Had not the sight of Evelina first inspired him with a sudden solicitude for the welfare of the clock? And what charms but Evelina's could have induced him to repeat his visit? Grief held up its torch to the frail fabric of Ann Eliza's illusions, and with a firm heart she watched them shrivel into ashes; then, rising from her knees full of the chill joy of renunciation, she laid a kiss on the crimping pins of the sleeping Evelina and crept under the bedspread at her side.

V

During the months that followed, Mr. Ramy visited the sisters with increasing frequency. It became his habit to call on them every Sunday evening, and occasionally during the week he would find an excuse for dropping in unannounced as they were settling down to their work beside the lamp. Ann Eliza noticed that Evelina now took the precaution of putting on her crimson bow every evening before supper, and that she had refurbished with a bit of carefully washed lace the black silk which they still called new because it had been bought a year after Ann Eliza's.

Mr. Ramy, as he grew more intimate, became less conversational, and after the sisters had blushingly accorded him the privilege of a pipe he began to permit himself long stretches of meditative silence that were not without charm to his hostesses. There was something at once fortifying and pacific in the sense of that tranquil male presence in an atmosphere which had so long quivered with little feminine doubts and distresses; and the sisters fell into the habit of saying to each other, in moments of uncertainty: "We'll ask Mr. Ramy when he comes," and of accepting his verdict, whatever it might be, with a fatalistic readiness that relieved them of all responsibility.

When Mr. Ramy drew the pipe from his mouth and became, in his turn, confidential, the acuteness of their sympathy grew almost painful to the sisters. With passionate participation they listened to the story of his early struggles in Germany, and of the long illness which had been the cause of his recent misfortunes. The name of the Mrs. Hochmüller (an old comrade's widow) who had nursed him through his fever was greeted with reverential sighs and an inward pang of envy whenever it recurred in his biographical monologues, and once when the sisters were alone Evelina called a responsive flush to Ann Eliza's brow by saying suddenly, without the mention of any name: "I wonder what she's like?"

One day toward spring Mr. Ramy, who had by this time become as much a part of their lives as the letter-carrier or the milkman, ventured the suggestion that the ladies should accompany him to an exhibition of stereopticon views which was to take place at Chickering Hall on the following evening.

After their first breathless "Oh!" of pleasure there was a silence of mutual consultation, which Ann Eliza at last broke by saying: "You better go with Mr. Ramy, Evelina. I guess we don't both want to leave the store at night."

Evelina, with such protests as politeness demanded, acquiesced in this opinion, and spent the next day in trimming a white chip bonnet with forget-me-nots of her own making. Ann Eliza brought out her mosaic brooch, a cashmere scarf of their mother's was taken from its linen cerements, and thus adorned Evelina blushingly departed with Mr. Ramy, while the elder sister sat down in her place at the pinking-machine.

It seemed to Ann Eliza that she was alone for hours, and she was surprised, when she heard Evelina tap on the door, to find that the clock marked only half-past ten.

"It must have gone wrong again," she reflected as she rose to let her sister in.

The evening had been brilliantly interesting, and several striking stereopticon views of Berlin had afforded Mr. Ramy the opportunity of enlarging on the marvels of his native city.

"He said he'd love to show it all to me!" Evelina declared as Ann Eliza conned her glowing face. "Did you ever hear anything so silly? I didn't know which way to look."

Ann Eliza received this confidence with a sympathetic murmur.

"My bonnet *is* becoming, isn't it"? Evelina went on irrelevantly, smiling at her reflection in the cracked glass above the chest of drawers.

"You're jest lovely," said Ann Eliza.

Spring was making itself unmistakably known to the distrustful New Yorker by an increased harshness of wind and prevalence of dust, when one day Evelina entered the back room at supper-time with a cluster of jonquils in her hand.

"I was just that foolish," she answered Ann Eliza's wondering glance, "I couldn't help buyin' 'em. I felt as if I must have something pretty to look at right away."

"Oh, sister," said Ann Eliza, in trembling sympathy. She felt that special indulgence must be conceded to those in Evelina's state since she had had her own fleeting vision of such mysterious longings as the words betrayed.

Evelina, meanwhile, had taken the bundle of dried grasses out of the broken china vase, and was putting the jonquils in their place with touches that lingered down their smooth stems and blade-like leaves.

"Ain't they pretty?" she kept repeating as she gathered the flowers into a starry circle. "Seems as if spring was really here, don't it?"

Ann Eliza remembered that it was Mr. Ramy's evening.

When he came, the Teutonic eye for anything that blooms made him turn at once to the jonquils.

"Ain't dey pretty?" he said. "Seems like as if de spring was really here."

"Don't it?" Evelina exclaimed, thrilled by the coincidence of their thought. "It's just what I was saying to my sister."

Ann Eliza got up suddenly and moved away: she remembered that she had not wound the clock the day before. Evelina was sitting at the table; the jonquils rose slenderly between herself and Mr. Ramy.

"Oh," she murmured with vague eyes, "how I'd love to get away somewheres into the country this very minute—somewheres where it was green and quiet. Seems as if I couldn't stand the city another day." But Ann Eliza noticed that she was looking at Mr. Ramy, and not at the flowers.

"I guess we might go to Cendral Park some Sunday," their visitor suggested. "Do you ever go there, Miss Evelina?"

"No, we don't very often; leastways we ain't been for a good while." She sparkled at the prospect. "It would be lovely, wouldn't it, Ann Eliza?"

"Why, yes," said the elder sister, coming back to her seat.

"Well, why don't we go next Sunday?" Mr. Ramy continued. "And we'll invite Miss Mellins too—that'll make a gosy little party."

That night when Evelina undressed she took a jonquil from the vase and pressed it with a certain ostentation between the leaves of her prayer-book. Ann Eliza, covertly observing her, felt that Evelina was not sorry to be observed, and that her own acute consciousness of the act was somehow regarded as magnifying its significance.

The following Sunday broke blue and warm. The Bunner sisters were habitual church-goers, but for once they left their prayer-books on the what-not, and ten o'clock found them, gloved and bonneted, awaiting Miss Mellins's knock. Miss Mellins presently appeared in a glitter of jet sequins and spangles, with a tale of having seen a strange man prowling under her windows till he was called off at dawn by a confederate's whistle; and shortly afterward came Mr. Ramy, his hair brushed with more than usual care, his broad hands encased in gloves of olive-green kid.

The little party set out for the nearest street-car, and a flutter of mingled gratification and embarrassment stirred Ann Eliza's bosom when it was found that Mr. Ramy intended to pay their fares. Nor did he fail to live up to this opening liberality; for after guiding them through the Mall and the Ramble he led the way to a rustic restaurant where, also at his expense, they fared idyllically on milk and lemon-pie.

After this they resumed their walk, strolling on with the slowness of unaccustomed holiday-makers from one path to another—through budding shrubberies, past grass-banks sprinkled with lilac crocuses, and under rocks on which the forsythia lay like sudden sunshine. Everything about her seemed new and miraculously lovely to Ann Eliza; but she kept her feelings to herself, leaving it to Evelina to exclaim at the hepaticas under the shady ledges, and to Miss Mellins, less interested in the vegetable than in the human world, to remark significantly on the probable history of the persons they met. All the alleys were thronged with promenaders and obstructed by perambulators; and Miss Mellins's running commentary threw a glare of lurid possibilities over the placid family groups and their romping progeny.

Ann Eliza was in no mood for such interpretations of life; but, knowing that Miss Mellins had been invited for the sole purpose of keeping her company she continued to cling to the dress-maker's side, letting Mr. Ramy lead the way with Evelina. Miss Mellins, stimulated by the excitement of the occasion, grew more and more discursive, and her ceaseless talk, and the kaleidoscopic whirl of the crowd, were unspeakably bewildering to Ann Eliza. Her feet, accustomed to the slippered ease of the shop, ached with the unfamiliar effort of walking, and her ears with the din of the dress-maker's anecdotes; but every nerve in her was aware of Evelina's enjoyment, and she was determined that no weariness of hers should curtail it. Yet even her heroism shrank from the significant glances which Miss Mellins presently began to cast at the couple in front of them: Ann Eliza could bear to connive at Evelina's bliss, but not to acknowledge it to others.

At length Evelina's feet also failed her, and she turned to suggest that they ought to be going home. Her flushed face had grown pale with fatigue, but her eyes were radiant.

The return lived in Ann Eliza's memory with the persistence of an evil dream. The horse-cars were packed with the returning throng, and they had to let a dozen go by before they could push their way into one that was already crowded. Ann Eliza had never before felt so tired. Even Miss Mellins's flow of narrative ran dry, and they sat silent, wedged between a negro woman and a pock-marked man with a bandaged head, while the car rumbled slowly down a squalid avenue to their corner. Evelina and Mr. Ramy sat together in the forward part of the car, and Ann Eliza could catch only an occasional glimpse of the forget-me-not bonnet and the clock-maker's shiny coat-collar; but when the little party got out at their corner the crowd swept them together again, and they walked back in the effortless silence of tired children to the Bunner sisters' basement. As Miss Mellins and Mr. Ramy turned to go their various ways Evelina mustered a last display of smiles; but Ann Eliza crossed the threshold in silence, feeling the stillness of the little shop reach out to her like consoling arms.

That night she could not sleep; but as she lay cold and rigid at her sister's side, she suddenly felt the pressure of Evelina's arms, and heard her whisper: "Oh, Ann Eliza, warn't it heavenly?"

VI

For four days after their Sunday in the Park the Bunner sisters had no news of Mr. Ramy. At first neither one betrayed her disappointment and anxiety to the other; but on the fifth morning Evelina, always the first to yield to her feelings, said, as she turned from her untasted tea: "I thought you'd oughter take that money out by now, Ann Eliza."

Ann Eliza understood and reddened. The winter had been a fairly prosperous one for the sisters, and their slowly accumulated savings had now reached the handsome sum of two hundred dollars; but the satisfaction they might have felt in this unwonted opulence had been clouded by a suggestion of Miss Mellins's that there were dark rumours concerning the savings bank in which their funds were deposited. They knew Miss Mellins was given to vain alarms; but her words, by the sheer force of repetition, had so shaken Ann Eliza's peace that after long hours of midnight counsel the sisters had decided to advise with Mr. Ramy; and on Ann Eliza, as the head of the house, this duty had devolved. Mr. Ramy, when consulted, had not only confirmed the dress-maker's report, but had offered to find some safe investment which should give the sisters a higher rate of interest than the suspected savings bank; and Ann Eliza knew that Evelina alluded to the suggested transfer.

"Why, yes, to be sure," she agreed. "Mr. Ramy said if he was us he wouldn't want to leave his money there any longer'n he could help."

"It was over a week ago he said it," Evelina reminded her.

"I know; but he told me to wait till he'd found out for sure about that other investment; and we ain't seen him since then."

Ann Eliza's words released their secret fear. "I wonder what's happened to him," Evelina said. "You don't suppose he could be sick?"

"I was wondering too," Ann Eliza rejoined; and the sisters looked down at their plates.

"I should think you'd oughter do something about that money pretty soon," Evelina began again.

"Well, I know I'd oughter. What would you do if you was me?"

"If I was *you*," said her sister, with perceptible emphasis and a rising blush, "I'd go right round and see if Mr. Ramy was sick. *You* could."

The words pierced Ann Eliza like a blade. "Yes, that's so," she said.

"It would only seem friendly, if he really *is* sick. If I was you I'd go to-day," Evelina continued; and after dinner Ann Eliza went.

On the way she had to leave a parcel at the dyer's, and having performed that errand she turned toward Mr. Ramy's shop. Never before had she felt so old, so hopeless and humble. She knew she was bound on a love-errand of Evelina's, and the knowledge seemed to dry the last drop of young blood in her veins. It took from her, too, all her faded virginal shyness; and with a brisk composure she turned the handle of the clock-maker's door.

But as she entered her heart began to tremble, for she saw
Mr. Ramy, his face hidden in his hands, sitting behind the
counter in an attitude of strange dejection. At the click of the
latch he looked up slowly, fixing a lustreless stare on Ann
Eliza. For a moment she thought he did not know her.

"Oh, you're sick!" she exclaimed; and the sound of her
voice seemed to recall his wandering senses.

"Why, if it ain't Miss Bunner!" he said, in a low thick tone;
but he made no attempt to move, and she noticed that his
face was the colour of yellow ashes.

"You *are* sick," she persisted, emboldened by his evident
need of help. "Mr. Ramy, it was real unfriendly of you not to
let us know."

He continued to look at her with dull eyes. "I ain't been
sick," he said. "Leastways not very: only one of my old
turns." He spoke in a slow laboured way, as if he had difficulty in getting his words together.

"Rheumatism?" she ventured, seeing how unwillingly he
seemed to move.

"Well—somethin' like, maybe. I couldn't hardly put a
name to it."

"If it *was* anything like rheumatism, my grandmother used
to make a tea—" Ann Eliza began: she had forgotten, in the
warmth of the moment, that she had only come as Evelina's
messenger.

At the mention of tea an expression of uncontrollable re-
pugnance passed over Mr. Ramy's face. "Oh, I guess I'm getting on all right. I've just got a headache to-day."

Ann Eliza's courage dropped at the note of refusal in his
voice.

"I'm sorry," she said gently. "My sister and me'd have been
glad to do anything we could for you."

"Thank you kindly," said Mr. Ramy wearily; then, as she
turned to the door, he added with an effort: "Maybe I'll step
round to-morrow."

"We'll be real glad," Ann Eliza repeated. Her eyes were
fixed on a dusty bronze clock in the window. She was unaware of looking at it at the time, but long afterward she remembered that it represented a Newfoundland dog with his
paw on an open book.

When she reached home there was a purchaser in the shop, turning over hooks and eyes under Evelina's absent-minded supervision. Ann Eliza passed hastily into the back room, but in an instant she heard her sister at her side.

"Quick! I told her I was goin' to look for some smaller hooks—how is he?" Evelina gasped.

"He ain't been very well," said Ann Eliza slowly, her eyes on Evelina's eager face; "but he says he'll be sure to be round to-morrow night."

"He will? Are you telling me the truth?"

"Why, Evelina Bunner!"

"Oh, I don't care!" cried the younger recklessly, rushing back into the shop.

Ann Eliza stood burning with the shame of Evelina's self-exposure. She was shocked that, even to her, Evelina should lay bare the nakedness of her emotion; and she tried to turn her thoughts from it as though its recollection made her a sharer in her sister's debasement.

The next evening, Mr. Ramy reappeared, still somewhat sallow and red-lidded, but otherwise like his usual self. Ann Eliza consulted him about the investment he had recommended, and after it had been settled that he should attend to the matter for her he took up the illustrated volume of Longfellow—for, as the sisters had learned, his culture soared beyond the newspapers—and read aloud, with a fine confusion of consonants, the poem on "Maidenhood." Evelina lowered her lids while he read. It was a very beautiful evening, and Ann Eliza thought afterward how different life might have been with a companion who read poetry like Mr. Ramy.

VII

During the ensuing weeks Mr. Ramy, though his visits were as frequent as ever, did not seem to regain his usual spirits. He complained frequently of headache, but rejected Ann Eliza's tentatively proffered remedies, and seemed to shrink from any prolonged investigation of his symptoms. July had come, with a sudden ardour of heat, and one evening, as the three sat together by the open window in the back room,

Evelina said: "I dunno what I wouldn't give, a night like this, for a breath of real country air."

"So would I," said Mr. Ramy, knocking the ashes from his pipe. "I'd like to be setting in an arbour dis very minute."

"Oh, wouldn't it be lovely?"

"I always think it's real cool here—we'd be heaps hotter up where Miss Mellins is," said Ann Eliza.

"Oh, I daresay—but we'd be heaps cooler somewhere else," her sister snapped: she was not infrequently exasperated by Ann Eliza's furtive attempts to mollify Providence.

A few days later Mr. Ramy appeared with a suggestion which enchanted Evelina. He had gone the day before to see his friend, Mrs. Hochmüller, who lived in the outskirts of Hoboken, and Mrs. Hochmüller had proposed that on the following Sunday he should bring the Bunner sisters to spend the day with her.

"She's got a real garden, you know," Mr. Ramy explained, "wid trees and a real summer-house to set in; and hens and chickens too. And it's an elegant sail over on de ferry-boat."

The proposal drew no response from Ann Eliza. She was still oppressed by the recollection of her interminable Sunday in the Park; but, obedient to Evelina's imperious glance, she finally faltered out an acceptance.

The Sunday was a very hot one, and once on the ferry-boat Ann Eliza revived at the touch of the salt breeze, and the spectacle of the crowded waters; but when they reached the other shore, and stepped out on the dirty wharf, she began to ache with anticipated weariness. They got into a street-car, and were jolted from one mean street to another, till at length Mr. Ramy pulled the conductor's sleeve and they got out again; then they stood in the blazing sun, near the door of a crowded beer-saloon, waiting for another car to come; and that carried them out to a thinly settled district, past vacant lots and narrow brick houses standing in unsupported solitude, till they finally reached an almost rural region of scattered cottages and low wooden buildings that looked like village "stores." Here the car finally stopped of its own accord, and they walked along a rutty road, past a stone-cutter's yard with a high fence tapestried with theatrical advertisements, to a little red house with green blinds and a garden paling. Really, Mr. Ramy had not deceived them. Clumps of dielytra and day-lilies bloomed behind the paling, and a crooked elm hung romantically over the gable of the house.

At the gate Mrs. Hochmüller, a broad woman in brick-brown merino, met them with nods and smiles, while her daughter Linda, a flaxen-haired girl with mottled red cheeks and a sidelong stare, hovered inquisitively behind her. Mrs. Hochmüller, leading the way into the house, conducted the Bunner sisters the way to her bedroom. Here they were invited to spread out on a mountainous white feather-bed the cashmere mantles under which the solemnity of the occasion had compelled them to swelter, and when they had given their black silks the necessary twitch of readjustment, and Evelina had fluffed out her hair before a looking-glass framed in pink-shell work, their hostess led them to a stuffy parlour smelling of ginger-bread. After another ceremonial pause, broken by polite enquiries and shy ejaculations, they were shown into the kitchen, where the table was already spread with strange-looking spice-cakes and stewed fruits, and where they presently found themselves seated between Mrs. Hochmüller and Mr. Ramy, while the staring Linda bumped back and forth from the stove with steaming dishes.

To Ann Eliza the dinner seemed endless, and the rich fare strangely unappetizing. She was abashed by the easy intimacy of her hostess's voice and eye. With Mr. Ramy Mrs. Hochmüller was almost flippantly familiar, and it was only when Ann Eliza pictured her generous form bent above his sick-bed that she could forgive her for tersely addressing him as "Ramy." During one of the pauses of the meal Mrs. Hochmüller laid her knife and fork against the edges of her plate, and, fixing her eyes on the clock-maker's face, said accusingly: "You hat one of dem turns again, Ramy."

"I dunno as I had," he returned evasively.

Evelina glanced from one to the other. "Mr. Ramy *has* been sick," she said at length, as though to show that she also was in a position to speak with authority. "He's complained very frequently of headaches."

"Ho!—I know him," said Mrs. Hochmüller with a laugh, her eyes still on the clock-maker. "Ain't you ashamed of yourself, Ramy?"

Mr. Ramy, who was looking at his plate, said suddenly one word which the sisters could not understand; it sounded to Ann Eliza like "Shwike."

Mrs. Hochmüller laughed again. "My, my," she said, "wouldn't you think he'd be ashamed to go and be sick and never dell me, me that nursed him troo dat awful fever?"

"Yes, I *should*," said Evelina, with a spirited glance at Ramy; but he was looking at the sausages that Linda had just put on the table.

When dinner was over Mrs. Hochmüller invited her guests to step out of the kitchen-door, and they found themselves in a green enclosure, half garden, half orchard. Grey hens followed by golden broods clucked under the twisted apple-boughs, a cat dozed on the edge of an old well, and from tree to tree ran the network of clothes-line that denoted Mrs. Hochmüller's calling. Beyond the apple trees stood a yellow summer-house festooned with scarlet runners; and below it, on the farther side of a rough fence, the land dipped down, holding a bit of woodland in its hollow. It was all strangely sweet and still on that hot Sunday afternoon, and as she moved across the grass under the apple-boughs Ann Eliza thought of quiet afternoons in church, and of the hymns her mother had sung to her when she was a baby.

Evelina was more restless. She wandered from the well to the summer-house and back, she tossed crumbs to the chickens and disturbed the cat with arch caresses; and at last she expressed a desire to go down into the wood.

"I guess you got to go round by the road, then," said Mrs. Hochmüller. "My Linda she goes troo a hole in de fence, but I guess you'd tear your dress if you was to dry."

"I'll help you," said Mr. Ramy; and guided by Linda the pair walked along the fence till they reached a narrow gap in its boards. Through this they disappeared, watched curiously in their descent by the grinning Linda, while Mrs. Hochmüller and Ann Eliza were left alone in the summer-house.

Mrs. Hochmüller looked at her guest with a confidential smile. "I guess dey'll be gone quite a while," she remarked, jerking her double chin toward the gap in the fence. "Folks like dat don't never remember about de dime." And she drew out her knitting.

Ann Eliza could think of nothing to say.

"Your sister she thinks a great lot of him, don't she?" her hostess continued.

Ann Eliza's cheeks grew hot. "Ain't you a teeny bit lonesome away out here sometimes?" she asked. "I should think you'd be scared nights, all alone with your daughter."

"Oh, no, I ain't," said Mrs. Hochmüller. "You see I take in washing—dat's my business—and it's a lot cheaper doing it out here dan in de city: where'd I get a drying-ground like dis in Hobucken? And den it's safer for Linda too; it geeps her outer de streets."

"Oh," said Ann Eliza, shrinking. She began to feel a distinct aversion for her hostess, and her eyes turned with involuntary annoyance to the square-backed form of Linda, still inquisitively suspended on the fence. It seemed to Ann Eliza that Evelina and her companion would never return from the wood; but they came at length, Mr. Ramy's brow pearled with perspiration, Evelina pink and conscious, a drooping bunch of ferns in her hand; and it was clear that, to her at least, the moments had been winged.

"D'you suppose they'll revive?" she asked, holding up the ferns; but Ann Eliza, rising at her approach, said stiffly: "We'd better be getting home, Evelina."

"Mercy me! Ain't you going to take your coffee first?" Mrs. Hochmüller protested; and Ann Eliza found to her dismay that another long gastronomic ceremony must intervene before politeness permitted them to leave. At length, however, they found themselves again on the ferry-boat. Water and sky were grey, with a dividing gleam of sunset that sent sleek opal waves in the boat's wake. The wind had a cool tarry breath, as though it had travelled over miles of shipping, and the hiss of the water about the paddles was as delicious as though it had been splashed into their tired faces.

Ann Eliza sat apart, looking away from the others. She had made up her mind that Mr. Ramy had proposed to Evelina in the wood, and she was silently preparing herself to receive her sister's confidence that evening.

But Evelina was apparently in no mood for confidences. When they reached home she put her faded ferns in water, and after supper, when she had laid aside her silk dress and the forget-me-not bonnet, she remained silently seated in her rocking-chair near the open window. It was long since Ann Eliza had seen her in so uncommunicative a mood.

The following Saturday Ann Eliza was sitting alone in the shop when the door opened and Mr. Ramy entered. He had never before called at that hour, and she wondered a little anxiously what had brought him.

"Has anything happened?" she asked, pushing aside the basketful of buttons she had been sorting.

"Not's I know of," said Mr. Ramy tranquilly. "But I always close up the store at two o'clock Saturdays at this season, so I thought I might as well call round and see you."

"I'm real glad, I'm sure," said Ann Eliza; "but Evelina's out."

"I know dat," Mr. Ramy answered. "I met her round de corner. She told me she got to go to dat new dyer's up in Forty-eighth Street. She won't be back for a couple of hours, har'ly, will she?"

Ann Eliza looked at him with rising bewilderment. "No, I guess not," she answered; her instinctive hospitality prompting her to add: "Won't you set down jest the same?"

Mr. Ramy sat down on the stool beside the counter, and Ann Eliza returned to her place behind it.

"I can't leave the store," she explained.

"Well, I guess we're very well here." Ann Eliza had become suddenly aware that Mr. Ramy was looking at her with unusual intentness. Involuntarily her hand strayed to the thin streaks of hair on her temples, and thence descended to straighten the brooch beneath her collar.

"You're looking very well to-day, Miss Bunner," said Mr. Ramy, following her gesture with a smile.

"Oh," said Ann Eliza nervously. "I'm always well in health," she added.

"I guess you're healthier than your sister, even if you are less sizeable."

"Oh, I don't know. Evelina's a mite nervous sometimes, but she ain't a bit sickly."

"She eats heartier than you do; but that don't mean nothing," said Mr. Ramy.

Ann Eliza was silent. She could not follow the trend of his thought, and she did not care to commit herself farther about Evelina before she had ascertained if Mr. Ramy considered nervousness interesting or the reverse.

But Mr. Ramy spared her all farther indecision.

"Well, Miss Bunner," he said, drawing his stool closer to the counter, "I guess I might as well tell you fust as last what I come here for to-day. I want to get married."

Ann Eliza, in many a prayerful midnight hour, had sought to strengthen herself for the hearing of this avowal, but now that it had come she felt pitifully frightened and unprepared. Mr. Ramy was leaning with both elbows on the counter, and she noticed that his nails were clean and that he had brushed his hat; yet even these signs had not prepared her!

At last she heard herself say, with a dry throat in which her heart was hammering: "Mercy me, Mr. Ramy!"

"I want to get married," he repeated. "I'm too lonesome. It ain't good for a man to live all alone, and eat noding but cold meat every day."

"No," said Ann Eliza softly.

"And the dust fairly beats me."

"Oh, the dust—I know!"

Mr. Ramy stretched one of his blunt-fingered hands toward her. "I wisht you'd take me."

Still Ann Eliza did not understand. She rose hesitatingly from her seat, pushing aside the basket of buttons which lay between them; then she perceived that Mr. Ramy was trying to take her hand, and as their fingers met a flood of joy swept over her. Never afterward, though every other word of their interview was stamped on her memory beyond all possible forgetting, could she recall what he said while their hands touched; she only knew that she seemed to be floating on a summer sea, and that all its waves were in her ears.

"Me—me?" she gasped.

"I guess so," said her suitor placidly. "You suit me right down to the ground, Miss Bunner. Dat's the truth."

A woman passing along the street paused to look at the shop-window, and Ann Eliza half hoped she would come in; but after a desultory inspection she went on.

"Maybe you don't fancy me?" Mr. Ramy suggested, discountenanced by Ann Eliza's silence.

A word of assent was on her tongue, but her lips refused it. She must find some other way of telling him.

"I don't say that."

"Well, I always kinder thought we was suited to one another," Mr. Ramy continued, eased of his momentary doubt. "I always liked de quiet style—no fuss and airs, and not afraid of work." He spoke as though dispassionately cataloguing her charms.

Ann Eliza felt that she must make an end. "But, Mr. Ramy, you don't understand. I've never thought of marrying."

Mr. Ramy looked at her in surprise. "Why not?"

"Well, I don't know, har'ly." She moistened her twitching lips. "The fact is, I ain't as active as I look. Maybe I couldn't stand the care. I ain't as spry as Evelina—nor as young," she added, with a last great effort.

"But you do most of de work here, anyways," said her suitor doubtfully.

"Oh, well, that's because Evelina's busy outside; and where there's only two women the work don't amount to much. Besides, I'm the oldest; I have to look after things," she hastened on, half pained that her simple ruse should so readily deceive him.

"Well, I guess you're active enough for me," he persisted. His calm determination began to frighten her; she trembled lest her own should be less staunch.

"No, no," she repeated, feeling the tears on her lashes. "I couldn't, Mr. Ramy, I couldn't marry. I'm so surprised. I always thought it was Evelina—always. And so did everybody else. She's so bright and pretty—it seemed so natural."

"Well, you was all mistaken," said Mr. Ramy obstinately.

"I'm so sorry."

He rose, pushing back his chair.

"You'd better think it over," he said, in the large tone of a man who feels he may safely wait.

"Oh, no, no. It ain't any sorter use, Mr. Ramy. I don't never mean to marry. I get tired so easily—I'd be afraid of the work. And I have such awful headaches." She paused, racking her brain for more convincing infirmities.

"Headaches, do you?" said Mr. Ramy, turning back.

"My, yes, awful ones, that I have to give right up to. Evelina has to do everything when I have one of them headaches. She has to bring me my tea in the mornings."

"Well, I'm sorry to hear it," said Mr. Ramy.

"Thank you kindly all the same," Ann Eliza murmured. "And please don't—don't—" She stopped suddenly, looking at him through her tears.

"Oh, that's all right," he answered. "Don't you fret, Miss Bunner. Folks have got to suit themselves." She thought his tone had grown more resigned since she had spoken of her headaches.

For some moments he stood looking at her with a hesitating eye, as though uncertain how to end their conversation; and at length she found courage to say (in the words of a novel she had once read): "I don't want this should make any difference between us."

"Oh, my, no," said Mr. Ramy, absently picking up his hat.

"You'll come in just the same?" she continued, nerving herself to the effort. "We'd miss you awfully if you didn't. Evelina, she—" She paused, torn between her desire to turn his thoughts to Evelina, and the dread of prematurely disclosing her sister's secret.

"Don't Miss Evelina have no headaches?" Mr. Ramy suddenly asked.

"My, no, never—well, not to speak of, anyway. She ain't had one for ages, and when Evelina *is* sick she won't never give in to it," Ann Eliza declared, making some hurried adjustments with her conscience.

"I wouldn't have thought that," said Mr. Ramy.

"I guess you don't know us as well as you thought you did."

"Well, no, that's so; maybe I don't. I'll wish you good day, Miss Bunner"; and Mr. Ramy moved toward the door.

"Good day, Mr. Ramy," Ann Eliza answered.

She felt unutterably thankful to be alone. She knew the crucial moment of her life had passed, and she was glad that she had not fallen below her own ideals. It had been a wonderful experience, full of undreamed-of fear and fascination; and in spite of the tears on her cheeks she was not sorry to have known it. Two facts, however, took the edge from its perfection: that it had happened in the shop, and that she had not had on her black silk.

She passed the next hour in a state of dreamy ecstasy. Something had entered into her life of which no subsequent empoverishment could rob it: she glowed with the same rich sense of possessorship that once, as a little girl, she had felt when her mother had given her a gold locket and she had sat up in bed in the dark to draw it from its hiding-place beneath her night-gown.

At length a dread of Evelina's return began to mingle with these musings. How could she meet her younger sister's eye without betraying what had happened? She felt as though a visible glory lay on her, and she was glad that dusk had fallen when Evelina entered. But her fears were superfluous. Evelina, always self-absorbed, had of late lost all interest in the simple happenings of the shop, and Ann Eliza, with mingled mortification and relief, perceived that she was in no danger of being cross-questioned as to the events of the afternoon. She was glad of this; yet there was a touch of humiliation in finding that the portentous secret in her bosom did not visibly shine forth. It struck her as dull, and even slightly absurd, of Evelina not to know at last that they were equals.

VIII

Mr. Ramy, after a decent interval, returned to the shop; and Ann Eliza, when they met, was unable to detect whether the emotions which seethed under her black alpaca found an echo in his bosom. Outwardly he made no sign. He lit his pipe as placidly as ever and seemed to relapse without effort into the unruffled intimacy of old. Yet to Ann Eliza's initiated eye a change became gradually perceptible. She saw that he was beginning to look at her sister as he had looked at her on that momentous afternoon: she even discerned a secret significance in the turn of his talk with Evelina. Once he asked her abruptly if she should like to travel, and Ann Eliza saw that the flush on Evelina's cheek was reflected from the same fire which had scorched her own.

So they drifted on through the sultry weeks of July. At that season the business of the little shop almost ceased, and one Saturday morning Mr. Ramy proposed that the sisters should lock up early and go with him for a sail down the bay in one of the Coney Island boats.

Ann Eliza saw the light in Evelina's eye and her resolve was instantly taken.

"I guess I won't go, thank you kindly; but I'm sure my sister will be happy to."

She was pained by the perfunctory phrase with which Evelina urged her to accompany them; and still more by Mr. Ramy's silence.

"No, I guess I won't go," she repeated, rather in answer to herself than to them. "It's dreadfully hot and I've got a kinder headache."

"Oh, well, I wouldn't then," said her sister hurriedly. "You'd better jest set here quietly and rest."

"Yes, I'll rest," Ann Eliza assented.

At two o'clock Mr. Ramy returned, and a moment later he and Evelina left the shop. Evelina had made herself another new bonnet for the occasion, a bonnet, Ann Eliza thought, almost too youthful in shape and colour. It was the first time it had ever occurred to her to criticize Evelina's taste, and she was frightened at the insidious change in her attitude toward her sister.

When Ann Eliza, in later days, looked back on that afternoon she felt that there had been something prophetic in the quality of its solitude; it seemed to distill the triple essence of loneliness in which all her after-life was to be lived. No purchasers came; not a hand fell on the door-latch; and the tick of the clock in the back room ironically emphasized the passing of the empty hours.

Evelina returned late and alone. Ann Eliza felt the coming crisis in the sound of her footstep, which wavered along as if not knowing on what it trod. The elder sister's affection had so passionately projected itself into her junior's fate that at such moments she seemed to be living two lives, her own and Evelina's; and her private longings shrank into silence at the sight of the other's hungry bliss. But it was evident that Evelina, never acutely alive to the emotional atmosphere

about her, had no idea that her secret was suspected; and with
an assumption of unconcern that would have made Ann Eliza
smile if the pang had been less piercing, the younger sister
prepared to confess herself.

"What are you so busy about?" she said impatiently, as Ann
Eliza, beneath the gas-jet, fumbled for the matches. "Ain't
you even got time to ask me if I'd had a pleasant day?"

Ann Eliza turned with a quiet smile. "I guess I don't have
to. Seems to me it's pretty plain you have."

"Well, I don't know. I don't know *how* I feel—it's all so
queer. I almost think I'd like to scream."

"I guess you're tired."

"No, I ain't. It's not that. But it all happened so suddenly,
and the boat was so crowded I thought everybody'd hear
what he was saying.—Ann Eliza," she broke out, "why on
earth don't you ask me what I'm talking about?"

Ann Eliza, with a last effort of heroism, feigned a fond incomprehension.

"What *are* you?"

"Why, I'm engaged to be married—so there! Now it's out!
And it happened right on the boat; only to think of it! Of course
I wasn't exactly surprised—I've known right along he was
going to sooner or later—on'y somehow I didn't think of its
happening to-day. I thought he'd never get up his courage. He
said he was so 'fraid I'd say no—that's what kep' him so long
from asking me. Well, I ain't said yes *yet*—leastways I told him
I'd have to think it over; but I guess he knows. Oh, Ann Eliza,
I'm so happy!" She hid the blinding brightness of her face.

Ann Eliza, just then, would only let herself feel that she was
glad. She drew down Evelina's hands and kissed her, and they
held each other. When Evelina regained her voice she had a
tale to tell which carried their vigil far into the night. Not a
syllable, not a glance or gesture of Ramy's, was the elder sister spared; and with unconscious irony she found herself com-
paring the details of his proposal to her with those which
Evelina was imparting with merciless prolixity.

The next few days were taken up with the embarrassed adjustment of their new relation to Mr. Ramy and to each other.
Ann Eliza's ardour carried her to new heights of self-effacement, and she invented late duties in the shop in order to

leave Evelina and her suitor longer alone in the back room. Later on, when she tried to remember the details of those first days, few came back to her: she knew only that she got up each morning with the sense of having to push the leaden hours up the same long steep of pain.

Mr. Ramy came daily now. Every evening he and his betrothed went out for a stroll around the Square, and when Evelina came in her cheeks were always pink. "He's kissed her under that tree at the corner, away from the lamp-post," Ann Eliza said to herself, with sudden insight into unconjectured things. On Sundays they usually went for the whole afternoon to the Central Park, and Ann Eliza, from her seat in the mortal hush of the back room, followed step by step their long slow beatific walk.

There had been, as yet, no allusion to their marriage, except that Evelina had once told her sister that Mr. Ramy wished them to invite Mrs. Hochmüller and Linda to the wedding. The mention of the laundress raised a half-forgotten fear in Ann Eliza, and she said in a tone of tentative appeal: "I guess if I was you I wouldn't want to be very great friends with Mrs. Hochmüller."

Evelina glanced at her compassionately. "I guess if you was me you'd want to do everything you could to please the man you loved. It's lucky," she added with glacial irony, "that I'm not too grand for Herman's friends."

"Oh," Ann Eliza protested, "that ain't what I mean—and you know it ain't. Only somehow the day we saw her I didn't think she seemed like the kinder person you'd want for a friend."

"I guess a married woman's the best judge of such matters," Evelina replied, as though she already walked in the light of her future state.

Ann Eliza, after that, kept her own counsel. She saw that Evelina wanted her sympathy as little as her admonitions, and that already she counted for nothing in her sister's scheme of life. To Ann Eliza's idolatrous acceptance of the cruelties of fate this exclusion seemed both natural and just; but it caused her the most lively pain. She could not divest her love for Evelina of its passionate motherliness; no breath of reason could lower it to the cool temperature of sisterly affection.

She was then passing, as she thought, through the novitiate of her pain; preparing, in a hundred experimental ways, for the solitude awaiting her when Evelina left. It was true that it would be a tempered loneliness. They would not be far apart. Evelina would "run in" daily from the clock-maker's; they would doubtless take supper with her on Sundays. But already Ann Eliza guessed with what growing perfunctoriness her sister would fulfill these obligations; she even foresaw the day when, to get news of Evelina, she should have to lock the shop at nightfall and go herself to Mr. Ramy's door. But on that contingency she would not dwell. "They can come to me when they want to—they'll always find me here," she simply said to herself.

One evening Evelina came in flushed and agitated from her stroll around the Square. Ann Eliza saw at once that something had happened; but the new habit of reticence checked her question.

She had not long to wait. "Oh, Ann Eliza, on'y to think what he says—" (the pronoun stood exclusively for Mr. Ramy). "I declare I'm so upset I thought the people in the Square would notice me. Don't I look queer? He wants to get married right off—this very next week."

"Next week?"

"Yes. So's we can move out to St. Louis right away."

"Him and you—move out to St. Louis?"

"Well, I don't know as it would be natural for him to want to go out there without me," Evelina simpered. "But it's all so sudden I don't know what to think. He only got the letter this morning. *Do* I look queer, Ann Eliza?" Her eye was roving for the mirror.

"No, you don't," said Ann Eliza almost harshly.

"Well, it's a mercy," Evelina pursued with a tinge of disappointment. "It's a regular miracle I didn't faint right out there in the Square. Herman's so thoughtless—he just put the letter into my hand without a word. It's from a big firm out there—the Tiff'ny of St. Louis, he says it is—offering him a place in their clock-department. Seems they heard of him through a German friend of his that's settled out there. It's a splendid opening, and if he gives satisfaction they'll raise him at the end of the year."

She paused, flushed with the importance of the situation, which seemed to lift her once for all above the dull level of her former life.

"Then you'll have to go?" came at last from Ann Eliza.

Evelina stared. "You wouldn't have me interfere with his prospects, would you?"

"No—no. I on'y meant—has it got to be so soon?"

"Right away, I tell you—next week. Ain't it awful?" blushed the bride.

Well, this was what happened to mothers. They bore it, Ann Eliza mused; so why not she? Ah, but they had their own chance first; she had had no chance at all. And now this life which she had made her own was going from her forever; had gone, already, in the inner and deeper sense, and was soon to vanish in even its outward nearness, its surface-communion of voice and eye. At that moment even the thought of Evelina's happiness refused her its consolatory ray; or its light, if she saw it, was too remote to warm her. The thirst for a personal and inalienable tie, for pangs and problems of her own, was parching Ann Eliza's soul: it seemed to her that she could never again gather strength to look her loneliness in the face.

The trivial obligations of the moment came to her aid. Nursed in idleness her grief would have mastered her; but the needs of the shop and the back room, and the preparations for Evelina's marriage, kept the tyrant under.

Miss Mellins, true to her anticipations, had been called on to aid in the making of the wedding dress, and she and Ann Eliza were bending one evening over the breadths of pearl-grey cashmere which, in spite of the dress-maker's prophetic vision of gored satin, had been judged most suitable, when Evelina came into the room alone.

Ann Eliza had already had occasion to notice that it was a bad sign when Mr. Ramy left his affianced at the door. It generally meant that Evelina had something disturbing to communicate, and Ann Eliza's first glance told her that this time the news was grave.

Miss Mellins, who sat with her back to the door and her head bent over her sewing, started as Evelina came around to the opposite side of the table.

"Mercy, Miss Evelina! I declare I thought you was a ghost, the way you crep' in. I had a customer once up in Forty-ninth Street—a lovely young woman with a thirty-six bust and a waist you could ha' put into her wedding ring—and her husband, he crep' up behind her that way jest for a joke, and frightened her into a fit, and when she come to she was a raving maniac, and had to be taken to Bloomingdale with two doctors and a nurse to hold her in the carriage, and a lovely baby on'y six weeks old—and there she is to this day, poor creature."

"I didn't mean to startle you," said Evelina.

She sat down on the nearest chair, and as the lamp-light fell on her face Ann Eliza saw that she had been crying.

"You do look dead-beat," Miss Mellins resumed, after a pause of soul-probing scrutiny. "I guess Mr. Ramy lugs you round that Square too often. You'll walk your legs off if you ain't careful. Men don't never consider—they're all alike. Why, I had a cousin once that was engaged to a book-agent—"

"Maybe we'd better put away the work for to-night, Miss Mellins," Ann Eliza interposed. "I guess what Evelina wants is a good night's rest."

"That's so," assented the dress-maker. "Have you got the back breadths run together, Miss Bunner? Here's the sleeves. I'll pin 'em together." She drew a cluster of pins from her mouth, in which she seemed to secrete them as squirrels stow away nuts. "There," she said, rolling up her work, "you go right away to bed, Miss Evelina, and we'll set up a little later to-morrow night. I guess you're a mite nervous, ain't you? I know when my turn comes I'll be scared to death."

With this arch forecast she withdrew, and Ann Eliza, returning to the back room, found Evelina still listlessly seated by the table. True to her new policy of silence, the elder sister set about folding up the bridal dress; but suddenly Evelina said in a harsh unnatural voice: "There ain't any use in going on with that."

The folds slipped from Ann Eliza's hands.

"Evelina Bunner—what you mean?"

"Jest what I say. It's put off."

"Put off—what's put off?"

"Our getting married. He can't take me to St. Louis. He ain't got money enough." She brought the words out in the monotonous tone of a child reciting a lesson.

Ann Eliza picked up another breadth of cashmere and began to smooth it out. "I don't understand," she said at length.

"Well, it's plain enough. The journey's fearfully expensive, and we've got to have something left to start with when we get out there. We've counted up, and he ain't got the money to do it—that's all."

"But I thought he was going right into a splendid place."

"So he is; but the salary's pretty low the first year, and board's very high in St. Louis. He's jest got another letter from his German friend, and he's been figuring it out, and he's afraid to chance it. He'll have to go alone."

"But there's your money—have you forgotten that? The hundred dollars in the bank."

Evelina made an impatient movement. "Of course I ain't forgotten it. On'y it ain't enough. It would all have to go into buying furniture, and if he was took sick and lost his place again we wouldn't have a cent left. He says he's got to lay by another hundred dollars before he'll be willing to take me out there."

For a while Ann Eliza pondered this surprising statement; then she ventured: "Seems to me he might have thought of it before."

In an instant Evelina was aflame. "I guess he knows what's right as well as you or me. I'd sooner die than be a burden to him."

Ann Eliza made no answer. The clutch of an unformulated doubt had checked the words on her lips. She had meant, on the day of her sister's marriage, to give Evelina the other half of their common savings; but something warned her not to say so now.

The sisters undressed without farther words. After they had gone to bed, and the light had been put out, the sound of Evelina's weeping came to Ann Eliza in the darkness, but she lay motionless on her own side of the bed, out of contact with her sister's shaken body. Never had she felt so coldly remote from Evelina.

The hours of the night moved slowly, ticked off with wearisome insistence by the clock which had played so prominent a part in their lives. Evelina's sobs still stirred the bed at gradually lengthening intervals, till at length Ann Eliza thought she slept. But with the dawn the eyes of the sisters met, and Ann Eliza's courage failed her as she looked in Evelina's face.

She sat up in bed and put out a pleading hand.

"Don't cry so, dearie. Don't."

"Oh, I can't bear it, I can't bear it," Evelina moaned.

Ann Eliza stroked her quivering shoulder. "Don't, don't," she repeated. "If you take the other hundred, won't that be enough? I always meant to give it to you. On'y I didn't want to tell you till your wedding day."

IX

Evelina's marriage took place on the appointed day. It was celebrated in the evening, in the chantry of the church which the sisters attended, and after it was over the few guests who had been present repaired to the Bunner Sisters' basement, where a wedding supper awaited them. Ann Eliza, aided by Miss Mellins and Mrs. Hawkins, and consciously supported by the sentimental interest of the whole street, had expended her utmost energy on the decoration of the shop and the back room. On the table a vase of white chrysanthemums stood between a dish of oranges and bananas and an iced wedding-cake wreathed with orange-blossoms of the bride's own making. Autumn leaves studded with paper roses festooned the what-not and the chromo of the Rock of Ages, and a wreath of yellow immortelles was twined about the clock which Evelina revered as the mysterious agent of her happiness.

At the table sat Miss Mellins, profusely spangled and bangled, her head sewing-girl, a pale young thing who had helped with Evelina's outfit, Mr. and Mrs. Hawkins, with Johnny, their eldest boy, and Mrs. Hochmüller and her daughter.

Mrs. Hochmüller's large blonde personality seemed to pervade the room to the effacement of the less amply-proportioned guests. It was rendered more impressive by a dress of crimson poplin that stood out from her in organ-like folds;

and Linda, whom Ann Eliza had remembered as an uncouth
child with a sly look about the eyes, surprised her by a sudden
blossoming into feminine grace such as sometimes follows on
a gawky girlhood. The Hochmüllers, in fact, struck the dominant note in the entertainment. Beside them Evelina, unusually pale in her grey cashmere and white bonnet, looked like a
faintly washed sketch beside a brilliant chromo; and Mr.
Ramy, doomed to the traditional insignificance of the bridegroom's part, made no attempt to rise above his situation.
Even Miss Mellins sparkled and jingled in vain in the shadow
of Mrs. Hochmüller's crimson bulk; and Ann Eliza, with a
sense of vague foreboding, saw that the wedding feast centred
about the two guests she had most wished to exclude from it.
What was said or done while they all sat about the table she
never afterward recalled: the long hours remained in her
memory as a whirl of high colours and loud voices, from
which the pale presence of Evelina now and then emerged
like a drowned face on a sunset-dabbled sea.

The next morning Mr. Ramy and his wife started for St.
Louis, and Ann Eliza was left alone. Outwardly the first strain
of parting was tempered by the arrival of Miss Mellins, Mrs.
Hawkins and Johnny, who dropped in to help in the ungar-
landing and tidying up of the back room. Ann Eliza was duly
grateful for their kindness, but the "talking over" on which
they had evidently counted was Dead Sea fruit on her lips;
and just beyond the familiar warmth of their presences she
saw the form of Solitude at her door.

Ann Eliza was but a small person to harbour so great a
guest, and a trembling sense of insufficiency possessed her.
She had no high musings to offer to the new companion of
her hearth. Every one of her thoughts had hitherto turned to
Evelina and shaped itself in homely easy words; of the mighty
speech of silence she knew not the earliest syllable.

Everything in the back room and the shop, on the second
day after Evelina's going, seemed to have grown coldly unfamiliar. The whole aspect of the place had changed with the
changed conditions of Ann Eliza's life. The first customer
who opened the shop-door startled her like a ghost; and all
night she lay tossing on her side of the bed, sinking now and
then into an uncertain doze from which she would suddenly

wake to reach out her hand for Evelina. In the new silence surrounding her the walls and furniture found voice, frightening her at dusk and midnight with strange sighs and stealthy whispers. Ghostly hands shook the window shutters or rattled at the outer latch, and once she grew cold at the sound of a step like Evelina's stealing through the dark shop to die out on the threshold. In time, of course, she found an explanation for these noises, telling herself that the bedstead was warping, that Miss Mellins trod heavily overhead, or that the thunder of passing beer-waggons shook the door-latch; but the hours leading up to these conclusions were full of the floating terrors that harden into fixed foreboding. Worst of all were the solitary meals, when she absently continued to set aside the largest slice of pie for Evelina, and to let the tea grow cold while she waited for her sister to help herself to the first cup. Miss Mellins, coming in on one of these sad repasts, suggested the acquisition of a cat; but Ann Eliza shook her head. She had never been used to animals, and she felt the vague shrinking of the pious from creatures divided from her by the abyss of soullessness.

At length, after ten empty days, Evelina's first letter came.

"My dear Sister," she wrote, in her pinched Spencerian hand, "it seems strange to be in this great City so far from home alone with him I have chosen for life, but marriage has its solemn duties which those who are not can never hope to understand, and happier perhaps for this reason, life for them has only simple tasks and pleasures, but those who must take thought for others must be prepared to do their duty in whatever station it has pleased the Almighty to call them. Not that I have cause to complain, my dear Husband is all love and devotion, but being absent all day at his business how can I help but feel lonesome at times, as the poet says it is hard for they that love to live apart, and I often wonder, my dear Sister, how you are getting along alone in the store, may you never experience the feelings of solitude I have underwent since I came here. We are boarding now, but soon expect to find rooms and change our place of Residence, then I shall have all the care of a household to bear, but such is the fate of those who join their Lot with others, they cannot hope to escape from the burdens of Life, nor would I ask it, I would not live alway, but while I live would always pray for strength to do my duty. This city is not near as large or handsome as New York, but had my lot been cast in a Wilderness I hope I should not repine, such never was my nature, and they who exchange their independence for the sweet name of Wife must be prepared to find all is not gold that glitters, nor I would not expect like you to drift down the stream of Life unfettered and serene as a Summer cloud, such is not my fate, but come what may will always find in me a resigned and prayerful Spirit, and hoping this finds you as well as it leaves me, I remain, my dear Sister,

"Yours truly,
"Evelina B. Ramy."

Ann Eliza had always secretly admired the oratorical and impersonal tone of Evelina's letters; but the few she had previously read, having been addressed to school-mates or distant relatives, had appeared in the light of literary compositions rather than as records of personal experience. Now she could not but wish that Evelina had laid aside her swelling periods for a style more suited to the chronicling of homely incidents. She read the letter again and again, seeking for a clue to what her sister was really doing and thinking; but after each reading she emerged impressed but unenlightened from the labyrinth of Evelina's eloquence.

During the early winter she received two or three more letters of the same kind, each enclosing in its loose husk of rhetoric a smaller kernel of fact. By dint of patient interlinear study, Ann Eliza gathered from them that Evelina and her husband, after various costly experiments in boarding, had been reduced to a tenement-house flat; that living in St. Louis was more expensive than they had supposed, and that Mr. Ramy was kept out late at night (why, at a jeweller's, Ann Eliza wondered?) and found his position less satisfactory than he had been led to expect. Toward February the letters fell off; and finally they ceased to come.

At first Ann Eliza wrote, shyly but persistently, entreating for more frequent news; then, as one appeal after another was swallowed up in the mystery of Evelina's protracted silence, vague fears began to assail the elder sister. Perhaps Evelina was ill, and with no one to nurse her but a man who could not even make himself a cup of tea! Ann Eliza recalled the layer of dust in Mr. Ramy's shop, and pictures of domestic disorder mingled with the more poignant vision of her sister's illness. But surely if Evelina were ill Mr. Ramy would have written. He wrote a small neat hand, and epistolary communication was not an insuperable embarrassment to him. The too probable alternative was that both the unhappy pair had been prostrated by some disease which left them powerless to summon her—for summon her they surely would, Ann Eliza with unconscious cynicism reflected, if she or her small economies could be of use to them! The more she strained her eyes into the mystery, the darker it grew; and her lack of initiative, her inability to imagine what steps might be taken to trace the lost in distant places, left her benumbed and helpless.

At last there floated up from some depth of troubled memory the name of the firm of St. Louis jewellers by whom Mr. Ramy was employed. After much hesitation, and considerable effort, she addressed to them a timid request for news of her brother-in-law; and sooner than she could have hoped the answer reached her.

"DEAR MADAM,

"In reply to yours of the 29th ult. we beg to state that the party you refer to was discharged from our employ a month ago. We are sorry we are unable to furnish you with his address.

"Yours respectfully,
                    "LUDWIG AND HAMMERBUSCH."

Ann Eliza read and re-read the curt statement in a stupor of distress. She had lost her last trace of Evelina. All that night she lay awake, revolving the stupendous project of going to St. Louis in search of her sister; but though she pieced together her few financial possibilities with the ingenuity of a brain used to fitting odd scraps into patch-work quilts, she woke to the cold daylight fact that she could not raise the money for her fare. Her wedding gift to Evelina had left her without any resources beyond her daily earnings, and these had steadily dwindled as the winter passed. She had long since renounced her weekly visit to the butcher, and had reduced her other expenses to the narrowest measure; but the most systematic frugality had not enabled her to put by any money. In spite of her dogged efforts to maintain the prosperity of the little shop, her sister's absence had already told on its business. Now that Ann Eliza had to carry the bundles to the dyer's herself, the customers who called in her absence, finding the shop locked, too often went elsewhere. Moreover, after several stern but unavailing efforts, she had had to give up the trimming of bonnets, which in Evelina's hands had been the most lucrative as well as the most interesting part of the business. This change, to the passing female eye, robbed the shop window of its chief attraction; and when painful experience had convinced the regular customers of the Bunner Sisters of Ann Eliza's lack of millinery skill they began to lose faith in her ability to curl a feather or even "freshen up" a bunch of flowers. The time came when Ann Eliza had almost made up her mind to speak to the lady with puffed sleeves, who had always looked at her so kindly, and had once ordered a hat of Evelina. Perhaps the lady with puffed sleeves would be able to get her a little plain sewing to do; or she might recommend the shop to friends. Ann Eliza, with this possibility in view, rummaged out of a drawer the fly-blown remainder of the business cards which the sisters had ordered in the first flush of their commercial adventure; but when the lady with puffed sleeves finally appeared she was in deep mourning, and wore so sad a look that Ann Eliza dared not speak. She came in to buy some spools of black thread and silk, and in the doorway she turned back to say: "I am going away to-morrow for a long time. I hope you will have a pleasant winter." And the door shut on her.

One day not long after this it occurred to Ann Eliza to go to Hoboken in quest of Mrs. Hochmüller. Much as she shrank from pouring her distress into that particular ear, her anxiety had carried her beyond such reluctances; but when she began to think the matter over she was faced by a new difficulty. On the occasion of her only visit to Mrs. Hochmüller, she and Evelina had suffered themselves to be led there by Mr. Ramy; and Ann Eliza now perceived that she did not

even know the name of the laundress's suburb, much less that
of the street in which she lived. But she must have news of
Evelina, and no obstacle was great enough to thwart her.

Though she longed to turn to some one for advice she disliked to expose her situation to Miss Mellins's searching eye,
and at first she could think of no other confidant. Then she
remembered Mrs. Hawkins, or rather her husband, who,
though Ann Eliza had always thought him a dull uneducated
man, was probably gifted with the mysterious masculine faculty of finding out people's addresses. It went hard with Ann
Eliza to trust her secret even to the mild ear of Mrs. Hawkins,
but at least she was spared the cross-examination to which the
dress-maker would have subjected her. The accumulating
pressure of domestic cares had so crushed in Mrs. Hawkins
any curiosity concerning the affairs of others that she received
her visitor's confidence with an almost masculine indifference,
while she rocked her teething baby on one arm and with the
other tried to check the acrobatic impulses of the next in age.

"My, my," she simply said as Ann Eliza ended. "Keep still
now, Arthur: Miss Bunner don't want you to jump up and
down on her foot to-day. And what are you gaping at,
Johnny? Run right off and play," she added, turning sternly to
her eldest, who, because he was the least naughty, usually
bore the brunt of her wrath against the others.

"Well, perhaps Mr. Hawkins can help you," Mrs. Hawkins
continued meditatively, while the children, after scattering at
her bidding, returned to their previous pursuits like flies settling down on the spot from which an exasperated hand has
swept them. "I'll send him right round the minute he comes
in, and you can tell him the whole story. I wouldn't wonder
but what he can find that Mrs. Hochmüller's address in the
d'rectory. I know they've got one where he works."

"I'd be real thankful if he could," Ann Eliza murmured,
rising from her seat with the factitious sense of lightness that
comes from imparting a long-hidden dread.

X

Mr. Hawkins proved himself worthy of his wife's faith in his
capacity. He learned from Ann Eliza as much as she could tell

him about Mrs. Hochmüller and returned the next evening
with a scrap of paper bearing her address, beneath which
Johnny (the family scribe) had written in a large round hand
the names of the streets that led there from the ferry.

Ann Eliza lay awake all that night, repeating over and over
again the directions Mr. Hawkins had given her. He was a
kind man, and she knew he would willingly have gone with
her to Hoboken; indeed she read in his timid eye the half-
formed intention of offering to accompany her—but on such
an errand she preferred to go alone.

The next Sunday, accordingly, she set out early, and without much trouble found her way to the ferry. Nearly a year
had passed since her previous visit to Mrs. Hochmüller, and a
chilly April breeze smote her face as she stepped on the boat.
Most of the passengers were huddled together in the cabin,
and Ann Eliza shrank into its obscurest corner, shivering under the thin black mantle which had seemed so hot in July.
She began to feel a little bewildered as she stepped ashore,
but a paternal policeman put her into the right car, and as in
a dream she found herself retracing the way to Mrs.
Hochmüller's door. She had told the conductor the name of
the street at which she wished to get out, and presently she
stood in the biting wind at the corner near the beer-saloon,
where the sun had once beat down on her so fiercely. At
length an empty car appeared, its yellow flank emblazoned
with the name of Mrs. Hochmüller's suburb, and Ann Eliza
was presently jolting past the narrow brick houses islanded
between vacant lots like giant piles in a desolate lagoon.
When the car reached the end of its journey she got out and
stood for some time trying to remember which turn Mr.
Ramy had taken. She had just made up her mind to ask the
car-driver when he shook the reins on the backs of his lean
horses, and the car, still empty, jogged away toward
Hoboken.

Ann Eliza, left alone by the roadside, began to move cautiously forward, looking about for a small red house with a
gable overhung by an elm-tree; but everything about her
seemed unfamiliar and forbidding. One or two surly looking
men slouched past with inquisitive glances, and she could not
make up her mind to stop and speak to them.

At length a tow-headed boy came out of a swinging door suggestive of illicit conviviality, and to him Ann Eliza ventured to confide her difficulty. The offer of five cents fired him with an instant willingness to lead her to Mrs. Hochmüller, and he was soon trotting past the stone-cutter's yard with Ann Eliza in his wake.

Another turn in the road brought them to the little red house, and having rewarded her guide, Ann Eliza unlatched the gate and walked up to the door. Her heart was beating violently, and she had to lean against the door-post to compose her twitching lips: she had not known till that moment how much it was going to hurt her to speak of Evelina to Mrs. Hochmüller. As her agitation subsided she began to notice how much the appearance of the house had changed. It was not only that winter had stripped the elm, and blackened the flower-borders: the house itself had a debased and deserted air. The window-panes were cracked and dirty, and one or two shutters swung dismally on loosened hinges.

She rang several times before the door was opened. At length an Irish woman with a shawl over her head and a baby in her arms appeared on the threshold, and glancing past her into the narrow passage Ann Eliza saw that Mrs. Hochmüller's neat abode had deteriorated as much within as without.

At the mention of the name the woman stared. "Mrs. who, did ye say?"

"Mrs. Hochmüller. This is surely her house?"

"No, it ain't neither," said the woman turning away.

"Oh, but wait, please," Ann Eliza entreated. "I can't be mistaken. I mean the Mrs. Hochmüller who takes in washing. I came out to see her last June."

"Oh, the Dutch washerwoman is it—her that used to live here? She's been gone two months and more. It's Mike McNulty lives here now. Whisht!" to the baby, who had squared his mouth for a howl.

Ann Eliza's knees grew weak. "Mrs. Hochmüller gone? But where has she gone? She must be somewhere round here. Can't you tell me?"

"Sure an' I can't," said the woman. "She wint away before iver we come."

"Dalia Geoghegan, will ye bring the choild in out av the cowld?" cried an irate voice from within.

"Please wait—oh, please wait," Ann Eliza insisted. "You see I must find Mrs. Hochmüller."

"Why don't ye go and look for her thin?" the woman returned, slamming the door in her face.

She stood motionless on the door-step, dazed by the immensity of her disappointment, till a burst of loud voices inside the house drove her down the path and out of the gate.

Even then she could not grasp what had happened, and pausing in the road she looked back at the house, half hoping that Mrs. Hochmüller's once detested face might appear at one of the grimy windows.

She was roused by an icy wind that seemed to spring up suddenly from the desolate scene, piercing her thin dress like gauze; and turning away she began to retrace her steps. She thought of enquiring for Mrs. Hochmüller at some of the neighbouring houses, but their look was so unfriendly that she walked on without making up her mind at which door to ring. When she reached the horse-car terminus a car was just moving off toward Hoboken, and for nearly an hour she had to wait on the corner in the bitter wind. Her hands and feet were stiff with cold when the car at length loomed into sight again, and she thought of stopping somewhere on the way to the ferry for a cup of tea; but before the region of lunch-rooms was reached she had grown so sick and dizzy that the thought of food was repulsive. At length she found herself on the ferry-boat, in the soothing stuffiness of the crowded cabin; then came another interval of shivering on a street-corner, another long jolting journey in a "cross-town" car that smelt of damp straw and tobacco; and lastly, in the cold spring dusk, she unlocked her door and groped her way through the shop to her fireless bedroom.

The next morning Mrs. Hawkins, dropping in to hear the result of the trip, found Ann Eliza sitting behind the counter wrapped in an old shawl.

"Why, Miss Bunner, you're sick! You must have fever—your face is just as red!"

"It's nothing. I guess I caught cold yesterday on the ferry-boat," Ann Eliza acknowledged.

"And it's jest like a vault in here!" Mrs. Hawkins rebuked her. "Let me feel your hand—it's burning. Now, Miss Bunner, you've got to go right to bed this very minute."

"Oh, but I can't, Mrs. Hawkins." Ann Eliza attempted a wan smile. "You forget there ain't nobody but me to tend the store."

"I guess you won't tend it long neither, if you ain't careful," Mrs. Hawkins grimly rejoined. Beneath her placid exterior she cherished a morbid passion for disease and death, and the sight of Ann Eliza's suffering had roused her from her habitual indifference. "There ain't so many folks comes to the store anyhow," she went on with unconscious cruelty, "and I'll go right up and see if Miss Mellins can't spare one of her girls."

Ann Eliza, too weary to resist, allowed Mrs. Hawkins to put her to bed and make a cup of tea over the stove, while Miss Mellins, always good-naturedly responsive to any appeal for help, sent down the weak-eyed little girl to deal with hypothetical customers.

Ann Eliza, having so far abdicated her independence, sank into sudden apathy. As far as she could remember, it was the first time in her life that she had been taken care of instead of taking care, and there was a momentary relief in the surrender. She swallowed the tea like an obedient child, allowed a poultice to be applied to her aching chest and uttered no protest when a fire was kindled in the rarely used grate; but as Mrs. Hawkins bent over to "settle" her pillows she raised herself on her elbow to whisper: "Oh, Mrs. Hawkins, Mrs. Hochmüller warn't there." The tears rolled down her cheeks.

"She warn't there? Has she moved?"

"Over two months ago—and they don't know where she's gone. Oh what'll I do, Mrs. Hawkins?"

"There, there, Miss Bunner. You lay still and don't fret. I'll ask Mr. Hawkins soon as ever he comes home."

Ann Eliza murmured her gratitude, and Mrs. Hawkins, bending down, kissed her on the forehead. "Don't you fret," she repeated, in the voice with which she soothed her children.

For over a week Ann Eliza lay in bed, faithfully nursed by her two neighbours, while the weak-eyed child, and the pale sewing girl who had helped to finish Evelina's wedding dress, took turns in minding the shop. Every morning, when her friends appeared, Ann Eliza lifted her head to ask: "Is there a letter?" and at their gentle negative sank back in silence. Mrs. Hawkins, for several days, spoke no more of her promise to consult her husband as to the best way of tracing Mrs. Hochmüller; and dread of fresh disappointment kept Ann Eliza from bringing up the subject.

But the following Sunday evening, as she sat for the first time bolstered up in her rocking-chair near the stove, while Miss Mellins studied the *Police Gazette* beneath the lamp, there came a knock on the shop-door and Mr. Hawkins entered.

Ann Eliza's first glance at his plain friendly face showed her he had news to give, but though she no longer attempted to hide her anxiety from Miss Mellins, her lips trembled too much to let her speak.

"Good evening, Miss Bunner," said Mr. Hawkins in his dragging voice. "I've been over to Hoboken all day looking round for Mrs. Hochmüller."

"Oh, Mr. Hawkins—you *have*?"

"I made a thorough search, but I'm sorry to say it was no use. She's left Hoboken—moved clear away, and nobody seems to know where."

"It was real good of you, Mr. Hawkins." Ann Eliza's voice struggled up in a faint whisper through the submerging tide of her disappointment.

Mr. Hawkins, in his embarrassed sense of being the bringer of bad news, stood before her uncertainly; then he turned to go. "No trouble at all," he paused to assure her from the doorway.

She wanted to speak again, to detain him, to ask him to advise her; but the words caught in her throat and she lay back silent.

The next day she got up early, and dressed and bonneted herself with twitching fingers. She waited till the weak-eyed child appeared, and having laid on her minute instructions as to the care of the shop, she slipped out into the street. It had occurred to her in one of the weary watches of the previous night that she might go to Tiffany's and make enquiries about

Ramy's past. Possibly in that way she might obtain some information that would suggest a new way of reaching Evelina. She was guiltily aware that Mrs. Hawkins and Miss Mellins would be angry with her for venturing out of doors, but she knew she should never feel any better till she had news of Evelina.

The morning air was sharp, and as she turned to face the wind she felt so weak and unsteady that she wondered if she should ever get as far as Union Square; but by walking very slowly, and standing still now and then when she could do so without being noticed, she found herself at last before the jeweller's great glass doors.

It was still so early that there were no purchasers in the shop, and she felt herself the centre of innumerable unemployed eyes as she moved forward between long lines of show-cases glittering with diamonds and silver.

She was glancing about in the hope of finding the clock-department without having to approach one of the impressive gentlemen who paced the empty aisles, when she attracted the attention of one of the most impressive of the number.

The formidable benevolence with which he enquired what he could do for her made her almost despair of explaining herself; but she finally disentangled from a flurry of wrong beginnings the request to the shown to the clock-department.

The gentleman considered her thoughtfully. "May I ask what style of clock you are looking for? Would it be for a wedding-present, or—"

The irony of the allusion filled Ann Eliza's veins with sudden strength. "I don't want to buy a clock at all. I want to see the head of the department."

"Mr. Loomis?" His stare still weighed her—then he seemed to brush aside the problem she presented as beneath his notice. "Oh, certainly. Take the elevator to the second floor. Next aisle to the left." He waved her down the endless perspective of show-cases.

Ann Eliza followed the line of his lordly gesture, and a swift ascent brought her to a great hall full of the buzzing and booming of thousands of clocks. Whichever way she looked, clocks stretched away from her in glittering interminable vistas: clocks of all sizes and voices, from the bell-throated giant of the hallway to the chirping dressing-table toy; tall clocks of mahogany and brass with cathedral chimes; clocks of bronze, glass, porcelain, of every possible size, voice and configuration; and between their serried ranks, along the polished floor of the aisles, moved the languid forms of other gentlemanly floor-walkers, waiting for their duties to begin.

One of them soon approached, and Ann Eliza repeated her request. He received it affably.

"Mr. Loomis? Go right down to the office at the other end." He pointed to a kind of box of ground glass and highly polished panelling.

As she thanked him he turned to one of his companions and said something in which she caught the name of Mr. Loomis, and which was received with an appreciative chuckle. She suspected herself of being the object of the pleasantry, and straightened her thin shoulders under her mantle.

The door of the office stood open, and within sat a gray-bearded man at a desk. He looked up kindly, and again she asked for Mr. Loomis.

"I'm Mr. Loomis. What can I do for you?"

He was much less portentous than the others, though she guessed him to be above them in authority; and encouraged by his tone she seated herself on the edge of the chair he waved her to.

"I hope you'll excuse my troubling you, sir. I came to ask if you could tell me anything about Mr. Herman Ramy. He was employed here in the clock-department two or three years ago."

Mr. Loomis showed no recognition of the name.

"Ramy? When was he discharged?"

"I don't har'ly know. He was very sick, and when he got well his place had been filled. He married my sister last October and they went to St. Louis, I ain't had any news of them for over two months, and she's my only sister, and I'm most crazy worrying about her."

"I see." Mr. Loomis reflected. "In what capacity was Ramy employed here?" he asked after a moment.

"He—he told us that he was one of the heads of the clock-department," Ann Eliza stammered, overswept by a sudden doubt.

"That was probably a slight exaggeration. But I can tell you about him by referring to our books. The name again?"

"Ramy—Herman Ramy."

There ensued a long silence, broken only by the flutter of leaves as Mr. Loomis turned over his ledgers. Presently he looked up, keeping his finger between the pages.

"Here it is—Herman Ramy. He was one of our ordinary workmen, and left us three years and a half ago last June."

"On account of sickness?" Ann Eliza faltered.

Mr. Loomis appeared to hesitate; then he said: "I see no mention of sickness." Ann Eliza felt his compassionate eyes on her again. "Perhaps I'd better tell you the truth. He was discharged for drug-taking. A capable workman, but we couldn't keep him straight. I'm sorry to have to tell you this, but it seems fairer, since you say you're anxious about your sister."

The polished sides of the office vanished from Ann Eliza's sight, and the cackle of the innumerable clocks came to her like the yell of waves in a storm. She tried to speak but could not; tried to get her to her feet, but the floor was gone.

"I'm very sorry," Mr. Loomis repeated, closing the ledger. "I remember the man perfectly now. He used to disappear every now and then, and turn up again in a state that made him useless for days."

As she listened, Ann Eliza recalled the day when she had come on Mr. Ramy sitting in abject dejection behind his counter. She saw again the blurred unrecognizing eyes he had raised to her, the layer of dust over everything in the shop, and the green bronze clock in the window representing a Newfoundland dog with his paw on a book. She stood up slowly.

"Thank you. I'm sorry to have troubled you."

"It was no trouble. You say Ramy married your sister last October?"

"Yes, sir; and they went to St. Louis right afterward. I don't know how to find her. I thought maybe somebody here might know about him."

"Well, possibly some of the workmen might. Leave me your name and I'll send you word if I get on his track."

He handed her a pencil, and she wrote down her address; then she walked away blindly between the clocks.

XI

Mr. Loomis, true to his word, wrote a few days later that he had enquired in vain in the work-shop for any news of Ramy; and as she folded this letter and laid it between the leaves of her Bible, Ann Eliza felt that her last hope was gone. Miss Mellins, of course, had long since suggested the mediation of the police, and cited from her favourite literature convincing instances of the supernatural ability of the Pinkerton detective; but Mr. Hawkins, when called in council, dashed this project by remarking that detectives cost something like twenty dollars a day; and a vague fear of the law, some half-formed vision of Evelina in the clutch of a blue-coated "officer," kept Ann Eliza from invoking the aid of the police.

After the arrival of Mr. Loomis's note the weeks followed each other uneventfully. Ann Eliza's cough clung to her till late in the spring, the reflection in her looking-glass grew more bent and meagre, and her forehead sloped back farther toward the twist of hair that was fastened above her parting by a comb of black India-rubber.

Toward spring a lady who was expecting a baby took up her abode at the Mendoza Family Hotel, and through the friendly intervention of Miss Mellins the making of some of the baby-clothes was entrusted to Ann Eliza. This eased her of anxiety for the immediate future; but she had to rouse herself to feel any sense of relief. Her personal welfare was what least concerned her. Sometimes she thought of giving up the shop altogether; and only the fear that, if she changed her address, Evelina might not be able to find her, kept her from carrying out this plan.

Since she had lost her last hope of tracing her sister, all the activities of her lonely imagination had been concentrated on the possibility of Evelina's coming back to her. The discovery of Ramy's secret filled her with dreadful fears. In the solitude of the shop and the back room she was tortured by vague pictures of Evelina's sufferings. What horrors might not be hidden beneath her silence? Ann Eliza's great dread was that Miss Mellins should worm out of her what she had learned from Mr. Loomis. She was sure Miss Mellins must have abominable things to tell about drug-fiends—things she did not have the strength to hear. "Drug-fiend"—the very word was Satanic: she could hear Miss Mellins roll it on her tongue. But Ann Eliza's own imagination, left to itself, had begun to people the long hours with evil visions. Sometimes, in the night, she thought she heard herself called: the voice was her sister's, but faint with a nameless terror. Her most peaceful moments were those in which she managed to convince herself that Evelina was dead. She thought of her then, mournfully but more calmly, as thrust away under the neglected mound of some unknown cemetery, where no headstone marked her name, no mourner with flowers for another grave paused in pity to lay a blossom on hers. But this vision did not often give Ann Eliza its negative relief: and always, beneath its hazy lines, lurked the dark conviction that Evelina was alive, in misery and longing for her.

So the summer wore on. Ann Eliza was conscious that Mrs. Hawkins and Miss Mellins were watching her with affectionate anxiety, but the knowledge brought no comfort. She no longer cared what they felt or thought about her. Her grief lay far beyond touch of human healing, and after a while she became aware that they knew they could not help her. They still came in as often as their busy lives permitted, but their visits grew shorter, and Mrs. Hawkins always brought Arthur or the baby, so that there should be something to talk about, and some one whom she could scold.

The autumn came, and the winter. Business had fallen off again, and but few purchasers came to the little shop in the basement. In January Ann Eliza pawned her mother's cashmere scarf, her mosaic brooch, and the rosewood what-not on which the clock had always stood; she would have sold the bedstead too, but for the persistent vision of Evelina returning weak and weary, and not knowing where to lay her head.

The winter passed in its turn, and March reappeared with its galaxies of yellow jonquils at the windy street corners, reminding Ann Eliza of the spring day when Evelina had come home with a bunch of jonquils in her hand. In spite of the flowers which lent such a premature brightness to the streets the month was fierce and stormy, and Ann Eliza could get no warmth into her bones. Nevertheless, she was insensibly beginning to take up the healing routine of life. Little by little she had grown used to being alone, she had begun to take a languid interest in the one or two new purchasers the season had brought, and though the thought of Evelina was as poignant as ever, it was less persistently in the foreground of her mind.

Late one afternoon she was sitting behind the counter, wrapped in her shawl, and wondering how soon she might draw down the blinds and retreat into the comparative cosiness of the back room. She was not thinking of anything in particular, except perhaps in a hazy way of the lady with the puffed sleeves, who after her long eclipse had reappeared the day before in sleeves of a new cut, and bought some tape and needles. The lady still wore mourning, but she was evidently lightening it, and Ann Eliza saw in this the hope of future orders. The lady had left the shop about an hour before, walking away with her graceful step toward Fifth Avenue. She had wished Ann Eliza good day in her usual affable way, and Ann Eliza thought how odd it was that they should have been acquainted so long, and yet that she should not know the lady's name. From this consideration her mind wandered to the cut of the lady's new sleeves, and she was vexed with herself for not having noted it more carefully. She felt Miss Mellins might have liked to know about it. Ann Eliza's powers of observation had never been as keen as Evelina's, when the latter was not too self-absorbed to exert them. As Miss Mellins always said, Evelina could "take patterns with her eyes": she could have cut that new sleeve out of a folded newspaper in a trice! Musing on these things, Ann Eliza wished the lady would come back and give her another look at the sleeve. It was not unlikely that she might pass that way, for she certainly lived in or about the Square. Suddenly Ann Eliza remarked a small neat handkerchief on the counter: it must have dropped from the lady's purse, and she would probably come back to get it. Ann Eliza, pleased at the idea, sat on behind the counter and watched the darkening street. She always lit the gas as late as possible, keeping the box of matches at her elbow, so that if any one came she could apply a quick flame to the gas-jet. At length through the deepening dusk she distinguished a slim dark figure coming down the steps to the shop.

With a little warmth of pleasure about her heart she reached up to light the gas. "I do believe I'll ask her name this time," she thought. She raised the flame to its full height, and saw her sister standing in the door.

There she was at last, the poor pale shade of Evelina, her thin face blanched of its faint pink, the stiff ripples gone from her hair, and a mantle shabbier than Ann Eliza's drawn about her narrow shoulders. The glare of the gas beat full on her as she stood and looked at Ann Eliza.

"Sister—oh, Evelina! I knowed you'd come!"

Ann Eliza had caught her close with a long moan of triumph. Vague words poured from her as she laid her cheek against Evelina's—trivial inarticulate endearments caught from Mrs. Hawkins's long discourses to her baby.

For a while Evelina let herself be passively held; then she drew back from her sister's clasp and looked about the shop. "I'm dead tired. Ain't there any fire?" she asked.

"Of course there is!" Ann Eliza, holding her hand fast, drew her into the back room. She did not want to ask any questions yet: she simply wanted to feel the emptiness of the room brimmed full again by the one presence that was warmth and light to her.

She knelt down before the grate, scraped some bits of coal and kindling from the bottom of the coal-scuttle, and drew one of the rocking-chairs up to the weak flame. "There— that'll blaze up in a minute," she said. She pressed Evelina down on the faded cushions of the rocking-chair, and, kneeling beside her, began to rub her hands.

"You're stone-cold, ain't you? Just sit still and warm yourself while I run and get the kettle. I've got something you always used to fancy for supper." She laid her hand on Evelina's shoulder. "Don't talk—oh, don't talk yet!" she implored. She wanted to keep that one frail second of happiness between herself and what she knew must come.

Evelina, without a word, bent over the fire, stretching her thin hands to the blaze and watching Ann Eliza fill the kettle and set the supper table. Her gaze had the dreamy fixity of a half-awakened child's.

Ann Eliza, with a smile of triumph, brought a slice of custard pie from the cupboard and put it by her sister's plate.

"You do like that, don't you? Miss Mellins sent it down to me this morning. She had her aunt from Brooklyn to dinner. Ain't it funny it just so happened?"

"I ain't hungry," said Evelina, rising to approach the table.

She sat down in her usual place, looked about her with the same wondering stare, and then, as of old, poured herself out the first cup of tea.

"Where's the what-not gone to?" she suddenly asked.

Ann Eliza set down the teapot and rose to get a spoon from the cupboard. With her back to the room she said: "The what-not? Why, you see, dearie, living here all alone by myself it only made one more thing to dust; so I sold it."

Evelina's eyes were still travelling about the familiar room. Though it was against all the traditions of the Bunner family to sell any household possession, she showed no surprise at her sister's answer.

"And the clock? The clock's gone too."

"Oh, I gave that away—I gave it to Mrs. Hawkins. She's kep' awake so nights with that last baby."

"I wish you'd never bought it," said Evelina harshly.

Ann Eliza's heart grew faint with fear. Without answering, she crossed over to her sister's seat and poured her out a second cup of tea. Then another thought struck her, and she went back to the cupboard and took out the cordial. In Evelina's absence considerable draughts had been drawn from it by invalid neighbours; but a glassful of the precious liquid still remained.

"Here, drink this right off—it'll warm you up quicker than anything," Ann Eliza said.

Evelina obeyed, and a slight spark of colour came into her cheeks. She turned to the custard pie and began to eat with a silent voracity distressing to watch. She did not even look to see what was left for Ann Eliza.

"I ain't hungry," she said at last as she laid down her fork. "I'm only so dead tired—that's the trouble."

"Then you'd better get right into bed. Here's my old plaid dressing-gown—you remember it, don't you?" Ann Eliza laughed, recalling Evelina's ironies on the subject of the anti-quated garment. With trembling fingers she began to undo her sister's cloak. The dress beneath it told a tale of poverty that Ann Eliza dared not pause to note. She drew it gently off, and as it slipped from Evelina's shoulders it revealed a tiny black bag hanging on a ribbon about her neck. Evelina lifted her hand as though to screen the bag from Ann Eliza; and the elder sister, seeing the gesture, continued her task with lowered eyes. She undressed Evelina as quickly as she could, and wrapping her in the plaid dressing-gown put her to bed, and spread her own shawl and her sister's cloak above the blanket.

"Where's the old red comfortable?" Evelina asked, as she sank down on the pillow.

"The comfortable? Oh, it was so hot and heavy I never used it after you went—so I sold that too. I never could sleep under much clothes."

She became aware that her sister was looking at her more attentively.

"I guess you've been in trouble too," Evelina said.

"Me? In trouble? What do you mean, Evelina?"

"You've had to pawn the things, I suppose," Evelina continued in a weary unmoved tone. "Well, I've been through worse than that. I've been to hell and back."

"Oh, Evelina—don't say it, sister!" Ann Eliza implored, shrinking from the unholy word. She knelt down and began to rub her sister's feet beneath the bed-clothes.

"I've been to hell and back—if I *am* back," Evelina repeated. She lifted her head from the pillow and began to talk with a sudden feverish volubility. "It began right away, less than a month after we were married. I've been in hell all that time, Ann Eliza." She fixed her eyes with passionate intentness on Ann Eliza's face. "He took opium. I didn't find it out till long afterward—at first, when he acted so strange, I thought he drank. But it was worse, much worse than drinking."

"Oh, sister, don't say it—don't say it yet! It's so sweet just to have you here with me again."

"I must say it," Evelina insisted, her flushed face burning with a kind of bitter cruelty. "You don't know what life's like—you don't know anything about it—setting here safe all the while in this peaceful place."

"Oh, Evelina—why didn't you write and send for me if it was like that?"

"That's why I couldn't write. Didn't you guess I was ashamed?"

"How could you be? Ashamed to write to Ann Eliza?"

Evelina raised herself on her thin elbow, while Ann Eliza, bending over, drew a corner of the shawl about her shoulder.

"Do lay down again. You'll catch your death."

"My death? That don't frighten me! You don't know what I've been through." And sitting upright in the old mahogany bed, with flushed cheeks and chattering teeth, and Ann Eliza's trembling arm clasping the shawl about her neck, Evelina poured out her story. It was a tale of misery and humiliation so remote from the elder sister's innocent experiences that much of it was hardly intelligible to her. Evelina's dreadful familiarity with it all, her fluency about things which Ann Eliza half-guessed and quickly shuddered back from, seemed even more alien and terrible than the actual tale she told. It was one thing—and heaven knew it was bad enough! —to learn that one's sister's husband was a drug-fiend; it was another, and much worse thing, to learn from that sister's pallid lips what vileness lay behind the word.

Evelina, unconscious of any distress but her own, sat upright, shivering in Ann Eliza's hold, while she piled up, detail by detail, her dreary narrative.

"The minute we got out there, and he found the job wasn't as good as he expected, he changed. At first I thought he was sick—I used to try to keep him home and nurse him. Then I saw it was something different. He used to go off for hours at a time, and when he came back his eyes kinder had a fog over them. Sometimes he didn't har'ly know me, and when he did he seemed to hate me. Once he hit me here." She touched her breast. "Do you remember, Ann Eliza, that time he didn't come to see us for a week—the time after we all went to Central Park together—and you and I thought he must be sick?"

Ann Eliza nodded.

"Well, that was the trouble—he'd been at it then. But nothing like as bad. After we'd been out there about a month he disappeared for a whole week. They took him back at the store, and gave him another chance; but the second time they discharged him, and he drifted round for ever so long before he could get another job. We spent all our money and had to move to a cheaper place. Then he got something to do, but they hardly paid him anything, and he didn't stay there long. When he found out about the baby—"

"The baby?" Ann Eliza faltered.

"It's dead—it only lived a day. When he found out about it, he got mad, and said he hadn't any money to pay doctors' bills, and I'd better write to you to help us. He had an idea you had money hidden away that I didn't know about." She turned to her sister with remorseful eyes. "It was him that made me get that hundred dollars out of you."

"Hush, hush. I always meant it for you anyhow."

"Yes, but I wouldn't have taken it if he hadn't been at me the whole time. He used to make me do just what he wanted. Well, when I said I wouldn't write to you for more money he said I'd better try and earn some myself. That was when he struck me. . . . Oh, you don't know what I'm talking about yet! . . . I tried to get work at a milliner's, but I was so sick I couldn't stay. I was sick all the time. I wisht I'd ha' died, Ann Eliza."

"No, no, Evelina."

"Yes, I do. It kept getting worse and worse. We pawned the furniture, and they turned us out because we couldn't pay the rent; and so then we went to board with Mrs. Hochmüller."

Ann Eliza pressed her closer to dissemble her own tremor. "Mrs. Hochmüller?"

"Didn't you know she was out there? She moved out a month after we did. She wasn't bad to me, and I think she tried to keep him straight—but Linda—"

"Linda—?"

"Well, when I kep' getting worse, and he was always off, for days at a time, the doctor had me sent to a hospital."

"A hospital? Sister—sister!"

"It was better than being with him; and the doctors were real kind to me. After the baby was born I was very sick and had to stay there a good while. And one day when I was laying there Mrs. Hochmüller came in as white as a sheet, and told me him and Linda had gone off together and taken all her money. That's the last I ever saw of him." She broke off with a laugh and began to cough again.

Ann Eliza tried to persuade her to lie down and sleep, but the rest of her story had to be told before she could be soothed into consent. After the news of Ramy's flight she had had brain fever, and had been sent to another hospital where she stayed a long time—how long she couldn't remember. Dates and days meant nothing to her in the shapeless ruin of her life. When she left the hospital she found that Mrs. Hochmüller had gone too. She was penniless, and had no one to turn to. A lady visitor at the hospital was kind, and found her a place where she did housework; but she was so weak they couldn't keep her. Then she got a job as waitress in a down-town lunch-room, but one day she fainted while she was handing a dish, and that evening when they paid her they told her she needn't come again.

"After that I begged in the streets"—(Ann Eliza's grasp again grew tight)—"and one afternoon last week, when the matinées was coming out, I met a man with a pleasant face, something like Mr. Hawkins, and he stopped and asked me what the trouble was. I told him if he'd give me five dollars I'd have money enough to buy a ticket back to New York, and he took a good look at me and said, well, if that was what I wanted he'd go straight to the station with me and give me the five dollars there. So he did—and he bought the ticket, and put me in the cars."

Evelina sank back, her face a sallow wedge in the white cleft of the pillow. Ann Eliza leaned over her, and for a long time they held each other without speaking.

They were still clasped in this dumb embrace when there was a step in the shop and Ann Eliza, starting up, saw Miss Mellins in the doorway.

"My sakes, Miss Bunner! What in the land are you doing? Miss Evelina—Mrs. Ramy—it ain't you?"

Miss Mellins's eyes, bursting from their sockets, sprang from Evelina's pallid face to the disordered supper table and the heap of worn clothes on the floor; then they turned back to Ann Eliza, who had placed herself on the defensive between her sister and the dress-maker.

"My sister Evelina has come back—come back on a visit. She was taken sick in the cars on the way home—I guess she caught cold—so I made her go right to bed as soon as ever she got here."

Ann Eliza was surprised at the strength and steadiness of her voice. Fortified by its sound she went on, her eyes on Miss Mellins's baffled countenance: "Mr. Ramy has gone west on a trip—a trip connected with his business; and Evelina is going to stay with me till he comes back."

XII

What measure of belief her explanation of Evelina's return obtained in the small circle of her friends Ann Eliza did not pause to enquire. Though she could not remember ever having told a lie before, she adhered with rigid tenacity to the consequences of her first lapse from truth, and fortified her original statement with additional details whenever a questioner sought to take her unawares.

But other and more serious burdens lay on her startled conscience. For the first time in her life she dimly faced the awful problem of the inutility of self-sacrifice. Hitherto she had never thought of questioning the inherited principles which had guided her life. Self-effacement for the good of others had always seemed to her both natural and necessary; but then she had taken it for granted that it implied the securing of that good. Now she perceived that to refuse the gifts of life does not ensure their transmission to those for whom they have been surrendered; and her familiar heaven was unpeopled. She felt she could no longer trust in the goodness of God, and that if he was not good he was not God, and there was only a black abyss above the roof of Bunner Sisters.

But there was little time to brood upon such problems. The care of Evelina filled Ann Eliza's days and nights. The hastily summoned doctor had pronounced her to be suffering from pneumonia, and under his care the first stress of the disease was relieved. But her recovery was only partial, and long after the doctor's visits had ceased she continued to lie in bed, too weak to move, and seemingly indifferent to everything about her.

At length one evening, about six weeks after her return, she said to her sister: "I don't feel's if I'd ever get up again."

Ann Eliza turned from the kettle she was placing on the stove. She was startled by the echo the words woke in her own breast.

"Don't you talk like that, Evelina! I guess you're on'y tired out—and disheartened."

"Yes, I'm disheartened," Evelina murmured.

A few months earlier Ann Eliza would have met the confession with a word of pious admonition; now she accepted it in silence.

"Maybe you'll brighten up when your cough gets better," she suggested.

"Yes—or my cough'll get better when I brighten up," Evelina retorted with a touch of her old tartness.

"Does your cough keep on hurting you jest as much?"

"I don't see's there's much difference."

"Well, I guess I'll get the doctor to come round again," Ann Eliza said, trying for the matter-of-course tone in which one might speak of sending for the plumber or the gas-fitter.

"It ain't any use sending for the doctor—and who's going to pay him?"

"I am," answered the elder sister. "Here's your tea, and a mite of toast. Don't that tempt you?"

Already, in the watches of the night, Ann Eliza had been tormented by that same question—who was to pay the doctor?—and a few days before she had temporarily silenced it by borrowing twenty dollars of Miss Mellins. The transaction had cost her one of the bitterest struggles of her life. She had never borrowed a penny of any one before, and the possibility of having to do so had always been classed in her mind among those shameful extremities to which Providence does not let decent people come. But nowadays she no longer believed in the personal supervision of Providence; and had she been compelled to steal the money instead of borrowing it, she would have felt that her conscience was the only tribunal before which she had to answer. Nevertheless, the actual humiliation of having to ask for the money was no less bitter; and she could hardly hope that Miss Mellins would view the case with the same detachment as herself. Miss Mellins was very kind; but she not unnaturally felt that her kindness should be rewarded by according her the right to ask questions; and bit by bit Ann Eliza saw Evelina's miserable secret slipping into the dress-maker's possession.

When the doctor came she left him alone with Evelina,

busying herself in the shop that she might have an opportunity of seeing him alone on his way out. To steady herself she began to sort a trayful of buttons, and when the doctor appeared she was reciting under her breath: "Twenty-four horn, two and a half cards fancy pearl. . . ." She saw at once that his look was grave.

He sat down on the chair beside the counter, and her mind travelled miles before he spoke.

"Miss Bunner, the best thing you can do is to let me get a bed for your sister at St. Luke's."

"The hospital?"

"Come now, you're above that sort of prejudice, aren't you?" The doctor spoke in the tone of one who coaxes a spoiled child. "I know how devoted you are—but Mrs. Ramy can be much better cared for there than here. You really haven't time to look after her and attend to your business as well. There'll be no expense, you understand—"

Ann Eliza made no answer. "You think my sister's going to be sick a good while, then?" she asked.

"Well, yes—possibly."

"You think she's very sick?"

"Well, yes. She's very sick."

His face had grown still graver; he sat there as though he had never known what it was to hurry.

Ann Eliza continued to separate the pearl and horn buttons. Suddenly she lifted her eyes and looked at him. "Is she going to die?"

The doctor laid a kindly hand on hers. "We never say that, Miss Bunner. Human skill works wonders—and at the hospital Mrs. Ramy would have every chance."

"What is it? What's she dying of?"

The doctor hesitated, seeking to substitute a popular phrase for the scientific terminology which rose to his lips.

"I want to know," Ann Eliza persisted.

"Yes, of course; I understand. Well, your sister has had a hard time lately, and there is a complication of causes, resulting in consumption—rapid consumption. At the hospital—"

"I'll keep her here," said Ann Eliza quietly.

After the doctor had gone she went on for some time sorting the buttons; then she slipped the tray into its place on a shelf behind the counter and went into the back room. She found Evelina propped upright against the pillows, a flush of agitation on her cheeks. Ann Eliza pulled up the shawl which had slipped from her sister's shoulders.

"How long you've been! What's he been saying?"

"Oh, he went long ago—he on'y stopped to give me a prescription. I was sorting out that tray of buttons. Miss Mellins's girl got them all mixed up."

She felt Evelina's eyes upon her.

"He must have said something: what was it?"

"Why, he said you'd have to be careful—and stay in bed—and take this new medicine he's given you."

"Did he say I was going to get well?"

"Why, Evelina!"

"What's the use, Ann Eliza? You can't deceive me. I've just been up to look at myself in the glass; and I saw plenty of 'em in the hospital that looked like me. They didn't get well, and I ain't going to." Her head dropped back. "It don't much matter—I'm about tired. On'y there's one thing—Ann Eliza—"

The elder sister drew near to the bed.

"There's one thing I ain't told you. I didn't want to tell you yet because I was afraid you might be sorry—but if he says I'm going to die I've got to say it." She stopped to cough, and to Ann Eliza it now seemed as though every cough struck a minute from the hours remaining to her.

"Don't talk now—you're tired."

"I'll be tireder to-morrow, I guess. And I want you should know. Sit down close to me—there."

Ann Eliza sat down in silence, stroking her shrunken hand.

"I'm a Roman Catholic, Ann Eliza."

"Evelina—oh, Evelina Bunner! A Roman Catholic—*you?* Oh, Evelina, did *he* make you?"

Evelina shook her head. "I guess he didn't have no religion; he never spoke of it. But you see Mrs. Hochmüller was a Catholic, and so when I was sick she got the doctor to send me to a Roman Catholic hospital, and the sisters was so good to me there—and the priest used to come and talk to me; and the things he said kep' me from going crazy. He seemed to make everything easier."

"Oh, sister, how could you?" Ann Eliza wailed. She knew little of the Catholic religion except that "Papists" believed in it—in itself a sufficient indictment. Her spiritual rebellion had not freed her from the formal part of her religious belief, and apostasy had always seemed to her one of the sins from which the pure in mind avert their thoughts.

"And then when the baby was born," Evelina continued, "he christened it right away, so it could go to heaven; and after that, you see, I had to be a Catholic."

"I don't see—"

"Don't I have to be where the baby is? I couldn't ever ha' gone there if I hadn't been made a Catholic. Don't you understand that?"

Ann Eliza sat speechless, drawing her hand away. Once more she found herself shut out of Evelina's heart, an exile from her closest affections.

"I've got to go where the baby is," Evelina feverishly insisted.

Ann Eliza could think of nothing to say; she could only feel that Evelina was dying, and dying as a stranger in her arms. Ramy and the day-old baby had parted her forever from her sister.

Evelina began again. "If I get worse I want you to send for a priest. Miss Mellins'll know where to send—she's got an aunt that's a Catholic. Promise me faithful you will."

"I promise," said Ann Eliza.

After that they spoke no more of the matter; but Ann Eliza now understood that the little black bag about her sister's neck, which she had innocently taken for a memento of Ramy, was some kind of sacrilegious amulet, and her fingers shrank from its contact when she bathed and dressed Evelina. It seemed to her the diabolical instrument of their estrangement.

XIII

Spring had really come at last. There were leaves on the ailanthus-tree that Evelina could see from her bed, gentle clouds floated over it in the blue, and now and then the cry of a flower-seller sounded from the street.

One day there was a shy knock on the back-room door, and Johnny Hawkins came in with two yellow jonquils in his fist. He was getting bigger and squarer, and his round freckled face was growing into a smaller copy of his father's. He walked up to Evelina and held out the flowers.

"They blew off the cart and the fellow said I could keep 'em. But you can have 'em," he announced.

Ann Eliza rose from her seat at the sewing-machine and tried to take the flowers from him.

"They ain't for you; they're for her," he sturdily objected; and Evelina held out her hand for the jonquils.

After Johnny had gone she lay and looked at them without speaking. Ann Eliza, who had gone back to the machine, bent her head over the seam she was stitching; the click, click, click of the machine sounded in her ear like the tick of Ramy's clock, and it seemed to her that life had gone backward, and that Evelina, radiant and foolish, had just come into the room with the yellow flowers in her hand.

When at last she ventured to look up, she saw that her sister's head had drooped against the pillow, and that she was sleeping quietly. Her relaxed hand still held the jonquils, but it was evident that they had awakened no memories; she had dozed off almost as soon as Johnny had given them to her. The discovery gave Ann Eliza a startled sense of the ruins that must be piled upon her past. "I don't believe I could have forgotten that day, though," she said to herself. But she was glad that Evelina had forgotten.

Evelina's disease moved on along the usual course, now lifting her on a brief wave of elation, now sinking her to new depths of weakness. There was little to be done, and the doctor came only at lengthening intervals. On his way out he always repeated his first friendly suggestion about sending Evelina to the hospital; and Ann Eliza always answered: "I guess we can manage."

The hours passed for her with the fierce rapidity that great joy or anguish lends them. She went through the days with a sternly smiling precision, but she hardly knew what was happening, and when night-fall released her from the shop, and she could carry her work to Evelina's bedside, the same sense of unreality accompanied her, and she still seemed to be accomplishing a task whose object had escaped her memory.

Once, when Evelina felt better, she expressed a desire to make some artificial flowers, and Ann Eliza, deluded by this awakening interest, got out the faded bundles of stems and petals and the little tools and spools of wire. But after a few minutes the work dropped from Evelina's hands and she said: "I'll wait till to-morrow."

She never again spoke of the flower-making, but one day, after watching Ann Eliza's laboured attempt to trim a spring hat for Mrs. Hawkins, she demanded impatiently that the hat should be brought to her, and in a trice had galvanized the lifeless bow and given the brim the twist it needed.

These were rare gleams; and more frequent were the days of speechless lassitude, when she lay for hours silently staring at the window, shaken only by the hard incessant cough that sounded to Ann Eliza like the hammering of nails into a coffin.

At length one morning Ann Eliza, starting up from the mattress at the foot of the bed, hastily called Miss Mellins down, and ran through the smoky dawn for the doctor. He came back with her and did what he could to give Evelina momentary relief; then he went away, promising to look in again before night. Miss Mellins, her head still covered with curl-papers, disappeared in his wake, and when the sisters were alone Evelina beckoned to Ann Eliza.

"You promised," she whispered, grasping her sister's arm; and Ann Eliza understood. She had not yet dared to tell Miss Mellins of Evelina's change of faith; it had seemed even more difficult than borrowing the money; but now it had to be done. She ran upstairs after the dress-maker and detained her on the landing.

"Miss Mellins, can you tell me where to send for a priest—a Roman Catholic priest?"

"A priest, Miss Bunner?"

"Yes. My sister became a Roman Catholic while she was away. They were kind to her in her sickness—and now she wants a priest." Ann Eliza faced Miss Mellins with unflinching eyes.

"My aunt Dugan'll know. I'll run right round to her the minute I get my papers off," the dress-maker promised; and Ann Eliza thanked her.

An hour or two later the priest appeared. Ann Eliza, who was watching, saw him coming down the steps to the shop-door and went to meet him. His expression was kind, but she shrank from his peculiar dress, and from his pale face with its bluish chin and enigmatic smile. Ann Eliza remained in the shop. Miss Mellins's girl had mixed the buttons again and she set herself to sort them. The priest stayed a long time with Evelina. When he again carried his enigmatic smile past the counter, and Ann Eliza rejoined her sister, Evelina was smiling with something of the same mystery; but she did not tell her secret.

After that it seemed to Ann Eliza that the shop and the back room no longer belonged to her. It was as though she were there on sufferance, indulgently tolerated by the unseen power which hovered over Evelina even in the absence of its minister. The priest came almost daily; and at last a day arrived when he was called to administer some rite of which Ann Eliza but dimly grasped the sacramental meaning. All she knew was that it meant that Evelina was going, and going, under this alien guidance, even farther from her than to the dark places of death.

When the priest came, with something covered in his hands, she crept into the shop, closing the door of the back room to leave him alone with Evelina.

It was a warm afternoon in May, and the crooked ailanthus-tree rooted in a fissure of the opposite pavement was a fountain of tender green. Women in light dresses passed with the languid step of spring; and presently there came a man with a hand-cart full of pansy and geranium plants who stopped outside the window, signalling to Ann Eliza to buy.

An hour went by before the door of the back room opened and the priest reappeared with that mysterious covered something in his hands. Ann Eliza had risen, drawing back as he passed. He had doubtless divined her antipathy, for he had hitherto only bowed in going in and out; but to-day he paused and looked at her compassionately.

"I have left your sister in a very beautiful state of mind," he said in a low voice like a woman's. "She is full of spiritual consolation."

Ann Eliza was silent, and he bowed and went out. She hastened back to Evelina's bed, and knelt down beside it.

Evelina's eyes were very large and bright; she turned them on Ann Eliza with a look of inner illumination.

"I shall see the baby," she said; then her eyelids fell and she dozed.

The doctor came again at nightfall, administering some last palliatives; and after he had gone Ann Eliza, refusing to have her vigil shared by Miss Mellins or Mrs. Hawkins, sat down to keep watch alone.

It was a very quiet night. Evelina never spoke or opened her eyes, but in the still hour before dawn Ann Eliza saw that the restless hand outside the bed-clothes had stopped its twitching. She stooped over and felt no breath on her sister's lips.

The funeral took place three days later. Evelina was buried in Calvary Cemetery, the priest assuming the whole care of the necessary arrangements, while Ann Eliza, a passive spectator, beheld with stony indifference this last negation of her past.

A week afterward she stood in her bonnet and mantle in the doorway of the little shop. Its whole aspect had changed. Counter and shelves were bare, the window was stripped of its familiar miscellany of artificial flowers, note-paper, wire hat-frames, and limp garments from the dyer's; and against the glass pane of the doorway hung a sign: "This store to let."

Ann Eliza turned her eyes from the sign as she went out and locked the door behind her. Evelina's funeral had been very expensive, and Ann Eliza, having sold her stock-in-trade and the few articles of furniture that remained to her, was leaving the shop for the last time. She had not been able to buy any mourning, but Miss Mellins had sewed some crape on her old black mantle and bonnet, and having no gloves she slipped her bare hands under the folds of the mantle.

It was a beautiful morning, and the air was full of a warm sunshine that had coaxed open nearly every window in the street, and summoned to the window-sills the sickly plants nurtured indoors in winter. Ann Eliza's way lay westward, toward Broadway; but at the corner she paused and looked back down the familiar length of the street. Her eyes rested a moment on the blotched "Bunner Sisters" above the empty

window of the shop; then they travelled on to the overflowing foliage of the Square, above which was the church tower
with the dial that had marked the hours for the sisters before
Ann Eliza had bought the nickel clock. She looked at it all as
though it had been the scene of some unknown life, of which
the vague report had reached her: she felt for herself the only
remote pity that busy people accord to the misfortunes which
come to them by hearsay.

She walked to Broadway and down to the office of the
house-agent to whom she had entrusted the sub-letting of the
shop. She left the key with one of his clerks, who took it from
her as if it had been any one of a thousand others, and
remarked that the weather looked as if spring was really
coming; then she turned and began to move up the great
thoroughfare, which was just beginning to wake to its multi-
tudinous activities.

She walked less rapidly now, studying each shop window as
she passed, but not with the desultory eye of enjoyment: the
watchful fixity of her gaze overlooked everything but the object of its quest. At length she stopped before a small window
wedged between two mammoth buildings, and displaying,
behind its shining plate-glass festooned with muslin, a varied
assortment of sofa-cushions, tea-cloths, pen-wipers, painted
calendars and other specimens of feminine industry. In a
corner of the window she had read, on a slip of paper pasted
against the pane: "Wanted, a Saleslady," and after studying
the display of fancy articles beneath it, she gave her mantle a
twitch, straightened her shoulders and went in.

Behind a counter crowded with pin-cushions, watch-hold-
ers and other needle-work trifles, a plump young woman with
smooth hair sat sewing bows of ribbon on a scrap basket. The
little shop was about the size of the one on which Ann Eliza
had just closed the door; and it looked as fresh and gay and
thriving as she and Evelina had once dreamed of making
Bunner Sisters. The friendly air of the place made her pluck
up courage to speak.

"Saleslady? Yes, we do want one. Have you any one to recommend?" the young woman asked, not unkindly.

Ann Eliza hesitated, disconcerted by the unexpected question; and the other, cocking her head on one side to study the

effect of the bow she had just sewed on the basket, continued: "We can't afford more than thirty dollars a month, but the work is light. She would be expected to do a little fancy sewing between times. We want a bright girl: stylish, and pleasant manners. You know what I mean. Not over thirty, anyhow; and nice-looking. Will you write down the name?"

Ann Eliza looked at her confusedly. She opened her lips to explain, and then, without speaking, turned toward the crisply-curtained door.

"Ain't you going to leave the *ad*-dress?" the young woman called out after her. Ann Eliza went out into the thronged street. The great city, under the fair spring sky, seemed to throb with the stir of innumerable beginnings. She walked on, looking for another shop window with a sign in it.

Writing a War Story

MISS IVY SPANG of Cornwall-on-Hudson had published a little volume of verse before the war.

It was called "Vibrations," and was preceded by a "Foreword" in which the author stated that she had yielded to the urgent request of "friends" in exposing her first-born to the public gaze. The public had not gazed very hard or very long, but the Cornwall-on-Hudson "News-Dispatch" had a flattering notice by the wife of the rector of St. Dunstan's (signed "Asterisk"), in which, while the somewhat unconventional sentiment of the poems was gently deprecated, a graceful and lady-like tribute was paid to the "brilliant daughter of one of our most prominent and influential citizens, who has voluntarily abandoned *the primrose way of pleasure* to scale *the rugged heights of Parnassus.*"

Also, after sitting one evening next to him at a bohemian dinner in New York, Miss Spang was honored by an article by the editor of "Zig-zag," the new "Weekly Journal of Defiance," in which that gentleman hinted that there was more than she knew in Ivy Spang's poems, and that their esoteric significance showed that she was a *vers-librist* in thought as well as in technique. He added that they would "gain incommensurably in meaning" when she abandoned the superannuated habit of beginning each line with a capital letter.

The editor sent a heavily-marked copy to Miss Spang, who was immensely flattered, and felt that at last she had been understood. But nobody she knew read "Zig-zag," and nobody who read "Zig-zag" seemed to care to know her. So nothing in particular resulted from this tribute to her genius.

Then the war came, and she forgot all about writing poetry.

The war was two years old, and she had been pouring tea once a week for a whole winter in a big Anglo-American hospital in Paris, when one day, as she was passing through the flower-edged court on her way to her ward, she heard one of the doctors say to a pale gentleman in civilian clothes and spectacles, "But I believe that pretty Miss Spang writes. If you want an American contributor, why not ask her?" And the next moment the pale gentleman had been introduced and, beaming anxiously at her through his spectacles, was urging her to contribute a rattling war story to "The Man-at-Arms," a monthly publication that was to bring joy to the wounded and disabled in British hospitals.

"A good rousing story, Miss Spang; a dash of sentiment of course, but nothing to depress or discourage. I'm sure you catch my meaning? A tragedy with a happy ending—that's about the idea. But I leave it to you; with your large experience of hospital work of course you know just what hits the poor fellows' taste. Do you think you could have it ready for our first number? And have you a portrait—if possible in nurse's dress—to publish with it? The Queen of Norromania has promised us a poem, with a picture of herself giving the baby Crown Prince his morning tub. We want the first number to be an 'actuality,' as the French say; all the articles written by people who've done the thing themselves, or seen it done. You've been at the front, I suppose? As far as Rheims, once? That's capital! Give us a good stirring trench story, with a Coming-Home scene to close with . . . a Christmas scene, if you can manage it, as we hope to be out in November. Yes—that's the very thing; and I'll try to get Sargent to do us the wounded V. C. coming back to the old home on Christmas Eve—snow effect."

It was lucky that Ivy Spang's leave was due about that time, for, devoted though she was to her patients, the tea she poured for them might have suffered from her absorption in her new task.

Was it any wonder that she took it seriously?

She, Ivy Spang, of Cornwall-on-Hudson, had been asked to write a war story for the opening number of "The Man-at Arms," to which Queens and Archbishops and Field Marshals were to contribute poetry and photographs and patriotic sentiment in autograph! And her full-length photograph in nurse's dress was to precede her prose; and in the table of contents she was to figure as "Ivy Spang, author of *Vibrations: A Book of Verse.*"

She was dizzy with triumph, and went off to hide her exultation in a quiet corner of Brittany, where she happened to have an old governess, who took her in and promised to defend at all costs the sacredness of her mornings—for Ivy knew that the morning hours of great authors were always "sacred."

She shut herself up in her room with a ream of mauve paper, and began to think.

At first the process was less exhilarating than she had expected. She knew so much about the war that she hardly knew where to begin; she found herself suffering from a plethora of impressions.

Moreover, the more she thought of the matter, the less she seemed to understand how a war story—or any story, for that matter—was written. Why did stories ever begin, and why did they ever leave off? Life didn't—it just went on and on.

This unforeseen problem troubled her exceedingly, and on the second morning she stealthily broke from her seclusion and slipped out for a walk on the beach. She had been ashamed to make known her projected escapade, and went alone, leaving her faithful governess to mount guard on her threshold while she sneaked out by a back way.

There were plenty of people on the beach, and among them some whom she knew; but she dared not join them lest they should frighten away her "Inspiration." She knew that "Inspirations" were fussy and contrarious, and she felt rather as if she were dragging along a reluctant dog on a string.

"If you wanted to stay indoors, why didn't you say so?" she grumbled to it. But the Inspiration continued to sulk.

She wandered about under the cliff till she came to an empty bench, where she sat down and gazed at the sea. After a while her eyes were dazzled by the light, and she turned them toward the bench and saw lying on it a battered magazine—the midsummer "All-Story" number of "Fact and Fiction." Ivy pounced upon it.

She had heard a good deal about not allowing one's self to be "influenced," about jealously guarding one's originality, and so forth; the editor of "Zig-zag" had been particularly strong on that theme. But her story had to be written, and she didn't know how to begin it; so she decided just to glance casually at a few beginnings.

The first tale in the magazine was signed by a name great in fiction, one of the most famous names of the past genera-

tion of novelists. The opening sentence ran: "In the month of
October, 1914—" and Ivy turned the page impatiently. She
may not have known much about story-writing, but she did
know that *that* kind of a beginning was played out. She
turned to the next.

" 'My God!' roared the engineer, tightening his grasp on the
lever, while the white, sneering face under the red lamp . . ."

No; that was beginning to be out of date, too.

"They sat there and stared at it in silence. Neither spoke;
but the woman's heart ticked like a watch."

That was better; but best of all she liked: "Lee Lorimer
leaned to him across the flowers. She had always known that
this was coming . . ." Ivy could imagine tying a story on to
that.

But she had promised to write a war story; and in a war
story the flowers must be at the end and not at the beginning.

At any rate, there was one clear conclusion to be drawn
from the successive study of all these opening paragraphs; and
that was that you must begin in the middle, and take for
granted that your reader knew what you were talking about.

Yes; but where was the middle, and how could your reader
know what you were talking about when you didn't know
yourself?

After some reflection, and more furtive scrutiny of "Fact
and Fiction," the puzzled authoress decided that perhaps, if
you pretended hard enough that you knew what your story
was about, you might end by finding out toward the last
page. "After all, if the reader can pretend, the author ought
to be able to," she reflected. And she decided (after a cautious
glance over her shoulder) to steal the magazine and take it
home with her for private dissection.

On the threshold she met her governess, who beamed on
her tenderly.

"Chérie, I saw you slip off, but I didn't follow. I knew you
wanted to be alone with your Inspiration." Mademoiselle
lowered her voice to add: "Have you found your plot?"

Ivy tapped her gently on the wrinkled cheek. "Dear old
Madsy! People don't bother with plots nowadays."

"Oh, don't they, darling? Then it must be very much
easier," said Mademoiselle. But Ivy was not so sure—

After a day's brooding over "Fact and Fiction," she decided to begin on the empiric system. ("It's sure to come to me as I go along," she thought.) So she sat down before the mauve paper and wrote "A shot rang out—"

But just as she was appealing to her Inspiration to suggest the next phrase a horrible doubt assailed her, and she got up and turned to "Fact and Fiction." Yes, it was just as she had feared, the last story in "Fact and Fiction" began: "A shot rang out—"

Its place on the list showed what the editor and his public thought of that kind of an opening, and her contempt for it was increased by reading the author's name. The story was signed "Edda Clubber Hump." Poor thing!

Ivy sat down and gazed at the page which she had polluted with that silly sentence.

And now (as they often said in "Fact and Fiction") a strange thing happened. The sentence was there—she had written it— it was the first sentence on the first page of her story, it *was* the first sentence of her story. It was there, it had gone out of her, got away from her, and she seemed to have no further control of it. She could imagine no other way of beginning, now that she had made the effort of beginning in that way.

She supposed that was what authors meant when they talked about being "mastered by their Inspiration." She began to hate her Inspiration.

On the fifth day an abased and dejected Ivy confided to her old governess that she didn't believe she knew how to write a short story.

"If they'd only asked me for poetry!" she wailed.

She wrote to the editor of "The Man-at-Arms," begging for permission to substitute a sonnet; but he replied firmly, if flatteringly, that they counted on a story, and had measured their space accordingly—adding that they already had rather more poetry than the first number could hold. He concluded by reminding her that he counted on receiving her contribution not later than September first; and it was now the tenth of August.

"It's all so sudden," she murmured to Mademoiselle, as if she were announcing her engagement.

"Of course, dearest—of course! I quite understand. How could the editor expect you to be tied to a date? But so few people know what the artistic temperament is; they seem to think one can dash off a story as easily as one makes an omelet."

Ivy smiled in spite of herself. "Dear Madsy, what an unlucky simile! So few people make good omelets."

"Not in France," said Mademoiselle firmly.

Her former pupil reflected. "In France a good many people have written good short stories, too—but I'm sure they were given more than three weeks to learn how. Oh, what shall I do?" she groaned.

The two pondered long and anxiously; and at last the governess modestly suggested: "Supposing you were to begin by thinking of a subject?"

"Oh, my dear, the subject's nothing!" exclaimed Ivy, remembering some contemptuous statement to that effect by the editor of "Zig-zag."

"Still—in writing a story, one has to have a subject. Of course I know it's only the treatment that really matters; but the treatment, naturally, would be yours, quite yours. . . ."

The authoress lifted a troubled gaze upon her Mentor. "What are you driving at, Madsy?"

"Only that during my year's work in the hospital here I picked up a good many stories—pathetic, thrilling, moving stories of our poor poilus; and in the evening, sometimes, I used to jot them down, just as the soldiers told them to me—oh, without any art at all . . . simply for myself, you understand. . . ."

Ivy was on her feet in an instant. Since even Mademoiselle admitted that "only the treatment really mattered," why should she not seize on one of these artless tales and transform it into Literature? The more she considered the idea, the more it appealed to her; she remembered Shakespeare and Molière, and said gayly to her governess: "You darling Madsy! Do lend me your book to look over—and we'll be collaborators!"

"Oh—collaborators!" blushed the governess, overcome. But she finally yielded to her charge's affectionate insistence, and brought out her shabby copybook, which began with lecture notes on Mr. Bergson's course at the Sorbonne in 1913, and suddenly switched off to "Military Hospital No. 13. November, 1914. Long talk with the Chasseur Alpin Emile Durand, wounded through the knee and the left lung at the Hautes Chaumes. I have decided to write down his story. . . ."

Ivy carried the little book off to bed with her, inwardly smiling at the fact that the narrative, written in a close, tremulous hand, covered each side of the page, and poured on and on without a paragraph—a good deal like life. Decidedly, poor Mademoiselle did not even know the rudiments of literature!

The story, not without effort, gradually built itself up about the adventures of Emile Durand. Notwithstanding her protests, Mademoiselle, after a day or two, found herself called upon in an advisory capacity, and finally as a collaborator. She gave the tale a certain consecutiveness, and kept Ivy to the main point when her pupil showed a tendency to wander; but she carefully revised and polished the rustic speech in which she had originally transcribed the tale, so that it finally issued forth in the language that a young lady writing a composition on the Battle of Hastings would have used in Mademoiselle's school days.

Ivy decided to add a touch of sentiment to the anecdote, which was purely military, both because she knew the reader was entitled to a certain proportion of "heart interest," and because she wished to make the subject her own by this original addition. The revisions and transpositions which these changes necessitated made the work one of uncommon difficulty; and one day, in a fit of discouragement, Ivy privately decided to notify the editor of "The Man-at-Arms" that she was ill and could not fulfill her engagement.

But that very afternoon the "artistic" photographer to whom she had posed for her portrait sent home the proofs; and she saw herself, exceedingly long, narrow and sinuous, robed in white and monastically veiled, holding out a refreshing beverage to an invisible sufferer with a gesture half way between Mélisande lowering her braid over the balcony and Florence Nightingale advancing with the lamp.

The photograph was really too charming to be wasted, and Ivy, feeling herself forced onward by an inexorable fate, sat down again to battle with the art of fiction. Her perseverance was rewarded, and after a while the fellow authors (though Mademoiselle disclaimed any right to the honors of literary partnership) arrived at what seemed to both a satisfactory result.

"You've written a very beautiful story, my dear," Mademoiselle sighed with moist eyes; and Ivy modestly agreed that she had.

The task was finished on the last day of her leave; and the next morning she traveled back to Paris, clutching the manuscript to her bosom, and forgetting to keep an eye on the bag that contained her passport and money, in her terror lest the precious pages should be stolen.

As soon as the tale was typed she did it up in a heavily-sealed envelope (she knew that only silly girls used blue ribbon for the purpose), and dispatched it to the pale gentleman in spectacles, accompanied by the Mélisande-Nightingale photograph. The receipt of both was acknowledged by a courteous note (she had secretly hoped for more enthusiasm), and thereafter life became a desert waste of suspense. The very globe seemed to cease to turn on its axis while she waited for "The Man-at-Arms" to appear.

Finally one day a thick packet bearing an English publisher's name was brought to her: she undid it with trembling fingers, and there, beautifully printed on the large rough pages, her story stood out before her.

At first, in that heavy text, on those heavy pages, it seemed to her a pitifully small thing, hopelessly insignificant and yet pitilessly conspicuous. It was as though words meant to be murmured to sympathetic friends were being megaphoned into the ear of a heedless universe.

Then she began to turn the pages of the review: she analyzed the poems, she read the Queen of Norromania's domestic confidences, and she looked at the portraits of the authors. The latter experience was peculiarly comforting. The Queen was rather good-looking—for a Queen—but her hair was drawn back from the temples as if it were wound round a windlass, and stuck out over her forehead in the good old-fashioned Royal Highness fuzz; and her prose was oddly built out of London drawing-room phrases grafted onto German genitives and datives. It was evident that neither Ivy's portrait nor her story would suffer by comparison with the royal contribution.

But most of all was she comforted by the poems. They were nearly all written on Kipling rhythms that broke down after two or three wheezy attempts to "carry on," and their knowing mixture of slang and pathos seemed oddly old-fashioned to the author of "Vibrations." Altogether, it struck her that "The Man-at-Arms" was made up in equal parts of tired compositions by people who knew how to write, and artless prattle by people who didn't. Against such a background "His Letter Home" began to loom up rather large.

At any rate, it took such a place in her consciousness for the next day or two that it was bewildering to find that no one about her seemed to have heard of it. "The Man-at-Arms" was conspicuously shown in the windows of the principal English and American book shops, but she failed to see it lying on her friends' tables, and finally, when her tea-pouring day came round, she bought a dozen copies and took them up to the English ward of her hospital, which happened to be full at the time.

It was not long before Christmas, and the men and officers were rather busy with home correspondence and the undoing and doing-up of seasonable parcels; but they all received "The Man-at-Arms" with an appreciative smile, and were most awfully pleased to know that Miss Spang had written something in it. After the distribution of her tale Miss Spang became suddenly hot and shy, and slipped away before they had begun to read her.

The intervening week seemed long; and it was marked only by the appearance of a review of "The Man-at-Arms" in the "Times"—a long and laudatory article—in which, by some odd accident, "His Letter Home" and its author were not so much as mentioned. Abridged versions of this notice appeared in the English and American newspapers published in Paris, and one anecdotic and intimate article in a French journal celebrated the maternal graces and literary art of the Queen of Norromania. It was signed "Fleur-de-Lys," and described a banquet at the Court of Norromania at which the writer hinted that she had assisted.

The following week, Ivy reëntered her ward with a beating heart. On the threshold one of the nurses detained her with a smile.

"Do be a dear and make yourself specially nice to the new officer in Number 5; he's only been here two days, and he's rather down on his luck. Oh, by the way—he's the novelist, Harold Harbard; you know, the man who wrote the book they made such a fuss about."

Harold Harbard—the book they made such a fuss about! What a poor fool the woman was—not even to remember the title of "Broken Wings!" Ivy's heart stood still with the shock of the discovery; she remembered that she had left a copy of "The Man-at-Arms" in Number 5, and the blood coursed through her veins and flooded her to the forehead at the idea that Harold Harbard might at that very moment be reading "His Letter Home."

To collect herself, she decided to remain a while in the ward, serving tea to the soldiers and N.C.O.'s, before venturing into Number 5, which the previous week had been occupied only by a polo-player drowsy with chloroform and uninterested in anything but his speciality. Think of Harold Harbard lying in the bed next to that man!

Ivy passed into the ward, and as she glanced down the long line of beds she saw several copies of "The Man-at-Arms" lying on them, and one special favorite of hers, a young lance-corporal, deep in its pages.

She walked down the ward, distributing tea and greetings; and she saw that her patients were all very glad to see her. They always were; but this time there was a certain unmistakable emphasis in their gladness; and she fancied they wanted her to notice it.

"Why," she cried gayly, "how uncommonly cheerful you all look!"

She was handing his tea to the young lance-corporal, who was usually the spokesman of the ward on momentous occasions. He lifted his eyes from the absorbed perusal of "The Man-at-Arms," and as he did so she saw that it was open at the first page of her story.

"I say, you know," he said, "it's simply topping—and we're so awfully obliged to you for letting us see it."

She laughed, but would not affect incomprehension.

"That?" She laid a light finger on the review. "Oh, I'm glad—I'm awfully pleased, of course—you *do* really like it?" she stammered.

"Rather—all of us—most tremendously—!" came a chorus from the long line of beds.

Ivy tasted her highest moment of triumph. She drew a deep breath and shone on them with glowing cheeks.

"There couldn't be higher praise . . . there couldn't be better judges. . . . You think it's really like, do you?"

"Really like? Rather! It's just topping," rang out the unanimous response.

She choked with emotion. "Coming from you—from all of you—it makes me most awfully glad."

They all laughed together shyly, and then the lance-corporal spoke up.

"We admire it so much that we're going to ask you a most tremendous favor—"

"Oh, yes," came from the other beds.

"A favor—?"

"Yes; if it's not too much." The lance-corporal became eloquent. "To remember you by, and all your kindness; we want to know if you won't give one to each of us—"

("Why, of course, of course," Ivy glowed.)

"—to frame and take away with us," the lance-corporal continued sentimentally. "There's a chap here who makes rather jolly frames out of Vichy corks."

"Oh—" said Ivy, with a protracted gasp.

"You see, in your nurse's dress, it'll always be such a jolly reminder," said the lance-corporal, concluding his lesson.

"I never saw a jollier photo," spoke up a bold spirit.

"Oh, do say yes, nurse," the shyest of the patients softly whispered; and Ivy, bewildered between tears and laughter, said, "Yes."

It was evident that not one of them had read her story.

She stopped on the threshold of Number 5, her heart beating uncomfortably.

She had already recovered from her passing mortification: it was absurd to have imagined that the inmates of the ward, dear, gallant young fellows, would feel the subtle meaning of a story like "His Letter Home." But with Harold Harbard it was different. Now, indeed, she was to be face to face with a critic.

She stopped on the threshold, and as she did so she heard a burst of hearty, healthy laughter from within. It was not the voice of the polo-player; could it be that of the novelist?

She opened the door resolutely and walked in with her tray. The polo-player's bed was empty, and the face on the pillow of the adjoining cot was the brown, ugly, tumultuous-locked head of Harold Harbard, well-known to her from frequent photographs in the literary weeklies. He looked up as she came in, and said in a voice that seemed to continue his laugh: "Tea? Come, that's something like!" And he began to laugh again.

It was evident that he was still carrying on the thread of his joke, and as she approached with the tea she saw that a copy of "The Man-at-Arms" lay on the bed at his side, and that he had his hand between the open pages.

Her heart gave an apprehensive twitch, but she determined to carry off the situation with a high hand.

"How do you do, Captain Harbard? I suppose you're laughing at the way the Queen of Norromania's hair is done."

He met her glance with a humorous look, and shook his head, while the laughter still rippled the muscles of his throat.

"No—no; I've finished laughing at that. It was the next thing; what's it called? 'His Letter Home,' by—" The review dropped abruptly from his hands, his brown cheek paled, and he fixed her with a stricken stare.

"Good lord," he stammered out, "but it's *you!*"

She blushed all colors, and dropped into a seat at his side. "After all," she faltered, half-laughing too, "at least you read the story instead of looking at my photograph."

He continued to scrutinize her with a reviving eye. "Why— do you mean that everybody else—"

"All the ward over there," she assented, nodding in the direction of the door.

"They all forgot to read the story for gazing at its author?"

"Apparently." There was a painful pause. The review dropped from his lax hand.

"Your tea—?" she suggested, stiffly.

"Oh, yes; to be sure. . . . Thanks."

There was another silence, during which the act of pouring out the milk, and the dropping of the sugar into the cup, seemed to assume enormous magnitude, and make an echoing noise. At length Ivy said, with an effort at lightness, "Since I know who you are, Mr. Harbard,—would you mind telling me what you were laughing at in my story?"

He leaned back against the pillows and wrinkled his forehead anxiously.

"My dear Miss Spang, not in the least—if I *could*."

"If you could?"

"Yes; I mean in any understandable way."

"In other words, you think it so silly that you don't dare to tell me anything more?"

He shook his head. "No; but it's queer—it's puzzling. You've got hold of a wonderfully good subject; and that's the main thing, of course—"

Ivy interrupted him eagerly. "The subject is the main thing?"

"Why, naturally; it's only the people without invention who tell you it isn't."

"Oh," she gasped, trying to readjust her carefully acquired theory of esthetics.

"You've got hold of an awfully good subject," Harbard continued; "but you've rather mauled it, haven't you?"

She sat before him with her head drooping, and the blood running back from her pale cheeks. Two tears had gathered on her lashes.

"There!" the novelist cried out irritably. "I knew that as soon as I was frank you'd resent it! What was the earthly use of asking me?"

She made no answer, and he added, lowering his voice a little, "Are you very angry with me, really?"

"No, of course not," she declared with a stony gayety.

"I'm so glad you're not; because I do want most awfully to ask you for one of these photographs," he concluded.

She rose abruptly from her seat. To save her life she could not conceal her disappointment. But she picked up the tray with feverish animation.

"A photograph? Of course—with pleasure. And now, if you've quite finished, I'm afraid I must run back to my teapot."

Harold Harbard lay on the bed and looked at her. As she reached the door he said, "Miss Spang!"

"Yes?" she rejoined, pausing reluctantly.

"You were angry just now because I didn't admire your story; and now you're angrier still because I do admire your photograph. Do you wonder that we novelists find such an inexhaustible field in Woman?"

The Marne

TO THE MEMORY OF
CAPTAIN RONALD SIMMONS, A.E.F.
WHO DIED FOR FRANCE
AUGUST 12, 1918.

CHAPTER I

EVER SINCE the age of six Troy Belknap of New York had embarked for Europe every June on the fastest steamer of one of the most expensive lines.

With his family he had descended at the dock from a large noiseless motor, had kissed his father good-bye, turned back to shake hands with the chauffeur (a particular friend), and trotted up the gang-plank behind his mother's maid, while one welcoming steward captured Mrs. Belknap's bag and another led away her miniature French bull-dog—also a particular friend of Troy's.

From that hour all had been delight. For six golden days Troy had ranged the decks, splashed in the blue salt water brimming his huge porcelain tub, lunched and dined with the grown-ups in the Ritz restaurant, and swaggered about in front of the children who had never crossed before and didn't know the stewards, or the purser, or the captain's cat, or on which deck you might exercise your dog, or how to induce the officer on the watch to let you scramble up for a minute to the bridge. Then, when these joys began to pall, he had lost himself in others deeper and dearer. Another of his cronies, the library steward, had unlocked the book-case doors for him, and buried for hours in the depths of a huge library armchair (there weren't any to compare with it on land) he had ranged through the length and breadth of several literatures.

These six days of bliss would have been too soon over if they had not been the mere prelude to intenser sensations. On the seventh morning—generally at Cherbourg—Troy

Belknap followed his mother, and his mother's maid, and the French bull, up the gang-plank and into another large noise-less motor, with another chauffeur (French this one) to whom he was also deeply attached, and who sat grinning and cap-touching at the wheel. And then—in a few minutes, so swiftly and smilingly was the way of Mrs. Belknap smoothed—the noiseless motor was off, and they were rushing eastward through the orchards of Normandy.

The little boy's happiness would have been complete if there had been more time to give to the beautiful things that flew past them; thatched villages with square-towered churches in hollows of the deep green country, or grey shining towns above rivers on which cathedrals seemed to be moored like ships; miles and miles of field and hedge and park falling away from high terraced houses, and little embroidered stone manors reflected in reed-grown moats under ancient trees.

Unfortunately Mrs. Belknap always had pressing engage-ments in Paris. She had made appointments beforehand with all her dressmakers, and, as Troy was well aware, it was im-possible, at the height of the season, to break such engage-ments without losing one's turn, and having to wait weeks and weeks to get a lot of nasty rags that one had seen, by that time, on the back of every other woman in the place.

Luckily, however, even Mrs. Belknap had to eat; and during the halts in the shining towns, where a succulent luncheon was served in a garden or a flowery court-yard, Troy had time (as he grew bigger) to slip away alone, and climb to the height where the cathedral stood, or at least to loiter and gaze in the narrow crooked streets, between gabled cross-beamed houses, each more picture-bookishly quaint than its neigh-bours.

In Paris, in their brightly-lit and beflowered hotel drawing-room, he was welcomed by Madame Lebuc, an old French lady smelling of crape, who gave him lessons and took him and the bull-dog for walks, and who, as he grew older, was supplemented, and then replaced, by an ugly vehement young tutor, of half-English descent, whose companionship opened fresh fields and pastures to Troy's dawning imagination.

Then in July—always at the same date—Mr. Belknap was deposited at the door by the noiseless motor, which had been down to Havre to fetch him; and a few days later they all got into it, and while Madame Lebuc (pressing a packet of chocolates into her pupil's hand) waved a damp farewell from the doorway, the Pegasus motor flew up the Champs Elysées, devoured the leafy alleys of the Bois, and soared away to new horizons.

Most often they were mountain horizons, for the tour invariably ended in the Swiss Alps. But there always seemed to be new ways (looked out by Mr. Belknap on the map) of reaching their destination; ways lovelier, more winding, more wonderful, that took in vast sweeping visions of France from the Seine to the Rhone. And when Troy grew older the vehement young tutor went with them; and once they all stopped and lunched at his father's house, on the edge of a gabled village in the Argonne, with a view stretching away for miles toward the Vosges and Alsace. Mr. and Mrs. Belknap were very kind people, and it would never have occurred to them to refuse M. Gantier's invitation to lunch with his family; but they had no idea of the emotions stirred in their son's eager bosom by what seemed to them merely a rather inconvenient deviation from their course. Troy himself was hardly aware of these emotions at the time, though his hungry interest in life always made him welcome the least deflection from the expected. He had simply thought what kind jolly people the Gantiers were, and what fun it was to be inside one of the quaint stone houses, with small window-panes looking on old box-gardens that he was always being whisked past in the motor. But later he was to re-live that day in all its homely details.

CHAPTER II

They were at St. Moritz—as usual. He and M. Gantier had been for a tramp through the Val Suvretta, and, coming home late, were rushing into their evening clothes to join Mr. and Mrs. Belknap at dinner (as they did now regularly, Troy having reached the virile age of fifteen, and having to justify the possession of a smoking-jacket and patent leather shoes). He was just out of his bath, and smothered in towels, when the tutor opened the door and thrust in a newspaper.

"There will be war—I must leave tomorrow."

Troy dropped the towels.

War! War! War against his beautiful France! And this young man, his dearest friend and companion, was to be torn from him suddenly, senselessly, torn from their endless talks, their long walks in the mountains, their elaborately planned courses of study—archæology, French literature, mediæval philosophy, the Divine Comedy, and vistas and vistas beyond—to be torn from all this, and to disappear from Troy Belknap's life into the black gulf of this unfathomable thing called War, that seemed suddenly to have escaped out of the history books like a dangerous lunatic escaping from the asylum in which he was supposed to be securely confined!

Troy Belknap was stunned.

He pulled himself together to bid a valiant farewell to M. Gantier (the air was full of the "Marseillaise" and "Sambre-et-Meuse") and everybody knew the Russians would be in Berlin in six weeks; but, once his tutor was gone, the mystery and horror again closed in on him.

France, his France, attacked, invaded, outraged—and he, a poor helpless American boy, who adored her, and could do nothing for her—not even cry, as a girl might! It was bitter.

His parents, too, were dreadfully upset; and so were all their friends. But what chiefly troubled them was that they could get no money, no seats in the trains, no assurance that the Swiss frontier would not be closed before they could cross the border. These preoccupations seemed to leave them, for the moment, no time to think about France; and Troy, during those first days, felt as if he were an infant Winkelried with all the shafts of the world's woe gathered into his inadequate breast.

For France was his holiday world, the world of his fancy and imagination, a great traceried window opening on the universe. And now, in the hour of her need, all he heard about him was the worried talk of people planning to desert her!

Safe in Paris, Mr. and Mrs. Belknap regained their balance. Having secured (for a sum that would have fitted up an ambulance) their passages on a steamer sailing from England, they could at length look about them, feel sorry, and subscribe to all the budding war charities. They even remembered poor Madame Lebuc, stranded by the flight of all her pupils, and found a job for her in a refugee bureau.

Then, just as they were about to sail, Mrs. Belknap had a touch of pneumonia, and was obliged to postpone her departure; while Mr. Belknap, jamming his possessions into a single suit case, dashed down to Spain to take ship at Malaga. The turn affairs were taking made it advisable for him to get back as quickly as possible, and his wife and son were to follow from England in a month.

All the while there came no news of M. Gantier. He had rejoined his dépôt at once, and Troy had had a post-card from him, dated the sixth of August, and saying that he was leaving for the front. After that, silence.

Troy, poring over the morning papers, and slipping out alone to watch for the noon communiqués in the windows of the Paris *Herald*, read of the rash French advance in Alsace, and the enemy's retaliatory descent on the region the Belknaps had so often sped over. And one day, among the names of the ruined villages, he lit on that of the little town where they had all lunched with the Gantiers. He saw the box-garden with the hornbeam arbour where they had gone to drink coffee, old M. Gantier ceremoniously leading the way with Mrs. Belknap; he saw Mme. Gantier, lame and stout, hobbling after with Mr. Belknap; a little old aunt with bobbing curls; the round-faced Gantier girl, shy and rosy; an incredibly dried and smoked and aged grandfather, with Voltairean eyes and sly snuff-taking gestures; and his own friend, the eldest of the four brothers. He saw all these modest beaming people grouped about Mme. Gantier's coffee, and Papa Gantier's best bottle of "*Fine*"; he smelt the lime-blossoms and box, he heard the bees in the lavender, he looked out on the rich fields and woods and the blue hills bathed in summer light. And he read: "Not a house is standing. The curé has been shot. A number of old people were burnt in the hospice. The mayor and five of the principal inhabitants have been taken to Germany as hostages."

The year before the war, he remembered, old M. Gantier was mayor!

He wrote and wrote, after that, to his tutor; wrote to his

dépôt, to his Paris address, to the ruin that had been his home; but had no answer. And finally, amid the crowding horrors of that dread August, he forgot even M. Gantier, and M. Gantier's family, forgot everything but the spectacle of the allied armies swept back from Liège, from Charleroi, from Mons, from Laon, and the hosts of evil surging nearer and ever nearer to the heart of France.

His father, with whom he might have talked, was gone; and Troy could not talk to his mother. Not that Mrs. Belknap was not kind and full of sympathy: as fast as the bank at home cabled funds she poured them out for war-charities. But most of her time was spent in agitated conference with her compatriots, and Troy could not bear to listen to their endlessly reiterated tales of flight from Nauheim or Baden or Brussels, their difficulties in drawing money, hiring motors, bribing hotel-porters, battling for seats in trains, recovering lost luggage, cabling for funds, and their general tendency to regard the war as a mere background to their personal grievances.

"You were exceedingly rude to Mrs. Sampson, Troy," his mother said to him, surprised one day by an explosion of temper. "It is natural she should be nervous at not being able to get staterooms; and she had just given me five hundred dollars for the American Ambulance."

"Giving money's no use," the boy growled, obscurely irritated; and when Mrs. Belknap exclaimed: "Why, Troy, how callous—with all this suffering!" he slunk out without answering, and went downstairs to lie in wait for the evening papers.

The misery of feeling himself a big boy, long-limbed, strong-limbed, old enough for evening clothes, champagne, the classics, biology and views on international politics, and yet able to do nothing but hang about marble hotels and pore over newspapers, while rank on rank, and regiment on regiment, the youth of France and England swung through the dazed streets and packed the endless trains—the misery of this was so great to Troy that he became, as the days dragged on, more than ever what his mother called "callous," sullen, humiliated, resentful at being associated with all the rich Americans flying from France.

At last the turn of the Belknaps came too; but, as they were preparing to start, news came that the German army was at Lille, and civilian travel to England interrupted.

It was the fateful week, and every name in the bulletins—Amiens, Compiègne, Rheims, Meaux, Senlis—evoked in Troy Belknap's tortured imagination visions of ancient beauty and stability. He had done that bit of France alone with M. Gantier the year before, while Mrs. Belknap waited in Paris for belated clothes; and the thought of the great stretch of desolation spreading and spreading like a leprosy over a land so full of the poetry of the past, and so rich in a happy prosperous present, was added to the crueller vision of the tragic and magnificent armies that had failed to defend it.

Troy, as soon as he was reassured about his mother's health, had secretly rejoiced at the accident which had kept them in France. But now his joy was turned to bitterness. Mrs. Belknap, in her horrified surprise at seeing her plans again obstructed, lost all sense of the impending calamity except as it affected her safety and Troy's, and joined in the indignant chorus of compatriots stranded in Paris, and obscurely convinced that France ought to have seen them safely home before turning her attention to the invader.

"Of course I don't pretend to be a strategist," whimpering or wrathful ladies used to declare, their jewel-boxes clutched in one hand, their passports in the other, "but one can't help feeling that if only the French government had told our Ambassador in *time* trains might have been provided . . ."

"Or why couldn't *Germany* have let our government know? After all, Germany has no grievance against *America* . . ."

"And we've really spent enough money in Europe for some consideration to be shown us . . ." the woeful chorus went on.

The choristers were all good and kindly persons, shaken out of the rut of right feeling by the first real fright of their lives. But Troy was too young to understand this, and to foresee that, once in safety, they would become the passionate advocates of France, all the more fervent in their championship because of their reluctant participation in her peril. ("What did I do?—Why, I just simply *stayed in Paris*. . . Not to run away was the only thing one *could* do to show one's sympathy," he heard one of the passport-clutchers declare, a year later, in a New York drawing-room.)

Troy, from the height of his youthful indignation, regarded them all as heartless egoists, and fled away into the streets from the sound of their lamentations.

But in the streets was fresh food for misery; for every day the once empty vistas were filled with trains of farm-wagons, drawn by slow country horses, and heaped with furniture and household utensils; and beside the carts walked lines of haggard people, old men and women with vacant faces, mothers hugging hungry babies, and children limping after them with heavy bundles. The fugitives of the Marne were pouring into Paris.

Troy dashed into the nearest shops, bought them cakes and fruit, followed them to the big hippodrome where they were engulphed in the dusty arena, and finally, in despair at his inability to do more than gape and pity, tried to avoid the streets they followed on their way into Paris from St. Denis and Vincennes.

Then one day, in the sunny desert of the Place de la Concorde, he came on a more cheering sight. A motley band of civilians, young, middle-aged and even gray-headed, were shambling along together, badged and beribboned, in the direction of the Invalides; and above them floated the American flag. Troy flew after it, and caught up with the last marchers.

"Where are we going? . . . Foreign Legion," an olive-faced "dago" answered joyously in broken American. "All 'nited States citizens. . . Come and join up, sonnie . . ." And for one mad moment Troy thought of risking the adventure.

But he was too visibly only a school-boy still; and with tears of envy in his smarting eyes he stood, small and useless, on the pavement, and watched the heterogeneous band under the beloved flag disappearing in the doorway of the registration office.

When he got back to his mother's drawing-room the tea-table was still surrounded, and a lady was saying: "I've offered *anything* for a special train, but they won't listen . . ." and another, in a stricken whisper: "If they *do* come, what do you mean to do about your pearls?"

CHAPTER III

Then came the Marne, and suddenly the foreigners caught in Paris by the German advance became heroes—or mostly heroines—who had stayed there to reassure their beloved city in her hour of need.

"We all owe so much to Paris," murmured Mrs. Belknap, in lovely convalescent clothes, from her sofa-corner. "I'm sure we can none of us ever cease to be thankful for this chance of showing it . . ."

She had sold her staterooms to a compatriot who happened to be in England, and was now cabling home to suggest to Mr. Belknap that she should spend the winter in France and take a job on a war charity. She was not strong enough for nursing, but she thought it would be delightful to take convalescent officers for drives in the Bois in the noiseless motor. "Troy would love it too," she cabled.

Mr. Belknap, however, was unmoved by these arguments. "Future too doubtful," he cabled back. "Insist on your sailing. Staterooms November tenth paid for. Troy must return to school."

"Future too doubtful" impressed Mrs. Belknap more than "Insist," though she made a larger use of the latter word in explaining to her friends why, after all, she was obliged to give up her projected war-work. Meanwhile, having quite recovered, she rose from her cushions, donned a nurse's garb, poured tea once or twice at a fashionable hospital, and, on the strength of this effort, obtained permission to carry supplies (in her own motor) to the devastated regions.

Troy, of course, went with her, and thus had his first glimpse of war.

Fresh in his mind was a delicious July day at Rheims with his tutor, and the memory of every detail noted on the way, along the green windings of the Marne, by Meaux, Mont-mirail and Epernay. Now, traversing the same towns, he seemed to be looking into murdered faces, vacant and stony. Where he had seen the sociable gossiping life of the narrow streets, young men lounging at the blacksmith's, blue-sleeved carters sitting in the wine-shops while their horses shook off the flies in the hot sunshine of the village square, black-

pinafored children coming home from school, the fat curé
stopping to talk to little old ladies under the church porch,
girls with sleek hair calling to each other from the doorways
of the shops, and women in sun-burnt gingham bending over
the village wash-trough, or leaning on their rakes among the
hayricks—where all this had been, now only a few incalculably old people sat in the doorways and looked with bewildered eyes at strange soldiers fulfilling the familiar tasks.

This was what war did! It emptied towns of their inhabitants as it emptied veins of their blood; it killed houses and
lands as well as men. Out there, a few miles beyond the sunny
vineyards and the low hills, men were dying at that very
moment by hundreds, by thousands—and their motionless
young bodies must have the same unnatural look as these wan
ruins, these gutted houses and sterile fields. . . War meant
Death, Death, Death—Death everywhere, and to everything.

By a special favour, the staff-officer who accompanied them
managed to extend their trip to the ruined château of
Mondement, the pivot on which the battle had turned. He
had himself been in the thick of the fight, and standing before
the shattered walls of the old house he explained the struggle
for the spur of Mondement: the advance of the gray masses
across the plain, their capture of the ridge, which was the key
to the road to Paris; then the impetuous rush of General
Humbert's infantry, repulsed, returning, repulsed again, and
again attacking; the hand-to-hand fighting in court and gardens; the French infantry's last irresistible dash, the batteries
rattling up, getting into place on the ridge, and flinging back
the gray battalions from the hillside into the marshes.

Mrs. Belknap smiled and exclaimed, with vague comments
and a wandering eye (for the officer, carried away by his subject, had forgotten her and become technical); while Troy, his
map spread on the top of a shot-riddled wall, followed every
word and gesture with a devouring gaze that absorbed at the
same time all the details of the immortal landscape.

The Marne—this was the actual setting of the battle of the
Marne! This happy temperate landscape with its sheltering
woods, its friendly fields and downs flowing away to a mild
sky, had looked on at the most awful conflict in history.
Scenes of anguish and heroism that ought to have had some

Titanic background of cliff and chasm had unrolled themselves among harmless fields, and along wood-roads where wild strawberries grew, and children cut hazel-switches to drive home their geese. A name of glory and woe was attached to every copse and hollow, and to each gray steeple above the village roofs.

Troy listened, his heart beating higher at each exploit, till he forgot the horror of war, and thought only of its splendours. Oh, to have been there too! To have had even the smallest share in those great hours! To be able to say, as this young man could say: "Yes, I was in the battle of the Marne"; to be able to break off, and step back a yard or two, correcting one's self critically: "No . . . it was *here* the General stood when I told him our batteries had got through . . ." or: "This is the very spot where the first seventy-five was trained on the valley. I can see the swathes it cut in the Bavarians as they swarmed up at us a third and fourth time . . ."

Troy suddenly remembered a bit of Henry the Fifth that M. Gantier had been fond of quoting:

> *And gentlemen in England now a-bed*
> *Shall think themselves accursed they were not here,*
> *And hold their manhoods cheap whiles any speaks*
> *That fought with us.*

Ah, yes—ah, yes—to have been in the battle of the Marne!

On the way back, below the crest of the hill, the motor stopped at the village church and the officer jumped down.

"Some of our men are buried here," he said.

Mrs. Belknap, with a murmur of sympathy, caught up the bunch of roses she had gathered in the ravaged garden of the château, and they picked their way among the smashed and slanting stones of the cemetery to a corner behind the church where wooden crosses marked a row of fresh graves. Half-faded flowers in bottles were thrust into the loose earth, and a few tin wreaths hung on the arms of the crosses.

Some of the graves bore only the date of the battle, with "Pour la France" or "Priez pour lui," but on others names and numbers had been roughly burnt into the crosses.

Suddenly Troy stopped short with a cry.

"What is it?" his mother asked.

She had walked ahead of him to the parapet overhanging the valley, and forgetting her roses she leaned against the low cemetery wall while the officer took up his story.

Troy made no answer. Mrs. Belknap stood with her back to him, and he did not ask her to turn. He did not want her, or anyone else, to read the name he had just read; of a sudden there had been revealed to him the deep secretiveness of sorrow. But he stole up to her and drew the flowers from her hand while she continued, with vague inattentive murmurs, to follow the officer's explanations. She took no notice of Troy, and he went back to the grave and laid the roses on it.

On the cross he had read: "September 8th, 1914. Paul Gantier, ——th Chasseurs à pied."

"Oh, poor fellows . . . poor fellows. Yes, that's right, Troy; put the roses on their graves," Mrs. Belknap assented approvingly, as she picked her way back to the motor.

CHAPTER IV

The tenth of November came, and they sailed.

The week in the steamer was intolerable, not only because they were packed like herrings, and Troy (who had never known discomfort before) had to share his narrow cabin with two young German-Americans full of open brag about the Fatherland; but also because of the same eternally renewed anecdotes among the genuine Americans about the perils and discomforts they had undergone, and the general disturbance of their plans.

Most of the passengers were in ardent sympathy with the allies, and hung anxiously on the meagre wirelesses; but a flat-faced professor with lank hair, having announced that "there were two sides to every case," immediately raised up a following of unnoticed ladies who "couldn't believe all that was said of the Germans" and hoped that America would never be "drawn in"; while, even among the right-minded, there subsisted a vague feeling that war was an avoidable thing which one had only to reprobate enough to prevent its recurrence.

They found New York—Mrs. Belknap's New York— buzzing with war-charities, yet apparently unaware of the war.

That at least was Troy's impression during the twenty-four hours before he was packed off to school to catch up with his interrupted studies.

At school he heard the same incessant war-talk, and found the same fundamental unawareness of the meaning of the war. At first the boys were very keen to hear his story, but he described what he had seen so often—and especially his haunting impressions of the Marne—that they named him "Marny Belknap," and finally asked him to cut it out.

The masters were mostly frankly for the allies, but the Rector had given out that neutrality was the attitude approved by the government, and therefore a patriotic duty; and one Sunday after chapel he gave a little talk to explain why the President thought it right to try to keep his people out of the dreadful struggle. The words duty and responsibility and fortunate privilege recurred often in this address, and it struck Troy as odd that the lesson of the day happened to be the story of the Good Samaritan.

When he went home for the Christmas holidays everybody was sending toys and sugar-plums to the Belgian war-orphans, with little notes from "Happy American children," requesting to have their gifts acknowledged.

"It makes us so happy to help," beaming young women declared with a kind of ghoulish glee, doing up parcels, planning war-tableaux and charity dances, rushing to "propaganda" lectures given by handsome French officers, and keeping up a kind of continuous picnic on the ruins of civilization.

Mr. and Mrs. Belknap had inevitably been affected by the surrounding atmosphere.

"The tragedy of it—the tragedy—no one can tell who hasn't seen it, and been through it," Mrs. Belknap would begin, looking down her long dinner table between the orchids and the candelabra; and the pretty women and prosperous men would interrupt their talk, and listen for a moment, half absently, with spurts of easy indignation that faded out again as they heard the story oftener.

After all, Mrs. Belknap wasn't the only person who had seen a battlefield! Lots and lots more were pouring home all the time with fresh tales of tragedy: the Marne had become—

in a way—an old story. People wanted something newer . . . different . . .

And then, why hadn't Joffre followed up the offensive? The Germans were wonderful soldiers, after all. . . Yes, but such beasts . . . sheer devils. . . Here was Mr. So-and-So, just back from Belgium—such horrible stories—really unrepeatable! "Don't you want to come and hear them, my dear? Dine with us tomorrow: he's promised to come unless he's summoned to Washington. But do come anyhow: the Jim Cottages are going to dance after dinner . . ."

In time Mrs. Belknap, finding herself hopelessly outstoried, out-adventured, out-charitied, began insensibly to take a calmer and more distant view of the war. What was the use of trying to keep up her own enthusiasm when that of her audience had flagged? Wherever she went she was sure to meet other ladies who had arrived from France much more recently, and had done and seen much more than she had. One after another she saw them received with the same eagerness.

"Of course we all know about the marvellous things you've been doing in France—your wonderful war-work"—then, like herself, they were superseded by some later arrival, who had been nearer the front, or had raised more money, or had had an audience of the Queen of the Belgians, or an autograph letter from Lord Kitchener. No one was listened to for long, and the most eagerly sought-for were like the figures in a moving-picture show, forever breathlessly whisking past to make way for others.

Mr. Belknap had always been less eloquent about the war than his wife; but somehow Troy had fancied he felt it more deeply. Gradually, however, he too seemed to accept the situation as a matter of course, and Troy, coming home for the Easter holidays, found at the family table a large sonorous personage—a Senator, just back from Europe—who, after rolling out vague praises of France and England insidiously began to hint that it was a pity to see such wasted heroism, such suicidal determination on the part of the allies to resist all offers of peace from an enemy so obviously their superior.

"She wouldn't be if America came in!" Troy blurted out, reddening at the sound of his voice.

"*America?*" someone playfully interjected; and the Senator laughed, and said something about geographical immunity. "They can't touch us. This isn't our war, young man."

"It may be by the time I'm grown up," Troy persisted, burning redder.

"Well," returned the Senator good-humouredly, "you'll have to hurry, for the economists all say it can't last more than a year longer. Lord Reading told me—"

"There's been misery enough, in all conscience!" sighed a lady, playing with her pearls; and Mr. Belknap added gravely: "By the time Troy grows up I hope wars and war-talk will be over for good and all."

"Oh, well—at his age every fellow wants to go out and kill something," remarked one of his uncles sympathetically.

Troy shuddered at the well-meant words. *To go out and kill something!* They thought he regarded the war as a sport, just as they regarded it as a moving-picture show! As if anyone who had had even a glimpse of it could ever again think with joy of killing! His boy's mind was sorely exercised to define the urgent emotions with which it laboured. *To save France—* that was the clear duty of the world, as he saw it. But none of these kindly careless people about him knew what he meant when he said "France." Bits of M. Gantier's talk came back to him, embodying that meaning.

"Whatever happens, keep your mind keen and clear; open as many windows on the universe as you can." To Troy France had been the biggest of those windows.

The young tutor had never declaimed about his country: he had simply told her story, and embodied her ideals in his own impatient, questioning and yet ardent spirit. "*Le monde est aux enthousiastes,*" he had once quoted; and he had shown Troy how France had always been alive in every fibre, and how her inexhaustible vitality had been perpetually nourished on criticism, analysis and dissatisfaction.

"Self-satisfaction is death," he had said; "France is the phœnix-country, always rising from the ashes of her recognized mistakes."

Troy felt what a wonderful help it must be to have that long rich past in one's blood. Every stone that France had carved, every song she had sung, every new idea she had struck out, every beauty she had created in her thousand fruitful years, was a tie between her and her children. These things were more glorious than her battles, for it was because of them that all civilization was bound up in her, and that nothing that concerned her could concern her only.

CHAPTER V

"It seems too absurd," said Mrs. Belknap; "but Troy will be eighteen this week. And that means," she added with a sigh, "that this horrible war has been going on for three whole years. Do you remember, dearest, your fifteenth birthday was on the very day that odious Archduke was assassinated? We had a picnic on the Morteratsch."

"Oh, dear," cried Sophy Wicks, flinging her tennis racket into the air with a swing that landed it in the middle of the empty court—"perhaps that's the reason he's never stopped talking about the war for a single minute since!"

Round the big tea-table under the trees there was a faint hush of disapproval. A year before, Sophy Wicks' airy indifference to the events that were agitating the world had amused some people and won the frank approval of others. She did not exasperate her friends by professions of pacifism, she simply declared that the war bored her; and after three years of vain tension, of effort in the void, something in the baffled American heart whispered that, things being as they were, she was perhaps right.

But now things were no longer as they had been. Looking back Troy surveyed the gradual development of the war-feeling as it entered into a schoolboy's range of vision. He had begun to notice the change before the sinking of the *Lusitania*. Even in the early days, when his school-fellows had laughed at him, and called him "Marny," some of them had listened to him and imitated him. It had become the fashion to have a collection of war-trophies from the battle-fields. The boys' sisters were "adopting war-orphans" at long distance, and when Troy went home for the holidays he heard more and more talk of war-charities, and noticed that the funds collected were no longer raised by dancing and fancy-balls. People who used the war as an opportunity to have fun were beginning to be treated almost as coldly as the pacifists.

But the two great factors in the national change of feeling were the *Lusitania* and the training-camps.

The *Lusitania* showed America what the Germans were, Plattsburg tried to show her the only way of dealing with them.

Both events called forth a great deal of agitated discussion, for, if they focused the popular feeling for war, they also gave the opponents of war in general a point of departure for their arguments. For a while feeling ran high, and Troy, listening to the heated talk at his parents' table, perceived with disgust and wonder that at the bottom of the anti-war sentiment, whatever specious impartiality it put on, there was always the odd belief that life-in-itself—just the mere raw fact of being alive—was the one thing that mattered, and getting killed the one thing to be avoided.

This new standard of human dignity plunged Troy into the lowest depths of pessimism. And it bewildered him as much as it disgusted him, since it did away at a stroke with all that gave any interest to the fact of living. It killed romance, it killed poetry and adventure, it took all the meaning out of history and conduct and civilization. There had never been anything worth while in the world that had not had to be died for, and it was as clear as day that a world which no one would die for could never be a world worth being alive in.

Luckily most people did not require to reason the matter out in order to feel as Troy did, and in the long run the *Lusitania* and Plattsburg won the day. America tore the gag of neutrality from her lips, and with all the strength of her liberated lungs claimed her right to a place in the struggle. The pacifists crept into their holes, and only Sophy Wicks remained unconverted.

Troy Belknap, tall and shy and awkward, lay at her feet, and blushed and groaned inwardly at her wrong-headedness. All the other girls were war-mad; with the rupture of diplomatic relations the country had burst into flame, and with the declaration of war the flame had become a conflagration. And now, having at last a definite and personal concern in the affair, everyone was not only happier but more sensible than when a perpetually thwarted indignation had had to expend itself in vague philanthropy.

It was a peculiar cruelty of Fate that made Troy feel Miss Wicks' indifference more than the zeal of all the other young women gathered about the Belknap tennis-court. In spite of everything, he found her more interesting, more inexhaustible, more "his size" (as they said at school) than any of the gay young war-goddesses who sped their tennis balls across the Belknap court.

It was a Long Island Sunday in June. A caressing warmth was in the air, and a sea-breeze stirred the tops of the lime-branches. The smell of fresh hay-cocks blew across the lawn, and a sparkle of blue water and a dipping of white sails showed through the trees beyond the hay-fields.

Mrs. Belknap smiled indulgently on the pleasant scene: her judgment of Sophy Wicks was less severe than that of the young lady's contemporaries. What did it matter if a chit of eighteen, having taken up a foolish attitude, was too self-conscious to renounce it?

"Sophy will feel differently when she has nursed some of our own soldiers in a French base-hospital," she said, addressing herself to the disapproving group.

The young girl raised her merry eyebrows. "Who'll stay and nurse Granny if I go to a French base-hospital? Troy, will you?" she suggested.

The other girls about the tea-table laughed. Though they were only Troy's age, or younger, they did not mind his being teased, for he seemed only a little boy to them, now that they all had friends or brothers in the training camps or on the way to France. Besides, though they disapproved of Sophy's tone, her argument was unanswerable. They knew that her precocious wisdom and self-confidence had been acquired at the head of her grandmother's household, and that there was no one else to look after poor old paralytic Mrs. Wicks and the orphan brothers and sisters to whom Sophy was mother and guardian.

Two or three of the young men present were in uniform, and one of them, Mrs. Belknap's nephew, had a captain's double bar on his shoulder. What did Troy Belknap and Sophy Wicks matter to young women playing a last tennis match with heroes on their way to France?

The game began again, with much noise and cheerful wrangling. Mrs. Belknap walked toward the house to welcome a group of visitors, and Miss Wicks remained beside the tea-table, alone with Troy. She was leaning back in a wide basket-chair, her thin ankles in white open-work stockings thrust out under her short skirt, her arms locked behind her thrown-back head. Troy lay on the ground and plucked at the tufts of grass at his elbow. Why was it that, with all the currents of vitality flowing between this group of animated girls and youths, he could feel no nearness but hers? The feeling was not particularly agreeable, but there was no shaking it off; it was like a scent that has got into one's clothes. He was not sure that he liked her, but he wanted to watch her, to listen to her, to defend her against the mockery and criticism in the eyes of the others. At this point his powers of analysis gave out, and his somewhat extensive vocabulary failed him. After all, he had to fall back on the stupid old school phrase. She was "his size"—that was all.

"Why do you always say the war bores you?" he asked abruptly, without looking up.

"Because it does, my boy; and so do you, when you hold forth about it."

He was silent, and she touched his arm with the tip of her swinging tennis-shoe. "Don't you see, Troy, it's not our job—not just now, anyhow. So what's the use of always jawing about it?"

She jumped up, recovered her racket, and ran to take her place in a new set beside Troy's cousin, the captain . . .

CHAPTER VI

It was not "his job"—that was the bitter drop in all the gladness.

At last what Troy longed for had come: his country was playing her part. And he, who had so watched and hoped and longed for the divine far-off event, had talked of it early and late, to old and young, had got himself laughed at, scolded, snubbed, ridiculed, nicknamed, commemorated in a school-magazine skit in which "Marne" and "yarn" and "oh, darn," formed the refrain of a lyric beginning "Oh *say*, have you *heard*

Belknap *flap* in the *breeze?*", he, who had borne all the scold-
ings and all the ridicule, sustained by a mysterious secret faith
in the strength of his cause, now saw that cause triumph, and
all his country waving with flags and swarming with khaki,
while he had to stand aside and look on, because his coming
birthday was only his nineteenth. . . He remembered the anguish of regret with which he had seen M. Gantier leave St.
Moritz to join his regiment, and thought now with passionate envy of his tutor's fate. "Dulce et decorum est . . ." The
old hackneyed phrase had taken on a beauty that filled his
eyes with tears.

Eighteen—and "nothing doing" till he was twenty-one! He
could have killed the cousins and uncles strutting about in
uniform and saying: "Don't fret, old man—there's lots of
time. The war is sure to last another four years."

To say that, and laugh, how little they must know of what
war meant!

It was an old custom in the Belknap family to ask Troy
what he wanted for his birthday. The custom (according to
tradition) had originated on his sixth anniversary, when, being
given a rabbit with ears that wiggled, he had grown very red
and stammered out: "I *did* so want a 'cyclopædia . . .'"

Since then, he had always been consulted on the subject
with a good deal of ceremony, and had spent no little time
and thought in making a judicious choice in advance. But this
year his choice took no thinking over.

"I want to go to France," he said immediately.

"To France—?"

It instantly struck his keen ears that there was less surprise
than he had feared in Mr. Belknap's voice.

"To France, my boy? The government doesn't encourage
foreign travel just now."

"I want to volunteer in the Foreign Legion," said Troy,
feeling as if the veins of his forehead would burst.

Mrs. Belknap groaned, but Mr. Belknap retained his composure.

"My dear chap, I don't think you know much about the
Foreign Legion. It's a pretty rough berth for a fellow like

you. And they're as likely as not," he added carelessly, "to send you to Morocco or the Kamerun."

Troy, knowing this to be true, hung his head.

"Now," Mr. Belknap continued, taking advantage of his silence, "my counter-proposition is that you should go to Brazil for three months with your uncle Tom Jarvice, who is being sent down there on a big engineering job. It's a wonderful opportunity to see the country—see it like a prince, too, for he'll have a special train at his disposal.—Then, when you come back," he continued, his voice weakening a little under the strain of Troy's visible inattention, "we'll see . . ."

"See what?"

"Well—I don't know . . . a camp . . . till it's time for Harvard . . ."

"I want to go to France at once, father," said Troy, with the voice of a man.

"To do *what?*" wailed his mother.

"Oh, any old thing—drive an ambulance," Troy struck out at random.

"But, dearest," she protested, "you could never even learn to drive a Ford car!"

"That's only because it never interested me."

"But one of those huge ambulances—you'll be killed!"

"*Father!*" exclaimed Troy, in a tone that seemed to say: "Aren't we out of the nursery, at least?"

"Don't talk to him like that, Josephine," said Mr. Belknap, visibly wishing that he knew how to talk to his son himself, but perceiving that his wife was on the wrong tack.

"Don't you see, father, that there's no use talking at all? I'm going to get to France, anyhow."

"In defiance of our wishes?"

"Oh, you'll forget all that later," said Troy.

Mrs. Belknap began to cry, and her husband turned on her.

"My dear, you're really—really—*I understand Troy!*" he blurted out, his veins swelling too.

But, if the Red Cross is to send you on that mission to Italy, why shouldn't Troy wait, and go as your secretary?" Mrs. Belknap said, tacking skilfully.

Mr. Belknap, who had not yet made up his mind to accept

the mission, made it up on the instant. "Yes, Troy—why not? I shall be going myself—in a month or so."

"I want to go to France," said his son. And he added, laughing with sudden courage: "You see, you've never refused me a birthday present yet."

CHAPTER VII

France again—France at last! As the cliffs grew green across the bay he could have knelt to greet them—as he hurried down the gang-plank with the eager jostling crowd he could have kissed the sacred soil they were treading.

The very difficulties and delays of the arrival thrilled and stimulated him, gave him a keener sense of his being already a humble participant in the conflict. Passports, identification papers, sharp interrogatories, examinations, the enforced surrendering of keys and papers; how different it all was from the old tame easy landings, with the noiseless motor waiting at the dock, and France lying safe and open before them whichever way they chose to turn!

On the way over, many things had surprised and irritated him—not least the attitude of some of his fellow passengers. The boat swarmed with young civilians, too young for military service, or having, for some more or less valid reason, been exempted from it. They were all pledged to some form of relief-work, and all overflowing with zeal. "France" was as often on their lips as on Troy's. But some of them seemed to be mainly concerned with questions of uniform and rank. The steamer seethed with wrangles and rivalries between their various organizations, and now and then the young crusaders seemed to lose sight of the object of their crusade—as had too frequently been the case with their predecessors.

Very few of the number knew France or could speak French, and most of them were full of the importance of America's mission. This was Liberty's chance to Enlighten the World; and all these earnest youths apparently regarded themselves as her chosen torch-bearers.

"We must teach France efficiency," they all said with a glowing condescension.

The women were even more sure of their mission; and

there were plenty of them, middle-aged as well as young, in uniform too, cocked-hatted, badged and gaitered—though most of them, apparently, were going to sit in the offices of Paris war charities; and Troy had never noticed that French-women had donned khaki for that purpose.

"France must be purified," these young Columbias pro-claimed. "Frenchmen must be taught to respect Women. We must protect our boys from contamination . . . the dreadful theatres . . . and the novels . . . and the Boulevards. . . Of course, we mustn't be hard on the French, . . . for they've never known Home Life or the Family, but we must show them . . . we must set the example . . ."

Troy, sickened by their blatancy, had kept to himself for the greater part of the trip; but during the last days he had been drawn into talk by a girl who reminded him of Miss Wicks, though she was in truth infinitely prettier. The evenings be-low decks were long, and he sat at her side in the saloon and listened to her.

Her name was Hinda Warlick, and she came from the Middle West. He gathered from her easy confidences that she was singing in a suburban church choir while waiting for a vaudeville engagement. Her studies had probably been cur-tailed by the need of preparing a repertory, for she appeared to think that Joan of Arc was a Revolutionary hero, who had been guillotined with Marie Antoinette for blowing up the Bastille; and her notions of French history did not extend be-yond this striking episode. But she was ready and eager to ex-plain France to Troy, and to the group of young men who gathered about her, listening to her piercing accents and gaz-ing into her deep blue eyes.

"We must carry America right into the heart of France—for she has got a great big splendid heart, in spite of *everything*," Miss Warlick declared. "We must teach her to love children and home and the outdoor life; and you American boys must teach the young Frenchmen to love their mothers. You must set the example. . . Oh, boys, do you know what my ambi-tion is? It's to organize an Old Home Week just like ours, all over France, from Harver right down to Marseilles. And all through the devastated regions too. Wouldn't it be lovely if we could get General Pershing to let us keep Home Week

right up at the front, at 'Eep and Leal and Rams, and all those
martyr cities—right close up in the trenches? So that even the
Germans would see us and hear us, and perhaps learn from us
too?—for you know we mustn't despair of teaching even the
Germans!"

Troy, as he crept away, heard one young man, pink and
shock-headed, murmur shyly to the prophetess: "Hearing you
say this has made it all so clear to me"—and an elderly gentleman, adjusting his eye-glasses, added with nasal emphasis:
"Yes, Miss Warlick has expressed in a very lovely way what we
all feel; that America's mission is to contribute the *human
element* to this war."

"Oh, good God," Troy groaned, crawling to his darkened
cabin. He remembered M. Gantier's phrase: "Self-satisfaction
is death," and felt a sudden yearning for Sophy Wicks' ironic
eyes and her curt: "What's the use of jawing?"

He had been for six months on his job, and was beginning
to know something about it: to know, for instance, that
nature had never meant him for an ambulance-driver.
Nevertheless he had stuck to his task with such a dogged determination to succeed that after several months about the
Paris hospitals he was beginning to be sent to exposed sectors.

His first sight of the desolated country he had traversed
three years earlier roused old memories of the Gantier family,
and he wrote once more to their little town, but again without result. Then one day he was sent to a sector of the Vosges
which was held by American troops. His heart was beating
hard as the motor rattled over the hills, through villages
empty of their inhabitants, like those of the Marne, but
swarming with big fair-haired soldiers. The land lifted and
dipped again, and he saw ahead of him the ridge once
crowned by M. Gantier's village, and the wall of the terraced
garden, with the horn-beam arbour putting forth its early
green. Everything else was in ruins: pale weather-bleached
ruins over which the rains and suns of three years had passed
effacingly. The church, once so firm and four-square on the hill,
was now a mere tracery against the clouds; the hospice roof-
less, the houses all gutted and bulging, with black smears of
smoke on their inner walls. At the head of the street a few old

women and children were hoeing vegetables before a row of tin-roofed shanties, and a Y.M.C.A. hut flew the stars and stripes across the way.

Troy jumped down, and began to ask questions. At first the only person who recognized the name of Gantier was an old woman too frightened and feeble-minded to answer intelligibly. Then a French territorial who was hoeing with the women came forward. He belonged to the place and knew the story.

"M. Gantier—the old gentleman? He was mayor, and the Germans took him. He died in Germany. The young girl—Mlle. Gantier—was taken with him. No, she's not dead. . . I don't know. . . She's shut up somewhere in Germany . . . queer in the head, they say. . . . The sons—ah, you knew Monsieur Paul? He went first . . . What, the others? . . . Yes; the three others—Louis at Notre Dame de Lorette; Jean on a submarine; poor little Félix, the youngest, of the fever at Salonika. *Voilà.* . . The old lady? Ah, she and her sister went away . . . some charitable people took them, I don't know where. . . I've got the address somewhere . . ."

He fumbled, and brought out a strip of paper on which was written the name of a town in the centre of France.

"There's where they were a year ago. . . . Yes, you may say: there's a family gone—wiped out. How often I've seen them all sitting there, laughing and drinking coffee under the arbour! They were not rich, but they were happy, and proud of each other. That's over."

He went back to his hoeing.

After that, whenever Troy Belknap got back to Paris, he hunted for the surviving Gantiers. For a long time he could get no trace of them; then he remembered his old governess, Mme. Lebuc, for whom Mrs. Belknap had found employment in a refugee bureau.

He ran down Mme. Lebuc, who was still at her desk in the same big room, facing a row of horse-hair benches packed with tired people waiting their turn for a clothing-ticket or a restaurant card.

Mme. Lebuc had grown much older, and her filmy eyes peered anxiously through large spectacles before she recognized Troy. Then, after tears and raptures, he set forth his errand, and she began to peer again anxiously, shuffling about the bits of paper on the desk, and confusing her records hopelessly.

"Why, is that you?" cried a gay young voice; and there, on the other side of the room, sat one of the young war-goddesses of the Belknap tennis court, trim, uniformed, important, with a row of bent backs in shabby black before her desk.

"Ah, Miss Batchford will tell you—she's so quick and clever," Mme. Lebuc sighed, resigning herself to chronic bewilderment.

Troy crossed to the other desk. An old woman sat before it, in threadbare mourning, a crape veil on her twitching head. She spoke in a low voice, slowly, taking a long time to explain; each one of Miss Batchford's quick questions put her back, and she had to begin all over again.

"Oh, these refugees!" cried Miss Batchford, stretching a bangled arm above the crape veil to clasp Troy's hand. "Do sit down, Mr. Belknap. Dépêchez-vous, s'il vous plaît," she said, not too unkindly, to the old woman; and added, to Troy: "There's no satisfying them."

At the sound of Troy's name, the old woman had turned her twitching head, putting back her veil. Her eyes met Troy's, and they looked at each other doubtfully. Then— "Madame Gantier!" he exclaimed.

"Yes, yes," she said, the tears running down her face.

Troy was not sure if she recognized him, though his name had evidently called up some vague association. He saw that most things had grown far off to her, and that for the moment her whole mind was centred on the painful and humiliating effort of putting her case to this strange young woman who snapped out questions like a machine.

"Do you know her?" asked Miss Batchford, surprised.

"I used to, I believe," Troy answered.

"You can't think what she wants—just everything! They're all alike. She wants to borrow five hundred francs to furnish a flat for herself and her sister."

"Well, why not?"

"Why, we don't lend money, of course. It's against all our principles. We give work, or relief in kind—that's what I'm telling her."

"I see. Could I give it to her?"

"What—all that money? Certainly *not*. You don't know them!"

Troy shook hands and went out into the street to wait for Mme. Gantier; and when she came he told her who he was. She cried and shook a great deal, and he called a cab and drove her home to the poor lodging where she and her sister lived. The sister had become weak-minded, and the room was dirty and untidy because, as Mme. Gantier explained, her lameness prevented her from keeping it clean, and they could not afford a char-woman. The pictures of the four dead sons hung on the wall, a wisp of crape above each, with all their ribbons and citations. But when Troy spoke of old M. Gantier and the daughter Mme. Gantier's face grew like a stone, and her sister began to whimper like an animal.

Troy remembered the territorial's phrase: "You may say: there's a family wiped out."

He went away, too shy to give the five hundred francs in his pocket.

One of his first cares on getting back to France had been to order a head-stone for Paul Gantier's grave at Mondement. A week or two after his meeting with Mme. Gantier his ambulance was ordered to Epernay, and he managed to get out to Mondement and have the stone set up and the grave photographed. He had brought some flowers to lay on it, and he borrowed two tin wreaths from the neighbouring crosses, so that Paul Gantier's mound should seem the most fondly tended of all. He sent the photograph to Mme. Gantier, with a five hundred franc bill; but after a long time his letter came back from the post-office.

The two old women had gone . . .

CHAPTER VIII

In February Mr. Belknap arrived in Paris on a mission. Tightly buttoned into his Red Cross uniform, he looked to his son older and fatter, but more important and impressive, than usual.

He was on his way to Italy, where he was to remain for three months, and Troy learned with dismay that he needed a secretary, and had brought none with him because he counted on his son to fill the post.

"You've had nearly a year of this, old man, and the front's as quiet as a church. As for Paris, isn't it too frivolous for you? It's much farther from the war than New York nowadays. I haven't had a dinner like this since your mother joined the Voluntary 'Rationing League.'" Mr. Belknap smiled at him across their little table at the Nouveau Luxe.

"I'm glad to hear it—about New York, I mean," Troy answered composedly. "It's our turn now. But Paris isn't a bit too frivolous for me. Which shall it be, father—the Palais Royal or the Capucines? They say the new *revue* there is great fun."

Mr. Belknap was genuinely shocked. He had caught the war fever late in life, and late in the war, and his son's flippancy surprised and pained him.

"The theatre? We don't go to the theatre. . ." He paused to light his cigar, and added, embarrassed: "Really, Troy, now there's so little doing here, don't you think you might be more useful in Italy?"

Troy was anxious, for he was not sure that Mr. Belknap's influence might not be sufficient to detach him from his job on a temporary mission; but long experience in dealing with parents made him assume a greater air of coolness as his fears increased.

"Well, you see, father, so many other chaps have taken advantage of the lull to go off on leave that if I asked to be detached now—well, it wouldn't do me much good with my chief," he said cunningly, guessing that if he appeared to yield his father might postpone action.

"Yes, I see," Mr. Belknap rejoined, impressed by the military character of the argument. He was still trying to get used to the fact that he was himself under orders, and nervous visions of a sort of mitigated court-martial came to him in the middle of pleasant dinners, or jumped him out of his morning sleep like an alarm-clock.

Troy saw that his point was gained; but he regretted having proposed the Capucines to his father. He himself was not shocked by the seeming indifference of Paris: he thought the gay theatres, the crowded shops, the restaurants groaning with abundance, were all healthy signs of the nation's irrepressible vitality. But he understood that America's young zeal might well be chilled by the first contact with this careless exuberance so close to the lines where young men like himself were dying day by day in order that the curtain might ring up punctually on low-necked *revues*, and fat neutrals feast undisturbed on lobster and champagne. Only now and then he asked himself what had become of the Paris of the Marne, and what would happen if ever again—— But that, of course, was nonsense . . .

Mr. Belknap left for Italy—and two days afterward Troy's ambulance was roused from semi-inaction and hurried to Beauvais. The retreat from St. Quentin had begun, and Paris was once again the Paris of the Marne.

The same—but how different!—were the tense days that followed. Troy Belknap, instead of hanging miserably about marble hotels and waiting with restless crowds for the communiqués to appear in the windows of the newspaper offices, was in the thick of the retreat, swept back on its tragic tide, his heart wrung, but his imagination hushed by the fact of participating in the struggle, playing a small dumb indefatigable part, relieving a little fraction of the immense anguish and the dreadful disarray.

The mere fact of lifting a wounded man "so that it wouldn't hurt"; of stiffening one's lips to a smile as the ambulance pulled up in the market-place of a terror-stricken village; or calling out "*Nous les tenons!*" to whimpering women and bewildered old people; of giving a lift to a family of footsore refugees; of prying open a tin of condensed milk for the baby, or taking down the address of a sister in Paris, with the promise to bring her news of the fugitives: the heat and the burden and the individual effort of each minute carried one along through the endless yet breathless hours—backward and forward, backward and forward, between Paris and the fluctuating front, till in Troy's weary brain the ambulance took on the semblance of a tireless gray shuttle humming in the hands of Fate . . .

It was on one of these trips that, for the first time, he saw a train-load of American soldiers on the way to the battle front. He had, of course, seen plenty of them in Paris during the months since his arrival; seen them vaguely roaming the streets, or sitting in front of cafés, or wooed by polyglot sirens in the obscure promiscuity of cinema-palaces.

At first he had seized every chance of talking to them; but either his own shyness or theirs seemed to paralyze him. He found them, as a rule, bewildered, depressed and unresponsive. They wanted to kill Germans all right, they said; but this hanging around Paris wasn't what they'd bargained for, and there was a good deal more doing back home at Podunk or Tombstone or Deposit.

It was not only the soldiers who took this depreciatory view of France. Some of the officers whom Troy met at his friends' houses discouraged him more than the enlisted men with whom he tried to make friends in the cafés. They had more definite and more unfavourable opinions as to the country they had come to defend. They wanted to know, in God's name, where in the blasted place you could get fried hominy and a real porter-house steak for breakfast, and when the ball-game season began, and whether it rained every day all the year round; and Troy's timid efforts to point out some of the compensating advantages of Paris failed to excite any lasting interest.

But now he seemed to see a different race of men. The faces leaning from the windows of the train glowed with youthful resolution. The soldiers were out on their real business at last, and as Troy looked at them, so alike and so innumerable, he had the sense of a force inexorable and exhaustless, poured forth from the reservoirs of the new world to replenish the wasted veins of the old.

"Hooray!" he shouted frantically, waving his cap at the passing train; but as it disappeared he hung his head and swore under his breath. There they went, his friends and fellows, as he had so often dreamed of seeing them, racing in their hundreds of thousands to the rescue of France; and he was still too young to be among them, and could only yearn after them with all his aching heart!

After a hard fortnight of day-and-night work he was ordered a few days off, and sulkily resigned himself to inaction. For the first twenty-four hours he slept the leaden sleep of weary youth, and for the next he moped on his bed in the infirmary; but the third day he crawled out to take a look at Paris.

The long-distance bombardment was going on, and now and then, at irregular intervals, there was a more or less remote crash, followed by a long reverberation. But the life of the streets was not affected. People went about their business as usual, and it was obvious that the strained look on every face was not caused by the random fall of a few shells, but by the perpetual vision of that swaying and receding line on which all men's thoughts were fixed. It was sorrow, not fear, that Troy read in all those anxious eyes: sorrow over so much wasted effort, such high hopes thwarted, so many dear-bought miles of France once more under the German heel.

That night when he came home he found a letter from his mother. At the very end, in a crossed postscript, he read: "Who do you suppose sailed last week? Sophy Wicks. Soon there'll be nobody left! Old Mrs. Wicks died in January—did I tell you?—and Sophy has sent the children to Long Island with their governess and rushed over to do Red Cross nursing. It seems she had taken a course at the Presbyterian without anyone's knowing it. I've promised to keep an eye on the children. Let me know if you see her."

Sophy Wicks in France! There was hardly room in his troubled mind for the news. What Sophy Wicks did or did not do had shrunk to utter insignificance in the crash of falling worlds. He was rather sorry to have to class her with the other hysterical girls fighting for a pretext to get to France; but what did it all matter, anyhow? On the way home he had overheard an officer in the street telling a friend that the Germans were at Creil . . .

Then came the day when the advance was checked. General Mangin's glorious counter-attack gave France new faith in her armies, and Paris, irrepressibly, burst at once into abounding life. It was as if she were ashamed of having doubted, as if she wanted, by a livelier renewal of activities, to proclaim her unshakable faith in her defenders. In the perpetual sunshine of the most golden of springs she basked and decked herself, and mirrored her recovered beauty in the Seine.

And still the cloudless weeks succeeded each other, days of blue warmth and nights of silver lustre; and still, behind the impenetrable wall of the front, the Beast dumbly lowered and waited. Then one morning, toward the end of May, Troy, waking late after an unusually hard day, read: "The new German offensive has begun. The Chemin des Dames has been retaken by the enemy. Our valiant troops are resisting heroically . . ."

Ah, now indeed they were on the road to Paris!

In a flash of horror he saw it all. The bitter history of the war was re-enacting itself, and the battle of the Marne was to be fought again . . .

The misery of the succeeding days would have been intolerable if there had been time to think of it. But day and night there was no respite for Troy's service; and, being at this time a practised hand, he had to be continually on the road.

On the second day he received orders to evacuate wounded from an American base hospital near the Marne. It was actually the old battle-ground he was to traverse; only, before he had traversed it in the wake of the German retreat, and now it was the allied troops who, slowly, methodically, and selling every inch dear, were falling back across the sacred soil. Troy faced eastward with a heavy heart . . .

CHAPTER IX

The next morning at daylight they started for the front.

Troy's breast swelled with the sense of the approach to something bigger than he had yet known. The air of Paris, that day, was heavy with doom. There was no mistaking its taste on the lips. It was the air of the Marne that he was breathing . . .

Here he was, once more involved in one of the great convulsions of destiny, and still almost as helpless a spectator as when, four years before, he had strayed the burning desert of Paris, and cried out in his boy's heart for a share in the drama. Almost as helpless, yes: in spite of his four more years, his grown-up responsibilities, and the blessed uniform thanks to which he, even he, a poor little ambulance-driver of nineteen, ranked as a soldier of the great untried army of his country. It was something—it was a great deal—to be even the humblest part, the most infinitesimal cog, in that mighty machinery of the future; but it was not enough, at this turning point of history, for one who had so lived it all in advance, who was so aware of it now that it had come, who had carried so long on his lips the taste of its scarcely breathable air . . .

As the ambulance left the gates of Paris, and hurried eastward in the gray dawn, this sense of going toward something new and overwhelming continued to grow in Troy. It was probably the greatest hour of the war that was about to strike—and he was still too young to give himself to the cause he had so long dreamed of serving . . .

From the moment they left the gates the road was encumbered with huge gray motor-trucks, limousines, motorcycles, long trains of artillery, army kitchens, supply waggons, all the familiar elements of the procession he had so often watched unrolling itself endlessly east and west from the Atlantic to the Alps. Nothing new in the sight—but something new in the faces! A look of having got beyond the accident of living, and accepted what lay over the edge, in the dim land of the final. He had seen that look too in the days before the Marne . . .

Most of the faces on the way were French: as far as Epernay they met their compatriots only in isolated groups. But whenever one of the motor-trucks lumbering by bore a big U.S. on its rear panel Troy pushed his light ambulance ahead and skimmed past, just for the joy of seeing the fresh young heads rising pyramid-wise above the sides of the lorry, hearing the snatches of familiar songs—"Hail, hail, the gang's all here!" and "We won't come back till it's over over here!"—and shouting back in reply to a stentorian "Hi, kid, beat it!", "Bet your life I will, old man!"

Hubert Jacks, the young fellow who was with him, shouted back too, as lustily; but between times he was more occupied with the details of their own particular job—to which he was newer than Troy—and seemed not to feel so intensely the weight of impending events.

As they neared the Montmirail monument: "Ever been over this ground before?" Troy asked carelessly.

And Jacks answered: "N-no."

"Ah—I have. I was here just after the battle of the Marne, in September, 'fourteen."

"That so? You must have been quite a kid," said Jacks with indifference, filling his pipe.

"Well—not *quite*," Troy rejoined sulkily; and they said no more.

At Epernay they stopped for lunch, and found the place swarming with troops. Troy's soul was bursting within him: he wanted to talk and remember and compare. But his companion was unimaginative, and perhaps a little jealous of his greater experience. "He doesn't want to show that he's new at the job," Troy decided.

They lunched together in a corner of the packed restaurant, and while they were taking coffee some French officers came up and chatted with Troy. To all of them he felt the desperate need of explaining that he was driving an ambulance only because he was still too young to be among the combatants.

"But I sha'n't be—soon!" he always added, in the tone of one who affirms: "It's merely a matter of a few weeks now."

"Oh, you all look like babies—but you all fight like devils," said a young French lieutenant seasoned by four years at the front; and another officer added gravely: "Make haste to be old enough, *cher Monsieur*. We need you all—every one of you . . ."

"Oh, we're coming—we're all coming!" Troy cried.

That evening after a hard and harrowing day's work between *postes de secours* and a base hospital, they found themselves in a darkened village, where, after a summary meal under flying shells, someone suggested ending up at the Y.M.C.A. hut.

The shelling had ceased, and there seemed nothing better to do than to wander down the dark street to the underground shelter packed with American soldiers. Troy was sleepy and tired, and would have preferred to crawl into his bed at the inn; he felt, more keenly than ever, the humiliation (the word was stupid, but he could find no other) of being among all these young men, only a year or two his seniors, and none, he was sure, more passionately eager than himself for the work that lay ahead, and yet so hopelessly divided from him by that stupid difference in age. But Hubert Jacks was seemingly unconscious of this, and only desirous of ending his night cheerfully. It would have looked unfriendly not to accompany him, so they pushed their way together through the cellar door surmounted by the sociable red triangle.

It was a big cellar, but brown uniforms and ruddy faces crowded it from wall to wall. In one corner the men were sitting on packing boxes at a long table made of boards laid across barrels, the smoky light of little oil-lamps reddening their cheeks and deepening the furrows in their white foreheads as they laboured over their correspondence. Others were playing checkers, or looking at the illustrated papers, and everybody was smoking and talking—not in large groups, but quietly, by twos or threes. Young women in trig uniforms, with fresh innocent faces, moved among the barrels and boxes, distributing stamps or books, chatting with the soldiers, and being generally home-like and sisterly. The men gave them back glances as honest, and almost as innocent, and an air of simple daylight friendliness pervaded the Avernian cave.

It was the first time that Troy had ever seen a large group of his compatriots so close to the fighting front, and in an hour of ease, and he was struck by the gravity of the young faces, and the low tones of their talk. Everything was in a minor key. No one was laughing or singing or larking; the note was that which might have prevailed in a club of quiet elderly men, or in a drawing-room where the guests did not know each other well. Troy was all the more surprised because he remembered the jolly calls of the young soldiers in the motor-trucks, and the songs and horse-play of the gangs of trench-diggers and hut-builders he had passed on the way. Was it that his compatriots did not know how to laugh when they were at leisure, or was it rather that in the intervals of work the awe of the unknown laid its hand on these untried hearts?

Troy and Jacks perched on a packing box, and talked a little with their neighbours; but suddenly they were interrupted by the noise of a motor stopping outside. There was a stir at the mouth of the cavern, and a girl said eagerly: "Here she comes!"

Instantly the cellar woke up. The soldiers' faces grew young again, they flattened themselves laughingly against the walls of the entrance, the door above was cautiously opened, and a girl in a long blue cloak appeared at the head of the stairs.

"Well, boys—you see I managed it!" she cried; and Troy instantly recognized the piercing accents and azure gaze of Miss Hinda Warlick.

"*She* managed it!" the whole cellar roared as one man, drowning her answer in a cheer: and "Of course I did!" she continued, laughing and nodding right and left as she made her triumphant way down the lane of khaki to what, at her appearance, had somehow instantly become the stage at the farther end of a packed theatre. The elderly Y.M.C.A. official who accompanied her puffed out his chest like a general, and blinked knowingly behind his gold eye-glasses.

Troy's first movement had been one of impatience. He hated all that Miss Warlick personified, and hated it most of all on this sacred soil, and at this fateful moment, with the iron wings of doom clanging so close above their heads. But it would have been almost impossible to fight his way out through the crowd that had closed in behind her—and he stayed.

The cheering subsided, she gained her improvised plat-form—a door laid on some biscuit-boxes—and the recitation began.

She gave them all sorts of things, ranging from grave to gay, and extracting from the sentimental numbers a peculiarly piercing effect that hurt Troy like the twinge of a dental instrument. And her audience loved it all, indiscriminately and voraciously, with souls hungry for the home-flavour and long nurtured on what Troy called "cereal-fiction." One had to admit that Miss Warlick knew her public, and could play on every cord.

It might have been funny, if it had not been so infinitely touching. They were all so young, so serious, so far from home, and bound on a quest so glorious! And there overhead, just above them, brooded and clanged the black wings of their doom. . . Troy's mockery was softened to tenderness, and he felt, under the hard shell of his youthful omniscience, the stir of all the things to which the others were unconsciously responding.

"And now, by special request, Miss Warlick is going to say a few words,"—the elderly eye-glassed officer importantly announced.

Ah, what a pity! If only she had ended on that last jolly chorus, so full of artless laughter and tears! Troy remembered her dissertations on the steamer, and winced at a fresh display of such fatuity, in such a scene.

She had let the cloak slip from her shoulders, and stepped to the edge of her unsteady stage. Her eyes burned large in a face grown suddenly grave. . . For a moment she reminded him again of Sophy Wicks. "Only a few words, really," she began, apologetically; and the cellar started a cheer of protest.

"No—not that kind. Something different . . ."

She paused long enough to let the silence prepare them: sharp little artist that she was! Then she leaned forward. "This is what I want to say: I've come from the French front— pretty near the edge. They're dying there, boys—dying by thousands, *now*, this minute. . . . But that's not it. I know: you want me to cut it out—and I'm going to. . . But this is why I began that way: because it was my first sight of—things of that sort. And I had to tell you—"

She stopped, pale, her pretty mouth twitching.

"What I really wanted to say is this: Since I came to Europe, nearly a year ago, I've got to know the country they're dying for—and I understand why they mean to go on and on dying—if they have to—till there isn't one of them left. Boys—I know France now—and she's worth it! Don't you make any mistake! I have to laugh now when I remember what I thought of France when I landed. My! How d'you suppose she got on so long without us? Done a few things too—poor little toddler! Well—it was time we took her by the hand, and showed her how to behave. And I wasn't the only one either. I guess most of us thought we'd have to teach her her letters. Maybe some of you boys right here felt that way too?"

A guilty laugh, and loud applause.

"Thought so," said Miss Warlick smiling.

"Well," she continued, "there wasn't hardly anything I wasn't ready to teach them. On the steamer coming out with us there was a lot of those Amb'lance boys. My! How I gassed to them. I said the French had got to be taught how to love their mothers—I said they hadn't any home-feeling— and didn't love children the way we do. I've been round among them some since then, in the hospitals, and I've seen fellows lying there shot 'most to death, and their little old mothers in white caps arriving from 'way off at the other end of France. Well, those fellows know how to see their mothers coming even if they're blind, and how to hug 'em even if their arms are off. . . . And the children—the way they go on about the children! Ever seen a French soldier yet that didn't have a photograph of a baby stowed away somewhere in his dirty uniform? *I* never have. I tell you, they're *white*! And they're fighting as only people can who feel that way about mothers and babies. The way we're going to fight; and maybe we'll prove it to 'em sooner than any of us think . . .

"Anyhow, I wanted to get this off my chest tonight; not for *you*, only for myself. I didn't want to have a shell get me before I'd said 'Veever la France!' before all of you.

"See here, boys—the Marsellaze!"

She snatched a flag from the wall, drawing herself up to heroic height; and the whole cellar joined her in a roar.

CHAPTER X

The next morning Jacks dragged Troy out of bed by the feet. The room was still dark, and through the square of the low window glittered a bunch of stars.

"Hurry call to Montmirail—step lively!" Jacks ordered, his voice thick with sleep.

All the old names: with every turn of the wheel they seemed to be drawing nearer and nearer to the ravaged spot of earth where Paul Gantier slept his faithful sleep. Strange if, today, of all days, Troy should again stand by his friend's grave!

They pushed along eastward under the last stars, the roll of the cannon crashing through the quiet dawn. The birds flew up with frightened cries from the trees along the roadside: rooks cawed their warning from clump to clump, and gathered in the sky in dark triangles flying before the danger.

The east began to redden through the dust-haze of the cloudless air. As they advanced the road became more and more crowded, and the ambulance was caught in the usual dense traffic of the front: artillery, field-kitchens, motor-trucks, horse-waggons, hay-carts packed with refugees, and popping motor-cycles zig-zagging through the tangle of vehicles. The movement seemed more feverish and uncertain than usual, and now and then the road was jammed, and curses, shouts, and the crack of heavy whips sounded against the incessant cannonade that hung its iron curtain above the hills to the north-east. The faces of soldiers and officers were unshaved, sallow, drawn with fatigue and anxiety. Women sat sobbing on their piled-up baggage, and here and there, by the roadside, a little country cart had broken down, and the occupants sat on the bank watching the confusion like impassive lookers-on.

Suddenly, in the thickest of the struggle, a heavy lorry smashed into Troy's ambulance, and he felt the unmistakable wrench of the steering-gear. The car shook like a careening boat, and then righted herself and stopped.

"Oh, hell!" shouted Jacks in a fury.

The two lads jumped down, and in a few minutes they saw that they were stranded beyond remedy. Tears of anger rushed into Troy's eyes. On this day of days he was not even to accomplish his own humble job!

Another ambulance of their own formation overtook them, and it was agreed that Jacks, who was the sharper of the two, was to get a lift to the nearest town, and try to bring back a spare part, or, failing that, pick up some sort of car, in which they could continue their work.

Troy was left by the roadside. Hour after hour he sat there waiting and cursing his fate. When would Jacks be back again? Not at all, most likely; it was ten to one he would be caught on the way and turned into some pressing job. He knew, and Troy knew, that their ambulance was for the time being a hopeless wreck, and would probably have to stick ignominiously in its ditch till someone could go and fetch a new axle from Paris. And meanwhile, what might not be happening nearer by?

The rumble and thump of the cannonade grew more intense: a violent engagement was evidently going on not far off. Troy pulled out his map and tried to calculate how far he was from the front; but the front at that point was a wavering and incalculable line. He had an idea that the fighting was much nearer than he or Jacks had imagined. The place at which they had broken down must be about fifteen miles from the Marne. But could it be possible that the Germans had crossed the Marne?

Troy grew hungry, and thrust his hand in his pocket to pull out a sandwich. With it came a letter of his mother's, carried off in haste when he left Paris the previous morning. He re-read it with a mournful smile. "Of course we all know the Allies must win; but the preparations here seem so slow and blundering; and the Germans are still so strong. . ." (Thump, thump, the artillery echoed: "*Strong!*") And just at the end of the letter, again, "I do wonder if you'll run across Sophy . . ."

He lit a cigarette and shut his eyes and thought. The sight of Miss Warlick had made Sophy Wicks' presence singularly vivid to him; he had fallen asleep thinking of her the night before. How like her to have taken a course at the Presbyterian Hospital without letting anyone know! He wondered that he had not suspected, under her mocking indifference, an ardour as deep as his own, and he was ashamed of having judged her as others had, when, for so long, the thought of her had been his torment and his joy. Where was she now, he wondered? Probably in some hospital in the south of the centre: the authorities did not let beginners get near the front, though of course it was what all the girls were mad for. . . Well, Sophy would do her work wherever it was assigned to her: he did not see her intriguing for a showy post.

Troy began to marvel again at the spell of France—his France! Here was a girl who had certainly not come in quest of vulgar excitement, as so many did: Sophy had always kept herself scornfully aloof from the pretty ghouls who danced and picnicked on the ruins of the world. He knew that her motives, so jealously concealed, must have been as pure and urgent as his own. France, which she hardly knew, had merely guessed at through the golden blur of a six weeks' midsummer trip, France had drawn her with an irresistible pressure; and the moment she had felt herself free she had come. "Whither thou goest I will go; . . . thy people shall be my people . . ." Yes, France was the Naomi-country that had but to beckon, and her children rose and came . . .

Troy was exceedingly tired; he stretched himself on the dusty bank, and the noise of the road traffic began to blend with the cannonade in his whirling brain. Suddenly he fancied the Germans were upon him. He thought he heard the peppering volley of machine-guns, shouts, screams, rifle-shots close at hand . . .

He sat up and rubbed his eyes.

What he had heard was the cracking of whips and the shouting of carters urging tired farm-horses along. Down a by-road to his left a stream of haggard country people was pouring from the direction of the Marne. This time only a few were in carts: the greater number were flying on their feet, the women carrying their babies, the old people bent under preposterous bundles, blankets, garden utensils, cages with rabbits, an agricultural prize framed and glazed, a wax wedding-wreath under a broken globe. Sick and infirm people were dragged and shoved along by the older children: a goitred idiot sat in a wheel-barrow pushed by a girl, and laughed and pulled its tongue . . .

In among the throng Troy began to see the torn blue uniform of wounded soldiers limping on bandaged legs. . . Others too, not wounded, elderly haggard territorials, with powder-black faces, bristling beards, and the horror of the shell-roar in their eyes. . . One of them stopped near Troy, and in a thick voice begged for a drink . . . just a drop of anything, for God's sake. Others followed, pleading for food and drink. "Gas, gas," . . a young artilleryman gasped at him through distorted lips. . . The Germans were over the Marne, they told him, the Germans were coming. It was hell back there, no one could stand it . . .

Troy ransacked the ambulance, found water, brandy, biscuits, condensed milk, and set up an impromptu canteen. But the people who had clustered about him were pushed forward by others, crying: "Are you mad to stay here? The Germans are coming!"—and in a feeble panic they pressed on.

One old man trembling with fatigue, and dragging a shaking little old woman, had spied the stretcher beds inside the ambulance, and without asking leave, scrambled in and pulled his wife after him. They fell like logs onto the gray blankets, and a livid territorial with a bandaged arm drenched in blood crawled in after them and sank on the floor. The rest of the crowd had surged by.

As he was helping the wounded soldier to settle himself in the ambulance, Troy heard a new sound down the road. It was a deep, continuous rumble, the rhythmic growl of a long train of army-trucks. The way must have been cleared to let them by, for there was no break or faltering in the ever-deepening roar of their approach.

A cloud of dust rolled ahead, growing in volume with the growing noise; now the first trucks were in sight, huge square olive-brown motor-trucks stacked high with scores and scores of bronzed soldiers. Troy jumped to his feet with a shout. It was an American regiment being rushed to the front!

The refugees and the worn-out blue soldiers fell back before the triumphant advance, and a weak shout went up. The bronzed soldiers shouted back, but their faces were grave and set. It was clear that they knew where they were going, and to what work they had been so hurriedly summoned.

"It's hell back there!" a wounded territorial called out, pointing backward over his bandaged shoulder, and another cried: "*Vive l'Amérique!*"

"*Vive la France!*" shouted the truckful abreast of Troy, and the same cry burst from his own lungs. A few miles off the battle of the Marne was being fought again, and there were his own brothers rushing forward to help! He felt that his greatest hour had struck.

One of the trucks had halted for a minute just in front of him, marking time, and the lads leaning over its side had seen him, and were calling out friendly college yells.

"Come along and help!" cried one, as the truck got under way again.

Troy glanced at his broken-down motor; then his eye lit on a rifle lying close by in the dust of the road-side. He supposed it belonged to the wounded territorial who had crawled into the ambulance.

He caught up the rifle, scrambled up over the side with the soldier's help, and was engulfed among his brothers. Furtively, he had pulled the ambulance badge from his collar . . . but a moment later he realized the uselessness of the precaution. All that mattered to anyone just then was that he was one more rifle for the front . . .

CHAPTER XI

On the way he tried to call up half-remembered snatches of military lore. If only he did not disgrace them by a blunder!

He had talked enough to soldiers, French and American, in the last year: he recalled odd bits of professional wisdom, but he was too excited to piece them together. He was not in the least afraid of being afraid, but his heart sank at the dread of doing something stupid, inopportune, idiotic. His envy of the youths beside him turned to veneration. They had all been in the front line, and knew its vocabulary, its dangers and its dodges. All he could do was to watch and imitate . . .

Presently they were all tumbled out of the motors and drawn up by the roadside. An officer bawled unintelligible orders, and the men executed mysterious movements in obedience.

Troy crept close to the nearest soldier and copied his gestures awkwardly—but no one noticed. Night had fallen, and he was thankful for the darkness. Perhaps by tomorrow morning he would have picked up a few of their tricks. Meanwhile, apparently, all he had to do was to march, march, march, at a sort of break-neck trot that the others took as lightly as one skims the earth in a dream. If it had not been for his pumping heart and his aching bursting feet Troy at moments would have thought it was a dream . . .

Rank by rank they pressed forward in the night toward a sky-line torn with intermittent flame.

"We're going toward a battle," Troy sang to himself, "toward a battle, toward a battle . . ." But the words meant no more to him than the doggerel the soldier was chanting at his elbow . . .

They were in a wood, slipping forward cautiously, beating their way through the under-growth. The night had grown cloudy, but now and then the clouds broke, and a knot of stars clung to a branch like swarming bees.

At length a halt was called in a clearing, and then the group to which Troy had attached himself was ordered forward. He did not understand the order, but seeing the men moving he followed, like a mascot dog trotting after its company; and they began to beat their way onward, still more cautiously, in little crawling lines of three or four. It reminded Troy of "playing Indian" in his childhood.

"Careful . . . watch out for 'em!" the soldier next to him whispered, clutching his arm at a noise in the underbrush; and Troy's heart jerked back violently, though his legs were still pressing forward.

They were here, then: they might be close by in the blackness, behind the next tree-bole, in the next clump of bushes— the destroyers of France, old M. Gantier's murderers, the enemy to whom Paul Gantier had given his life! These thoughts slipped confusedly through Troy's mind, scarcely brushing it with a chill wing. His main feeling was one of a base physical fear, and of a newly-awakened moral energy which had the fear by the throat and held it down with shaking hands. Which of the two would conquer, how many yards farther would the resolute Troy drag on the limp coward through this murderous wood? That was the one thing that mattered . . .

At length they dropped down into a kind of rocky hollow, overhung with bushes, and lay there, finger on trigger, hardly breathing. "Sleep a bit if you can—you look beat," whispered the friendly soldier.

Sleep!

Troy's mind was whirling like a machine in a factory blazing with lights. His thoughts rushed back over the miles he had travelled since he had caught up the rifle by the roadside.

"My God!" he suddenly thought, "What am I doing here, anyhow? I'm a deserter."

Yes: that was the name he would go by if ever his story became known. And how should it not become known? He had deserted—deserted not only his job, and his ambulance, and Jacks, who might come back at any moment—it was a dead certainty to him now that Jacks would come back—but also (incredible perfidy!) the poor worn-out old couple and the wounded territorial who had crawled into the ambulance. He, Troy Belknap, United States Army Ambulance driver, and sworn servant of France, had deserted three sick and helpless people who, if things continued to go badly, would almost certainly fall into the hands of the Germans. . . It was too horrible to think of—and so, after a minute or two, he ceased to think of it—at least with the surface of his mind.

"If it's a court-martial it's a court-martial," he reflected; and began to stretch his ears again for the sound of men slipping up in the darkness through the bushes . . .

But he was really horribly tired, and in the midst of the tension the blaze of lights in his head went out, and he fell into a half-conscious doze. When he started into full consciousness again the men were stirring, and he became aware that the sergeant was calling for volunteers.

Volunteers for what? He didn't know and was afraid to ask. But it became clear to him that the one chance to wash his guilt away (was that funny old-fashioned phrase a quotation, and where did it come from?) was to offer himself for the job, whatever it might be.

The decision once taken, he became instantly calm, happy and alert. He observed the gesture made by the other volunteers and imitated it. It was too dark for the sergeant to distinguish one man from another, and without comment he let Troy fall into the line of men who were creeping up out of the hollow. He understood now that they were being sent out on a scouting expedition.

The awful cannonade had ceased, and as they crawled along single file between the trees the before-dawn twitter of birds rained down on them like dew, and the woods smelt like the woods at home.

They came to the end of the trees, and guessed that the dark wavering wall ahead was the edge of a wheat-field. Someone whispered that the Marne was just beyond the wheat-field, and that the red flares they saw must be over Château-Thierry.

The momentary stillness laid a reassuring touch on Troy's nerves, and he slipped along adroitly at the tail of the line, alert but cool. Far off the red flares still flecked the darkness, but they did not frighten him. He said to himself: "People are always afraid in their first battle. I'm not the least afraid, so I suppose this is not a battle . . ." and at the same moment there was a small shrieking explosion, followed by a horrible rattle of projectiles that seemed to spring up out of the wheat at their feet.

The men dropped on their bellies and crawled away from it, and Troy crawled after, sweating with fear. He had not looked back, but he knew that some of the men must be lying where they had dropped, and suddenly it occurred to him that it was his business to go back and see . . .

Was it, though? Or would that be disobeying orders again?

He did not stop to consider. The Ambulance driver's instinct was uppermost, and he turned and crawled back, straight back to the place that the horrible explosion had come from. The firing had stopped, but in the thin darkness he saw a body lying in front of him in the flattened wheat. He looked back, and saw that the sergeant and the rest of the men were disappearing at the right; then he ramped forward again, forward and forward, till he touched the arm of the motionless man and whispered: "Hi, kid, it's me . . ."

He tried to rouse the wounded man, to pull him forward, to tow him like a barge along the beaten path in the wheat. But the man groaned and resisted. He was evidently in great pain, and Troy, whom a year's experience in ambulance work had enlightened, understood that he must be either carried away or left where he was.

To carry him it was necessary to stand up, and the night was growing transparent, and the wheat was not more than waist high.

Troy raised his head an inch or two and looked about him. In the east, beyond the wheat, a pallor was creeping upward, drowning the last stars. Anyone standing up would be distinctly visible against that pallor. With a sense of horror and reluctance and dismay he lifted the wounded man and stood up. As he did so he felt a small tap on his back, between the shoulders, as if someone had touched him from behind. He half turned to see who it was, and doubled up, slipping down with the wounded soldier in his arms . . .

CHAPTER XII

Troy, burning with fever, lay on a hospital bed.

He was not very clear where the hospital was, or how he had got there; and he did not greatly care. All that was left of clearness in his brain was filled with the bitter sense of his failure. He had abandoned his job to plunge into battle, and before he had seen a German or fired a shot he found himself ignominiously laid by the heels in a strange place full of benevolent looking hypocrites whose least touch hurt him a million times more than the German bullet.

It was all a stupid agitating muddle, in the midst of which he tried in vain to discover what had become of Jacks, what had happened to the ambulance, and whether the old people and the wounded territorial had been heard of. He insisted particularly on the latter point to the cruel shaved faces that were always stooping over him, but they seemed unable to give him a clear answer—or else their cruelty prompted them to withhold what they knew. He groaned and tossed and got no comfort, till suddenly, opening his eyes, he found Jacks sitting by his bed.

He poured out his story to Jacks in floods and torrents: there was no time to listen to what his friend had to say. He went in and out of the whole business with him, explaining, arguing, and answering his own arguments. Jacks, passive and bewildered, sat by the bed and murmured "All right—all right" at intervals. Then he too disappeared, giving way to other unknown faces.

The third night (someone said it was the third night) the fever dropped a little. Troy felt more quiet, and Jacks, who had turned up again, sat beside him, and told him all the things he had not been able to listen to the first day—all the great things in which he had played an unconscious part.

"Battle of the Marne? Sure you were in it—in it up to the hilt, you lucky kid!"

And what a battle it had been! The Americans had taken Vaux and driven the Germans back across the bridge at Château-Thierry, the French were pressing hard on their left flank, the advance on Paris had been checked—and the poor old couple and the territorial in the ambulance had not fallen into enemy hands, but had been discovered by Jacks where Troy had left them, and hurried off to places of safety the same night . . .

As Troy lay and listened, tears of weakness and joy ran down his face. The Germans were back across the Marne, and he had really been in the action that had sent them there! The road to Paris was barred—and Sophy Wicks was somewhere in France. . . He felt as light as a feather, and if it had not been for his deathly weakness he would have jumped out of bed and insisted on rejoining the ambulance. But as it was he could only lie flat and feebly return Jacks' grin . . .

There was just one thing he had not told Jacks: a little thing that Jacks would not have understood. Out in the wheat, when he had felt that tap on the shoulder, he had turned round quickly, thinking a friend had touched him. At the same instant he had stumbled and fallen, and his eyes had grown dark; but through the darkness he still felt confusedly that a friend was near, if only he could lift his lids and look . . .

He did lift them at last; and there, in the dawn, he saw a French soldier, haggard and battle-worn, looking down at him. The soldier wore the uniform of the *chasseurs à pied*, and his face was the face of Paul Gantier, bending low and whispering: "*Mon petit—mon pauvre petit gars. . .*" Troy heard the words distinctly, he knew the voice as well as he knew his mother's. His eyes shut again, but he felt Gantier's arms under his body, felt himself lifted, lifted, till he seemed to float in the arms of his friend . . .

He said nothing of that to Jacks or anyone, and now that the fever had dropped he was glad he had held his tongue. Someone told him that a sergeant of the *chasseurs à pied* had found him and brought him in to the nearest *poste de secours*, where Jacks, providentially, had run across him and carried him back to the base. They told him that his rescue had been wonderful, but that nobody knew what the sergeant's name was, or where he had gone to . . .

("If *ever* a man ought to have had the Croix de Guerre—!" one of the nurses interjected emotionally.)

Troy listened and shut his lips. It was really none of his business to tell these people where the sergeant had gone to: but he smiled a little when the doctor said: "Chances are a man like that hasn't got much use for decorations . . ."

And then the emotional nurse added: "Well, you must just devote the rest of your life to trying to find him."

Ah, yes, he would do that, Troy swore—he would do it on the battle-fields of France.

Miss Mary Pask

I T WAS not till the following spring that I plucked up courage to tell Mrs. Bridgeworth what had happened to me that night at Morgat.

In the first place, Mrs. Bridgeworth was in America; and after the night in question I lingered on abroad for several months—not for pleasure, God knows, but because of a nervous collapse supposed to be the result of having taken up my work again too soon after my touch of fever in Egypt. But, in any case, if I had been door to door with Grace Bridgeworth I could not have spoken of the affair before, to her or to any one else; not till I had been rest-cured and built up again at one of those wonderful Swiss sanatoria where they clean the cobwebs out of you. I could not even have written to her—not to save my life. The happenings of that night had to be overlaid with layer upon layer of time and forgetfulness before I could tolerate any return to them.

The beginning was idiotically simple; just the sudden reflex of a New England conscience acting on an enfeebled constitution. I had been painting in Brittany, in lovely but uncertain autumn weather, one day all blue and silver, the next shrieking gales or driving fog. There is a rough little white-washed inn out on the Pointe du Raz, swarmed over by tourists in summer but a sea-washed solitude in autumn; and there I was staying and trying to do waves, when some one said: "You ought to go over to Cape something else, beyond Morgat."

I went, and had a silver-and-blue day there; and on the way back the name of Morgat set up an unexpected association of ideas: Morgat—Grace Bridgeworth—Grace's sister, Mary Pask—"You know my darling Mary has a little place now near Morgat; if you ever go to Brittany do go to see her. She lives such a lonely life—it makes me so unhappy."

That was the way it came about. I had known Mrs. Bridgeworth well for years, but had only a hazy intermittent acquaintance with Mary Pask, her older and unmarried sister. Grace and she were greatly attached to each other, I knew; it had been Grace's chief sorrow, when she married my old friend Horace Bridgeworth, and went to live in New York, that Mary, from whom she had never before been separated, obstinately lingered on in Europe, where the two sisters had been travelling since their mother's death. I never quite understood why Mary Pask refused to join Grace in America. Grace said it was because she was "too artistic"—but, knowing the elder Miss Pask, and the extremely elementary nature of her interest in art, I wondered whether it were not rather because she disliked Horace Bridgeworth. There was a third alternative—more conceivable if one knew Horace—and that was that she may have liked him too much. But that again became untenable (at least I supposed it did) when one knew Miss Pask: Miss Pask with her round flushed face, her innocent bulging eyes, her old-maidish flat decorated with art-tidies, and her vague and timid philanthropy. Aspire to Horace—!

Well, it was all rather puzzling, or would have been if it had been interesting enough to be worth puzzling over. But it was not. Mary Pask was like hundreds of other dowdy old maids, cheerful derelicts content with their innumerable little substitutes for living. Even Grace would not have interested me particularly if she hadn't happened to marry one of my oldest friends, and to be kind to his friends. She was a handsome capable and rather dull woman, absorbed in her husband and children, and without an ounce of imagination; and between her attachment to her sister and Mary Pask's worship of her there lay the inevitable gulf between the feelings of the sentimentally unemployed and those whose affections are satisfied. But a close intimacy had linked the two sisters before Grace's marriage, and Grace was one of the sweet conscientious women who go on using the language of devotion about people whom they live happily without seeing; so that when she said: "You know it's years since Mary and I have been together—not since little Molly was born. If only she'd come to America! Just think . . . Molly is six, and has never seen her darling auntie . . ." when she said this, and added: "If you go to Brittany promise me you'll look up my Mary," I was moved in that dim depth of one where unnecessary obligations are contracted.

And so it came about that, on that silver-and-blue after-noon, the idea "Morgat—Mary Pask—to please Grace" sud-denly unlocked the sense of duty in me. Very well: I would chuck a few things into my bag, do my day's painting, go to see Miss Pask when the light faded, and spend the night at the inn at Morgat. To this end I ordered a rickety one-horse vehicle to await me at the inn when I got back from my paint-ing, and in it I started out toward sunset to hunt for Mary Pask. . .

As suddenly as a pair of hands clapped over one's eyes, the sea-fog shut down on us. A minute before we had been dri-ving over a wide bare upland, our backs turned to a sunset that crimsoned the road ahead; now the densest night en-veloped us. No one had been able to tell me exactly where Miss Pask lived; but I thought it likely that I should find out at the fishers' hamlet toward which we were trying to make our way. And I was right . . . an old man in a doorway said: Yes—over the next rise, and then down a lane to the left that led to the sea; the American lady who always used to dress in white. Oh, *he* knew . . . near the *Baie des Trépassés*.

"Yes; but how can we see to find it? I don't know the place," grumbled the reluctant boy who was driving me.

"You will when we get there," I remarked.

"Yes—and the horse foundered meantime! I can't risk it, sir; I'll get into trouble with the *patron*."

Finally an opportune argument induced him to get out and lead the stumbling horse, and we continued on our way. We seemed to crawl on for a long time through a wet blackness impenetrable to the glimmer of our only lamp. But now and then the pall lifted or its folds divided; and then our feeble light would drag out of the night some perfectly common-place object—a white gate, a cow's staring face, a heap of roadside stones—made portentous and incredible by being thus detached from its setting, capriciously thrust at us, and as suddenly withdrawn. After each of these projections the dark-ness grew three times as thick; and the sense I had had for some time of descending a gradual slope now became that of scrambling down a precipice. I jumped out hurriedly and joined my young driver at the horse's head.

"I can't go on—I won't, sir!" he whimpered.

"Why, see, there's a light over there—just ahead!"

The veil swayed aside, and we beheld two faintly illuminated squares in a low mass that was surely the front of a house.

"Get me as far as that—then you can go back if you like."

The veil dropped again; but the boy had seen the lights and took heart. Certainly there was a house ahead of us; and certainly it must be Miss Pask's, since there could hardly be two in such a desert. Besides, the old man in the hamlet had said: "Near the sea"; and those endless modulations of the ocean's voice, so familiar in every corner of the Breton land that one gets to measure distances by them rather than by visual means, had told me for some time past that we must be making for the shore. The boy continued to lead the horse on without making any answer. The fog had shut in more closely than ever, and our lamp merely showed us the big round drops of wet on the horse's shaggy quarters.

The boy stopped with a jerk. "There's no house—we're going straight down to the sea."

"But you saw those lights, didn't you?"

"I thought I did. But where are they now? The fog's thinner again. Look—I can make out trees ahead. But there are no lights any more."

"Perhaps the people have gone to bed," I suggested jocosely.

"Then hadn't we better turn back, sir?"

"What—two yards from the gate?"

The boy was silent: certainly there was a gate ahead, and presumably, behind the dripping trees, some sort of dwelling. Unless there was just a field and the sea . . . the sea whose hungry voice I heard asking and asking, close below us. No wonder the place was called the Bay of the Dead! But what could have induced the rosy benevolent Mary Pask to come and bury herself there? Of course the boy wouldn't wait for me. . . I knew that . . . the *Baie des Trépassés* indeed! The sea whined down there as if it were feeding-time, and the Furies, its keepers, had forgotten it. . .

There *was* the gate! My hand had struck against it. I felt along to the latch, undid it, and brushed between wet bushes to the house-front. Not a candle-glint anywhere. If the house were indeed Miss Pask's, she certainly kept early hours. . .

II

Night and fog were now one, and the darkness as thick as a blanket. I felt vainly about for a bell. At last my hand came in contact with a knocker and I lifted it. The clatter with which it fell sent a prolonged echo through the silence; but for a minute or two nothing else happened.

"There's no one there, I tell you!" the boy called impatiently from the gate.

But there was. I had heard no steps inside, but presently a bolt shot back, and an old woman in a peasant's cap pushed her head out. She had set her candle down on a table behind her, so that her face, aureoled with lacy wings, was in obscurity; but I knew she was old by the stoop of her shoulders and her fumbling movements. The candle-light, which made her invisible, fell full on my face, and she looked at me.

"This is Miss Mary Pask's house?"

"Yes, sir." Her voice—a very old voice—was pleasant enough, unsurprised and even friendly.

"I'll tell her," she added, shuffling off.

"Do you think she'll see me?" I threw after her.

"Oh, why not? The idea!" she almost chuckled. As she retreated I saw that she was wrapped in a shawl and had a cotton umbrella under her arm. Obviously she was going out—perhaps going home for the night. I wondered if Mary Pask lived all alone in her hermitage.

The old woman disappeared with the candle and I was left in total darkness. After an interval I heard a door shut at the back of the house and then a slow clumping of aged *sabots* along the flags outside. The old woman had evidently picked up her *sabots* in the kitchen and left the house. I wondered if she had told Miss Pask of my presence before going, or whether she had just left me there, the butt of some grim practical joke of her own. Certainly there was no sound within doors. The footsteps died out, I heard a gate click—then complete silence closed in again like the fog.

"I wonder—" I began within myself; and at that moment a smothered memory struggled abruptly to the surface of my languid mind.

"But she's *dead*—Mary Pask is *dead*!" I almost screamed it aloud in my amazement.

It was incredible, the tricks my memory had played on me since my fever! I had known for nearly a year that Mary Pask was dead—had died suddenly the previous autumn—and though I had been thinking of her almost continuously for the last two or three days it was only now that the forgotten fact of her death suddenly burst up again to consciousness.

Dead! But hadn't I found Grace Bridgeworth in tears and crape the very day I had gone to bid her good-bye before sailing for Egypt? Hadn't she laid the cable before my eyes, her own streaming with tears while I read: "Sister died suddenly this morning requested burial in garden of house particulars by letter"—with the signature of the American Consul at Brest, a friend of Bridgeworth's I seemed to recall? I could see the very words of the message printed on the darkness before me.

As I stood there I was a good deal more disturbed by the discovery of the gap in my memory than by the fact of being alone in a pitch-dark house, either empty or else inhabited by strangers. Once before of late I had noted this queer temporary blotting-out of some well-known fact; and here was a second instance of it. Decidedly, I wasn't as well over my illness as the doctors had told me. . . Well, I would get back to Morgat and lie up there for a day or two, doing nothing, just eating and sleeping. . .

In my self-absorption I had lost my bearings, and no longer remembered where the door was. I felt in every pocket in turn for a match—but since the doctors had made me give up smoking, why should I have found one?

The failure to find a match increased my sense of irritated helplessness, and I was groping clumsily about the hall among the angles of unseen furniture when a light slanted along the rough-cast wall of the stairs. I followed its direction, and on the landing above me I saw a figure in white shading a candle with one hand and looking down. A chill ran along my spine, for the figure bore a strange resemblance to that of Mary Pask as I used to know her.

"Oh, it's *you*!" she exclaimed in the cracked twittering voice which was at one moment like an old woman's quaver, at another like a boy's falsetto. She came shuffling down in her baggy white garments, with her usual clumsy swaying movements; but I noticed that her steps on the wooden stairs were soundless. Well—they would be, naturally!

I stood without a word, gazing up at the strange vision above me, and saying to myself: "There's nothing there, nothing whatever. It's your digestion, or your eyes, or some damned thing wrong with you somewhere—"

But there was the candle, at any rate; and as it drew nearer, and lit up the place about me, I turned and caught hold of the door-latch. For, remember, I had seen the cable, and Grace in crape. . .

"Why, what's the matter? I assure you, you don't disturb me!" the white figure twittered; adding, with a faint laugh: "I don't have so many visitors nowadays—"

She had reached the hall, and stood before me, lifting her candle shakily and peering up into my face. "You haven't changed—not as much as I should have thought. But *I* have, haven't I?" she appealed to me with another laugh; and abruptly she laid her hand on my arm. I looked down at the hand, and thought to myself: "*That* can't deceive me."

I have always been a noticer of hands. The key to character that other people seek in the eyes, the mouth, the modelling of the skull, I find in the curve of the nails, the cut of the finger-tips, the way the palm, rosy or sallow, smooth or seamed, swells up from its base. I remembered Mary Pask's hand vividly because it was so like a caricature of herself; round, puffy, pink, yet prematurely old and useless. And there, unmistakably, it lay on my sleeve: but changed and shrivelled—somehow like one of those pale freckled toadstools that the least touch resolves to dust. . . Well—to dust? Of course. . .

I looked at the soft wrinkled fingers, with their foolish little oval finger-tips that used to be so innocently and naturally pink, and now were blue under the yellowing nails—and my flesh rose in ridges of fear.

"Come in, come in," she fluted, cocking her white untidy head on one side and rolling her bulging blue eyes at me. The horrible thing was that she still practised the same arts, all the childish wiles of a clumsy capering coquetry. I felt her pull on my sleeve and it drew me in her wake like a steel cable.

The room she led me into was—well, "unchanged" is the term generally used in such cases. For as a rule, after people die, things are tidied up, furniture is sold, remembrances are despatched to the family. But some morbid piety (or Grace's instructions, perhaps) had kept this room looking exactly as I supposed it had in Miss Pask's lifetime. I wasn't in the mood for noting details; but in the faint dabble of moving candle-light I was half aware of bedraggled cushions, odds and ends of copper pots, and a jar holding a faded branch of some late-flowering shrub. A real Mary Pask "interior"!

The white figure flitted spectrally to the chimney-piece, lit two more candles, and set down the third on a table. I hadn't supposed I was superstitious—but those three candles! Hardly knowing what I did, I hurriedly bent and blew one out. Her laugh sounded behind me.

"Three candles—you still mind that sort of thing? I've got beyond all that, you know," she chuckled. "Such a comfort . . . such a sense of freedom. . ." A fresh shiver joined the others already coursing over me .

"Come and sit down by me," she entreated, sinking to a sofa. "It's such an age since I've seen a living being!"

Her choice of terms was certainly strange, and as she leaned back on the white slippery sofa and beckoned me with one of those unburied hands my impulse was to turn and run. But her old face, hovering there in the candle-light, with the un-naturally red cheeks like varnished apples and the blue eyes swimming in vague kindliness, seemed to appeal to me against my cowardice, to remind me that, dead or alive, Mary Pask would never harm a fly.

"Do sit down!" she repeated, and I took the other corner of the sofa.

"It's so wonderfully good of you—I suppose Grace asked you to come?" She laughed again—her conversation had always been punctuated by rambling laughter. "It's an event—quite an event! I've had so few visitors since my death, you see."

Another bucketful of cold water ran over me; but I looked at her resolutely, and again the innocence of her face disarmed me.

I cleared my throat and spoke—with a huge panting effort, as if I had been heaving up a grave-stone. "You live here alone?" I brought out.

"Ah, I'm glad to hear your voice—I still remember voices, though I hear so few," she murmured dreamily. "Yes—I live here alone. The old woman you saw goes away at night. She won't stay after dark . . . she says she can't. Isn't it funny? But it doesn't matter; I like the darkness." She leaned to me with one of her irrelevant smiles. "The dead," she said, "naturally get used to it."

Once more I cleared my throat; but nothing followed.

She continued to gaze at me with confidential blinks. "And Grace? Tell me all about my darling. I wish I could have seen her again . . . just once." Her laugh came out grotesquely. "When she got the news of my death—were you with her? Was she terribly upset?"

I stumbled to my feet with a meaningless stammer. I couldn't answer—I couldn't go on looking at her.

"Ah, I see . . . it's too painful," she acquiesced, her eyes brimming, and she turned her shaking head away.

"But after all . . . I'm glad she was so sorry. . . It's what I've been longing to be told, and hardly hoped for. Grace forgets. . ." She stood up too and flitted across the room, wavering nearer and nearer to the door.

"Thank God," I thought, "she's going."

"Do you know this place by daylight?" she asked abruptly. I shook my head.

"It's very beautiful. But you wouldn't have seen *me* then. You'd have had to take your choice between me and the landscape. I hate the light—it makes my head ache. And so I sleep all day. I was just waking up when you came." She smiled at me with an increasing air of confidence. "Do you know where I usually sleep? Down below there—in the garden!" Her laugh shrilled out again. "There's a shady corner down at the bottom where the sun never bothers one. Sometimes I sleep there till the stars come out."

The phrase about the garden, in the consul's cable, came back to me and I thought: "After all, it's not such an unhappy state. I wonder if she isn't better off than when she was alive?"

Perhaps she was—but I was sure *I* wasn't, in her company. And her way of sidling nearer to the door made me distinctly want to reach it before she did. In a rush of cowardice I strode

ahead of her—but a second later she had the latch in her hand
and was leaning against the panels, her long white raiment
hanging about her like grave-clothes. She drooped her head a
little sideways and peered at me under her lashless lids.

"You're not going?" she reproached me.

I dived down in vain for my missing voice, and silently
signed that I was.

"Going—going away? Altogether?" Her eyes were still
fixed on me, and I saw two tears gather in their corners and
run down over the red glistening circles on her cheeks. "Oh,
but you mustn't," she said gently. "I'm too lonely. . ."

I stammered something inarticulate, my eyes on the blue-
nailed hand that grasped the latch. Suddenly the window behind us crashed open, and a gust of wind, surging in out
of the blackness, extinguished the candle on the nearest
chimney-corner. I glanced back nervously to see if the other
candle were going out too.

"You don't like the noise of the wind? *I* do. It's all I have
to talk to. . . People don't like me much since I've been
dead. Queer, isn't it? The peasants are so superstitious. At
times I'm really lonely. . ." Her voice cracked in a last effort
at laughter, and she swayed toward me, one hand still on the
latch.

"Lonely, lonely! If you *knew* how lonely! It was a lie when
I told you I wasn't! And now you come, and your face looks
friendly . . . and you say you're going to leave me! No—no
—no—you shan't! Or else, why did you come? It's cruel. . .
I used to think I knew what loneliness was . . . after Grace
married, you know. Grace thought she was always thinking of
me, but she wasn't. She called me 'darling,' but she was
thinking of her husband and children. I said to myself then:
'You couldn't be lonelier if you were dead.' But I know better now. . . There's been no loneliness like this last year's . . .
none! And sometimes I sit here and think: 'If a man came
along some day and took a fancy to you?'" She gave another
wavering cackle. "Well, such things *have* happened, you know,
even after youth's gone . . . a man who'd had his troubles
too. But no one came till to-night . . . and now you say
you're going!" Suddenly she flung herself toward me. "Oh,
stay with me, stay with me . . . just tonight. . . It's so sweet

and quiet here. . . No one need know . . . no one will ever come and trouble us."

I ought to have shut the window when the first gust came. I might have known there would soon be another, fiercer one. It came now, slamming back the loose-hinged lattice, filling the room with the noise of the sea and with wet swirls of fog, and dashing the other candle to the floor. The light went out, and I stood there—we stood there—lost to each other in the roaring coiling darkness. My heart seemed to stop beating; I had to fetch up my breath with great heaves that covered me with sweat. The door—the door—well, I knew I had been facing it when the candle went. Something white and wraithlike seemed to melt and crumple up before me in the night, and avoiding the spot where it had sunk away I stumbled around it in a wide circle, got the latch in my hand, caught my foot in a scarf or sleeve, trailing loose and invisible, and freed myself with a jerk from this last obstacle. I had the door open now. As I got into the hall I heard a whimper from the blackness behind me; but I scrambled on to the hall door, dragged it open and bolted out into the night. I slammed the door on that pitiful low whimper, and the fog and wind enveloped me in healing arms.

III

When I was well enough to trust myself to think about it all again I found that a very little thinking got my temperature up, and my heart hammering in my throat. No use. . . I simply couldn't stand it . . . for I'd seen Grace Bridgeworth in crape, weeping over the cable, and yet I'd sat and talked with her sister, on the same sofa—her sister who'd been dead a year!

The circle was a vicious one; I couldn't break through it. The fact that I was down with fever the next morning might have explained it; yet I couldn't get away from the clinging reality of the vision. Supposing it *was* a ghost I had been talking to, and not a mere projection of my fever? Supposing something survived of Mary Pask—enough to cry out to me the unuttered loneliness of a lifetime, to express at last what the living woman had always had to keep dumb and hidden? The thought moved me curiously—in my weakness I lay and wept over it. No end of women were like that, I supposed, and perhaps, after death, if they got their chance they tried to use it. . . Old tales and legends floated through my mind; the bride of Corinth, the mediaeval vampire—but what names to attach to the plaintive image of Mary Pask!

My weak mind wandered in and out among these visions and conjectures, and the longer I lived with them the more convinced I became that something *which had been Mary Pask* had talked with me that night . . . I made up my mind, when I was up again, to drive back to the place (in broad daylight, this time), to hunt out the grave in the garden—that "shady corner where the sun never bothers one"—and appease the poor ghost with a few flowers. But the doctors decided otherwise; and perhaps my weak will unknowingly abetted them. At any rate, I yielded to their insistence that I should be driven straight from my hotel to the train for Paris, and thence transshipped, like a piece of luggage, to the Swiss sanatorium they had in view for me. Of course I meant to come back when I was patched up again . . . and meanwhile, more and more tenderly, but more intermittently, my thoughts went back from my snow-mountain to that wailing autumn night above the *Baie des Trépassés*, and the revelation of the dead Mary Pask who was so much more real to me than ever the living one had been.

IV

After all, why should I tell Grace Bridgeworth—ever? I had had a glimpse of things that were really no business of hers. If the revelation had been vouchsafed to me, ought I not to bury it in those deepest depths where the inexplicable and the unforgettable sleep together? And besides, what interest could there be to a woman like Grace in a tale she could neither understand nor believe in? She would just set me down as "queer"—and enough people had done that already. My first object, when I finally did get back to New York, was to convince everybody of my complete return to mental and physical soundness; and into this scheme of evidence my experience with Mary Pask did not seem to fit. All things considered, I would hold my tongue.

But after a while the thought of the grave began to trouble me. I wondered if Grace had ever had a proper grave-stone put on it. The queer neglected look of the house gave me the idea that perhaps she had done nothing—had brushed the whole matter aside, to be attended to when she next went abroad. "Grace forgets," I heard the poor ghost quaver. . . No, decidedly, there could be no harm in putting (tactfully) just that one question about the care of the grave; the more so as I was beginning to reproach myself for not having gone back to see with my own eyes how it was kept. . .

Grace and Horace welcomed me with all their old friendliness, and I soon slipped into the habit of dropping in on them for a meal when I thought they were likely to be alone. Nevertheless my opportunity didn't come at once—I had to wait for some weeks. And then one evening, when Horace was dining out and I sat alone with Grace, my glance lit on a photograph of her sister—an old faded photograph which seemed to meet my eyes reproachfully.

"By the way, Grace," I began with a jerk, "I don't believe I ever told you: I went down to that little place of . . . of your sister's the day before I had that bad relapse."

At once her face lit up emotionally. "No, you never told me. How sweet of you to go!" The ready tears overbrimmed her eyes. "I'm *so* glad you did." She lowered her voice and added softly: "And did you see her?"

The question sent one of my old shudders over me. I looked with amazement at Mrs. Bridgeworth's plump face, smiling at me through a veil of painless tears. "I do reproach myself more and more about darling Mary," she added tremulously. "But tell me—tell me everything."

There was a knot in my throat; I felt almost as uncomfortable as I had in Mary Pask's own presence. Yet I had never before noticed anything uncanny about Grace Bridgeworth. I forced my voice up to my lips.

"Everything? Oh, I can't—." I tried to smile.

"But you did see her?"

I managed to nod, still smiling.

Her face grew suddenly haggard—yes, haggard! "And the change was so dreadful that you can't speak of it? Tell me—was that it?"

I shook my head. After all, what had shocked me was that the change was so slight—that between being dead and alive there seemed after all to be so little difference, except that of a mysterious increase in reality. But Grace's eyes were still searching me insistently. "You must tell me," she reiterated. "I know I ought to have gone there long ago—"

"Yes; perhaps you ought." I hesitated. "To see about the grave, at least. . ."

She sat silent, her eyes still on my face. Her tears had stopped, but her look of solicitude slowly grew into a stare of something like terror. Hesitatingly, almost reluctantly, she stretched out her hand and laid it on mine for an instant. "Dear old friend—" she began.

"Unfortunately," I interrupted, "I couldn't get back myself to see the grave . . . because I was taken ill the next day. . ."

"Yes, yes; of course. I know." She paused. "Are you *sure* you went there at all?" she asked abruptly.

"Sure? Good Lord—" It was my turn to stare. "Do you suspect me of not being quite right yet?" I suggested with an uneasy laugh.

"No—no . . . of course not . . . but I don't understand."

"Understand what? I went into the house. . . I saw everything, in fact, *but* her grave. . ."

"Her grave?" Grace jumped up, clasping her hands on her breast and darting away from me. At the other end of the room she stood and gazed, and then moved slowly back.

"Then, after all—I wonder?" She held her eyes on me, half fearful and half reassured. "Could it be simply that you never heard?"

"Never heard?"

"But it was in all the papers! Don't you ever read them? I meant to write. . . I thought I *had* written . . . but I said: 'At any rate he'll see it in the papers'. . . You know I'm always lazy about letters. . ."

"See what in the papers?"

"Why, that she *didn't* die. . . She isn't dead! There isn't any grave, my dear man! It was only a cataleptic trance. . . An extraordinary case, the doctors say. . . But didn't she tell you all about it—if you say you saw her?" She burst into half-hysterical laughter: "Surely she must have told you that she wasn't dead?"

"No," I said slowly, "she didn't tell me that."

We talked about it together for a long time after that—talked on till Horace came back from his men's dinner, after midnight. Grace insisted on going in and out of the whole subject, over and over again. As she kept repeating, it was certainly the only time that poor Mary had ever been in the papers. But though I sat and listened patiently I couldn't get up any real interest in what she said. I felt I should never again be interested in Mary Pask, or in anything concerning her.

The Young Gentlemen

THE uniform newness of a new country gives peculiar relief to its few relics of antiquity—a term which, in America, may fairly enough be applied to any building already above ground when the colony became a republic.

Groups of such buildings, little settlements almost unmarred by later accretions, are still to be found here and there in the Eastern states; and they are always productive of inordinate pride in those who discover and live in them. A place of the sort, twenty years ago, was Harpledon, on the New England coast, somewhere between Salem and Newburyport. How intolerantly proud we all were of inhabiting it! How we resisted modern improvements, ridiculed fashionable "summer resorts," fought trolley-lines, overhead wires and telephones, wrote to the papers denouncing municipal vandalism, and bought up (those of us who could afford it) one little heavy-roofed house after another, as the land-speculator threatened them! All this, of course, was on a very small scale: Harpledon was, and is still, the smallest of towns, hardly more than a village, happily unmenaced by industry, and almost too remote for the week-end "flivver." And now that civic pride has taught Americans to preserve and adorn their modest monuments, setting them in smooth stretches of turf and nursing the elms of the village green, the place has become far more attractive, and far worthier of its romantic reputation, than when we artists and writers first knew it. Nevertheless, I hope I shall never see it again; certainly I shall not if I can help it. . .

II

The elders of the tribe of summer visitors nearly all professed to have "discovered" Harpledon. The only one of the number who never, to my knowledge, put forth this claim was Waldo Cranch; and he had lived there longer than any of us.

The one person in the village who could remember his coming to Harpledon, and opening and repairing the old

Cranch house (for his family had been India merchants when Harpledon was a thriving sea-port)—the only person who went back far enough to antedate Waldo Cranch was an aunt of mine, old Miss Lucilla Selwick, who lived in the Selwick house, itself a stout relic of India merchant days, and who had been sitting at the same window, watching the main street of Harpledon, for seventy years and more to my knowledge. But unfortunately the long range of Aunt Lucilla's memory often made it hit rather wide of the mark. She remembered heaps and heaps of far-off things; but she almost always remembered them wrongly. For instance, she used to say: "Poor Polly Everitt! How well I remember her, coming up from the beach one day screaming, and saying she'd seen her husband drowning before her eyes"—whereas every one knew that Mrs. Everitt was on a picnic when her husband was drowned at the other end of the world, and that no ghostly premonition of her loss had reached her. And whenever Aunt Lucilla mentioned Mr. Cranch's coming to live at Harpledon she used to say: "Dear me, I can see him now, driving by on that rainy afternoon in Denny Brine's old carry-all, with a great pile of bags and bundles, and on top of them a black and white hobby-horse with a real mane—the very handsomest hobby-horse I ever saw." No persuasion could induce her to dissociate the image of this prodigious toy from her first sight of Waldo Cranch, most incurable of bachelors, and least concerned with the amusing of other people's children, even those of his best friends. In this case, to be sure, her power of evocation had a certain success. Some one told Cranch—Mrs. Durant I think it must have been—and I can still hear his hearty laugh.

"What could it have been that she saw?" Mrs. Durant questioned; and he responded gaily: "Why not simply the symbol of my numerous tastes?" Which—as Cranch painted and gardened and made music (even composed it)—seemed so happy an explanation that for long afterward the Cranch house was known to us as Hobby-Horse Hall.

It will be seen that Aunt Lucilla's reminiscences, though they sometimes provoked a passing amusement, were neither accurate nor illuminating. Naturally, nobody paid much attention to them, and we had to content ourselves with regarding

Waldo Cranch, hale and hearty and social as he still was, as an Institution already venerable when the rest of us had first apprehended Harpledon. We knew, of course, the chief points in the family history: that the Cranches had been prosperous merchants for three centuries, and had intermarried with other prosperous families; that one of them, serving his business apprenticeship at Malaga in colonial days, had brought back a Spanish bride, to the bewilderment of Harpledon; and that Waldo Cranch himself had spent a studious and wandering youth in Europe. His Spanish great-grandmother's portrait still hung in the old house; and it was a long-standing joke at Harpledon that the young Cranch who went to Malaga, where he presumably had his pick of Spanish beauties, should have chosen so dour a specimen. The lady was a forbidding character on the canvas: very short and thickset, with a huge wig of black ringlets, a long harsh nose, and one shoulder perceptibly above the other. It was characteristic of Aunt Lucilla Selwick that in mentioning this swart virago she always took the tone of elegy. "Ah, poor thing, they say she never forgot the sunshine and orange blossoms, and pined off early, when her queer son Calvert was hardly out of petticoats. A strange man Calvert Cranch was; but he married Euphemia Waldo of Wood's Hole, the beauty, and had two sons, one exactly like Euphemia, the other made in his own image. And they do say that one was so afraid of his own face that he went back to Spain and died a monk—if you'll believe it," she always concluded with a Puritan shudder.

This was all we knew of Waldo Cranch's past; and he had been so long a part of Harpledon that our curiosity seldom ranged beyond his coming there. He was our local ancestor; but it was a mark of his studied cordiality and his native tact that he never made us feel his priority. It was never he who embittered us with allusions to the picturesqueness of the old light-house before it was rebuilt, or the paintability of the vanished water-mill; he carried his distinction so far as to take Harpledon itself for granted, carelessly, almost condescendingly—as if there had been rows and rows of them strung along the Atlantic coast.

Yet the Cranch house was really something to brag about. Architects and photographers had come in pursuit of it long

before the diffused quaintness of Harpledon made it the prey
of the magazine illustrator. The Cranch house was not quaint;
it owed little to the happy irregularities of later additions, and
needed no such help. Foursquare and stern, built of a dark
mountain granite (though all the other old houses in the
place were of brick or wood), it stood at the far end of the
green, where the elms were densest and the village street
faded away between blueberry pastures and oakwoods. A
door with a white classical portico was the only eighteenth
century addition. The house kept untouched its heavy slate
roof, its low windows, its sober cornice and plain interior panelling—even the old box garden at the back, and the pagoda-
roofed summer house, could not have been much later than
the house. I have said that the latter owed little to later additions; yet some people thought the wing on the garden side
was of more recent construction. If it was, its architect had
respected the dimensions and detail of the original house,
simply giving the wing one less story, and covering it with a
lower-pitched roof. The learned thought that the kitchen and
offices, and perhaps the slaves' quarters, had originally been in
this wing; they based their argument on the fact of there being no windows, but only blind arches, on the side toward the
garden, Waldo Cranch said he didn't know; he had found the
wing just as it was now, with a big empty room on the ground
floor, that he used for storing things, and a few low-studded
bedchambers above. The house was so big that he didn't need
any of these rooms, and had never bothered about them.
Once, I remember, I thought him a little short with a fashionable Boston architect who had insisted on Mrs. Durant's
bringing him to see the house, and who wanted to examine
the windows on the farther, the invisible, side of the wing.

"Certainly," Cranch had agreed. "But you see those windows look on the kitchen-court and the drying-ground. My
old house-keeper and the faithful retainers generally sit there
in the afternoons in hot weather, when their work is done,
and they've been with me so long that I respect their habits.
At some other hour, if you'll come again—. You're going
back to Boston tomorrow? So sorry! Yes, of course, you can
photograph the front as much as you like. It's used to it."
And he showed out Mrs. Durant and her protégé.

When he came back a frown still lingered on his handsome brows. "I'm getting sick of having this poor old house lionized. No one bothered about it or me when I first came back to live here," he said. But a moment later he added, in his usual kindly tone: "After all, I suppose I ought to be pleased."

If anyone could have soothed his annoyance, and even made it appear unreasonable, it was Mrs. Durant. The fact that it was to her he had betrayed his impatience struck us all, and caused me to remark, for the first time, that she was the only person at Harpledon who was not afraid of him. Yes; we all were, though he came and went among us with such a show of good-fellowship that it took this trifling incident to remind me of his real aloofness. Not one of us but would have felt a slight chill at his tone to the Boston architect; but then I doubt if any of us but Mrs. Durant would have dared to bring a stranger to the house.

Mrs. Durant was a widow who combined gray hair with a still-youthful face at a time when this happy union was less generally fashionable than now. She had come to Harpledon among the earliest summer colonists, and had soon struck up a friendship with Waldo Cranch. At first Harpledon was sure they would marry; then it became sure they wouldn't; for a number of years now it had wondered why they hadn't. These conjectures, of which the two themselves could hardly have been unaware, did not seem to trouble the even tenor of their friendship. They continued to meet as often as before, and Mrs. Durant continued to be the channel for transmitting any request or inquiry that the rest of us hesitated to put to Cranch. "We know he won't refuse you," I once said to her; and I recall the half-lift of her dark brows above a pinched little smile. "Perhaps," I thought, "he *has* refused her—once." If so, she had taken her failure gallantly, and Cranch appeared to find an undiminished pleasure in her company. Indeed, as the years went on their friendship grew closer; one would have said he was dependent on her if one could have pictured Cranch as dependent on anybody. But whenever I tried to do this I was driven back to the fundamental fact of his isolation.

"He could get on well enough without any of us," I thought to myself, wondering if this remoteness were inherited from the homesick Spanish ancestress. Yet I have seldom known a more superficially sociable man than Cranch. He had many talents, none of which perhaps went as far as he had once confidently hoped; but at least he used them as links with his kind instead of letting them seclude him in their jealous hold. He was always eager to show his sketches, to read aloud his occasional articles in the lesser literary reviews, and above all to play his new compositions to the musically-minded among us; or rather, since "eager" is hardly the term to apply to his calm balanced manner, I should say that he was affably ready to show off his accomplishments. But then he may have regarded doing so as one of the social obligations: I had felt from the first that, whatever Cranch did, he was always living up to some self-imposed and complicated standard. Even his way of taking off his hat struck me as the result of more thought than most people give to the act; his very absence of flourish lent it an odd importance.

III

It was the year of Harpledon's first "jumble sale" that all these odds and ends of observation first began to connect themselves in my mind.

Harpledon had decided that it ought to have a village hospital and dispensary, and Cranch was among the first to promise a subscription and to join the committee. A meeting was called at Mrs. Durant's and after much deliberation it was decided to hold a village fair and jumble sale in somebody's grounds; but whose? We all hoped Cranch would lend his garden; but no one dared to ask him. We sounded each other cautiously, before he arrived, and each tried to shift the enterprise to his neighbour; till at last Homer Davids, our chief celebrity as a painter, and one of the shrewdest heads in the community, said drily: "Oh, Cranch wouldn't care about it."

"How do you know he wouldn't?" some one queried.

"Just as you all do; if not, why is it that you all want some one else to ask him?"

Mrs. Durant hesitated. "I'm sure—" she began.

"Oh, well, all right, then! *You* ask him," rejoined Davids cheerfully.

"I can't always be the one—"

I saw her embarrassment, and volunteered: "If you think there's enough shade in *my* garden. . ."

By the way their faces lit up I saw the relief it was to them all not to have to tackle Cranch. Yet why, having a garden he was proud of, need he have been displeased at the request?

"Men don't like the bother," said one of our married ladies; which occasioned the proper outburst of praise for my unselfishness, and the observation that Cranch's maids, who had all been for years in his service, were probably set in their ways, and wouldn't care for the confusion and extra work. "Yes, old Catherine especially; she guards the place like a dragon," one of the ladies remarked; and at that moment Cranch appeared. Having been told what had been settled he joined with the others in complimenting me; and we began to plan for the jumble sale.

The men needed enlightenment on this point, I as much as the rest, but the prime mover immediately explained: "Oh, you just send any old rubbish you've got in the house."

We all welcomed this novel way of clearing out our cupboards, except Cranch who, after a moment, and with a whimsical wrinkling of his brows, said: "But I haven't got any old rubbish."

"Oh, well, children's cast-off toys for instance," a newcomer threw out at random.

There was a general smile, to which Cranch responded with one of his rare expressive gestures, as who should say: "*Toys*—in my house? But whose?"

I laughed, and one of the ladies, remembering our old joke, cried out: "Why, but the hobby-horse!"

Cranch's face became a well-bred blank. Long-suffering courtesy was the note of the voice in which he echoed: "Hobby-horse—?"

"Don't you remember?" It was Mrs. Durant who prompted him. "Our old joke? The wonderful black-and-white hobby-horse that Miss Lucilla Selwick said she saw you driving home with when you first arrived here? It had a real mane." Her colour rose a little as she spoke.

There was a moment's pause, while Cranch's brow remained puzzled; then a smile slowly cleared his face. "Of course!" he said. "I'd forgotten. Well, I feel now that I *was* young enough for toys thirty years ago; but I didn't feel so then. And we should have to apply to Miss Selwick to know what became of that hobby-horse. Meanwhile," he added, putting his hand in his pocket, "here's a small offering to supply some new ones for the fair."

The offering was not small: Cranch always gave liberally, yet always produced the impression of giving indifferently. Well, one couldn't have it both ways; some of our most gushing givers were the least lavish. The committee was delighted. . .

"It was queer," I said afterward to Mrs. Durant. "Why did the hobby-horse joke annoy Cranch? He used to like it."

She smiled. "He may think it's lasted long enough. Harpledon jokes *do* last, you know."

Yes; perhaps they did, though I had never thought of it before.

"There's one thing that puzzles me," I went on; "I never know beforehand what is going to annoy him."

She pondered. "I'll tell you, then," she said suddenly. "It has annoyed him that no one thought of asking him to give one of his water-colours to the sale."

"Didn't we?"

"No. Homer Davids was asked, and that made it . . . rather more marked. . ."

"Oh, of course! I suppose we all forgot—"

She looked away. "Well," she said, "I don't suppose he likes to be forgotten."

"You mean: to have his accomplishments forgotten?"

"Isn't that a little condescending? I should say, his *gifts*," she corrected a trifle sharply. Sharpness was so unusual in her that she may have seen my surprise, for she added, in her usual tone: "After all, I suppose he's our most brilliant man, isn't he?" She smiled a little, as if to take the sting from my doing so.

"Of course he is," I rejoined. "But all the more reason— how could a man of his kind resent such a trifling oversight? I'll write at once—"

"Oh, *don't*!" she cut me short, almost pleadingly.

Mrs. Durant's word was law: Cranch was not asked for a water-colour. Homer Davids's, I may add, sold for two thousand dollars, and paid for a heating-system for our hospital. A Boston millionaire came down on purpose to buy the picture. It was a great day for Harpledon.

IV

About a week after the fair I went one afternoon to call on Mrs. Durant, and found Cranch just leaving. His greeting, as he hurried by, was curt and almost hostile, and his handsome countenance so disturbed and pale that I hardly recognized him. I was sure there could be nothing personal in his manner; we had always been on good terms, and, next to Mrs. Durant, I suppose I was his nearest friend at Harpledon—if ever one could be said to get near Waldo Cranch! After he had passed me I stood hesitating at Mrs. Durant's open door—front doors at Harpledon were always open in those friendly days, except, by the way, Cranch's own, which the stern Catherine kept chained and bolted. Since meeting me could not have been the cause of his anger, it might have been excited by something which had passed between Mrs. Durant and himself; and if that were so, my call was probably inopportune. I decided not to go in, and was turning away when I heard hurried steps, and Mrs. Durant's voice. "Waldo!" she said.

I suppose I had always assumed that she called him so; yet the familiar appellation startled me, and made me feel more than ever in the way. None of us had ever given Cranch his Christian name.

Mrs. Durant checked her steps, perceiving that the back in the doorway was not Cranch's but mine. "Oh, do come in," she murmured, with an attempt at ease.

In the little drawing-room I turned and looked at her. She, too, was visibly disturbed; not angry, as he had been, but showing, on her white face and reddened lids, the pained reflection of his anger. Was it against her, then, that he had manifested it? Probably she guessed my thought, or felt her appearance needed to be explained, for she added quickly: "Mr. Cranch has just gone. Did he speak to you?"

"No. He seemed in a great hurry."

"Yes. . . I wanted to beg him to come back . . . to try to quiet him. . ."

She saw my bewilderment, and picked up a copy of an illustrated magazine which had been tossed on the sofa. "It's
that—" she said.

The pages fell apart at an article entitled: "Colonial
Harpledon," the greater part of which was taken up by a series of clever sketches signed by the Boston architect whom
she had brought to Cranch's a few months earlier.

Of the six or seven drawings, four were devoted to the
Cranch house. One represented the façade and its pillared
gates, a second the garden front with the windowless side of
the wing, the third a corner of the box garden surrounding
the Chinese summer-house; while the fourth, a full-page
drawing, was entitled: "The back of the slaves' quarters and
service-court: quaint window-grouping."

On that picture the magazine had opened; it was evidently
the one which had been the subject of discussion between my
hostess and her visitor.

"You see . . . you see . . ." she cried.

"This picture? Well, what of it? I suppose it's the far side of
the wing—the side we've never any of us seen."

"Yes; that's just it. He's horribly upset. . ."

"Upset about what? I heard him tell the architect he could
come back some other day and see the wing . . . some day
when the maids were not sitting in the court; wasn't that it?"

She shook her head tragically. "He didn't mean it.
Couldn't you tell by the sound of his voice that he didn't?"

Her tragedy airs were beginning to irritate me. "I don't
know that I pay as much attention as all that to the sound of
his voice."

She coloured, and choked back her tears. "I know him so
well; I'm always sorry to see him lose his self-control. And
then he considers me responsible."

"You?"

"It was I who took the wretched man there. And of course
it was an indiscretion to do that drawing; he was never really
authorized to come back. In fact, Mr. Cranch gave orders to
Catherine and all the other servants not to let him in if he did."

"Well—?"

"One of the maids seems to have disobeyed the order; Mr.
Cranch imagines she was bribed. He has been staying in

Boston, and this morning, on the way back, he saw this magazine at the book-stall at the station. He was so horrified that he
brought it to me. He came straight from the train without going home, so he doesn't yet know how the thing happened."

"It doesn't take much to horrify him," I said, again unable
to restrain a faint sneer. "What's the harm in the man's having made that sketch?"

"Harm?" She looked surprised at my lack of insight. "No
actual harm, I suppose; but it was very impertinent; and Mr.
Cranch resents such liberties intensely. He's so punctilious."

"Well, we Americans are not punctilious, and being one
himself, he ought to know it by this time."

She pondered again. "It's his Spanish blood, I suppose . . .
he's frightfully proud." As if this were a misfortune, she
added: "I'm very sorry for him."

"So am I, if such trifles upset him."

Her brows lightened. "Ah, that's what I tell him—such
things *are* trifles, aren't they? As I said just now: 'Your life's
been too fortunate, too prosperous. That's why you're so easily put out.' "

"And what did he answer?"

"Oh, it only made him angrier. He said: 'I never expected
that from *you*'—that was when he rushed out of the house."
Her tears flowed over, and seeing her so genuinely perturbed
I restrained my impatience, and took leave after a few words
of sympathy.

Never had Harpledon seemed to me more like a tea-cup
than with that silly tempest convulsing it. That there should
be grown-up men who could lose their self-command over
such rubbish, and women to tremble and weep with them!
For a moment I felt the instinctive irritation of normal man at
such foolishness; yet before I reached my own door I was as
mysteriously perturbed as Mrs. Durant.

The truth was, I had never thought of Cranch as likely to
lose his balance over trifles. He had never struck me as un-
manly; his quiet manner, his even temper, showed a sound
sense of the relative importance of things. How then could so
petty an annoyance have thrown him into such disorder?

I stopped short on my threshold, remembering his face as
he brushed past me. "Something *is* wrong; really wrong," I

thought. But what? Could it be jealousy of Mrs. Durant and the Boston architect? The idea would not bear a moment's consideration, for I remembered *her* face too. "Oh, well, if it's his silly punctilio," I grumbled, trying to reassure myself, and remaining, after all, as much perplexed as before.

All the next day it poured, and I sat at home among my books. It must have been after ten in the evening when I was startled by a ring. The maids had gone to bed, and I went to the door, and opened it to Mrs. Durant. Surprised at the lateness of her visit, I drew her in out of the storm. She had flung a cloak over her light dress, and the lace scarf on her head dripped with rain. Our houses were only a few hundred yards apart, and she had brought no umbrella, nor even exchanged her evening slippers for heavier shoes.

I took her wet cloak and scarf and led her into the library. She stood trembling and staring at me, her face like a marble mask in which the lips were too rigid for speech; then she laid a sheet of note-paper on the table between us. On it was written, in Waldo Cranch's beautiful hand: "My dear friend, I am going away on a journey. You will hear from me," with his initials beneath. Nothing more. The letter bore no date.

I looked at her, waiting for an explanation. None came. The first word she said was: "Will you come with me—now, at once?"

"Come with you—where?"

"To his house—before he leaves. I've only just got the letter, and I daren't go alone. . ."

"Go to Cranch's house? But I . . . at this hour. . . What is it you are afraid of?" I broke out, suddenly looking into her eyes.

She gave me back my look, and her rigid face melted. "I don't know—any more than you do! That's why I'm afraid."

"But I know nothing. What on earth has happened since I saw you yesterday?"

"Nothing till I got this letter."

"You haven't seen him?"

"Not since you saw him leave my house yesterday."

"Or had any message—any news of him?"

"Absolutely nothing. I've just sat and remembered his face."

My perplexity grew. "But surely you can't imagine. . . If you're as frightened as that you must have some other reason for it," I insisted.

She shook her head wearily. "It's the having none that frightens me. Oh, do come!"

"You think his leaving in this way means that he's in some kind of trouble?"

"In dreadful trouble."

"And you don't know why?"

"No more than you do!" she repeated.

I pondered, trying to avoid her entreating eyes. "But at this hour—come, do consider! I don't know Cranch so awfully well. How will he take it? You say he made a scene yesterday about that silly business of the architect's going to his house without leave. . ."

"That's just it. I feel as if his going away might be connected with that."

"But then he's mad!" I exclaimed.

"No; not mad. Only—desperate."

I stood irresolute. It was evident that I had to do with a woman whose nerves were in fiddle-strings. What had reduced them to that state I could not conjecture, unless, indeed, she were keeping back the vital part of her confession. But that, queerly enough, was not what I suspected. For some reason I felt her to be as much in the dark over the whole business as I was; and that added to the strangeness of my dilemma.

"Do you know in the least what you're going for?" I asked at length.

"No, no, no—but come!"

"If he's there, he'll kick us out, most likely; kick *me* out, at any rate."

She did not answer; I saw that in her anguish she was past speaking. "Wait till I get my coat," I said.

She took my arm, and side by side we hurried in the rain through the shuttered village. As we passed the Selwick house I saw a light burning in old Miss Selwick's bedroom window. It was on the tip of my tongue to say: "Hadn't we better stop and ask Aunt Lucilla what's wrong? She knows more about Cranch than any of us!"

Then I remembered Cranch's expression the last time Aunt Lucilla's legend of the hobby-horse had been mentioned before him—the day we were planning the jumble sale—and a sudden shiver checked my pleasantry. "He looked then as he did when he passed me in the doorway yesterday," I thought; and I had a vision of my ancient relative, sitting there propped up in her bed and looking quietly into the unknown while all the village slept. Was she aware, I wondered, that we were passing under her window at that moment, and did she know what would await us when we reached our destination?

V

Mrs. Durant, in her thin slippers, splashed on beside me through the mud.

"Oh," she exclaimed, stopping short with a gasp, "look at the lights!"

We had crossed the green, and were groping our way under the dense elm-shadows, and there before us stood the Cranch house, all its windows illuminated. It was the only house in the village except Miss Selwick's that was not darkened and shuttered.

"Well, he can't be gone; he's giving a party, you see," I said derisively.

My companion made no answer. She only pulled me forward, and yielding once more I pushed open the tall entrance gates. In the brick path I paused. "Do you still want to go in?" I asked.

"More than ever!" She kept her tight clutch on my arm, and I walked up the path at her side and rang the bell.

The sound went on jangling for a long time through the stillness; but no one came to the door. At length Mrs. Durant laid an impatient hand on the door-panel. "But it's open!" she exclaimed.

It was probably the first time since Waldo Cranch had come back to live in the house that unbidden visitors had been free to enter it. We looked at each other in surprise and I followed Mrs. Durant into the lamplit hall. It was empty.

With a common accord we stood for a moment listening; but not a sound came to us, though the doors of library and drawing-room stood open, and there were lighted lamps in both rooms.

"It's queer," I said, "all these lights, and no one about."

My companion had walked impulsively into the drawing-room and stood looking about at its familiar furniture. From the panelled wall, distorted by the wavering lamp-light, the old Spanish ancestress glared down duskily at us out of the shadows. Mrs. Durant had stopped short—a sound of voices, agitated, discordant, a strange man's voice among them, came to us from across the hall. Silently we retraced our steps, opened the dining-room door, and went in. But here also we found emptiness; the talking came from beyond, came, as we now perceived, from the wing which none of us had ever entered. Again we hesitated and looked at each other. Then "Come!" said Mrs. Durant in a resolute tone; and again I followed her.

She led the way into a large pantry, airy, orderly, well-stocked with china and glass. That too was empty; and two doors opened from it. Mrs. Durant passed through the one on the right, and we found ourselves, not, as I had expected, in the kitchen, but in a kind of vague unfurnished anteroom. The quarrelling voices had meanwhile died out; we seemed once more to have the mysterious place to ourselves. Suddenly, beyond another closed door, we heard a shrill crowing laugh. Mrs. Durant dashed at this last door and it let us into a large high-studded room. We paused and looked about us. Evidently we were in what Cranch had always described as the lumber-room on the ground floor of the wing. But there was no lumber in it now. It was scrupulously neat, and fitted up like a big and rather bare nursery; and in the middle of the floor, on a square of drugget, stood a great rearing black and white animal: my Aunt Lucilla's hobby-horse. . .

I gasped at the sight; but in spite of its strangeness it did not detain me long, for at the farther end of the room, before a fire protected by a tall nursery fender, I had seen something stranger still. Two little boys in old-fashioned round jackets and knickerbockers knelt by the hearth, absorbed in the building of a house of blocks. Mrs. Durant saw them at the same moment. She caught my arm as if she were about to fall, and uttered a faint cry.

The sound, low as it was, produced a terrifying effect on the two children. Both of them dropped their blocks, turned around as if to dart at us, and then stopped short, holding each other by the hand, and staring and trembling as if we had been ghosts.

At the opposite end of the room, we stood staring and trembling also; for it was they who were the ghosts to our terrified eyes. It must have been Mrs. Durant who spoke first.

"Oh . . . the poor things . . ." she said in a low choking voice.

The little boys stood there, motionless and far off, among the ruins of their house of blocks. But, as my eyes grew used to the faint light—there was only one lamp in the big room—and as my shaken nerves adjusted themselves to the strangeness of the scene, I perceived the meaning of Mrs. Durant's cry.

The children before us were not children; they were two tiny withered men, with frowning foreheads under their baby curls, and heavy-shouldered middle-aged bodies. The sight was horrible, and rendered more so by the sameness of their size and by their old-fashioned childish dress. I recoiled; but Mrs. Durant had let my arm go, and was moving softly forward. Her own arms out-stretched, she advanced toward the two strange beings. "You poor poor things, you," she repeated, the tears running down her face.

I thought her tender tone must have drawn the little creatures; but as she advanced they continued to stand motionless, and then suddenly—each with the same small falsetto scream—turned and dashed toward the door. As they reached it, old Catherine appeared and held out her arms to them.

"Oh, my God—how dare you, madam? My young gentlemen!" she cried.

They hid their dreadful little faces in the folds of her skirt, and kneeling down she put her arms about them and received them on her bosom. Then, slowly, she lifted up her head and looked at us.

I had always, like the rest of Harpledon, thought of Catherine as a morose old Englishwoman, civil enough in her cold way, but yet forbidding. Now it seemed to me that her worn brown face, in its harsh folds of gray hair, was the saddest I had ever looked upon.

"How could you, madam; oh, how could you? Haven't we got enough else to bear?" she asked, speaking low above the cowering heads on her breast. Her eyes were on Mrs. Durant.

The latter, white and trembling, gave back the look. "Enough else? Is there *more*, then?"

"There's everything—." The old servant got to her feet, keeping her two charges by the hand. She put her finger to her lips, and stooped again to the dwarfs. "Master Waldo, Master Donald, you'll come away now with your old Catherine. No one's going to harm us, my dears; you'll just go upstairs and let Janey Sampson put you to bed, for it's very late; and presently Catherine'll come up and hear your prayers like every night." She moved to the door; but one of the dwarfs hung back, his forehead puckering, his eyes still fixed on Mrs. Durant in indescribable horror.

"Good Dobbin," cried he abruptly, in a piercing pipe.

"No, dear, no; the lady won't touch good Dobbin," said Catherine. "It's the young gentlemen's great pet," she added, glancing at the Roman steed in the middle of the floor. She led the changelings away, and a moment later returned. Her face was ashen-white under its swarthiness, and she stood looking at us like a figure of doom.

"And now, perhaps," she said, "you'll be good enough to go away too."

"Go away?" Mrs. Durant, instead, came closer to her. "How can I—when I've just had this from your master?" She held out the letter she had brought to my house.

Catherine glanced coldly at the page and returned it to her.

"He says he's going on a journey. Well, he's been, madam; been and come back," she said.

"Come back? Already? He's in the house, then? Oh, do let me—" Mrs. Durant dropped back before the old woman's frozen gaze.

"He's lying overhead, dead on his bed, madam—just as they carried him up from the beach. Do you suppose, else, you'd have ever got in here and seen the young gentlemen? He rushed out and died sooner than have seen them, the poor lambs; him that was their father, madam. And here you and this gentleman come thrusting yourselves in. . ."

I thought Mrs. Durant would reel under the shock; but she stood quiet, very quiet—it was almost as if the blow had mysteriously strengthened her.

"He's dead? He's killed himself?" She looked slowly about the trivial tragic room. "Oh, now I understand," she said.

Old Catherine faced her with grim lips. "It's a pity you didn't understand sooner, then; you and the others, whoever they was, forever poking and prying; till at last that miserable girl brought in the police on us—"

"The police?"

"They was here, madam, in this house, not an hour ago, frightening my young gentlemen out of their senses. When word came that my master had been found on the beach they went down there to bring him back. Now they've gone to Hingham to report his death to the coroner. But there's one of them in the kitchen, mounting guard. Over what, I wonder? As if my young gentlemen could run away! Where in God's pity would they go? Wherever it is, I'll go with them; I'll never leave them. . . And here we were at peace for thirty years, till you brought that man to draw the pictures of the house. . . ."

For the first time Mrs. Durant's strength seemed to fail her; her body drooped, and she leaned her weight against the door. She and the housekeeper stood confronted, two stricken old women staring at each other; then Mrs. Durant's agony broke from her. "Don't say I did it—don't say that!"

But the other was relentless. As she faced us, her arms outstretched, she seemed still to be defending her two charges. "What else would you have me say, madam? You brought that man here, didn't you? And he was determined to see the other side of the wing, and my poor master was determined he shouldn't." She turned to me for the first time. "It was plain enough to you, sir, wasn't it? To me it was, just coming and going with the tea-things. And the minute your backs was turned, Mr. Cranch rang, and gave me the order: 'That man's never to set foot here again, you understand.' And I went out and told the other three; the cook, and Janey, and Hannah Oast, the parlour-maid. I was as sure of the cook and Janey as I was of myself; but Hannah was new, she hadn't been with us not above a year, and though I knew all about her, and had made sure before she came that she was a decent close-mouthed girl, and one that would respect our . . . our misfortune . . . yet I couldn't feel as safe about her as the others, and of her temper I wasn't sure from the first. I told Mr. Cranch so, often enough; I said: 'Remember, now, sir, not to put her pride up, won't you?' For she was jealous, and angry, I think, at never being allowed to see the young gentlemen, yet knowing they were there, as she *had* to know. But their father would never have any but me and Janey Sampson about them.

"Well—and then, in he came yesterday with those accursèd pictures. And however had the man got in? And where was Hannah? And it must have been her doing . . . and swearing and cursing at her . . . and me crying to him and saying: 'For God's sake, sir, let be, let be . . . don't stir the matter up . . . just let me talk to her. . .' And I went in to my little boys, to see about their supper; and before I was back, I heard a trunk bumping down the stairs, and the gardener's lad outside with a wheel-barrow, and Hannah Oast walking away out of the gate like a ramrod. 'Oh, sir, what have you done? Let me go after her!' I begged and besought him; but my master, very pale, but as calm as possible, held me back by the arm, and said: 'Don't you worry, Catherine. It passed off very quietly. We'll have no trouble from her.' 'No trouble, sir, from Hannah Oast? Oh, for pity's sake, call her back and let me smooth it over, sir!' But the girl was gone, and he wouldn't leave go of my arm nor yet listen to me, but stood there like a marble stone and saw her drive away, and wouldn't stop her. 'I'd die first, Catherine,' he said, his kind face all changed to me, and looking like that old Spanish she-devil on the parlour wall, that brought the curse on us. . . And this morning the police came. The gardener got wind of it, and let us know they was on the way; and my master sat and wrote a long time in his room, and then walked out, looking very quiet, and saying to me he was going to the post office, and would be back before they got here. And the next we knew of him was when they carried him up to his bed just now. . . And perhaps we'd best give thanks that he's at rest in it. But, oh, my young gentlemen . . . my young gentlemen!"

VI

I never saw the "young gentlemen" again. I suppose most men are cowards about calamities of that sort, the irremediable kind that have to be faced anew every morning. It takes a woman to shoulder such a lasting tragedy, and hug it to her . . . as I had seen Catherine doing; as I saw Mrs. Durant yearning to do. . .

It was about that very matter that I interviewed the old housekeeper the day after the funeral. Among the papers which the police found on poor Cranch's desk was a letter addressed to me. Like his message to Mrs. Durant it was of the briefest. "I have appointed no one to care for my sons; I expected to outlive them. Their mother would have wished Catherine to stay with them. Will you try to settle all this mercifully? There is plenty of money, but my brain won't work. Good-bye."

It was a matter, first of all, for the law; but before we entered on that phase I wanted to have a talk with old Catherine. She came to me, very decent in her new black; I hadn't the heart to go to that dreadful house again, and I think perhaps it was easier for her to speak out under another roof. At any rate, I soon saw that, after all the years of silence, speech was a relief; as it might have been to him too, poor fellow, if only he had dared! But he couldn't; there was that pride of his, his "Spanish pride" as she called it. . .

"Not but what he would have hated me to say so, sir; for the Spanish blood in him, and all that went with it, was what he most abominated. . . But there it was, closer to him than his marrow. . . Oh, what that old woman done to us! He told me why, once, long ago—it was about the time when he began to understand that our little boys were never going to grow up like other young gentlemen. 'It's her doing, the devil,' he said to me; and then he told me how she'd been a great Spanish heiress, a rich merchant's daughter, and had been promised, in that foreign way they have, to a young nobleman who'd never set eyes on her; and when the bridegroom came to the city where she lived, and saw her sitting in her father's box across the theatre, he turned about and mounted his horse and rode off the same night; and never a word came from him—the shame of it! It nigh killed her, I believe, and she swore then and there she'd marry a foreigner and leave Spain; and that was how she took up with young Mr. Cranch that was in her father's bank; and the old gentleman put a big sum into the Cranch shipping business, and packed off the young couple to Harpledon. . . But the poor misbuilt thing, it seems, couldn't ever rightly get over the hurt to her pride, nor get used to the cold climate, and the snow and the strange faces; she would go about pining for the orange-flowers and the sunshine; and though she brought her husband a son, I do believe she hated him, and was glad to die and get out of Harpledon. . . That was my Mr. Cranch's story. . .

"Well, sir, he despised his great-grandfather more than he hated the Spanish woman. 'Marry that twisted stick for her money, and put her poisoned blood in us!' He used to put it that way, sir, in his bad moments. And when he was twenty-one, and travelling abroad, he met the young English lady I was maid to, the loveliest soundest young creature you ever set eyes on. They loved and married, and the next year—oh, the pity—the next year she brought him our young gentlemen . . . twins, they were . . . When she died, a few weeks after, he was desperate . . . more desperate than I've ever seen him till the other day. But as the years passed, and he began to understand about our little boys—well, then he was thankful she was gone. And that thankfulness was the bitterest part of his grief.

"It was when they was about nine or ten that *he* first saw it; though I'd been certain long before that. We were living in Italy then. And one day—oh, what a day, sir!—he got a letter, Mr. Cranch did, from a circus-man who'd heard somehow of our poor little children. . . Oh, sir! . . . Then it was that he decided to leave Europe, and come back to Harpledon to live. It was a lonely lost place at that time; and there was all the big wing for our little gentlemen. We were happy in the old house, in our way; but it was a solitary life for so young a man as Mr. Cranch was then, and when the summer folk began to settle here I was glad of it, and I said to him: 'You go out, sir, now, and make friends, and invite your friends here. I'll see to it that our secret is kept.' And so I did, sir, so I did . . . and he always trusted me. He needed life and company himself; but he would never separate himself from the little boys. He was so proud—and yet so soft-hearted! And where could he have put the little things? They never grew past their toys—there's the worst of it. Heaps and heaps of them he brought home to them, year after year. Pets he tried too . . . but animals were afraid of them—just as I expect you were, sir, when you saw them," she added suddenly, "but with no reason; there were never gentler beings. Little Waldo especially—it's as if they were trying to make up for being a burden. . . Oh, for pity's sake, let them stay on in their father's house, and me with them, won't you, sir?"

As she wished it, so it was. The legal side of the matter did not take long to settle, for the Cranches were almost extinct; there were only some distant cousins, long since gone from Harpledon. Old Catherine was suffered to remain on with her charges in the Cranch house, and one of the guardians appointed by the courts was Mrs. Durant.

Would you have believed it? She wanted it—the horror, the responsibility and all. After that she lived all the year round at Harpledon; I believe she saw Cranch's sons every day. I never went back there; but she used sometimes to come up and see me in Boston. The first time she appeared—it must have been about a year after the events I have related—I scarcely knew her when she walked into my library. She was an old bent woman; her white hair now seemed an attribute of age, not a form of coquetry. After that, each time I saw her she seemed older and more bowed. But she told me once she was not unhappy—"not as unhappy as I used to be," she added, qualifying the phrase.

On the same occasion—it was only a few months ago—she also told me that one of the twins was ill. She did not think he would last long, she said; and old Catherine did not think so either. "It's little Waldo; he was the one who felt his father's death the most; the dark one; I really think he understands. And when he goes, Donald won't last long either." Her eyes filled with tears. "Presently I shall be alone again," she added.

I asked her then how old they were; and she thought for a moment, murmuring the years over slowly under her breath.

"Only forty-one," she said at length—as if she had said "Only four."

Women are strange. I am their other guardian; and I have never yet had the courage to go down to Harpledon and see them.

Bewitched

T HE SNOW was still falling thickly when Orrin Bosworth, who farmed the land south of Lonetop, drove up in his cutter to Saul Rutledge's gate. He was surprised to see two other cutters ahead of him. From them descended two muffled figures. Bosworth, with increasing surprise, recognized Deacon Hibben, from North Ashmore, and Sylvester Brand, the widower, from the old Bearcliff farm on the way to Lonetop.

It was not often that anybody in Hemlock County entered Saul Rutledge's gate; least of all in the dead of winter, and summoned (as Bosworth, at any rate, had been) by Mrs. Rutledge, who passed, even in that unsocial region, for a woman of cold manners and solitary character. The situation was enough to excite the curiosity of a less imaginative man than Orrin Bosworth.

As he drove in between the broken-down white gate-posts topped by fluted urns the two men ahead of him were leading their horses to the adjoining shed. Bosworth followed, and hitched his horse to a post. Then the three tossed off the snow from their shoulders, clapped their numb hands together, and greeted each other.

"Hallo, Deacon."

"Well, well, Orrin—." They shook hands.

" 'Day, Bosworth," said Sylvester Brand, with a brief nod. He seldom put any cordiality into his manner, and on this occasion he was still busy about his horse's bridle and blanket.

Orrin Bosworth, the youngest and most communicative of the three, turned back to Deacon Hibben, whose long face, queerly blotched and mouldy-looking, with blinking peering eyes, was yet less forbidding than Brand's heavily-hewn countenance.

"Queer, our all meeting here this way. Mrs. Rutledge sent me a message to come," Bosworth volunteered.

The Deacon nodded. "I got a word from her too—Andy Pond come with it yesterday noon. I hope there's no trouble here—"

347

He glanced through the thickening fall of snow at the desolate front of the Rutledge house, the more melancholy in its present neglected state because, like the gate-posts, it kept traces of former elegance. Bosworth had often wondered how such a house had come to be built in that lonely stretch between North Ashmore and Cold Corners. People said there had once been other houses like it, forming a little township called Ashmore, a sort of mountain colony created by the caprice of an English Royalist officer, one Colonel Ashmore, who had been murdered by the Indians, with all his family, long before the Revolution. This tale was confirmed by the fact that the ruined cellars of several smaller houses were still to be discovered under the wild growth of the adjoining slopes, and that the Communion plate of the moribund Episcopal church of Cold Corners was engraved with the name of Colonel Ashmore, who had given it to the church of Ashmore in the year 1723. Of the church itself no traces remained. Doubtless it had been a modest wooden edifice, built on piles, and the conflagration which had burnt the other houses to the ground's edge had reduced it utterly to ashes. The whole place, even in summer, wore a mournful solitary air, and people wondered why Saul Rutledge's father had gone there to settle.

"I never knew a place," Deacon Hibben said, "as seemed as far away from humanity. And yet it ain't so in miles."

"Miles ain't the only distance," Orrin Bosworth answered; and the two men, followed by Sylvester Brand, walked across the drive to the front door. People in Hemlock County did not usually come and go by their front doors, but all three men seemed to feel that, on an occasion which appeared to be so exceptional, the usual and more familiar approach by the kitchen would not be suitable.

They had judged rightly; the Deacon had hardly lifted the knocker when the door opened and Mrs. Rutledge stood before them.

"Walk right in," she said in her usual dead-level tone; and Bosworth, as he followed the others, thought to himself: "Whatever's happened, she's not going to let it show in her face."

It was doubtful, indeed, if anything unwonted could be made to show in Prudence Rutledge's face, so limited was its scope, so fixed were its features. She was dressed for the occasion in a black calico with white spots, a collar of crochet-lace fastened by a gold brooch, and a gray woollen shawl, crossed under her arms and tied at the back. In her small narrow head the only marked prominence was that of the brow projecting roundly over pale spectacled eyes. Her dark hair, parted above this prominence, passed tight and flat over the tips of her ears into a small braided coil at the nape; and her contracted head looked still narrower from being perched on a long hollow neck with cord-like throat-muscles. Her eyes were of a pale cold gray, her complexion was an even white. Her age might have been anywhere from thirty-five to sixty.

The room into which she led the three men had probably been the dining-room of the Ashmore house. It was now used as a front parlour, and a black stove planted on a sheet of zinc stuck out from the delicately fluted panels of an old wooden mantel. A newly-lit fire smouldered reluctantly, and the room was at once close and bitterly cold.

"Andy Pond," Mrs. Rutledge cried to some one at the back of the house, "step out and call Mr. Rutledge. You'll likely find him in the wood-shed, or round the barn somewheres." She rejoined her visitors. "Please suit yourselves to seats," she said.

The three men, with an increasing air of constraint, took the chairs she pointed out, and Mrs. Rutledge sat stiffly down upon a fourth, behind a rickety bead-work table. She glanced from one to the other of her visitors.

"I presume you folks are wondering what it is I asked you to come here for," she said in her dead-level voice. Orrin Bosworth and Deacon Hibben murmured an assent; Sylvester Brand sat silent, his eyes, under their great thicket of eyebrows, fixed on the huge boot-tip swinging before him.

"Well, I allow you didn't expect it was for a party," continued Mrs. Rutledge.

No one ventured to respond to this chill pleasantry, and she continued: "We're in trouble here, and that's the fact. And we need advice—Mr. Rutledge and myself do." She cleared her throat, and added in a lower tone, her pitilessly clear eyes looking straight before her: "There's a spell been cast over Mr. Rutledge."

The Deacon looked up sharply, an incredulous smile pinching his thin lips. "A spell?"

"That's what I said: he's bewitched."

Again the three visitors were silent; then Bosworth, more at ease or less tongue-tied than the others, asked with an attempt at humour: "Do you use the word in the strict Scripture sense, Mrs. Rutledge?"

She glanced at him before replying: "That's how *he* uses it."

The Deacon coughed and cleared his long rattling throat. "Do you care to give us more particulars before your husband joins us?"

Mrs. Rutledge looked down at her clasped hands, as if considering the question. Bosworth noticed that the inner fold of her lids was of the same uniform white as the rest of her skin, so that when she dropped them her rather prominent eyes looked like the sightless orbs of a marble statue. The impression was unpleasing, and he glanced away at the text over the mantelpiece, which read:

The Soul That Sinneth It Shall Die.

"No," she said at length, "I'll wait."

At this moment Sylvester Brand suddenly stood up and pushed back his chair. "I don't know," he said, in his rough bass voice, "as I've got any particular lights on Bible mysteries; and this happens to be the day I was to go down to Starkfield to close a deal with a man."

Mrs. Rutledge lifted one of her long thin hands. Withered and wrinkled by hard work and cold, it was nevertheless of the same leaden white as her face. "You won't be kept long," she said. "Won't you be seated?"

Farmer Brand stood irresolute, his purplish underlip twitching. "The Deacon here—such things is more in his line. . ."

"I want you should stay," said Mrs. Rutledge quietly; and Brand sat down again.

A silence fell, during which the four persons present seemed all to be listening for the sound of a step; but none was heard, and after a minute or two Mrs. Rutledge began to speak again.

"It's down by that old shack on Lamer's pond; that's where they meet," she said suddenly.

Bosworth, whose eyes were on Sylvester Brand's face, fancied he saw a sort of inner flush darken the farmer's heavy leathern skin. Deacon Hibben leaned forward, a glitter of curiosity in his eyes.

"They—*who*, Mrs. Rutledge?"

"My husband, Saul Rutledge . . . and her. . ."

Sylvester Brand again stirred in his seat. "Who do you mean by *her*?" he asked abruptly, as if roused out of some far-off musing.

Mrs. Rutledge's body did not move; she simply revolved her head on her long neck and looked at him.

"Your daughter, Sylvester Brand."

The man staggered to his feet with an explosion of inarticulate sounds. "My—my daughter? What the hell are you talking about? My daughter? It's a damned lie . . . it's . . . it's. . ."

"Your daughter *Ora*, Mr. Brand," said Mrs. Rutledge slowly.

Bosworth felt an icy chill down his spine. Instinctively he turned his eyes away from Brand, and they rested on the mildewed countenance of Deacon Hibben. Between the blotches it had become as white as Mrs. Rutledge's, and the Deacon's eyes burned in the whiteness like live embers among ashes.

Brand gave a laugh: the rusty creaking laugh of one whose springs of mirth are never moved by gaiety. "My daughter *Ora*?" he repeated.

"Yes."

"My *dead* daughter?"

"That's what he says."

"Your husband?"

"That's what Mr. Rutledge says."

Orrin Bosworth listened with a sense of suffocation; he felt as if he were wrestling with long-armed horrors in a dream. He could no longer resist letting his eyes return to Sylvester Brand's face. To his surprise it had resumed a natural imperturbable expression. Brand rose to his feet. "Is that all?" he queried contemptuously.

"All? Ain't it enough? How long is it since you folks seen Saul Rutledge, any of you?" Mrs. Rutledge flew out at them.

Bosworth, it appeared, had not seen him for nearly a year; the Deacon had only run across him once, for a minute, at the North Ashmore post office, the previous autumn, and acknowledged that he wasn't looking any too good then. Brand said nothing, but stood irresolute.

"Well, if you wait a minute you'll see with your own eyes; and he'll tell you with his own words. That's what I've got you here for—to see for yourselves what's come over him. Then you'll talk different," she added, twisting her head abruptly toward Sylvester Brand.

The Deacon raised a lean hand of interrogation.

"Does your husband know we've been sent for on this business, Mrs. Rutledge?"

Mrs. Rutledge signed assent.

"It was with his consent, then—?"

She looked coldly at her questioner. "I guess it had to be," she said. Again Bosworth felt the chill down his spine. He tried to dissipate the sensation by speaking with an affectation of energy.

"Can you tell us, Mrs. Rutledge, how this trouble you speak of shows itself . . . what makes you think . . . ?"

She looked at him for a moment; then she leaned forward across the rickety bead-work table. A thin smile of disdain narrowed her colourless lips. "I don't think—I know."

"Well—but how?"

She leaned closer, both elbows on the table, her voice dropping. "I seen 'em."

In the ashen light from the veiling of snow beyond the windows the Deacon's little screwed-up eyes seemed to give out red sparks. "Him and the dead?"

"Him and the dead."

"Saul Rutledge and—and Ora Brand?"

"That's so."

Sylvester Brand's chair fell backward with a crash. He was on his feet again, crimson and cursing. "It's a God-damned fiend-begotten lie. . ."

"Friend Brand . . . friend Brand . . ." the Deacon protested.

"Here, let me get out of this. I want to see Saul Rutledge himself, and tell him—"

"Well, here he is," said Mrs. Rutledge.

The outer door had opened; they heard the familiar stamping and shaking of a man who rids his garments of their last snowflakes before penetrating to the sacred precincts of the best parlour. Then Saul Rutledge entered.

II

As he came in he faced the light from the north window, and Bosworth's first thought was that he looked like a drowned man fished out from under the ice—"self-drowned," he added. But the snow-light plays cruel tricks with a man's colour, and even with the shape of his features; it must have been partly that, Bosworth reflected, which transformed Saul Rutledge from the straight muscular fellow he had been a year before into the haggard wretch now before them.

The Deacon sought for a word to ease the horror. "Well, now, Saul—you look's if you'd ought to set right up to the stove. Had a touch of ague, maybe?"

The feeble attempt was unavailing. Rutledge neither moved nor answered. He stood among them silent, incommunicable, like one risen from the dead.

Brand grasped him roughly by the shoulder. "See here, Saul Rutledge, what's this dirty lie your wife tells us you've been putting about?"

Still Rutledge did not move. "It's no lie," he said.

Brand's hand dropped from his shoulder. In spite of the man's rough bullying power he seemed to be undefinably awed by Rutledge's look and tone.

"No lie? You've gone plumb crazy, then, have you?"

Mrs. Rutledge spoke. "My husband's not lying, nor he ain't gone crazy. Don't I tell you I seen 'em?"

Brand laughed again. "Him and the dead?"

"Yes."

"Down by the Lamer pond, you say?"

"Yes."

"And when was that, if I might ask?"

"Day before yesterday."

A silence fell on the strangely assembled group. The Deacon at length broke it to say to Mr. Brand: "Brand, in my opinion we've got to see this thing through."

Brand stood for a moment in speechless contemplation: there was something animal and primitive about him, Bosworth thought, as he hung thus, lowering and dumb, a little foam beading the corners of that heavy purplish underlip. He let himself slowly down into his chair. "I'll see it through."

The two other men and Mrs. Rutledge had remained seated. Saul Rutledge stood before them, like a prisoner at the bar, or rather like a sick man before the physicians who were to heal him. As Bosworth scrutinized that hollow face, so wan under the dark sunburn, so sucked inward and consumed by some hidden fever, there stole over the sound healthy man the thought that perhaps, after all, husband and wife spoke the truth, and that they were all at that moment really standing on the edge of some forbidden mystery. Things that the rational mind would reject without a thought seemed no longer so easy to dispose of as one looked at the actual Saul Rutledge and remembered the man he had been a year before. Yes; as the Deacon said, they would have to see it through. . .

"Sit down then, Saul; draw up to us, won't you?" the Deacon suggested, trying again for a natural tone.

Mrs. Rutledge pushed a chair forward, and her husband sat down on it. He stretched out his arms and grasped his knees in his brown bony fingers; in that attitude he remained, turning neither his head nor his eyes.

"Well, Saul," the Deacon continued, "your wife says you thought mebbe we could do something to help you through this trouble, whatever it is."

Rutledge's gray eyes widened a little. "No; I didn't think that. It was her idea to try what could be done."

"I presume, though, since you've agreed to our coming, that you don't object to our putting a few questions?"

Rutledge was silent for a moment; then he said with a visible effort: "No; I don't object."

"Well—you've heard what your wife says?"

Rutledge made a slight motion of assent.

"And—what have you got to answer? How do you explain. . . ?"

Mrs. Rutledge intervened. "How can he explain? I seen 'em."

There was a silence; then Bosworth, trying to speak in an easy reassuring tone, queried: "That so, Saul?"

"That's so."

Brand lifted up his brooding head. "You mean to say you . . . you sit here before us all and say. . ."

The Deacon's hand again checked him. "Hold on, friend Brand. We're all of us trying for the facts, ain't we?" He turned to Rutledge. "We've heard what Mrs. Rutledge says. What's your answer?"

"I don't know as there's any answer. She found us."

"And you mean to tell me the person with you was . . . was what you took to be . . ." the Deacon's thin voice grew thinner: "Ora Brand?"

Saul Rutledge nodded.

"You knew . . . or thought you knew . . . you were meeting with the dead?"

Rutledge bent his head again. The snow continued to fall in a steady unwavering sheet against the window, and Bosworth felt as if a winding-sheet were descending from the sky to envelop them all in a common grave.

"Think what you're saying! It's against our religion! Ora . . . poor child! . . . died over a year ago. I saw you at her funeral, Saul. How can you make such a statement?"

"What else can he do?" thrust in Mrs. Rutledge.

There was another pause. Bosworth's resources had failed him, and Brand once more sat plunged in dark meditation. The Deacon laid his quivering finger-tips together, and moistened his lips.

"Was the day before yesterday the first time?" he asked.

The movement of Rutledge's head was negative.

"Not the first? Then when. . ."

"Nigh on a year ago, I reckon."

"God! And you mean to tell us that ever since—?"

"Well . . . look at him," said his wife. The three men lowered their eyes.

After a moment Bosworth, trying to collect himself, glanced at the Deacon. "Why not ask Saul to make his own statement, if that's what we're here for?"

"That's so," the Deacon assented. He turned to Rutledge. "Will you try and give us your idea . . . of . . . of how it began?"

There was another silence. Then Rutledge tightened his grasp on his gaunt knees, and still looking straight ahead, with his curiously clear unseeing gaze: "Well," he said, "I guess it begun away back, afore even I was married to Mrs. Rutledge. . ." He spoke in a low automatic tone, as if some invisible agent were dictating his words, or even uttering them for him. "You know," he added, "Ora and me was to have been married."

Sylvester Brand lifted his head. "Straighten that statement out first, please," he interjected.

"What I mean is, we kept company. But Ora she was very young. Mr. Brand here he sent her away. She was gone nigh to three years, I guess. When she come back I was married."

"That's right," Brand said, relapsing once more into his sunken attitude.

"And after she came back did you meet her again?" the Deacon continued.

"Alive?" Rutledge questioned.

A perceptible shudder ran through the room.

"Well—of course," said the Deacon nervously.

Rutledge seemed to consider. "Once I did—only once. There was a lot of other people round. At Cold Corners fair it was."

"Did you talk with her then?"

"Only a minute."

"What did she say?"

His voice dropped. "She said she was sick and knew she was going to die, and when she was dead she'd come back to me."

"And what did you answer?"

"Nothing."

"Did you think anything of it at the time?"

"Well, no. Not till I heard she was dead I didn't. After that I thought of it—and I guess she drew me." He moistened his lips.

"Drew you down to that abandoned house by the pond?"

Rutledge made a faint motion of assent, and the Deacon added: "How did you know it was there she wanted you to come?"

"She . . . just drew me. . ."

There was a long pause. Bosworth felt, on himself and the other two men, the oppressive weight of the next question to be asked. Mrs. Rutledge opened and closed her narrow lips once or twice, like some beached shell-fish gasping for the tide. Rutledge waited.

"Well, now, Saul, won't you go on with what you was telling us?" the Deacon at length suggested.

"That's all. There's nothing else."

The Deacon lowered his voice. "She just draws you?"

"Yes."

"Often?"

"That's as it happens. . ."

"But if it's always there she draws you, man, haven't you the strength to keep away from the place?"

For the first time, Rutledge wearily turned his head toward his questioner. A spectral smile narrowed his colourless lips. "Ain't any use. She follers after me. . ."

There was another silence. What more could they ask, then and there? Mrs. Rutledge's presence checked the next question. The Deacon seemed hopelessly to revolve the matter. At length he spoke in a more authoritative tone. "These are forbidden things. You know that, Saul. Have you tried prayer?"

Rutledge shook his head.

"Will you pray with us now?"

Rutledge cast a glance of freezing indifference on his spiritual adviser. "If you folks want to pray, I'm agreeable," he said. But Mrs. Rutledge intervened.

"Prayer ain't any good. In this kind of thing it ain't no manner of use; you know it ain't. I called you here, Deacon, because you remember the last case in this parish. Thirty years ago it was, I guess; but you remember. Lefferts Nash—did praying help *him*? I was a little girl then, but I used to hear my folks talk of it winter nights. Lefferts Nash and Hannah Cory. They drove a stake through her breast. That's what cured him."

"Oh—" Orrin Bosworth exclaimed.

Sylvester Brand raised his head. "You're speaking of that old story as if this was the same sort of thing?"

"Ain't it? Ain't my husband pining away the same as Lefferts Nash did? The Deacon here knows—"

The Deacon stirred anxiously in his chair. "These are forbidden things," he repeated. "Supposing your husband is quite sincere in thinking himself haunted, as you might say. Well, even then, what proof have we that the . . . the dead woman . . . is the spectre of that poor girl?"

"Proof? Don't he say so? Didn't she tell him? Ain't I seen 'em?" Mrs. Rutledge almost screamed.

The three men sat silent, and suddenly the wife burst out: "A stake through the breast! That's the old way; and it's the only way. The Deacon knows it!"

"It's against our religion to disturb the dead."

"Ain't it against your religion to let the living perish as my husband is perishing?" She sprang up with one of her abrupt movements and took the family Bible from the what-not in a corner of the parlour. Putting the book on the table, and moistening a livid finger-tip, she turned the pages rapidly, till she came to one on which she laid her hand like a stony paper-weight. "See here," she said, and read out in her level chanting voice:

" *'Thou shalt not suffer a witch to live.'*

"That's in Exodus, that's where it is," she added, leaving the book open as if to confirm the statement.

Bosworth continued to glance anxiously from one to the other of the four people about the table. He was younger than any of them, and had had more contact with the modern world; down in Starkfield, in the bar of the Fielding House, he could hear himself laughing with the rest of the men at such old wives' tales. But it was not for nothing that he had been born under the icy shadow of Lonetop, and had shivered and hungered as a lad through the bitter Hemlock County winters. After his parents died, and he had taken hold of the farm himself, he had got more out of it by using improved methods, and by supplying the increasing throng of summer-boarders over Stotesbury way with milk and vegetables. He had been made a selectman of North Ashmore; for so young a man he had a standing in the county. But the roots of the old life were still in him. He could remember, as a little boy, going twice a year with his mother to that bleak hill-farm out beyond Sylvester Brand's, where Mrs. Bosworth's aunt, Cressidora Cheney, had been shut up for years in a cold clean room with iron bars in the windows. When little Orrin first saw Aunt Cressidora she was a small white old woman, whom her sisters used to "make decent" for visitors the day that Orrin and his mother were expected. The child wondered why there were bars to the window. "Like a canary-bird," he said to his mother. The phrase made Mrs. Bosworth reflect. "I do believe they keep Aunt Cressidora too lonesome," she said; and the next time she went up the mountain with the little boy he carried to his great-aunt a canary in a little wooden cage. It was a great excitement; he knew it would make her happy.

The old woman's motionless face lit up when she saw the bird, and her eyes began to glitter. "It belongs to me," she said instantly, stretching her soft bony hand over the cage.

"Of course it does, Aunt Cressy," said Mrs. Bosworth, her eyes filling.

But the bird, startled by the shadow of the old woman's hand, began to flutter and beat its wings distractedly. At the sight, Aunt Cressidora's calm face suddenly became a coil of twitching features. "You she-devil, you!" she cried in a high squealing voice; and thrusting her hand into the cage she dragged out the terrified bird and wrung its neck. She was plucking the hot body, and squealing "she-devil, she-devil!" as they drew little Orrin from the room. On the way down the mountain his mother wept a great deal, and said: "You must never tell anybody that poor Auntie's crazy, or the men would come and take her down to the asylum at Starkfield, and the shame of it would kill us all. Now promise." The child promised.

He remembered the scene now, with its deep fringe of mystery, secrecy and rumour. It seemed related to a great many other things below the surface of his thoughts, things which stole up anew, making him feel that all the old people he had known, and who "believed in these things," might after all be right. Hadn't a witch been burned at North Ashmore? Didn't the summer folk still drive over in jolly buckboard loads to see the meeting-house where the trial had been held, the pond where they had ducked her and she had floated? . . . Deacon Hibben believed; Bosworth was sure of it. If he didn't, why did people from all over the place come to him when their

animals had queer sicknesses, or when there was a child in the
family that had to be kept shut up because it fell down flat
and foamed? Yes, in spite of his religion, Deacon Hibben
knew. . .

And Brand? Well, it came to Bosworth in a flash: that
North Ashmore woman who was burned had the name of
Brand. The same stock, no doubt; there had been Brands in
Hemlock County ever since the white men had come there.
And Orrin, when he was a child, remembered hearing his
parents say that Sylvester Brand hadn't ever oughter married
his own cousin, because of the blood. Yet the couple had
had two healthy girls, and when Mrs. Brand pined away and
died nobody suggested that anything had been wrong with
her mind. And Vanessa and Ora were the handsomest girls
anywhere round. Brand knew it, and scrimped and saved all
he could to send Ora, the eldest, down to Starkfield to learn
book-keeping. "When she's married I'll send you," he used
to say to little Venny, who was his favourite. But Ora never
married. She was away three years, during which Venny ran
wild on the slopes of Lonetop; and when Ora came back she
sickened and died—poor girl! Since then Brand had grown
more savage and morose. He was a hard-working farmer, but
there wasn't much to be got out of those barren Bearcliff
acres. He was said to have taken to drink since his wife's
death; now and then men ran across him in the "dives" of
Stotesbury. But not often. And between times he laboured
hard on his stony acres and did his best for his daughters. In
the neglected grave-yard of Cold Corners there was a slanting head-stone marked with his wife's name; near it, a year
since, he had laid his eldest daughter. And sometimes, at
dusk, in the autumn, the village people saw him walk slowly
by, turn in between the graves, and stand looking down on
the two stones. But he never brought a flower there, or
planted a bush; nor Venny either. She was too wild and ignorant. . .

Mrs. Rutledge repeated: "That's in Exodus."

The three visitors remained silent, turning about their hats
in reluctant hands. Rutledge faced them, still with that empty
pellucid gaze which frightened Bosworth. What was he
seeing?

"Ain't any of you folks got the grit—?" his wife burst out again, half hysterically.

Deacon Hibben held up his hand. "That's no way, Mrs. Rutledge. This ain't a question of having grit. What we want first of all is . . . proof. . ."

"That's so," said Bosworth, with an explosion of relief, as if the words had lifted something black and crouching from his breast. Involuntarily the eyes of both men had turned to Brand. He stood there smiling grimly, but did not speak.

"Ain't it so, Brand?" the Deacon prompted him.

"Proof that spooks walk?" the other sneered.

"Well—I presume you want this business settled too?"

The old farmer squared his shoulders. "Yes—I do. But I ain't a sperritualist. How the hell are you going to settle it?"

Deacon Hibben hesitated; then he said, in a low incisive tone: "I don't see but one way—Mrs. Rutledge's."

There was a silence.

"What?" Brand sneered again. "Spying?"

The Deacon's voice sank lower. "If the poor girl *does* walk . . . her that's your child . . . wouldn't you be the first to want her laid quiet? We all know there've been such cases . . . mysterious visitations . . . Can any one of us here deny it?"

"I seen 'em," Mrs. Rutledge interjected.

There was another heavy pause. Suddenly Brand fixed his gaze on Rutledge. "See here, Saul Rutledge, you've got to clear up this damned calumny, or I'll know why. You say my dead girl comes to you." He laboured with his breath, and then jerked out: "When? You tell me that, and I'll be there."

Rutledge's head drooped a little, and his eyes wandered to the window. "Round about sunset, mostly."

"You know beforehand?"

Rutledge made a sign of assent.

"Well, then—tomorrow, will it be?"

Rutledge made the same sign.

Brand turned to the door. "I'll be there." That was all he said. He strode out between them without another glance or word. Deacon Hibben looked at Mrs. Rutledge. "We'll be there too," he said, as if she had asked him; but she had not spoken, and Bosworth saw that her thin body was trembling all over. He was glad when he and Hibben were out again in the snow.

III

They thought that Brand wanted to be left to himself, and to give him time to unhitch his horse they made a pretense of hanging about in the doorway while Bosworth searched his pockets for a pipe he had no mind to light.

But Brand turned back to them as they lingered. "You'll meet me down by Lamer's pond tomorrow?" he suggested. "I want witnesses. Round about sunset."

They nodded their acquiescence, and he got into his sleigh, gave the horse a cut across the flanks, and drove off under the snow-smothered hemlocks. The other two men went to the shed.

"What do you make of this business, Deacon?" Bosworth asked, to break the silence.

The Deacon shook his head. "The man's a sick man—that's sure. Something's sucking the life clean out of him."

But already, in the biting outer air, Bosworth was getting himself under better control. "Looks to me like a bad case of the ague, as you said."

"Well—ague of the mind, then. It's his brain that's sick."

Bosworth shrugged. "He ain't the first in Hemlock County."

"That's so," the Deacon agreed. "It's a worm in the brain, solitude is."

"Well, we'll know this time tomorrow, maybe," said Bosworth. He scrambled into his sleigh, and was driving off in his turn when he heard his companion calling after him. The Deacon explained that his horse had cast a shoe; would Bosworth drive him down to the forge near North Ashmore, if it wasn't too much out of his way? He didn't want the mare slipping about on the freezing snow, and he could probably get the blacksmith to drive him back and shoe her in Rutledge's shed. Bosworth made room for him under the bearskin, and the two men drove off, pursued by a puzzled whinny from the Deacon's old mare.

The road they took was not the one that Bosworth would have followed to reach his own home. But he did not mind that. The shortest way to the forge passed close by Lamer's pond, and Bosworth, since he was in for the business, was not sorry to look the ground over. They drove on in silence.

The snow had ceased, and a green sunset was spreading upward into the crystal sky. A stinging wind barbed with ice-flakes caught them in the face on the open ridges, but when they dropped down into the hollow by Lamer's pond the air was as soundless and empty as an unswung bell. They jogged along slowly, each thinking his own thoughts.

"That's the house . . . that tumble-down shack over there, I suppose?" the Deacon said, as the road drew near the edge of the frozen pond.

"Yes: that's the house. A queer hermit-fellow built it years ago, my father used to tell me. Since then I don't believe it's ever been used but by the gipsies."

Bosworth had reined in his horse, and sat looking through pine-trunks purpled by the sunset at the crumbling structure. Twilight already lay under the trees, though day lingered in the open. Between two sharply-patterned pine-boughs he saw the evening star, like a white boat in a sea of green.

His gaze dropped from that fathomless sky and followed the blue-white undulations of the snow. It gave him a curious agitated feeling to think that here, in this icy solitude, in the tumble-down house he had so often passed without heeding it, a dark mystery, too deep for thought, was being enacted. Down that very slope, coming from the grave-yard at Cold Corners, the being they called "Ora" must pass toward the pond. His heart began to beat stiflingly. Suddenly he gave an exclamation: "Look!"

He had jumped out of the cutter and was stumbling up the bank toward the slope of snow. On it, turned in the direction of the house by the pond, he had detected a woman's foot-prints; two; then three; then more. The Deacon scrambled out after him, and they stood and stared.

"God—barefoot!" Hibben gasped. "Then it *is* . . . the dead. . ."

Bosworth said nothing. But he knew that no live woman would travel with naked feet across that freezing wilderness. Here, then, was the proof the Deacon had asked for—they held it. What should they do with it?

"Supposing we was to drive up nearer—round the turn of the pond, till we get close to the house," the Deacon proposed in a colourless voice. "Mebbe then. . ."

Postponement was a relief. They got into the sleigh and drove on. Two or three hundred yards farther the road, a mere lane under steep bushy banks, turned sharply to the right, following the bend of the pond. As they rounded the turn they saw Brand's cutter ahead of them. It was empty, the horse tied to a tree-trunk. The two men looked at each other again. This was not Brand's nearest way home.

Evidently he had been actuated by the same impulse which had made them rein in their horse by the pond-side, and then hasten on to the deserted hovel. Had he too discovered those spectral foot-prints? Perhaps it was for that very reason that he had left his cutter and vanished in the direction of the house. Bosworth found himself shivering all over under his bearskin. "I wish to God the dark wasn't coming on," he muttered. He tethered his own horse near Brand's, and without a word he and the Deacon ploughed through the snow, in the track of Brand's huge feet. They had only a few yards to walk to overtake him. He did not hear them following him, and when Bosworth spoke his name, and he stopped short and turned, his heavy face was dim and confused, like a darker blot on the dusk. He looked at them dully, but without surprise.

"I wanted to see the place," he merely said.

The Deacon cleared his throat. "Just take a look . . . yes. . . We thought so. . . But I guess there won't be anything to *see*. . ." He attempted a chuckle.

The other did not seem to hear him, but laboured on ahead through the pines. The three men came out together in the cleared space before the house. As they emerged from beneath the trees they seemed to have left night behind. The evening star shed a lustre on the speckless snow, and Brand, in that lucid circle, stopped with a jerk, and pointed to the same light foot-prints turned toward the house—the track of a woman in the snow. He stood still, his face working. "Bare feet . . ." he said.

The Deacon piped up in a quavering voice: "The feet of the dead."

Brand remained motionless. "The feet of the dead," he echoed.

Deacon Hibben laid a frightened hand on his arm. "Come away now, Brand; for the love of God come away."

The father hung there, gazing down at those light tracks on the snow—light as fox or squirrel trails they seemed, on the white immensity. Bosworth thought to himself: "The living couldn't walk so light—not even Ora Brand couldn't have, when she lived. . ." The cold seemed to have entered into his very marrow. His teeth were chattering.

Brand swung about on them abruptly. "*Now!*" he said, moving on as if to an assault, his head bowed forward on his bull neck.

"Now—now? Not in there?" gasped the Deacon. "What's the use? It was tomorrow he said—." He shook like a leaf.

"It's now," said Brand. He went up to the door of the crazy house, pushed it inward, and meeting with an unexpected resistance, thrust his heavy shoulder against the panel. The door collapsed like a playing-card, and Brand stumbled after it into the darkness of the hut. The others, after a moment's hesitation, followed.

Bosworth was never quite sure in what order the events that succeeded took place. Coming in out of the snow-dazzle, he seemed to be plunging into total blackness. He groped his way across the threshold, caught a sharp splinter of the fallen door in his palm, seemed to see something white and wraith-like surge up out of the darkest corner of the hut, and then heard a revolver shot at his elbow, and a cry—

Brand had turned back, and was staggering past him out into the lingering daylight. The sunset, suddenly flushing through the trees, crimsoned his face like blood. He held a revolver in his hand and looked about him in his stupid way.

"They *do* walk, then," he said and began to laugh. He bent his head to examine his weapon. "Better here than in the church-yard. They shan't dig her up *now*," he shouted out. The two men caught him by the arms, and Bosworth got the revolver away from him.

IV

The next day Bosworth's sister Loretta, who kept house for him, asked him, when he came in for his midday dinner, if he had heard the news.

Bosworth had been sawing wood all the morning, and in spite of the cold and the driving snow, which had begun again in the night, he was covered with an icy sweat, like a man getting over a fever.

"What news?"

"Venny Brand's down sick with pneumonia. The Deacon's been there. I guess she's dying."

Bosworth looked at her with listless eyes. She seemed far off from him, miles away. "Venny Brand?" he echoed.

"You never liked her, Orrin."

"She's a child. I never knew much about her."

"Well," repeated his sister, with the guileless relish of the unimaginative for bad news, "I guess she's dying." After a pause she added: "It'll kill Sylvester Brand, all alone up there."

Bosworth got up and said: "I've got to see to poulticing the gray's fetlock." He walked out into the steadily falling snow.

Venny Brand was buried three days later. The Deacon read the service; Bosworth was one of the pall-bearers. The whole countryside turned out, for the snow had stopped falling, and at any season a funeral offered an opportunity for an outing that was not to be missed. Besides, Venny Brand was young and handsome—at least some people thought her handsome, though she was so swarthy—and her dying like that, so suddenly, had the fascination of tragedy.

"They say her lungs filled right up. . . Seems she'd had bronchial troubles before . . . I always said both them girls was frail . . . Look at Ora, how she took and wasted away! And it's colder'n all outdoors up there to Brand's. . . Their mother, too, *she* pined away just the same. They don't ever make old bones on the mother's side of the family. . . There's that young Bedlow over there; they say Venny was engaged to him. . . Oh, Mrs. Rutledge, excuse *me*. . . Step right into the pew; there's a seat for you alongside of grandma. . ."

Mrs. Rutledge was advancing with deliberate step down the narrow aisle of the bleak wooden church. She had on her best bonnet, a monumental structure which no one had seen out of her trunk since old Mrs. Silsee's funeral, three years before. All the women remembered it. Under its perpendicular pile her narrow face, swaying on the long thin neck, seemed whiter than ever; but her air of fretfulness had been composed into a suitable expression of mournful immobility.

"Looks as if the stone-mason had carved her to put atop of Venny's grave," Bosworth thought as she glided past him; and then shivered at his own sepulchral fancy. When she bent over her hymn book her lowered lids reminded him again of marble eye-balls; the bony hands clasping the book were bloodless. Bosworth had never seen such hands since he had seen old Aunt Cressidora Cheney strangle the canary-bird because it fluttered.

The service was over, the coffin of Venny Brand had been lowered into her sister's grave, and the neighbours were slowly dispersing. Bosworth, as pall-bearer, felt obliged to linger and say a word to the stricken father. He waited till Brand had turned from the grave with the Deacon at his side. The three men stood together for a moment; but not one of them spoke. Brand's face was the closed door of a vault, barred with wrinkles like bands of iron.

Finally the Deacon took his hand and said: "The Lord gave—"

Brand nodded and turned away toward the shed where the horses were hitched. Bosworth followed him. "Let me drive along home with you," he suggested.

Brand did not so much as turn his head. "Home? What home?" he said; and the other fell back.

Loretta Bosworth was talking with the other women while the men unblanketed their horses and backed the cutters out into the heavy snow. As Bosworth waited for her, a few feet off, he saw Mrs. Rutledge's tall bonnet lording it above the group. Andy Pond, the Rutledge farm-hand, was backing out the sleigh.

"Saul ain't here today, Mrs. Rutledge, is he?" one of the village elders piped, turning a benevolent old tortoise-head

about on a loose neck, and blinking up into Mrs. Rutledge's
marble face.

Bosworth heard her measure out her answer in slow incisive
words. "No. Mr. Rutledge he ain't here. He would 'a' come
for certain, but his aunt Minorca Cummins is being buried
down to Stotesbury this very day and he had to go down
there. Don't it sometimes seem zif we was all walking right in
the Shadow of Death?"

As she walked toward the cutter, in which Andy Pond was
already seated, the Deacon went up to her with visible hesitation. Involuntarily Bosworth also moved nearer. He heard the
Deacon say: "I'm glad to hear that Saul is able to be up and
around."

She turned her small head on her rigid neck, and lifted the
lids of marble.

"Yes, I guess he'll sleep quieter now.—And *her* too, maybe,
now she don't lay there alone any longer," she added in a low
voice, with a sudden twist of her chin toward the fresh black
stain in the grave-yard snow. She got into the cutter, and said
in a clear tone to Andy Pond: " 'S long as we're down here I
don't know but what I'll just call round and get a box of soap
at Hiram Pringle's."

The Seed of the Faith

THE BLINDING June sky of Africa hung over the town. In the doorway of an Arab coffee-house a young man stood listening to the remarks exchanged by the patrons of the establishment, who lay in torpid heaps on the low shelf bordering the room.

The young man's caftan was faded to a dingy brown, but the muslin garment covering it was clean, and so was the turban wound about his shabby fez.

Cleanliness was not the most marked characteristic of the conversation to which he lent a listless ear. It was no prurient curiosity that fixed his attention on this placid exchange of obscenities: he had lived too long in Morocco for obscenities not to have lost their savour. But he had never quite overcome the fascinated disgust with which he listened, nor the hope that one among the talkers would suddenly reveal some sense of a higher ideal, of what, at home, the earnest women he knew used solemnly to call a Purpose. He was sure that, some day, such a sign would come, and then—

Meanwhile, at that hour, there was nothing on earth to do in Eloued but to stand and listen—

The bazaar was beginning to fill up. Looking down the vaulted tunnel which led to the coffee-house the young man watched the thickening throng of shoppers and idlers. The fat merchant whose shop faced the end of the tunnel had just ridden up and rolled off his mule, while his black boy unbarred the door of the niche hung with embroidered slippers where the master throned. The young man in the faded caftan, watching the merchant scramble up and sink into his cushions, wondered for the thousandth time what he thought about all day in his dim stifling kennel, and what he did when he was away from it . . . for no length of residence in that dark land seemed to bring one nearer to finding out what the heathen thought and did when the eye of the Christian was off him.

Suddenly a wave of excitement ran through the crowd. Every head turned in the same direction, and even the camels

bent their frowning faces and stretched their necks all one
way, as animals do before a storm. A wild hoot had penetrated
the bazaar, howling through the long white tunnels and under the reed-woven roofs like a Djinn among dishonoured
graves. The heart of the young man began to beat.

"It sounds," he thought, "like a motor. . ."

But a motor at Eloued! There was one, every one knew, in
the Sultan's Palace. It had been brought there years ago by a
foreign Ambassador, as a gift from his sovereign, and was var-
iously reported to be made entirely of aluminium, platinum
or silver. But the parts had never been put together, the body
had long been used for breeding silk-worms in—a not wholly
successful experiment—and the acetylene lamps adorned the
Pasha's gardens on state occasions. As for the horn, it had
been sent as a gift, with a choice panoply of arms, to the Caïd
of the Red Mountain; but as the india-rubber bulb had accidentally been left behind, it was certainly not the Caïd's visit
which the present discordant cries announced. . .

"Hullo, you old dromedary! How's the folks up state?"
cried a ringing voice. The awestruck populace gave way, and
a young man in linen duster and motor cap, slipping under
the interwoven necks of the astonished camels, strode down
the tunnel with an air of authority and clapped a hand on the
dreamer in the doorway.

"Harry Spink!" the latter gasped in a startled whisper, and
with an intonation as un-African as his friend's. At the same
instant he glanced over his shoulder, and his mild lips formed
a cautious: " 'sh."

"Who'd you take me for—Gabby Deslys?" asked the newcomer gaily; then, seeing that this topical allusion hung fire:
"And what the dickens are you 'hushing' for, anyhow? You
don't suppose, do you, that anybody in the bazaar thinks
you're a *native*? D'y' ever look at your chin? Or that Adam's
apple running up and down you like a bead on a billiard
marker's wire? See here, Willard Bent. . ."

The young man in the caftan blushed distressfully, not so
much at the graphic reference to his looks as at the doubt cast
on his disguise.

"I do assure you, Harry, I pick up a great deal of . . . of
useful information . . . in this way. . ."

"Oh, get out," said Harry Spink cheerfully. "You believe all that still, do you? What's the good of it all, anyway?"

Willard Bent passed a hand under the other's arm and led him through the coffee-house into an empty room at the back. They sat down on a shelf covered with matting and looked at each other earnestly.

"Don't *you* believe any longer, Harry Spink?" asked Willard Bent.

"Don't have to. I'm travelling for rubber now."

"Oh, merciful heaven! Was that your automobile?"

"Sure."

There was a long silence, during which Bent sat with bowed head gazing on the earthen floor, while the bead in his throat performed its most active gymnastics. At last he lifted his eyes and fixed them on the tight red face of his companion.

"When did your faith fail you?" he asked.

The other considered him humorously. "Why—when I got onto this job, I guess."

Willard Bent rose and held out his hand.

"Good-bye. . . I must go. . . If I can be of any use . . . you know where to find me. . ."

"Any use? Say, old man, what's wrong? Are you trying to shake me?" Bent was silent, and Harry Spink continued insidiously: "Ain't you a mite hard on me? I thought the heathen was just what you was laying for."

Bent smiled mournfully. "There's no use trying to convert a renegade."

"That what I am? Well—all right. But how about the others? Say—let's order a lap of tea and have it out right here."

Bent seemed to hesitate; but at length he rose, put back the matting that screened the inner room, and said a word to the proprietor. Presently a scrofulous boy with gazelle eyes brought a brass tray bearing glasses and pipes of *kif*, gazed earnestly at the stranger in the linen duster, and slid back behind the matting.

"Of course," Bent began, "a good many people know I am a Baptist missionary"—(*"No?"* from Spink, incredulously)—"but in the crowd of the bazaar they don't notice me, and I hear things. . ."

"Golly! I should suppose you did."

"I mean, things that may be useful. You know Mr. Bland-horn's idea. . ."

A tinge of respectful commiseration veiled the easy impudence of the drummer's look. "The old man still here, is he?"

"Oh, yes; of course. He will never leave Eloued."

"And the missus—?"

Bent again lowered his naturally low voice. "She died—a year ago—of the climate. The doctor had warned her; but Mr. Blandhorn felt a call to remain here."

"And she wouldn't leave without him?"

"Oh, *she* felt a call too . . . among the women. . ."

Spink pondered. "How many years you been here, Willard?"

"Ten next July," the other responded, as if he had added up the weeks and months so often that the reply was always on his lips.

"And the old man?"

"Twenty-five last April. We had planned a celebration . . . before Mrs. Blandhorn died. There was to have been a testimonial offered . . . but, owing to her death, Mr. Blandhorn preferred to devote the sum to our dispensary."

"I see. How much?" said Spink sharply.

"It wouldn't seem much to you. I believe about fifty pesetas. . ."

"Two pesetas a year? Lucky the Society looks after you, ain't it?"

Willard Bent met his ironic glance steadily. "We're not here to trade," he said with dignity.

"No—that's right too—" Spink reddened slightly. "Well, all I meant was—look at here, Willard, we're old friends, even if I did go wrong, as I suppose you'd call it. I was in this thing near on a year myself, and what always tormented me was this: *What does it all amount to?*"

"Amount to?"

"Yes. I mean, what's the results? Supposing you was a fisherman. Well, if you fished a bit of river year after year, and never had a nibble, you'd do one of two things, wouldn't you? Move away—or lie about it. See?"

Bent nodded without speaking. Spink set down his glass and busied himself with the lighting of his long slender pipe. "Say, this mint-julep feels like old times," he remarked.

Bent continued to gaze frowningly into his untouched glass. At length he swallowed the sweet decoction at a gulp, and turned to his companion.

"I'd never lie . . ." he murmured.

"Well—"

"I'm—I'm still—waiting. . ."

"Waiting—?"

"Yes. The wind bloweth where it listeth. If St. Paul had stopped to count . . . in Corinth, say. As I take it—" he looked long and passionately at the drummer—"as I take it, the thing is to *be* St. Paul."

Harry Spink remained unimpressed. "That's all talk—I heard all that when I was here before. What I want to know is: What's your bag? How many?"

"It's difficult—"

"I see: like the pigs. They run around so!"

Both the young men were silent, Spink pulling at his pipe, the other sitting with bent head, his eyes obstinately fixed on the beaten floor. At length Spink rose and tapped the missionary on the shoulder.

"Say—s'posin' we take a look around Corinth? I got to get onto my job tomorrow, but I'd like to take a turn round the old place first."

Willard Bent rose also. He felt singularly old and tired, and his mind was full of doubt as to what he ought to do. If he refused to accompany Harry Spink, a former friend and fellow-worker, it might look like running away from his questions. . .

They went out together.

II

The bazaar was seething. It seemed impossible that two more people should penetrate the throng of beggars, pilgrims, traders, slave-women, water-sellers, hawkers of dates and sweetmeats, leather-gaitered country-people carrying bunches of hens head-downward, jugglers' touts from the market-place, Jews in black caftans and greasy turbans, and scrofulous children reaching up to the high counters to fill their jars and baskets. But every now and then the Arab "Look out!" made the crowd divide and flatten itself against the stalls, and a long line of donkeys loaded with water-barrels or bundles of reeds, a string of musk-scented camels swaying their necks like horizontal question marks, or a great man perched on a pink-saddled mule and followed by slaves and clients, swept through the narrow passage without other peril to the pedestrians than that of a fresh exchange of vermin.

As the two young men drew back to make way for one of these processions, Willard Bent lifted his head and looked at his friend with a smile. "That's what Mr. Blandhorn says we ought to remember—it's one of his favourite images."

"What is?" asked Harry Spink, following with attentive gaze the movements of a young Jewess whose uncovered face and bright head-dress stood out against a group of muffled Arab women.

Instinctively Willard's voice took on a hortatory roll.

"Why, the way this dense mass of people, so heedless, so preoccupied, is imperceptibly penetrated—"

"By a handful of asses? That's so. But the asses have got some kick in 'em, remember!"

The missionary flushed to the edge of his fez, and his mild eyes grew dim. It was the old story: Harry Spink invariably got the better of him in bandying words—and the interpretation of allegories had never been his strong point. Mr. Blandhorn always managed to make them sound unanswerable, whereas on his disciple's lips they fell to pieces at a touch. What *was* it that Willard always left out?

A mournful sense of his unworthiness overcame him, and with it the discouraged vision of all the long months and years spent in the struggle with heat and dust and flies and filth and wickedness, the long lonely years of his youth that would never come back to him. It was the vision he most dreaded, and turning from it he tried to forget himself in watching his friend.

"Golly! The vacuum-cleaner ain't been round since my last visit," Mr. Spink observed, as they slipped in a mass of offal beneath a butcher's stall. "Let's get into another soukh—the flies here beat me."

They turned into another long lane chequered with a criss-cross of black reed-shadows. It was the saddlers' quarter, and here an even thicker crowd wriggled and swayed between the cramped stalls hung with bright leather and spangled ornaments.

"Say! It might be a good idea to import some of this stuff for Fourth of July processions—Knights of Pythias and Secret Societies' kinder thing," Spink mused, pausing before the brilliant spectacle. At the same moment a lad in an almond-green caftan sidled up and touched his arm.

Willard's face brightened. "Ah, that's little Ahmed—you don't remember him? Surely—the water-carrier's boy. Mrs. Blandhorn saved his mother's life when he was born, and he still comes to prayers. Yes, Ahmed, this is your old friend Mr. Spink."

Ahmed raised prodigious lashes from seraphic eyes and reverently surveyed the face of his old friend. "Me 'member."

"Hullo, old chap . . . why, of course . . . so do I," the drummer beamed. The missionary laid a brotherly hand on the boy's shoulder. It was really providential that Ahmed—whom they hadn't seen at the Mission for more weeks than Willard cared to count—should have "happened by" at that moment: Willard took it as a rebuke to his own doubts.

"You'll be in this evening for prayers, won't you, Ahmed?" he said, as if Ahmed never failed them. "Mr. Spink will be with us."

"Yessir," said Ahmed with unction. He slipped from under Willard's hand, and out-flanking the drummer approached him from the farther side.

"Show you Souss boys dance? Down to old Jewess's, Bab-el-Soukh," he breathed angelically.

Willard saw his companion turn from red to a wrathful purple.

"Get out, you young swine, you—do you hear me?"

Ahmed grinned, wavered and vanished, engulfed in the careless crowd. The young men walked on without speaking.

III

In the market-place they parted. Willard Bent, after some hesitation, had asked Harry Spink to come to the Mission that evening. "You'd better come to supper—then we can talk quietly afterward. Mr. Blandhorn will want to see you," he suggested; and Mr. Spink had affably acquiesced.

The prayer-meeting was before supper, and Willard would have liked to propose that his friend should come to that also; but he did not dare. He said to himself that Harry Spink, who had been merely a lay assistant, might have lost the habit of reverence, and that it would be too painful to risk his scandalizing Mr. Blandhorn. But that was only a sham reason; and Willard, with his incorrigible habit of self-exploration, fished up the real one from a lower depth. What he had most feared was that there would be no one at the meeting.

During Mrs. Blandhorn's lifetime there had been no reason for such apprehension: they could always count on a few people. Mrs. Blandhorn, who had studied medicine at Ann Arbor, Michigan, had early gained renown in Eloued by her miraculous healing powers. The dispensary, in those days, had been beset by anxious-eyed women who unwound skinny fig-coloured children from their dirty draperies; and there had even been a time when Mr. Blandhorn had appealed to the Society for a young lady missionary to assist his wife. But, for reasons not quite clear to Willard Bent, Mrs. Blandhorn, a thin-lipped determined little woman, had energetically opposed the coming of this youthful "Sister," and had declared that their Jewish maid-servant, old Myriem, could give her all the aid she needed.

Mr. Blandhorn yielded, as he usually did—as he had yielded, for instance, when one day, in a white inarticulate fury, his wife had banished her godson, little Ahmed (whose life she had saved), and issued orders that he should never show himself again except at prayer-meeting, and accompanied by his father. Mrs. Blandhorn, small, silent and passionate, had always—as Bent made out in his long retrospective musings—ended by having her way in the conflicts that occasionally shook the monotony of life at the Mission. After her death the young man had even suspected, beneath his superior's sincere and vehement sorrow, a lurking sense of relief. Mr. Blandhorn had snuffed the air of freedom, and had been, for the moment, slightly intoxicated by it. But not for long. Very soon his wife's loss made itself felt as a lasting void.

She had been (as Spink would have put it) "the whole show"; had led, inspired, organized her husband's work, held it together, and given it the brave front it presented to the unheeding heathen. Now the heathen had almost entirely fallen away, and the too evident inference was that they had come rather for Mrs. Blandhorn's pills than for her husband's preaching. Neither of the missionaries had avowed this discovery to the other, but to Willard at least it was implied in all the circumlocutions and evasions of their endless talks.

The young man's situation had been greatly changed by Mrs. Blandhorn's death. His superior had grown touchingly dependent on him. Their conversation, formerly confined to parochial matters, now ranged from abstruse doctrinal problems to the question of how to induce Myriem, who had deplorably "relapsed," to keep the kitchen cleaner and spend less time on the roofs. Bent felt that Mr. Blandhorn needed him at every moment, and that, during any prolonged absence, something vaguely "unfortunate" might happen at the Mission.

"I'm glad Spink has come; it will do him good to see somebody from outside," Willard thought, nervously hoping that Spink (a good fellow at bottom) would not trouble Mr. Blandhorn by any of his "unsettling" questions.

At the end of a labyrinth of lanes, on the farther side of the Jewish quarter, a wall of heat-cracked clay bore the inscription: "American Evangelical Mission." Underneath it a door opened into a court where an old woman in a bright headdress sat under a fig-tree pounding something in a mortar.

She looked up, and, rising, touched Bent's draperies with her lips. Her small face, withered as a dry medlar, was full of an ancient wisdom: Mrs. Blandhorn had certainly been right in trusting Myriem.

A narrow house-front looked upon the court. Bent climbed the stairs to Mr. Blandhorn's study. It was a small room with a few dog-eared books on a set of rough shelves, the table at which Mr. Blandhorn wrote his reports for the Society, and a mattress covered with a bit of faded carpet, on which he slept. Near the window stood Mrs. Blandhorn's sewing-machine; it had never been moved since her death.

The missionary was sitting in the middle of the room, in the rocking chair which had also been his wife's. His large veined hands were clasped about its arms and his head rested against a patch-work cushion tied to the back by a shoe-lace. His mouth was slightly open, and a deep breath, occasionally rising to a whistle, proceeded with rhythmic regularity from his delicately-cut nostrils. Even surprised in sleep he was a fine man to look upon; and when, at the sound of Bent's approach, he opened his eyes and pulled himself out of his chair, he became magnificent. He had taken off his turban, and thrown a handkerchief over his head, which was shaved like an Arab's for coolness. His long beard was white, with the smoker's yellow tinge about the lips; but his eyebrows were jet-black, arched and restless. The gray eyes beneath them shed a mild benedictory beam, confirmed by the smile of a mouth which might have seemed weak if the beard had not so nearly concealed it. But the forehead menaced, fulminated or awed with the ever-varying play of the eyebrows. Willard Bent never beheld that forehead without thinking of Sinai.

Mr. Blandhorn brushed some shreds of tobacco from his white djellabah and looked impressively at his assistant.

"The heat is really overwhelming," he said, as if excusing himself. He readjusted his turban, and then asked: "Is everything ready downstairs?"

Bent assented, and they went down to the long bare room where the prayer-meetings were held. In Mrs. Blandhorn's day it had also served as the dispensary, and a cupboard containing drugs and bandages stood against the wall under the text: *"Come unto me, all ye that labour and are heavy laden."*

Myriem, abandoning her mortar, was vaguely tidying the Arab tracts and leaflets that lay on the divan against the wall. At one end of the room stood a table covered with a white cloth, with a Bible lying on it; and to the left a sort of pulpit-lectern, from which Mr. Blandhorn addressed his flock. In the doorway squatted Ayoub, a silent gray-headed negro; Bent, on his own arrival at Eloued, ten years earlier, had found him there in the same place and the same attitude. Ayoub was supposed to be a rescued slave from the Soudan, and was shown to visitors as "our first convert." He manifested no interest at the approach of the missionaries, but continued to gaze out into the sun-baked court cut in half by the shadow of the fig-tree.

Mr. Blandhorn, after looking about the empty room as if he were surveying the upturned faces of an attentive congregation, placed himself at the lectern, put on his spectacles, and turned over the pages of his prayer-book. Then he knelt and bowed his head in prayer. His devotions ended, he rose and seated himself in the cane arm-chair that faced the lectern. Willard Bent sat opposite in another arm-chair. Mr. Blandhorn leaned back, breathing heavily, and passing his handkerchief over his face and brow. Now and then he drew out his watch, now and then he said: "The heat is really overwhelming."

Myriem had drifted back to her fig-tree, and the sound of the pestle mingled with the drone of flies on the windowpane. Occasionally the curses of a muleteer or the rhythmic chant of a water-carrier broke the silence; once there came from a neighbouring roof the noise of a short cat-like squabble ending in female howls; then the afternoon heat laid its leaden hush on all things.

Mr. Blandhorn opened his mouth and slept.

Willard Bent, watching him, thought with wonder and admiration of his past. What had he not seen, what secrets were not hidden in his bosom? By dint of sheer "sticking it out" he had acquired to the younger man a sort of visible sanctity. Twenty-five years of Eloued! He had known the old mad torturing Sultan, he had seen, after the defeat of the rebels, the long line of prisoners staggering in under a torrid sky, chained wrist to wrist, and dragging between them the putrefying bodies of those who had died on the march. He had seen the Great Massacre, when the rivers were red with French blood, and the Blandhorns had hidden an officer's wife and children in the rat-haunted drain under the court; he had known robbery and murder and intrigue, and all the dark maleficence of Africa; and he remained as serene, as confident and guileless, as on the day when he had first set foot on that evil soil, saying to himself (as he had told Willard): *"I will tread upon the lion and the adder, the young lion and the dragon will I tread under foot."*

Willard Bent hated Africa; but it awed and fascinated him. And as he contemplated the splendid old man sleeping opposite him, so mysterious, so childlike and so weak (Mrs. Blandhorn had left him no doubts on that point), the disciple marvelled at the power of the faith which had armed his master with a sort of infantile strength against such dark and manifold perils.

Suddenly a shadow fell in the doorway, and Bent, roused from his dream, saw Harry Spink tiptoeing past the unmoved Ayoub. The drummer paused and looked with astonishment from one of the missionaries to the other. "Say," he asked, "is prayer-meeting over? I thought I'd be round in time."

He spoke seriously, even respectfully; it was plain that he felt flippancy to be out of place. But Bent suspected a lurking malice under his astonishment: he was sure Harry Spink had come to "count heads."

Mr. Blandhorn, wakened by the voice, stood up heavily.

"Harry Spink! Is it possible you are amongst us?"

"Why, yes, sir—I'm amongst. Didn't Willard tell you? I guess Willard Bent's ashamed of me."

Spink, with a laugh, shook Mr. Blandhorn's hand, and glanced about the empty room.

"I'm only here for a day or so—on business. Willard'll explain. But I wanted to come round to meeting—like old times. Sorry it's over."

The missionary looked at him with a grave candour. "It's not over—it has not begun. The overwhelming heat has probably kept away our little flock."

"I see," interpolated Spink.

"But now," continued Mr. Blandhorn with majesty, "that two or three are gathered together in His name, there is no reason why we should wait.—Myriem! Ayoub!"

He took his place behind the lectern and began: "Almighty and merciful Father—"

IV

The night was exceedingly close. Willard Bent, after Spink's departure, had undressed and stretched himself on his camp bed; but the mosquitoes roared like lions, and lying down made him more wakeful.

"In any Christian country," he mused, "this would mean a thunderstorm and a cool-off. Here it just means months and months more of the same thing." And he thought enviously of Spink, who, in two or three days, his "deal" concluded, would be at sea again, heading for the north.

Bent was honestly distressed at his own state of mind: he had feared that Harry Spink would "unsettle" Mr. Blandhorn, and, instead, it was he himself who had been unsettled. Old slumbering distrusts and doubts, bursting through his surface-apathy, had shot up under the drummer's ironic eye. It was not so much Spink, individually, who had loosened the crust of Bent's indifference; it was the fact of feeling his whole problem suddenly viewed and judged from the outside. At Eloued, he was aware, nobody, for a long time, had thought much about the missionaries. The French authorities were friendly, the Pacha was tolerant, the American Consul at Mogador had always stood by them in any small difficulties. But beyond that they were virtually non-existent. Nobody's view of life was really affected by their presence in the great swarming mysterious city: if they should pack up and leave that night, the story-tellers of the market would not interrupt their tales, or one less bargain be struck in the bazaar. Ayoub would still doze in the door, and old Myriem continue her secret life on the roofs. . .

The roofs were of course forbidden to the missionaries, as they are to men in all Moslem cities. But the Mission-house stood close to the walls, and Mr. Blandhorn's room, across the passage, gave on a small terrace overhanging the court of a caravansary upon which it was no sin to look. Willard wondered if it were any cooler on the terrace.

Some one tapped on his open door, and Mr. Blandhorn, in turban and caftan, entered the room, shading a small lamp.

"My dear Willard—can you sleep?"

"No, sir." The young man stumbled to his feet.

"Nor I. The heat is really. . . Shall we seek relief on the terrace?"

Bent followed him, and having extinguished the lamp Mr. Blandhorn led the way out. He dragged a strip of matting to the edge of the parapet, and the two men sat down on it side by side.

There was no moon, but a sky so full of stars that the city was outlined beneath it in great blue-gray masses. The air was motionless, but every now and then a wandering tremor stirred it and died out. Close under the parapet lay the bales and saddle-packs of the caravansary, between vaguer heaps, presumably of sleeping camels. In one corner, the star-glitter picked out the shape of a trough brimming with water, and stabbed it with long silver beams. Beyond the court rose the crenellations of the city walls, and above them one palm stood up like a tree of bronze.

"Africa—" sighed Mr. Blandhorn.

Willard Bent started at the secret echo of his own thoughts.

"Yes. Never anything else, sir—"

"Ah—" said the old man.

A tang-tang of stringed instruments, accompanied by the lowing of an earthenware drum, rose exasperatingly through the night. It was the kind of noise that, one knew, had been going on for hours before one began to notice it, and would go on, unchecked and unchanging, for endless hours more: like the heat, like the drought—like Africa.

Willard slapped at a mosquito.

"It's a party at the wool-merchant's, Myriem tells me," Mr. Blandhorn remarked. It really seemed as if, that night, the thoughts of the two men met without the need of words. Willard Bent was aware that, for both, the casual phrase had called up all the details of the scene: fat merchants in white bunches on their cushions, negresses coming and going with trays of sweets, champagne clandestinely poured, ugly singing-girls yowling, slim boys in petticoats dancing—perhaps little Ahmed among them.

"I went down to the court just now. Ayoub has disappeared," Mr. Blandhorn continued.

"Of course. When I heard in the bazaar that a black caravan was in from the south I knew he'd be off. . ."

Mr. Blandhorn lowered his voice. "Willard—have you reason to think . . . that Ayoub joins in their rites?"

"Myriem has always said he was a Hamatcha, sir. Look at those queer cuts and scars on him. . . It's a much bloodier sect than the Aissaouas."

Through the nagging throb of the instruments came a sound of human wailing, cadenced, terrible, relentless, carried from a long way off on a lift of the air. Then the air died, and the wailing with it.

"From somewhere near the Potters' Field . . . there's where the caravan is camping," Willard murmured.

The old man made no answer. He sat with his head bowed, his veined hands grasping his knees; he seemed to his disciple to be whispering fragments of Scripture.

"Willard, my son, this is our fault," he said at length.

"What—? Ayoub?"

"Ayoub is a poor ignorant creature, hardly more than an animal. Even when he witnessed for Jesus I was not very sure the Word reached him. I refer to—to what Harry Spink said this evening. . . It has kept me from sleeping, Willard Bent."

"Yes—I know, sir."

"Harry Spink is a worldly-minded man. But he is not a bad man. He did a manly thing when he left us, since he did not feel the call. But we have felt the call, Willard, you and I—and when a man like Spink puts us a question such as he put this evening we ought to be able to answer it. And we ought not to want to avoid answering it."

"You mean when he said: *'What is there in it for Jesus?'*"

"The phrase was irreverent, but the meaning reached me. He meant, I take it: 'What have your long years here profited to Christ?' You understood it so—?"

"Yes. He said to me in the bazaar: 'What's your bag?' "

Mr. Blandhorn sighed heavily. For a few minutes Willard fancied he had fallen asleep; but he lifted his head and, stretching his hand out, laid it on his disciple's arm.

"The Lord chooses His messengers as it pleaseth Him: I have been awaiting this for a long time." The young man felt his arm strongly grasped. "Willard, you have been much to me all these years; but that is nothing. All that matters is what you are to Christ . . . and the test of that, at this moment, is your willingness to tell me the exact truth, as you see it."

Willard Bent felt as if he were a very tall building, and his heart a lift suddenly dropping down from the roof to the cellar. He stirred nervously, releasing his arm, and cleared his throat; but he made no answer. Mr. Blandhorn went on.

"Willard, this is the day of our accounting—of *my* accounting. What have I done with my twenty-five years in Africa? I might deceive myself as long as my wife lived—I cannot now." He added, after a pause: "Thank heaven *she* never doubted. . ."

The younger man, with an inward shiver, remembered some of Mrs. Blandhorn's confidences. "I suppose that's what marriage is," he mused—"just a fog, like everything else."

Aloud he asked: "Then why should *you* doubt, sir?"

"Because my eyes have been opened—"

"By Harry Spink?" the disciple sneered.

The old man raised his hand. " '*Out of the mouths of babes*—' But it is not Harry Spink who first set me thinking. He has merely loosened my tongue. He has been the humble instrument compelling me to exact the truth of you."

Again Bent felt his heart dropping down a long dark shaft. He found no words at the bottom of it, and Mr. Blandhorn continued: "The truth and the whole truth, Willard Bent. We have failed—*I* have failed. We have not reached the souls of these people. Those who still come to us do so from interested motives—or, even if I do some few of them an injustice, if there is in some a blind yearning for the light, is there one among them whose eyes we have really opened?"

Willard Bent sat silent, looking up and down the long years, as if to summon from the depths of memory some single incident that should permit him to say there was.

"You don't answer, my poor young friend. Perhaps you have been clearer-sighted; perhaps you saw long ago that we were not worthy of our hire."

"I never thought that of you, sir!"

"Nor of yourself? For we have been one—or so I have believed—in all our hopes and efforts. Have you been satisfied with *your* results?"

Willard saw the dialectical trap, but some roused force in him refused to evade it.

"No, sir—God knows."

"Then I am answered. We have failed: Africa has beaten us. It has always been my way, as you know, Willard, to face the truth squarely," added the old man who had lived so long in dreams; "and now that *this* truth has been borne in on me, painful as it is, I must act on it .   . . act in accordance with its discovery."

He drew a long breath, as if oppressed by the weight of his resolution, and sat silent for a moment, fanning his face with a corner of his white draperies.

"And here too—here too I must have your help, Willard," he began presently, his hand again weighing on the young man's arm. "I will tell you the conclusions I have reached; and you must answer me—as you would answer your Maker."

"Yes, sir."

The old man lowered his voice. "It is our lukewarmness, Willard—it is nothing else. We have not witnessed for Christ as His saints and martyrs witnessed for Him. What have we done to fix the attention of these people, to convince them of our zeal, to overwhelm them with the irresistibleness of the Truth? Answer me on your word—what have we done?"

Willard pondered. "But the saints and martyrs . . . were persecuted, sir."

"*Persecuted!* You have spoken the word I wanted."

"But the people here," Willard argued, "don't *want* to persecute anybody. They're not fanatical unless you insult their religion."

Mr. Blandhorn's grasp grew tighter. "Insult their religion! That's it . . . tonight you find just the words. . ."

Willard felt his arm shake with the tremor that passed through the other's body. "The saints and martyrs insulted the religion of the heathen—they spat on it, Willard—they rushed into the temples and knocked down the idols. They said to the heathen: 'Turn away your faces from all your abominations'; and after the manner of men they fought with beasts at Ephesus. What is the Church on earth called? The Church Militant! You and I are soldiers of the Cross."

The missionary had risen and stood leaning against the parapet, his right arm lifted as if he spoke from a pulpit. The music at the wool-merchant's had ceased, but now and then, through the midnight silence, there came an echo of ritual howls from the Potters' Field.

Willard was still seated, his head thrown back against the parapet, his eyes raised to Mr. Blandhorn. Following the gesture of the missionary's lifted hand, from which the muslin fell back like the sleeve of a surplice, the young man's gaze was led upward to another white figure, hovering small and remote above their heads. It was a muezzin leaning from his airy balcony to drop on the blue-gray masses of the starlit city the cry: "Only Allah is great."

Mr. Blandhorn saw the white figure too, and stood facing it with motionless raised arm.

"Only Christ is great, only Christ crucified!" he suddenly shouted in Arabic with all the strength of his broad lungs.

The figure paused, and seemed to Willard to bend over, as if peering down in their direction; but a moment later it had moved to the other corner of the balcony, and the cry fell again on the sleeping roofs:

"Allah—Allah—only Allah!"

"Christ—Christ—only Christ crucified!" roared Mr. Bland-horn, exalted with wrath and shaking his fist at the aerial puppet.

The puppet once more paused and peered; then it moved on and vanished behind the flank of the minaret.

The missionary, still towering with lifted arm, dusky-faced in the starlight, seemed to Willard to have grown in majesty and stature. But presently his arm fell and his head sank into his hands. The young man knelt down, hiding his face also, and they prayed in silence, side by side, while from the farther corners of the minaret, less audibly, fell the infidel call.

Willard, his prayer ended, looked up, and saw that the old man's garments were stirred as if by a ripple of air. But the air was quite still, and the disciple perceived that the tremor of the muslin was communicated to it by Mr. Blandhorn's body.

"He's trembling—trembling all over. He's afraid of something. What's he afraid of?" And in the same breath Willard had answered his own question: "He's afraid of what he's made up his mind to do."

V

Two days later Willard Bent sat in the shade of a ruined tomb outside the Gate of the Graves, and watched the people streaming in to Eloued. It was the eve of the feast of the local saint, Sidi Oman, who slept in a corner of the Great Mosque, under a segment of green-tiled cupola, and was held in deep reverence by the country people, many of whom belonged to the powerful fraternity founded in his name.

The ruin stood on a hillock beyond the outer wall. From where the missionary sat he overlooked the fortified gate and the irregular expanse of the Potters' Field, with its primitive furnaces built into hollows of the ground, between ridges shaded by stunted olive-trees. On the farther side of the trail which the pilgrims followed on entering the gate lay a sun-blistered expanse dotted with crooked grave-stones, where hucksters traded, and the humblest caravans camped in a waste of refuse, offal and stripped date-branches. A cloud of dust, perpetually subsiding and gathering again, hid these sordid details from Bent's eyes, but not from his imagination.

"Nowhere in Eloued," he thought with a shudder, "are the flies as fat and blue as they are inside that gate."

But this was a fugitive reflection: his mind was wholly absorbed in what had happened in the last forty-eight hours, and what was likely to happen in the next.

"To think," he mused, "that after ten years I don't really know him! . . . A labourer in the Lord's vineyard—shows how much good I am!"

His thoughts were moody and oppressed with fear. Never, since his first meeting with Mr. Blandhorn, had he pondered so deeply the problem of his superior's character. He tried to deduce from the past some inference as to what Mr. Blandhorn was likely to do next; but, as far as he knew, there was nothing in the old man's previous history resembling the midnight scene on the Mission terrace.

That scene had already had its repercussion.

On the following morning, Willard, drifting as usual about the bazaar, had met a friendly French official, who, taking him aside, had told him there were strange reports abroad— which he hoped Mr. Bent would be able to deny. . . In short, as it had never been Mr. Blandhorn's policy to offend the native population, or insult their religion, the Administration was confident that. . .

Surprised by Willard's silence, and visibly annoyed at being obliged to pursue the subject, the friendly official, growing graver, had then asked what had really occurred; and, on Willard's replying, had charged him with an earnest recommendation to his superior—a warning, if necessary—that the government would not, under any circumstances, tolerate a repetition. . . "But I daresay it was the heat?" he concluded; and Willard weakly acquiesced.

He was ashamed now of having done so; yet, after all, how did he know it was *not* the heat? A heavy sanguine man like Mr. Blandhorn would probably never quite accustom himself to the long strain of the African summer. "Or his wife's death—" he had murmured to the sympathetic official, who smiled with relief at the suggestion.

And now he sat overlooking the enigmatic city, and asking himself again what he really knew of his superior. Mr. Blandhorn had come to Eloued as a young man, extremely poor, and dependent on the pittance which the Missionary Society at that time gave to its representatives. To ingratiate himself among the people (the expression was his own), and also to earn a few pesetas, he had worked as a carpenter in the bazaar, first in the soukh of the ploughshares and then in that of the cabinet-makers. His skill in carpentry had not been great, for his large eloquent hands were meant to wave from a pulpit, and not to use the adze or the chisel; but he had picked up a little Arabic (Willard always marvelled that it remained so little), and had made many acquaintances—and, as he thought, some converts. At any rate, no one, either then or later, appeared to wish him ill, and during the massacre his house had been respected, and the insurgents had even winked at the aid he had courageously given to the French.

Yes—he had certainly been courageous. There was in him, in spite of his weaknesses and his vacillations, a streak of moral heroism that perhaps only waited its hour. . . But hitherto his principle had always been that the missionary must win converts by kindness, by tolerance, and by the example of a blameless life.

Could it really be Harry Spink's question that had shaken him in this belief? Or was it the long-accumulated sense of inefficiency that so often weighed on his disciple? Or was it simply the call—did it just mean that their hour had come?

Shivering a little in spite of the heat, Willard pulled himself together and descended into the city. He had been seized with a sudden desire to know what Mr. Blandhorn was about, and avoiding the crowd he hurried back by circuitous lanes to the Mission. On the way he paused at a certain corner and looked into a court full of the murmur of water. Beyond it was an arcade detached against depths of shadow, in which a few lights glimmered. White figures, all facing one way, crouched and touched their foreheads to the tiles, the soles of their bare feet, wet with recent ablutions, turning up as their bodies swayed forward. Willard caught the scowl of a beggar on the threshold, and hurried past the forbidden scene.

He found Mr. Blandhorn in the meeting-room, tying up Ayoub's head.

"I do it awkwardly," the missionary mumbled, a safety-pin between his teeth. "Alas, my hands are not *hers*."

"What's he done to himself?" Willard growled; and above the bandaged head Mr. Blandhorn's expressive eyebrows answered.

There was a dark stain on the back of Ayoub's faded shirt, and another on the blue scarf he wore about his head.

"Ugh—it's like cats slinking back after a gutter-fight," the young man muttered.

Ayoub wound his scarf over the bandages, shambled back to the doorway, and squatted down to watch the fig-tree.

The missionaries looked at each other across the empty room.

"What's the use, sir?" was on Willard's lips; but instead of speaking he threw himself down on the divan. There was to be no prayer-meeting that afternoon, and the two men sat silent, gazing at the back of Ayoub's head. A smell of disinfectants hung in the heavy air. . .

"Where's Myriem?" Willard asked, to say something.

"I believe she had a ceremony of some sort . . . a family affair. . ."

"A circumcision, I suppose?"

Mr. Blandhorn did not answer, and Willard was sorry he had made the suggestion. It would simply serve as another reminder of their failure. . .

He stole a furtive glance at Mr. Blandhorn, nervously wondering if the time had come to speak of the French official's warning. He had put off doing so, half-hoping it would not be necessary. The old man seemed so calm, so like his usual self, that it might be wiser to let the matter drop. Perhaps he had already forgotten the scene on the terrace; or perhaps he thought he had sufficiently witnessed for the Lord in shouting his insult to the muezzin. But Willard did not really believe this: he remembered the tremor which had shaken Mr. Blandhorn after the challenge, and he felt sure it was not a retrospective fear.

"Our friend Spink has been with me," said Mr. Blandhorn suddenly. "He came in soon after you left."

"Ah? I'm sorry I missed him. I thought he'd gone, from his not coming in yesterday."

"No; he leaves tomorrow morning for Mogador." Mr Blandhorn paused, still absently staring at the back of Ayoub's neck; then he added: "I have asked him to take you with him."

"To take me—Harry Spink? In his automobile?" Willard gasped. His heart began to beat excitedly.

"Yes. You'll enjoy the ride. It's a long time since you've been away, and you're looking a little pulled down."

"You're very kind, sir: so is Harry." He paused. "But I'd rather not."

Mr. Blandhorn, turning slightly, examined him between half-dropped lids.

"I have business for you—with the Consul," he said with a certain sternness. "I don't suppose you will object—"

"Oh, of course not." There was another pause. "Could you tell me—give me an idea—of what the business is, sir?"

It was Mr. Blandhorn's turn to appear perturbed. He coughed, passed his hand once or twice over his beard, and again fixed his gaze on Ayoub's inscrutable nape.

"I wish to send a letter to the Consul."

"A letter? If it's only a letter, couldn't Spink take it?"

"Undoubtedly. I might also send it by post—if I cared to transmit it in that manner. I presumed," added Mr. Blandhorn with threatening brows, "that you would understand I had my reasons—"

"Oh, in that case, of course, sir—" Willard hesitated, and then spoke with a rush. "I saw Lieutenant Lourdenay in the bazaar yesterday—" he began.

When he had finished his tale Mr. Blandhorn meditated for a long time in silence. At length he spoke in a calm voice. "And what did you answer, Willard?"

"I—I said I'd tell you—"

"Nothing more?"

"No. Nothing."

"Very well. We'll talk of all this more fully . . . when you get back from Mogador. Remember that Mr. Spink will be here before sunrise. I advised him to get away as early as possible on account of the Feast of Sidi Oman. It's always a poor day for foreigners to be seen about the streets."

VI

At a quarter before four on the morning of the Feast of Sidi Oman, Willard Bent stood waiting at the door of the Mission.

He had taken leave of Mr. Blandhorn the previous night, and stumbled down the dark stairs on bare feet, his bundle under his arm, just as the sky began to whiten around the morning star.

The air was full of a mocking coolness which the first ray of the sun would burn up; and a hush as deceptive lay on the city that was so soon to blaze with religious frenzy. Ayoub lay curled up on his door-step like a dog, and old Myriem, presumably, was still stretched on her mattress on the roof.

What a day for a flight across the desert in Harry's tough little car! And after the hours of heat and dust and glare, how good, at twilight, to see the cool welter of the Atlantic, a spent sun dropping into it, and the rush of the stars. . . Dizzy with the vision, Willard leaned against the door-post with closed eyes.

A subdued hoot aroused him, and he hurried out to the car, which was quivering and growling at the nearest corner. The drummer nodded a welcome, and they began to wind cautiously between sleeping animals and huddled heaps of humanity till they reached the nearest gate.

On the waste land beyond the walls the people of the caravans were already stirring, and pilgrims from the hills streaming across the palmetto scrub under emblazoned banners. As the sun rose the air took on a bright transparency in which distant objects became unnaturally near and vivid, like pebbles seen through clear water: a little turban-shaped tomb far off in the waste looked as lustrous as ivory, and a tiled minaret in an angle of the walls seemed to be carved out of turquoise. How Eloued lied to eyes looking back on it at sunrise!

"Something wrong," said Harry Spink, putting on the brake and stopping in the thin shade of a cork-tree. They got out and Willard leaned against the tree and gazed at the red walls of Eloued. They were already about two miles from the town, and all around them was the wilderness. Spink shoved his head into the bonnet, screwed and greased and hammered, and finally wiped his hands on a black rag and called out: "I thought so—. Jump in!"

Willard did not move.

"Hurry up, old man. She's all right, I tell you. It was just the carburettor."

The missionary fumbled under his draperies and pulled out Mr. Blandhorn's letter.

"Will you see that the Consul gets this tomorrow?"

"Will I—what the hell's the matter, Willard?" Spink dropped his rag and stared.

"I'm not coming. I never meant to."

The young men exchanged a long look.

"It's no time to leave Mr. Blandhorn—a day like this," Willard continued, moistening his dry lips.

Spink shrugged, and sounded a faint whistle. "Queer—!"

"What's queer?"

"He said just the same thing to me about *you*—wanted to get you out of Eloued on account of the goings on today. He said you'd been rather worked up lately about religious matters, and might do something rash that would get you both into trouble."

"Ah—" Willard murmured.

"And I believe you might, you know—you look sorter funny." Willard laughed.

"Oh, come along," his friend urged, disappointed.

"I'm sorry—I can't. I had to come this far so that he wouldn't know. But now I've got to go back. Of course what he told you was just a joke—but I must be there today to see that nobody bothers him."

Spink scanned his companion's face with friendly flippant eyes. "Well, I give up—. What's the *use*, when he don't want you?—Say," he broke off, "what's the truth of that story about the old man's having insulted a marabout in a mosque night before last? It was all over the bazaar—"

Willard felt himself turn pale. "Not a marabout. It was—where did you hear it?" he stammered.

"All over—the way you hear stories in these places."

"Well—it's not true." Willard lifted his bundle from the motor and tucked it under his arm. "I'm sorry, Harry—I've got to go back," he repeated.

"What? The Call, eh?" The sneer died on Spink's lips, and he held out his hand. "Well, I'm sorry too. So long." He turned the crank, scrambled into his seat, and cried back over his shoulder: "What's the *use*, when he don't want you?"

Willard was already labouring home across the plain.

After struggling along for half an hour in the sand he crawled under the shade of an abandoned well and sat down to ponder. Two courses were open to him, and he had not yet been able to decide between them. His first impulse was to go straight to the Mission, and present himself to Mr. Blandhorn. He felt sure, from what Spink had told him, that the old missionary had sent him away purposely, and the fact seemed to confirm his apprehensions. If Mr. Blandhorn wanted him away, it was not through any fear of his imprudence, but to be free from his restraining influence. But what act did the old man contemplate, in which he feared to involve his disciple? And if he were really resolved on some rash measure, might not Willard's unauthorized return merely serve to exasperate this resolve, and hasten whatever action he had planned?

The other step the young man had in mind was to go secretly to the French Administration, and there drop a hint of what he feared. It was the course his sober judgment commended. The echo of Spink's "What's the use?" was in his ears: it was the expression of his own secret doubt. What *was* the use? If dying could bring any of these darkened souls to the light . . . well, that would have been different. But what least sign was there that it would do anything but rouse their sleeping blood-lust?

Willard was oppressed by the thought that had always lurked beneath his other doubts. They talked, he and Mr. Blandhorn, of the poor ignorant heathen—but were not they themselves equally ignorant in everything that concerned the heathen? What did they know of these people, of their antecedents, the origin of their beliefs and superstitions, the meaning of their habits and passions and precautions? Mr. Blandhorn seemed never to have been troubled by this question, but it had weighed on Willard ever since he had come across a quiet French ethnologist who was studying the tribes of the Middle Atlas. Two or three talks with this traveller—or listenings to him—had shown Willard the extent of his own ignorance. He would have liked to borrow books, to read, to study; but he knew little French and no German, and he felt confusedly that there was in him no soil sufficiently prepared for facts so overwhelmingly new to root in it. . . And the heat lay on him, and the little semblance of his missionary duties deluded him . . . and he drifted. . .

As for Mr. Blandhorn, he never read anything but the Scriptures, a volume of his own sermons (printed by subscription, to commemorate his departure for Morocco), and—occasionally—a back number of the missionary journal that arrived at Eloued at long intervals, in thick mouldy batches. Consequently no doubts disturbed him, and Willard felt the hopelessness of grappling with an ignorance so much deeper and denser than his own. Whichever way his mind turned, it seemed to bring up against the blank wall of Harry Spink's: "What's the use?"

He slipped through the crowds in the congested gateway, and made straight for the Mission. He had decided to go to the French Administration, but he wanted first to find out from the servants what Mr. Blandhorn was doing, and what his state of mind appeared to be.

The Mission door was locked, but Willard was not surprised; he knew the precaution was sometimes taken on feast days, though seldom so early. He rang, and waited impatiently for Myriem's old face in the crack; but no one came, and below his breath he cursed her with expurgated curses.

"Ayoub—*Ayoub!*" he cried, rattling at the door; but still no answer. Ayoub, apparently, was off too. Willard rang the bell again, giving the three long pulls of the "emergency call"; it was the summons which always roused Mr. Blandhorn. But no one came.

Willard shook and pounded, and hung on the bell till it tinkled its life out in a squeak . . . but all in vain. The house was empty: Mr. Blandhorn was evidently out with the others.

Disconcerted, the young man turned, and plunged into the red clay purlieus behind the Mission. He entered a mud-hut where an emaciated dog, dozing on the threshold, lifted a recognizing lid, and let him by. It was the house of Ahmed's father, the water-carrier, and Willard knew it would be empty at that hour.

A few minutes later there emerged into the crowded streets a young American dressed in a black coat of vaguely clerical cut, with a soft felt hat shading his flushed cheek-bones, and a bead running up and down his nervous throat.

The bazaar was already full of a deep holiday rumour, like the rattle of wind in the palm-tops. The young man in the clerical coat, sharply examined as he passed by hundreds of long Arab eyes, slipped into the lanes behind the soukhs, and by circuitous passages gained the neighbourhood of the Great Mosque. His heart was hammering against his black coat, and under the buzz in his brain there boomed out insistently the old question: "What's the use?"

Suddenly, near the fountain that faced one of the doors of the Great Mosque, he saw the figure of a man dressed like himself. The eyes of the two men met across the crowd, and Willard pushed his way to Mr. Blandhorn's side.

"Sir, why did you—why are you—? I'm back—I couldn't help it," he gasped out disconnectedly.

He had expected a vehement rebuke; but the old missionary only smiled on him sadly. "It was noble of you, Willard . . . I understand. . ." He looked at the young man's coat. "We had the same thought—again—at the same hour." He paused, and drew Willard into the empty passage of a ruined building behind the fountain. "But what's the use,—what's the use?" he exclaimed.

The blood rushed to the young man's forehead. "Ah—then you feel it too?"

Mr. Blandhorn continued, grasping his arm: "I've been out—in this dress—ever since you left; I've hung about the doors of the Medersas, I've walked up to the very threshold of the Mosque, I've leaned against the wall of Sidi Oman's shrine; once the police warned me, and I pretended to go away . . . but I came back. . . I pushed up closer. . . I stood in the doorway of the Mosque, and they saw me . . . the people inside saw me . . . and no one touched me . . . I'm too harmless . . . *they don't believe in me!*"

He broke off, and under his struggling eyebrows Willard saw the tears on his old lids.

The young man gathered courage. "But don't you see, sir, that that's the reason it's no use? We don't understand them any more than they do us; they know it, and all our witnessing for Christ will make no difference."

Mr. Blandhorn looked at him sternly. "Young man, no Christian has the right to say that."

Willard ignored the rebuke. "Come home, sir, come home . . . it's no use. . ."

"It was because I foresaw you would take this view that I sent you to Mogador. Since I was right," exclaimed Mr. Blandhorn, facing round on him fiercely, "how is it you have disobeyed me and come back?"

Willard was looking at him with new eyes. All his majesty seemed to have fallen from him with his Arab draperies. How short and heavy and weak he looked in his scant European clothes! The coat, tightly strained across the stomach, hung above it in loose wrinkles, and the ill-fitting trousers revealed their wearer's impressive legs as slightly bowed at the knees. This diminution in his physical prestige was strangely moving to his disciple. What was there left, with that gone—?

"Oh, do come home, sir," the young man groaned. "Of course they don't care what we do—of course—"

"Ah—" cried Mr. Blandhorn, suddenly dashing past him into the open.

The rumour of the crowd had become a sort of roaring chant. Over the thousands of bobbing heads that packed every cranny of the streets leading to the space before the

Mosque there ran the mysterious sense of something new, invisible, but already imminent. Then, with the strange Oriental elasticity, the immense throng divided, and a new throng poured through it, headed by riders ritually draped, and overhung with banners which seemed to be lifted and floated aloft on the shouts of innumerable throats. It was the Pasha of Eloued coming to pray at the tomb of Sidi Oman.

Into this mass Mr. Blandhorn plunged and disappeared, while Willard Bent, for an endless minute, hung back in the shelter of the passage, the old "What's the use?" in his ears.

A hand touched his sleeve, and a cracked voice echoed the words.

"What's the use, master?" It was old Myriem, clutching him with scared face and pulling out a limp djellabah from under her holiday shawl.

"I saw you . . . Ahmed's father told me. . ." (How everything was known in the bazaars!) "Here, put this on quick, and slip away. They won't trouble you. . ."

"Oh, but they will—they *shall!*" roared Willard, in a voice unknown to his own ears, as he flung off the old woman's hand and, trampling on the djellabah in his flight, dashed into the crowd at the spot where it had swallowed up his master.

They would—they *should!* No more doubting and weighing and conjecturing! The sight of the weak unwieldy old man, so ignorant, so defenceless and so convinced, disappearing alone into that red furnace of fanaticism, swept from the disciple's mind every thought but the single passion of devotion.

That he lay down his life for his friend— If he couldn't bring himself to believe in any other reason for what he was doing, that one seemed suddenly to be enough. . .

The crowd let him through, still apparently indifferent to his advance. Closer, closer he pushed to the doors of the Mosque, struggling and elbowing through a mass of people so densely jammed that the heat of their breathing was in his face, the rank taste of their bodies on his parched lips—closer, closer, till a last effort of his own thin body, which seemed a mere cage of ribs with a wild heart dashing against it, brought him to the doorway of the Mosque, where Mr. Blandhorn, his head thrown back, his arms crossed on his chest, stood steadily facing the heathen multitude.

As Willard reached his side their glances met, and the old man, glaring out under prophetic brows, whispered without moving his lips: "Now—*now!*"

Willard took it as a signal to follow, he knew not where or why: at that moment he had no wish to know.

Mr. Blandhorn, without waiting for an answer, had turned, and, doubling on himself, sprung into the great court of the Mosque. Willard breathlessly followed, the glitter of tiles and the blinding sparkle of fountains in his dazzled eyes. . .

The court was almost empty, the few who had been praying having shortened their devotions and joined the Pasha's train, which was skirting the outer walls of the Mosque to reach the shrine of Sidi Oman. Willard was conscious of a moment of detached reconnoitring: once or twice, from the roof of a deserted college to which the government architect had taken him, he had looked down furtively on the forbidden scene, and his sense of direction told him that the black figure speeding across the blazing mirror of wet tiles was making for the hall where the Koran was expounded to students.

Even now, as he followed, through the impending sense of something dangerous and tremendous he had the feeling that after all perhaps no one would bother them, that all the effort of will pumped up by his storming heart to his lucid brain might conceivably end in some pitiful anti-climax in the French Administration offices.

"They'll treat us like whipped puppies—"

But Mr. Blandhorn had reached the school, had disappeared under its shadowy arcade, and emerged again into the blaze of sunlight, clutching a great parchment Koran.

"Ah," thought Willard, *"now—!"*

He found himself standing at the missionary's side, so close that they must have made one black blot against the white-hot quiver of tiles. Mr. Blandhorn lifted up the Book and spoke.

"The God whom ye ignorantly worship, Him declare I unto you," he cried in halting Arabic.

A deep murmur came from the turbaned figures gathered under the arcade of the Mosque. Swarthy faces lowered, eyes gleamed like agate, teeth blazed under snarling lips; but the group stood motionless, holding back, visibly restrained by the menace of the long arm of the Administration.

"Him declare I unto you—Christ crucified!" cried Mr. Blandhorn.

An old man, detaching himself from the group, advanced across the tiles and laid his hand on the missionary's arm. Willard recognized the Cadi of the Mosque.

"You must restore the Book," the Cadi said gravely to Mr. Blandhorn, "and leave this court immediately; if not—"

He held out his hand to take the Koran. Mr. Blandhorn, in a flash, dodged the restraining arm, and, with a strange new elasticity of his cumbrous body, rolling and bouncing across the court between the dazed spectators, gained the gateway opening on the market-place behind the Mosque. The centre of the great dusty space was at the moment almost deserted. Mr. Blandhorn sprang forward, the Koran clutched to him, Willard panting at his heels, and the turbaned crowd after them, menacing but still visibly restrained.

In the middle of the square Mr. Blandhorn halted, faced about and lifted the Koran high above his head. Willard, rigid at his side, was obliquely conscious of the gesture, and at the same time aware that the free space about them was rapidly diminishing under the mounting tide of people swarming in from every quarter. The faces closest were no longer the gravely wrathful countenances of the Mosque, but lean fanatical masks of pilgrims, beggars, wandering "saints" and miracle-makers, and dark tribesmen of the hills careless of their creed but hot to join in the halloo against the hated stranger. Far off in the throng, bobbing like a float on the fierce sea of turbans, Willard saw the round brown face of a native officer frantically fighting his way through. Now and then the face bobbed nearer, and now and then a tug of the tide rolled it back.

Willard felt Mr. Blandhorn's touch on his arm.

"You're with me—?"

"Yes—"

The old man's voice sank and broke. "Say a word to . . . strengthen me. . . I can't find any . . . Willard," he whispered.

Willard's brain was a blank. But against the blank a phrase suddenly flashed out in letters of fire, and he turned and spoke it to his master. *"Say among the heathen that the Lord reigneth!"*

"Ah—." Mr. Blandhorn, with a gasp, drew himself to his full height and hurled the Koran down at his feet in the dung-strown dust.

"Him, Him declare I unto you—Christ crucified!" he thundered: and to Willard, in a fierce aside: "Now spit!"

Dazed a moment, the young man stood uncertain; then he saw the old missionary draw back a step, bend forward, and deliberately spit upon the sacred pages.

"This . . . is abominable . . ." the disciple thought; and, sucking up the last drop of saliva from his dry throat, he also bent and spat.

"Now trample—*trample!*" commanded Mr. Blandhorn, his arms stretched out, towering black and immense, as if crucified against the flaming sky; and his foot came down on the polluted Book.

Willard, seized with the communicative frenzy, fell on his knees, tearing at the pages, and scattering them about him, smirched and defiled in the dust.

"Spit—spit! Trample—trample! . . . Christ! I see the heavens opened!" shrieked the old missionary, covering his eyes with his hands. But what he said next was lost to his disciple in the rising roar of the mob which had closed in on them. Far off, Willard caught a glimpse of the native officer's bobbing head, and then of Lieutenant Lourdenay's scared face. But a moment later he had veiled his own face from the sight of the struggle at his side. Mr. Blandhorn had fallen on his knees, and Willard heard him cry out once: "Sadie—*Sadie!*" It was Mrs. Blandhorn's name.

Then the young man was himself borne down, and darkness descended on him. Through it he felt the sting of separate pangs indescribable, melting at last into a general mist of pain. He remembered Stephen, and thought: "Now they're stoning me—" and tried to struggle up and reach out to Mr. Blandhorn. . .

But the market-place seemed suddenly empty, as though the throng of their assailants had been demons of the desert, the thin spirits of evil that dance on the noonday heat. Now the dusk seemed to have dispersed them, and Willard looked up and saw a quiet star above a wall, and heard the cry of the muezzin dropping down from a near-by minaret: "Allah—Allah—only Allah is great!"

Willard closed his eyes, and in his great weakness felt the tears run down between his lids. A hand wiped them away, and he looked again, and saw the face of Harry Spink stooping over him.

He supposed it was a dream-Spink, and smiled a little, and the dream smiled back.

"Where am I?" Willard wondered to himself; and the dream-Spink answered: "In the hospital, you infernal fool. I got back too late—"

"You came back—?"

"Of course. Lucky I did—! I saw this morning you were off your base."

Willard, for a long time, lay still. Impressions reached him slowly, and he had to deal with them one by one, like a puzzled child.

At length he said: "Mr. Blandhorn—?"

Spink bent his head, and his voice was grave in the twilight.

"They did for him in no time; I guess his heart was weak. I don't think he suffered. Anyhow, if he did he wasn't sorry; I know, because I saw his face before they buried him. . . Now you lie still, and I'll get you out of this tomorrow," he commanded, waving a fly-cloth above Willard's sunken head.

Velvet Ear-Pads

P ROFESSOR LORING G. HIBBART, of Purewater University, Clio, N.Y., settled himself in the corner of his compartment in the Marseilles-Ventimiglia express, drew his velvet ear-pads from his pocket, slipped them over his ears, and began to think.

It was nearly three weeks since he had been able to indulge undisturbed in this enchanting operation. On the steamer which had brought him from Boston to Marseilles considerable opportunity had in truth been afforded him, for though he had instantly discovered his fellow-passengers to be insinuating and pervasive, an extremely rough passage had soon reduced them to inoffensiveness. Unluckily the same cause had in like manner affected the Professor; and when the ship approached calmer waters, and he began to revive, the others revived also, and proceeded to pervade, to insinuate and even to multiply—since a lady gave birth to twins as they entered the Mediterranean.

As for the tumultuous twenty-four hours since his landing, the Professor preferred not to include them in his retrospect. It was enough that they were over. "All I want is *quiet*," he had said to the doctors who, after his alarming attack of influenza, followed by bronchial pneumonia, had ordered an immediate departure for warmer climes; and they had thrust him onto an excursion-steamer jammed with noisy sight-seers, and shipped him to a port whither all the rest of the world appeared to be bound at the same moment! His own fault, perhaps? Well—he never could plan or decide in a hurry, and when, still shaken by illness, he had suddenly been told that he must spend six months in a mild climate, and been faced with the alternatives of southern California or southern France, he had chosen the latter because it meant a more complete escape from professional associations and the terror of meeting people one knew. As far as climate went, he understood the chances to be equal; and all he wanted was to recover from his pulmonary trouble and employ his enforced leisure in writing a refutation of Einstein's newly published book on Relativity.

Once the Professor had decided on the south of France, there remained the difficulty of finding, in that populous region, a spot quiet enough to suit him; but after much anxious consultation with colleagues who shared his dread of noise and of promiscuous human intercourse, he had decided on a secluded *pension* high up in the hills, between Monte Carlo and Mentone. In this favoured spot, he was told, no dogs barked, cocks crew or cats courted. There were no waterfalls, or other sonorous natural phenomena, and it was utterly impossible for a motor (even with its muffler knocked off) to ascend the precipitous lane which led to the *pension*. If, in short, it were possible to refute Einstein's theory, it was in just such a place, and there only, that the feat might be accomplished.

Once settled in the train, the Professor breathed more freely. Most of his fellow-passengers had stayed on the ship, which was carrying them on to swarm over a succession of other places as he had just left them swarming over Marseilles. The train he got into was not very crowded, and should other travellers enter the compartment, his ear-pads would secure him from interruption. At last he could revert to the absorbing thought of the book he was planning; could plunge into it like a diver into the ocean. He drew a deep breath and plunged. . .

Certainly the compartment had been empty when the train left Marseilles—he was sure of that; but he seemed to remember now that a man had got in at a later station, though he couldn't have said where or when; for once he began to think, time vanished from him as utterly as space.

He became conscious of the intruding presence only from the smell of tobacco gradually insinuating itself into his nostrils. Very gradually; for when the Professor had withdrawn into his inner stronghold of Pure Reason, and pulled up the ladder, it was not easy for any appeal to reach him through the channel of the senses. Not that these were defective in him. Far from it: he could smell and see, taste and hear, with any man alive; but for many years past he had refrained from exercising these faculties except in so far as they conduced to the maintenance of life and security. He would have preferred that the world should contain nothing to see, nothing to smell, nothing to hear; and by negativing persistently every superfluous hint of his visual, auditive or olfactory organs he had sheathed himself in a general impenetrability of which the ear-pads were merely a restricted symbol.

His noticing the whiff of tobacco was an accident, a symptom of his still disorganized state; he put the smell resolutely from him, registered "A Man Opposite," and plunged again into the Abstract.

Once—about an hour later, he fancied—the train stopped with a jerk which flung him abruptly out of his corner. His mental balance was disturbed, and for one irritating instant his gaze unwillingly rested on silver groves, purple promontories and a blue sea. "Ugh—*scenery!*" he muttered; and with a renewed effort of the will he dropped his mental curtain between that inconsequent jumble of phenomena and the absolutely featureless area in which the pure intellect thrones. The incident had brought back the smell of his neighbour's cigarette; but the Professor sternly excluded that also, and the train moved on. . .

Professor Hibbart was in truth a man of passionately excitable nature: no one was ever, by temperament, less adapted to the lofty intellectual labours in which his mind delighted. He asked only to live in the empyrean; but he was perpetually being dragged back to earth by the pity, wrath or contempt excited in him by the slipshod course of human affairs. There were only two objects on which he flattered himself he could always look with a perfectly unseeing eye; and these were a romantic landscape and a pretty woman. And he was not absolutely sure about the landscape.

Suddenly a touch, soft yet peremptory, was laid on his arm. Looking down, he beheld a gloved hand; looking up he saw that the man opposite him was a woman.

To this awkward discovery he was still prepared to oppose the blank wall of the most complete imperception. But a sharp pinch proved that the lady who had taken hold of his arm had done so with the fixed determination to attract his attention, at the cost of whatever pain or inconvenience to himself. As she appeared also to be saying something—probably asking if the next station were the one at which she ought to get out—he formed with soundless lips the word

"Deaf," and pointed to his ears. The lady's reply was to release his wrist, and with her free hand flick off an ear-pad.

"Deaf? Oh, no," she said briskly, in fluent but exotic English. "You wouldn't need ear-pads if you were. You don't want to be bothered—that's all. I know the trick; you got it out of Herbert Spencer!"

The assault had nearly disabled the Professor for farther resistance; but he rallied his wits and answered stonily: "I have no time-table. You'd better consult the guard."

The lady threw her spent cigarette out of the window. As the smoke drifted away from her features he became uneasily aware that they were youthful, and that the muscles about her lips and eyes were contracted into what is currently known as a smile. In another moment, he realized with dismay, he was going to know what she looked like. He averted his eyes.

"I don't want to consult the guard—I want to consult *you*," said the lady.

His ears took reluctant note of an intonation at once gay and appealing, which caressed the "You" as if it were a new pronoun rich in vowels, and the only one of its kind in the world.

"Eeee-you," she repeated.

He shook his averted head. "I don't know the name of a single station on this line."

"Dear me, don't you?" The idea seemed to shock her, to make a peculiar appeal to her sympathy. "But I do—every one of them! With my eyes shut. Listen: I'll begin at the beginning. Paris—"

"But I don't *want* to know them!" he almost screamed.

"Well, neither do I. What I want is to ask you a favour—just one tiny little enormous favour."

The Professor still looked away. "I have been in very bad health until recently," he volunteered.

"Oh, I'm so glad—glad, I mean," she corrected herself hastily, "that you're all right again now! And glad too that you've been ill, since that just confirms it—"

Here the Professor fell. "Confirms what?" he snapped, and saw too late the trap into which he had plunged.

"My belief that you are predestined to help me," replied his neighbour with joyful conviction.

"Oh, but that's quite a mistake—a complete mistake. I never in my life helped anybody, in any way. I've always made it a rule not to."

"Not even a Russian refugee?"

"Never!"

"Oh, yes, you have. You've helped *me!*"

The Professor turned an ireful glance upon her, and she nodded. "I am a Russian refugee."

"You?" he exclaimed. His eyes, by this time, had definitely escaped from his control, and were recording with an irrepressible activity and an exasperating precision the details of her appearance and her dress. Both were harmonious and opulent. He laughed incredulously.

"Why do you laugh? Can't you *see* that I'm a refugee; by my clothes, I mean? Who has such pearls but Russian refugees? Or such sables? We have to have them—to sell, of course! You don't care to buy my sables, do you? For you they would be only six thousand pounds cash. No, I thought not. It's my duty to ask—but I didn't suppose they would interest you. The Paris and London jewellers farm out the pearls to us; the big dressmakers supply the furs. For of course we've all sold the originals long ago. And really I've been rather successful. I placed two sets of silver fox and a rope of pearls last week at Monte Carlo. Ah, that fatal place! I gambled away the whole of my commission the same night. . . But I'm forgetting to tell you how you've already helped me. . ."

She paused to draw breath, and in the pause the Professor, who had kept his hand on his loosened ear-pad, slipped it back over his ear.

"I wear these," he said coldly, "to avoid argument."

With a flick she had it off again. "I wasn't going to argue— I was only going to thank you."

"I can't conceive for what. In any case, I don't want to be thanked."

Her brows gathered resentfully. "Why did you *ask* to be, then?" she snapped; and opening a bejewelled wrist-bag she drew forth from a smother of cigarette-papers and pawn-tickets a slip of paper on which her astonished companion read a phrase written in a pointed feminine hand, but signed with his own name.

"There!"

The Professor took the paper and scanned it indignantly. "This copy of 'The Elimination of Phenomena' was presented by Professor Loring G. Hibbart of Purewater University, Clio, N.Y., to the library of the American Y.M.C.A. Refugee Centre at Odessa.

"A word of appreciation, sent by any reader to the above address, would greatly gratify Loring G. Hibbart."

"There!" she repeated. "Why did you ask to be thanked if you didn't want to be? What else does 'greatly gratify' mean? I couldn't write to you from Odessa because I hadn't the money to buy a stamp; but I've longed ever since to tell you what your book did for me. It simply changed my whole life —books do sometimes, you know. I saw everything differently—even our Refugee Centre! I decided at once to give up my lover and divorce my husband. Those were my two first Eliminations." She smiled retrospectively. "But you mustn't think I'm a frivolous person. I have my degree as a Doctor of Philosophy—I took it at sixteen, at the University of Moscow. I gave up philosophy the year after for sculpture; the next year I gave up sculpture for mathematics and love. For a year I loved. After that I married Prince Balalatinsky. He was my cousin, and enormously wealthy. I need not have divorced him, as it turned out, for he was soon afterward buried alive by the Bolsheviks. But how could I have foreseen it? And your book had made me feel—"

"Good gracious!" the author of the book interrupted desperately. "You don't suppose *I* wrote that rubbish about wanting to be thanked, do you?"

"Didn't you? How could I tell? Almost all the things sent from America to the refugee camp came with little labels like that. You all seemed to think we were sitting before perfectly appointed desks, with fountain pens and stamp-cases from Bond Street in our pockets. I remember once getting a lipstick and a Bernard Shaw calendar labelled: 'If the refugee who receives these would write a line of thanks to little Sadie Burt of Meropee Junction, Ga., who bought them out of her own savings by giving up chewing-gum for a whole month, it would make a little American girl very happy.' Of course I was sorry not to be able to write to little Sadie." She broke off, and then added: "Do you know, I was sure you were my Professor as soon as I saw your name on your suit-case?"

"Good Lord!" groaned the Professor. He had forgotten to remove the obligatory steamer-labels! Instinctively he reached out a hand to tear off the offending member; but again a gesture of the Princess's arrested him. "It's too late now. And you can't surely grudge me the pleasure of thanking you for your book?"

"But I *didn't* ask—"

"No; but I wanted to. You see, at that time I had quite discarded philosophy. I was living in the Actual—with a young officer of Preobrajensky—when the war broke out. And of course in our camp at Odessa the Actual was the very thing one wanted to get away from. And your book took me straight back into that other world where I had known my only pure happiness. Purity—what a wonderful thing it is! What a pity it is so hard to keep; like money, and everything else really valuable! But I'm thankful for any little morsel of it that I've had. When I was only ten years old—"

But suddenly she drew back and nestled down into her lustrous furs. "You thought I was going to tell you the story of my life? No. Put your ear-pads on again. I know now why you wear them—because you're planning a new book. Is it not so? You see I can read your thoughts. Go on—do! I would rather assist at the birth of a masterpiece than chatter about my own insignificant affairs."

The Professor smiled. If she thought masterpieces were born in that way—between railway stations, and in a whirl of prattle! Yet he was not wholly angry. Either because it had been unexpectedly agreeable to hear his book praised, or because of that harmonious impression which, now that he actually saw her, a protracted scrutiny confirmed, he began to feel more tolerantly toward his neighbour. Deliberately, his eyes still on hers, he pushed the other ear-pad away.

"Oh—" she said with a little gasp. "Does that mean I may go on talking?" But before he could answer, her face clouded. "I know—it only means that I might as well, now that I've broken in on your meditations. I'm dreadfully penitent; but luckily you won't have me for long, for I'm getting out at

Cannes, and Cannes is the next station. And that reminds me
of the enormous little favour I have to ask."

The Professor's face clouded also: he had a nervous apprehension of being asked favours. "My fountain pen," he said,
regaining firmness of tone, "is broken."

"Ah—you thought I meant to ask for your autograph? Or
perhaps for a cheque?" (Lord, how quick she was!) She shook
her head. "No, I don't care for compulsory autographs. And
I'm not going to ask for money—I'm going to give you
some."

He faced her with renewed dismay. Could it be—? After all,
he was not more than fifty-seven; and the blameless life he
had led had perhaps helped to preserve a certain . . . at least
that was *one* theory. . . In these corrupt European societies
what might a man not find himself exposed to? With some
difficulty he executed a pinched smile.

"Money?"

She nodded again. "Oh, don't laugh! Don't think I'm joking. It's your ear-pads," she disconcertingly added.

"My—?"

"Yes. If you hadn't put them on I should never have spoken to you; for it wasn't till afterward that I saw your name
on the suit-case. And after that I should have been too shy to
break in on the meditations of a Great Philosopher. But you
see I have been watching—oh, for years!—for your ear-pads."

He stared at her helplessly. "You want to buy them from
me?" he asked in terror, wondering how on earth he would
be able to get others in a country of which he did not speak
the language.

She burst into a laugh that ran up and down the whole
scale of friendly derision and tender mockery.

"Buy them? Gracious, no! I could make myself a better pair
in five minutes." She smiled at his visible relief. "But you see
I'm ruined—stony broke; isn't that what they call it? I have a
young American friend who is always saying that about himself. And once in the Caucasus, years ago, a gipsy told me that
if ever I had gambled away my last penny (and I nearly *have*)
it would all be won back by a pale intellectual looking man in
velvet ear-pads, if only I could induce him to put a stake on

the tables for me." She leaned forward and scrutinized him. "You *are* very pale, you know," she said, "and very intellectual looking. I was sure it was you when you told me you'd been ill."

Professor Loring D. Hibbart looked about him desperately. He knew now that he was shut up with a madwoman. A harmless one, probably; but what if, in the depths of that jewelled bag, a toy revolver lurked under the pawn-tickets and the cigarette papers? The Professor's life had been so guarded from what are known as "exciting situations" that he was not sure of his ability to meet one with becoming tact and energy.

"I suppose I'm a physical coward," he reflected bitterly, an uncomfortable dampness breaking out all over him. "And I *know*," he added in self-extenuation, "that I'm in no condition yet for any sort of a struggle. . ."

But what did one do with lunatics? If only he could remember! And suddenly he did: one humoured them!

Fortified by the thought, he made shift to glance more kindly toward the Princess Balalatinsky. "So you want me to gamble for you?" he said, in the playful tone he might have adopted in addressing little Sadie Burt of Meropee.

"Oh, how glorious of you! You will? I *knew* you would! But first," she broke off, "you must let me explain—"

"Oh, do explain, of course," he agreed, rapidly calculating that her volubility might make the explanation last until they reached the next station, where, as she had declared, she was to leave the train.

Already her eye was less wild; and he drew an inward breath of relief.

"You angel, you! I *do*," she confessed, "simply love to talk about myself. And I'm sure you'll be interested when I tell you that, if you'll only do as I ask, I shall be able to marry one of your own compatriots—such a beautiful heroic youth! It is for him, for him only, that I long to be wealthy again. If you loved, could you bear to see your beloved threatened with starvation?"

"But I thought," he gently reminded her, "that it was you who were threatened with starvation?"

"We *both* are. Isn't it terrible? You see, when we met and loved, we each had the same thought—to make the other

wealthy! It was not possible, at the moment, for either of us
to attain our end by the natural expedient of a rich marriage
with reasonable prospect of a quick divorce—so we staked our
all at those accursed tables, and we both lost! My poor betrothed has only a few hundred francs left, and as for me, I
have had to take a miserably paid job as a dressmaker's *mannequin* at Cannes. But I see you are going on to Monte Carlo
(yes, that's on your luggage too); and as I don't suppose you
will spend a night there without visiting the rooms, I—" She
was pulling forth the hundred francs from her inexhaustible
bag when the Professor checked her with dismay. Mad
though she might be, he could not even make believe to take
her money.

"I'm *not* spending a night at Monte Carlo," he protested.
"I'm only getting out there to take a motorbus for a quiet
place up in the hills; I've the name written down somewhere;
my room is engaged, so I couldn't possibly wait over," he argued gently.

She looked at him with what seemed to his inflamed imagination the craftiness of a maniac. "Don't you know that our
train is nearly two hours late? I don't suppose you noticed
that we ran over a crowded excursion charabanc near Toulon?
Didn't you even hear the ambulances rushing up? Your motorbus will certainly have left Monte Carlo when you arrive,
so you'll *have* to spend the night there! And even if you
don't," she added persuasively, "the station's only two steps
from the Casino, and you surely can't refuse just to nip in for
half an hour." She clasped her hands in entreaty. "You
wouldn't refuse if you knew my betrothed—your young compatriot! If only we had a few thousands all would go smoothly.
We should be married at once and go to live on his ancestral
estate of Kansas. It appears the climate is that of Africa in
summer and of the Government of Omsk in winter; so our
plan is to grow oranges and breed sables. You see, we can
hardly fail to succeed with two such crops. All we ask is enough
money to make a start. And that you will get for me tonight.
You have only to stake this hundred franc note; you'll win on
the first turn, and you'll go on winning. You'll see!"

With one of her sudden plunges she pried open his contracted fist and pressed into it a banknote wrapped in a torn

envelope. "Now listen; this is my address at Cannes. Princess Balala—oh, here's the station. Good-bye, guardian angel. No, *au revoir*, I shall see you soon. They call me Betsy at the dressmaker's. . ."

Before he could open his convulsed fingers, or dash out after her, she had vanished, bag and baggage, in the crowd and confusion of the platform; other people, pushing and chattering and tearing themselves from the embrace of friends, had piled into her place, and were waving from the window, and blocking the way out; and now the train was moving on, and there he sat in his corner, aghast, clutching the banknote. . .

II

At Monte Carlo the Professor captured a porter and rescued his luggage. Exhausted by this effort, and by the attempt to communicate with the porter, first in Latin and then in French as practised at Purewater, he withdrew to a corner of the waiting-room and fished in his pockets for the address of the quiet *pension* in the hills. He found it at last, and handed it wearily to the porter. The latter threw up his hands. "*Parti! Parti! Autobus* gone." That devil of a woman had been right!

When would there be another, the Professor asked.

Not till tomorrow morning at 8:30. To confirm his statement the porter pointed to a large time-table on the wall of the waiting-room. The Professor scanned it and sat down again with a groan. He was about to consult his companion as to the possibility of finding a night's lodging in a respectable *pension* (fantastic as the idea seemed in such a place); but hardly had he begun: "Can you tell me where—" when, with a nod of comprehension and a wink of complicity, the porter returned in fluent English: "Pretty ladies? Turkish bath? Fottographs?"

The Professor repudiated these suggestions with a shudder, and leaving his bags in the cloak-room set forth on his quest. He had hardly taken two steps when another stranger of obviously doubtful morality offered him a pamphlet which he was indignantly rejecting when he noticed its title: "The

Theory of Chance in Roulette." The theory of chance was deeply interesting to the Professor, and the idea of its application to roulette not without an abstract attraction. He bought the pamphlet and sat down on the nearest bench.

His study was so absorbing that he was roused only by the fall of twilight, and the scattered twinkle of many lamps all radiating up to the central focus of the Casino. The Professor started to his feet, remembering that he had still to find a lodging. "And I must be up early to catch the bus," he reminded himself. He took his way down a wide empty street apparently leading to a quieter and less illuminated quarter. This street he followed for some distance, vainly scrutinizing the houses, which seemed all to be private dwellings, till at length he ran against a slim well-set-up young fellow in tennis flannels, with a bright conversational eye, who was strolling along from the opposite direction.

"Excuse me, sir," said the Professor.

"What for?" rejoined the other, in a pleasant tone made doubly pleasant by the familiar burr of the last word, which he pronounced like *fur*.

"Why, you're an American!" exclaimed the Professor.

"Sher*lock!*" exulted the young man, extending his hand. "I diagnose the same complaint in yourself."

The Professor sighed pleasurably. "Oh, yes. What I want," he added, "is to find a plain quiet boarding-house or family hotel."

"Same as mother used to make 'em?" The young man reflected. "Well, it's a queer place in which to prosecute your search; but there *is* one at Monte, and I'm about the only person that knows it. My name's Taber Tring. Come along."

For a second the Professor's eye rested doubtfully on Mr. Tring. He knew, of course—even at Purewater it was known —that in the corrupt capitals of Europe one could not always rely implicitly on the information given by strangers casually encountered; no, not even when it was offered with affability, and in the reassuring twang of the Western States. But after all Monte Carlo was not a capital; it was just an absurd little joke of a town crammed on a ledge between sea and mountain; and a second glance at the young man convinced the Professor that he was as harmless as the town.

Mr. Tring, who seemed quick at thought-reading, returned his look with an amused glance.

"Not much like our big and breezy land, is it? These Riviera resorts always remind me of the subway at rush hours; everybody strap-hanging. But my landlady is an old friend, and I know one of her boarders left this morning, because I heard her trying to seize his luggage. He got away; so I don't see why you shouldn't have his room. See?"

The Professor saw. But he became immediately apprehensive of having his own luggage seized, an experience unprecedented in his history.

"Are such things liable to occur in this place?" he enquired.

"What? A scrap with your landlady? Not if you pay up regularly; or if she likes you. I guess she didn't like that other fellow; and I know he was always on the wrong side of the tables."

"The tables—do you refer to the gambling tables?" The Professor stopped short to put the question.

"That's it," said the other.

"And do you yourself sometimes visit the gambling-rooms?" the Professor next enquired.

"Oh, hell," said Taber Tring expressively.

The Professor scrutinized him with growing interest. "And have you a theory of chance?"

The young man met his gaze squarely. "I have; but it can't be put into language that would pass the censor."

"Ah—you refer, no doubt, to your personal experience. But, as regards the theory—"

"Well, the theory has let me down to bedrock; and I came down on it devilish hard." His expression turned from apathy to animation. "I'm stony broke; but if you'd like to lend me a hundred francs to have another try—"

"Oh, no," said the Professor hastily; "I don't possess it." And his doubts began to stir again.

Taber Tring laughed. "Of course you don't; not for lending purposes. I was only joking; everybody makes that joke here. Well, here's the house; I'll go ahead and rout out our hostess."

They stopped before a pleasant-looking little house at the end of the street. A palm-tree, a couple of rose-bushes and a gateway surmounted by the word *Arcadie* divided it from the pavement; the Professor drew a breath of relief as a stout lady in an orange wig bustled out to receive him.

In spite of the orange wig her face was so full of a shrewd benevolence that the Professor felt sure he had reached a haven of rest. She welcomed him affably, informed him that she had a room, and offered to lead him up to it. "Only for tonight, though? For it is promised to a Siamese nobleman for tomorrow."

This, the Professor assured her, made no difference, as he would be leaving at daylight. But on the lowest step of the stair he turned and addressed himself to Mr. Tring.

"Perhaps the lady would be good enough to have my bags brought up from the station? If you would kindly explain that I'm going out now to take a little stroll. As I'm leaving so early tomorrow it's my only chance to have a look around."

"That's so; I'll tell her," the young man rejoined sympathetically; and as the Professor's hand was on the gate, he heard Mr. Tring call out, mimicking the stentorian tones of a megaphone man on a sight-seeing motorbus: "Third street to the left, then first right to the tables"; after which he added, in his natural tone: "Say, Arcadia locks up at midnight."

The Professor smiled at the superfluous hint.

III

Having satisfied a polyglot door-keeper as to his nationality, and the fact that he was not a minor, the Professor found himself in the gambling-rooms. They were not particularly crowded, for people were beginning to go out for dinner, and he was able to draw fairly near to the first roulette table he encountered.

As he stood looking over the shoulders of the players he understood that no study of abstract theories could be worth the experience acquired by thus observing the humours of the goddess in her very temple. Her caprices, so ably seconded by the inconceivable stupidity, timidity or rashness of her votaries, first amused and finally exasperated the Professor; he began to feel toward her something of the annoyance excited in him by the sight of a pretty woman, or any other vain superfluity, combined with the secret sense that if he chose he could make her dance to his tune, and that it might be mildly amusing to do so. He had felt the same once or twice—but only for a fugitive instant—about pretty women.

None, however, had ever attracted him as strongly as this veiled divinity. The longing to twitch the veil from her cryptic features became violent, irresistible. "Not one of these fools has any idea of the theory of chance," he muttered to himself, elbowing his way to a seat near one of the croupiers. As he did so, he put his hand into his pocket, and found to his disgust that it contained only a single five franc piece and a few *sous*. All the rest of his money—a matter of four or five hundred francs—lay locked up in his suit-case at *Arcadie*. He anathematized his luck in expurgated language, and was about to rise from the table when the croupier called out: *"Faites vos jeux, Messieurs."*

The Professor, with a murmured expletive which was to a real oath what Postum is to coffee, dropped back into his place and flung his five franc piece on the last three numbers. He lost.

Of course—in his excitement he had gone exactly contrary to his own theory! It was on the first three that he had meant to stake his paltry bet. Well; now it was too late. But stay—

Diving into another pocket, he came with surprise on a hundred franc note. Could it really be his? But no; he had an exact memorandum of his funds, and he knew this banknote was not to be thus accounted for. He made a violent effort to shake off his abstraction, and finally recalled that the note in question had been pressed into his hand that very afternoon as he left the train. But by whom—?

"Messieurs, faites vos jeux! Faites vos jeux! Le jeu est fait. Rien ne va plus."

The hundred francs, escaping from his hand, had fluttered of themselves to a number in the middle of the table. That number came up. Across the green board thirty-six other hundred franc notes flew swiftly back in the direction of the Professor. Should he put them all back on the same number? "Yes," he nodded calmly to the croupier's question; and the three-thousand seven hundred francs were guided to their place by the croupier's rake.

The number came up again, and another argosy of notes sailed into the haven of the happy gambler's pocket. This time he knew he ought to settle down quietly to his theory; and he did so. He staked a thousand and tripled it, then let the three thousand lie, and won again. He doubled that stake, and began to feel his neighbours watching him with mingled interest and envy as the winnings once more flowed his way. But to whom did this mounting pile really belong?

No time to think of that now; he was fast in the clutches of his theory. It seemed to guide him like some superior being seated at the helm of his intelligence: his private dæmon pitted against the veiled goddess! It was exciting, undoubtedly; considerably more so, for example, than taking tea with the President's wife at Purewater. He was beginning to feel like Napoleon, disposing his battalions to right and left, advancing, retreating, reinforcing or redistributing his troops. Ah, the veiled goddess was getting what she deserved for once!

At a late hour of the evening, when the Professor had become the centre of an ever-thickening crowd of fascinated observers, it suddenly came back to him that a woman had given him that original hundred franc note. A woman in the train that afternoon. . .

But what did he care for that? He was playing the limit at every stake; and his mind had never worked more clearly and with a more exquisite sense of complete detachment. He was in his own particular seventh heaven of lucidity. He even recalled, at the precise moment when cognizance of the fact became useful, that the doors of *Arcadie* closed at midnight, and that he had only just time to get back if he wished to sleep with a roof over his head.

As he did wish to, he pocketed his gains quietly and composedly, rose from the table and walked out of the rooms. He felt hungry, cheerful and alert. Perhaps, after all, excitement had been what he needed—pleasurable excitement, that is, not the kind occasioned by the small daily irritations of life, such as the presence of that woman in the train whose name he was still unable to remember. What he would have liked best of all would have been to sit down in one of the brightly lit cafés he was passing, before a bottle of beer and a ham sandwich; or perhaps what he had heard spoken of as a Welsh rabbit. But he did not want to sleep on a bench, for the night air was sharp; so he continued self-denyingly on his way to *Arcadie*.

A sleepy boy in a dirty apron let him in, locked up after him, and led him to a small bare room on the second floor. The stairs creaked and rattled as they mounted, and the rumblings of sleep sounded through the doors of the rooms they passed. *Arcadie* was a cramped and ramshackle construction, and the Professor hoped to heaven that his *pension* in the hills would be more solidly built and less densely inhabited. However, for one night it didn't matter—or so he imagined.

His guide left him, and he turned on the electric light, threw down on the table the notes with which all his pockets were bulging, and began to unstrap his portmanteaux.

Though he had so little luggage he always found the process of unpacking a long and laborious one; for he never could remember where he had put anything, and invariably passed through all the successive phases of apprehension and despair before he finally discovered his bedroom slippers in his sponge-bag, and the sponge itself (still dripping) rolled up inside his pyjamas.

But tonight he sought for neither sponge nor pyjamas, for as he opened his first suit-case his hand lit on a ream of spotless foolscap—the kind he always used for his literary work. The table on which he had tossed his winnings held a crusty hotel inkstand, and was directly overhung by a vacillating electric bulb. Before it was a chair; through the open window flowed the silence of the night, interwoven with the murmurs of a sleeping sea and hardly disturbed by the occasional far-off hoot of a motor horn. In his own brain was the same nocturnal quiet and serenity. A curious thing had happened to him. His bout with the veiled goddess had sharpened his wits and dragged him suddenly and completely out of the intellectual apathy into which he had been gradually immersed by his illness and the harassing discomforts of the last few weeks. He was no longer thinking now about the gambling tables or the theory of chance; but with all the strength of his freshly stimulated faculties was grappling the mighty monster with whom he meant to try a fall.

"Einstein!" he cried, as a Crusader might have shouted his battle-cry. He sat down at the table, shoved aside the bank-notes, plunged his pen into the blue mud of the inkstand, and began.

The silence was delicious, mysterious. Link by link the chain of his argument unrolled itself, travelling across his pages with the unending flow of a trail of migratory caterpillars. Not a break; not a hesitation. It was years since his mental machinery had worked with that smooth consecutiveness. He began to wonder whether, after all, it might not be better to give up the idea of a remote and doubtful *pension* in the hills, and settle himself for the winter in a place apparently so propitious to his intellectual activities.

It was then that the noises in the next room suddenly began. First there was the brutal slam of the door, followed by a silly bad-tempered struggle with a reluctant lock. Then a pair of shoes were flung down on the tiled floor. Water was next poured into an unsteady basin, and a water-jug set down with a hideous clatter on a rickety washstand which seemed to be placed against the communicating door between the two rooms. Turbulent ablutions ensued. These over, there succeeded a moment of deceptive calm, almost immediately succeeded by a series of whistled scales, emitted just above the whistler's breath, and merging into the exact though subdued reproduction of various barn-yard gutturals, ending up with the raucous yelp of a parrot proclaiming again and again: "I'm stony broke, I am!"

All the while Professor Hibbart's brain continued to marshal its arguments, and try to press them into the hard mould of words. But the struggle became more and more unequal as the repressed cacophony next door increased. At last he jumped up, rummaged in every pocket for his ear-pads and snapped them furiously over his ears. But this measure, instead of silencing the tenuous insistent noises from the next room, only made him strain for them more attentively through the protecting pads, giving them the super-natural shrillness of sounds heard at midnight in a sleeping house, the secret crackings and creakings against which heaped-up pillows and drawn-up bedclothes are a vain defence.

Finally the Professor noticed that there was a wide crack under the communicating door. Not till that crack was filled would work be possible. He jumped up again and dived at the washstand for towels. But he found that in the hasty preparation of the room the towels had been forgotten. A newspaper, then—but no; he cast about him in vain for a newspaper. . .

The noises had now sunk to a whisper, broken by irritating intervals of silence; but in the exasperated state of the Professor's nerves these irregular lulls, and the tension of watching for the sounds that broke them, were more trying than what had gone before. He sent a despairing glance about him, and his eye lit on the pile of banknotes on the table. He sprang up again, seized the notes, and crammed them into the crack.

After that the silence became suddenly and almost miraculously complete, and he went on with his writing.

IV

After his first twenty-four hours in the hills the Professor was ready to swear that this final refuge was all he had hoped for. The situation (though he had hardly looked out on it) seemed high yet sheltered; he had a vague impression of sunshine in his room; and when he went down on the first morning, after a deep and curative sleep, he at once found himself in a congenial atmosphere. No effusive compatriots; no bowing and scraping French; only four or five English people, as much in dread of being spoken to as he was of their speaking to him. He consumed the necessary number of square inches of proteins and carbohydrates and withdrew to his room, as stubbornly ignored as if the other guests had all thought he was trying to catch their eyes. An hour later he was lost in his work.

If only life could ever remain on an even keel! But something had made him suspect it from the first: *there was a baby in the house.* Of course everybody denied it: the cook said the bowl of pap left by accident on the stairs was for the cat; the landlady said she had been a widow twenty years, and did he suppose—? And the *bonne* denied that there was a smell of paregoric on the landing, and said that was the way the scent of mimosa sometimes affected people.

That night, after a constitutional in the garden (ear-pads on), the Professor went up to his room to resume his writing. For two hours he wrote uninterruptedly; then he was disturbed by a faint wail. He clapped on the pads, and continued; but the wail, low as it was, pierced them like a corkscrew. Finally he laid down his pen and listened, furiously. Every five minutes the sound came again. "I suppose they'll say it's a kitten!" he growled. No such pretence could deceive him for a moment; he remembered now that at the moment of entering the house he had noticed a smell of nursery. If only he had turned straight around and gone elsewhere! But where?

The idea of a fresh plunge into the unknown made him feel as weak as in the first stages of convalescence. And then his book had already sunk such talons into him; he could feel it sucking at his brain like some hungry animal. And all those people downstairs had been as cold and stony at dinner as they had at lunch. After two such encounters he was sure they would never bother him. A Paradise indeed, but for that serpent!

The wail continued, and he turned in his chair and looked slowly and desperately about him. The room was small and bare, and had only one door, the one leading into the passage. He vaguely recalled that, two nights before, at Monte Carlo, he had been disturbed in much the same way, and had found means to end the disturbance. What had he done? If only he could remember!

His eye went back to the door. There was a light under it now; no doubt someone was up with the child. Slowly his mind dropped from the empyrean to the level of the crack under the door.

"A couple of towels. . . Ah, but, there are no towels!" Almost as the words formed themselves, his glance lit on a well-garnished rack. What had made him think there were no towels? Why, he had been reliving the night at Monte Carlo, where in fact, he now remembered, he could find none, and to protect himself from the noise next door had had to. . .

"Oh, my God!" shouted the Professor. His pen clattered to the floor. He jumped up, and his chair crashed after it. The baby, terror-struck, ceased to cry. There was an awful silence.

"Oh, my God!" shouted the Professor.

Slowly the vision of that other room came back: he saw himself jumping up just as wildly, dashing for towels and finding none, and then seizing a pile of papers and cramming them into the crack under the door. Papers, indeed! "Oh, my God. . ."

It was money that he had seized that other night: hundreds of hundred franc bills; or hundreds of thousands, were they? How furiously he had crushed and crumpled them in his haste to cram enough stuffing into the crack! Money—an unbelievable amount of it. But how in the world had it got there, to whom on earth did it belong?

The Professor sat down on the edge of the bed and took his bursting head between his hands.

Daylight found him still labouring to reconstitute the succession of incredible episodes leading up to his mad act. Of all the piles of notes he had stuffed under the door not one franc had belonged to him. Of that he was now sure. He recalled also, but less clearly, that some one had given him a banknote —a hundred francs, he thought; was it on the steamer at Marseilles, or in the train?—given it with some mysterious injunction about gambling . . . that was as far as he could go at present. . . His mind had come down from the empyrean with a crash, and was still dazed from its abrupt contact with reality. At any rate, not a penny of the money was his, and he had left it all under the door in his hotel bedroom at Monte Carlo. And that was two days ago. . .

The baby was again crying, but the rest of the house still slept when, unkempt, unshorn, and with as many loose ends to his raiment as Hamlet, Professor Hibbart dashed out past an affrighted *bonne*, who cried after him that he might still catch the *autobus* if he took the short cut to the village.

To the Professor any abrupt emergence from his work was like coming to after a severe operation. He floated in a world as empty of ideas as of facts, and hemmed with slippery perpendicular walls. All the way to Monte Carlo those walls were made of the faces in the motorbus, blank inscrutable faces, smooth secret surfaces up which his mind struggled to clamber back to the actual. Only one definite emotion survived: hatred of the being—a woman, was it?—who had given him that fatal hundred franc note. He clung to that feeling as to a life-belt, waiting doggedly till it should lift him back to reality. If only he could have recalled his enemy's name!

Arrived at Monte Carlo he hailed a taxi and pronounced the one name he did recall: *Arcadie!* But what chance was there that the first chauffeur he met would know the title, or remember the site, of that undistinguished family hotel?

"*Arcadie?* But, of course! It's the place they're all asking for!" cried the chauffeur, turning without a moment's hesitation in what seemed to his fare to be the right direction. Yet how could that obscure pension be the place "they" were all asking for, and who in the name of madness were "they"?

"Are you sure—?" the Professor faltered.

"Of finding the way? *Allons donc;* we have only to follow the crowd!"

This was a slight exaggeration, for at that early hour the residential quarter of Monte Carlo was hardly more populous than when the Professor had last seen it; but if he had doubted being on the right road his doubt was presently dispelled by the sight of a well-set-up young man in tennis flannels, with a bright conversational eye, who came swinging along from the opposite direction.

"Taber Tring!" cried a voice from the depths of the Professor's sub-consciousness; and the Professor nearly flung himself over the side of the taxi in the effort to attract his friend's notice.

Apparently he had been mistaken; for the young man, arrested by his signals, gave back a blank stare from eyes grown suddenly speechless, and then, turning on his heels, disappeared double-quick down a side-street. The Professor, thrown back into his habitual uncertainty, wavered over the question of pursuit; but the taxi was still moving forward, and before he could decide what to do it had worked its way through a throng of gaping people and drawn up before a gate surmounted by the well-remembered *Arcadie.*

"There you are!" the chauffeur gestured, with the air of a parent humouring a spoilt child.

There he was! The Professor started to jump out, and pushing through the crowd was confronted with a smoking ruin. The garden gate, under its lying inscription, led straight into chaos; and behind where *Arcadie* had stood, other houses, blank unknown houses, were also shouldering up to gape at the disaster.

"But this is not the place!" remonstrated the Professor. "This is a house that has burnt down!"

"*Parbleu,*" replied the chauffeur, still humouring him.

The Professor's temples were bursting. "But was it—*was* it —was *this* Hotel *Arcadie*?"

The chauffeur shrugged again and pointed to the name.

"When—did it burn?"

"Early yesterday."

"And the landlady—the person who kept it?"

"*Ah, ça. . .*"

"But how, in the name of pity, can I find out?"

The chauffeur seemed moved by his distress. "Let Monsieur reassure himself. There was no loss of life. If Monsieur had friends or relations. . ."

The Professor waved away the suggestion.

"We could, of course, address ourselves to the police," the chauffeur continued.

The police! The mere sound of the word filled his hearer with dismay. Explain to the police about that money? How could he—and in his French? He turned cold at the idea, and in his dread of seeing himself transported to the *commissariat* by the too-sympathetic driver, he hurriedly paid the latter off, and remained alone gazing through the gate at the drenched and smoking monument of his folly.

The money—try to get back the money? It had seemed almost hopeless before; now the attempt could only expose him to all the mysterious perils of an alien law. He saw himself interrogated, investigated, his passport seized, his manuscript confiscated, and every hope of rational repose and work annihilated for months to come. He felt himself curiously eyed by the policeman who was guarding the ruins, and turned from the scene of the disaster almost as hurriedly as the young man whom he had taken—no doubt erroneously—for Taber Tring.

Having reached another quarter of the town, he sat down on a bench to take stock of his situation.

It was exactly what he had done two days before when, on arriving at Monte Carlo, he had found that he had missed the

motorbus; and the associations of ideas once more came to
his rescue.

Gradually there arose in his mind a faint wavering vision of
a young woman, pearled and furred and scented, precipitately
descending from his compartment, and, as she did so, cramming a banknote into his hand.

"The Princess . . . the Princess . . . *they call me Betsy at the
dressmaker's. . .*" That was as far as the clue went; but
presently the Professor remembered that his companion had
got out of the train at Cannes, and it became certain to him
that his only hope of clearing his overburdened conscience
would be to take the train to that place, and there prosecute
his almost hopeless search.

V

Not until he found himself seated in the train, and on the
point of starting for Cannes, did the full horror of his situation break on the Professor. Then, for an hour, he contemplated it in all its intricate enormity, saw himself as a man
dishonoured, ruined (for he now remembered the full
amount of the sum he had to account for), and, worse still,
severed from his best-loved work for a period incalculably
long. For after he had struggled through the preliminary difficulties he would have to settle down to the slow task of re-
imbursement, and he knew that, to earn enough money to
repay what he had lost, he must abandon serious scientific
work such as he was now engaged in, and probably stoop—
abominable thought!—to writing popular "science" articles in
one of the illustrated magazines. Such a job had once been
offered him on very handsome terms, and contemptuously rejected; and the best he could now hope was that there was
still an opening for him somewhere between the Etiquette
Column and the notes on Rachel powder and bathing tights.

Arrived at Cannes, he found his way to what appeared to be
the fashionable shopping-street, and exteriorising his attention by an extreme effort of the will he began to go the
rounds of the dressmaking establishments.

At every one he was received with distinguished politeness,
and every one, by some curious coincidence, had a Betsy to

offer him. As the Betsies were all young, fluffy and rosy, considerable offence was caused by his rapid rejection of them, and it was in vain that he tried to close his ears to the crude and disobliging comments which on each occasion attended his retreat. But he had by this time regained a sufficiently clear vision of the Princess to be sure that she was not concealed behind any of the youthful substitutes proposed to him. In despair he issued from the last shop, and again sat himself down to consider.

As he did so, his mind gave a queer click, and the doors of his inner consciousness again swung open. But this time it was only to draw him back into the creative world from which he had been so violently ejected. He had suddenly seen a point to be made in the Einstein controversy, and he began to fumble for a paper on which to jot it down. He found only one, the closely-scribbled flap of a torn envelope on which, during the journey to Cannes, he had calculated and re-calculated the extent of the sum he would have to raise to reimburse the Princess; but possibly there might be a clear space on the other side. He turned it over, and there read, in a tall slanting hand:

Princesse Balalatinsky,

Villa *Mon Caprice*, Route de Californie.

He started to his feet, and glanced about him frantically for a taxi. He had no idea where the Route de Californie was, but in his desperate circumstances, it seemed as easy to hire a taxi for a five minutes' transit as for a long expedition. Besides, it was the only way he knew of being sure of reaching his destination; and to do so as soon as possible was now a fixed idea.

The taxi carried him a long way; back through the whole length of the town, out on a flat white dusty road, and then up and up between walls overhung with luxuriant verdure till, at a turn, it stood still with a violent jerk.

The Professor looked out, and saw himself confronted by the expressive countenance of Mr. Taber Tring.

"Oh, my God—you again!" shrieked the young man, turning suddenly white with fury—or was it rather with fear?

"Why do you say *again*?" questioned the Professor; but his interlocutor, taking to his heels with unaccountable velocity, had already disappeared down a verdant by-way.

The Professor leaned back in the taxi in speechless amazement. He was sure now that the "again" referred to their previous encounter that morning at Monte Carlo, and he could
only conclude that it had become a fixed habit of Taber Tring's
to run away whenever they met, and that he ran a great deal
too fast for the Professor ever to hope to overtake him.

"Well," said the driver, "there's a gentleman who isn't
pleased. He thought I had no fare, and expected to get a lift
up to the top of this mountain."

"I should have been happy to give him a lift," said the
Professor rather wistfully; to which the driver replied: "He
must be a mile off by this time. He didn't seem to fancy your
looks."

There was no controverting this statement, mortifying as it
was, and they continued their ascent till a gateway impressively crowned by heraldic lions admitted them to terraced
gardens above which a villa of ample proportions looked forth
upon the landscape.

The Professor was by this time so steeled to the unexpected
that he hardly paused to consider the strange incongruity between the Princess's account of her fortunes and the setting
in which she lived. He had read *Mon Caprice* on the gate, and
that was the name on the envelope he had found in his
pocket. With a resolute hand he rang the bell and asked a resplendent footman if the Princess Balalatinsky were at home.

He was shown through a long succession of drawing-
rooms, in the last of which the Princess rose from the depths
of a broad divan. She was dressed in black draperies, half-
transparent—no, half-translucent; and she stood before the
Professor in all the formidable completeness of her beauty.

Instantly his mind clicked again, and a voice shrilled up at
him from the depths: "You always *knew* you could still recognize a beautiful woman when you saw one"; but he closed his
ears to the suggestion and advanced toward the lady.

Before he could take more than three steps she was at his
side, almost at his feet; her burning clasp was on his wrists,
and her eyes were consuming him like coals of fire.

"Master! *Maestro!* Disguise is useless! You choose to come
to me unannounced; but I was sure you would answer my appeal, and I should have recognized you anywhere, and among

any number of people." She lifted his astonished hand to her lips. "It is the penalty of genius," she breathed.

"But—" gasped the Professor.

A scented finger was laid across his lips. "Hush: not yet. Let me tell you first why I ventured to write to you." She drew him gently down to an arm-chair beside the divan, and herself sank orientally into its pillows. "I thought I had exhausted all the emotions of life. At *my* age—is it not a tragedy? But I was mistaken. It is true that I had tried philosophy, marriage, mathematics, divorce, sculpture and love; but I had never attempted the stage. How long it sometimes takes to discover one's real vocation! No doubt you may have gone through the same uncertainties yourself. At any rate, my gift for the drama did not reveal itself till three months ago, and I have only just completed my play, 'The Scarlet Cataract,' a picture of my life, as the title suggests—and which, my friends tell me, is not without dramatic merit. In fact, if I were to listen to them. . ."

The Professor struggled from his seat. His old fear of her madness had returned. He began very mildly: "It is quite natural that you should mistake me for some one else—"

With an inimitable gesture she waved the interruption aside. "But what I want to explain is that, of course, the leading rôle can have but one interpreter—Myself. The things happened to *Me*: who else could possibly know how to act them? Therefore, if I appeal to you—on my knees, Illustrious Impresario!—it is in my double character as dramatist and tragédienne; for in spite of appearances my life *has* been a tragedy, as you will acknowledge if you will let me outline its principal events in a few words. . ."

But here she had to pause a second for breath, and the Professor, on his feet, actually shouted his protest. "Madam, I cannot let you go on another moment, first because I've heard the story of your life already, and secondly because I'm not the man you suppose."

The Princess turned deadly pale. "Impostor!" she hissed, and reached for an embroidered bell-rope.

Her agitation had the curious effect of calming the Professor. "You had better not send me away," he said, "till you learn why I am here. I am the unhappy man to whom, the day before yesterday, you entrusted a hundred franc note which you asked him to stake for you at Monte Carlo. Unfortunately I could not recall your name or address, and I have been hunting for you through all the dressmakers' establishments in Cannes."

The instant lighting-up of her face was a sight so lovely that he almost forgot his apprehensions and his shame.

"The dressmakers' shops? Ah—in search of 'Betsy'! It is true, I was obliged to act as a *mannequin* for one day; but since then my fortunes have miraculously changed—changed thanks to you; for now," the Princess continued with enthusiasm, "I do at last recognise my good angel, my benefactor of the other day, and ask myself how I could have failed to know you again, how I could have taken you for a vulgar theatrical manager, you, a man of genius and a Philosopher. Can you ever forgive me? For I owe you everything—everything—everything!" she sobbed out, again almost at his knees.

His self-possession continued to increase in proportion to her agitation. He actually risked laying a hand on her arm and pressing her mildly back among her cushions.

"Only a change of pronouns," he said sighing, "is necessary to the complete accuracy of your last statement."

But she was off again on a new tack. "That blessed hundred franc note! From the moment when you took it from me, as I got out of the train, my luck miraculously and completely changed. I knew you were going to win some money for me; but how could I have imagined the extent of the fortune you were to heap at my feet?"

A cold sweat broke out over the Professor. She knew, then—once again her infernal intuition had pierced his secret! In the train had she not discovered his name, identified him as the author of "The Elimination of Phenomena," and guessed that he was actually engaged in the composition of another work? At the moment he had fancied that there was a plausible explanation for each of these discoveries; but he now felt that her powers of divination were in need of no outward aid. She had risen from her seat and was once more in possession of his hands.

"You have come to be thanked—and I *do* thank you!" Her heavy lashes glittered with tears which threatened to merge

with the drops of moisture rolling down the Professor's ago-
nized brow.

"Don't—don't, I beg!" He freed himself and shrank back.
"If you'll only let me speak . . . let me explain. . ."

She raised a reproachful finger. "Let you belittle yourself?
Let you reject my gratitude? No—no! Nothing that you can
say can make any difference. The gipsy in the Caucasus told me
long ago what you were going to do for me. And now that
you have done it you want to stifle the thanks on my lips!"

"But you have nothing to thank me for. I have made no
money for you—on the contrary, I—"

"Hush, hush! Such words are blasphemy. Look about you
at all this luxury, this beauty. I expected to have to leave it tomorrow. And thanks to you, wealth has poured in on me at
the moment when I thought I was face to face with ruin."

"Madam, you must let me undeceive you. I don't know
who can have brought you such an erroneous report." The
Professor glanced about him in acute distress, seeking to escape from her devouring scrutiny. "It is true that I did make
a considerable sum for you, but I—I afterward lost it. To my
shame be it said."

The Princess hardly appeared to hear him. Tears of gratitude still rained down her face. "Lost it? A little more, a little
less—what does it matter? In my present pecuniary situation
nothing of that sort counts. I am rich—rich for life! I should,
in fact," she continued with a gush of candour, "be an absolutely happy woman if I could only find an impresario who
would stage my play." She lifted her enchanting eyes to his. "I
wonder, by the way, dear friend," she proposed, "if you
would let me read it to you *now*?"

"Oh, no, no," the Professor protested; and then, becoming
aware of the offence his words were likely to give, he added
precipitately: "Before we turn to any other subject you must
really let me tell you just how much money I owe you, and
what were the unfortunate circumstances in which. . ."

But he was conscious that the Princess was no longer listening to him. A new light had dawned in her face, and the
glow of it was already drying her tears. Slim, palpitating and
girlish, she turned toward one of the tall French windows
opening upon the terrace.

"My fiancé—your young compatriot! Here he is! Oh, how happy I am to bring you together!" she exclaimed.

The Professor followed her glance with a stare of fresh amazement. Through the half-open window a young man in tennis flannels had strolled into the room.

"My Taber," the Princess breathed, "this is my benefactor —*our* benefactor—this is. . ."

Taber Tring gently removed the perfect arms which were already tightening about his neck. "I know who he is," he said in a hard high tone. "That's why I've been running away from him ever since early this morning."

His good-humoured boyish face was absolutely decomposed by distress. Without vouchsafing the least attention to the Princess he stood pallidly but resolutely facing her visitor.

"I've been running for all I was worth; at least till a quarter of an hour ago. Then I suddenly pulled up short and said to myself: 'Taber Tring, this won't do. You were born in the Middle West, but your parents came from New England, and now's the time to prove it if you're ever going to. Stern and rockbound coast, and *Mayflower* and all the rest of it. If there's anything in it, it ought to come out now.' And, by George it *did*; and here I am, ready to make a clean breast of it."

He drew a silk handkerchief from his pocket, and wiped his brow, which was as damp with agony as the Professor's.

But the Professor's patience had reached its final limit, and he was determined, whatever happened, to hold all interrupters at bay till he had made a clean breast of his own.

"I don't know, sir," he said, "why you avoided my presence this morning nor why you now seek it; but since you are connected with this lady by so close a tie, there is no reason why I should not continue in your presence what I had begun to tell her. I repeat then, Madam, that with your hundred franc note in my hand, I approached a table and staked the sum with results so unexpectedly and incredibly favourable that I left the gaming-rooms just before midnight in possession of—"

"Ninety-nine thousand seven hundred francs and no centimes," Taber Tring interposed.

The Professor received this with a gasp of astonishment; but everything which was happening was so foreign to all the laws of probability as experienced at Purewater that it did not long arrest his attention.

"You have stated the sum accurately," he said; "but you do not know that I am no longer in possession of a penny of it."

"Oh, don't I?" groaned Taber Tring, wiping a fresh outbreak of moisture from his forehead.

The Professor stopped short. "You do know? Ah, but to be sure. You were yourself a fellow-boarder at *Arcadie*. You were perhaps under its roof when that disastrous fire broke out and destroyed the whole of the large sum of money I had so negligently left—"

"Under the door!" shrieked Taber Tring. "Under the door of your room, which happened to be the one next to mine."

A light began to dawn on the Professor. "Is it possible that you were the neighbour whose unseasonable agitation during the small hours of the night caused me, in the total absence of towels or other available material, to stuff the money in question under the crack of the door in order to continue my intellectual labours undisturbed?"

"That's me," said Taber Tring sullenly.

But the Princess, who had been listening to the Professor's disquisition with a look of lovely bewilderment gradually verging on boredom, here intervened with a sudden flash of attention.

"What sort of noises proceeded from my Taber's room at that advanced hour of the night?" she inquisitorially demanded of the Professor.

"Oh, shucks," said her betrothed in a weary tone. "Aren't they all alike, every one of 'em?" He turned to the Professor. "I daresay I *was* making a noise. I was about desperate. Stony broke, and didn't know which way to turn next. I guess *you*'d have made a noise in my place."

The Professor felt a stirring of sympathy for the stricken youth. "I'm sorry for you—very sorry," he said. "If I had known your situation I should have tried to master my impatience, and should probably not have crammed the money under the door; in which case it would not have been destroyed in the fire. . ."

("How like the reflexions of a Chinese sage!" the Princess admiringly murmured.)

"Destroyed in the fire? It wasn't," said Taber Tring.

The Professor reeled back and was obliged to support himself upon the nearest chair.

"It wasn't?"

"Trust me," said the young man. "I was there, and I stole it."

"You stole it—his money?" The Princess instantly flung herself on his bosom. "To save your beloved from ruin? Oh, how Christlike—how Dostoyevskian!" She addressed herself with streaming eyes to the Professor. "Oh, spare him, sir, for heaven's sake spare him! What shall I do to avert your vengeance? Shall I prostitute myself in the streets of Cannes? I will do anything to atone to you for his heroic gesture in stealing your money—"

Taber Tring again put her gently aside. "Do drop it, Betsy. This is not a woman's job. I stole that money in order to gamble with it, and I've got to pay it back, and all that I won with it too." He paused and faced about on the Professor. "Isn't that so, sir?" he questioned. "I've been puzzling over it day and night for the last two days, and I can't figure it out any other way. Hard on you, Betsy, just as we thought our fortune was made; but my firm conviction, Professor Hibbart, as a man of New England stock, is that at this moment I owe you the sum of one million seven hundred and fifty thousand francs."

"My God," screamed the Professor, "what system did you play?"

Mr. Tring's open countenance snapped shut like a steel trap. "That's my secret," he said politely; and the Professor had to acknowledge that it was.

"I must ask you," the young man pursued, "to be good enough either to disprove or to confirm my estimate of my indebtedness to you. How much should you consider that you owed if you had stolen anybody's money and made a lot more with it? Only the sum stolen or the whole amount? There's my point."

"But I did! I have!" cried the Professor.

"Did what?"

"Exactly what you have done. Stole—that is, gambled with a sum of money entrusted to me for the purpose, and won the large amount you have correctly stated. It is true," the Professor continued, "that I had no intention of appropriating a penny of it; but, believing that my culpable negligence had caused the whole sum to be destroyed by fire, I considered myself—"

"Well?" panted Taber Tring.

"As indebted for the entire amount to this lady here—"

Taber Tring's face became illuminated with sudden comprehension.

"Holy Moses! You don't mean to say all that money under the door belonged to Betsy?"

"Every cent of it, in my opinion," said the Professor firmly; and the two men stood and stared at each other.

"But, good gracious," the Princess intervened, "then nobody has stolen anything!"

The load which had crushed the Professor to earth rolled from his shoulders, and he lifted the head of a free man. "So it would seem."

But Taber Tring could only ejaculate once again: "Holy Moses!"

"Then we are rich once more—is it not so, my Taber?" The Princess leaned a thoughtful head upon her hand. "Do you know, I could almost regret it? Yes, I regret, dear friends, that you are both blameless, and that no sacrifice will be demanded of me. It would have been so beautiful if you had both sinned, and I had also had to sin to save you. But, on the other hand," she reflected, with lifted eyes and a smile like heaven, "I shall now be able to have my play brought out at my own expense. And for that," she cried, again possessing herself of Professor Hibbart's hands, "for that too I have to thank you! And this is the only way I know of doing it."

She flung her arms around his neck and lifted her lips to his; and the exonerated and emancipated Professor took what she offered like a man.

"And now," she cried, "for my other hero!" and caught her betrothed to her heart.

These effusions were interrupted by the entrance of the resplendent footman, who surveyed them without surprise or disapproval.

"There is at the door," he announced, "a young lady of the name of Betsy who is asking for Monsieur." He indicated the Professor. "She would give no other name; she said that was enough. She knows Monsieur has been seeking her everywhere in Cannes, and she is in despair at having missed him; but at the time she was engaged with another client."

The Professor turned pale, and Taber Tring's left lid sketched a tentative wink.

But the Princess intervened in her most princely manner. "Of course! My name is Betsy, and you were seeking for *me* at all the dressmakers'!" She turned to the footman with her smile of benediction. "Tell the young lady," she said, "that Monsieur in his turn is engaged with another client, who begs her to accept this slight compensation for her trouble." She slipped from her wrist a hoop of jade and brilliants, and the footman withdrew with the token.

"And now," said the Princess, "as it is past three o'clock, we ought really to be thinking of *zakouska*."

Atrophy

NORA FRENWAY settled down furtively in her corner of
the Pullman and, as the express plunged out of the Grand
Central Station, wondered at herself for being where she was.
The porter came along. "Ticket?" "Westover." She had instinctively lowered her voice and glanced about her. But neither the porter nor her nearest neighbours—fortunately none
of them known to her—seemed in the least surprised or interested by the statement that she was travelling to Westover.

Yet what an earth-shaking announcement it was! Not that
she cared, now; not that anything mattered except the one
overwhelming fact which had convulsed her life, hurled her
out of her easy velvet-lined rut, and flung her thus naked to
the public scrutiny. . . Cautiously, again, she glanced about
her to make doubly sure that there was no one, absolutely no
one, in the Pullman whom she knew by sight.

Her life had been so carefully guarded, so inwardly conventional in a world where all the outer conventions were tottering, that no one had ever known she had a lover. No one
—of that she was absolutely sure. All the circumstances of the
case had made it necessary that she should conceal her real
life—her only real life—from everyone about her; from her
half-invalid irascible husband, his prying envious sisters, and
the terrible monumental old chieftainess, her mother-in-law,
before whom all the family quailed and humbugged and
fibbed and fawned.

What nonsense to pretend that nowadays, even in big cities,
in the world's greatest social centres, the severe old-fashioned
standards had given place to tolerance, laxity and ease! You
took up the morning paper, and you read of girl bandits,
movie-star divorces, "hold-ups" at balls, murder and suicide
and elopement, and a general welter of disjointed discon-
nected impulses and appetites; then you turned your eyes
onto your own daily life, and found yourself as cribbed and
cabined, as beset by vigilant family eyes, observant friends, all
sorts of embodied standards, as any white-muslin novel heroine of the 'sixties!

In a different way, of course. To the casual eye Mrs. Frenway herself might have seemed as free as any of the young married women of her group. Poker playing, smoking, cocktail drinking, dancing, painting, short skirts, bobbed hair and the rest—when had these been denied to her? If by any outward sign she had differed too markedly from her kind— lengthened her skirts, refused to play for money, let her hair grow, or ceased to make up—her husband would have been the first to notice it, and to say: "Are you ill? What's the matter? How queer you look! What's the sense of making yourself conspicuous?" For he and his kind had adopted all the old inhibitions and sanctions, blindly transferring them to a new ritual, as the receptive Romans did when strange gods were brought into their temples. . .

The train had escaped from the ugly fringes of the city, and the soft spring landscape was gliding past her: glimpses of green lawns, budding hedges, pretty irregular roofs, and miles and miles of alluring tarred roads slipping away into mystery. How often she had dreamed of dashing off down an unknown road with Christopher!

Not that she was a woman to be awed by the conventions. She knew she wasn't. She had always taken their measure, smiled at them—and conformed. On account of poor George Frenway, to begin with. Her husband, in a sense, was a man to be pitied; his weak health, his bad temper, his unsatisfied vanity, all made him a rather forlornly comic figure. But it was chiefly on account of the two children that she had always resisted the temptation to do anything reckless. The least self-betrayal would have been the end of everything. Too many eyes were watching her, and her husband's family was so strong, so united—when there was anybody for them to hate —and at all times so influential, that she would have been defeated at every point, and her husband would have kept the children.

At the mere thought she felt herself on the brink of an abyss. "The children are my religion," she had once said to herself; and she had no other.

Yet here she was on her way to Westover. . . Oh, what did it matter now? That was the worst of it—it was too late for anything between her and Christopher to matter! She was

sure he was dying. The way in which his cousin, Gladys
Brincker, had blurted it out the day before at Kate Salmer's
dance: "You didn't know—poor Kit? Thought you and he
were such pals! Yes; awfully bad, I'm afraid. Return of the old
trouble! I know there've been two consultations—they had
Knowlton down. They say there's not much hope; and nobody but that forlorn frightened Jane mounting guard. . ."

Poor Christopher! His sister Jane Aldis, Nora suspected,
forlorn and frightened as she was, had played in his life a part
nearly as dominant as Frenway and the children in Nora's.
Loyally, Christopher always pretended that she didn't; talked
of her indulgently as "poor Jenny". But didn't she, Nora, always think of her husband as "poor George"? Jane Aldis, of
course, was much less self-assertive, less demanding, than
George Frenway; but perhaps for that very reason she would
appeal all the more to a man's compassion. And somehow,
under her unobtrusive air, Nora had—on the rare occasions
when they met—imagined that Miss Aldis was watching and
drawing her inferences. But then Nora always felt, where
Christopher was concerned, as if her breast were a pane of
glass through which her trembling palpitating heart could be
seen as plainly as holy viscera in a reliquary. Her sober after-
thought was that Jane Aldis was just a dowdy self-effacing old
maid whose life was filled to the brim by looking after the
Westover place for her brother, and seeing that the fires were
lit and the rooms full of flowers when he brought down his
friends for a week-end.

Ah, how often he had said to Nora: "If I could have you to
myself for a week-end at Westover"—quite as if it were the
easiest thing imaginable, as far as his arrangements were concerned! And they had even pretended to discuss how it could
be done. But somehow she fancied he said it because he knew
that the plan, for her, was about as feasible as a week-end in
the moon. And in reality her only visits to Westover had been
made in the company of her husband, and that of other
friends, two or three times, at the beginning. . . For after
that she wouldn't. It was three years now since she had been
there.

Gladys Brincker, in speaking of Christopher's illness, had
looked at Nora queerly, as though suspecting something. But

no—what nonsense! No one had ever suspected Nora
Frenway. Didn't she know what her friends said of her?
"Nora? No more temperament than a lamp-post. Always
buried in her books. . . Never very attractive to men, in spite
of her looks." Hadn't she said that of other women, who perhaps, in secret, like herself. . . ?

The train was slowing down as it approached a station. She
sat up with a jerk and looked at her wrist-watch. It was half-
past two, the station was Ockham; the next would be
Westover. In less than an hour she would be under his roof,
Jane Aldis would be receiving her in that low panelled room
full of books, and she would be saying—what would she be
saying?

She had gone over their conversation so often that she
knew not only her own part in it but Miss Aldis's by heart.
The first moments would of course be painful, difficult; but
then a great wave of emotion, breaking down the barriers between the two anxious women, would fling them together.
She wouldn't have to say much, to explain; Miss Aldis would
just take her by the hand and lead her upstairs to the room.

That room! She shut her eyes, and remembered other
rooms where she and he had been together in their joy and
their strength. . . No, not that; she must not think of that
now. For the man she had met in those other rooms was dying; the man she was going to was some one so different from
that other man that it was like a profanation to associate their
images. . . And yet the man she was going to was her own
Christopher, the one who had lived in her soul; and how his
soul must be needing hers, now that it hung alone on the
dark brink! As if anything else mattered at such a moment!
She neither thought nor cared what Jane Aldis might say or
suspect; she wouldn't have cared if the Pullman had been full
of prying acquaintances, or if George and all George's family
had got in at that last station.

She wouldn't have cared a fig for any of them. Yet at the
same moment she remembered having felt glad that her old
governess, whom she used to go and see twice a year, lived at
Ockham—so that if George did begin to ask questions, she
could always say: "Yes, I went to see poor old Fraülein; she's
absolutely crippled now. I shall have to give her a Bath chair.

Could you get me a catalogue of prices?" There wasn't a pre-caution she hadn't thought of—and now she was ready to scatter them all to the winds. . .

Westover—*Junction!*

She started up and pushed her way out of the train. All the people seemed to be obstructing her, putting bags and suit-cases in her way. And the express stopped for only two min-utes. Suppose she should be carried on to Albany?

Westover Junction was a growing place, and she was fairly sure there would be a taxi at the station. There was one—she just managed to get to it ahead of a travelling man with a sample case and a new straw hat. As she opened the door a smell of damp hay and bad tobacco greeted her. She sprang in and gasped: "To Oakfield. You know? Mr. Aldis's place near Westover."

II

It began exactly as she had expected. A surprised parlour maid—why surprised?—showed her into the low panelled room that was so full of his presence, his books, his pipes, his terrier dozing on the shabby rug. The parlour maid said she would go and see if Miss Aldis could come down. Nora wanted to ask if she were with her brother—and how he was. But she found herself unable to speak the words. She was afraid her voice might tremble. And why should she question the parlour maid, when in a moment, she hoped, she was to see Miss Aldis?

The woman moved away with a hushed step—the step which denotes illness in the house. She did not immediately return, and the interval of waiting in that room, so strange yet so intimately known, was a new torture to Nora. It was unlike anything she had imagined. The writing table with his scat-tered pens and letters was more than she could bear. His dog looked at her amicably from the hearth, but made no ad-vances; and though she longed to stroke him, to let her hand rest where Christopher's had rested, she dared not for fear he should bark and disturb the peculiar hush of that dumb watchful house. She stood in the window and looked out at the budding shrubs and the bulbs pushing up through the swollen earth.

"This way, please."

Her heart gave a plunge. Was the woman actually taking her upstairs to his room? Her eyes filled, she felt herself swept forward on a great wave of passion and anguish. . . But she was only being led across the hall into a stiff lifeless drawing-room—the kind that bachelors get an upholsterer to do for them, and then turn their backs on forever. The chairs and sofas looked at her with an undisguised hostility, and then resumed the moping expression common to furniture in unfrequented rooms. Even the spring sun slanting in through the windows on the pale marquetry of a useless table seemed to bring no heat or light with it.

The rush of emotion subsided, leaving in Nora a sense of emptiness and apprehension. Supposing Jane Aldis should look at her with the cold eyes of this resentful room? She began to wish she had been friendlier and more cordial to Jane Aldis in the past. In her intense desire to conceal from everyone the tie between herself and Christopher she had avoided all show of interest in his family; and perhaps, as she now saw, excited curiosity by her very affectation of indifference.

No doubt it would have been more politic to establish an intimacy with Jane Aldis; and today, how much easier and more natural her position would have been! Instead of groping about—as she was again doing—for an explanation of her visit, she could have said: "My dear, I came to see if there was anything in the world I could do to help you."

She heard a hesitating step in the hall—a hushed step like the parlour maid's—and saw Miss Aldis pause near the half-open door. How old she had grown since their last meeting! Her hair, untidily pinned up, was gray and lanky. Her eyelids, always reddish, were swollen and heavy, her face sallow with anxiety and fatigue. It was odd to have feared so defenseless an adversary. Nora, for an instant, had the impression that Miss Aldis had wavered in the hall to catch a glimpse of her, take the measure of the situation. But perhaps she had only stopped to push back a strand of hair as she passed in front of a mirror.

"Mrs. Frenway—how good of you!" She spoke in a cool detached voice, as if her real self were elsewhere and she were simply an automaton wound up to repeat the familiar forms of hospitality. "Do sit down," she said.

She pushed forward one of the sulky arm-chairs, and Nora seated herself stiffly, her hand-bag clutched on her knee, in the self-conscious attitude of a country caller.

"I came—"

"So good of you," Miss Aldis repeated. "I had no idea you were in this part of the world. Not the slightest."

Was it a lead she was giving? Or did she know everything, and wish to extend to her visitor the decent shelter of a pretext? Or was she really so stupid—

"You're staying with the Brinckers, I suppose. Or the Northrups? I remember the last time you came to lunch here you motored over with Mr. Frenway from the Northrups'. That must have been two years ago, wasn't it?" She put the question with an almost sprightly show of interest.

"No—three years," said Nora, mechanically.

"Was it? As long ago as that? Yes—you're right. That was the year we moved the big fern-leaved beech. I remember Mr. Frenway was interested in tree moving, and I took him out to show him where the tree had come from. He *is* interested in tree moving, isn't he?"

"Oh yes; very much."

"We had those wonderful experts down to do it. 'Tree doctors,' they call themselves. They have special appliances, you know. The tree is growing better than it did before they moved it. But I suppose you've done a great deal of transplanting on Long Island."

"Yes. My husband does a good deal of transplanting."

"So you've come over from the Northrups'? I didn't even know they were down at Maybrook yet. I see so few people."

"No; not from the Northrups'."

"Oh—the Brinckers'? Hal Brincker was here yesterday, but he didn't tell me you were staying there."

Nora hesitated. "No. The fact is, I have an old governess who lives at Ockham. I go to see her sometimes. And so I came on to Westover—" She paused, and Miss Aldis interrogated brightly: "Yes?" as if prompting her in a lesson she was repeating.

"Because I saw Gladys Brincker the other day, and she told me that your brother was ill."

"Oh." Miss Aldis gave the syllable its full weight, and set a full stop after it. Her eyebrows went up, as if in a faint surprise. The silent room seemed to close in on the two speakers, listening. A resuscitated fly buzzed against the sunny window pane. "Yes; he's ill," she conceded at length.

"I'm so sorry; I . . . he has been . . . such a friend of ours . . . so long . . ."

"Yes; I've often heard him speak of you and Mr. Frenway." Another full stop sealed this announcement. ("No, she knows nothing," Nora thought.) "I remember his telling me that he thought a great deal of Mr. Frenway's advice about moving trees. But then you see our soil is so different from yours. I suppose Mr. Frenway has had your soil analyzed?"

"Yes; I think he has."

"Christopher's always been a great gardener."

"I hope he's not—not very ill? Gladys seemed to be afraid—"

"Illness is always something to be afraid of, isn't it?"

"But you're not—I mean, not anxious . . . not seriously?"

"It's so kind of you to ask. The doctors seem to think there's no particular change since yesterday."

"And yesterday?"

"Well, yesterday they seemed to think there might be."

"A change, you mean?"

"Well, yes."

"A change—I hope for the better?"

"They said they weren't sure; they couldn't say."

The fly's buzzing had become so insistent in the still room that it seemed to be going on inside of Nora's head, and in the confusion of sound she found it more and more difficult to regain a lead in the conversation. And the minutes were slipping by, and upstairs the man she loved was lying. It was absurd and lamentable to make a pretense of keeping up this twaddle. She would cut through it, no matter how.

"I suppose you've had—a consultation?"

"Oh, yes; Dr. Knowlton's been down twice."

"And what does he—"

"Well; he seems to agree with the others."

There was another pause, and then Miss Aldis glanced out of the window. "Why, who's that driving up?" she enquired. "Oh, it's your taxi, I suppose, coming up the drive."

"Yes. I got out at the gate." She dared not add: "For fear the noise might disturb him."

"I hope you had no difficulty in finding a taxi at the Junction?"

"Oh, no; I had no difficulty."

"I think it was so kind of you to come—not even knowing whether you'd find a carriage to bring you out all this way. And I know how busy you are. There's always so much going on in town, isn't there, even at this time of year?"

"Yes; I suppose so. But your brother—"

"Oh, of course my brother won't be up to any sort of gaiety; not for a long time."

"A long time; no. But you do hope—"

"I think everybody about a sick bed ought to hope, don't you?"

"Yes; but I mean—"

Nora stood up suddenly, her brain whirling. Was it possible that she and that woman had sat thus facing each other for half an hour, piling up this conversational rubbish, while up-stairs, out of sight, the truth, the meaning of their two lives hung on the frail thread of one man's intermittent pulse? She could not imagine why she felt so powerless and baffled. What had a woman who was young and handsome and beloved to fear from a dowdy and insignificant old maid? Why, the antagonism that these very graces and superiorities would create in the other's breast, especially if she knew they were all spent in charming the being on whom her life depended. Weak in herself, but powerful from her circumstances, she stood at bay on the ruins of all that Nora had ever loved. "How she must hate me—and I never thought of it," mused Nora, who had imagined that she had thought of everything where her relation to her lover was concerned. Well, it was too late now to remedy her omission; but at least she must assert herself, must say something to save the precious minutes that remained and break through the stifling web of platitudes which her enemy's tremulous hand was weaving around her.

"Miss Aldis—I must tell you—I came to see—"

"How he was? So very friendly of you. He would appreciate it, I know. Christopher is so devoted to his friends."

"But you'll—you'll tell him that I—"

"Of course. That you came on purpose to ask about him. As soon as he's a little bit stronger."

"But I mean—now?"

"Tell him now that you called to enquire? How good of you to think of that too! Perhaps tomorrow morning, if he's feeling a little bit brighter. . ."

Nora felt her lips drying as if a hot wind had parched them. They would hardly move. "But now—now—today." Her voice sank to a whisper as she added: "Isn't he conscious?"

"Oh, yes; he's conscious; he's perfectly conscious." Miss Aldis emphasized this with another of her long pauses. "He shall certainly be told that you called." Suddenly she too got up from her seat and moved toward the window. "I must seem dreadfully inhospitable, not even offering you a cup of tea. But the fact is, perhaps I ought to tell you—if you're thinking of getting back to Ockham this afternoon there's only one train that stops at the Junction after three o'clock." She pulled out an old-fashioned enamelled watch with a wreath of roses about the dial, and turned almost apologetically to Mrs. Frenway. "You ought to be at the station by four o'clock at the latest; and with one of those old Junction taxis . . . I'm so sorry; I know I must appear to be driving you away." A wan smile drew up her pale lips.

Nora knew just how long the drive from Westover Junction had taken, and understood that she was being delicately dismissed. Dismissed from life—from hope—even from the dear anguish of filling her eyes for the last time with the face which was the one face in the world to her! ("But then she does know everything," she thought.)

"I mustn't make you miss your train, you know."

"Miss Aldis, is he—has he seen any one?" Nora hazarded in a painful whisper.

"Seen any one? Well, there've been all the doctors—five of them! And then the nurses. Oh, but you mean friends, of course. Naturally." She seemed to reflect. "Hal Brincker, yes; he saw our cousin Hal yesterday—but not for very long."

Hal Brincker! Nora knew what Christopher thought of his Brincker cousins—blighting bores, one and all of them, he always said. And in the extremity of his illness the one person privileged to see him had been—Hal Brincker! Nora's eyes filled; she had to turn them away for a moment from Miss Aldis's timid inexorable face.

"But today?" she finally brought out.

"No. Today he hasn't seen any one; not yet." The two women stood and looked at each other; then Miss Aldis glanced uncertainly about the room. "But couldn't I— Yes, I ought at least to have asked you if you won't have a cup of tea. So stupid of me! There might still be time. I never take tea myself." Once more she referred anxiously to her watch. "The water is sure to be boiling, because the nurses' tea is just being taken up. If you'll excuse me a moment I'll go and see."

"Oh, no; no!" Nora drew in a quick sob. "How can you? . . . I mean, I don't want any. . ."

Miss Aldis looked relieved. "Then I shall be quite sure that you won't reach the station too late." She waited again, and then held out a long stony hand. "So kind—I shall never forget your kindness. Coming all this way, when you might so easily have telephoned from town. Do please tell Mr. Frenway how I appreciated it. You will remember to tell him, won't you? He sent me such an interesting collection of pamphlets about tree moving. I should like him to know how much I feel his kindness in letting you come." She paused again, and pulled in her lips so that they became a narrow thread, a mere line drawn across her face by a ruler. "But, no; I won't trouble you; I'll write to thank him myself." Her hand ran out to an electric bell on the nearest table. It shrilled through the silence, and the parlour maid appeared with a stage-like promptness.

"The taxi, please? Mrs. Frenway's taxi."

The room became silent again. Nora thought: "Yes; she knows everything." Miss Aldis peeped for the third time at her watch, and then uttered a slight unmeaning laugh. The blue-bottle banged against the window, and once more it seemed to Nora that its sonorities were reverberating inside her head. They were deafeningly mingled there with the explosion of the taxi's reluctant starting-up and its convulsed halt at the front door. The driver sounded his horn as if to summon her.

"He's afraid too that you'll be late!" Miss Aldis smiled.

The smooth slippery floor of the hall seemed to Nora to extend away in front of her for miles. At its far end she saw a little tunnel of light, a miniature maid, a toy taxi. Somehow she managed to travel the distance that separated her from them, though her bones ached with weariness, and at every step she seemed to be lifting a leaden weight. The taxi was close to her now, its door was open, she was getting in. The same smell of damp hay and bad tobacco greeted her. She saw her hostess standing on the threshold. "To the Junction, driver—back to the Junction," she heard Miss Aldis say. The taxi began to roll toward the gate. As it moved away Nora heard Miss Aldis calling: "I'll be sure to write and thank Mr. Frenway."

A Bottle of Perrier

A TWO DAYS' struggle over the treacherous trails in a well-intentioned but short-winded "flivver", and a ride of two more on a hired mount of unamiable temper, had disposed young Medford, of the American School of Archæology at Athens, to wonder why his queer English friend, Henry Almodham, had chosen to live in the desert.

Now he understood.

He was leaning against the roof parapet of the old building, half Christian fortress, half Arab palace, which had been Almodham's pretext; or one of them. Below, in an inner court, a little wind, rising as the sun sank, sent through a knot of palms the rain-like rattle so cooling to the pilgrims of the desert. An ancient fig tree, enormous, exuberant, writhed over a whitewashed well-head, sucking life from what appeared to be the only source of moisture within the walls. Beyond these, on every side, stretched away the mystery of the sands, all golden with promise, all livid with menace, as the sun alternately touched or abandoned them.

Young Medford, somewhat weary after his journey from the coast, and awed by his first intimate sense of the omnipresence of the desert, shivered and drew back. Undoubtedly, for a scholar and a misogynist, it was a wonderful refuge; but one would have to be, incurably, both.

"Let's take a look at the house," Medford said to himself, as if speedy contact with man's handiwork were necessary to his reassurance.

The house, he already knew, was empty save for the quick cosmopolitan man-servant, who spoke a sort of palimpsest Cockney lined with Mediterranean tongues and desert dialects—English, Italian or Greek, which was he?—and two or three burnoused underlings who, having carried Medford's bags to his room, had relieved the place of their gliding presences. Mr. Almodham, the servant told him, was away; suddenly summoned by a friendly chief to visit some unexplored ruins to the south, he had ridden off at dawn, too hurriedly to write, but leaving messages of excuse and regret. That evening late he might be back, or next morning. Meanwhile Mr. Medford was to make himself at home.

Almodham, as young Medford knew, was always making these archæological explorations; they had been his ostensible reason for settling in that remote place, and his desultory search had already resulted in the discovery of several early Christian ruins of great interest.

Medford was glad that his host had not stood on ceremony, and rather relieved, on the whole, to have the next few hours to himself. He had had a malarial fever the previous summer, and in spite of his cork helmet he had probably caught a touch of the sun; he felt curiously, helplessly tired, yet deeply content.

And what a place it was to rest in! The silence, the remoteness, the illimitable air! And in the heart of the wilderness green leafage, water, comfort—he had already caught a glimpse of wide wicker chairs under the palms—a humane and welcoming habitation. Yes, he began to understand Almodham. To anyone sick of the Western fret and fever the very walls of this desert fortress exuded peace.

As his foot was on the ladder-like stair leading down from the roof, Medford saw the man-servant's head rising toward him. It rose slowly and Medford had time to remark that it was sallow, bald on the top, diagonally dented with a long white scar, and ringed with thick ash-blond hair. Hitherto Medford had noticed only the man's face—youngish, but sallow also—and been chiefly struck by its wearing an odd expression which could best be defined as surprise.

The servant, moving aside, looked up, and Medford perceived that his air of surprise was produced by the fact that his intensely blue eyes were rather wider open than most eyes, and fringed with thick ash-blond lashes; otherwise there was nothing noticeable about him.

"Just to ask—what wine for dinner, sir? Champagne, or—"

"No wine, thanks."

The man's disciplined lips were played over by a faint flicker of deprecation or irony, or both.

"Not any at all, sir?"

Medford smiled back. "It's not out of respect for Prohibition." He was sure that the man, of whatever nationality, would understand that; and he did.

"Oh, I didn't suppose, sir—"

"Well, no; but I've been rather seedy, and wine's forbidden."

The servant remained incredulous. "Just a little light Moselle, though, to colour the water, sir?"

"No wine at all," said Medford, growing bored. He was still in the stage of convalescence when it is irritating to be argued with about one's dietary.

"Oh—what's your name, by the way?" he added, to soften the curtness of his refusal.

"Gosling," said the other unexpectedly, though Medford didn't in the least know what he had expected him to be called.

"You're English, then?"

"Oh, yes, sir."

"You've been in these parts a good many years, though?"

Yes, he had, Gosling said; rather too long for his own liking; and added that he had been born at Malta. "But I know England well too." His deprecating look returned. "I will confess, sir, I'd like to have 'ad a look at Wembley.* Mr. Almodham 'ad promised me—but there—" As if to minimize the *abandon* of this confidence, he followed it up by a ceremonious request for Medford's keys, and an enquiry as to when he would like to dine. Having received a reply, he still lingered, looking more surprised than ever.

"Just a mineral water, then, sir?"

"Oh, yes—anything."

"Shall we say a bottle of Perrier?"

Perrier in the desert! Medford smiled assentingly, surrendered his keys and strolled away.

The house turned out to be smaller than he had imagined, or at least the habitable part of it; for above this towered mighty dilapidated walls of yellow stone, and in their crevices clung plaster chambers, one above the other, cedar-beamed,

*The famous exhibition at Wembley, near London, took place in 1924.

crimson-shuttered but crumbling. Out of this jumble of masonry and stucco, Christian and Moslem, the latest tenant of the fortress had chosen a cluster of rooms tucked into an angle of the ancient keep. These apartments opened on the uppermost court, where the palms chattered and the fig tree coiled above the well. On the broken marble pavement, chairs and a low table were grouped, and a few geraniums and blue morning-glories had been coaxed to grow between the slabs.

A white-skirted boy with watchful eyes was watering the plants; but at Medford's approach he vanished like a wisp of vapour.

There was something vaporous and insubstantial about the whole scene; even the long arcaded room opening on the court, furnished with saddlebag cushions, divans with gazelle skins and rough indigenous rugs; even the table piled with old *Timeses* and ultra-modern French and English reviews—all seemed, in that clear mocking air, born of the delusion of some desert wayfarer.

A seat under the fig tree invited Medford to doze, and when he woke the hard blue dome above him was gemmed with stars and the night breeze gossiped with the palms.

Rest—beauty—peace. Wise Almodham!

II

Wise Almodham! Having carried out—with somewhat disappointing results—the excavation with which an archæological society had charged him twenty-five years ago, he had lingered on, taken possession of the Crusaders' stronghold, and turned his attention from ancient to mediæval remains. But even these investigations, Medford suspected, he prosecuted only at intervals, when the enchantment of his leisure did not lie on him too heavily.

The young American had met Henry Almodham at Luxor the previous winter; had dined with him at old Colonel Swordsley's, on that perfumed starlit terrace above the Nile; and, having somehow awakened the archæologist's interest, had been invited to look him up in the desert the following year.

They had spent only that one evening together, with old Swordsley blinking at them under memory-laden lids, and two or three charming women from the Winter Palace chattering and exclaiming; but the two men had ridden back to Luxor together in the moonlight, and during that ride Medford fancied he had puzzled out the essential lines of Henry Almodham's character. A nature saturnine yet sentimental; chronic indolence alternating with spurts of highly intelligent activity; gnawing self-distrust soothed by intimate self-appreciation; a craving for complete solitude coupled with the inability to tolerate it for long.

There was more, too, Medford suspected; a dash of Victorian romance, gratified by the setting, the remoteness, the inaccessibility of his retreat, and by being known as *the* Henry Almodham—"the one who lives in a Crusaders' castle, you know"—the gradual imprisonment in a pose assumed in youth, and into which middle age had slowly stiffened; and something deeper, darker, too, perhaps, though the young man doubted that; probably just the fact that living in that particular way had brought healing to an old wound, an old mortification, something which years ago had touched a vital part and left him writhing. Above all, in Almodham's hesitating movements and the dreaming look of his long well-featured brown face with its shock of gray hair, Medford detected an inertia, mental and moral, which life in this castle of romance must have fostered and excused.

"Once here, how easy not to leave!" he mused, sinking deeper into his deep chair.

"Dinner, sir," Gosling announced.

The table stood in an open arch of the living-room; shaded candles made a rosy pool in the dusk. Each time he emerged into their light the servant, white-jacketed, velvet-footed, looked more competent and more surprised than ever. Such dishes, too—the cook also a Maltese? Ah, they were geniuses, these Maltese! Gosling bridled, smiled his acknowledgment, and started to fill the guest's glass with Chablis.

"No wine," said Medford patiently.

"Sorry, sir. But the fact is—"

"You said there was Perrier?"

"Yes, sir; but I find there's none left. It's been awfully hot, and Mr. Almodham has been and drank it all up. The new supply isn't due till next week. We 'ave to depend on the caravans going south."

"No matter. Water, then. I really prefer it."

Gosling's surprise widened to amazement. "Not water, sir? Water—in these parts?"

Medford's irritability stirred again. "Something wrong with your water? Boil it then, can't you? I won't—" He pushed away the half-filled wineglass.

"Oh—boiled? Certainly, sir." The man's voice dropped almost to a whisper. He placed on the table a succulent mess of rice and mutton, and vanished.

Medford leaned back, surrendering himself to the night, the coolness, the ripple of wind in the palms.

One agreeable dish succeeded another. As the last appeared, the diner began to feel the pangs of thirst, and at the same moment a beaker of water was placed at his elbow. "Boiled, sir, and I squeezed a lemon into it."

"Right. I suppose at the end of the summer your water gets a bit muddy?"

"That's it, sir. But you'll find this all right, sir."

Medford tasted. "Better than Perrier." He emptied the glass, leaned back and groped in his pocket. A tray was instantly at his hand with cigars and cigarettes.

"You don't—smoke, sir?"

Medford, for answer, held up his cigar to the man's light. "What do you call this?"

"Oh, just so. I meant the other style." Gosling glanced discreetly at the opium pipes of jade and amber laid out on a low table.

Medford shrugged away the invitation—and wondered. Was that perhaps Almodham's other secret—or one of them? For he began to think there might be many; and all, he was sure, safely stored away behind Gosling's vigilant brow.

"No news yet of Mr. Almodham?"

Gosling was gathering up the dishes with dexterous gestures. For a moment he seemed not to hear. Then—from beyond the candle gleam—"News, sir? There couldn't 'ardly be, could there? There's no wireless in the desert, sir; not like London." His respectful tone tempered the slight irony. "But tomorrow evening ought to see him riding in." Gosling paused, drew nearer, swept one of his swift hands across the table in pursuit of the last crumbs, and added tentatively: "You'll surely be able, sir, to stay till then?"

Medford laughed. The night was too rich in healing; it sank on his spirit like wings. Time vanished, fret and trouble were no more. "Stay? I'll stay a year if I have to!"

"Oh—a year?" Gosling echoed it playfully, gathered up the dessert dishes and was gone.

III

Medford had said that he would wait for Almodham a year; but the next morning he found that such arbitrary terms had lost their meaning. There were no time measures in a place like this. The silly face of his watch told its daily tale to emptiness. The wheeling of the constellations over those ruined walls marked only the revolutions of the earth; the spasmodic motions of man meant nothing.

The very fact of being hungry, that stroke of the inward clock, was minimized by the slightness of the sensation—just the ghost of a pang, that might have been quieted by dried fruit and honey. Life had the light monotonous smoothness of eternity.

Toward sunset Medford shook off this queer sense of otherwhereness and climbed to the roof. Across the desert he spied for Almodham. Southward the Mountains of Alabaster hung like a blue veil lined with light. In the west a great column of fire shot up, spraying into plumy cloudlets which turned the sky to a fountain of rose-leaves, the sands beneath to gold.

No riders specked them. Medford watched in vain for his absent host till night fell, and the punctual Gosling invited him once more to table.

In the evening Medford absently fingered the ultra-modern reviews—three months old, and already so stale to the touch —then tossed them aside, flung himself on a divan and dreamed. Almodham must spend a lot of time in dreaming; that was it. Then, just as he felt himself sinking down into torpor, he would be off on one of these dashes across the desert in quest of unknown ruins. Not such a bad life.

Gosling appeared with Turkish coffee in a cup cased in filigree.

"Are there any horses in the stable?" Medford suddenly asked.

"Horses? Only what you might call pack-horses, sir. Mr. Almodham has the two best saddle-horses with him."

"I was thinking I might ride out to meet him."

Gosling considered. "So you might, sir."

"Do you know which way he went?"

"Not rightly, sir. The caid's man was to guide them."

"Them? Who went with him?"

"Just one of our men, sir. They've got the two thorough-breds. There's a third, but he's lame." Gosling paused. "Do you know the trails, sir? Excuse me, but I don't think I ever saw you here before."

"No," Medford acquiesced, "I've never been here before."

"Oh, then"—Gosling's gesture added: "In that case, even the best thoroughbred wouldn't help you."

"I suppose he may still turn up tonight?"

"Oh, easily, sir. I expect to see you both breakfasting here tomorrow morning," said Gosling cheerfully.

Medford sipped his coffee. "You said you'd never seen me here before. How long have you been here yourself?"

Gosling answered instantly, as though the figures were never long out of his memory: "Eleven years and seven months altogether, sir."

"Nearly twelve years! That's a longish time."

"Yes, it is."

"And I don't suppose you often get away?"

Gosling was moving off with the tray. He halted, turned back, and said with sudden emphasis: "I've never once been away. Not since Mr. Almodham first brought me here."

"Good Lord! Not a single holiday?"

"Not one, sir."

"But Mr. Almodham goes off occasionally. I met him at Luxor last year."

"Just so, sir. But when he's here he needs me for himself; and when he's away he needs me to watch over the others. So you see—"

"Yes, I see. But it must seem to you devilish long."

"It seems long, sir."

"But the others? You mean they're not—wholly trustworthy?"

"Well, sir, they're just Arabs," said Gosling with careless contempt.

"I see. And not a single old reliable among them?"

"The term isn't in their language, sir."

Medford was busy lighting his cigar. When he looked up he found that Gosling still stood a few feet off.

"It wasn't as if it 'adn't been a promise, you know, sir," he said, almost passionately.

"A promise?"

"To let me 'ave my holiday, sir. A promise—agine and agine."

"And the time never came?"

"No, sir. The days just drifted by—"

"Ah. They would, here. Don't sit up for me," Medford added. "I think I shall wait up—wait for Mr. Almodham."

Gosling's stare widened. "Here, sir? Here in the court?"

The young man nodded, and the servant stood still regarding him, turned by the moonlight to a white spectral figure, the unquiet ghost of a patient butler who might have died without his holiday.

"Down here in this court all night, sir? It's a lonely spot. I couldn't 'ear you if you was to call. You're best in bed, sir. The air's bad. You might bring your fever on again."

Medford laughed and stretched himself in his long chair. "Decidedly," he thought, "the fellow needs a change." Aloud he remarked: "Oh, I'm all right. It's you who are nervous, Gosling. When Mr. Almodham comes back I mean to put in a word for you. You shall have your holiday."

Gosling still stood motionless. For a minute he did not speak. "You would, sir, you would?" He gasped it out on a high cracked note, and the last word ran into a laugh—a brief shrill cackle, the laugh of one long unused to such indulgences.

"Thank you, sir. Good night, sir." He was gone.

IV

"You do boil my drinking-water, always?" Medford questioned, his hand clasping the glass without lifting it.

The tone was amicable, almost confidential; Medford felt that since his rash promise to secure a holiday for Gosling he and Gosling were on terms of real friendship.

"Boil it? Always, sir. Naturally." Gosling spoke with a slight note of reproach, as though Medford's question implied a slur—unconscious, he hoped—on their newly established relation. He scrutinized Medford with his astonished eyes, in which a genuine concern showed itself through the glaze of professional indifference.

"Because, you know, my bath this morning—"

Gosling was in the act of receiving from the hands of a gliding Arab a fragrant dish of *kuskus*. Under his breath he hissed to the native: "You damned aboriginy, you, can't you even 'old a dish steady? Ugh!" The Arab vanished before the imprecation, and Gosling, with a calm deliberate hand, set the dish before Medford. "All alike, they are." Fastidiously he wiped a trail of grease from his linen sleeve.

"Because, you know, my bath this morning simply stank," said Medford, plunging fork and spoon into the dish.

"Your bath, sir?" Gosling stressed the word. Astonishment, to the exclusion of all other emotion, again filled his eyes as he rested them on Medford. "Now, I wouldn't 'ave 'ad that 'appen for the world," he said self-reproachfully.

"There's only the one well here, eh? The one in the court?"

Gosling aroused himself from absorbed consideration of the visitor's complaint. "Yes, sir; only the one."

"What sort of a well is it? Where does the water come from?"

"Oh, it's just a cistern, sir. Rain-water. There's never been any other here. Not that I ever knew it to fail; but at this season sometimes it does turn queer. Ask any o' them Arabs, sir; they'll tell you. Liars as they are, they won't trouble to lie about that."

Medford was cautiously tasting the water in his glass. "This seems all right," he pronounced.

Sincere satisfaction was depicted on Gosling's countenance. "I seen to its being boiled myself, sir. I always do. I 'ope that Perrier'll turn up tomorrow, sir."

"Oh, tomorrow"—Medford shrugged, taking a second helping. "Tomorrow I may not be here to drink it."

"What—going away, sir?" cried Gosling.

Medford, wheeling round abruptly, caught a new and incomprehensible look in Gosling's eyes. The man had seemed to feel a sort of dog-like affection for him; had wanted, Medford could have sworn, to keep him on, persuade him to patience and delay; yet now, Medford could equally have sworn, there was relief in his look, satisfaction, almost, in his voice.

"So soon, sir?"

"Well, this is the fifth day since my arrival. And as there's no news yet of Mr. Almodham, and you say he may very well have forgotten all about my coming—"

"Oh, I don't say that, sir; not forgotten! Only, when one of those old piles of stones takes 'old of him, he does forget about the time, sir. That's what I meant. The days drift by—'e's in a dream. Very likely he thinks you're just due now, sir." A small thin smile sharpened the lustreless gravity of Gosling's features. It was the first time that Medford had seen him smile.

"Oh, I understand. But still—" Medford paused. Through the spell of inertia laid on him by the drowsy place and its easeful comforts his instinct of alertness was struggling back. "It's odd—"

"What's odd?" Gosling echoed unexpectedly, setting the dried dates and figs on the table.

"Everything," said Medford.

He leaned back in his chair and glanced up through the arch at the lofty sky from which noon was pouring down in cataracts of blue and gold. Almodham was out there somewhere under that canopy of fire, perhaps, as the servant said, absorbed in his dream. The land was full of spells.

"Coffee, sir?" Gosling reminded him. Medford took it.

"It's odd that you say you don't trust any of these fellows —these Arabs—and yet that you don't seem to feel worried at Mr. Almodham's being off God knows where, all alone with them."

Gosling received this attentively, impartially; he saw the point. "Well, sir, no—you wouldn't understand. It's the very thing that can't be taught, when to trust 'em and when not. It's 'ow their interests lie, of course, sir; and their religion, as they call it." His contempt was unlimited. "But even to begin to understand why I'm not worried about Mr. Almodham, you'd 'ave to 'ave lived among them, sir, and you'd 'ave to speak their language."

"But I—" Medford began. He pulled himself up short and bent above his coffee.

"Yes, sir?"

"But I've travelled among them more or less."

"Oh, travelled!" Even Gosling's intonation could hardly conciliate respect with derision in his reception of this boast.

"This makes the fifth day, though," Medford continued argumentatively. The midday heat lay heavy even on the shaded side of the court, and the sinews of his will were weakening.

"I can understand, sir, a gentleman like you 'aving other engagements—being pressed for time, as it were," Gosling reasonably conceded.

He cleared the table, committed its freight to a pair of Arab arms that just showed and vanished, and finally took himself off while Medford sank into the divan. A land of dreams. . .

The afternoon hung over the place like a great velarium of cloth-of-gold stretched across the battlements and drooping down in ever slacker folds upon the heavy-headed palms. When at length the gold turned to violet, and the west to a bow of crystal clasping the dark sands, Medford shook off his sleep and wandered out. But this time, instead of mounting to the roof, he took another direction.

He was surprised to find how little he knew of the place after five days of loitering and waiting. Perhaps this was to be his last evening alone in it. He passed out of the court by a vaulted stone passage which led to another walled enclosure. At his approach two or three Arabs who had been squatting there rose and melted out of sight. It was as if the solid masonry had received them.

Beyond, Medford heard a stamping of hoofs, the stir of a stable at night-fall. He went under another archway and found himself among horses and mules. In the fading light an Arab was rubbing down one of the horses, a powerful young chestnut. He too seemed about to vanish; but Medford caught him by the sleeve.

"Go on with your work," he said in Arabic.

The man, who was young and muscular, with a lean Bedouin face, stopped and looked at him.

"I didn't know your Excellency spoke our language."

"Oh, yes," said Medford.

The man was silent, one hand on the horse's restless neck, the other thrust into his woollen girdle. He and Medford examined each other in the faint light.

"Is that the horse that's lame?" Medford asked.

"Lame?" The Arab's eyes ran down the animal's legs. "Oh, yes; lame," he answered vaguely.

Medford stooped and felt the horse's knees and fetlocks. "He seems pretty fit. Couldn't he carry me for a canter this evening if I felt like it?"

The Arab considered; he was evidently perplexed by the weight of responsibility which the question placed on him.

"Your Excellency would like to go for a ride this evening?"

"Oh, just a fancy. I might or I might not." Medford lit a cigarette and offered one to the groom, whose white teeth flashed his gratification. Over the shared match they drew nearer and the Arab's diffidence seemed to lessen.

"Is this one of Mr. Almodham's own mounts?" Medford asked.

"Yes, sir; it's his favourite," said the groom, his hand passing proudly down the horse's bright shoulder.

"His favourite? Yet he didn't take him on this long expedition?"

The Arab fell silent and stared at the ground.

"Weren't you surprised at that?" Medford queried.

The man's gesture declared that it was not his business to be surprised.

The two remained without speaking while the quick blue night descended.

At length Medford said carelessly: "Where do you suppose your master is at this moment?"

The moon, unperceived in the radiant fall of day, had now suddenly possessed the world, and a broad white beam lay full on the Arab's white smock, his brown face and the turban of camel's hair knotted above it. His agitated eyeballs glistened like jewels.

"If Allah would vouchsafe to let us know!"

"But you suppose he's safe enough, don't you? You don't think it's necessary yet for a party to go out in search of him?"

The Arab appeared to ponder this deeply. The question must have taken him by surprise. He flung a brown arm about the horse's neck and continued to scrutinize the stones of the court.

"When the master is away Mr. Gosling is our master."

"And he doesn't think it necessary?"

The Arab signed: "Not yet."

"But if Mr. Almodham were away much longer—"

The man was again silent, and Medford continued: "You're the head groom, I suppose?"

"Yes, Excellency."

There was another pause. Medford half turned away; then, over his shoulder: "I suppose you know the direction Mr. Almodham took? The place he's gone to?"

"Oh, assuredly, Excellency."

"Then you and I are going to ride after him. Be ready an hour before daylight. Say nothing to any one—Mr. Gosling or anybody else. We two ought to be able to find him without other help."

The Arab's face was all a responsive flash of eyes and teeth. "Oh, sir, I undertake that you and my master shall meet before tomorrow night. And none shall know of it."

"He's as anxious about Almodham as I am," Medford thought; and a faint shiver ran down his back. "All right. Be ready," he repeated.

He strolled back and found the court empty of life, but fantastically peopled by palms of beaten silver and a white marble fig tree.

"After all," he thought irrelevantly, "I'm glad I didn't tell Gosling that I speak Arabic."

He sat down and waited till Gosling, approaching from the living-room, ceremoniously announced for the fifth time that dinner was served.

V

Medford sat up in bed with the jerk which resembles no other. Someone was in his room. The fact reached him not by sight or sound—for the moon had set, and the silence of the night was complete—but by a peculiar faint disturbance of the invisible currents that enclose us.

He was awake in an instant, caught up his electric hand-lamp and flashed it into two astonished eyes. Gosling stood above the bed.

"Mr. Almodham—he's back?" Medford exclaimed.

"No, sir; he's not back." Gosling spoke in low controlled tones. His extreme self-possession gave Medford a sense of danger—he couldn't say why, or of what nature. He sat upright, looking hard at the man.

"Then what's the matter?"

"Well, sir, you might have told me you talk Arabic"—Gosling's tone was now wistfully reproachful—"before you got 'obnobbing with that Selim. Making randy-voos with 'im by night in the desert."

Medford reached for his matches and lit the candle by the bed. He did not know whether to kick Gosling out of the room or to listen to what the man had to say; but a quick movement of curiosity made him determine on the latter course.

"Such folly! First I thought I'd lock you in. I might 'ave." Gosling drew a key from his pocket and held it up. "Or again I might 'ave let you go. Easier than not. But there was Wembley."

"Wembley?" Medford echoed. He began to think the man was going mad. One might, so conceivably, in that place of postponements and enchantments! He wondered whether Almodham himself were not a little mad—if, indeed, Almodham were still in a world where such a fate is possible.

"Wembley. You promised to get Mr. Almodham to give me an 'oliday—to let me go back to England in time for a look at Wembley. Every man 'as 'is fancies, 'asn't 'e, sir? And that's mine. I've told Mr. Almodham so, agine and agine. He'd never listen, or only make believe to; say: 'We'll see, now, Gosling, we'll see'; and no more 'eard of it. But you was different, sir. You said it, and I knew you meant it—about my 'oliday. So I'm going to lock you in."

Gosling spoke composedly, but with an under-thrill of emotion in his queer Mediterranean-Cockney voice.

"Lock me in?"

"Prevent you somehow from going off with that murderer. You don't suppose you'd ever 'ave come back alive from that ride, do you?"

A shiver ran over Medford, as it had the evening before when he had said to himself that the Arab was as anxious as he was about Almodham. He gave a slight laugh.

"I don't know what you're talking about. But you're not going to lock me in."

The effect of this was unexpected. Gosling's face was drawn up into a convulsive grimace and two tears rose to his pale eyelashes and ran down his cheeks.

"You don't trust me, after all," he said plaintively.

Medford leaned on his pillow and considered. Nothing as queer had ever before happened to him. The fellow looked almost ridiculous enough to laugh at; yet his tears were certainly not simulated. Was he weeping for Almodham, already dead, or for Medford, about to be committed to the same grave?

"I should trust you at once," said Medford, "if you'd tell me where your master is."

Gosling's face resumed its usual guarded expression, though the trace of the tears still glittered on it.

"I can't do that, sir."

"Ah, I thought so!"

"Because—'ow do I know?"

Medford thrust a leg out of bed. One hand, under the blanket, lay on his revolver.

"Well, you may go now. Put that key down on the table first. And don't try to do anything to interfere with my plans. If you do I'll shoot you," he added concisely.

"Oh, no, you wouldn't shoot a British subject; it makes such a fuss. Not that I'd care—I've often thought of doing it myself. Sometimes in the sirocco season. That don't scare me. And you shan't go."

Medford was on his feet now, the revolver visible. Gosling eyed it with indifference.

"Then you do know where Mr. Almodham is? And you're determined that I shan't find out?" Medford challenged him.

"Selim's determined," said Gosling, "and all the others are. They all want you out of the way. That's why I've kept 'em to their quarters—done all the waiting on you myself. Now will you stay here? For God's sake, sir! The return caravan is going through to the coast the day after tomorrow. Join it, sir— it's the only safe way! I darsn't let you go with one of our men, not even if you was to swear you'd ride straight for the coast and let this business be."

"This business? What business?"

"This worrying about where Mr. Almodham is, sir. Not that there's anything to worry about. The men all know that. But the plain fact is they've stolen some money from his box, since he's been gone, and if I hadn't winked at it they'd 'ave killed me; and all they want is to get you to ride out after 'im, and put you safe away under a 'eap of sand somewhere off the caravan trails. Easy job. There; that's all, sir. My word it is."

There was a long silence. In the weak candle-light the two men stood considering each other.

Medford's wits began to clear as the sense of peril closed in on him. His mind reached out on all sides into the enfolding mystery, but it was everywhere impenetrable. The odd thing was that, though he did not believe half of what Gosling had told him, the man yet inspired him with a queer sense of confidence as far as their mutual relation was concerned. "He may be lying about Almodham, to hide God knows what; but I don't believe he's lying about Selim."

Medford laid his revolver on the table. "Very well," he said. "I won't ride out to look for Mr. Almodham, since you advise me not to. But I won't leave by the caravan; I'll wait here till he comes back."

He saw Gosling whiten under his sallowness. "Oh, don't do that, sir; I couldn't answer for them if you was to wait. The caravan'll take you to the coast the day after tomorrow as easy as if you was riding in Rotten Row."

"Ah, then you know that Mr. Almodham won't be back by the day after tomorrow?" Medford caught him up.

"I don't know anything, sir."

"Not even where he is now?"

Gosling reflected. "He's been gone too long, sir, for me to know that," he said from the threshold.

The door closed on him.

Medford found sleep unrecoverable. He leaned in his window and watched the stars fade and the dawn break in all its holiness. As the stir of life rose among the ancient walls he marvelled at the contrast between that fountain of purity welling up into the heavens and the evil secrets clinging bat-like to the nest of masonry below.

He no longer knew what to believe or whom. Had some enemy of Almodham's lured him into the desert and bought the connivance of his people? Or had the servants had some reason of their own for spiriting him away, and was Gosling possibly telling the truth when he said that the same fate would befall Medford if he refused to leave?

Medford, as the light brightened, felt his energy return. The very impenetrableness of the mystery stimulated him. He would stay, and he would find out the truth.

VI

It was always Gosling himself who brought up the water for Medford's bath; but this morning he failed to appear with it, and when he came it was to bring the breakfast tray. Medford noticed that his face was of a pasty pallor, and that his lids were reddened as if with weeping. The contrast was unpleasant, and a dislike for Gosling began to shape itself in the young man's breast.

"My bath?" he queried.

"Well, sir, you complained yesterday of the water—"

"Can't you boil it?"

"I 'ave, sir."

"Well, then—"

Gosling went out sullenly and presently returned with a brass jug. "It's the time of year—we're dying for rain," he grumbled, pouring a scant measure of water into the tub.

Yes, the well must be pretty low, Medford thought. Even boiled, the water had the disagreeable smell that he had noticed the day before, though of course in a slighter degree.

But a bath was a necessity in that climate. He splashed the few cupfuls over himself as best as he could.

He spent the day in rather fruitlessly considering his situation. He had hoped the morning would bring counsel, but it brought only courage and resolution, and these were of small use without enlightenment. Suddenly he remembered that the caravan going south from the coast would pass near the castle that afternoon. Gosling had dwelt on the date often enough, for it was the caravan which was to bring the box of Perrier water.

"Well, I'm not sorry for that," Medford reflected, with a slight shrinking of the flesh. Something sick and viscous, half smell, half substance, seemed to have clung to his skin since his morning bath, and the idea of having to drink that water again was nauseating.

But his chief reason for welcoming the caravan was the hope of finding in it some European, or at any rate some native official from the coast, to whom he might confide his anxiety. He hung about, listening and waiting, and then mounted to the roof to gaze northward along the trail. But in the afternoon glow he saw only three Bedouins guiding laden pack-mules toward the castle.

As they mounted the steep path he recognized some of Almodham's men, and guessed at once that the southward caravan trail did not actually pass under the walls and that the men had been out to meet it, probably at a small oasis behind some fold of the sand-hills. Vexed at his own thoughtlessness in not foreseeing such a possibility, Medford dashed down to the court, hoping the men might have brought back some news of Almodham, though, as the latter had ridden south, he could at best only have crossed the trail by which the caravan had come. Still, even so, some one might know something, some report might have been heard—since everything was always known in the desert.

As Medford reached the court, angry vociferations, and retorts as vehement, rose from the stable-yard. He leaned over the wall and listened. Hitherto nothing had surprised him more than the silence of the place. Gosling must have had a strong arm to subdue the shrill voices of his underlings. Now they had all broken loose, and it was Gosling's own voice—usually so discreet and measured—which dominated them.

Gosling, master of all the desert dialects, was cursing his subordinates in a half-dozen.

"And you didn't bring it—and you tell me it wasn't there, and I tell you it was, and that you know it, and that you either left it on a sand-heap while you were jawing with some of those slimy fellows from the coast, or else fastened it on to the horse so carelessly that it fell off on the way—and all of you too sleepy to notice. Oh, you sons of females I wouldn't soil my lips by naming! Well, back you go to hunt it up, that's all!"

"By Allah and the tomb of his Prophet, you wrong us unpardonably. There was nothing left at the oasis, nor yet dropped off on the way back. It was not there, and that is the truth in its purity."

"Truth! Purity! You miserable lot of shirks and liars, you—and the gentleman here not touching a drop of anything but water—as you profess to do, you liquor-swilling humbugs!"

Medford drew back from the parapet with a smile of relief. It was nothing but a case of Perrier—the missing case—which had raised the passions of these grown men to the pitch of frenzy! The anti-climax lifted a load from his breast. If Gosling, the calm and self-controlled, could waste his wrath on so slight a hitch in the working of the commissariat, he at least must have a free mind. How absurd this homely incident made Medford's speculations seem!

He was at once touched by Gosling's solicitude, and annoyed that he should have been so duped by the hallucinating fancies of the East.

Almodham was off on his own business; very likely the men knew where and what the business was; and even if they had robbed him in his absence, and quarrelled over the spoils, Medford did not see what he could do. It might even be that his eccentric host—with whom, after all, he had had but one evening's acquaintance—repenting of an invitation too rashly given, had ridden away to escape the boredom of entertaining him. As this alternative occurred to Medford it seemed so plausible that he began to wonder if Almodham had not simply withdrawn to some secret suite of that intricate dwelling, and were waiting there for his guest's departure.

So well would this explain Gosling's solicitude to see the visitor off—so completely account for the man's nervous and contradictory behaviour—that Medford, smiling at his own obtuseness, hastily resolved to leave on the morrow. Tranquillized by this decision, he lingered about the court till dusk fell, and then, as usual, went up to the roof. But today his eyes, instead of raking the horizon, fastened on the clustering edifice of which, after six days' residence, he knew so little. Aerial chambers, jutting out at capricious angles, baffled him with closely shuttered windows, or here and there with the enigma of painted panes. Behind which window was his host concealed, spying, it might be, at this very moment on the movements of his lingering guest?

The idea that that strange moody man, with his long brown face and shock of white hair, his half-guessed selfishness and tyranny, and his morbid self-absorption, might be actually within a stone's throw, gave Medford, for the first time, a sharp sense of isolation. He felt himself shut out, unwanted—the place, now that he imagined someone might be living in it unknown to him, became lonely, inhospitable, dangerous.

"Fool that I am—he probably expected me to pack up and go as soon as I found he was away!" the young man reflected. Yes; decidedly, he would leave the next morning.

Gosling had not shown himself all the afternoon. When at length, belatedly, he came to set the table, he wore a look of sullen, almost surly, reserve which Medford had not yet seen on his face. He hardly returned the young man's friendly "Hallo—dinner?" and when Medford was seated handed him the first dish in silence. Medford's glass remained unfilled till he touched its brim.

"Oh, there's nothing to drink, sir. The men lost the case of Perrier—or dropped it and smashed the bottles. They say it never came. 'Ow do I know, when they never open their 'eathen lips but to lie?" Gosling burst out with sudden violence.

He set down the dish he was handing, and Medford saw that he had been obliged to do so because his whole body was shaking as if with fever.

"My dear man, what does it matter? You're going to be ill," Medford exclaimed, laying his hand on the servant's arm. But the latter, muttering: "Oh, God, if I'd only 'a' gone for it my-self," jerked away and vanished from the room.

Medford sat pondering; it certainly looked as if poor Gosling were on the edge of a break-down. No wonder, when Medford himself was so oppressed by the uncanniness of the place. Gosling reappeared after an interval, correct, close-lipped, with the dessert and a bottle of white wine. "Sorry, sir."

To pacify him, Medford sipped the wine and then pushed his chair away and returned to the court. He was making for the fig tree by the well when Gosling, slipping ahead, trans-ferred his chair and wicker table to the other end of the court.

"You'll be better here—there'll be a breeze presently," he said. "I'll fetch your coffee."

He disappeared again, and Medford sat gazing up at the pile of masonry and plaster, and wondering whether he had not been moved away from his favourite corner to get him out of—or into?—the angle of vision of the invisible watcher. Gosling, having brought the coffee, went away and Medford sat on.

At length he rose and began to pace up and down as he smoked. The moon was not yet up, and darkness fell solemnly on the ancient walls. Presently the breeze arose and began its secret commerce with the palms.

Medford went back to his seat; but as soon as he had re-sumed it he fancied that the gaze of his hidden watcher was jealously fixed on the red spark of his cigar. The sensation be-came increasingly distasteful; he could almost feel Almodham reaching out long ghostly arms from somewhere above him in the darkness. He moved back into the living-room, where a shaded light hung from the ceiling; but the room was airless, and finally he went out again and dragged his seat to its old place under the fig tree. From there the windows which he suspected could not command him, and he felt easier, though the corner was out of the breeze and the heavy air seemed tainted with the exhalation of the adjoining well.

"The water must be very low," Medford mused. The smell, though faint, was unpleasant; it smirched the purity of the night. But he felt safer there, somehow, farther from those unseen eyes which seemed mysteriously to have become his enemies.

"If one of the men had knifed me in the desert, I shouldn't wonder if it would have been at Almodham's orders," Medford thought. He drowsed.

When he woke the moon was pushing up its ponderous orange disk above the walls, and the darkness in the court was less dense. He must have slept for an hour or more. The night was delicious, or would have been anywhere but there. Medford felt a shiver of his old fever and remembered that Gosling had warned him that the court was unhealthy at night.

"On account of the well, I suppose. I've been sitting too close to it," he reflected. His head ached, and he fancied that the sweetish foulish smell clung to his face as it had after his bath. He stood up and approached the well to see how much water was left in it. But the moon was not yet high enough to light those depths, and he peered down into blackness.

Suddenly he felt both shoulders gripped from behind and forcibly pressed forward, as if by someone seeking to push him over the edge. An instant later, almost coinciding with his own swift resistance, the push became a strong tug backward, and he swung round to confront Gosling, whose hands immediately dropped from his shoulders.

"I thought you had the fever, sir—I seemed to see you pitching over," the man stammered.

Medford's wits returned. "We must both have it, for I fancied you were pitching me," he said with a laugh.

"Me, sir?" Gosling gasped. "I pulled you back as 'ard as ever—"

"Of course. I know."

"Whatever are you doing here, anyhow, sir? I warned you it was un'ealthy at night," Gosling continued irritably.

Medford leaned against the well-head and contemplated him. "I believe the whole place is unhealthy."

Gosling was silent. At length he asked: "Aren't you going up to bed, sir?"

"No," said Medford, "I prefer to stay here."

Gosling's face took on an expression of dogged anger. "Well, then, I prefer that you shouldn't."

Medford laughed again. "Why? Because it's the hour when Mr. Almodham comes out to take the air?"

The effect of this question was unexpected. Gosling dropped back a step or two and flung up his hands, pressing them to his lips as if to stifle a low outcry.

"What's the matter?" Medford queried. The man's antics were beginning to get on his nerves.

"Matter?" Gosling still stood away from him, out of the rising slant of moonlight.

"Come! Own up that he's here and have done with it!" cried Medford impatiently.

"Here? What do you mean by 'here'? You 'aven't seen 'im, 'ave you?" Before the words were out of the man's lips he flung up his arms again, stumbled forward and fell in a heap at Medford's feet.

Medford, still leaning against the well-head, smiled down contemptuously at the stricken wretch. His conjecture had been the right one, then; he had not been Gosling's dupe after all.

"Get up, man. Don't be a fool! It's not your fault if I guessed that Mr. Almodham walks here at night—"

"Walks here!" wailed the other, still cowering.

"Well, doesn't he? He won't kill you for owning up, will he?"

"Kill me? Kill me? I wish I'd killed *you*!" Gosling half got to his feet, his head thrown back in ashen terror. "And I might 'ave, too, so easy! You felt me pushing of you over, didn't you? Coming 'ere spying and sniffing—" His anguish seemed to choke him.

Medford had not changed his position. The very abjectness of the creature at his feet gave him an easy sense of power. But Gosling's last cry had suddenly deflected the course of his speculations. Almodham was here, then; that was certain; but just where was he, and in what shape? A new fear scuttled down Medford's spine.

"So you did want to push me over?" he said. "Why? As the quickest way of joining your master?"

The effect was more immediate than he had foreseen.

Gosling, getting to his feet, stood there bowed and shrunken in the accusing moonlight.

"Oh, God—and I 'ad you 'arf over! You know I did! And then—it was what you said about Wembley. So help me, sir, I felt you meant it, and it 'eld me back." The man's face was again wet with tears, but this time Medford recoiled from them as if they had been drops splashed up by a falling body from the foul waters below.

Medford was silent. He did not know if Gosling were armed or not, but he was no longer afraid; only aghast, and yet shudderingly lucid.

Gosling continued to ramble on half deliriously:

"And if only that Perrier 'ad of come. I don't believe it'd ever 'ave crossed your mind, if only you'd 'ave had your Perrier regular, now would it? But you say 'e walks—and I knew he would! Only—what was I to do with him, with you turning up like that the very day?"

Still Medford did not move.

"And 'im driving me to madness, sir, sheer madness, that same morning. Will you believe it? The very week before you come, I was to sail for England and 'ave my 'oliday, a 'ole month, sir—and I was entitled to six, if there was any justice—a 'ole month in 'Ammersmith, sir, in a cousin's 'ouse, and the chance to see Wembley thoroughly; and then 'e 'eard you was coming, sir, and 'e was bored and lonely 'ere, you understand—'e 'ad to have new excitements provided for 'im or 'e'd go off 'is bat—and when 'e 'eard you were coming, 'e come out of his black mood in a flash and was 'arf crazy with pleasure, and said: 'I'll keep 'im 'ere all winter—a remarkable young man, Gosling—just my kind.' And when I says to him: 'And 'ow about my 'oliday?' he stares at me with those stony eyes of 'is and says: ''Oliday? Oh, to be sure; why, next year—we'll see what can be done about it next year.' Next year, sir, as if 'e was doing me a favour! And that's the way it 'ad been for nigh on twelve years.

"But this time, if you 'adn't 'ave come I do believe I'd 'ave got away, for he was getting used to 'aving Selim about 'im and his 'ealth was never better—and, well, I told 'im as much, and 'ow a man 'ad his rights after all, and my youth was going, and me that 'ad served him so well chained up 'ere like 'is watch-dog, and always next year and next year—and, well, sir, 'e just laughed, sneering-like, and lit 'is cigarette. 'Oh, Gosling, cut it out,' 'e says.

"He was standing on the very spot where you are now, sir; and he turned to walk into the 'ouse. And it was then I 'it 'im. He was a heavy man, and he fell against the well kerb. And just when you were expected any minute—oh, my God!"

Gosling's voice died out in a strangled murmur.

Medford, at his last words, had unvoluntarily shrunk back a few feet. The two men stood in the middle of the court and stared at each other without speaking. The moon, swinging high above the battlements, sent a searching spear of light down into the guilty darkness of the well.

After Holbein

ANSON WARLEY had had his moments of being a rather remarkable man; but they were only intermittent; they recurred at ever-lengthening intervals; and between times he was a small poor creature, chattering with cold inside, in spite of his agreeable and even distinguished exterior.

He had always been perfectly aware of these two sides of himself (which, even in the privacy of his own mind, he contemptuously refused to dub a dual personality); and as the rather remarkable man could take fairly good care of himself, most of Warley's attention was devoted to ministering to the poor wretch who took longer and longer turns at bearing his name, and was more and more insistent in accepting the invitations which New York, for over thirty years, had tirelessly poured out on him. It was in the interest of this lonely fidgety unemployed self that Warley, in his younger days, had frequented the gaudiest restaurants and the most glittering Palace Hotels of two hemispheres, subscribed to the most advanced literary and artistic reviews, bought the pictures of the young painters who were being the most vehemently discussed, missed few of the showiest first nights in New York, London or Paris, sought the company of the men and women —especially the women—most conspicuous in fashion, scandal, or any other form of social notoriety, and thus tried to warm the shivering soul within him at all the passing bonfires of success.

The original Anson Warley had begun by staying at home in his little flat, with his books and his thoughts, when the other poor creature went forth; but gradually—he hardly knew when or how—he had slipped into the way of going too, till finally he made the bitter discovery that he and the creature had become one, except on the increasingly rare occasions when, detaching himself from all casual contingencies, he mounted to the lofty water-shed which fed the sources of his scorn. The view from there was vast and glorious, the air was icy but exhilarating; but soon he began to find the place too lonely, and too difficult to get to, especially as the lesser

Anson not only refused to go up with him but began to sneer, at first ever so faintly, then with increasing insolence, at this affectation of a taste for the heights.

"What's the use of scrambling up there, anyhow? I could understand it if you brought down anything worth while—a poem or a picture of your own. But just climbing and staring: what does it lead to? Fellows with the creative gift have got to have their occasional Sinaïs; I can see that. But for a mere looker-on like you, isn't that sort of thing rather a pose? You talk awfully well—brilliantly, even (oh, my dear fellow, no false modesty between you and *me*, please!) But who the devil is there to listen to you, up there among the glaciers? And sometimes, when you come down, I notice that you're rather—well, heavy and tongue-tied. Look out, or they'll stop asking us to dine! And sitting at home every evening—brr! Look here, by the way; if you've got nothing better for tonight, come along with me to Chrissy Torrance's—or the Bob Briggses'—or Princess Kate's; anywhere where there's lots of racket and sparkle, places that people go to in Rollses, and that are smart and hot and overcrowded, and you have to pay a lot—in one way or another—to get in."

Once and again, it is true, Warley still dodged his double and slipped off on a tour to remote uncomfortable places, where there were churches or pictures to be seen, or shut himself up at home for a good bout of reading, or just, in sheer disgust at his companion's platitude, spent an evening with people who were doing or thinking real things. This happened seldomer than of old, however, and more clandestinely; so that at last he used to sneak away to spend two or three days with an archæologically-minded friend, or an evening with a quiet scholar, as furtively as if he were stealing to a lover's tryst; which, as lovers' trysts were now always kept in the lime-light, was after all a fair exchange. But he always felt rather apologetic to the other Warley about these escapades—and, if the truth were known, rather bored and restless before they were over. And in the back of his mind there lurked an increasing dread of missing something hot and noisy and overcrowded when he went off to one of his mountain-tops. "After all, that high-brow business has been awfully overdone—now hasn't it?" the little Warley would insinuate, rummaging for his pearl studs, and consulting his flat evening watch as nervously as if it were a railway time-table. "If only we haven't missed something really jolly by all this backing and filling . . ."

"Oh, you poor creature, you! Always afraid of being left out, aren't you? Well—just for once, to humour you, and because I happen to be feeling rather stale myself. But only to think of a sane man's wanting to go to places just because they're hot and smart and overcrowded!" And off they would dash together. . .

II

All that was long ago. It was years now since there had been two distinct Anson Warleys. The lesser one had made away with the other, done him softly to death without shedding of blood; and only a few people suspected (and they no longer cared) that the pale white-haired man, with the small slim figure, the ironic smile and the perfect evening clothes, whom New York still indefatigably invited, was nothing less than a murderer.

Anson Warley—Anson Warley! No party was complete without Anson Warley. He no longer went abroad now; too stiff in the joints; and there had been two or three slight attacks of dizziness. . . Nothing to speak of, nothing to think of, even; but somehow one dug one's self into one's comfortable quarters, and felt less and less like moving out of them, except to motor down to Long Island for week-ends, or to Newport for a few visits in summer. A trip to the Hot Springs, to get rid of the stiffness, had not helped much, and the ageing Anson Warley (who really, otherwise, felt as young as ever) had developed a growing dislike for the promiscuities of hotel life and the monotony of hotel food.

Yes; he was growing more fastidious as he grew older. A good sign, he thought. Fastidious not only about food and comfort but about people also. It was still a privilege, a distinction, to have him to dine. His old friends were faithful, and the new people fought for him, and often failed to get him; to do so they had to offer very special inducements in the way of *cuisine*, conversation or beauty. Young beauty; yes, that would do it. He did like to sit and watch a lovely face, and call laughter into lovely eyes. But no dull dinners for *him*, not even if they fed you off gold. As to that he was as firm as the other Warley, the distant aloof one with whom he had— er, well, parted company, oh, quite amicably, a good many years ago. . .

On the whole, since that parting, life had been much easier and pleasanter; and by the time the little Warley was sixty-three he found himself looking forward with equanimity to an eternity of New York dinners.

Oh, but only at the right houses—always at the right houses; that was understood! The right people—the right setting—the right wines. . . He smiled a little over his perennial enjoyment of them; said "Nonsense, Filmore," to his devoted tiresome man-servant, who was beginning to hint that really, every night, sir, and sometimes a dance afterward, was too much, especially when you kept at it for months on end; and Dr.——

"Oh, damn your doctors!" Warley snapped. He was seldom ill-tempered; he knew it was foolish and upsetting to lose one's self-control. But Filmore began to be a nuisance, nagging him, preaching at him. As if he himself wasn't the best judge. . .

Besides, he chose his company. He'd stay at home any time rather than risk a boring evening. Damned rot, what Filmore had said about his going out every night. Not like poor old Mrs. Jaspar, for instance. . . He smiled self-approvingly as he evoked her tottering image. "That's the kind of fool Filmore takes me for," he chuckled, his good-humour restored by an analogy that was so much to his advantage.

Poor old Evelina Jaspar! In his youth, and even in his prime, she had been New York's chief entertainer—"leading hostess", the newspapers called her. Her big house in Fifth Avenue had been an entertaining machine. She had lived, breathed, invested and reinvested her millions, to no other end. At first her pretext had been that she had to marry her daughters and amuse her sons; but when sons and daughters had married and left her she had seemed hardly aware of it; she had just gone on entertaining. Hundreds, no, thousands of dinners (on gold plate, of course, and with orchids, and all the delicacies that were out of season), had been served in that vast pompous dining-room, which one had only to close one's eyes to transform into a railway buffet for millionaires, at a big junction, before the invention of restaurant trains. . .

Warley closed his eyes, and did so picture it. He lost himself in amused computation of the annual number of guests, of saddles of mutton, of legs of lamb, of terrapin, canvasbacks, magnums of champagne and pyramids of hot-house fruit that must have passed through that room in the last forty years.

And even now, he thought—hadn't one of old Evelina's nieces told him the other day, half bantering, half shivering at the avowal, that the poor old lady, who was gently dying of softening of the brain, still imagined herself to be New York's leading hostess, still sent out invitations (which of course were never delivered), still ordered terrapin, champagne and orchids, and still came down every evening to her great shrouded drawing-rooms, with her tiara askew on her purple wig, to receive a stream of imaginary guests?

Rubbish, of course—a macabre pleasantry of the extravagant Nelly Pierce, who had always had her joke at Aunt Evelina's expense. . . But Warley could not help smiling at the thought that those dull monotonous dinners were still going on in their hostess's clouded imagination. Poor old Evelina, he thought! In a way she was right. There was really no reason why that kind of standardized entertaining should ever cease; a performance so undiscriminating, so undifferentiated, that one could almost imagine, in the hostess's tired brain, all the dinners she had ever given merging into one Gargantuan pyramid of food and drink, with the same faces, perpetually the same faces, gathered stolidly about the same gold plate.

Thank heaven, Anson Warley had never conceived of social values in terms of mass and volume. It was years since he had dined at Mrs. Jaspar's. He even felt that he was not above reproach in that respect. Two or three times, in the past, he had accepted her invitations (always sent out weeks ahead), and then chucked her at the eleventh hour for something more amusing. Finally, to avoid such risks, he had made it a rule always to refuse her dinners. He had even—he remembered—

been rather funny about it once, when someone had told him that Mrs. Jaspar couldn't understand . . . was a little hurt . . . said it couldn't be true that he always had another engagement the nights she asked him. . . "*True?* Is the truth what she wants? All right! Then the next time I get a 'Mrs. Jaspar requests the pleasure' I'll answer it with a 'Mr. Warley declines the boredom.' Think she'll understand that, eh?" And the phrase became a catchword in his little set that winter. " 'Mr. Warley declines the boredom'—good, good, *good!*" "Dear Anson, I do hope you won't decline the boredom of coming to lunch next Sunday to meet the new Hindu Yoghi"—or the new saxophone soloist, or that genius of a mulatto boy who plays negro spirituals on a toothbrush; and so on and so on. He only hoped poor old Evelina never heard of it. . .

"Certainly I shall *not* stay at home tonight—why, what's wrong with me?" he snapped, swinging round on Filmore.

The valet's long face grew longer. His way of answering such questions was always to pull out his face; it was his only means of putting any expression into it. He turned away into the bedroom, and Warley sat alone by his library fire. . . Now what did the man see that was wrong with him, he wondered? He had felt a little confusion that morning, when he was doing his daily sprint around the Park (his exercise was reduced to that!); but it had been only a passing flurry, of which Filmore could of course know nothing. And as soon as it was over his mind had seemed more lucid, his eye keener, than ever; as sometimes (he reflected) the electric light in his library lamps would blaze up too brightly after a break in the current, and he would say to himself, wincing a little at the sudden glare on the page he was reading: "That means that it'll go out again in a minute."

Yes; his mind, at that moment, had been quite piercingly clear and perceptive; his eye had passed with a renovating glitter over every detail of the daily scene. He stood still for a minute under the leafless trees of the Mall, and looking about him with the sudden insight of age, understood that he had reached the time of life when Alps and cathedrals become as transient as flowers.

Everything was fleeting, fleeting . . . yes, that was what
had given him the vertigo. The doctors, poor fools, called it
the stomach, or high blood-pressure; but it was only the dizzy
plunge of the sands in the hour-glass, the everlasting plunge
that emptied one of heart and bowels, like the drop of an elevator from the top floor of a sky-scraper.

Certainly, after that moment of revelation, he had felt a little more tired than usual for the rest of the day; the light had
flagged in his mind as it sometimes did in his lamps. At
Chrissy Torrance's, where he had lunched, they had accused
him of being silent, his hostess had said that he looked pale;
but he had retorted with a joke, and thrown himself into the
talk with a feverish loquacity. It was the only thing to do; for
he could not tell all these people at the lunch table that very
morning he had arrived at the turn in the path from which
mountains look as transient as flowers—and that one after another they would all arrive there too.

He leaned his head back and closed his eyes, but not in
sleep. He did not feel sleepy, but keyed up and alert. In the
next room he heard Filmore reluctantly, protestingly, laying
out his evening clothes. . . He had no fear about the dinner tonight; a quiet intimate little affair at an old friend's
house. Just two or three congenial men, and Elfmann, the
pianist (who would probably play), and that lovely Elfrida
Flight. The fact that people asked him to dine to meet
Elfrida Flight seemed to prove pretty conclusively that he
was still in the running! He chuckled softly at Filmore's
pessimism, and thought: "Well, after all, I suppose no man
seems young to his valet. . . Time to dress very soon," he
thought; and luxuriously postponed getting up out of his
chair. . .

III

"She's worse than usual tonight," said the day nurse, laying
down the evening paper as her colleague joined her.
"Absolutely determined to have her jewels out."

The night nurse, fresh from a long sleep and an afternoon
at the movies with a gentleman friend, threw down her fancy
bag, tossed off her hat and rumpled up her hair before old

Mrs. Jaspar's tall toilet mirror. "Oh, I'll settle that—don't you worry," she said brightly.

"Don't you fret her, though, Miss Cress," said the other, getting wearily out of her chair. "We're very well off here, take it as a whole, and I don't want her pressure rushed up for nothing."

Miss Cress, still looking at herself in the glass, smiled reassuringly at Miss Dunn's pale reflection behind her. She and Miss Dunn got on very well together, and knew on which side their bread was buttered. But at the end of the day Miss Dunn was always fagged out and fearing the worst. The patient wasn't as hard to handle as all that. Just let her ring for her old maid, old Lavinia, and say: "My sapphire velvet tonight, with the diamond stars"—and Lavinia would know exactly how to manage her.

Miss Dunn had put on her hat and coat, and crammed her knitting, and the newspaper, into her bag, which, unlike Miss Cress's, was capacious and shabby; but she still loitered undecided on the threshold. "I could stay with you till ten as easy as not. . ." She looked almost reluctantly about the big high-studded dressing-room (everything in the house was high-studded), with its rich dusky carpet and curtains, and its monumental dressing-table draped with lace and laden with gold-backed brushes and combs, gold-stoppered toilet-bottles, and all the charming paraphernalia of beauty at her glass. Old Lavinia even renewed every morning the roses and carnations in the slim crystal vases between the powder boxes and the nail polishers. Since the family had shut down the hot-houses at the uninhabited country place on the Hudson, Miss Cress suspected that old Lavinia bought these flowers out of her own pocket.

"Cold out tonight?" queried Miss Dunn from the door.

"Fierce. . . Reg'lar blizzard at the corners. Say, shall I lend you my fur scarf?" Miss Cress, pleased with the memory of her afternoon (they'd be engaged soon, she thought), and with the drowsy prospect of an evening in a deep arm-chair near the warm gleam of the dressing-room fire, was disposed to kindliness toward that poor thin Dunn girl, who supported her mother, and her brother's idiot twins. And she wanted Miss Dunn to notice her new fur.

"My! Isn't it too lovely? No, not for worlds, thank you. . ." Her hand on the door-knob, Miss Dunn repeated: "Don't you cross her now," and was gone.

Lavinia's bell rang furiously, twice; then the door between the dressing-room and Mrs. Jaspar's bedroom opened, and Mrs. Jaspar herself emerged.

"Lavinia!" she called, in a high irritated voice; then, seeing the nurse, who had slipped into her print dress and starched cap, she added in a lower tone: "Oh, Miss Lemoine, good evening." Her first nurse, it appeared, had been called Miss Lemoine; and she gave the same name to all the others, quite unaware that there had been any changes in the staff.

"I heard talking, and carriages driving up. Have people begun to arrive?" she asked nervously. "Where is Lavinia? I still have my jewels to put on."

She stood before the nurse, the same petrifying apparition which always, at this hour, struck Miss Cress to silence. Mrs. Jaspar was tall; she had been broad; and her bones remained impressive though the flesh had withered on them. Lavinia had encased her, as usual, in her low-necked purple velvet dress, nipped in at the waist in the old-fashioned way, expanding in voluminous folds about the hips and flowing in a long train over the darker velvet of the carpet. Mrs. Jaspar's swollen feet could no longer be pushed into the high-heeled satin slippers which went with the dress; but her skirts were so long and spreading that, by taking short steps, she managed (so Lavinia daily assured her) entirely to conceal the broad round tips of her black orthopædic shoes.

"Your jewels, Mrs. Jaspar? Why, you've got them on," said Miss Cress brightly.

Mrs. Jaspar turned her porphyry-tinted face to Miss Cress, and looked at her with a glassy incredulous gaze. Her eyes, Miss Cress thought, were the worst. . . She lifted one old hand, veined and knobbed as a raised map, to her elaborate purple-black wig, groped among the puffs and curls and undulations (queer, Miss Cress thought, that it never occurred to her to look into the glass), and after an interval affirmed: "You must be mistaken, my dear. Don't you think you ought to have your eyes examined?"

The door opened again, and a very old woman, so old as to make Mrs. Jaspar appear almost young, hobbled in with side-long steps. "Excuse me, madam. I was downstairs when the bell rang."

Lavinia had probably always been small and slight; now, beside her towering mistress, she looked a mere feather, a straw. Everything about her had dried, contracted, been volatilized into nothingness, except her watchful gray eyes, in which intelligence and comprehension burned like two fixed stars. "Do excuse me, madam," she repeated.

Mrs. Jaspar looked at her despairingly. "I hear carriages driving up. And Miss Lemoine says I have my jewels on; and I know I haven't."

"With that lovely necklace!" Miss Cress ejaculated.

Mrs. Jaspar's twisted hand rose again, this time to her denuded shoulders, which were as stark and barren as the rock from which the hand might have been broken. She felt and felt, and tears rose in her eyes. . . .

"Why do you lie to me?" she burst out passionately.

Lavinia softly intervened. "Miss Lemoine meant, how lovely you'll be when you get the necklace on, madam."

"Diamonds, diamonds," said Mrs. Jaspar with an awful smile.

"Of course, madam."

Mrs. Jaspar sat down at the dressing-table, and Lavinia, with eager random hands, began to adjust the *point de Venise* about her mistress's shoulders, and to repair the havoc wrought in the purple-black wig by its wearer's gropings for her tiara.

"Now you do look lovely, madam," she sighed.

Mrs. Jaspar was on her feet again, stiff but incredibly active. ("Like a cat she is," Miss Cress used to relate.) "I do hear carriages—or is it an automobile? The Magraws, I know, have one of those new-fangled automobiles. And now I hear the front door opening. Quick, Lavinia! My fan, my gloves, my handkerchief . . . how often have I got to tell you? I used to have a *perfect* maid—"

Lavinia's eyes brimmed. "That was me, madam," she said, bending to straighten out the folds of the long purple velvet train. ("To watch the two of 'em," Miss Cress used to tell a circle of appreciative friends, "is a lot better than any circus.")

Mrs. Jaspar paid no attention. She twitched the train out of Lavinia's vacillating hold, swept to the door, and then paused there as if stopped by a jerk of her constricted muscles. "Oh, but my diamonds—you cruel woman, you! You're letting me go down without my diamonds!" Her ruined face puckered up in a grimace like a new-born baby's, and she began to sob despairingly. "Everybody. . . Every . . . body's . . . against me . . ." she wept in her powerless misery.

Lavinia helped herself to her feet and tottered across the floor. It was almost more than she could bear to see her mistress in distress. "Madam, madam—if you'll just wait till they're got out of the safe," she entreated.

The woman she saw before her, the woman she was entreating and consoling, was not the old petrified Mrs. Jaspar with porphyry face and wig awry whom Miss Cress stood watching with a smile, but a young proud creature, commanding and splendid in her Paris gown of amber *moiré*, who, years ago, had burst into just such furious sobs because, as she was sweeping down to receive her guests, the doctor had told her that little Grace, with whom she had been playing all the afternoon, had a diphtheritic throat, and no one must be allowed to enter. "Everybody's against me, everybody . . ." she had sobbed in her fury; and the young Lavinia, stricken by such Olympian anger, had stood speechless, longing to comfort her, and secretly indignant with little Grace and the doctor. . .

"If you'll just wait, madam, while I go down and ask Munson to open the safe. There's no one come yet, I do assure you. . ."

Munson was the old butler, the only person who knew the combination of the safe in Mrs. Jaspar's bedroom. Lavinia had once known it too, but now she was no longer able to remember it. The worst of it was that she feared lest Munson, who had been spending the day in the Bronx, might not have returned. Munson was growing old too, and he did sometimes forget about these dinner-parties of Mrs. Jaspar's, and then the stupid footman, George, had to announce the names; and you couldn't be sure that Mrs. Jaspar wouldn't notice Munson's absence, and be excited and angry. These dinner-party nights were killing old Lavinia, and she did so want to keep alive; she wanted to live long enough to wait on Mrs. Jaspar to the last.

She disappeared, and Miss Cress poked up the fire, and persuaded Mrs. Jaspar to sit down in an arm-chair and "tell her who was coming". It always amused Mrs. Jaspar to say over the long list of her guests' names, and generally she remembered them fairly well, for they were always the same—the last people, Lavinia and Munson said, who had dined at the house, on the very night before her stroke. With recovered complacency she began, counting over one after another on her ring-laden fingers: "The Italian Ambassador, the Bishop, Mr. and Mrs. Torrington Bligh, Mr. and Mrs. Fred Amesworth, Mr. and Mrs. Mitchell Magraw, Mr. and Mrs. Torrington Bligh . . ." ("You've said them before," Miss Cress interpolated, getting out her fancy knitting—a necktie for her friend—and beginning to count the stitches.) And Mrs. Jaspar, distressed and bewildered by the interruption, had to repeat over and over: "Torrington Bligh, Torrington Bligh," till the connection was re-established, and she went on again swimmingly with "Mr. and Mrs. Fred Amesworth, Mr. and Mrs. Mitchell Magraw, Miss Laura Ladew, Mr. Harold Ladew, Mr. and Mrs. Benjamin Bronx, Mr. and Mrs. Torrington Bl—no, I mean, Mr. Anson Warley. Yes, Mr. Anson Warley; that's it," she ended complacently.

Miss Cress smiled and interrupted her counting. "No, that's *not* it."

"What do you mean, my dear—not it?"

"Mr. Anson Warley. He's not coming."

Mrs. Jaspar's jaw fell, and she stared at the nurse's coldly smiling face. "Not coming?"

"No. He's not coming. He's not on the list." (That old list! As if Miss Cress didn't know it by heart! Everybody in the house did, except the booby, George, who heard it reeled off every other night by Munson, and who was always stumbling over the names, and having to refer to the written paper.)

"Not on the list?" Mrs. Jaspar gasped.

Miss Cress shook her pretty head.

Signs of uneasiness gathered on Mrs. Jaspar's face and her lip began to tremble. It always amused Miss Cress to give her these little jolts, though she knew Miss Dunn and the doctors didn't approve of her doing so. She knew also that it was against her own interests, and she did try to bear in mind Miss Dunn's oft-repeated admonition about not sending up the patient's blood pressure; but when she was in high spirits, as she was tonight (they would certainly be engaged), it was irresistible to get a rise out of the old lady. And she thought it funny, this new figure unexpectedly appearing among those time-worn guests. ("I wonder what the rest of 'em 'll say to him," she giggled inwardly.)

"No; he's not on the list." Mrs. Jaspar, after pondering deeply, announced the fact with an air of recovered composure.

"That's what I told you," snapped Miss Cress.

"He's not on the list; but he promised me to come. I saw him yesterday," continued Mrs. Jaspar, mysteriously.

"You *saw* him—where?"

She considered. "Last night, at the Fred Amesworths' dance."

"Ah," said Miss Cress, with a little shiver; for she knew that Mrs. Amesworth was dead, and she was the intimate friend of the trained nurse who was keeping alive, by dint of *piqûres* and high frequency, the inarticulate and inanimate Mr. Amesworth. "It's funny," she remarked to Mrs. Jaspar, "that you'd never invited Mr. Warley before."

"No, I hadn't; not for a long time. I believe he felt I'd neglected him; for he came up to me last night, and said he was so sorry he hadn't been able to call. It seems he's been ill, poor fellow. Not as young as he was! So of course I invited him. He was very much gratified."

Mrs. Jaspar smiled at the remembrance of her little triumph; but Miss Cress's attention had wandered, as it always did when the patient became docile and reasonable. She thought: "Where's old Lavinia? I bet she can't find Munson." And she got up and crossed the floor to look into Mrs. Jaspar's bedroom, where the safe was.

There an astonishing sight met her. Munson, as she had expected, was nowhere visible; but Lavinia, on her knees before the safe, was in the act of opening it herself, her twitching hand slowly moving about the mysterious dial.

"Why, I thought you'd forgotten the combination!" Miss Cress exclaimed.

Lavinia turned a startled face over her shoulder. "So I had, Miss. But I've managed to remember it, thank God. I *had* to, you see, because Munson's forgot to come home."

"Oh," said the nurse incredulously. ("Old fox," she thought, "I wonder why she's always pretended she'd forgotten it.") For Miss Cress did not know that the age of miracles is not yet past.

Joyous, trembling, her cheeks wet with grateful tears, the little old woman was on her feet again, clutching to her breast the diamond stars, the necklace of *solitaires*, the tiara, the earrings. One by one she spread them out on the velvet-lined tray in which they always used to be carried from the safe to the dressing-room; then, with rambling fingers, she managed to lock the safe again, and put the keys in the drawer where they belonged, while Miss Cress continued to stare at her in amazement. "I don't believe the old witch is as shaky as she makes out," was her reflection as Lavinia passed her, bearing the jewels to the dressing-room where Mrs. Jaspar, lost in pleasant memories, was still computing: "The Italian Ambassador, the Bishop, the Torrington Blighs, the Mitchell Magraws, the Fred Amesworths. . ."

Mrs. Jaspar was allowed to go down to the drawing-room alone on dinner-party evenings because it would have mortified her too much to receive her guests with a maid or a nurse at her elbow; but Miss Cress and Lavinia always leaned over the stair-rail to watch her descent, and make sure it was accomplished in safety.

"She do look lovely yet, when all her diamonds is on," Lavinia sighed, her purblind eyes bedewed with memories, as the bedizened wig and purple velvet disappeared at the last bend of the stairs. Miss Cress, with a shrug, turned back to the fire and picked up her knitting, while Lavinia set about the slow ritual of tidying up her mistress's room. From below they heard the sound of George's stentorian monologue: "Mr. and Mrs. Torrington Bligh, Mr. and Mrs. Mitchell Magraw . . . Mr. Ladew, Miss Laura Ladew. . ."

IV

Anson Warley, who had always prided himself on his
equable temper, was conscious of being on edge that evening.
But it was an irritability which did not frighten him (in spite
of what those doctors always said about the importance of
keeping calm) because he knew it was due merely to the unusual lucidity of his mind. He was in fact feeling uncommonly
well, his brain clear and all his perceptions so alert that he
could positively hear the thoughts passing through his man-
servant's mind on the other side of the door, as Filmore
grudgingly laid out the evening clothes.

Smiling at the man's obstinacy, he thought: "I shall have to
tell them tonight that Filmore thinks I'm no longer fit to go
into society." It was always pleasant to hear the incredulous
laugh with which his younger friends received any allusion to
his supposed senility. "What, *you?* Well, that's a good one!"
And he thought it was, himself.

And then, the moment he was in his bedroom, dressing,
the sight of Filmore made him lose his temper again. "No;
not those studs, confound it. The black onyx ones—haven't I
told you a hundred times? Lost them, I suppose? Sent them
to the wash again in a soiled shirt? That it?" He laughed nervously, and sitting down before his dressing-table began to
brush back his hair with short angry strokes.

"Above all," he shouted out suddenly, "don't stand there
staring at me as if you were watching to see exactly at what
minute to telephone for the undertaker!"

"The under—? Oh, sir!" gasped Filmore.

"The—the—damn it, are you *deaf* too? Who said undertaker? I said *taxi;* can't you hear what I say?"

"You want me to call a taxi, sir?"

"No; I don't. I've already told you so. I'm going to walk."
Warley straightened his tie, rose and held out his arms toward
his dress-coat.

"It's bitter cold, sir; better let me call a taxi all the same."

Warley gave a short laugh. "Out with it, now! What you'd
really like to suggest is that I should telephone to say I can't
dine out. You'd scramble me some eggs instead, eh?"

"I wish you would stay in, sir. There's eggs in the house."

"My overcoat," snapped Warley.

"Or else let me call a taxi; now do, sir."

Warley slipped his arms into his overcoat, tapped his chest to see if his watch (the thin evening watch) and his note-case were in their proper pockets, turned back to put a dash of lavender on his handkerchief, and walked with stiff quick steps toward the front door of his flat.

Filmore, abashed, preceded him to ring for the lift; and then, as it quivered upward through the long shaft, said again: "It's a bitter cold night, sir; and you've had a good deal of exercise today."

Warley levelled a contemptuous glance at him. "Daresay that's why I'm feeling so fit," he retorted as he entered the lift.

It *was* bitter cold; the icy air hit him in the chest when he stepped out of the overheated building, and he halted on the doorstep and took a long breath. "Filmore's missed his vocation; ought to be nurse to a paralytic," he thought. "He'd love to have to wheel me about in a chair."

After the first shock of the biting air he began to find it exhilarating, and walked along at a good pace, dragging one leg ever so little after the other. (The *masseur* had promised him that he'd soon be rid of that stiffness.) Yes—decidedly a fellow like himself ought to have a younger valet; a more cheerful one, anyhow. He felt like a young'un himself this evening; as he turned into Fifth Avenue he rather wished he could meet some one he knew, some man who'd say afterward at his club: "Warley? Why, I saw him sprinting up Fifth Avenue the other night like a two-year-old; that night it was four or five below. . ." He needed a good counter-irritant for Filmore's gloom. "Always have young people about you," he thought as he walked along; and at the words his mind turned to Elfrida Flight, next to whom he would soon be sitting in a warm pleasantly lit dining-room—*where?*

It came as abruptly as that: the gap in his memory. He pulled up at it as if his advance had been checked by a chasm in the pavement at his feet. Where the dickens was he going to dine? And with whom was he going to dine? God! But things didn't happen in that way; a sound strong man didn't suddenly have to stop in the middle of the street and ask himself where he was going to dine. . .

"Perfect in mind, body and understanding." The old legal phrase bobbed up inconsequently into his thoughts. Less than two minutes ago he had answered in every particular to that description; what was he now? He put his hand to his forehead, which was bursting; then he lifted his hat and let the cold air blow for a while on his overheated temples. It was queer, how hot he'd got, walking. Fact was, he'd been sprinting along at a damned good pace. In future he must try to remember not to hurry. . . Hang it—one more thing to remember! . . Well, but what was all the fuss about? Of course, as people got older their memories were subject to these momentary lapses; he'd noticed it often enough among his contemporaries. And, brisk and alert though he still was, it wouldn't do to imagine himself totally exempt from human ills. . .

Where was it he was dining? Why, somewhere farther up Fifth Avenue; he was perfectly sure of that. With that lovely . . . that lovely. . . No; better not make any effort for the moment. Just keep calm, and stroll slowly along. When he came to the right street corner of course he'd spot it; and then everything would be perfectly clear again. He walked on, more deliberately, trying to empty his mind of all thoughts. "Above all," he said to himself, "don't worry."

He tried to beguile his nervousness by thinking of amusing things. "Decline the boredom—" He thought he might get off that joke tonight. "Mrs. Jaspar requests the pleasure—Mr. Warley declines the boredom." Not so bad, really; and he had an idea he'd never told it to the people . . . what in hell *was* their name? . . . the people he was on his way to dine with. . . *Mrs. Jaspar requests the pleasure.* Poor old Mrs. Jaspar; again it occurred to him that he hadn't always been very civil to her in old times. When everybody's running after a fellow it's pardonable now and then to chuck a boring dinner at the last minute; but all the same, as one grew older one understood better how an unintentional slight of that sort might cause offense, cause even pain. And he hated to cause people pain. . . He thought perhaps he'd better call on Mrs. Jaspar some afternoon. She'd be surprised! Or ring her up, poor old girl, and propose himself, just informally, for dinner. One dull evening wouldn't kill him—and how pleased she'd be! Yes—he thought decidedly. . . When he got to be her age, he could imagine how much he'd like it if somebody still in the running should ring him up unexpectedly and say—

He stopped, and looked up, slowly, wonderingly, at the wide illuminated façade of the house he was approaching. Queer coincidence—it was the Jaspar house. And all lit up; for a dinner evidently. And that was queerer yet; almost uncanny; for here he was, in front of the door, as the clock struck a quarter past eight; and of course—he remembered it quite clearly now—it was just here, it was with Mrs. Jaspar, that he was dining. . . Those little lapses of memory never lasted more than a second or two. How right he'd been not to let himself worry. He pressed his hand on the door-bell.

"God," he thought, as the double doors swung open, "but it's good to get in out of the cold."

V

In that hushed sonorous house the sound of the door-bell was as loud to the two women upstairs as if it had been rung in the next room.

Miss Cress raised her head in surprise, and Lavinia dropped Mrs. Jaspar's other false set (the more comfortable one) with a clatter on the marble wash-stand. She stumbled across the dressing-room, and hastened out to the landing. With Munson absent, there was no knowing how George might muddle things. . .

Miss Cress joined her. "Who is it?" she whispered excitedly. Below, they heard the sound of a hat and a walking stick being laid down on the big marble-topped table in the hall, and then George's stentorian drone: "Mr. Anson Warley."

"It is—it *is!* I can see him—a gentleman in evening clothes," Miss Cress whispered, hanging over the stair-rail.

"Good gracious—mercy me! And Munson not here! Oh, whatever, whatever shall we do?" Lavinia was trembling so violently that she had to clutch the stair-rail to prevent herself from falling. Miss Cress thought, with her cold lucidity: "She's a good deal sicker than the old woman."

"What shall we do, Miss Cress? That fool of a George— he's showing him in! Who could have thought it?" Miss Cress

knew the images that were whirling through Lavinia's brain:
the vision of Mrs. Jaspar's having another stroke at the sight
of this mysterious intruder, of Mr. Anson Warley's seeing her
there, in her impotence and her abasement, of the family's being summoned, and rushing in to exclaim, to question, to be
horrified and furious—and all because poor old Munson's
memory was going, like his mistress's, like Lavinia's, and because he had forgotten that it was one of the *dinner nights*.
Oh, misery! . . . The tears were running down Lavinia's
cheeks, and Miss Cress knew she was thinking: "If the daughters send him off—and they will—where's he going to, old
and deaf as he is, and all his people dead? Oh, if only he can
hold on till she dies, and get his pension. . ."

Lavinia recovered herself with one of her supreme efforts.
"Miss Cress, we must go down at once, at once! Something
dreadful's going to happen. . ." She began to totter toward
the little velvet-lined lift in the corner of the landing.

Miss Cress took pity on her. "Come along," she said. "But
nothing dreadful's going to happen. You'll see."

"Oh, thank you, Miss Cress. But the shock—the awful
shock to her—of seeing that strange gentleman walk in."

"Not a bit of it." Miss Cress laughed as she stepped into
the lift. "He's not a stranger. She's expecting him."

"Expecting him? Expecting Mr. Warley?"

"Sure she is. She told me so just now. She says she invited
him yesterday."

"But, Miss Cress, what are you thinking of? Invite him—
how? When you know she can't write nor telephone?"

"Well, she says she saw him; she saw him last night at a
dance."

"Oh, God," murmured Lavinia, covering her eyes with her
hands.

"At a dance at the Fred Amesworths'—that's what she
said," Miss Cress pursued, feeling the same little shiver run
down her back as when Mrs. Jaspar had made the statement
to her.

"The Amesworths—oh, not the Amesworths?" Lavinia
echoed, shivering too. She dropped her hands from her face,
and followed Miss Cress out of the lift. Her expression had
become less anguished, and the nurse wondered why. In

reality, she was thinking, in a sort of dreary beatitude: "But if she's suddenly got as much worse as this, she'll go before me, after all, my poor lady, and I'll be able to see to it that she's properly laid out and dressed, and nobody but Lavinia's hands'll touch her."

"You'll see—if she was expecting him, as she says, it won't give her a shock, anyhow. Only, how did *he* know?" Miss Cress whispered, with an acuter renewal of her shiver. She followed Lavinia with muffled steps down the passage to the pantry, and from there the two women stole into the dining-room, and placed themselves noiselessly at its farther end, behind the tall Coromandel screen through the cracks of which they could peep into the empty room.

The long table was set, as Mrs. Jaspar always insisted that it should be on these occasions; but old Munson not having returned, the gold plate (which his mistress also insisted on) had not been got out, and all down the table, as Lavinia saw with horror, George had laid the coarse blue and white plates from the servants' hall. The electric wall-lights were on, and the candles lit in the branching Sèvres candelabra—so much at least had been done. But the flowers in the great central dish of Rose Dubarry porcelain, and in the smaller dishes which accompanied it—the flowers, oh shame, had been forgotten! They were no longer real flowers; the family had long since suppressed that expense; and no wonder, for Mrs. Jaspar always insisted on orchids. But Grace, the youngest daughter, who was the kindest, had hit on the clever device of arranging three beautiful clusters of artificial orchids and maiden-hair, which had only to be lifted from their shelf in the pantry and set in the dishes—only, of course, that imbecile footman had forgotten, or had not known where to find them. And, oh, horror, realizing his oversight too late, no doubt, to appeal to Lavinia, he had taken some old newspapers and bunched them up into something that he probably thought resembled a bouquet, and crammed one into each of the priceless Rose Dubarry dishes.

Lavinia clutched at Miss Cress's arm. "Oh, look—look what he's done; I shall die of the shame of it. . . Oh, Miss, hadn't we better slip around to the drawing-room and try to coax my poor lady upstairs again, afore she ever notices?"

Miss Cress, peering through the crack of the screen, could hardly suppress a giggle. For at that moment the double doors of the dining-room were thrown open, and George, shuffling about in a baggy livery inherited from a long-departed predecessor of more commanding build, bawled out in his loud sing-song: "Dinner is served, madam."

"Oh, it's too late," moaned Lavinia. Miss Cress signed to her to keep silent, and the two watchers glued their eyes to their respective cracks of the screen.

What they saw, far off down the vista of empty drawing-rooms, and after an interval during which (as Lavinia knew) the imaginary guests were supposed to file in and take their seats, was the entrance, at the end of the ghostly cortège, of a very old woman, still tall and towering, on the arm of a man somewhat smaller than herself, with a fixed smile on a darkly pink face, and a slim erect figure clad in perfect evening clothes, who advanced with short measured steps, profiting (Miss Cress noticed) by the support of the arm he was supposed to sustain. "Well—I never!" was the nurse's inward comment.

The couple continued to advance, with rigid smiles and eyes staring straight ahead. Neither turned to the other, neither spoke. All their attention was concentrated on the immense, the almost unachievable effort of reaching that point, half way down the long dinner table, opposite the big Dubarry dish, where George was drawing back a gilt armchair for Mrs. Jaspar. At last they reached it, and Mrs. Jaspar seated herself, and waved a stony hand to Mr. Warley. "On my right." He gave a little bow, like the bend of a jointed doll, and with infinite precaution let himself down into his chair. Beads of perspiration were standing on his forehead, and Miss Cress saw him draw out his handkerchief and wipe them stealthily away. He then turned his head somewhat stiffly toward his hostess.

"Beautiful flowers," he said, with great precision and perfect gravity, waving his hand toward the bunched-up newspaper in the bowl of Sèvres.

Mrs. Jaspar received the tribute with complacency. "So glad . . . orchids . . . From High Lawn . . . every morning," she simpered.

"Mar-vellous," Mr. Warley completed.

"I always say to the Bishop. . ." Mrs. Jaspar continued.

"Ha—of course," Mr. Warley warmly assented.

"Not that I don't think. . ."

"Ha—rather!"

George had reappeared from the pantry with a blue crockery dish of mashed potatoes. This he handed in turn to one after another of the imaginary guests, and finally presented to Mrs. Jaspar and her right-hand neighbour.

They both helped themselves cautiously, and Mrs. Jaspar addressed an arch smile to Mr. Warley. " 'Nother month—no more oysters."

"Ha—no more!"

George, with a bottle of Apollinaris wrapped in a napkin, was saying to each guest in turn: "Perrier-Jouet, 'ninety-five." (He had picked that up, thought Miss Cress, from hearing old Munson repeat it so often.)

"Hang it—well, then just a sip," murmured Mr. Warley.

"Old times," bantered Mrs. Jaspar; and the two turned to each other and bowed their heads and touched glasses.

"I often tell Mrs. Amesworth. . ." Mrs. Jaspar continued, bending to an imaginary presence across the table.

"Ha—*ha!*" Mr. Warley approved.

George reappeared and slowly encircled the table with a dish of spinach. After the spinach the Apollinaris also went the rounds again, announced successively as Château Lafite, 'seventy-four, and "the old Newbold Madeira". Each time that George approached his glass, Mr. Warley made a feint of lifting a defensive hand, and then smiled and yielded. "Might as well—hanged for a sheep. . ." he remarked gaily; and Mrs. Jaspar giggled.

Finally a dish of Malaga grapes and apples was handed. Mrs. Jaspar, now growing perceptibly languid, and nodding with more and more effort at Mr. Warley's pleasantries, transferred a bunch of grapes to her plate, but nibbled only two or three. "Tired," she said suddenly, in a whimper like a child's; and she rose, lifting herself up by the arms of her chair, and leaning over to catch the eye of an invisible lady, presumably Mrs. Amesworth, seated opposite to her. Mr. Warley was on his feet too, supporting himself by resting one hand on the table in a jaunty attitude. Mrs. Jaspar waved to him to be re-seated. "Join us—after cigars," she smilingly ordained; and with a great and concentrated effort he bowed to her as she passed toward the double doors which George was throwing open. Slowly, majestically, the purple velvet train disappeared down the long enfilade of illuminated rooms, and the last door closed behind her.

"Well, I do believe she's enjoyed it!" chuckled Miss Cress, taking Lavinia by the arm to help her back to the hall. Lavinia, for weeping, could not answer.

VI

Anson Warley found himself in the hall again, getting into his fur-lined overcoat. He remembered suddenly thinking that the rooms had been intensely over-heated, and that all the other guests had talked very loud and laughed inordinately. "Very good talk though, I must say," he had to acknowledge.

In the hall, as he got his arms into his coat (rather a job, too, after that Perrier-Jouet) he remembered saying to some-body (perhaps it was to the old butler): "Slipping off early—going on; 'nother engagement," and thinking to himself the while that when he got out into the fresh air again he would certainly remember where the other engagement was. He smiled a little while the servant, who seemed a clumsy fellow, fumbled with the fastening of the door. "And Filmore, who thought I wasn't even well enough to dine out! Damned ass! What would he say if he knew I was going on?"

The door opened, and with an immense sense of exhilara-tion Mr. Warley issued forth from the house and drew in a first deep breath of night air. He heard the door closed and bolted behind him, and continued to stand motionless on the step, expanding his chest, and drinking in the icy draught.

" 'Spose it's about the last house where they give you 'ninety-five Perrier-Jouet," he thought; and then: "Never heard better talk either. . ."

He smiled again with satisfaction at the memory of the wine and the wit. Then he took a step forward, to where a moment before the pavement had been—and where now there was nothing.

Mr. Jones

LADY JANE LYNKE was unlike other people: when she heard that she had inherited Bells, the beautiful old place which had belonged to the Lynkes of Thudeney for something like six hundred years, the fancy took her to go and see it unannounced. She was staying at a friend's near by, in Kent, and the next morning she borrowed a motor and slipped away alone to Thudeney-Blazes, the adjacent village.

It was a lustrous motionless day. Autumn bloom lay on the Sussex downs, on the heavy trees of the weald, on streams moving indolently, far off across the marshes. Farther still, Dungeness, a fitful streak, floated on an immaterial sea which was perhaps, after all, only sky.

In the softness Thudeney-Blazes slept: a few aged houses bowed about a duck-pond, a silvery spire, orchards thick with dew. Did Thudeney-Blazes ever wake?

Lady Jane left the motor to the care of the geese on a miniature common, pushed open a white gate into a field (the griffoned portals being padlocked), and struck across the park toward a group of carved chimney-stacks. No one seemed aware of her.

In a dip of the land, the long low house, its ripe brick masonry overhanging a moat deeply sunk about its roots, resembled an aged cedar spreading immemorial red branches. Lady Jane held her breath and gazed.

A silence distilled from years of solitude lay on lawns and gardens. No one had lived at Bells since the last Lord Thudeney, then a penniless younger son, had forsaken it sixty years before to seek his fortune in Canada. And before that, he and his widowed mother, distant poor relations, were housed in one of the lodges, and the great place, even in their day, had been as mute and solitary as the family vault.

Lady Jane, daughter of another branch, to which an earldom and considerable possessions had accrued, had never seen Bells, hardly heard its name. A succession of deaths, and the whim of an old man she had never known, now made her heir to all this beauty; and as she stood and looked she was

glad she had come to it from so far, from impressions so remote and different. "It would be dreadful to be used to it—
to be thinking already about the state of the roof, or the cost
of a heating system."

Till this her thirty-fifth year, Lady Jane had led an active,
independent and decided life. One of several daughters, mod-
erately but sufficiently provided for, she had gone early from
home, lived in London lodgings, travelled in tropic lands,
spent studious summers in Spain and Italy, and written two or
three brisk business-like little books about cities usually dealt
with sentimentally. And now, just back from a summer in the
south of France, she stood ankle-deep in wet bracken, and
gazed at Bells lying there under a September sun that looked
like moonlight.

"I shall never leave it!" she ejaculated, her heart swelling as
if she had taken the vow to a lover.

She ran down the last slope of the park and entered the
faded formality of gardens with clipped yews as ornate as architecture, and holly hedges as solid as walls. Adjoining the
house rose a low deep-buttressed chapel. Its door was ajar,
and she thought this of good augury: her forebears were waiting for her. In the porch she remarked fly-blown notices of
services, an umbrella stand, a dishevelled door-mat: no doubt
the chapel served as the village church. The thought gave her
a sense of warmth and neighbourliness. Across the damp flags
of the chancel, monuments and brasses showed through a
traceried screen. She examined them curiously. Some hailed
her with vocal memories, others whispered out of the remote
and the unknown: it was a shame to know so little about her
own family. But neither Crofts nor Lynkes had ever greatly
distinguished themselves; they had gathered substance simply
by holding on to what they had, and slowly accumulating
privileges and acres. "Mostly by clever marriages," Lady Jane
thought with a faint contempt.

At that moment her eyes lit on one of the less ornate monuments: a plain sarcophagus of gray marble niched in the wall
and surmounted by the bust of a young man with a fine ar-
rogant head, a Byronic throat and tossed-back curls.

"Peregrine Vincent Theobald Lynke, Baron Clouds, fifteenth Viscount Thudeney of Bells, Lord of the Manors of

Thudeney, Thudeney-Blazes, Upper Lynke, Lynke-Linnet—"
so it ran, with the usual tedious enumeration of honours, titles, court and county offices, ending with: "Born on May 1st,
1790, perished of the plague at Aleppo in 1828." And underneath, in small cramped characters, as if crowded as an after-
thought into an insufficient space: "Also His Wife."

That was all. No name, dates, honours, epithets, for the
Viscountess Thudeney. Did she too die of the plague at
Aleppo? Or did the "also" imply her actual presence in the
sarcophagus which her husband's pride had no doubt prepared for his own last sleep, little guessing that some Syrian
drain was to receive him? Lady Jane racked her memory in
vain. All she knew was that the death without issue of this
Lord Thudeney had caused the property to revert to the
Croft-Lynkes, and so, in the end, brought her to the chancel
step where, shyly, she knelt a moment, vowing to the dead to
carry on their trust.

She passed on to the entrance court, and stood at last at
the door of her new home, a blunt tweed figure in heavy
mud-stained shoes. She felt as intrusive as a tripper, and her
hand hesitated on the door-bell. "I ought to have brought
some one with me," she thought; an odd admission on the
part of a young woman who, when she was doing her
books of travel, had prided herself on forcing single-handed
the most closely guarded doors. But those other places, as
she looked back, seemed easy and accessible compared to
Bells.

She rang, and a tinkle answered, carried on by a flurried
echo which seemed to ask what in the world was happening.
Lady Jane, through the nearest window, caught the spectral
vista of a long room with shrouded furniture. She could not
see its farther end, but she had the feeling that someone stationed there might very well be seeing her.

"Just at first," she thought, "I shall have to invite people
here—to take the chill off."

She rang again, and the tinkle again prolonged itself; but
no one came.

At last she reflected that the care-takers probably lived at
the back of the house, and pushing open a door in the courtyard wall she worked her way around to what seemed a stable-

yard. Against the purple brick sprawled a neglected magnolia, bearing one late flower as big as a planet. Lady Jane rang at a door marked "Service." This bell, though also languid, had a wakefuller sound, as if it were more used to being rung, and still knew what was likely to follow; and after a delay during which Lady Jane again had the sense of being peered at— from above, through a lowered blind—a bolt shot, and a woman looked out. She was youngish, unhealthy, respectable and frightened; and she blinked at Lady Jane like someone waking out of sleep.

"Oh," said Lady Jane—"do you think I might visit the house?"

"The house?"

"I'm staying near here—I'm interested in old houses. Mightn't I take a look?"

The young woman drew back. "The house isn't shown."

"Oh, but not to—not to—" Jane weighed the case. "You see," she explained, "I know some of the family: the Northumberland branch."

"You're related, madam?"

"Well—distantly, yes." It was exactly what she had not meant to say; but there seemed no other way.

The woman twisted her apron-strings in perplexity. "Come, you know," Lady Jane urged, producing half-a-crown. The woman turned pale.

"I couldn't, madam; not without asking." It was clear that she was sorely tempted.

"Well, ask, won't you?" Lady Jane pressed the tip into a hesitating hand. The young woman shut the door and vanished. She was away so long that the visitor concluded her half-crown had been pocketed, and there was an end; and she began to be angry with herself, which was more often her habit than to be so with others.

"Well, for a fool, Jane, you're a complete one," she grumbled.

A returning footstep, listless, reluctant—the tread of one who was not going to let her in. It began to be rather comic.

The door opened, and the young woman said in her dull sing-song: "Mr. Jones says that no one is allowed to visit the house."

She and Lady Jane looked at each other for a moment, and Lady Jane read the apprehension in the other's eyes.

"Mr. Jones? Oh?— Yes; of course, keep it. . ." She waved away the woman's hand.

"Thank you, madam." The door closed again, and Lady Jane stood and gazed up at the inexorable face of her old home.

II

"But you didn't get in? You actually came back without so much as a peep?"

Her story was received, that evening at dinner, with mingled mirth and incredulity.

"But, my dear! You mean to say you asked to see the house, and they wouldn't let you? *Who* wouldn't?" Lady Jane's hostess insisted.

"Mr. Jones."

"Mr. Jones?"

"He said no one was allowed to visit it."

"Who on earth is Mr. Jones?"

"The care-taker, I suppose. I didn't see him."

"Didn't see him either? But I never heard such nonsense! Why in the world didn't you insist?"

"Yes; why didn't you?" they all chorused; and she could only answer, a little lamely: "I think I was afraid."

"Afraid? *You*, darling?" There was fresh hilarity. "Of Mr. Jones?"

"I suppose so." She joined in the laugh, yet she knew it was true: she had been afraid.

Edward Stramer, the novelist, an old friend of her family, had been listening with an air of abstraction, his eyes on his empty coffee-cup. Suddenly, as the mistress of the house pushed back her chair, he looked across the table at Lady Jane. "It's odd: I've just remembered something. Once, when I was a youngster, I tried to see Bells; over thirty years ago it must have been." He glanced at his host. "Your mother drove me over. And we were not let in."

There was a certain flatness in this conclusion, and someone remarked that Bells had always been known as harder to get into than any other house thereabouts.

"Yes," said Stramer; "but the point is that we were refused in exactly the same words. Mr. Jones said no one was allowed to visit the house."

"Ah—he was in possession already? Thirty years ago? Unsociable fellow, Jones. Well, Jane, you've got a good watch-dog."

They moved to the drawing-room, and the talk drifted to other topics. But Stramer came and sat down beside Lady Jane. "It is queer, though, that at such a distance of time we should have been given exactly the same answer."

She glanced up at him curiously. "Yes; and you didn't try to force your way in either?"

"Oh, no: it was not possible."

"So I felt," she agreed.

"Well, next week, my dear, I hope we shall see it all, in spite of Mr. Jones," their hostess intervened, catching their last words as she moved toward the piano.

"I wonder if we shall see Mr. Jones," said Stramer.

III

Bells was not nearly as large as it looked; like many old houses it was very narrow, and but one storey high, with servants' rooms in the low attics, and much space wasted in crooked passages and superfluous stairs. If she closed the great saloon, Jane thought, she might live there comfortably with the small staff which was the most she could afford. It was a relief to find the place less important than she had feared.

For already, in that first hour of arrival, she had decided to give up everything else for Bells. Her previous plans and ambitions—except such as might fit in with living there—had fallen from her like a discarded garment, and things she had hardly thought about, or had shrugged away with the hasty subversiveness of youth, were already laying quiet hands on her; all the lives from which her life had issued, with what they bore of example or admonishment. The very shabbiness of the house moved her more than splendours, made it, after its long abandonment, seem full of the careless daily coming and going of people long dead, people to whom it had not been a museum, or a page of history, but cradle, nursery, home, and sometimes, no doubt, a prison. If those marble lips in the chapel could speak! If she could hear some of their comments on the old house which had spread its silent shelter over their sins and sorrows, their follies and submissions! A long tale, to which she was about to add another chapter, subdued and humdrum beside some of those earlier annals, yet probably freer and more varied than the unchronicled lives of the great-aunts and great-grandmothers buried there so completely that they must hardly have known when they passed from their beds to their graves. "Piled up like dead leaves," Jane thought, "layers and layers of them, to preserve something forever budding underneath."

Well, all these piled-up lives had at least preserved the old house in its integrity; and that was worth while. She was satisfied to carry on such a trust.

She sat in the garden looking up at those rosy walls, iridescent with damp and age. She decided which windows should be hers, which rooms given to the friends from Kent who were motoring over, Stramer among them, for a modest house-warming; then she got up and went in.

The hour had come for domestic questions; for she had arrived alone, unsupported even by the old family housemaid her mother had offered her. She preferred to start afresh, convinced that her small household could be staffed from the neighbourhood. Mrs. Clemm, the rosy-cheeked old person who had curtsied her across the threshold, would doubtless know.

Mrs. Clemm, summoned to the library, curtsied again. She wore black silk, gathered and spreading as to skirt, flat and perpendicular as to bodice. On her glossy false front was a black lace cap with ribbons which had faded from violet to ash-colour, and a heavy watch-chain descended from the lava brooch under her crochet collar. Her small round face rested on the collar like a red apple on a white plate: neat, smooth, circular, with a pursed-up mouth, eyes like black seeds, and round ruddy cheeks with the skin so taut that one had to look close to see that it was as wrinkled as a piece of old crackly.

Mrs. Clemm was sure there would be no trouble about servants. She herself could do a little cooking: though her hand might be a bit out. But there was her niece to help; and she was quite of her ladyship's opinion, that there was no need to get in strangers. They were mostly a poor lot; and besides, they might not take to Bells. There were persons who didn't. Mrs. Clemm smiled a sharp little smile, like the scratch of a pin, as she added that she hoped her ladyship wouldn't be one of them.

As for under-servants . . . well, a boy, perhaps? She had a great-nephew she might send for. But about women—under-housemaids—if her ladyship thought they couldn't manage as they were; well, she really didn't know. Thudeney-Blazes? Oh, she didn't think so. . . There was more dead than living at Thudeney-Blazes . . . everyone was leaving there . . . or in the church-yard . . . one house after another being shut . . . death was everywhere, wasn't it, my lady? Mrs. Clemm said it with another of her short sharp smiles, which provoked the appearance of a frosty dimple.

"But my niece Georgiana is a hard worker, my lady; her that let you in the other day. . ."

"That didn't," Lady Jane corrected.

"Oh, my lady, it was too unfortunate. If only your ladyship had have said . . . poor Georgiana had ought to have seen; but she never *did* have her wits about her, not for answering the door."

"But she was only obeying orders. She went to ask Mr. Jones."

Mrs. Clemm was silent. Her small hands, wrinkled and resolute, fumbled with the folds of her apron, and her quick eyes made the circuit of the room and then came back to Lady Jane's.

"Just so, my lady; but, as I told her, she'd ought to have known—"

"And who is Mr. Jones?"

Mrs. Clemm's smile snapped out again, deprecating, respectful. "Well, my lady, he's more dead than living, too . . . if I may say so," was her surprising answer.

"Is he? I'm sorry to hear that; but who is he?"

"Well, my lady, he's . . . he's my great-uncle, as it were . . . my grandmother's own brother, as you might say."

"Ah; I see." Lady Jane considered her with growing curiosity. "He must have reached a great age, then."

"Yes, my lady; he has that. Though I'm not," Mrs. Clemm added, the dimple showing, "as old myself as your ladyship might suppose. Living at Bells all these years has been ageing to me; it would be to anybody."

"I suppose so. And yet," Lady Jane continued, "Mr. Jones has survived; has stood it well—as you certainly have?"

"Oh, not as well as I have," Mrs. Clemm interjected, as if resentful of the comparison.

"At any rate, he still mounts guard; mounts it as well as he did thirty years ago."

"Thirty years ago?" Mrs. Clemm echoed, her hands dropping from her apron to her sides.

"Wasn't he here thirty years ago?"

"Oh, yes, my lady; certainly; he's never once been away that I know of."

"What a wonderful record! And what exactly are his duties?"

Mrs. Clemm paused again, her hands still motionless in the folds of her skirt. Lady Jane noticed that the fingers were tightly clenched, as if to check an involuntary gesture.

"He began as pantry-boy; then footman; then butler, my lady; but it's hard to say, isn't it, what an old servant's duties are, when he's stayed on in the same house so many years?"

"Yes; and that house always empty."

"Just so, my lady. Everything came to depend on him; one thing after another. His late lordship thought the world of him."

"His late lordship? But he was never here! He spent all his life in Canada."

Mrs. Clemm seemed slightly disconcerted. "Certainly, my lady." (Her voice said: "Who are you, to set me right as to the chronicles of Bells?") "But by letter, my lady; I can show you the letters. And there was his lordship before, the sixteenth Viscount. He *did* come here once."

"Ah, did he?" Lady Jane was embarrassed to find how little she knew of them all. She rose from her seat. "They were lucky, all these absentees, to have some one to watch over their interests so faithfully. I should like to see Mr. Jones—to thank him. Will you take me to him now?"

"Now?" Mrs. Clemm moved back a step or two; Lady Jane fancied her cheeks paled a little under their ruddy varnish. "Oh, not today, my lady."

"Why? Isn't he well enough?"

"Not nearly. He's between life and death, as it were," Mrs. Clemm repeated, as if the phrase were the nearest approach she could find to a definition of Mr. Jones's state.

"He wouldn't even know who I was?"

Mrs. Clemm considered a moment. "I don't say *that*, my lady;" her tone implied that to do so might appear disrespectful. "He'd know you, my lady; but you wouldn't know *him*." She broke off and added hastily: "I mean, for what he is: he's in no state for you to see him."

"He's so very ill? Poor man! And is everything possible being done?"

"Oh, everything; and more too, my lady. But perhaps," Mrs. Clemm suggested, with a clink of keys, "this would be a good time for your ladyship to take a look about the house. If your ladyship has no objection, I should like to begin with the linen."

IV

"And Mr. Jones?" Stramer queried, a few days later, as they sat, Lady Jane and the party from Kent, about an improvised tea-table in a recess of one of the great holly-hedges.

The day was as hushed and warm as that on which she had first come to Bells, and Lady Jane looked up with a smile of ownership at the old walls which seemed to smile back, the windows which now looked at her with friendly eyes.

"Mr. Jones? Who's Mr. Jones?" the others asked; only Stramer recalled their former talk.

Lady Jane hesitated. "Mr. Jones is my invisible guardian; or rather, the guardian of Bells."

They remembered then. "Invisible? You don't mean to say you haven't seen him yet?"

"Not yet; perhaps I never shall. He's very old—and very ill, I'm afraid."

"And he still rules here?"

"Oh, absolutely. The fact is," Lady Jane added, "I believe he's the only person left who really knows all about Bells."

"Jane, my *dear!* That big shrub over there against the wall! I verily believe it's *Templetonia retusa.* It *is!* Did any one ever hear of its standing an English winter?" Gardeners all, they dashed off towards the shrub in its sheltered angle. "I shall certainly try it on a south wall at Dipway," cried the hostess from Kent.

Tea over, they moved on to inspect the house. The short autumn day was drawing to a close; but the party had been able to come only for an afternoon, instead of staying over the week-end, and having lingered so long in the gardens they had only time, indoors, to puzzle out what they could through the shadows. Perhaps, Lady Jane thought, it was the best hour to see a house like Bells, so long abandoned, and not yet warmed into new life.

The fire she had had lit in the saloon sent its radiance to meet them, giving the great room an air of expectancy and welcome. The portraits, the Italian cabinets, the shabby arm-chairs and rugs, all looked as if life had but lately left them; and Lady Jane said to herself: "Perhaps Mrs. Clemm is right in advising me to live here and close the blue parlour."

"My dear, what a fine room! Pity it faces north. Of course you'll have to shut it in winter. It would cost a fortune to heat."

Lady Jane hesitated. "I don't know: I *had* meant to. But there seems to be no other. . ."

"No other? In all this house?" They laughed; and one of the visitors, going ahead and crossing a panelled anteroom, cried out: "But here! A delicious room; windows south—yes, and west. The warmest of the house. This is perfect."

They followed, and the blue room echoed with exclamations. "Those charming curtains with the parrots . . . and the blue of that *petit point* fire-screen! But, Jane, of course you must live here. Look at this citron-wood desk!"

Lady Jane stood on the threshold. "It seems that the chimney smokes hopelessly."

"Hopelessly? Nonsense! Have you consulted anybody? I'll send you a wonderful man. . ."

"Besides, if you put in one of those one-pipe heaters. . . At Dipway. . ."

Stramer was looking over Lady Jane's shoulder. "What does Mr. Jones say about it?"

"He says no one has ever been able to use this room; not for ages. It was the housekeeper who told me. She's his great-niece, and seems simply to transmit his oracles."

Stramer shrugged. "Well, he's lived at Bells longer than you have. Perhaps he's right."

"How absurd!" one of the ladies cried. "The housekeeper and Mr. Jones probably spend their evenings here, and don't want to be disturbed. Look—ashes on the hearth! What did I tell you?"

Lady Jane echoed the laugh as they turned away. They had still to see the library, damp and dilapidated, the panelled dining-room, the breakfast-parlour, and such bedrooms as had any old furniture left; not many, for the late lords of Bells, at one time or another, had evidently sold most of its removable treasures.

When the visitors came down their motors were waiting. A lamp had been placed in the hall, but the rooms beyond were lit only by the broad clear band of western sky showing through uncurtained casements. On the doorstep one of the ladies exclaimed that she had lost her hand-bag—no, she remembered; she had laid it on the desk in the blue room. Which way was the blue room?

"I'll get it," Jane said, turning back. She heard Stramer following. He asked if he should bring the lamp.

"Oh, no; I can see."

She crossed the threshold of the blue room, guided by the light from its western window; then she stopped. Some one was in the room already; she felt rather than saw another presence. Stramer, behind her, paused also; he did not speak or move. What she saw, or thought she saw, was simply an old man with bent shoulders turning away from the citron-wood desk. Almost before she had received the impression there was no one there; only the slightest stir of the needlework curtain over the farther door. She heard no step or other sound.

"There's the bag," she said, as if the act of speaking, and saying something obvious, were a relief.

In the hall her glance crossed Stramer's, but failed to find there the reflection of what her own had registered.

He shook hands, smiling. "Well, goodbye. I commit you to Mr. Jones's care; only don't let him say that *you're* not shown to visitors."

She smiled: "Come back and try," and then shivered a little as the lights of the last motor vanished beyond the great black hedges.

V

Lady Jane had exulted in her resolve to keep Bells to herself till she and the old house should have had time to make friends. But after a few days she recalled the uneasy feeling which had come over her as she stood on the threshold after her first tentative ring. Yes; she had been right in thinking she would have to have people about her to take the chill off. The house was too old, too mysterious, too much withdrawn into its own secret past, for her poor little present to fit into it without uneasiness.

But it was not a time of year when, among Lady Jane's friends, it was easy to find people free. Her own family were all in the north, and impossible to dislodge. One of her sisters, when invited, simply sent her back a list of shooting-dates; and her mother wrote: "Why not come to us? What can you have to do all alone in that empty house at this time of year? Next summer we're all coming."

Having tried one or two friends with the same result, Lady Jane bethought her of Stramer. He was finishing a novel, she knew, and at such times he liked to settle down somewhere in the country where he could be sure of not being disturbed. Bells was a perfect asylum, and though it was probable that some other friend had anticipated her, and provided the requisite seclusion, Lady Jane decided to invite him. "Do bring your work and stay till it's finished—and don't be in a hurry to finish. I promise that no one shall bother you—" and she added, half-nervously: "Not even Mr. Jones." As she wrote she felt an absurd impulse to blot the words out. "He might not like it," she thought; and the "he" did not refer to Stramer.

Was the solitude already making her superstitious? She thrust the letter into an envelope, and carried it herself to the post-office at Thudeney-Blazes. Two days later a wire from Stramer announced his arrival.

He came on a cold stormy afternoon, just before dinner, and as they went up to dress Lady Jane called after him: "We shall sit in the blue parlour this evening." The housemaid Georgiana was crossing the passage with hot water for the visitor. She stopped and cast a vacant glance at Lady Jane. The latter met it, and said carelessly: "You hear, Georgiana? The fire in the blue parlour."

While Lady Jane was dressing she heard a knock, and saw Mrs. Clemm's round face just inside the door, like a red apple on a garden wall.

"Is there anything wrong about the saloon, my lady? Georgiana understood—"

"That I want the fire in the blue parlour. Yes. What's wrong with the saloon is that one freezes there."

"But the chimney smokes in the blue parlour."

"Well, we'll give it a trial, and if it does I'll send for some one to arrange it."

"Nothing can be done, my lady. Everything has been tried, and—"

Lady Jane swung about suddenly. She had heard Stramer singing a cheerful hunting-song in a cracked voice, in his dressing-room at the other end of the corridor.

"That will do, Mrs. Clemm. I want the fire in the blue parlour."

"Yes, my lady." The door closed on the housekeeper.

"So you decided on the saloon after all?" Stramer said, as Lady Jane led the way there after their brief repast.

"Yes: I hope you won't be frozen. Mr. Jones swears that the chimney in the blue parlour isn't safe; so, until I can fetch the mason over from Strawbridge—"

"Oh, I see." Stramer drew up to the blaze in the great fireplace. "We're very well off here; though heating this room is going to be ruinous. Meanwhile, I note that Mr. Jones still rules."

Lady Jane gave a slight laugh.

"Tell me," Stramer continued, as she bent over the mixing of the Turkish coffee, "what is there about him? I'm getting curious."

Lady Jane laughed again, and heard the embarrassment in her laugh. "So am I."

"Why—you don't mean to say you haven't seen him yet?"

"No. He's still too ill."

"What's the matter with him? What does the doctor say?"

"He won't see the doctor."

"But look here—if things take a worse turn—I don't know; but mightn't you be held to have been negligent?"

"What can I do? Mrs. Clemm says he has a doctor who treats him by correspondence. I don't see that I can interfere."

"Isn't there some one beside Mrs. Clemm whom you can consult?"

She considered: certainly, as yet, she had not made much effort to get into relation with her neighbours. "I expected the vicar to call. But I've enquired: there's no vicar any longer at Thudeney-Blazes. A curate comes from Strawbridge every other Sunday. And the one who comes now is new: nobody about the place seems to know him."

"But I thought the chapel here was in use? It looked so when you showed it to us the other day."

"I thought so too. It used to be the parish church of Lynke-Linnet and Lower-Lynke; but it seems that was years ago. The parishioners objected to coming so far; and there weren't enough of them. Mrs. Clemm says that nearly everybody has died off or left. It's the same at Thudeney-Blazes."

Stramer glanced about the great room, with its circle of warmth and light by the hearth, and the sullen shadows huddled at its farther end, as if hungrily listening. "With this emptiness at the centre, life was bound to cease gradually on the outskirts."

Lady Jane followed his glance. "Yes; it's all wrong. I must try to wake the place up."

"Why not open it to the public? Have a visitors' day?"

She thought a moment. In itself the suggestion was distasteful; she could imagine few things that would bore her more. Yet to do so might be a duty, a first step toward reëstablishing relations between the lifeless house and its neighbourhood. Secretly, she felt that even the coming and going of indifferent unknown people would help to take the chill from those rooms, to brush from their walls the dust of too-heavy memories.

"Who's that?" asked Stramer. Lady Jane started in spite of herself, and glanced over her shoulder; but he was only looking past her at a portrait which a dart of flame from the hearth had momentarily called from its obscurity.

"That's a Lady Thudeney." She got up and went toward the picture with a lamp. "Might be an Opie, don't you think? It's a strange face, under the smirk of the period."

Stramer took the lamp and held it up. The portrait was that of a young woman in a short-waisted muslin gown caught beneath the breast by a cameo. Between clusters of beribboned curls a long fair oval looked out dumbly, inexpressively, in a stare of frozen beauty. "It's as if the house had been too empty even then," Lady Jane murmured. "I wonder which she was? Oh, I know: it must be *'Also His Wife'*."

Stramer stared.

"It's the only name on her monument. The wife of Peregrine Vincent Theobald, who perished of the plague at Aleppo in 1828. Perhaps she was very fond of him, and this was painted when she was an inconsolable widow."

"They didn't dress like that as late as 1828." Stramer holding the lamp closer, deciphered the inscription on the border of the lady's India scarf; *Juliana, Viscountess Thudeney, 1818.* "She must have been inconsolable before his death, then."

Lady Jane smiled. "Let's hope she grew less so after it."

Stramer passed the lamp across the canvas. "Do you see where she was painted? In the blue parlour. Look: the old panelling; and she's leaning on the citron-wood desk. They evidently used the room in winter then." The lamp paused on the background of the picture: a window framing snow-laden paths and hedges in icy perspective.

"Curious," Stramer said—"and rather melancholy: to be painted against that wintry desolation. I wish you could find out more about her. Have you dipped into your archives?"

"No. Mr. Jones—"

"He won't allow that either?"

"Yes; but he's lost the key of the muniment-room. Mrs. Clemm has been trying to get a locksmith."

"Surely the neighbourhood can still produce one?"

"There *was* one at Thudeney-Blazes; but he died the week before I came."

"Of course!"

"Of course?"

"Well, in Mrs. Clemm's hands keys get lost, chimneys smoke, locksmiths die. . ." Stramer stood, light in hand, looking down the shadowy length of the saloon. "I say, let's go and see what's happening now in the blue parlour."

Lady Jane laughed: a laugh seemed easy with another voice near by to echo it. "Let's—"

She followed him out of the saloon, across the hall in which a single candle burned on a far-off table, and past the stairway yawning like a black funnel above them. In the doorway of the blue parlour Stramer paused. "Now, then, Mr. Jones!"

It was stupid, but Lady Jane's heart gave a jerk: she hoped the challenge would not evoke the shadowy figure she had half seen that other day.

"Lord, it's cold!" Stramer stood looking about him. "Those ashes are still on the hearth. Well, it's all very queer." He crossed over to the citron-wood desk. "There's where she sat for her picture—and in this very arm-chair—look!"

"Oh, don't!" Lady Jane exclaimed. The words slipped out unawares.

"Don't—what?"

"Try those drawers—" she wanted to reply; for his hand was stretched toward the desk.

"I'm frozen; I think I'm starting a cold. Do come away," she grumbled, backing toward the door.

Stramer lighted her out without comment. As the lamp-light slid along the walls Lady Jane fancied that the needle-work curtain over the farther door stirred as it had that other day. But it may have been the wind rising outside. . .

The saloon seemed like home when they got back to it.

"There *is* no Mr. Jones!"

Stramer proclaimed it triumphantly when they met the next morning. Lady Jane had motored off early to Strawbridge in quest of a mason and a locksmith. The quest had taken longer than she had expected, for everybody in Strawbridge was busy on jobs nearer by, and unaccustomed to the idea of going to Bells, with which the town seemed to have had no communication within living memory. The younger workmen did not even know where the place was, and the best Lady Jane could do was to coax a locksmith's apprentice to come with her, on the understanding that he would be driven back to the nearest station as soon as his job was over. As for the mason, he had merely taken note of her request, and promised half-heartedly to send somebody when he could. "Rather off our beat, though."

She returned, discouraged and somewhat weary, as Stramer was coming downstairs after his morning's work.

"No Mr. Jones?" she echoed.

"Not a trace! I've been trying the old Glamis experiment —situating his room by its window. Luckily the house is smaller. . ."

Lady Jane smiled. "Is this what you call locking yourself up with your work?"

"I can't work: that's the trouble. Not till this is settled. Bells is a fidgety place."

"Yes," she agreed.

"Well, I wasn't going to be beaten; so I went to try to find the head-gardener."

"But there isn't—"

"No. Mrs. Clemm told me. The head-gardener died last year. That woman positively glows with life whenever she announces a death. Have you noticed?"

Yes: Lady Jane had.

"Well—I said to myself that if there wasn't a head-gardener there must be an underling; at least one. I'd seen somebody in the distance, raking leaves, and I ran him down. Of course he'd never seen Mr. Jones."

"You mean that poor old half-blind Jacob? He couldn't see anybody."

"Perhaps not. At any rate, he told me that Mr. Jones wouldn't let the leaves be buried for leaf-mould—I forget why. Mr. Jones's authority extends even to the gardens."

"Yet you say he doesn't exist!"

"Wait. Jacob is half-blind, but he's been here for years, and knows more about the place than you'd think. I got him talking about the house, and I pointed to one window after another, and he told me each time whose the room was, or had been. But he couldn't situate Mr. Jones."

"I beg your ladyship's pardon—" Mrs. Clemm was on the threshold, cheeks shining, skirt rustling, her eyes like drills. "The locksmith your ladyship brought back; I understand it was for the lock of the muniment-room—"

"Well?"

"He's lost one of his tools, and can't do anything without it. So he's gone. The butcher's boy gave him a lift back."

Lady Jane caught Stramer's faint chuckle. She stood and stared at Mrs. Clemm, and Mrs. Clemm stared back, deferential but unflinching.

"Gone? Very well; I'll motor after him."

"Oh, my lady, it's too late. The butcher's boy had his motor-cycle. . . Besides, what could he do?"

"Break the lock," exclaimed Lady Jane, exasperated.

"Oh, my lady—" Mrs. Clemm's intonation marked the most respectful incredulity. She waited another moment, and then withdrew, while Lady Jane and Stramer considered each other.

"But this is absurd," Lady Jane declared when they had lunched, waited on, as usual, by the flustered Georgiana. "I'll break in that door myself, if I have to.—Be careful please, Georgiana," she added; "I was speaking of doors, not dishes." For Georgiana had let fall with a crash the dish she was removing from the table. She gathered up the pieces in her tremulous fingers, and vanished. Jane and Stramer returned to the saloon.

"Queer!" the novelist commented.

"Yes." Lady Jane, facing the door, started slightly. Mrs. Clemm was there again; but this time subdued, unrustling, bathed in that odd pallour which enclosed but seemed unable to penetrate the solid crimson of her cheeks.

"I beg pardon, my lady. The key is found." Her hand, as she held it out, trembled like Georgiana's.

VII

"It's not here," Stramer announced, a couple of hours later.

"What isn't?" Lady Jane queried, looking up from a heap of disordered papers. Her eyes blinked at him through the fog of yellow dust raised by her manipulations.

"The clue.— I've got all the 1800 to 1840 papers here; and there's a gap."

She moved over to the table above which he was bending. "A gap?"

"A big one. Nothing between 1815 and 1835. No mention of Peregrine or of Juliana."

They looked at each other across the tossed papers, and suddenly Stramer exclaimed: "Some one has been here before us—just lately."

Lady Jane stared, incredulous, and then followed the direction of his downward pointing hand.

"Do you wear flat heelless shoes?" he questioned. "And of that size? Even my feet are too small to fit into those footprints. Luckily there wasn't time to sweep the floor!"

Lady Jane felt a slight chill, a chill of a different and more inward quality than the shock of stuffy coldness which had met them as they entered the unaired attic set apart for the storing of the Thudeney archives.

"But how absurd! Of course when Mrs. Clemm found we were coming up she came—or sent some one—to open the shutters."

"That's not Mrs. Clemm's foot, or the other woman's. She must have sent a man—an old man with a shaky uncertain step. Look how it wanders."

"Mr. Jones, then!" said Lady Jane, half impatiently.

"Mr. Jones. And he got what he wanted, and put it— where?"

"Ah, *that*—! I'm freezing, you know; let's give this up for the present." She rose, and Stramer followed her without protest; the muniment-room was really untenable.

"I must catalogue all this stuff some day, I suppose," Lady Jane continued, as they went down the stairs. "But meanwhile, what do you say to a good tramp, to get the dust out of our lungs?"

He agreed, and turned back to his room to get some letters he wanted to post at Thudeney-Blazes.

Lady Jane went down alone. It was a fine afternoon, and the sun, which had made the dust-clouds of the muniment-room so dazzling, sent a long shaft through the west window of the blue parlour, and across the floor of the hall.

Certainly Georgiana kept the oak floors remarkably well; considering how much else she had to do, it was surp—

Lady Jane stopped as if an unseen hand had jerked her violently back. On the smooth parquet before her she had caught the trace of dusty foot-prints—the prints of broad-soled heelless shoes—making for the blue parlour and crossing its threshold. She stood still with the same inward shiver that she had felt upstairs; then, avoiding the foot-prints, she too stole very softly toward the blue parlour, pushed the door wider, and saw, in the long dazzle of autumn light, as if translucid, edged with the glitter, an old man at the desk.

"Mr. Jones!"

A step came up behind her: Mrs. Clemm with the post-bag. "You called, my lady?"

"I . . . yes. . ."

When she turned back to the desk there was no one there. She faced about on the housekeeper. "Who was that?"

"Where, my lady?"

Lady Jane, without answering, moved toward the needle-work curtain, in which she had detected the same faint tremor as before. "Where does that door go to—behind the curtain?"

"Nowhere, my lady. I mean; there is no door."

Mrs. Clemm had followed; her step sounded quick and assured. She lifted up the curtain with a firm hand. Behind it was a rectangle of roughly plastered wall, where an opening had visibly been bricked up.

"When was that done?"

"The wall built up? I couldn't say. I've never known it otherwise," replied the housekeeper.

The two women stood for an instant measuring each other with level eyes; then the housekeeper's were slowly lowered, and she let the curtain fall from her hand. "There are a great many things in old houses that nobody knows about," she said.

"There shall be as few as possible in mine," said Lady Jane.

"My lady!" The housekeeper stepped quickly in front of her. "My lady, what are you doing?" she gasped.

Lady Jane had turned back to the desk at which she had just seen—or fancied she had seen—the bending figure of Mr. Jones.

"I am going to look through these drawers," she said.

The housekeeper still stood in pale immobility between her and the desk. "No, my lady—no. You won't do that."

"Because—?"

Mrs. Clemm crumpled up her black silk apron with a despairing gesture. "Because—if you *will* have it—that's where Mr. Jones keeps his private papers. I know he'd oughtn't to. . ."

"Ah—then it was Mr. Jones I saw here?"

The housekeeper's arms sank to her sides and her mouth hung open on an unspoken word. "You *saw* him?" The question came out in a confused whisper; and before Lady Jane could answer, Mrs. Clemm's arms rose again, stretched before her face as if to fend off a blaze of intolerable light, or some forbidden sight she had long since disciplined herself not to see. Thus screening her eyes she hurried across the hall to the door of the servants' wing.

Lady Jane stood for a moment looking after her; then, with a slightly shaking hand, she opened the desk and hurriedly took out from it all the papers—a small bundle—that it contained. With them she passed back into the saloon.

As she entered it her eye was caught by the portrait of the melancholy lady in the short-waisted gown whom she and Stramer had christened "Also His Wife." The lady's eyes, usually so empty of all awareness save of her own frozen beauty, seemed suddenly waking to an anguished participation in the scene.

"Fudge!" muttered Lady Jane, shaking off the spectral suggestion as she turned to meet Stramer on the threshold.

VIII

The missing papers were all there. Stramer and she spread them out hurriedly on a table and at once proceeded to gloat

over their find. Not a particularly important one, indeed; in
the long history of the Lynkes and Crofts it took up hardly
more space than the little handful of documents did, in actual
bulk, among the stacks of the muniment-room. But the fact
that these papers filled a gap in the chronicles of the house,
and situated the sad-faced beauty as veritably the wife of the
Peregrine Vincent Theobald Lynke who had "perished of the
plague at Aleppo in 1828"—this was a discovery sufficiently
exciting to whet amateur appetites, and to put out of Lady
Jane's mind the strange incident which had attended the
opening of the cabinet.

For a while she and Stramer sat silently and methodically
going through their respective piles of correspondence; but
presently Lady Jane, after glancing over one of the yellowing
pages, uttered a startled exclamation.

"How strange! Mr. Jones again—always Mr. Jones!"

Stramer looked up from the papers he was sorting. "You
too? I've got a lot of letters here addressed to a Mr. Jones
by Peregrine Vincent, who seems to have been always dis-
porting himself abroad, and chronically in want of money.
Gambling debts, apparently . . . ah and women . . . a dirty
record altogether. . ."

"Yes? My letter is not written to a Mr. Jones; but it's
about one. Listen." Lady Jane began to read. " 'Bells,
February 20th, 1826. . .' (It's from poor 'Also His Wife' to
her husband.) 'My dear Lord, Acknowledging as I ever do
the burden of the sad impediment which denies me the happiness of being more frequently in your company, I yet fail
to conceive how anything in my state obliges that close
seclusion in which Mr. Jones persists—and by your express
orders, so he declares—in confining me. Surely, my lord, had
you found it possible to spend more time with me since the
day of our marriage, you would yourself have seen it to be
unnecessary to put this restraint upon me. It is true, alas,
that my unhappy infirmity denies me the happiness to speak
with you, or to hear the accents of the voice I should love
above all others could it but reach me; but, my dear husband, I would have you consider that my mind is in no way
affected by this obstacle, but goes out to you, as my heart
does, in a perpetual eagerness of attention, and that to sit in

this great house alone, day after day, month after month, deprived of your company, and debarred also from any intercourse but that of the servants you have chosen to put about me, is a fate more cruel than I deserve and more painful than I can bear. I have entreated Mr. Jones, since he seems all-powerful with you, to represent this to you, and to transmit this my last request—for should I fail I am resolved to make no other—that you should consent to my making the acquaintance of a few of your friends and neighbours, among whom I cannot but think there must be some kind hearts that would take pity on my unhappy situation, and afford me such companionship as would give me more courage to bear your continual absence. . .' "

Lady Jane folded up the letter. "Deaf and dumb—ah, poor creature! That explains the look—"

"And this explains the marriage," Stramer continued, unfolding a stiff parchment document. "Here are the Viscountess Thudeney's marriage settlements. She appears to have been a Miss Portallo, daughter of Obadiah Portallo Esqre, of Purflew Castle, Caermarthenshire, and Bombay House, Twickenham, East India merchant, senior member of the banking house of Portallo and Prest—and so on and so on. And the figures run up into hundreds of thousands."

"It's rather ghastly—putting the two things together. All the millions and—imprisonment in the blue parlour. I suppose her Viscount had to have the money, and was ashamed to have it known how he had got it. . ." Lady Jane shivered. "Think of it—day after day, winter after winter, year after year . . . speechless, soundless, alone . . . under Mr. Jones's guardianship. Let me see: what year were they married?"

"In 1817."

"And only a year later that portrait was painted. And she had the frozen look already."

Stramer mused: "Yes; it's grim enough. But the strangest figure in the whole case is still—Mr. Jones."

"Mr. Jones—yes. Her keeper," Lady Jane mused "I suppose he must have been this one's ancestor. The office seems to have been hereditary at Bells."

"Well—I don't know."

Stramer's voice was so odd that Lady Jane looked up at him with a stare of surprise. "What if it were the same one?" suggested Stramer with a queer smile.

"The same?" Lady Jane laughed. "You're not good at figures are you? If poor Lady Thudeney's Mr. Jones were alive now he'd be—"

"I didn't say ours was alive now," said Stramer.

"Oh—why, what . . . ?" she faltered.

But Stramer did not answer; his eyes had been arrested by the precipitate opening of the door behind his hostess, and the entry of Georgiana, a livid, dishevelled Georgiana, more than usually bereft of her faculties, and gasping out something inarticulate.

"Oh, my lady—it's my aunt—she won't answer me," Georgiana stammered in a voice of terror.

Lady Jane uttered an impatient exclamation. "Answer you? Why—what do you want her to answer?"

"Only whether she's alive, my lady," said Georgiana with streaming eyes.

Lady Jane continued to look at her severely. "Alive? Alive? Why on earth shouldn't she be?"

"She might as well be dead—by the way she just lies there."

"Your aunt dead? I saw her alive enough in the blue parlour half an hour ago," Lady Jane returned. She was growing rather *blasé* with regard to Georgiana's panics; but suddenly she felt this to be of a different nature from any of the others. "Where is it your aunt's lying?"

"In her own bedroom, on her bed," the other wailed, "and won't say why."

Lady Jane got to her feet, pushing aside the heaped-up papers, and hastening to the door with Stramer in her wake.

As they went up the stairs she realized that she had seen the housekeeper's bedroom only once, on the day of her first obligatory round of inspection, when she had taken possession of Bells. She did not even remember very clearly where it was, but followed Georgiana down the passage and through a door which communicated, rather surprisingly, with a narrow walled-in staircase that was unfamiliar to her. At its top she and Stramer found themselves on a small landing upon which

two doors opened. Through the confusion of her mind Lady
Jane noticed that these rooms, with their special staircase
leading down to what had always been called his lordship's
suite, must obviously have been occupied by his lordship's confidential servants. In one of them, presumably, had been
lodged the original Mr. Jones, the Mr. Jones of the yellow letters, the letters purloined by Lady Jane. As she crossed the
threshold, Lady Jane remembered the housekeeper's attempt
to prevent her touching the contents of the desk.

Mrs. Clemm's room, like herself, was neat, glossy and extremely cold. Only Mrs. Clemm herself was no longer like
Mrs. Clemm. The red-apple glaze had barely faded from her
cheeks, and not a lock was disarranged in the unnatural lustre
of her false front; even her cap ribbons hung symmetrically
along either cheek. But death had happened to her, and had
made her into someone else. At first glance it was impossible
to say if the unspeakable horror in her wide-open eyes were
only the reflection of that change, or of the agent by whom it
had come. Lady Jane, shuddering, paused a moment while
Stramer went up to the bed.

"Her hand is warm still—but no pulse." He glanced about
the room. "A glass anywhere?" The cowering Georgiana took
a hand-glass from the neat chest of drawers, and Stramer held
it over the housekeeper's drawn-back lip. . .

"She's dead," he pronounced.

"Oh, poor thing! But how—?" Lady Jane drew near, and
was kneeling down, taking the inanimate hand in hers,
when Stramer touched her on the arm, and then silently
raised a finger of warning. Georgiana was crouching in the
farther corner of the room, her face buried in her lifted
arms.

"Look here," Stramer whispered. He pointed to Mrs.
Clemm's throat, and Lady Jane, bending over, distinctly saw
a circle of red marks on it—the marks of recent bruises. She
looked again into the awful eyes.

"She's been strangled," Stramer whispered.

Lady Jane, with a shiver of fear, drew down the housekeeper's lids. Georgiana, her face hidden, was still sobbing
convulsively in the corner. There seemed, in the air of the
cold orderly room, something that forbade wonderment and

silenced conjecture. Lady Jane and Stramer stood and looked at each other without speaking. At length Stramer crossed over to Georgiana, and touched her on the shoulder. She appeared unaware of the touch, and he grasped her shoulder and shook it. "Where is Mr. Jones?" he asked.

The girl looked up, her face blurred and distorted with weeping, her eyes dilated as if with the vision of some latent terror. "Oh, sir, she's not really dead, is she?"

Stramer repeated his question in a loud authoritative tone; and slowly she echoed it in a scarce-heard whisper. "Mr. Jones—?"

"Get up, my girl, and send him here to us at once, or tell us where to find him."

Georgiana, moved by the old habit of obedience, struggled to her feet and stood unsteadily, her heaving shoulders braced against the wall. Stramer asked her sharply if she had not heard what he had said.

"Oh, poor thing, she's so upset—" Lady Jane intervened compassionately. "Tell me, Georgiana: where shall we find Mr. Jones?"

The girl turned to her with eyes as fixed as the dead woman's. "You won't find him anywhere," she slowly said.

"Why not?"

"Because he's not here."

"Not here? Where is he, then?" Stramer broke in.

Georgiana did not seem to notice the interruption. She continued to stare at Lady Jane with Mrs. Clemm's awful eyes. "He's in his grave in the church-yard—these years and years he is. Long before ever I was born . . . my aunt hadn't ever seen him herself, not since she was a tiny child. . . That's the terror of it . . . that's why she always had to do what he told her to . . . because you couldn't ever answer him back. . ." Her horrified gaze turned from Lady Jane to the stony face and fast-glazing pupils of the dead woman. "You hadn't ought to have meddled with his papers, my lady. . . That's what he's punished her for. . . When it came to those papers he wouldn't ever listen to human reason . . . he wouldn't. . ." Then, flinging her arms above her head, Georgiana straightened herself to her full height before falling in a swoon at Stramer's feet.

Her Son

I DID not recognise Mrs. Stephen Glenn when I first saw her on the deck of the *Scythian*.

The voyage was more than half over, and we were counting on Cherbourg within forty-eight hours, when she appeared on deck and sat down beside me. She was as handsome as ever, and not a day older looking than when we had last met—toward the end of the war, in 1917 it must have been, not long before her only son, the aviator, was killed. Yet now, five years later, I was looking at her as if she were a stranger. Why? Not, certainly, because of her white hair. She had had the American woman's frequent luck of acquiring it while the face beneath was still fresh, and a dozen years earlier, when we used to meet at dinners, at the Opera, that silver diadem already crowned her. Now, looking more closely, I saw that the face beneath was still untouched; what then had so altered her? Perhaps it was the faint line of anxiety between her dark strongly-drawn eyebrows; or the setting of the eyes themselves, those sombre starlit eyes which seemed to have sunk deeper into their lids, and showed like glimpses of night through the arch of a cavern. But what a gloomy image to apply to eyes as tender as Catherine Glenn's! Yet it was immediately suggested by the look of the lady in deep mourning who had settled herself beside me, and now turned to say: "So you don't know me, Mr. Norcutt—Catherine Glenn?"

The fact was flagrant. I acknowledged it, and added: "But why didn't I? I can't imagine. Do you mind my saying that I believe it's because you're even more beautiful now than when I last saw you?"

She replied with perfect simplicity: "No; I don't mind—because I ought to be; that is, if there's any meaning in anything."

"Any meaning—?"

She seemed to hesitate; she had never been a woman who found words easily. "Any meaning in life. You see, since we've met I've lost everything: my son, my husband." She bent her head slightly, as though the words she pronounced were holy.

Then she added, with the air of striving for more scrupulous accuracy: "Or, at least, almost everything."

The "almost" puzzled me. Mrs. Glenn, as far as I knew, had had no child but the son she had lost in the war; and the old uncle who had brought her up had died years earlier. I wondered if, in thus qualifying her loneliness, she alluded to the consolations of religion.

I murmured that I knew of her double mourning; and she surprised me still farther by saying: "Yes; I saw you at my husband's funeral. I've always wanted to thank you for being there."

"But of course I was there."

She continued: "I noticed all of Stephen's friends who came. I was very grateful to them, and especially to the younger ones." (This was meant for me.) "You see," she added, "a funeral is—is a very great comfort."

Again I looked my surprise.

"My son—my son Philip—" (why should she think it necessary to mention his name, since he was her only child?)— "my son Philip's funeral took place just where his aeroplane fell. A little village in the Somme; his father and I went there immediately after the Armistice. One of our army chaplains read the service. The people from the village were there— they were so kind to us. But there was no one else—no personal friends; at that time only the nearest relations could get passes. Our boy would have wished it . . . he would have wanted to stay where he fell. But it's not the same as feeling one's friends about one, as I did at my husband's funeral."

While she spoke she kept her eyes intently, almost embarrassingly, on mine. It had never occurred to me that Mrs. Stephen Glenn was the kind of woman who would attach any particular importance to the list of names at her husband's funeral. She had always seemed aloof and abstracted, shut off from the world behind the high walls of a happy domesticity. But on adding this new indication of character to the fragments of information I had gathered concerning her first appearance in New York, and to the vague impression she used to produce on me when we met, I began to see that lists of names were probably just what she would care about. And then I asked myself what I really knew of her. Very little, I perceived; but no doubt just as much as she wished me to. For, as I sat there, listening to her voice, and catching unguarded glimpses of her crape-shadowed profile, I began to suspect that what had seemed in her a rather dull simplicity might be the vigilance of a secretive person; or perhaps of a person who had a secret. There is a world of difference between them, for the secretive person is seldom interesting and seldom has a secret; but I felt inclined—though nothing I knew of her justified it—to put her in the other class.

I began to think over the years of our intermittent acquaintance—it had never been more, for I had never known the Glenns well. She had appeared in New York when I was a very young man, in the 'nineties, as a beautiful girl—from Kentucky or Alabama—a niece of old Colonel Reamer's. Left an orphan, and penniless, when she was still almost a child, she had been passed about from one reluctant relation to another, and had finally (the legend ran) gone on the stage, and followed a strolling company across the continent. The manager had deserted his troupe in some far-off state, and Colonel Reamer, fatuous, impecunious, and no doubt perplexed as to how to deal with the situation, had yet faced it manfully, and shaking off his bachelor selfishness had taken the girl into his house. Such a past, though it looks dovecoloured now, seemed hectic in the 'nineties, and gave a touch of romance and mystery to the beautiful Catherine Reamer, who appeared so aloof and distinguished, yet had been snatched out of such promiscuities and perils.

Colonel Reamer was a ridiculous old man: everything about him was ridiculous—his "toupee" (probably the last in existence), his vague military title, his anecdotes about southern chivalry, and duels between other gentlemen with military titles and civilian pursuits, and all the obsolete swagger of a character dropped out of Martin Chuzzlewit. He was the notorious bore of New York; tolerated only because he was old Mrs. So-and-so's second cousin, because he was poor, because he was kindly—and because, out of his poverty, he had managed, with a smile and a gay gesture, to shelter and clothe his starving niece. Old Reamer, I recalled, had always had a passion for lists of names; for seeing his own appear in the "society column" of the morning papers, for giving you those of the people he had dined with, or been unable to dine with because already bespoken by others even more important. The young people called him "Old Previous-Engagement," because he was so anxious to have you know that, if you hadn't met him at some particular party, it was because he had been previously engaged at another.

Perhaps, I thought, it was from her uncle that Mrs. Glenn had learned to attach such importance to names, to lists of names, to the presence of certain people on certain occasions, to a social suitability which could give a consecration even to death. The profile at my side, so marble-pure, so marble-sad, did not suggest such preoccupations; neither did the deep entreating gaze she bent on me; yet many details fitted into the theory.

Her very marriage to Stephen Glenn seemed to confirm it. I thought back, and began to reconstruct Stephen Glenn. He was considerably older than myself, and had been a familiar figure in my earliest New York; a man who was a permanent ornament to society, who looked precisely as he ought, spoke, behaved, received his friends, filled his space on the social stage, exactly as his world expected him to. While he was still a young man, old ladies in perplexity over some social problem (there were many in those draconian days) would consult Stephen Glenn as if he had been one of the Ancients of the community. Yet there was nothing precociously old or dry about him. He was one of the handsomest men of his day, a good shot, a leader of cotillions. He practised at the bar, and became a member of a reputed legal firm chiefly occupied with the management of old ponderous New York estates. In process of time the old ladies who had consulted him about social questions began to ask his advice about investments; and on this point he was considered equally reliable. Only one cloud shadowed his early life. He had married a distant cousin, an effaced sort of woman who bore him no children, and presently (on that account, it was said) fell into suicidal melancholia; so that for a good many years Stephen Glenn's handsome and once hospitable house must have been a grim place to go home to. But at last she died, and after a decent interval the widower married Miss Reamer. No one was greatly surprised. It had been observed that the handsome

Stephen Glenn and the beautiful Catherine Reamer were drawn to each other; and though the old ladies thought he might have done better, some of the more caustic remarked that he could hardly have done differently, after having made Colonel Reamer's niece so "conspicuous." The attentions of a married man, especially of one unhappily married, and virtually separated from his wife, were regarded in those days as likely to endanger a young lady's future. Catherine Reamer, however, rose above these hints as she had above the perils of her theatrical venture. One had only to look at her to see that, in that smooth marble surface there was no crack in which detraction could take root.

Stephen Glenn's house was opened again, and the couple began to entertain in a quiet way. It was thought natural that Glenn should want to put a little life into the house which had so long been a sort of tomb; but though the Glenn dinners were as good as the most carefully chosen food and wine could make them, neither of the pair had the gifts which make hospitality a success, and by the time I knew them, the younger set had come to regard dining with them as somewhat of a bore. Stephen Glenn was still handsome, his wife still beautiful, perhaps more beautiful than ever; but the apathy of prosperity seemed to have settled down on them, and they wore their beauty and affability like expensive clothes put on for the occasion. There was something static, unchanging in their appearance, as there was in their affability, their conversation, the *menus* of their carefully-planned dinners, the studied arrangement of the drawing-room furniture. They had a little boy, born after a year of marriage, and they were devoted parents, given to lengthy anecdotes about their son's doings and sayings; but one could not imagine their tumbling about with him on the nursery floor. Some one said they must go to bed with their crowns on, like the kings and queens on packs of cards; and gradually, from being thought distinguished and impressive, they came to be regarded as wooden, pompous and slightly absurd. But the old ladies still spoke of Stephen Glenn as a man who had done his family credit, and his wife began to acquire his figure-head attributes, and to be consulted, as he was, about the minuter social problems. And all the while—I thought as I looked back—

there seemed to have been no one in their lives with whom they were really intimate. . . .

Then, of a sudden, they again became interesting. It was when their only son was killed, attacked alone in mid-sky by a German air squadron. Young Phil Glenn was the first American aviator to fall; and when the news came people saw that the Mr. and Mrs. Glenn they had known was a mere *façade*, and that behind it were a passionate father and mother, crushed, rebellious, agonizing, but determined to face their loss dauntlessly, though they should die of it.

Stephen Glenn did die of it, barely two years later. The doctors ascribed his death to a specific disease; but everybody who knew him knew better. "It was the loss of the boy," they said; and added: "It's terrible to have only one child."

Since her husband's funeral I had not seen Mrs. Glenn; I had completely ceased to think of her. And now, on my way to take up a post at the American Consulate in Paris, I found myself sitting beside her and remembering these things. "Poor creatures—it's as if two marble busts had been knocked off their pedestals and smashed," I thought, recalling the faces of husband and wife after the boy's death; "and she's been smashed twice, poor woman. . . . Yet she says it has made her more beautiful. . . ." Again I lost myself in conjecture.

II

I was told that a lady in deep mourning wanted to see me on urgent business, and I looked out of my private den at the Paris Consulate into the room hung with maps and Presidents, where visitors were sifted out before being passed on to the Vice-Consul or the Chief.

The lady was Mrs. Stephen Glenn.

Six or seven months had passed since our meeting on the *Scythian*, and I had again forgotten her very existence. She was not a person who stuck in one's mind; and once more I wondered why, for in her statuesque weeds she looked nobler, more striking than ever. She glanced at the people awaiting their turn under the maps and the Presidents, and asked in a low tone if she could see me privately.

I was free at the moment, and I led her into my office and banished the typist.

Mrs. Glenn seemed disturbed by the signs of activity about me. "I'm afraid we shall be interrupted. I wanted to speak to you alone," she said.

I assured her we were not likely to be disturbed if she could put what she had to say in a few words—

"Ah, but that's just what I can't do. What I have to say can't be put in a few words." She fixed her splendid nocturnal eyes on me, and I read in them a distress so deep that I dared not suggest postponement.

I said I would do all I could to prevent our being interrupted, and in reply she just sat silent, and looked at me, as if after all she had nothing farther to communicate. The telephone clicked, and I rang for my secretary to take the message; then one of the clerks came in with papers for my signature. I said: "I'd better sign and get it over," and she sat motionless, her head slightly bent, as if secretly relieved by the delay. The clerk went off, I shut the door again, and when we were alone she lifted her head and spoke. "Mr. Norcutt," she asked, "have you ever had a child?"

I replied with a smile that I was not married. She murmured: "I'm sorry—excuse me," and looked down again at her black-gloved hands, which were clasped about a black bag richly embroidered with dull jet. Everything about her was as finished, as costly, as studied, as if she were a young beauty going forth in her joy; yet she looked like a heart-broken woman.

She began again: "My reason for coming is that I've promised to help a friend, a poor woman who's lost all trace of her son—her only surviving son—and is hunting for him." She paused, though my expectant silence seemed to encourage her to continue. "It's a very sad case: I must try to explain. Long ago, as a girl, my friend fell in love with a married man—a man unhappily married." She moistened her lips, which had become parched and colourless. "You mustn't judge them too severely. . . . He had great nobility of character—the highest standards—but the situation was too cruel. His wife was insane; at that time there was no legal release in such cases. If you were married to a lunatic only death could free you. It was a most unhappy affair—the poor girl pitied her friend profoundly. Their little boy . . ." Suddenly she stood up with a proud and noble movement and leaned to me across the desk. "I am that woman," she said.

She straightened herself and stood there, trembling, erect, like a swathed figure of woe on an illustrious grave. I thought: "What this inexpressive woman was meant to express is grief—" and marvelled at the wastefulness of Nature. But suddenly she dropped back into her chair, bowed her face against the desk, and burst into sobs. Her sobs were not violent; they were soft, low, almost rhythmical, with lengthening intervals between, like the last drops of rain after a long down-pour; and I said to myself: "She's cried so much that this must be the very end."

She opened the jet bag, took out a delicate handkerchief, and dried her eyes. Then she turned to me again. "It's the first time I've ever spoken of this . . . to any human being except one."

I laid my hand on hers. "It was no use—my pretending," she went on, as if appealing to me for justification.

"Is it ever? And why should you, with an old friend?" I rejoined, attempting to comfort her.

"Ah, but I've had to—for so many years; to be silent has become my second nature." She paused, and then continued in a softer tone: "My baby was so beautiful . . . do you know, Mr. Norcutt, I'm sure I should know him anywhere. . . . Just two years and one month older than my second boy, Philip . . . the one you knew." Again she hesitated, and then, in a warmer burst of confidence, and scarcely above a whisper: "We christened the eldest Stephen. We knew it was dangerous: it might give a clue—but I felt I must give him his father's name, the name I loved best. . . . It was all I could keep of my baby. And Stephen understood; he consented. . . ."

I sat and stared at her. What! This child of hers that she was telling me of was the child of Stephen Glenn? The two had had a child two years before the birth of their lawful son Philip? And consequently nearly a year before their marriage? I listened in a stupor, trying to reconstruct in my mind the image of a new, of another, Stephen Glenn, of the suffering reckless man behind the varnished image familiar to me. Now and then I murmured: "Yes . . . yes . . ." just to help her to go on.

"Of course it was impossible to keep the baby with me. Think—at my uncle's! My poor uncle . . . he would have died of it. . . ."

"And so you died instead?"

I had found the right word; her eyes filled again, and she stretched her hands to mine. "Ah, you've understood! Thank you. Yes; I died," She added: "Even when Philip was born I didn't come to life again—not wholly. Because there was always Stevie . . . part of me belonged to Stevie forever."

"But when you and Glenn were able to marry, why—?"

She hung her head, and the blood rose to her worn temples. "Ah, why? . . . Listen; you mustn't blame my husband. Try to remember what life was thirty years ago in New York. He had his professional standing to consider. A woman with a shadow on her was damned. . . . I couldn't discredit Stephen. . . . We knew *positively* that our baby was in the best of hands. . . ."

"You never saw him again?"

She shook her head. "It was part of the agreement—with the persons who took him. They wanted to imagine he was their own. We knew we were fortunate . . . to find such a safe home, so entirely beyond suspicion . . . we had to accept the conditions." She looked up with a faint flicker of reassurance in her eyes. "In a way it no longer makes any difference to me—the interval. It seems like yesterday. I know he's been well cared for, and I should recognise him anywhere. No child ever had such eyes. . . ." She fumbled in her bag, drew out a small morocco case, opened it, and showed me the miniature of a baby a few months old. "I managed, with the greatest difficulty, to get a photograph of him—and this was done from it. Beautiful? Yes. I shall be able to identify him anywhere. . . . It's only twenty-seven years. . . ."

III

Our talk was prolonged, the next day, at the quiet hotel where Mrs. Glenn was staying; but it led—it could lead—to nothing definite.

The unhappy woman could only repeat and amplify the strange confession stammered out at the Consulate. As soon as her child was born it had been entrusted with the utmost secrecy to a rich childless couple, who at once adopted it, and disappeared forever. Disappeared, that is, in the sense that (as I guessed) Stephen Glenn was as determined as they were that the child's parents should never hear of them again. Poor Catherine had been very ill at her baby's birth. Tortured by the need of concealment, of taking up her usual life at her uncle's as quickly as possible, of explaining her brief absence in such a way as to avert suspicion, she had lived in a blur of fear and suffering, and by the time she was herself again the child was gone, and the adoption irrevocable. Thereafter, I gathered, Glenn made it clear that he wished to avoid the subject, and she learned very little about the couple who had taken her child except that they were of good standing, and came from somewhere in Pennsylvania. They had gone to Europe almost immediately, it appeared, and no more was heard of them. Mrs. Glenn understood that Mr. Brown (their name was Brown) was a painter, and that they went first to Italy, then to Spain—unless it was the other way round. Stephen Glenn, it seemed, had heard of them through an old governess of his sister's, a family confidante, who was the sole recipient of poor Catherine's secret. Soon afterward the governess died, and with her disappeared the last trace of the mysterious couple; for it was not going to be easy to wander about Europe looking for a Mr. and Mrs. Brown who had gone to Italy or Spain with a baby twenty-seven years ago. But that was what Mrs. Glenn meant to do. She had a fair amount of money, she was desperately lonely, she had no aim or interest or occupation or duty—except to find the child she had lost.

What she wanted was some sort of official recommendation to our consuls in Italy and Spain, accompanied by a private letter hinting at the nature of her errand. I took these papers to her and when I did so I tried to point out the difficulties and risks of her quest, and suggested that she ought to be accompanied by some one who could advise her—hadn't she a man of business, or a relation, a cousin, a nephew? No, she said; there was no one; but for that matter she needed no one. If necessary she could apply to the police, or employ private detectives; and any American consul to whom she appealed would know how to advise her. "In any case," she added, "I couldn't be mistaken—I should always recognise him. He was the very image of his father. And if there were any possibility of my being in doubt, I have the miniature, and photographs of his father as a young man."

She drew out the little morocco case and offered it again for my contemplation. The vague presentment of a child a few months old—and by its help she expected to identify a man of nearly thirty!

Apparently she had no clue beyond the fact that, all those years ago, the adoptive parents were rumoured to have sojourned in Europe. She was starting for Italy because she thought she remembered that they were said to have gone there first—in itself a curious argument. Wherever there was an American consul she meant to apply to him. First at Genoa; then Milan; then Florence, Rome and Naples. In one or the other of these cities she would surely discover some one who could remember the passage there of an American couple named Brown with the most beautiful baby boy in the world. Even the long arm of coincidence could not have scattered so widely over southern Europe American couples of the name of Brown, with a matchlessly beautiful baby called Stephen.

Mrs. Glenn set forth in a mood of almost mystical exaltation. She promised that I should hear from her as soon as she had anything definite to communicate: "which means that you *will* hear—and soon!" she concluded with a happy laugh. But six months passed without my receiving any direct news, though I was kept on her track by a succession of letters addressed to my chief by various consuls who wrote to say that a Mrs. Stephen Glenn had called with a letter of recommendation, but that unluckily it had been impossible to give her any assistance "as she had absolutely no data to go upon." Alas poor lady—

And then, one day, about eight months after her departure, there was a telegram. "Found my boy. Unspeakably happy. Long to see you." It was signed Catherine Glenn, and dated from a mountain-cure in Switzerland.

IV

That summer, when the time came for my vacation, it was raining in Paris even harder than it had rained all the preceding winter, and I decided to make a dash for the sun.

I had read in the papers that the French Riviera was suffering from a six months' drought; and though I didn't half believe it, I took the next train for the south. I got out at Les Calanques, a small bathing-place between Marseilles and Toulon, where there was a fairish hotel, and pine-woods to walk in, and there, that very day, I saw seated on the beach the majestic figure of Mrs. Stephen Glenn. The first thing that struck me was that she had at last discarded her weeds. She wore a thin white dress, and a wide-brimmed hat of russet straw shaded the fine oval of her face. She saw me at once, and springing up advanced across the beach with a light step. The sun, striking on her hat brim, cast a warm shadow on her face; and in that semi-shade it glowed with recovered youth. "Dear Mr. Norcutt! How wonderful! Is it really you? I've been meaning to write for weeks; but I think happiness has made me lazy—and my days are so full," she declared with a joyous smile.

I looked at her with increased admiration. At the Consulate, I remembered, I had said to myself that grief was what Nature had meant her features to express; but that was only because I had never seen her happy. No; even when her husband and her son Philip were alive, and the circle of her well-being seemed unbroken, I had never seen her look as she looked now. And I understood that, during all those years, the unsatisfied longing for her eldest child, the shame at her own cowardice in disowning and deserting him, and perhaps her secret contempt for her husband for having abetted (or more probably exacted) that desertion, must have been eating into her soul, deeper, far deeper, than satisfied affections could reach. Now everything in her was satisfied; I could see it. . . . "How happy you look!" I exclaimed.

"But of course." She took it as simply as she had my former remark on her heightened beauty; and I perceived that what had illumined her face when we met on the steamer was not sorrow but the dawn of hope. Even then she had felt certain

that she was going to find her boy; now she had found him
and was transfigured. I sat down beside her on the sands.
"And now tell me how the incredible thing happened."

She shook her head. "Not incredible—inevitable. When
one has lived for more than half a life with one object in view
it's bound to become a reality. I *had* to find Stevie; and I
found him." She smiled with the inward brooding smile of a
Madonna—an image of the eternal mother who, when she
speaks of her children in old age, still feels them at the breast.

Of details, as I made out, there were few; or perhaps she
was too confused with happiness to give them. She had
hunted up and down Italy for her Mr. and Mrs. Brown, and
then suddenly, at Alassio, just as she was beginning to give up
hope, and had decided (in a less sanguine mood) to start for
Spain, the miracle had happened. Falling into talk, on her last
evening, with a lady in the hotel lounge, she had alluded
vaguely—she couldn't say why—to the object of her quest;
and the lady, snatching the miniature from her, and bursting
into tears, had identified the portrait as her adopted child's,
and herself as the long-sought Mrs. Brown. Papers had been
produced, dates compared, all to Mrs. Glenn's complete satisfaction. There could be no doubt that she had found her
Stevie (thank heaven, they had kept the name!); and the only
shadow on her joy was the discovery that he was lying ill,
menaced with tuberculosis, at some Swiss mountain-cure. Or
rather, that was part of another sadness; of the unfortunate
fact that his adopted parents had lost nearly all their money
just as he was leaving school, and hadn't been able to do
much for him in the way of medical attention or mountain
air—the very things he needed as he was growing up. Instead,
since he had a passion for painting, they had allowed him to
live in Paris, rather miserably, in the Latin Quarter, and work
all day in one of those big schools—Julian's, wasn't it? The
very worst thing for a boy whose lungs were slightly affected;
and this last year he had had to give up, and spend several
months in a cheap hole in Switzerland. Mrs. Glenn joined
him there at once—ah, that meeting!—and as soon as she had
seen him, and talked with the doctors, she became convinced
that all that was needed to ensure his recovery was comfort,
care and freedom from anxiety. His lungs, the doctors assured

her, were all right again; and he had such a passion for the sea
that after a few weeks in a good hotel at Montana he had persuaded Mrs. Glenn to come with him to the Mediterranean.
But she was firmly resolved on carrying him back to
Switzerland for another winter, no matter how much he objected; and Mr. and Mrs. Brown agreed that she was absolutely right—

"Ah; there's still a Mr. Brown?"

"Oh, yes." She smiled at me absently, her whole mind on
Stevie. "You'll see them both—they're here with us. I invited
them for a few weeks, poor souls. I can't altogether separate
them from Stevie—not yet." (It was clear that eventually she
hoped to.)

No, I assented; I supposed she couldn't; and just then she
exclaimed: "Ah, there's my boy!" and I saw a tall stooping
young man approaching us with the listless step of convalescence. As he came nearer I felt that I was going to like him a
good deal better than I had expected—though I don't know
why I had doubted his likeableness before knowing him. At
any rate, I was taken at once by the look of his dark-lashed
eyes, deep-set in a long thin face which I suspected of being
too pale under the carefully-acquired sunburn. The eyes were
friendly, humorous, ironical; I liked a little less the rather hard
lines of the mouth, until his smile relaxed them into boyish-
ness. His body, lank and loose-jointed, was too thin for his
suit of light striped flannel, and the untidy dark hair tumbling
over his forehead adhered to his temples as if they were perpetually damp. Yes, he looked ill, this young Glenn.

I remembered wondering, when Mrs. Glenn told me her
story, why it had not occurred to her that her oldest son had
probably joined the American forces and might have remained on the field with his junior. Apparently this tragic possibility had never troubled her. She seemed to have forgotten
that there had ever been a war, and that a son of her own,
with thousands of young Americans of his generation, had
lost his life in it. And now it looked as though she had been
gifted with a kind of prescience. The war did not last long
enough for America to be called on to give her weaklings, as
Europe had, and it was clear that Stephen Glenn, with his
narrow shoulders and hectic cheek-bones, could never have

been wanted for active service. I suspected him of having been ill for longer than his mother knew.

Mrs. Glenn shone on him as he dropped down beside us. "This is an old friend, Stephen; a very dear friend of your father's." She added, extravagantly, that but for me she and her son might never have found each other. I protested: "How absurd," and young Glenn, stretching out his long limbs against the sand-back, and crossing his arms behind his head, turned on me a glance of rather weary good-humour. "Better give me a longer trial, my dear, before you thank him."

Mrs. Glenn laughed contentedly, and continued, her eyes on her son: "I was telling him that Mr. and Mrs. Brown are with us."

"Ah, yes—" said Stephen indifferently. I was inclined to like him a little less for his undisguised indifference. Ought he to have allowed his poor and unlucky foster-parents to be so soon superseded by this beautiful and opulent new mother? But, after all, I mused, I had not yet seen the Browns; and though I had begun to suspect, from Catherine's tone as well as from Stephen's, that they both felt the presence of that couple to be vaguely oppressive, I decided that I must wait before drawing any conclusions. And then suddenly Mrs. Glenn said, in a tone of what I can only describe as icy cordiality: "Ah, here they come now. They must have hurried back on purpose—"

V

Mr. and Mrs. Brown advanced across the beach. Mrs. Brown led the way; she walked with a light springing step, and if I had been struck by Mrs. Glenn's recovered youthfulness, her co-mother, at a little distance, seemed to me positively girlish. She was smaller and much slighter than Mrs. Glenn, and looked so much younger that I had a moment's doubt as to the possibility of her having, twenty-seven years earlier, been of legal age to adopt a baby. Certainly she and Mr. Brown must have had exceptional reasons for concluding so early that Heaven was not likely to bless their union. I had to admit, when Mrs. Brown came up, that I had overrated her juvenility. Slim, active and girlish she remained; but the freshness of her face was largely due to artifice, and the golden glints in her chestnut hair were a thought too golden. Still, she was a very pretty woman, with the alert cosmopolitan air of one who had acquired her elegance in places where the very best counterfeits are found. It will be seen that my first impression was none too favourable; but for all I knew of Mrs. Brown it might turn out that she had made the best of meagre opportunities. She met my name with a conquering smile, said: "Ah, yes—dear Mr. Norcutt. Mrs. Glenn has told us all we owe you"—and at the "we" I detected a faint shadow on Mrs. Glenn's brow. Was it only maternal jealousy that provoked it? I suspected an even deeper antagonism. The women were so different, so diametrically opposed to each other in appearance, dress, manner, and all the inherited standards, that if they had met as strangers it would have been hard for them to find a common ground of understanding; and the fact of that ground being furnished by Stephen hardly seemed to ease the situation.

"Well, what's the matter with taking some notice of little me?" piped a small dry man dressed in too-smart flannels, and wearing a too-white Panama which he removed with an elaborate flourish.

"Oh, of course! My husband—Mr. Norcutt." Mrs. Brown laid a jewelled hand on Stephen's recumbent shoulder. "Steve, you rude boy, you ought to have introduced your dad." As she pressed his shoulder I noticed that her long oval nails were freshly lacquered with the last new shade of coral, and that the forefinger was darkly yellowed with nicotine. This familiar colour-scheme struck me at the moment as peculiarly distasteful.

Stephen vouchsafed no answer, and Mr. Brown remarked to me sardonically. "You know you won't lose your money or your morals in this secluded spot."

Mrs. Brown flashed a quick glance at him. "Don't be so silly! It's much better for Steve to be in a quiet place where he can just sleep and eat and bask. His mother and I are going to be firm with him about that—aren't we, dearest?" She transferred her lacquered talons to Mrs. Glenn's shoulder, and the latter, with a just perceptible shrinking, replied gaily: "As long as we can hold out against him!"

"Oh, this is the very place I was pining for," said Stephen placidly. ("Gosh—*pining!*" Mr. Brown interpolated.) Stephen tilted his hat forward over his sunburnt nose with the drawn nostrils, crossed his arms under his thin neck, and closed his eyes. Mrs. Brown bent over Mrs. Glenn with one of her quick gestures. "Darling—before we go in to lunch do let me fluff you out a little: so." With a flashing hand she loosened the soft white waves under Mrs. Glenn's spreading hat brim. "There—that's better; isn't it, Mr. Norcutt?"

Mrs. Glenn's face was a curious sight. The smile she had forced gave place to a marble rigidity; the old statuesqueness which had melted to flesh and blood stiffened her features again. "Thank you . . . I'm afraid I never think . . ."

"No, you never do; that's the trouble!" Mrs. Brown shot an arch glance at me. "With her looks, oughtn't she to think? But perhaps it's lucky for the rest of us poor women she don't—eh, Stevie?"

The colour rushed to Mrs. Glenn's face; she was going to retort; to snub the dreadful woman. But the new softness had returned, and she merely lifted a warning finger. "Oh, don't, please . . . speak to him. Can't you see that he's fallen asleep?"

O great King Solomon, I thought—and bowed my soul before the mystery.

I spent a fortnight at Les Calanques, and every day my perplexity deepened. The most conversible member of the little group was undoubtedly Stephen. Mrs. Glenn was as she had always been: beautiful, benevolent and inarticulate. When she sat on the beach beside the dozing Stephen, in her flowing white dress, her large white umbrella tilted to shelter him, she reminded me of a carven angel spreading broad wings above a tomb (I could never look at her without being reminded of statuary); and to converse with a marble angel so engaged can never have been easy. But I was perhaps not wrong in suspecting that her smiling silence concealed a reluctance to talk about the Browns. Like many perfectly unegotistical women Catherine Glenn had no subject of conversation except her own affairs; and these at present so visibly hinged on the Browns that it was easy to see why silence was simpler.

Mrs. Brown, I may as well confess, bored me acutely. She was a perfect specimen of the middle-aged flapper, with layers and layers of hard-headed feminine craft under her romping ways. All this I suffered from chiefly because I knew it was making Mrs. Glenn suffer. But after all it was thanks to Mrs. Brown that she had found her son; Mrs. Brown had brought up Stephen, had made him (one was obliged to suppose) the whimsical dreamy charming creature he was; and again and again, when Mrs. Brown outdid herself in girlish archness or middle-aged craft, Mrs. Glenn's wounded eyes said to mine: "Look at Stephen; isn't that enough?"

Certainly it was enough; enough even to excuse Mr. Brown's jocular allusions and arid anecdotes, his boredom at Les Calanques, and the too-liberal potations in which he drowned it. Mr. Brown, I may add, was not half as trying as his wife. For the first two or three days I was mildly diverted by his contempt for the quiet watering-place in which his women had confined him, and his lordly conception of the life of pleasure, as exemplified by intimacy with the head-waiters of gilt-edged restaurants and the lavishing of large sums on horse-racing and cards. "Damn it, Norcutt, I'm not used to being mewed up in this kind of place. Perhaps it's different with you—all depends on a man's standards, don't it? Now before I lost my money—" and so on. The odd thing was that, though this loss of fortune played a large part in the conversation of both husband and wife, I never somehow believed in it—I mean in the existence of the fortune. I hinted as much one day to Mrs. Glenn, but she only opened her noble eyes reproachfully, as if I had implied that it discredited the Browns to dream of a fortune they had never had. "They tell me Stephen was brought up with every luxury. And besides—their own tastes seem rather expensive, don't they?" she argued gently.

"That's the very reason."

"The reason—?"

"The only people I know who are totally without expensive tastes are the overwhelmingly wealthy. You see it when you visit palaces. They sleep on camp-beds and live on boiled potatoes."

Mrs. Glenn smiled. "Stevie wouldn't have liked that."

Stephen smiled also when I alluded to these past splendours. "It must have been before I cut my first teeth. I know Boy's always talking about it; but I've got to take it on faith, just as you have."

"Boy—?"

"Didn't you know? He's always called 'Boy.' Boydon Brown—abbreviated by friends and family to 'Boy.' The Boy Browns. Suits them, doesn't it?"

It did; but I was not sure that it suited him to say so.

"And you've always addressed your adopted father in that informal style?"

"Lord, yes; nobody's formal with Boy except head-waiters. They bow down to him; I don't know why. He's got the manner. I haven't. When I go to a restaurant they always give me the worst table and the stupidest waiter." He leaned back against the sand-bank and blinked contentedly seaward. "Got a cigarette?"

"You know you oughtn't to smoke," I protested.

"I know; but I do." He held out a lean hand with prominent knuckles. "As long as Kit's not about." He called the marble angel, his mother, "Kit"! And yet I was not offended—I let him do it, just as I let him have one of my cigarettes. If "Boy" had a way with head-waiters his adopted son undoubtedly had one with lesser beings; his smile, his faint hoarse laugh would have made me do his will even if his talk had not conquered me. We sat for hours on the sands, discussing and dreaming; not always undisturbed, for Mrs. Brown had a tiresome way of hovering and "listening in," as she archly called it—("I don't want Stevie to depreciate his poor ex-mamma to you," she explained one day); and whenever Mrs. Brown (who, even at Les Calanques, had contrived to create a social round for herself) was bathing, dancing, playing bridge, or being waved, massaged or manicured, the other mother, assuring herself from an upper window that the coast was clear, would descend in her gentle majesty and turn our sand-bank into a throne by sitting on it. But now and then Stephen and I had a half-hour to ourselves; and then I tried to lead his talk to the past.

He seemed willing enough that I should, but uninterested, and unable to recover many details. "I never can remember things that don't matter—and so far nothing about me has mattered," he said with a humorous melancholy. "I mean, not till I struck mother Kit."

He had vague recollections of continental travels as a little boy; had afterward been at a private school in Switzerland; had tried to pass himself off as a Canadian volunteer in 1915, and in 1917 to enlist in the American army, but had failed in each case—one had only to look at him to see why. The war over, he had worked for a time at Julian's, and then broken down; and after that it had been a hard row to hoe till mother Kit came along. By George, but he'd never forget what she'd done for him—never!

"Well, it's a way mothers have with their sons," I remarked.

He flushed under his bronze tanning, and said simply: "Yes—only you see I didn't know."

His view of the Browns, while not unkindly, was so detached that I suspected him of regarding his own mother with the same objectivity; but when we spoke of her there was a different note in his voice. "I didn't know"—it was a new experience to him to be really mothered. As a type, however, she clearly puzzled him. He was too sensitive to class her (as the Browns obviously did) as a simple-minded woman to whom nothing had ever happened; but he could not conceive what sort of things could happen to a woman of her kind. I gathered that she had explained the strange episode of his adoption by telling him that at the time of his birth she had been "secretly married"—poor Catherine!—to his father, but that "family circumstances" had made it needful to conceal his existence till the marriage could be announced; by which time he had vanished with his adopted parents. I guessed how it must have puzzled Stephen to adapt his interpretation of this ingenuous tale to what, in the light of Mrs. Glenn's character, he could make out of her past. Of obvious explanations there were plenty; but evidently none fitted into his vision of her. For a moment (I could see) he had suspected a sentimental tie, a tender past, between Mrs. Glenn and myself; but this his quick perceptions soon discarded, and he apparently resigned himself to regarding her as inscrutably proud and incorrigibly perfect. "I'd like to paint her some day—if ever I'm fit to," he said; and I wondered whether his scruples applied to his moral or artistic inadequacy.

At the doctor's orders he had dropped his painting altogether since his last breakdown; but it was manifestly the one thing he cared for, and perhaps the only reason he had for wanting to get well. "When you've dropped to a certain level, it's so damnably easy to keep on till you're altogether down and out. So much easier than dragging up hill again. But I do want to get well enough to paint mother Kit. She's a subject."

One day it rained, and he was confined to the house. I went up to sit with him, and he got out some of his sketches and studies. Instantly he was transformed from an amiably mocking dilettante into an absorbed and passionate professional. "This is the only life I've ever had. All the rest—!" He made a grimace that turned his thin face into a death's-head. "Cinders!"

The studies were brilliant—there was no doubt of that. The question was—the eternal question—what would they turn into when he was well enough to finish them? For the moment the problem did not present itself, and I could praise and encourage him in all sincerity. My words brought a glow into his face, but also, as it turned out, sent up his temperature. Mrs. Glenn reproached me mildly; she begged me not to let him get excited about his pictures. I promised not to, and reassured on that point she asked if I didn't think he had talent—real talent? "Very great talent, yes," I assured her; and she burst into tears—not of grief or agitation, but of a deep upwelling joy. "Oh, what have I done to deserve it all—to deserve such happiness? Yet I always knew if I could find him he'd make me happy!" She caught both my hands, and pressed her wet cheek on mine. That was one of her unclouded hours.

There were others not so radiant. I could see that the Browns were straining at the leash. With the seductions of Juan-les-Pins and Antibes in the offing, why, their frequent allusions implied, must they remain marooned at Les Calanques? Of course, for one thing, Mrs. Brown admitted, she hadn't the clothes to show herself on a smart *plage*. Though so few were worn they had to come from the big dressmakers; and the latter's charges, everybody knew, were in inverse ratio to the amount of material used. "So that to be really naked is ruinous," she concluded, laughing; and I saw the narrowing of Catherine's lips. As for Mr. Brown, he added morosely that if a man couldn't take a hand at baccarat, or offer his friends something decent to eat and drink, it was better to vegetate at Les Calanques, and be done with it. Only, when a fellow'd been used to having plenty of money . . .

I saw at once what had happened. Mrs. Glenn, whose material wants did not extend beyond the best plumbing and expensive clothes (and the latter were made to do for three seasons), did not fully understand the Browns' aspirations. Her fortune, though adequate, was not large, and she had settled on Stephen's adoptive parents an allowance which, converted into francs, made a generous showing. It was obvious, however, that what they hoped was to get more money. There had been debts in the background, perhaps; who knew but the handsome Stephen had had his share in them? One day I suggested discreetly to Mrs. Glenn that if she wished to be alone with her son she might offer the Browns a trip to Juan-les-Pins, or some such centre of gaiety. But I pointed out that the precedent might be dangerous, and advised her first to consult Stephen. "I suspect he's as anxious to have them go as you are," I said recklessly; and her flush of pleasure rewarded me. "Oh, you mustn't say that," she reproved me, laughing; and added that she would think over my advice. I am not sure if she did consult Stephen; but she offered the Browns a holiday, and they accepted it without false pride.

VI

After my departure from Les Calanques I had no news of Mrs. Glenn till she returned to Paris in October. Then she begged me to call at the hotel where I had previously seen her, and where she was now staying with Stephen—and the Browns.

She suggested, rather mysteriously, my dining with her on a particular evening, when, as she put it, "everybody" would be out; and when I arrived she explained that Stephen had

gone to the country for the week-end, with some old comrades from Julian's, and that the Browns were dining at a
smart night-club in Montmartre. "So we'll have a quiet time
all by ourselves." She added that Steve was so much better
that he was trying his best to persuade her to spend the winter in Paris, and let him get back to his painting; but in spite
of the good news I thought she looked worn and dissatisfied.

I was surprised to find the Browns still with her, and told
her so.

"Well, you see, it's difficult," she returned with a troubled
frown. "They love Stephen so much that they won't give him
up; and how can I blame them? What are my rights, compared with theirs?"

Finding this hard to answer, I put another question. "Did
you enjoy your quiet time with Stephen while they were at
Juan-les-Pins?"

"Oh, they didn't go; at least Mrs. Brown didn't—Chrissy
she likes me to call her," Mrs. Glenn corrected herself hurriedly. "She couldn't bear to leave Stephen."

"So she sacrificed Juan-les-Pins, and that handsome
cheque?"

"Not the cheque; she kept that. Boy went," Mrs. Glenn
added apologetically. Boy and Chrissy—it had come to that! I
looked away from my old friend's troubled face before
putting my next question. "And Stephen—?"

"Well, I can't exactly tell how he feels. But I sometimes
think he'd like to be alone with me." A passing radiance
smoothed away her frown. "He's hinted that, if we decide to
stay here, they might be tempted by winter sports, and go to
the Engadine later."

"So that they would have the benefit of the high air instead
of Stephen?" She coloured a little, looked down, and then
smiled at me. "What can I do?"

I resolved to sound Stephen on his adopted parents. The
present situation would have to be put an end to somehow;
but it had puzzling elements. Why had Mrs. Brown refused to
go to Juan-les-Pins? Was it, as I had suspected, because there
were debts, and more pressing uses for the money? Or was it
that she was so much attached to her adopted son as to be
jealous of his mother's influence? This was far more to be

feared; but it did not seem to fit in with what I knew of Mrs. Brown. The trouble was that what I knew was so little. Mrs. Brown, though in one way so intelligible, was in another as cryptic to me as Catherine Glenn was to Stephen. The surface was transparent enough; but what did the blur beneath conceal? Troubled waters, or just a mud-flat? My only hope was to try to get Stephen to tell me.

Stephen had hired a studio—against his doctor's advice, I gathered—and spent most of his hours there, in the company of his old group of painting friends. Mrs. Glenn had been there once or twice, but in spite of his being so sweet and dear to her she had felt herself in the way—as she undoubtedly was. "I can't keep up with their talk, you know," she explained. With whose talk could she, poor angel?

I suggested that, for the few weeks of their Paris sojourn, it would be kinder to let Stephen have his fling; and she agreed. Afterward, in the mountains, he could recuperate; youth had such powers of self-healing. But I urged her to insist on his spending another winter in the Engadine; not at one of the big fashionable places—

She interrupted me. "I'm afraid Boy and Chrissy wouldn't like—"

"Oh, for God's sake; can't you give Boy and Chrissy another cheque, and send them off to Egypt, or to Monte Carlo?"

She hesitated. "I could try; but I don't believe she'd go. Not without Stevie."

"And what does Stevie say?"

"What can he say? She brought him up. She was there—all the years when I'd failed him."

It was unanswerable, and I felt the uselessness of any advice I could give. The situation could be changed only by some internal readjustment. Still, out of pity for the poor mother, I determined to try a word with Stephen. She gave me the address of his studio, and the next day I went there.

It was in a smart-looking modern building in the Montparnasse quarter; lofty, well-lit and well-warmed. What a contrast to his earlier environment! I climbed to his door, rang the bell and waited. There were sounds of moving about within, but as no one came I rang again; and finally Stephen opened the door. His face lit up pleasantly when he saw me. "Oh, it's you, my dear fellow!" But I caught a hint of constraint in his voice.

"I'm not in the way? Don't mind throwing me out if I am."

"I've got a sitter—" he began, visibly hesitating.

"Oh, in that case—"

"No, no; it's only—the fact is, it's Chrissy. I was trying to do a study of her—"

He led me across the passage and into the studio. It was large and flooded with light. Divans against the walls; big oak tables; shaded lamps, a couple of tall screens. From behind one of them emerged Mrs. Brown, hatless and slim, in a pale summer-like frock, her chestnut hair becomingly tossed about her eyes. "Dear Mr. Norcutt. So glad you turned up! I was getting such a stiff neck—Stephen's merciless."

"May I see the result?" I asked; and "Oh, no," she protested in mock terror, "it's too frightful—it really is. I think he thought he was doing a *nature morte*—lemons and a bottle of beer, or something!"

"It's not fit for inspection," Stephen agreed.

The room was spacious, and not over-crowded. Glancing about, I could see only one easel with a painting on it. Stephen went up and turned the canvas face inward, with the familiar gesture of the artist who does not wish to challenge attention. But before he did so I had remarked that the painting was neither a portrait of Mrs. Brown nor a still-life. It was a rather brilliant three-quarter sketch of a woman's naked back and hips. A model, no doubt—but why did he wish to conceal it?

"I'm so glad you came," Mrs. Brown repeated, smiling intensely. I stood still, hoping she was about to go; but she dropped down on one of the divans, tossing back her tumbled curls. "He works too hard, you know; I wish you'd tell him so. Steve, come here and stretch out," she commanded, indicating the other end of the divan. "You ought to take a good nap."

The hint was so obvious that I said: "In that case I'd better come another time."

"No, no; wait till I give you a cock-tail. We all need cock-tails. Where's the shaker, darling?" Mrs. Brown was on her feet again, alert and gay. She dived behind the screen which had previously concealed her, and reappeared with the necessary appliances. "Bring up that little table, Mr. Norcutt, please. Oh, I know—dear Kit doesn't approve of cock-tails; and she's right. But look at him—dead beat! If he will slave at his painting, what's he to do? I was scolding him about it when you came in."

The shaker danced in her flashing hands, and in a trice she was holding a glass out to me, and another to Stephen, who had obediently flung himself down on the divan. As he took the glass she bent and laid her lips on his damp hair. "You bad boy, you!"

I looked at Stephen. "You ought to get out of this, and start straight off for Switzerland," I admonished him.

"Oh, hell," he groaned. "Can't you get Kit to drop all that?"

Mrs. Brown made an impatient gesture. "Isn't he too foolish? Of course he ought to go away. He looks like nothing on earth. But his only idea of Switzerland is one of those awful places we used to have to go to because they were cheap, where there's nothing to do in the evening but to sit with clergymen's wives looking at stereopticon views of glaciers. I tell him he'll love St. Moritz. There's a thrill there every minute."

Stephen closed his eyes and sank his head back in the cushions without speaking. His face was drawn and weary; I was startled at the change in him since we had parted at Les Calanques.

Mrs. Brown, following my glance, met it with warning brows and a finger on her painted lips. It was like a parody of Mrs. Glenn's maternal gesture, and I perceived that it meant: "Can't you see that he's falling asleep? Do be tactful and slip out without disturbing him."

What could I do but obey? A moment later the studio door had closed on me, and I was going down the long flights of stairs. The worst of it was that I was not at all sure that Stephen was really asleep.

VII

The next morning I received a telephone call from Stephen asking me to lunch. We met at a quiet restaurant near his studio, and when, after an admirably chosen meal, we settled down to coffee and cigars, he said carelessly: "Sorry you got thrown out that way yesterday."

"Oh, well—I saw you were tired, and I didn't want to interfere with your nap."

He looked down moodily at his plate. "Tired—yes, I'm tired. But I didn't want a nap. I merely simulated slumber to try and make Chrissy shut up."

"Ah—" I said.

He shot a quick glance at me, almost resentfully, I thought. Then he went on: "There are times when aimless talk nearly kills me. I wonder," he broke out suddenly, "if you can realize what it feels like for a man who's never—I mean for an orphan—suddenly to find himself with two mothers?"

I said I could see it might be arduous.

"Arduous! It's literally asphyxiating." He frowned, and then smiled whimsically. "When I need all the fresh air I can get!"

"My dear fellow—what you need first of all is to get away from cities and studios."

His frown deepened. "I know; I know all that. Only, you see—well, to begin with, before I turn up my toes I want to do something for mother Kit."

"Do something?"

"Something to show her that I was—was worth all this fuss." He paused, and turned his coffee-spoon absently between his long twitching fingers.

I shrugged. "Whatever you do, she'll always think that. Mothers do."

He murmured after me slowly: "Mothers—"

"What she wants you to do now is to get well," I insisted.

"Yes; I know; I'm pledged to get well. But somehow that bargain doesn't satisfy me. If I don't get well I want to leave something behind me that'll make her think: 'If he'd lived a little longer he'd have pulled it off'."

"If you left a gallery of masterpieces it wouldn't help her much."

His face clouded, and he looked at me wistfully. "What the devil else can I do?"

"Go to Switzerland, and let yourself be bored there for a whole winter. Then you can come back and paint, and enjoy your success instead of having the enjoyment done for you by your heirs."

"Oh, what a large order—" he sighed, and drew out his cigarettes.

For a moment we were both silent; then he raised his eyes and looked straight at me. "Supposing I don't get well, there's another thing . . ." He hesitated a moment. "Do you happen to know if my mother has made her will?"

I imagine my look must have surprised him, for he hurried on: "It's only this: if I should drop out—you can never tell—there are Chrissy and Boy, poor helpless devils. I can't forget what they've been to me . . . done for me . . . though sometimes I daresay I seem ungrateful. . . ."

I listened to his embarrassed phrases with an embarrassment at least as great. "You may be sure your mother won't forget either," I said.

"No; I suppose not. Of course not. Only sometimes—you can see for yourself that things are a little breezy . . . They feel that perhaps she doesn't always remember for how many years . . ." He brought the words out as though he were reciting a lesson. "I can't forget it . . . of course," he added, painfully.

I glanced at my watch and stood up. I wanted to spare him the evident effort of going on. "Mr. and Mrs. Brown's tastes don't always agree with your mother's. That's evident. If you could persuade them to go off somewhere—or to lead more independent lives when they're with her—mightn't that help?"

He cast a despairing glance at me. "Lord—I wish you'd try! But you see they're anxious—anxious about their future. . . ."

"I'm sure they needn't be," I answered shortly, more and more impatient to make an end.

His face lit up with a suddenness that hurt me. "Oh, well . . . it's sure to be all right if you say so. Of course you know."

"I know your mother," I said, holding out my hand for goodbye.

VIII

Shortly after my lunch with Stephen Glenn I was unexpectedly detached from my job in Paris and sent on a special mission to the other side of the world. I was sorry to bid goodbye to Mrs. Glenn, but relieved to be rid of the thankless task of acting as her counsellor. Not that she herself was not thankful, poor soul; but the situation abounded in problems, to not one of which could I find a solution; and I was embarrassed by her simple faith in my ability to do so. "Get rid of the Browns; pension them off," I could only repeat; but since my talk with Stephen I had little hope of his mother's acting on this suggestion. "You'll probably all end up together at St. Moritz," I prophesied; and a few months later a belated Paris *Herald*, overtaking me in my remote corner of the globe, informed me that among the guests of the new Ice Palace Hotel at St. Moritz were Mrs. Glenn of New York, Mr. Stephen Glenn, and Mr. and Mrs. Boydon Brown. From succeeding numbers of the same sheet I learned that Mr. and Mrs. Boydon Brown were among those entertaining on the opening night of the new *Restaurant des Glaciers*, that the Boydon Brown cup for the most original costume at the Annual Fancy Ball of the Skiers' Club had been won by Miss Thora Dacy (costume designed by the well-known artist, Stephen Glenn), and that Mr. Boydon Brown had been one of the stewards of the dinner given to the participants in the ice-hockey match between the St. Moritz and Suvretta teams. And on such items I was obliged to nourish my memory of my friends, for no direct news came to me from any of them.

When I bade Mrs. Glenn goodbye I had told her that I had hopes of a post in the State Department at the close of my temporary mission, and she said, a little wistfully: "How wonderful if we could meet next year in America! As soon as Stephen is strong enough I want him to come back and live with me in his father's house." This seemed a natural wish; and it struck me that it might also be the means of effecting a break with the Browns. But Mrs. Glenn shook her head.

"Chrissy says a winter in New York would amuse them both tremendously."

I was not so sure that it would amuse Stephen, and therefore did not base much hope on the plan. The one thing Stephen wanted was to get back to Paris and paint: it would presumably be his mother's lot to settle down there when his health permitted.

I heard nothing more until I got back to Washington the following spring; then I had a line from Stephen. The winter in the Engadine had been a deadly bore, but had really done him good, and his mother was just leaving for Paris to look for an apartment. She meant to take one on a long lease, and have the furniture of the New York house sent out—it would be jolly getting it arranged. As for him, the doctors said he was well enough to go on with his painting, and, as I knew, it was the one thing he cared for; so I might cast off all anxiety about the family. That was all—and perhaps I should have obeyed if Mrs. Glenn had also written. But no word, no message even, came from her; and as she always wrote when there was good news to give, her silence troubled me.

It was in the course of the same summer, during a visit to Bar Harbour, that one evening, dining with a friend, I found myself next to a slight pale girl with large gray eyes, who suddenly turned them on me reproachfully. "Then you don't know me? I'm Thora."

I looked my perplexity, and she added: "Aren't you Steve Glenn's great friend? He's always talking of you." My memory struggled with a tangle of oddments, from which I finally extricated the phrase in the *Herald* about Miss Thora Dacy and the fancy-dress ball at St. Moritz. "You're the young lady who won the Boydon Brown prize in a costume designed by the well-known artist, Mr. Stephen Glenn!"

Her charming face fell. "If you know me only through that newspaper rubbish . . . I had an idea the well-known artist might have told you about me."

"He's not much of a correspondent."

"No; but I thought—"

"Why won't you tell me yourself instead?"

Dinner was over, and the company had moved out to a wide, starlit verandah looking seaward. I found a corner for two, and installed myself there with my new friend, who was also Stephen's. "I like him awfully—don't you?" she began at once. I liked her way of saying it; I liked her direct gaze; I found myself thinking: "But this may turn out to be the solution!" For I felt sure that, if circumstances ever gave her the right to take part in the coming struggle over Stephen, Thora Dacy would be on the side of the angels.

As if she had guessed my thought she continued: "And I do love Mrs. Glenn too—don't you?"

I assured her that I did, and she added: "And Steve loves her—I'm sure he does!"

"Well, if he didn't—!" I exclaimed indignantly.

"That's the way I feel; he ought to. Only, you see, Mrs. Brown—the Browns adopted him when he was a baby, didn't they, and brought him up as if he'd been their own child? I suppose they must know him better than any of us do; and Mrs. Brown says he can't help feeling bitter about—I don't know all the circumstances, but his mother did desert him soon after he was born, didn't she? And if it hadn't been for the Browns—"

"The Browns—the Browns! It's a pity they don't leave it to other people to proclaim their merits! And I don't believe Stephen does feel as they'd like you to think. If he does, he ought to be kicked. If—if complicated family reasons obliged Mrs. Glenn to separate herself from him when he was a baby, the way she mourned for him all those years, and her devotion since they've come together again, have atoned a thousandfold for that old unhappiness; and no one knows it better than Stephen."

The girl received this without protesting. "I'm so glad—so glad." There was a new vibration in her voice; she looked up gravely. "I've always *wanted* to love Mrs. Glenn the best."

"Well, you'd better; especially if you love Stephen."

"Oh, I do love him," she said simply. "But of course I understand his feeling as he does about the Browns."

I hesitated, not knowing how I ought to answer the question I detected under this; but at length I said: "Stephen, at any rate, must feel that Mrs. Brown has no business to insinuate anything against his mother. He ought to put a stop to that." She met the suggestion with a sigh, and stood up to join another group. "Thora Dacy may yet save us!" I thought, as my gaze followed her light figure across the room.

I had half a mind to write of that meeting to Stephen or to his mother; but the weeks passed while I procrastinated, and one day I received a note from Stephen. He wrote (with many messages from Mrs. Glenn) to give me their new address, and to tell me that he was hard at work at his painting, and doing a "promising portrait of mother Kit." He signed himself my affectionate Steve, and added underneath: "So glad you've come across little Thora. She took a most tremendous shine to you. Do please be nice to her; she's a dear child. But don't encourage any illusions about me, please; marrying's not in my programme." "So that's that," I thought, and tore the letter up rather impatiently. I wondered if Thora Dacy already knew that her illusions were not to be encouraged.

IX

The months went by, and I heard no more from my friends. Summer came round again, and with it the date of my six weeks' holiday, which I purposed to take that year in Europe. Two years had passed since I had last seen Mrs. Glenn, and during that time I had received only two or three brief notes from her, thanking me for Christmas wishes, or telling me that Stephen was certainly better, though he would take no care of himself. But several months had passed since the date of her last report.

I had meant to spend my vacation in a trip in south-western France, and on the way over I decided to invite Stephen Glenn to join me. I therefore made direct for Paris, and the next morning rang him up at Mrs. Glenn's. Mrs. Brown's voice met me in reply, informing me that Stephen was no longer living with his mother. "Read the riot act to us all a few months ago—said he wanted to be independent. You know his fads. Dear Catherine was foolishly upset. As I said to her . . . yes, I'll give you his address; but poor Steve's not well just now . . . Oh, go on a trip with you? No; I'm afraid there's no chance of that. The truth is, he told us he didn't want to be bothered—rather warned us off the premises; even poor old Boy; and you know he adores Boy. I haven't seen him myself for several days. But you can try . . . oh, of course, you can try . . . No; I'm afraid you can't see Catherine either—not just at present. She's been ill too— feverish; worrying about her naughty Steve, I suspect. I'm mounting guard for a few days, and not letting her see anybody till her temperature goes down. And would you do me a favour? Don't write—don't let her know you're here. Not for a day or two, I mean . . . She'd be so distressed at not being able to see you. . . ."

She rang off, and left me to draw my own conclusions.

They were not of the pleasantest. I was perplexed by the apparent sequestration of both my friends, still more so by the disquieting mystery of Mrs. Glenn's remaining with the Browns while Stephen had left them. Why had she not followed her son? Was it because she had not been allowed to? I conjectured that Mrs. Brown, knowing I was likely to put these questions to the persons concerned, was manoeuvring to prevent my seeing them. If she could manoeuvre, so could I; but for the moment I had to consider what line to take. The fact of her giving me Stephen's address made me suspect that she had taken measures to prevent my seeing him; and if that were so there was not much use in making the attempt. And Mrs. Glenn was in bed, and "feverish," and not to be told of my arrival. . . .

After a day's pondering I reflected that telegrams sometimes penetrate where letters fail to, and decided to telegraph to Stephen. No reply came, but the following afternoon, as I was leaving my hotel a taxi drove up and Mrs. Glenn descended from it. She was dressed in black, with many hanging scarves and veils, as if she either feared the air or the searching eye of some one who might be interested in her movements. But for her white hair and heavy stooping lines she might have suggested the furtive figure of a young woman stealing to her lover. But when I looked at her the analogy seemed a profanation.

To women of Catherine Glenn's ripe beauty thinness gives a sudden look of age; and the face she raised among her thrown-back veils was emaciated. Illness and anxiety had

scarred her as years and weather scar some beautiful still image on a church-front. She took my hand, and I led her into
the empty reading-room. "You've been ill!" I said.

"Not very; just a bad cold." It was characteristic that while
she looked at me with grave beseeching eyes her words were
trivial, ordinary. "Chrissy's so devoted—takes such care of
me. She was afraid to have me go out. The weather's so unsettled, isn't it? But really I'm all right; and as it cleared this
morning I just ran off for a minute to see you." The entreaty
in her eyes became a prayer. "Only don't tell her, will you?
Dear Steve's been ill too—did you know? And so I just
slipped out while Chrissy went to see him. She sees him nearly
every day, and brings me the news." She gave a sigh and
added, hardly above a whisper: "He sent me your address.
She doesn't know."

I listened with a sense of vague oppression. Why this mystery, this watching, these evasions? Was it because Steve was
not allowed to write to me that he had smuggled my address
to his mother? Mystery clung about us in damp fog-like coils,
like the scarves and veils about Mrs. Glenn's thin body. But I
knew that I must let my visitor tell her tale in her own way;
and, of course, when it was told, most of the mystery subsided, for she was in it, enveloped in it, blinded by it. I gathered, however, that Stephen had been very unhappy. He had
met at St. Moritz a girl whom he wanted to marry: Thora
Dacy—ah, I'd heard of her, I'd met her? Mrs. Glenn's face lit
up. She had thought the child lovely; she had known the family in Washington—excellent people; she had been so happy
in the prospect of Stephen's happiness. And then something
had happened . . . she didn't know, she had an idea that
Chrissy hadn't liked the girl. The reason Stephen gave was
that in his state of health he oughtn't to marry; but at the
time he'd been perfectly well—the doctors had assured his
mother that his lungs were sound, and that there was no like-
lihood of a relapse. She couldn't imagine why he should have
had such scruples; still less why Chrissy should have encouraged them. For Chrissy had also put it on the ground of
health; she had approved his decision. And since then he had
been unsettled, irritable, difficult—oh, very difficult. Two or
three months ago the state of tension in which they had all

been living had reached a climax; Mrs. Glenn couldn't say how or why—it was still obscure to her. But she suspected that Stephen had quarrelled with the Browns. They had patched it up now, they saw each other; but for a time there had certainly been something wrong. And suddenly Stephen had left the apartment, and moved into a wretched studio in a shabby quarter. The only reason he gave for leaving was that he had too many mothers—that was a joke, of course, Mrs. Glenn explained . . . but her eyes filled as she said it.

Poor mother—and, alas, poor Stephen! All the sympathy I could spare from the mother went to the son. He had behaved harshly, cruelly, no doubt; the young do; but under what provocation! I understood his saying that he had too many mothers; and I suspected that what he had tried for—and failed to achieve—was a break with the Browns. Trust Chrissy to baffle that attempt, I thought bitterly; she had obviously deflected the dispute, and made the consequences fall upon his mother. And at bottom everything was unchanged.

Unchanged—except for that thickening of the fog. At the moment it was almost as impenetrable to me as to Mrs. Glenn. Certain things I could understand that she could not; for instance, why Stephen had left home. I could guess that the atmosphere had become unbreathable. But if so, it was certainly Mrs. Brown's doing, and what interest had she in sowing discord between Stephen and his mother? With a shock of apprehension my mind reverted to Stephen's enquiry about his mother's will. It had offended me at the time; now it frightened me. If I was right in suspecting that he had tried to break with his adopted parents—over the question of the will, no doubt, or at any rate over their general selfishness and rapacity—then his attempt had failed, since he and the Browns were still on good terms, and the only result of the dispute had been to separate him from his mother. At the thought my indignation burned afresh. "I mean to see Stephen," I declared, looking resolutely at Mrs. Glenn.

"But he's not well enough, I'm afraid; he told me to send you his love, and to say that perhaps when you come back—"

"Ah, you've seen him, then?"

She shook her head. "No; he telegraphed me this morning. He doesn't even write any longer." Her eyes filled, and she looked away from me.

He too used the telegraph! It gave me more to think about than poor Mrs. Glenn could know. I continued to look at her. "Don't you want to send him a telegram in return? You could write it here, and give it to me," I suggested. She hesitated, seemed half to assent, and then stood up abruptly.

"No; I'd better not. Chrissy takes my messages. If I telegraphed she might wonder—she might be hurt—"

"Yes; I see."

"But I must be off; I've stayed too long." She cast a nervous glance at her watch. "When you come back . . ." she repeated.

When we reached the door of the hotel rain was falling, and I drew her back into the vestibule while the porter went to call a taxi. "Why haven't you your own motor?" I asked.

"Oh, Chrissy wanted the motor. She had to go to see Stevie—and of course she didn't know I should be going out. You won't tell her, will you?" Mrs. Glenn cried back to me as the door of the taxi closed on her.

The taxi drove off, and I was standing on the pavement looking after it when a handsomely appointed private motor glided up to the hotel. The chauffeur sprang down, and I recognized him as the man who had driven Mrs. Glenn when we had been together at Les Calanques. I was therefore not surprised to see Mrs. Brown, golden-haired and slim, descending under his unfurled umbrella. She held a note in her hand, and looked at me with a start of surprise. "What luck! I was going to try to find out when you were likely to be in—and here you are! Concierges are always so secretive that I'd written as well." She held the envelope up with her brilliant smile. "Am I butting in? Or may I come and have a talk?"

I led her to the reading-room which Mrs. Glenn had so lately left, and suggested the cup of tea which I had forgotten to offer to her predecessor.

She made a gay grimace. "Tea? Oh, no—thanks. Perhaps we might go round presently to the Nouveau Luxe grill for a cock-tail. But it's rather early yet; there's nobody there at this hour. And I want to talk to you about Stevie."

She settled herself in Mrs. Glenn's corner, and as she sat there, slender and alert in her perfectly-cut dark coat and skirt, with her silver fox slung at the exact fashion-plate angle, I felt the irony of these two women succeeding each other in the same seat to talk to me on the same subject. Mrs. Brown groped in her bag for a jade cigarette-case, and lifted her smiling eyes to mine. "Catherine's just been here, hasn't she? I passed her in a taxi at the corner," she remarked lightly.

"She's been here; yes. I scolded her for not being in her own motor," I rejoined, with an attempt at the same tone.

Mrs. Brown laughed. "I knew you would! But I'd taken the motor on purpose to prevent her going out. She has a very bad cold, as I told you; and the doctor has absolutely forbidden—"

"Then why didn't you let me go to see her?"

"Because the doctor forbids her to see visitors. I told you that too. Didn't you notice how hoarse she is?"

I felt my anger rising. "I noticed how unhappy she is," I said bluntly.

"Oh, unhappy—why is she unhappy? If I were in her place I should just lie back and enjoy life," said Mrs. Brown, with a sort of cold impatience.

"She's unhappy about Stephen."

Mrs. Brown looked at me quickly. "She came here to tell you so, I suppose? Well—he *has* behaved badly."

"Why did you let him?"

She laughed again, this time ironically. "Let him? Ah, you believe in that legend? The legend that I do what I like with Stephen." She bent her head to light another cigarette. "He's behaved just as badly to me, my good man—and to Boy. And *we* don't go about complaining!"

"Why should you, when you see him every day?"

At this she bridled, with a flitting smile. "Can I help it—if it's me he wants?"

"Yes, I believe you can," I said resolutely.

"Oh, thanks! I suppose I ought to take that as a compliment."

"Take it as you like. Why don't you make Stephen see his mother?"

"Dear Mr. Norcutt, if I had any influence over Stephen, do

you suppose I'd let him quarrel with his bread-and-butter? To put it on utilitarian grounds, why should I?" She lifted her clear shallow eyes and looked straight into mine—and I found no answer. There was something impenetrable to me beneath that shallowness.

"But why did Stephen leave his mother?" I persisted.

She shrugged, and looked down at her rings, among which I fancied I saw a new one, a dark luminous stone in claws of platinum. She caught my glance. "You're admiring my brown diamond? A beauty, isn't it? Dear Catherine gave it to me for Christmas. The angel! Do you suppose I wouldn't do anything to spare her all this misery? I wish I could tell you why Stephen left her. Perhaps . . . perhaps because she *is* such an angel . . . Young men—you understand? She was always wrapping him up, lying awake to listen for his latch-key. . . . Steve's rather a Bohemian; suddenly he struck—that's all I know."

I saw at once that this contained a shred of truth wrapped round an impenetrable lie; and I saw also that to tell that lie had not been Mrs. Brown's main object. She had come for a still deeper reason, and I could only wait for her to reveal it.

She glanced up reproachfully. "How hard you are on me— always! From the very first day—don't I know? And never more than now. Don't you suppose I can guess what you're thinking? You're accusing me of trying to prevent your seeing Catherine; and in reality I came here to ask you to see her— to beg you to—as soon as she's well enough. If you'd only trusted me, instead of persuading her to slip off on the sly and come here in this awful weather . . ."

It was on the tip of my tongue to declare that I was guilt-less of such perfidy; but it occurred to me that my visitor might be trying to find out how Mrs. Glenn had known I was in Paris, and I decided to say nothing.

"At any rate, if she's no worse I'm sure she could see you tomorrow. Why not come and dine? I'll carry Boy off to a restaurant, and you and she can have a cosy evening to-gether, like old times. You'd like that, wouldn't you?" Mrs. Brown's face was veiled with a retrospective emotion; I saw that, less acute than Stephen, she still believed in a senti-mental past between myself and Catherine Glenn. "She must

have been one of the loveliest creatures that ever lived—
wasn't she? Even now no one can come up to her. You don't
know how I wish she liked me better; that she had more
confidence in me. If she had, she'd know that I love Stephen
as much as she does—perhaps more. For so many years he
was mine, all mine! But it's all so difficult—at this moment,
for instance . . ." She paused, jerked her silver fox back into
place, and gave me a prolonged view of meditative lashes. At
last she said: "Perhaps you don't know that Steve's final folly
has been to refuse his allowance. He returned the last cheque
to Catherine with a dreadful letter."

"Dreadful? How?"

"Telling her he was old enough to shift for himself—
that he refused to sell his independence any longer; perfect
madness."

"Atrocious cruelty—"

"Yes; that too. I told him so. But do you realise the result?"
The lashes, suddenly lifted, gave me the full appeal of wide,
transparent eyes. "Steve's starving—voluntarily starving himself. Or would be, if Boy and I hadn't scraped together our
last pennies . . ."

"If independence is what he wants, why should he take
your pennies when he won't take his mother's?"

"Ah—there's the point. He will." She looked down again,
fretting her rings. "Ill as he is, how could he live if he didn't
take somebody's pennies? If I could sell my brown diamond
without Catherine's missing it I'd have done it long ago, and
you need never have known of all this. But she's so sensitive—and she notices everything. She literally spies on me.
I'm at my wits' end. If you'd only help me!"

"How in the world can I?"

"You're the only person who can. If you'd persuade her, as
long as this queer mood of Stephen's lasts, to draw his
monthly cheque in my name, I'd see that he gets it—and that
he uses it. He would, you know, if he thought it came from
Boy and me."

I looked at her quickly. "That's why you want me to see
her. To get her to give you her son's allowance?"

Her lips parted as if she were about to return an irritated
answer; but she twisted them into a smile. "If you like to de-

scribe it in that way—I can't help your putting an unkind interpretation on whatever I do. I was prepared for that when I came here." She turned her bright inclement face on me. "If you think I enjoy humiliating myself! After all, it's not so much for Stephen that I ask it as for his mother. Have you thought of that? If she knew that in his crazy pride he was depriving himself of the most necessary things, wouldn't she do anything on earth to prevent it? She's his *real* mother . . . I'm nothing . . ."

"You're everything, if he sees you and listens to you."

She received this with the air of secret triumph that met every allusion to her power over Stephen. Was she right, I wondered, in saying that she loved him even more than his mother did? "Everything?" she murmured deprecatingly. "It's you who are everything, who can help us all. What can I do?"

I pondered a moment, and then said: "You can let me see Stephen."

The colour rushed up under her powder. "Much good that would do—if I could! But I'm afraid you'll find his door barricaded."

"That's a pity," I said coldly.

"It's very foolish of him," she assented.

Our conversation had reached a deadlock, and I saw that she was distinctly disappointed—perhaps even more than I was. I suspected that while I could afford to wait for a solution she could not.

"Of course, if Catherine is willing to sit by and see the boy starve"—she began.

"What else can she do? Shall we go over to the Nouveau Luxe bar and study the problem from the cock-tail angle?" I suggested.

Mrs. Brown's delicately pencilled brows gathered over her transparent eyes. "You're laughing at me—and at Steve. It's rather heartless of you, you know," she said, making a movement to rise from the deep armchair in which I had installed her. Her movements, as always, were quick and smooth; she got up and sat down with the ease of youth. But her face startled me—it had suddenly shrunk and withered, so that the glitter of cosmetics hung before it like a veil. A pang of compunction shot through me. I felt that it *was* heartless to make her look like that. I could no longer endure the part I was playing. "I'll—I'll see what I can do to arrange things," I stammered. "If only she's not too servile," I thought, feeling that my next move hung on the way in which she received my reassurance.

She stood up with a quick smile. "Ogre!" she just breathed, her lashes dancing. She was laughing at me under her breath—the one thing she could have done just then without offending me. "Come; we *do* need refreshment, don't we?" She slipped her arm through mine as we crossed the lounge and emerged on the wet pavement.

X

The cosy evening with which Mrs. Brown had tempted me was not productive of much enlightenment. I found Catherine Glenn tired and pale, but happy at my coming, with a sort of furtive school-girl happiness which suggested the same secret apprehension as I had seen in Mrs. Brown's face when she found I would not help her to capture Stephen's allowance. I had already perceived my mistake in letting Mrs. Brown see this, and during our cock-tail epilogue at the Nouveau Luxe had tried to restore her confidence; but her distrust had been aroused, and in spite of her recovered good-humour I felt that I should not be allowed to see Stephen.

In this respect poor Mrs. Glenn could not help me. She could only repeat the lesson which had evidently been drilled into her. "Why should I deny what's so evident—and so natural? When Stevie's ill and unhappy it's not to me he turns. During so many years he knew nothing of me, never even suspected my existence; and all the while *they* were there, watching over him, loving him, slaving for him. If he concealed his real feelings now it might be only on account of the—the financial inducements; and I like to think my boy's too proud for that. If you see him, you'll tell him so, won't you? You'll tell him that, unhappy as he's making me, mistaken as he is, I enter into his feelings as—as only his mother can." She broke down, and hid her face from me.

When she regained her composure she rose and went over

to the writing-table. From the blotting-book she drew an envelope. "I've drawn this cheque in your name—it may be
easier for you to get Stevie to accept a few bank-notes than a
cheque. You must try to persuade him—tell him his behaviour is making the Browns just as unhappy as it is me, and
that he has no right to be cruel to them, at any rate." She
lifted her head and looked into my eyes heroically.

I went home perplexed, and pondering on my next move;
but (not wholly to my surprise) the question was settled for
me the following morning by a telephone call from Mrs.
Brown. Her voice rang out cheerfully.

"Good news! I've had a talk with Steve's doctor—on the
sly, of course. Steve would kill me if he knew! The doctor says
he's really better; you can see him today if you'll promise to
stay only a few minutes. Of course I must first persuade Steve
himself, the silly boy. You can't think what a savage mood
he's in. But I'm sure I can bring him round—he's so fond of
you. Only before that I want to see you myself—" ("Of
course," I commented inwardly, feeling that here at last was
the gist of the communication.) "Can I come presently—before you go out? All right; I'll turn up in an hour."

Within the hour she was at my hotel; but before her arrival
I had decided on my course, and she on her side had probably guessed what it would be. Our first phrases, however,
were non-committal. As we exchanged them I saw that Mrs.
Brown's self-confidence was weakening, and this incited me
to prolong the exchange. Stephen's doctor, she assured me,
was most encouraging; one lung only was affected, and that
slightly; his recovery now depended on careful nursing, good
food, cheerful company—all the things of which, in his foolish obstinacy, he had chosen to deprive himself. She paused,
expectant—

"And if Mrs. Glenn handed over his allowance to you, you
could ensure his accepting what he's too obstinate to take
from his mother?"

Under her carefully prepared complexion the blood rushed
to her temples. "I always knew you were Steve's best friend!"
She looked away quickly, as if to hide the triumph in her eyes.

"Well, if I am, he's first got to recognise it by seeing me."

"Of course—of course!" She corrected her impetuosity. "I'll do all I can . . ."

"That's a great deal, as we know." Under their lowered lashes her eyes followed my movements as I turned my coat back to reach an inner pocket. She pressed her lips tight to control their twitching. "There, then!" I said.

"Oh, you angel, you! I should never have dared to ask Catherine," she stammered with a faint laugh as the banknotes passed from my hand to her bag.

"Mrs. Glenn understood—she always understands."

"She understands when *you* ask," Mrs. Brown insinuated, flashing her lifted gaze on mine. The sense of what was in the bag had already given her a draught of courage, and she added quickly: "Of course I needn't warn you not to speak of all this to Steve. If he knew of our talk it would wreck everything."

"I can see that," I remarked, and she dropped her lids again, as though I had caught her in a blunder.

"Well, I must go; I'll tell him his best friend's coming . . . I'll reason with him . . ." she murmured, trying to disguise her embarrassment in emotion. I saw her to the door, and into Mrs. Glenn's motor, from the interior of which she called back: "You know you're going to make Catherine as happy as I am."

Stephen Glenn's new habitation was in a narrow and unsavoury street, and the building itself contrasted mournfully with the quarters in which he had last received me. As I climbed the greasy stairs I felt as much perplexed as ever. I could not yet see why Stephen's quarrel with Mrs. Glenn should, even partially, have included the Browns, nor, if it had, why he should be willing to accept from their depleted purse the funds he was too proud to receive from his mother. It gave me a feeling of uneasy excitement to know that behind the door at which I stood the answer to these problems awaited me.

No one answered my knock, so I opened the door and went in. The studio was empty, but from the room beyond Stephen's voice called out irritably: "Who is it?" and then, in answer to my name: "Oh, Norcutt—come in."

Stephen Glenn lay in bed, in a small room with a window opening on a dimly-lit inner courtyard. The room was bare and untidy, the bed-clothes were tumbled, and he looked at me with the sick man's instinctive resentfulness at any intrusion on his lonely pain. "Above all," the look seemed to say, "don't try to be kind."

Seeing that moral pillow-smoothing would be resented I sat down beside him without any comment on the dismalness of the scene, or on his own aspect, much as it disquieted me.

"Well, old man—" I began, wondering how to go on; but he cut short my hesitation. "I've been wanting to see you for ever so long," he said.

In my surprise I had nearly replied: "That's not what I'd been told"—but, resolved to go warily, I rejoined with a sham gaiety: "Well, here I am!"

Stephen gave me the remote look which the sick turn on those arch-aliens, the healthy. "Only," he pursued, "I was afraid if you did come you'd begin and lecture me; and I couldn't stand that—I can't stand anything. I'm *raw*!" he burst out.

"You might have known me better than to think I'd lecture you."

"Oh, I don't know. Naturally the one person you care about in all this is—mother Kit."

"Your mother," I interposed.

He raised his eyebrows with the familiar ironic movement; then they drew together again over his sunken eyes. "I wanted to wait till I was up to discussing things. I wanted to get this fever out of me."

"You don't look feverish now."

"No; they've brought it down. But I'm down with it. I'm very low," he said, with a sort of chill impartiality, as though speaking of some one whose disabilities did not greatly move him. I replied that the best way for him to pull himself up again was to get out of his present quarters, and let himself be nursed and looked after.

"Oh, don't argue!" he interrupted.

"Argue—?"

"You're going to tell me to go back to—to my mother. To

let her fatten me up. Well, it's no use. I won't take another dollar from her—not one."

I met this in silence, and after a moment perceived that my silence irritated him more than any attempt at argument. I did not want to irritate him, and I began: "Then why don't you go off again with the Browns? There's nothing you can do that your mother won't understand—"

"And suffer from!" he interjected.

"Oh, as to suffering—she's seasoned."

He bent his slow feverish stare on me. "So am I."

"Well, at any rate, you can spare her by going off at once into good air, and trying your level best to get well. You know as well as I do that nothing else matters to her. She'll be glad to have you go away with the Browns—I'll answer for that."

He gave a short laugh, so harsh and disenchanted that I suddenly felt he was right: to laugh like that he must be suffering as much as his mother. I laid my hand on his thin wrist. "Old man—"

He jerked away. "No, no. Go away with the Browns? I'd rather be dead. I'd rather hang on here till I *am* dead."

The outburst was so unexpected that I sat in silent perplexity. Mrs. Brown had told the truth, then, when she said he hated them too? Yet he saw them, he accepted their money . . . The darkness deepened as I peered into it.

Stephen lay with half-closed lids, and I saw that whatever enlightenment he had to give would have to be forced from him. The perception made me take a sudden resolve.

"When one is physically down and out one *is* raw, as you say: one hates everybody. I know you don't really feel like that about the Browns; but if they've got on your nerves, and you want to go off by yourself, you might at least accept the money they're ready to give you—"

He raised himself on his elbow with an ironical stare. "Money? They borrow money; they don't give it."

"Ah—" I thought; but aloud I continued: "They're prepared to give it now. Mrs. Brown tells me—"

He lifted his hand with a gesture that cut me short; then he leaned back, and drew a painful breath or two. Beads of moisture came out on his forehead. "If she told you that, it means she's got more out of Kit. Or out of Kit through *you*—is that it?" he brought out roughly.

His clairvoyance frightened me almost as much as his physical distress—and the one seemed, somehow, a function of the other, as though the wearing down of his flesh had made other people's diaphanous to him, and he could see through it to their hearts. "Stephen—" I began imploringly.

Again his lifted hand checked me. "No, wait." He breathed hard again and shut his eyes. Then he opened them and looked into mine. "There's only one way out of this."

"For you to be reasonable."

"Call it that if you like. I've got to see mother Kit—and without their knowing it."

My perplexity grew, and my agitation with it. Could it be that the end of the Browns was in sight? I tried to remember that my first business was to avoid communicating my agitation to Stephen. In a tone that I did my best to keep steady I said: "Nothing could make your mother happier. You're all she lives for."

"She'll have to find something else soon."

"No, no. Only let her come, and she'll make you well. Mothers work miracles—"

His inscrutable gaze rested on mine. "So they say. Only, you see, she's not my mother."

He spoke so quietly, in such a low detached tone, that at first the words carried no meaning to me. If he had been excited I should have suspected fever, delirium; but voice and eyes were clear. "Now you understand," he added.

I sat beside him stupidly, speechless, unable to think. "I don't understand anything," I stammered. Such a possibility as his words suggested had never once occurred to me. Yet he wasn't delirious, he wasn't raving—it was I whose brain was reeling as if in fever.

"Well, I'm not the long-lost child. The Browns are not *her* Browns. It's all a lie and an imposture. We faked it up between us, Chrissy and I did—her simplicity made it so cursedly easy for us. Boy didn't have much to do with it; poor old Boy! He just sat back and took his share . . . *Now* you do see," he repeated, in the cool explanatory tone in which he might have set forth some one else's shortcomings.

My mind was still a blur while he poured out, in broken sentences, the details of the conspiracy—the sordid tale of a trio of society adventurers come to the end of their resources, and suddenly clutching at this unheard-of chance of rescue, affluence, peace. But gradually, as I listened, the glare of horror with which he was blinding me turned into a strangely clear and penetrating light, forcing its way into obscure crannies, elucidating the incomprehensible, picking out one by one the links that bound together his fragments of fact. I saw—but what I saw my gaze shrank from.

"Well," I heard him say, between his difficult breaths, "now do you begin to believe me?"

"I don't know. I can't tell. Why on earth," I broke out, suddenly relieved at the idea, "should you want to see your mother if this isn't all a ghastly invention?"

"To tell her what I've just told you—make a clean breast of it. Can't you see?"

"If that's the reason, I see you want to kill her—that's all."

He grew paler under his paleness. "Norcutt, I can't go on like this; I've got to tell her. I want to do it at once. I thought I could keep up the lie a little longer—let things go on drifting—but I can't. I held out because I wanted to get well first, and paint her picture—leave her that to be proud of, anyhow! Now that's all over, and there's nothing left but the naked shame . . ." He opened his eyes and fixed them again on mine. "I want you to bring her here today—without *their* knowing it. You've got to manage it somehow. It'll be the first decent thing I've done in years."

"It will be the most unpardonable," I interrupted angrily. "The time's past for trying to square your own conscience. What you've got to do now is to go on lying to her—you've got to get well, if only to go on lying to her!"

A thin smile flickered over his face. "I can't get well."

"That's as it may be. You can spare her, anyhow."

"By letting things go on like this?" He lay for a long time silent; then his lips drew up in a queer grimace. "It'll be horrible enough to be a sort of expiation—"

"It's the only one."

"It's the worst."

He sank back wearily. I saw that fatigue had silenced him,

and wondered if I ought to steal away. My presence could not but be agitating; yet in his present state it seemed almost as dangerous to leave him as to stay. I saw a flask of brandy on the table, a glass beside it. I poured out some brandy and held it to his lips. He emptied the glass slowly, and as his head fell back I heard him say: "Before I knew her I thought I could pull it off . . . But, you see, her sweetness . . ."

"If she heard you say that it would make up for everything."

"Even for what I've just told you?"

"Even for that. For God's sake hold your tongue, and just let her come here and nurse you."

He made no answer, but under his lids I saw a tear or two.

"Let her come—let her come," I pleaded, taking his dying hand in mine.

XI

Nature does not seem to care for dramatic climaxes. Instead of allowing Stephen to die at once, his secret on his lips, she laid on him the harsher task of living on through weary weeks, and keeping back the truth till the end.

As the result of my visit, he consented, the next day, to be carried back in an ambulance to Mrs. Glenn's; and when I saw their meeting it seemed to me that ties of blood were frail compared to what drew those two together. After she had fallen on her knees at his bedside, and drawn his head to her breast, I was almost sure he would not speak; and he did not.

I was able to stay with Mrs. Glenn till Stephen died; then I had to hurry back to my post in Washington. When I took leave of her she told me that she was following on the next steamer with Stephen's body. She wished her son to have a New York funeral, a funeral like his father's, at which all their old friends could be present. "Not like poor Phil's, you know—" and I recalled the importance she had attached to the presence of her husband's friends at his funeral. "It's something to remember afterwards," she said, with dry eyes. "And it will be their only way of knowing my Stephen . . ." It was of course impossible to exclude Mr. and Mrs. Brown

from these melancholy rites; and accordingly they sailed with
her.

If Stephen had recovered she had meant, as I knew, to re-
open her New York house; but now that was not to be
thought of. She sold the house, and all it contained, and a few
weeks later sailed once more for Paris—again with the
Browns.

I had resolved, after Stephen's death—when the first shock
was over—to do what I could toward relieving her of the
Browns' presence. Though I could not tell her the truth
about them, I might perhaps help her to effect some transaction which would relieve her of their company. But I soon
saw that this was out of the question; and the reason deepened my perplexity. It was simply that the Browns—or at least
Mrs. Brown—had become Mrs. Glenn's chief consolation in
her sorrow. The two women, so incessantly at odds while
Stephen lived, were now joined in a common desolation. It
seemed like profaning Catherine Glenn's grief to compare
Mrs. Brown's to it; yet, in the first weeks after Stephen's
death, I had to admit that Mrs. Brown mourned him as genuinely, as inconsolably, as his supposed mother. Indeed, it
would be nearer the truth to say that Mrs. Brown's grief was
more hopeless and rebellious than the other's. After all, as
Mrs. Glenn said, it was much worse for Chrissy. "She had so
little compared to me; and she gave as much, I suppose.
Think what I had that she's never known; those precious
months of waiting for him, when he was part of me, when we
were one body and one soul. And then, years afterward, when
I was searching for him, and knowing all the while I should
find him; and after that, our perfect life together—our perfect
understanding. All that—there's all that left to me! And what
did she have? Why, when she shows me his little socks and
shoes (she's kept them all so carefully) they're *my* baby's socks
and shoes, not hers—and I know she's thinking of it when we
cry over them. I see now that I've been unjust to her . . . and
cruel . . . For he *did* love me best; and that ought to have
made me kinder—"

Yes; I had to recognise that Mrs. Brown's grief was as genuine as her rival's, that she suffered more bleakly and bitterly.
Every turn of the strange story had been improbable and in-

calculable, and this new freak of fate was the most unexpected. But since it brought a softening to my poor friend's affliction, and offered a new pretext for her self-devotion, I could only hold my tongue and be thankful that the Browns were at last serving some humaner purpose.

The next time I returned to Paris the strange trio were still together, and still living in Mrs. Glenn's apartment. Its walls were now hung with Stephen's paintings and sketches—among them many unfinished attempts at a portrait of Mrs. Glenn—and the one mother seemed as eager as the other to tell me that a well-known collector of modern art had been so struck by their quality that there was already some talk of a posthumous exhibition. Mrs. Brown triumphed peculiarly in the affair. It was she who had brought the collector to see the pictures, she who had always known that Stephen had genius; it was with the Browns' meagre pennies that he had been able to carry on his studies at Julian's, long before Mrs. Glenn had appeared. "Catherine doesn't pretend to know much about art. Do you, my dear? But, as I tell her, when you're a picture yourself you don't have to bother about other people's pictures. There—your hat's crooked again! Just let me straighten it, darling—" I saw Mrs. Glenn wince a little, as she had winced the day at Les Calanques when Mrs. Brown, with an arch side-glance at me, had given a more artful twist to her friend's white hair.

It was evident that time, in drying up the source which had nourished the two women's sympathy, had revived their fundamental antagonism. It was equally clear, however, that Mrs. Brown was making every effort to keep on good terms with Mrs. Glenn. That substantial benefits thereby accrued to her I had no doubt; but at least she kept up in Catherine's mind the illusion of the tie between them.

Mrs. Brown had certainly sorrowed for Stephen as profoundly as a woman of her kind could sorrow; more profoundly, indeed, than I had thought possible. Even now, when she spoke of him, her metallic voice broke, her metallic mask softened. On the rare occasions when I found myself alone with her (and I had an idea she saw to it that they were rare), she spoke so tenderly of Stephen, so affectionately of Mrs. Glenn, that I could only suppose she knew nothing of

my last talk with the poor fellow. If she had, she would almost
certainly have tried to ensure my silence; unless, as I sometimes imagined, a supreme art led her to feign unawareness.
But, as always when I speculated on Mrs. Brown, I ended up
against a blank wall.

The exhibition of Stephen's pictures took place, and caused
(I learned from Mrs. Glenn) a little flutter in the inner circle
of connoisseurs. Mrs. Glenn deluged me with newspaper
rhapsodies which she doubtless never imagined had been
bought. But presently, as a result of the show, a new difference arose between the two women. The pictures had been
sufficiently remarked for several purchasers to present themselves, and their offers were so handsome that Mrs. Brown
thought they should be accepted. After all, Stephen would
have regarded the sale of the pictures as the best proof of his
success; if they remained hidden away at Mrs. Glenn's, she,
who had the custody of his name, was obviously dooming it
to obscurity. Nevertheless she persisted in refusing. If selling
her darling's pictures was the price of glory, then she must
cherish his genius in secret. Could any one imagine that she
would ever part with a single stroke of his brush? She was his
mother; no one else had a voice in the matter. I divined that
the struggle between herself and Mrs. Brown had been not
only sharp but prolonged, and marked by a painful interchange of taunts. "If it hadn't been for me," Mrs. Brown argued, "the pictures would never have existed"; and "If it
hadn't been for me," the other retorted, "my Stephen would
never have existed." It ended—as I had foreseen—in the
adoptive parents accepting from Mrs. Glenn a sum equivalent
to the value at which they estimated the pictures. The quarrel
quieted down, and a few months later Mrs. Glenn was re-
morsefully accusing herself of having been too hard on
Chrissy.

So the months passed. With their passage news came to me
more rarely; but I gathered from Mrs. Glenn's infrequent
letters that she had been ill, and from her almost illegible
writing that her poor hands were stiffening with rheumatism.
Finally, a year later, a letter announced that the doctors had
warned her against spending her winters in the damp climate
of Paris, and that the apartment had been disposed of, and its

contents (including, of course, Stephen's pictures) transported to a villa at Nice. The Browns had found the villa and
managed the translation—with their usual kindness. After that
there was a long silence.

It was not until over two years later that I returned to
Europe; and as my short holiday was taken in winter, and I
meant to spend it in Italy, I took steamer directly to
Villefranche. I had not announced my visit to Mrs. Glenn. I
was not sure till the last moment of being able to get off; but
that was not the chief cause of my silence. Though relations
between the incongruous trio seemed to have become harmonious, it was not without apprehension that I had seen
Mrs. Glenn leave New York with the Browns. She was old,
she was tired and stricken; how long would it be before she
became a burden to her beneficiaries? This was what I
wanted to find out without giving them time to prepare
themselves or their companion for my visit. Mrs. Glenn had
written that she wished very particularly to see me, and had
begged me to let her know if there were a chance of my
coming abroad; but though this increased my anxiety it
strengthened my resolve to arrive unannounced, and I merely
replied that she could count on seeing me as soon as I was
able to get away.

Though some months had since gone by I was fairly sure of
finding her still at Nice, for in the newspapers I had bought
on landing I had lit on several allusions to Mr. and Mrs.
Boydon Brown. Apparently the couple had an active press-
agent, for an attentive world was daily supplied with a minute
description of Mrs. "Boy" Brown's casino toilets, the value of
the golf or pigeon-shooting cups offered by Mr. "Boy"
Brown to various fashionable sporting clubs, and the names
of the titled guests whom they entertained at the local
"Lidos" and "Jardins Fleuris." I wondered how much the
chronicling of these events was costing Mrs. Glenn, but reminded myself that it was part of the price she had to pay for
the hours of communion over Stephen's little socks. At any
rate it proved that my old friend was still in the neighbourhood; and the next day I set out to find her.

I waited till the afternoon, on the chance of her being alone
at the hour when mundane affairs were most likely to engage

the Browns; but when my taxi-driver had brought me to the address I had given him I found a locked garden-gate and a shuttered house. The sudden fear of some new calamity seized me. My first thought was that Mrs. Glenn must have died; yet if her death had occurred before my sailing I could hardly have failed to hear of it, and if it was more recent I must have seen it announced in the papers I had read since landing. Besides, if the Browns had so lately lost their bene-factress they would hardly have played such a part in the so-cial chronicles I had been studying. There was no particular reason why a change of address should portend tragedy; and when at length a reluctant portress appeared in answer to my ringing she said, yes, if it was the Americans I was after, I was right: they had moved away a week ago. Moved—and where to? She shrugged and declared she didn't know; but probably not far, she thought, with the old white-haired lady so ill and helpless.

"Ill and helpless—then why did they move?"

She shrugged again. "When people don't pay their rent, they have to move, don't they? When they don't even settle with the butcher and baker before they go, or with the laun-dress who was fool enough to do their washing—and it's I who speak to you, Monsieur!"

This was worse than I had imagined. I produced a bank-note, and in return the victimized concierge admitted that she had secured the fugitives' new address—though they were naturally not anxious to have it known. As I had surmised, they had taken refuge within the kindly bounds of the princi-pality of Monaco; and the taxi carried me to a small shabby hotel in one of the steep streets above the Casino. I could imagine nothing less in harmony with Catherine Glenn or her condition than to be ill and unhappy in such a place. My only consolation was that now perhaps there might be an end to the disastrous adventure. "After all," I thought, as I looked up at the cheerless front of the hotel, "if the catastrophe has come the Browns can't have any reason for hanging on to her."

A red-faced lady with a false front and false teeth emerged from the back-office to receive me.

Madame Glenn—Madame Brown? Oh, yes; they were staying at the hotel—they were both upstairs now, she believed. Perhaps Monsieur was the gentleman that Madame Brown was expecting? She had left word that if he came he was to go up without being announced.

I was inspired to say that I was that gentleman; at which the landlady rejoined that she was sorry the lift was out of order, but that I would find the ladies at number 5 on the third floor. Before she had finished I was half way up.

A few steps down an unventilated corridor brought me to number 5; but I did not have to knock, for the door was ajar—perhaps in expectation of the other gentleman. I pushed it open, and entered a small plushy sitting-room, with faded mimosa in ornate vases, newspapers and cigarette-ends scattered on the dirty carpet, and a bronzed-over plaster Bayadère posturing before the mantelpiece mirror. If my first glance took such sharp note of these details it is because they seemed almost as much out of keeping with Catherine Glenn as the table laden with gin and bitters, empty cock-tail glasses and disks of sodden lemon.

It was not the first time it had occurred to me that I was partly responsible for Mrs. Glenn's unhappy situation. The growing sense of that responsibility had been one of my reasons for trying to keep an eye on her, for wanting her to feel that in case of need she could count on me. But on the whole my conscience had not been oppressed. The impulse which had made me exact from Stephen the promise never to undeceive her had necessarily governed my own conduct. I had only to recall Catherine Glenn as I had first known her to feel sure that, after all, her life had been richer and deeper than if she had spent it, childless and purposeless, in the solemn upholstery of her New York house. I had had nothing to do with her starting on her strange quest; but I was certain that in what had followed she had so far found more happiness than sorrow.

But now? As I stood in that wretched tawdry room I wondered if I had not laid too heavy a burden on my conscience in keeping the truth from her. Suddenly I said to myself: "The time has come—whatever happens I must get her away from these people." But then I remembered how Stephen's death had drawn the two ill-assorted women together, and wondered if to destroy that tie would not now be the crowning cruelty.

I was still uneasily deliberating when I heard a voice behind the door opposite the one by which I had entered. The room beyond must have been darkened, for I had not noticed before that this door was also partly open. "Well, have you had your nap?" a woman's voice said irritably. "Is there anything you want before I go out? I told you that the man who's going to arrange for the loan is coming for me. He'll be here in a minute." The voice was Mrs. Brown's, but so sharpened and altered that at first I had not known it. "This is how she speaks when she thinks there's no one listening," I thought.

I caught an indistinct murmur in reply; then the rattle of drawn-back curtain-rings; then Mrs. Brown continuing: "Well, you may as well sign the letter now. Here it is—you've only got to write your name . . . Your glasses? I don't know where your glasses are—you're always dropping your things about. I'm sorry I can't keep a maid to wait on you—but there's nothing in this letter you need be afraid of. I've told you before that it's only a formality. Boy's told you so too, hasn't he? I don't suppose you mean to suggest that we're trying to do you out of your money, do you? We've got to have enough to keep going. Here, let me hold your hand while you sign. My hand's shaky too . . . it's all this beastly worry . . . Don't you imagine you're the only person who's had a bad time of it . . . Why, what's the matter? Why are you pushing me away—?"

Till now I had stood motionless, unabashed by the fact that I was eaves-dropping. I was ready enough to stoop to that if there was no other way of getting at the truth. But at the question: "Why are you pushing me away?" I knocked hurriedly at the door of the inner room.

There was a silence after my knock. "There he is! You'll have to sign now," I heard Mrs. Brown exclaim; and I opened the door and went in. The room was a bedroom; like the other, it was untidy and shabby. I noticed a stack of canvases, framed and unframed, piled up against the wall. In an armchair near the window Mrs. Glenn was seated. She was wrapped in some sort of dark dressing-gown, and a lace cap covered her white hair. The face that looked out from it had still the same carven beauty; but its texture had dwindled from marble to worn ivory. Her body too had shrunk, so that, low in her chair, under her loose garments, she seemed to have turned into a little broken doll. Mrs. Brown, on the contrary, perhaps by contrast, appeared large and almost towering. At first glance I was more startled by the change in her appearance than in Mrs. Glenn's. The latter had merely followed, more quickly than I had hoped she would, the natural decline of the years; whereas Mrs. Brown seemed like another woman. It was not only that she had grown stout and heavy, or that her complexion had coarsened so noticeably under the skilful make-up. In spite of her good clothes and studied coiffure there was something haphazard and untidy in her appearance. Her hat, I noticed, had slipped a little side-ways on her smartly waved head, her bright shallow eyes looked blurred and red, and she held herself with a sort of vacillating erectness. Gradually the incredible fact was borne in on me; Mrs. Brown had been drinking.

"Why, where on earth—?" she broke out, bewildered, as my identity dawned on her. She put up a hand to straighten her hat, and in doing so dragged it over too far on the other side.

"I beg your pardon. I was told to come to number 5, and as there was no one in the sitting-room I knocked on this door."

"Oh, you knocked? I didn't hear you knock," said Mrs. Brown suspiciously; but I had no ears for her, for my old friend had also recognised me, and was holding out her trembling hands. "I knew you'd come—I said you'd come!" she cried out to me.

Mrs. Brown laughed. "Well, you've said he would often enough. But it's taken some time for it to come true."

"I knew you'd come," Mrs. Glenn repeated, and I felt her hand pass tremblingly over my hair as I stooped to kiss her.

"Lovers' meeting!" Mrs. Brown tossed at us with an unsteady gaiety; then she leaned against the door, and stood looking on ironically. "You didn't expect to find us in this palatial abode, did you?"

"No. I went to the villa first."

Mrs. Glenn's eyes dwelt on me softly. I sat down beside

her, and she put her hand in mine. Her withered fingers trembled incessantly.

"Perhaps," Mrs. Brown went on, "if you'd come sooner you might have arranged things so that we could have stayed there. I'm powerless—I can't do anything with her. The fact that for years I looked after the child she deserted weighs nothing with her. She doesn't seem to think she owes us anything."

Mrs. Glenn listened in silence, without looking at her accuser. She kept her large sunken eyes fixed on mine. "There's no money left," she said when the other ended.

"No money! No money! That's always the tune nowadays. There was always plenty of money for her precious—money for all his whims and fancies, for journeys, for motors, for doctors, for—well, what's the use of going on? But now that there's nobody left but Boy and me, who slaved for her darling for years, who spent our last penny on him when his mother'd forgotten his existence—now there's nothing left! Now she can't afford anything; now she won't even pay her own bills; now she'd sooner starve herself to death than let us have what she owes us . . ."

"My dear—my dear," Mrs. Glenn murmured, her eyes still on mine.

"Oh, don't 'my dear' me," Mrs. Brown retorted passionately. "What you mean is: 'How can you talk like that before him?' I suppose you think I wish he hadn't come. Well, you never were more mistaken. I'm glad he's here; I'm glad he's found out where you're living, and how you're living. Only this time I mean him to hear our side of the story instead of only yours."

Mrs. Glenn pressed my hand in her twitching fingers. "She wants me to sign a paper. I don't understand."

"You don't understand? Didn't Boy explain it to you? You said you understood then." Mrs. Brown turned to me with a shrug. "These whims and capers . . . all I want is money enough to pay the bills . . . so that we're not turned out of this hole too . . ."

"There is no money," Mrs. Glenn softly reiterated.

My heart stood still. The scene must at all costs be ended, yet I could think of no way of silencing the angry woman. At length I said: "If you'll leave me for a little while with Mrs. Glenn perhaps she'll be able to tell me—"

"How's she to tell you what she says she doesn't understand herself? If I leave her with you all she'll tell you is lies about us—I found that out long ago." Mrs. Brown took a few steps in my direction, and then, catching at the window-curtain, looked at me with a foolish laugh. "Not that I'm pining for her society. I have a good deal of it in the long run. But you'll excuse me for saying that, as far as this matter is concerned, it's entirely between Mrs. Glenn and me."

I tightened my hold on Mrs. Glenn's hand, and sat looking at Mrs. Brown in the hope that a silent exchange of glances might lead farther than the vain bandying of arguments. For a moment she seemed dominated; I began to think she had read in my eyes the warning I had tried to put there. If there was any money left I might be able to get it from Catherine after her own attempts had failed; that was what I was trying to remind her of, and what she understood my looks were saying. Once before I had done the trick; supposing she were to trust me to try again? I saw that she wavered; but her brain was not alert, as it had been on that other occasion. She continued to stare at me through a blur of drink and anger; I could see her thoughts clutching uneasily at my suggestion and then losing their hold on it. "Oh, we all know you think you're God Almighty!" she broke out with a contemptuous toss.

"I think I could help you if I could have a quiet talk with Mrs. Glenn."

"Well, you can have your quiet talk." She looked about her, and pulling up a chair plumped down into it heavily. "I'd love to hear what you've got to say to each other," she declared.

Mrs. Glenn's hand began to shake again. She turned her head toward Mrs. Brown. "My dear, I should like to see my friend alone."

" 'I should like! I should like!' I daresay you would. It's always been what *you'd* like—but now it's going to be what I choose. And I choose to assist at the conversation between Mrs. Glenn and Mr. Norcutt, instead of letting them quietly say horrors about me behind my back."

"Oh, Chrissy—" my old friend murmured; then she turned to me and said: "You'd better come back another day."

Mrs. Brown looked at me with a sort of feeble cunning. "Oh, you needn't send him away. I've told you my friend's coming—he'll be here in a minute. If you'll sign that letter I'll take it to the bank with him, and Mr. Norcutt can stay here and tell you all the news. Now wouldn't that be nice and cosy?" she concluded coaxingly.

Looking into Mrs. Glenn's pale frightened face I was on the point of saying: "Well, sign it then, whatever it is—anything to get her to go." But Mrs. Glenn straightened her drooping shoulders and repeated softly: "I can't sign it."

A flush rose to Mrs. Brown's forehead. "You can't? That's final, is it?" She turned to me. "It's all money she owed us, mind you—money we've advanced to her—in one way or another. Every penny of it. And now she sits there and says she won't pay us!"

Mrs. Glenn, twisting her fingers into mine, gave a barely audible laugh. "Now he's here I'm safe," she said.

The crimson of Mrs. Brown's face darkened to purple. Her lower lip trembled and I saw she was struggling for words that her dimmed brain could not supply. "God Almighty— you think he's God Almighty!" She evidently felt the inadequacy of this, for she stood up suddenly, and coming close to Mrs. Glenn's armchair, stood looking down on her in impotent anger. "Well, I'll show you—" She turned to me, moved by another impulse. "You know well enough you could make her sign if you chose to."

My eyes and Mrs. Brown's met again. Hers were saying: "It's your last chance—it's *her* last chance. I warn you—" and mine replying: "Nonsense, you can't frighten us; you can't even frighten *her* while I'm here. And if she doesn't want to sign you shan't force her to. I have something up my sleeve that would shut you up in five seconds if you knew."

She kept her thick stare on mine till I felt as if my silent signal must have penetrated it. But she said nothing, and at last I exclaimed: "You know well enough the risk you're running—"

Perhaps I had better not have spoken. But that dumb dialogue was getting on my nerves. If she wouldn't see, it was time to make her—

Ah, she saw now—she saw fast enough! My words seemed to have cleared the last fumes from her brain. She gave me back my look with one almost as steady; then she laughed.

"The risk I'm running? Oh, that's it, is it? That's the pull you thought you had over me? Well, I'm glad to know—and I'm glad to tell you that I've known all along that you knew. I'm sick and tired of all the humbug—if she won't sign I'm going to tell her everything myself. So now the cards are on the table, and you can take your choice. It's up to you. The risk's on your side now!"

The unaccountable woman—drunkenly incoherent a moment ago, and now hitting the nail on the head with such fiendish precision! I sat silent, meditating her hideous challenge without knowing how to meet it. And then I became aware that a quiver had passed over Mrs. Glenn's face, which had become smaller and more ivory-yellow than before. She leaned toward me as if Mrs. Brown, who stood close above us, could not hear what we were saying.

"What is it she means to tell me? I don't care unless it's something bad about Stevie. And it couldn't be that, could it? How does she know? No one can come between a son and his mother."

Mrs. Brown gave one of her sudden laughs. "A son and his mother? I daresay not! Only I'm just about fed up with having you think you're his mother."

It was the one thing I had not foreseen—that she would possess herself of my threat and turn it against me. The risk was too deadly; and so no doubt she would have felt if she had been in a state to measure it. She was not; and there lay the peril.

Mrs. Glenn sat quite still after the other's outcry, and I hoped it had blown past her like some mere rag of rhetoric. Then I saw that the meaning of the words had reached her, but without carrying conviction. She glanced at me with the flicker of a smile. "Now she says I'm not his mother—!" It's her last round of ammunition; but don't be afraid—it won't make me sign, the smile seemed to whisper to me.

Mrs. Brown caught the unspoken whisper, and her

exasperation rushed to meet it. "You don't believe me? I knew you wouldn't! Well, ask your friend here; ask Mr. Norcutt; you always believe everything he says. He's known the truth for ever so long—long before Stephen died he knew he wasn't your son."

I jumped up, as if to put myself between my friend and some bodily harm: but she held fast to my hand with her clinging twitching fingers. "As if she knew what it is to have a son! All those long months when he's one with you . . . *Mothers* know," she said.

"Mothers, yes! I don't say you didn't have a son and desert him. I say that son wasn't Stephen. Don't you suppose I know? Sometimes I've wanted to laugh in your face at the way you went on about him . . . Sometimes I used to have to rush out of the room, just to have my laugh out by myself . . ."

Mrs. Brown stopped with a gasp, as if the fury of the outburst had shaken her back to soberness, and she saw for the first time what she had done. Mrs. Glenn sat with her head bowed; her hand had grown cold in mine. I looked at Mrs. Brown and said: "Now won't you leave us? I suppose there's nothing left to say."

She blinked at me through her heavy lids; I saw she was wavering. But at the same moment Mrs. Glenn's clutch tightened; she drew me down to her, and looked at me out of her deep eyes. "What does she mean when she says you knew about Stevie?"

I pressed her hand without answering. All my mind was concentrated on the effort of silencing my antagonist and getting her out of the room. Mrs. Brown leaned in the window-frame and looked down on us. I could see that she was dismayed at what she had said, and yet exultant; and my business was to work on the dismay before the exultation mastered it. But Mrs. Glenn still held me down: her eyes seemed to be forcing their gaze into me. "Is it true?" she asked almost inaudibly.

"True?" Mrs. Brown burst out. "Ask him to swear to you it's not true—see what he looks like then! He was in the conspiracy, you old simpleton."

Mrs. Glenn's head straightened itself again on her

weak neck: her face wore a singular majesty. "You were my friend—" she appealed to me.

"I've always been your friend."

"Then I don't have to believe her."

Mrs. Brown seemed to have been gathering herself up for a last onslaught. She saw that I was afraid to try to force her from the room, and the discovery gave her a sense of hazy triumph, as if all that was left to her was to defy me. "Tell her I'm lying—why don't you tell her I'm lying?" she taunted me.

I knelt down by my old friend and put my arm about her. "Will you come away with me now—at once? I'll take you wherever you want to go . . . I'll look after you . . . I'll always look after you."

Mrs. Glenn's eyes grew wider. She seemed to weigh my words till their sense penetrated her; then she said, in the same low voice: "It is true, then?"

"Come away with me; come away with me," I repeated.

I felt her trying to rise; but her feet failed under her and she sank back. "Yes, take me away from her," she said.

Mrs. Brown laughed. "Oh, that's it, is it? 'Come away from that bad woman, and I'll explain everything, and make it all right' . . . Why don't you adopt *him* instead of Steve? I daresay that's what he's been after all the time. That's the reason he was so determined we shouldn't have your money . . ." She drew back, and pointed to the door. "You can go with him—who's to prevent you? I couldn't if I wanted to. I see now it's for him we've been nursing your precious millions . . . Well, go with him, and he'll tell you the whole story . . ." A strange secretive smile stole over her face. "All except one bit . . . there's one bit he doesn't know; but *you're* going to know it now."

She stepped nearer, and I held up my hand; but she hurried on, her eyes on Mrs. Glenn. "What he doesn't know is why we fixed the thing up. Steve wasn't my adopted son any more than he was your real one. Adopted son, indeed! How old do you suppose I am? He was my lover. There—do you understand? My Lover! That's why we faked up that ridiculous adoption story, and all the rest of it—because he was desperately ill, and down and out and we hadn't a penny, the three of us, and I had to have money for him, and didn't care how I got it, didn't care for anything on earth but seeing him well again, and happy." She stopped and drew a panting breath. "There—I'd rather have told you that than have your money. I'd rather you should know what Steve was to me than think any longer that you owned him . . ."

I was still kneeling by Mrs. Glenn, my arm about her. Once I felt her heart give a great shake; then it seemed to stop altogether. Her eyes were no longer turned to me, but fixed in a wide stare on Mrs. Brown. A tremor convulsed her face; then, to my amazement, it was smoothed into an expression of childish serenity, and a faint smile, half playful, half ironic, stole over it.

She raised her hand and pointed tremulously to the other's disordered headgear. "My dear—your hat's crooked," she said.

For a moment I was bewildered; then I saw that, very gently, she was at last returning the taunt that Mrs. Brown had so often addressed to her. The shot fired, she leaned back against me with the satisfied sigh of a child; and immediately I understood that Mrs. Brown's blow had gone wide. A pitying fate had darkened Catherine Glenn's intelligence at the exact moment when to see clearly would have been the final anguish.

Mrs. Brown understood too. She stood looking at us doubtfully; then she said in a tone of feeble defiance: "Well, I had to tell her."

She turned and went out of the room, and I continued to kneel by Mrs. Glenn. Her eyes had gradually clouded, and I doubted if she still knew me; but her lips nursed their soft smile, and I saw that she must have been waiting for years to launch that little shaft at her enemy.

The Day of the Funeral

HIS WIFE had said: "If you don't give her up I'll throw myself from the roof." He had not given her up, and his wife had thrown herself from the roof.

Nothing of this had of course come out at the inquest. Luckily Mrs. Trenham had left no letters or diary—no papers of any sort, in fact; not even a little mound of ashes on the clean hearth. She was the kind of woman who never seemed to have many material appurtenances or encumbrances. And Dr. Lanscomb, who had attended her ever since her husband had been called to his professorship at Kingsborough, testified that she had always been excessively emotional and high-strung, and never "quite right" since her only child had died. The doctor's evidence closed the inquiry; the whole business had not lasted more than ten minutes.

Then, after another endless interval of forty-eight hours, came the funeral. Ambrose Trenham could never afterward recall what he did during those forty-eight hours. His wife's relations lived at the other end of the continent, in California; he himself had no immediate family; and the house—suddenly become strange and unfamiliar, a house that seemed never to have been his—had been given over to benevolent neighbours, soft-stepping motherly women, and to glib, subservient men who looked like a cross between book-agents and revivalists. These men took measures, discussed technical questions in undertones with the motherly women, and presently came back with a coffin with plated handles. Some one asked Trenham what was to be engraved on the plate on the lid, and he said: "Nothing." He understood afterward that the answer had not been what was expected; but at the time every one evidently ascribed it to his being incapacitated by grief.

Before the funeral one horrible moment stood out from the others, though all were horrible. It was when Mrs. Cossett, the wife of the professor of English Literature, came to him and said: "Do you want to see her?"

"See her—?" Trenham gasped, not understanding.

587

Mrs. Cossett looked surprised, and a little shocked. "The time has come—they must close the coffin . . ."

"Oh, let them close it," was on the tip of the widower's tongue; but he saw from Mrs. Cossett's expression that something very different was expected of him. He got up and followed her out of the room and up the stairs. . . . He looked at his wife. Her face had been spared. . . .

That too was over now, and the funeral as well. Somehow, after all, the time had worn on. At the funeral, Trenham had discovered in himself—he, the absent-minded, the unobservant—an uncanny faculty for singling out every one whom he knew in the crowded church. It was incredible; sitting in the front pew, his head bowed forward on his hands, he seemed suddenly gifted with the power of knowing who was behind him and on either side. And when the service was over, and to the sound of O Paradise he turned to walk down the nave behind the coffin, though his head was still bowed, and he was not conscious of looking to the right or the left, face after face thrust itself forward into his field of vision—and among them, yes: of a sudden, Barbara Wake's!

The shock was terrible; Trenham had been so sure she would not come. Afterward he understood that she had had to—for the sake of appearances. "Appearances" still ruled at Kingsborough—where didn't they, in the University world, and more especially in New England? But at the moment, and for a long time, Trenham had felt horrified, and outraged in what now seemed his holiest feelings. What right had she? How dared she? It was indecent. . . . In the reaction produced by the shock of seeing her, his remorse for what had happened hardened into icy hate of the woman who had been the cause of the tragedy. The sole cause—for in a flash Trenham had thrown off his own share in the disaster. "The woman tempted me—" Yes, she had! It was what his poor wronged Milly had always said: "You're so weak; and she's always tempting you—"

He used to laugh at the idea of Barbara Wake as a temptress; one of poor Milly's delusions! It seemed to him, then, that he was always pursuing, the girl evading; but now he saw her as his wife had seen her, and despised her accordingly. The indecency of her coming to the funeral! To have another look at him, he supposed. . . . She was insatiable . . . it was as if she could never fill her eyes with him. But, if he could help it, they should never be laid on him again. . . .

II

His indignation grew; it filled the remaining hours of the endless day, the empty hours after the funeral was over; it occupied and sustained him. The President of the University, an old friend, had driven him back to his lonely house, had wanted to get out and come in with him. But Trenham had refused, had shaken hands at the gate, and walked alone up the path to his front door. A cold lunch was waiting on the dining-room table. He left it untouched, poured out some whisky and water, carried the glass into his study, lit his pipe and sat down in his armchair to think, not of his wife, with whom the inquest seemed somehow to have settled his account, but of Barbara Wake. With her he must settle his account himself. And he had known at once how he would do it; simply by tying up all her letters, and the little photograph he always carried in his note-case (the only likeness he had of her), and sending them back without a word.

A word! What word indeed could equal the emphasis of that silence? Barbara Wake had all the feminine passion for going over and over things; talking them inside out; in that respect she was as bad as poor Milly had been, and nothing would humiliate and exasperate her as much as an uncommented gesture of dismissal. It was so fortifying to visualize that scene—the scene of her opening the packet alone in her room—that Trenham's sense of weariness disappeared, his pulses began to drum excitedly, and he was torn by a pang of hunger, the first he had felt in days. Was the cold meat still on the table, he wondered? Shamefacedly he stole back to the dining-room. But the table had been cleared, of course—just today! On ordinary days the maid would leave the empty dishes for hours unremoved; it was one of poor Milly's household grievances. How often he had said to her, impatiently: "Good Lord, what does it matter?" and she had answered: "But, Ambrose, the flies!" . . . And now, of all days, the fool of a maid had cleared away everything. He went back to his study, sat down again, and suddenly felt too hungry to think of anything but his hunger. Even his vengeance no longer nourished him; he felt as if nothing would replace that slice of pressed beef, with potato salad and pickles, of which his eyes had rejected the disgusted glimpse an hour or two earlier.

He fought his hunger for a while longer; then he got up and rang. Promptly, attentively, Jane, the middle-aged disapproving maid, appeared—usually one had to rip out the bell before she disturbed herself. Trenham felt sheepish at having to confess his hunger to her, as if it made him appear unfeeling, unheroic; but he could not help himself. He stammered out that he supposed he ought to eat something . . . and Jane, at once, was all tearful sympathy. "That's right, sir; you must *try* . . . you must force yourself. . . ." Yes, he said; he realized that. He would force himself. "We were saying in the kitchen, Katy and me, that you couldn't go on any longer this way. . . ." He could hardly wait till she had used up her phrases and got back to the pantry. . . . Through the half-open dining-room door he listened avidly to her steps coming and going, to the clatter of china, the rattle of the knife-basket. He met her at the door when she returned to tell him that his lunch was ready . . . and that Katy had scrambled some eggs for him the way he liked them.

At the dining-room table, when the door had closed on her, he squared his elbows, bent his head over his plate, and emptied every dish. Had he ever before known the complex exquisiteness of a slice of pressed beef? He filled his glass again, leaned luxuriously, waited without hurry for the cheese and biscuits, the black coffee, and a slice of apple-pie apologetically added from the maids' dinner—and then—oh, resurrection!—felt for his cigar-case, and calmly, carelessly almost, under Jane's moist and thankful eyes, cut his Corona and lit it.

"Now he's saved," her devout look seemed to say.

III

The letters must be returned at once. But to whom could he entrust them? Certainly not to either one of the maid-servants. And there was no one else but the slow-witted man who looked after the garden and the furnace, and who would have been too much dazed by such a commission to execute it without first receiving the most elaborate and reiterated explanations, and then would probably have delivered the packet to Professor Wake, or posted it—the latter a possibility to be at all costs avoided, since Trenham's writing might have been recognised by someone at the post-office, one of the chief centres of gossip at Kingsborough. How it complicated everything to live in a small, prying community! He had no reason to suppose that any one divined the cause of his wife's death, yet he was aware that people had seen him more than once in out-of-the-way places, and at queer hours, with Barbara Wake; and if his wife knew, why should not others suspect? For a while, at any rate, it behoved him to avoid all appearance of wishing to communicate with the girl. Returning a packet to her on the very day of the funeral would seem particularly suspicious. . . .

Thus, after coffee and cigar, and a nip of old Cognac, argued the normal sensible man that Trenham had become again. But if his nerves had been steadied by food his will had been strengthened by it, and instead of a weak, vacillating wish to let Barbara Wake feel the weight of his scorn he was now animated by the furious resolution to crush her with it, and at once. That packet should be returned to her before night.

He shut the study door, drew out his keys, and unlocked the cabinet in which he kept the letters. He had no need now to listen for his wife's step, or to place himself between the cabinet and the door of the study, as he used to when he thought he heard her coming. Now, had he chosen, he could have spread the letters out all over the table. Jane and Katy were busy in the kitchen, and the rest of the house was his to do what he liked in. He could have sat down and read the serried pages one by one, lingeringly, gloatingly, as he had so often longed to do when the risk was too great—and now they were but so much noisome rubbish to him, to be crammed into a big envelope, and sealed up out of sight. He began to hunt for an envelope. . . .

God! What dozens and dozens of letters there were!

And all written within eighteen months. No wonder poor Milly . . . but what a blind reckless fool he had been! The reason of their abundance was, of course, the difficulty of meeting. . . . So often he and Barbara had had to write because they couldn't contrive to see each other . . . but still, this bombardment of letters was monstrous, inexcusable. . . . He hunted for a long time for an envelope big enough to contain them; finally found one, a huge linen-lined envelope meant for college documents, and jammed the letters into it with averted head. But what, he thought suddenly, if she mistook his silence, imagined he had sent her the letters simply as a measure of prudence? No—that was hardly likely, now that all need of prudence was over; but she might affect to think so, use the idea as a pretext to write and ask what he meant, what she was to understand by his returning her letters without a word. It might give her an opening, which was probably what she was hoping for, and certainly what he was most determined she should not have.

He found a sheet of note-paper, shook his fountain-pen, wrote a few words (hardly looking at the page as he did so), and thrust the note in among the letters. His hands turned clammy as he touched them; he felt cold and sick. . . . And the cursèd flap of the envelope wouldn't stick—those linen envelopes were always so stiff. And where the devil was the sealing-wax? He rummaged frantically among the odds and ends on his desk. A provision of sealing-wax used always to be kept in the lower left-hand drawer. He groped about in it and found only some yellowing newspaper cuttings. Milly used to be so careful about seeing that his writing-table was properly supplied; but lately—ah, his poor poor Milly! If she could only know how he was suffering and atoning already. . . . Some string, then. . . . He fished some string out of another drawer. He would have to make it do instead of sealing-wax; he would have to try to tie a double knot. But his fingers, always clumsy, were twitching like a drug-fiend's; the letters seemed to burn them through the envelope. With a shaking hand he addressed the packet, and sat there, his eyes turned from it, while he tried again to think out some safe means of having it delivered. . . .

IV

He dined hungrily, as he had lunched; and after dinner he took his hat from its peg in the hall, and said to Jane: "I think I'll smoke my cigar in the campus."

That was a good idea; he saw at once that she thought it a hopeful sign, his wanting to take the air after being mewed up in the house for so long. The night was cold and moonless, and the college grounds, at that hour, would be a desert. . . . After all, delivering the letters himself was the safest way: openly, at the girl's own door, without any mystery. . . . If Malvina, the Wakes' old maid, should chance to open the door, he'd pull the packet out and say at once: "Oh, Malvina, I've found some books that Miss Barbara lent me last year, and as I'm going away—" He had gradually learned that there was nothing as safe as simplicity.

He was reassured by the fact that the night was so dark. It felt queer, unnatural somehow, to be walking abroad again like the Ambrose Trenham he used to be; he was glad there were so few people about, and that the Kingsborough suburbs were so scantily lit. He walked on, his elbow hitting now and then against the bundle, which bulged out of his pocket. Every time he felt it a sort of nausea rose in him. Professor Wake's house stood half way down one of the quietest of Kingsborough's outlying streets. It was withdrawn from the road under the hanging boughs of old elms; he could just catch a glint of light from one or two windows. And suddenly, as he was almost abreast of the gate, Barbara Wake came out of it.

For a moment she stood glancing about her; then she turned in the direction of the narrow lane bounding the farther side of the property. What took her there, Trenham wondered? His first impulse had been to draw back, and let her go her way; then he saw how providential the encounter was. The lane was dark, deserted—a mere passage between widely scattered houses, all asleep in their gardens. The chilly night had sent people home early; there was not a soul in sight. In another moment the packet would be in her hands, and he would have left her, just silently raising his hat.

He remembered now where she was going. The garage, built in the far corner of the garden, opened into the lane. The Wakes had no chauffeur, and Barbara, who drove the car, was sole mistress of the garage and of its keys. Trenham and she had met there sometimes; a desolate trysting-place! But what could they do, in a town like Kingsborough? At one time she had talked of setting up a studio—she dabbled in painting; but the suggestion had alarmed him (he knew the talk it would create), and he had discouraged her. Most often they took the train and went to Ditson, a manufacturing town an hour away, where no one knew them. . . . But what could she be going to the garage for at this hour?

The thought of his wife rushed into Trenham's mind. The discovery that she had lived there beside him, knowing all, and that suddenly, when she found she could not regain his affection, life had seemed worthless, and without a moment's hesitation she had left it . . . why, if he had known the quiet woman at his side had such springs of passion in her, how differently he would have regarded her, how little this girl's insipid endearments would have mattered to him! He was a man who could not live without tenderness, without demonstrative tenderness; his own shyness and reticence had to be perpetually broken down, laughingly scattered to the winds. His wife, he now saw, had been too much like him, had secretly suffered from the same inhibitions. She had always seemed ashamed, and frightened by her feeling for him, and half-repelled, half-fascinated by his response. At times he imagined that she found him physically distasteful, and wondered how, that being the case, she could be so fiercely jealous of him. Now he understood that her cold reluctant surrender concealed a passion so violent that it humiliated her, and so incomprehensible that she had never mastered its language. She reminded him of a clumsy little girl he had once known at a dancing class he had been sent to as a boy—a little girl who had a feverish passion for dancing, but could never learn the steps. And because he too had felt the irresistible need to join in the immemorial love-dance he had ended by choosing a partner more skilled in its intricacies. . . .

These thoughts wandered through his mind as he stood

watching Barbara Wake. Slowly he took a few steps down the lane; then he halted again. He had not yet made up his mind what to do. If she were going to the garage to get something she had forgotten (as was most probable, at that hour) she would no doubt be coming back in a few moments, and he could meet her and hand her the letters. Above all, he wanted to avoid going into the garage. To do so at that moment would have been a profanation of Milly's memory. He would have liked to efface from his own all recollection of the furtive hours spent there; but the vision returned with intolerable acuity as the girl's slim figure, receding from him, reached the door. How often he had stood at that corner, under those heavy trees, watching for her to appear and slip in ahead of him—so that they should not be seen entering together. The elaborate precautions with which their meetings had been surrounded—how pitiably futile they now seemed! They had not even achieved their purpose, but had only belittled his love and robbed it of its spontaneity. Real passion ought to be free, reckless, audacious, unhampered by the fear of a wife's feelings, of the University's regulations, the President's friendship, the deadly risk of losing one's job and wrecking one's career. It seemed to him now that the love he had given to Barbara Wake was almost as niggardly as that which he had doled out to his wife. . . .

He walked down the lane and saw that Barbara was going into the garage. It was so dark that he could hardly make out her movements; but as he reached the door she drew out her electric lamp (that recalled memories too), and by its flash he saw her slim gloveless hand put the key into the lock. The key turned, the door creaked, and all was darkness. . . .

The glimpse of her hand reminded him of the first time he had dared to hold it in his and press a kiss on the palm. They had met accidentally in the train, both of them on their way home from Boston, and he had proposed that they should get off at the last station before Kingsborough, and walk back by a short cut he knew, through the woods and along the King river. It was a shining summer day, and the girl had been amused at the idea and had accepted. . . . He could see now every line, every curve of her hand, a quick strong young hand, with long fingers, slightly blunt at the tips, and a sensuous elastic palm. It would be queer to have to carry on life without ever again knowing the feel of that hand. . . .

Of course he would go away; he would have to. If possible he would leave the following week. Perhaps the Faculty would let him advance his Sabbatical year. If not, they would probably let him off for the winter term, and perhaps after that he might make up his mind to resign, and look for a professorship elsewhere—in the south, or in California—as far away from that girl as possible. Meanwhile what he wanted was to get away to some hot climate, steamy, tropical, where one could lie out all night on a white beach and hear the palms chatter to the waves, and the trade-winds blow from God knew where . . . one of those fiery flowery islands where marriage and love were not regarded so solemnly, and a man could follow his instinct without calling down a catastrophe, or feeling himself morally degraded. . . . Above all, he never wanted to see again a woman who argued and worried and reproached, and dramatized things that ought to be as simple as eating and drinking. . . .

Barbara, he had to admit, had never been frightened or worried, had never reproached him. The girl had the true sporting instinct; he never remembered her being afraid of risks, or nervous about "appearances." Once or twice, at moments when detection seemed imminent, she had half frightened him by her cool resourcefulness. He sneered at the remembrance. "An old hand, no doubt!" But the sneer did not help him. Whose fault was it if the girl had had to master the arts of dissimulation? Whose but his? He alone (he saw in sudden terror) was responsible for what he supposed would be called her downfall. Poor child—poor Barbara! Was it possible that he, the seducer, the corrupter, had presumed to judge her? The thought was monstrous. . . . His resentment had already vanished like a puff of mist. The feeling of his responsibility, which had seemed so abhorrent, was now almost sweet to him. He was responsible—he owed her something! Thank heaven for that! For now he could raise his passion into a duty, and thus disguised and moralized, could once more—oh, could he, dared he?—admit it openly into his life. The mere possibility made him suddenly feel less cold and desolate. That the something-not-himself that made for

Righteousness should take on the tender lineaments, the human warmth of love, should come to sit by his hearth in the shape of Barbara—how warm, how happy and reassured it made him! He had a swift vision of her, actually sitting there in the shabby old leather chair (he would have it recovered), her slim feet on the faded Turkey rug (he would have it replaced). It was almost a pity—he thought madly—that they would probably not be able to stay on at Kingsborough, there, in that very house where for so long he had not even dared to look at her letters. . . . Of course, if they did decide to, he would have it all done over for her.

V

The garage door creaked and again he saw the flash of the electric lamp on her bare hand as she turned the key; then she moved toward him in the darkness.

"Barbara!"

She stopped short at his whisper. They drew closer to each other. "You wanted to see me?" she whispered back. Her voice flowed over him like summer air.

"Can we go in there—?" he gestured.

"Into the garage? Yes—I suppose so."

They turned and walked in silence through the obscurity. The comfort of her nearness was indescribable.

She unlocked the door again, and he followed her in. "Take care; I left the wheel-jack somewhere," she warned him. Automatically he produced a match, and she lit the candle in an old broken-paned lantern that hung on a nail against the wall. How familiar it all was—how often he had brought out his match-box and she had lit that candle! In the little pool of yellowish light they stood and looked at each other.

"You didn't expect me?" he stammered.

"I'm not sure I didn't," she returned softly, and he just caught her smile in the half-light. The divineness of it!

"I didn't suppose I should see you. I just wandered out. . . ." He suddenly felt the difficulty of accounting for himself.

"My poor Ambrose!" She laid her hand on his arm. "How I've ached for you—"

Yes; that was right; the tender sympathizing friend . . . anything else, at that moment, would have been unthinkable. He drew a breath of relief and self-satisfaction. Her pity made him feel almost heroic—had he not lost sight of his own sufferings in the thought of hers? "It's been awful—" he muttered.

"Yes; I know."

She sat down on the step of the old Packard, and he found a wooden stool and dragged it into the candle-ray.

"I'm glad you came," she began, still in the same soft healing voice, "because I'm going away tomorrow early, and—"

He started to his feet, upsetting the stool with a crash. "Going away? Early tomorrow?" Why hadn't he known of this? He felt weak and injured. Where could she be going in this sudden way? If they hadn't happened to meet, would he have known nothing of it till she was gone? His heart grew small and cold.

She was saying quietly: "You must see—it's better. I'm going out to the Jim Southwicks, in California. They're always asking me. Mother and father think it's on account of my colds . . . the winter climate here . . . they think I'm right." She paused, but he could find nothing to say. The future had become a featureless desert. "I wanted to see you before going," she continued, "and I didn't exactly know . . . I hoped you'd come—"

"When are you coming back?" he interrupted desperately.

"Oh, I don't know; they want me for the winter, of course. There's a crazy plan about Hawaii and Samoa . . . sounds lovely, doesn't it? And from there on . . . But I don't know. . . ."

He felt a suffocation in his throat. If he didn't cry out, do something at once to stop her, he would choke. "You can't go—you can't leave me like this!" It seemed to him that his voice had risen to a shout.

"Ambrose—" she murmured, subdued, half-warning.

"You can't. How can you? It's madness. You don't understand. You say you ought to go—it's better you should go. What do you mean—why better? Are you afraid of what people might say? Is that it? How can they say anything when they know we're going to be married? Don't you know we're going to be married?" he burst out weakly, his words stumbling over each other in the effort to make her understand.

She hesitated a moment, and he stood waiting in an agony of suspense. How women loved to make men suffer! At last she said in a constrained voice: "I don't think we ought to talk of all this yet—"

Rebuking him—she was actually rebuking him for his magnanimity! But couldn't she see—couldn't she understand? Or was it that she really enjoyed torturing him? "How can I help talking of it, when you tell me you're going away tomorrow morning? Did you really mean to go without even telling me?"

"If I hadn't seen you I should have written," she faltered.

"Well, now I'm here you needn't write. All you've got to do is to answer me," he retorted almost angrily. The calm way in which she dealt with the situation was enough to madden a man—actually as if she hadn't made up her mind, good God! "What are you afraid of?" he burst out harshly.

"I'm not afraid—only I didn't expect . . . I thought we'd talk of all this later . . . if you feel the same when I come back—if we both do."

"If we both do!" Ah, there was the sting—the devil's claw! What was it? Was she being super-humanly magnanimous—or proud, over-sensitive, afraid that he might be making the proposal out of pity? Poor girl—poor child! That must be it. He loved her all the more for it, bless her! Or was it (ah, now again the claw tightened), was it that she really didn't want to commit herself, wanted to reserve her freedom for this crazy expedition, to see whether she couldn't do better by looking about out there—she, so young, so fresh and radiant—than by binding herself in advance to an elderly professor at Kingsborough? Hawaii—Samoa—swarming with rich idle yachtsmen and young naval officers (he had an excruciating vision of a throng of "Madame Butterfly" tenors in immaculate white duck and gold braid)—cock-tails, fox-trot, moonlight in the tropics . . . he felt suddenly middle-aged, round-shouldered, shabby, with thinning graying hair. . . . Of course what she wanted was to look round and see what her chances were! He retrieved the fallen stool, set it up again, and sat down on it.

"I suppose you're not sure you'll feel the same when you get back? Is that it?" he suggested bitterly.

Again she hesitated. "I don't think we ought to decide now—tonight. . . ."

His anger blazed. "Why oughtn't we? Tell me that! I've decided. Why shouldn't you?"

"You haven't really decided either," she returned gently.

"I haven't—haven't I? Now what do you mean by that?" He forced a laugh that was meant to be playful but sounded defiant. He was aware that his voice and words were getting out of hand—but what business had she to keep him on the stretch like this?

"I mean, after what you've been through. . . ."

"After what I've been through? But don't you see that's the very reason? I'm at the breaking-point—I can't bear any more."

"I know; I know." She got up and came close, laying a quiet hand on his shoulder. "I've suffered for you too. The shock it must have been. That's the reason why I don't want to say anything now that you might—"

He shook off her hand, and sprang up. "What hypocrisy!" He heard himself beginning to shout again. "I suppose what you mean is that you want to be free to marry out there if you see anybody you like better. Then why not admit it at once?"

"Because it's not what I mean. I don't want to marry any one else, Ambrose."

Oh, the melting music of it! He lifted his hands and hid his burning eyes in them. The sound of her voice wove magic passes above his forehead. Was it possible that such bliss could come out of such anguish? He forgot the place—forgot the day—and abruptly, blindly, caught her by the arm, and flung his own about her.

"Oh, Ambrose—" he heard her, reproachful, panting. He struggled with her, feverish for her lips.

In the semi-obscurity there was the sound of something crashing to the floor between them. They drew apart, and she looked at him, bewildered. "What was that?"

What was it? He knew well enough; a shiver of cold ran over him. The letters, of course—her letters! The bulging clumsily-tied envelope had dropped out of his pocket onto

the floor of the garage; in the fall the string had come undone, and the mass of papers had tumbled out, scattering
themselves like a pack of cards at Barbara's feet. She picked up
her electric lamp, and bending over shot its sharp ray on
them.

"Why, they're letters! Ambrose—are they my letters?" She
waited; but silence lay on him like lead. "Was that what you
came for?" she exclaimed.

If there was an answer to that he couldn't find it, and stupidly, without knowing what he was doing, he bent down and
began to gather up the letters.

For a while he was aware of her standing there motionless,
watching him; then she too bent over, and took up the gaping linen envelope. "Miss Barbara Wake," she read out; and
suddenly she began to laugh. "Why," she said, "there's something left in it! A letter for *me*? Is that it?"

He put his hand out. "Barbara—don't! Barbara—I implore
you!"

She turned the electric ray on the sheet of paper, which detached itself from the shadows with the solidity of a graven
tablet. Slowly she read out, in a cool measured voice, almost
as though she were parodying his poor phrases: " 'November
tenth. . . . You will probably feel as I do' (no—don't snatch!
Ambrose, I forbid you!) 'You will probably feel, as I do, that
after what has happened you and I can never'—" She broke
off and raised her eyes to Trenham's. " 'After what has happened'? I don't understand. What do you mean? What *has*
happened, Ambrose—between you and me?"

He had retreated a few steps, and stood leaning against the
side of the motor. "I didn't say 'between you and me.' "

"What did you say?" She turned the light once more on the
fatal page. " 'You and I can never wish to meet again.' " Her
hand sank, and she stood facing him in silence.

Feeling her gaze fixed on him, he muttered miserably: "I
asked you not to read the thing."

"But if it was meant for me why do you want me not to
read it?"

"Can't you see? It doesn't mean anything. I was raving
mad when I wrote it. . . ."

"But you wrote it only a few hours ago. It's dated today.

How can you have changed so in a few hours? And you say: 'After what has happened.' That must mean something. What does it mean? What *has* happened?"

He thought he would go mad indeed if she repeated the word again. "Oh, don't—!" he exclaimed.

"Don't what?"

"Say it over and over—'what has happened?' Can't you understand that just at first—"

He broke off, and she prompted him: "Just at first—?"

"I couldn't bear the horror alone. Like a miserable coward I let myself think you were partly responsible—I wanted to think so, you understand. . . ."

Her face seemed to grow white and wavering in the shadows. "What do you mean? Responsible for what?"

He straightened his shoulders and said slowly: "Responsible for her death. I was too weak to carry it alone."

"Her death?" There was a silence that seemed to make the shadowy place darker. He could hardly see her face now, she was so far off. "How could I be responsible?" she broke off, and then began again: "Are you—trying to tell me—that it wasn't an accident?"

"No—it wasn't an accident."

"She—"

"Well, can't you guess?" he stammered, panting.

"You mean—she killed herself?"

"Yes."

"Because of us?"

He could not speak, and after a moment she hurried on: "But what makes you think so? What proof have you? Did she tell any one? Did she leave a message—a letter?"

He summoned his voice to his dry throat. "No; nothing."

"Well, then—?"

"She'd told me beforehand; she'd warned me—"

"Warned you?"

"That if I went on seeing you . . . and I did go on seeing you . . . She warned me again and again. Do you understand now?" he exclaimed, twisting round on her fiercely, like an animal turning on its torturer.

There was an interval of silence—endless it seemed to him. She did not speak or move; but suddenly he heard a low sobbing sound. She was weeping, weeping like a frightened child. . . . Well, of all the unexpected turns of fate! A moment ago he had seemed to feel her strength flowing into his cold veins, had thought to himself: "I shall never again be alone with my horror—" and now the horror had spread from him to her, and he felt her inwardly recoiling as though she shuddered away from the contagion.

"Oh, how dreadful, how dreadful—" She began to cry again, like a child swept by a fresh gust of misery as the last subsides.

"Why dreadful?" he burst out, unnerved by the continuance of her soft unremitting sobs. "You must have known she didn't like it—didn't you?"

Through her lament a whisper issued: "I never dreamed she knew. . . ."

"You mean to say you thought we'd deceived her? All those months? In a one-horse place where everybody is on the watch to see what everybody else is doing? Likely, isn't it? My God—"

"I never dreamed . . . I never dreamed . . ." she reiterated.

His exasperation broke out again. "Well, now you begin to see what I've suffered—"

"Suffered? *You* suffered?" She uttered a low sound of derision. "I see what she must have suffered—what we both of us must have made her suffer."

"Ah, at least you say 'both of us'!"

She made no answer, and through her silence he felt again that she was inwardly shrinking, averting herself from him. What! His accomplice deserting him? She acknowledged that she was his accomplice—she said "both of us"—and yet she was drawing back from him, flying from him, leaving him alone! Ah, no—she shouldn't escape as easily as that, she shouldn't leave him; he couldn't face that sense of being alone again. "Barbara!" he cried out, as if the actual distance between them had already doubled.

She still remained silent, and he hurried on, almost cringingly: "Don't think I blame you, child—don't think . . ."

"Oh, what does it matter, when I blame myself?" she wailed out, her face in her hands.

"Blame yourself? What folly! When you say you didn't know—"

"Of course I didn't know! How can you imagine—? But this dreadful thing has happened; and *you* knew it might happen . . . you knew it all along . . . all the while it was in the back of your mind . . . the days when we used to meet here . . . and the days when we went to Ditson . . . oh, that horrible room at Ditson! All that time she was sitting at home alone, knowing everything, and hating me as if I'd been her murderess. . . ."

"Good God, Barbara! Don't you suppose I blame myself?"

"But if you blamed yourself how could you go on, how could you let me think she didn't care?"

"I didn't suppose she did," he muttered sullenly.

"But you say she told you—she warned you! Over and over again she warned you."

"Well, I didn't want to believe her—and so I didn't. When a man's infatuated . . . Don't you see it's hard enough to bear without all this? Haven't you any pity for me, Barbara?"

"Pity?" she repeated slowly. "The only pity I feel is for *her*—for what she must have gone through, day after day, week after week, sitting there all alone and knowing . . . imagining exactly what you were saying to me . . . the way you kissed me . . . and watching the clock, and counting the hours . . . and then having you come back, and explain, and pretend—I suppose you *did* pretend? . . . and all the while secretly knowing you were lying, and yet longing to believe you . . . and having warned you, and seeing that her warnings made no difference . . . that you didn't care if she died or not . . . that you were doing all you could to kill her . . . that you were probably counting the days till she was dead!" Her passionate apostrophe broke down in a sob, and again she stood weeping like an inconsolable child.

Trenham was struck silent. It was true. He had never been really able to enter into poor Milly's imaginings, the matter of her lonely musings; and here was this girl to whom, in a flash, that solitary mind lay bare. Yes; that must have been the way Milly felt—he knew it now—and the way poor Barbara herself would feel if he ever betrayed her. Ah, but he was never going to betray her—the thought was monstrous! Never for a moment would he cease to love her. This catastrophe had bound them together as a happy wooing could never have done. It was her love for him, her fear for their future, that was shaking her to the soul, giving her this unnatural power to enter into Milly's mind. If only he could find words to re-assure her, now, at once. But he could not think of any.

"Barbara—Barbara," he kept on repeating, as if her name were a sort of incantation.

"Oh, think of it—those lonely endless hours! I wonder if you ever did think of them before? When you used to go home after one of our meetings, did you remember each time what she'd told you, and begin to wonder, as you got near the house, if she'd done it *that day*?"

"Barbara—"

"Perhaps you did—perhaps you were even vexed with her for being so slow about it. Were you?"

"Oh, Barbara—Barbara . . ."

"And when the day came at last, were you surprised? Had you got so impatient waiting that you'd begun to believe she'd never do it? Were there days when you went almost mad at having to wait so long for your freedom? It was the way I used to feel when I was rushing for the train to Ditson, and father would call me at the last minute to write letters for him, or mother to replace her on some charity committee; there were days when I could have *killed* them, almost, for in-terfering with me, making me miss one of our precious hours together. *Killed them*, I say! Don't you suppose I know how murderers feel? How *you* feel—for you're a murderer, you know! And now you come here, when the earth's hardly cov-ered her, and try to kiss me, and ask me to marry you—and think, I suppose, that by doing so you're covering up her memory more securely, you're pounding down the earth on her a little harder. . . ."

She broke off, as if her own words terrified her, and hid her eyes from the vision they called up.

Trenham stood without moving. He had gathered up the letters, and they lay in a neat pile on the floor between him-self and her, because there seemed no other place to put them. He said to himself (reflecting how many million men must have said the same thing at such moments): "After this

she'll calm down, and by tomorrow she'll be telling me how
sorry she is. . . ." But the reflection did not seem to help
him. She might forget—but he would not. He had forgotten
too easily before; he had an idea that his future would be burdened with long arrears of remembrance. Just as the girl described Milly, so he would see her in the years to come. He
would have to pay the interest on his oblivion; and it would
not help much to have Barbara pay it with him. The job was
probably one that would have to be accomplished alone. At
last words shaped themselves without his knowing it. "I'd
better go," he said.

Unconsciously he had expected an answer; an appeal; a
protest, perhaps. But none came. He moved away a few steps
in the direction of the door. As he did so he heard Barbara
break into a laugh, and the sound, so unnatural in that place,
and at that moment, brought him abruptly to a halt.

"Yes—?" he said, half turning, as though she had called
him.

"And I sent a wreath—I sent her a wreath! It's on her grave
now—it hasn't even had time to fade!"

"Oh—" he gasped, as if she had struck him across the face.
They stood forlornly confronting each other. Her last words
seemed to have created an icy void between them. Within
himself a voice whispered: "She can't find anything worse
than that." But he saw by the faint twitch of her lips that she
was groping, groping—

"And the worst of it is," she broke out, "that if I didn't go
away, and we were to drag on here together, after a time I
might even drift into forgiving you."

Yes; she was right; that was certainly the worst of it.
Human imagination could not go beyond that, he thought.
He moved away again stiffly.

"Well, you *are* going away, aren't you?" he said.

"Yes; I'm going."

He walked back slowly through the dark deserted streets.
His brain, reeling with the shock of the encounter, gradually
cleared, and looked about on the new world within itself. At
first the inside of his head was like a deserted house out of
which all the furniture has been moved, down to the last

familiar encumbrances. It was empty, absolutely empty. But gradually a small speck of consciousness appeared in the dreary void, like a mouse scurrying across bare floors. He stopped on a street corner to say to himself: "But after all nothing is changed—absolutely nothing. I went there to tell her that we should probably never want to see each other again; and she agreed with me. She agreed with me—that's all."

It was a relief, almost, to have even that little thought stirring about in the resonant void of his brain. He walked on more quickly, reflecting, as he reached his own corner: "In a minute it's going to rain." He smiled a little at his unconscious precaution in hurrying home to escape the rain. "Jane will begin to fret—she'll be sure to notice that I didn't take my umbrella." And his cold heart felt a faint warmth at the thought that some one in the huge hostile world would really care whether he had taken his umbrella or not. "But probably she's in bed and asleep," he mused, despondently.

On his door-step he paused and began to grope for his latch-key. He felt impatiently in one pocket after another— but the key was not to be found. He had an idea that he had left it lying on his study table when he came in after—after what? Why, that very morning, after the funeral! He had flung the key down among his papers—and Jane would never notice that it was there. She would never think of looking; she had been bidden often enough on no account to meddle with the things on his desk. And besides she would take for granted that he had the key in his pocket. And here he stood, in the middle of the night, locked out of his own house—

A sudden exasperation possessed him. He was aware that he must have lost all sense of proportion, all perspective, for he felt as baffled and as angry as when Barbara's furious words had beaten down on him. Yes; it made him just as unhappy to find himself locked out of his house—he could have sat down on the door-step and cried. And here was the rain beginning. . . .

He put his hand to the bell; but did the front door bell ring in the far-off attic where the maids were lodged? And was there the least chance of the faint tinkle from the pantry mounting two flights, and penetrating to their sleep-muffled ears? Utterly improbable, he knew. And if he couldn't make them hear he would have to spend the night at a hotel—the night of his wife's funeral! And the next morning all Kingsborough would know of it, from the President of the University to the boy who delivered the milk. . . .

But his hand had hardly touched the bell when he felt a vibration of life in the house. First there was a faint flash of light through the transom above the front door; then, scarcely distinguishable from the noises of the night, a step sounded far off: it grew louder on the hall floor, and after an interval that seemed endless the door was flung open by a Jane still irreproachably capped and aproned.

"Why, Jane—I didn't think you'd be awake! I forgot my key. . . ."

"I know, sir. I found it. I was waiting." She took his wet coat from him. "Dear, dear! And you hadn't your umbrella."

He stepped into his own hall, and heard her close and bar the door behind him. He liked to listen to that familiar slipping of the bolts and clink of the chain. He liked to think that she minded about his not having his umbrella. It was his own house, after all—and this friendly hand was shutting him safely into it. The dreadful sense of loneliness melted a little at the old reassuring touch of habit.

"Thank you, Jane; sorry I kept you up," he muttered, nodding to her as he went upstairs.

A Glimpse

As John Kilvert got out of the motor at the Fusina landing-stage, and followed his neat suit-cases on board the evening boat for Venice, he growled to himself inconsequently: "Always on wheels! When what I really want is to walk—"

To walk? How absurd! Would he even have known how to, any longer? In youth he had excelled in the manly exercises then fashionable: lawn tennis, racquets, golf and the rest. He had even managed, till well over forty, to combine the more violent of these with his busy life of affairs in New York, and since then, with devout regularity and some success, had conformed to the national ritual of golf. But the muscles used for a mere walk were probably long since atrophied; and, indeed, so little did this modest form of exercise enter into the possibilities of his life that in his sudden outburst he had used the word metaphorically, meaning that all at once his existence seemed to him too cushioned, smooth and painless—he didn't know why.

Perhaps it was the lucky accident of finding himself on board the wrong boat—the unfashionable boat; an accident caused by the chauffeur's having mistaken a turn soon after they left Padua, missed the newly opened *"auto-strada,"* and slipped through reed-grown byways to the Fusina water-side. It was a hot Sunday afternoon in September, and a throng of dull and dingy-looking holiday-makers were streaming across the gang-plank onto the dirty deck, and settling down with fretful babies, withered flowers, and baskets stuffed with provisions from the mainland on the narrow uncomfortable bench along the rail. Perhaps it was that—at any rate the discomfort did not annoy John Kilvert; on the contrary, it gave him a vague glow of satisfaction. Camping for an hour on this populous garlicky boat would be almost the equivalent of walking from Padua to Fusina instead of gliding there in the commodious Fiat he had hired at Milan. And to begin with, why had he hired it? Why hadn't the train been good enough for him? What was the matter with him, anyhow? . . . He hadn't meant to include Venice in his holiday that summer. He had settled down in Paris to do some systematic sight-seeing in the Ile-de-France: French church architecture was his hobby, he had collected a library on the subject, and liked going on archæological trips (also in a commodious motor, with a pause for lunch at the most reputed restaurants) in company with a shy shabby French archæologist who could guide and explain, and save him the labour of reading all the books he bought. But he concealed his archæological interests from most of his American friends because they belonged to a cosmopolitan group who thought that motors were made for speeding, not sight-seeing, and that Paris existed merely to launch new fashions, new plays and new restaurants, for rich and easily bored Americans. John Kilvert, at fifty-five, had accepted this point of view with the weary tolerance which had long since replaced indignation in his moral make-up.

And now, after all, his plans had been upset by a telegram from Sara Roseneath, insisting that he should come to Venice at once to help her about her fancy-dress for the great historical ball which was to be given at the Ducal Palace (an unheard-of event, looming in cosmopolitan society far higher than declarations of war, or peace treaties). And he had started.

But why, again—why? Sara Roseneath was an old friend, of course; an old love. He had been half disposed to marry her once, when she was Sara Court; but she had chosen a richer man, and now that she was widowed, though he had no idea of succeeding to the late Roseneath, he and she had drifted into a semi-sentimental friendship, occasionally went on little tours together, and were expected by their group to foregather whenever they were both in New York, or when they met in Paris or London. A safe, prudent arrangement, gradually fading into an intimacy scarcely calmer than the romance that went before. It was all she wanted of the emotional life (practical life being so packed with entertainments, dressmakers, breathless travel and all sorts of fashionable rivalries); and it was all he had to give in return for what she was able to offer. What held him, then? Partly habit, a common stock of relations and allusions, the knowledge that her exactions would never be more serious than this urgent call to help her to design a fancy-dress—and partly, of course, what survived in her, carefully preserved by beauty-doctors and gymnastic trainers, of the physical graces which had first captured him.

Nevertheless he was faintly irritated with both himself and her for having suffered this journey to be imposed on him. Of course it was his own fault; if he had refused to come she would have found half a dozen whippersnappers to devise a fancy-dress for her. And she would not have been really angry; only gently surprised and disappointed. She would have said: "I thought I could *always* count on you in an emergency!" An emergency—this still handsome but middle-aged woman, to whom a fancy ball represented an event! There is no frivolity, he thought, like that of the elderly. . . . Venice in September was a place wholly detestable to him, and that he should be summoned there to assist a spoilt woman in the choice of a fancy-dress shed an ironic light on the contrast between his old ambitions and his present uses. The whole affair was silly and distasteful, and he wished he could shake off his social habits and break once for all with the trivial propinquities which had created them. . . .

The slatternly woman who sat crammed close against him moved a little to readjust the arm supporting her sleep-drunken baby, and her elbow pressed uncomfortably against Kilvert's ribs. He got up and wandered forward. As the passengers came on board he had noticed two people—a man and a woman—whose appearance singled them out from the workaday crowd. Not that they fitted in with his standard of personal seemliness; the woman was bare-headed, with blown hair, untidy and turning gray, and the man, in worn shapeless homespun, with a short beard turning gray also, was as careless in dress and bearing as his companion. Still, blowsy and shabby as they were, they were evidently persons of education and refinement, and Kilvert, having found a corner for himself in the forward part of the boat, began to watch them with a certain curiosity.

First he speculated about their nationality; but that was hard to determine. The woman was dusky, almost swarthy, under her sunburn; her untidy hair was still streaked with jet, and the eyes under her dense black eyebrows were of a rich burning brown. The man's eyes were gray, his nose was straight, his complexion and hair vaguely pepper-and-salt, like his clothes. He had taken off his stalking-cap, disclosing thick hair brushed back carelessly from a high wide forehead. His brow and his high cheekbones were burnt to a deeper bronze than his companion's, but his long nervous hands showed whiter at the wrists than hers. For the rest, they seemed of about the same age, and though there was no trace of youth about either of them their vigorous maturity seemed to give out a strong emotional glow. Such had been Kilvert's impression as they came on board, hurriedly, almost precipitately, after all the other passengers were seated. The woman had come first, and the man, after a perceptible interval, had scrambled over the side as the boat was actually beginning to put off. Where had they come from, Kilvert wondered, why such haste and such agitation? They had no luggage, no wraps, the woman, gloveless and cloakless, apparently had not even a hat.

For a while Kilvert had lost them in the crowd; but now, going forward, he found them wedged between the prow of the boat and the low sky-light of the forward cabin. They had not found seats, but they seemed hardly aware of it; the woman was perched on the edge of the closed sky-light, the man, facing her, leaned against the side of the boat, his hands braced against the rail. Both turned their backs to the low misty line along the horizon that was rapidly defining itself as a distant view of Venice. Kilvert's first thought was: "I don't believe they even know where they are."

A fat passenger perched on a coil of rope had spied the seat which Kilvert had left, and the latter was able to possess himself of the vacated rope. From where he sat he was only a few yards from the man and woman he had begun to watch; just too far to catch their words, or even to make quite sure of the language they were speaking (he wavered between Hungarian, and Austrian German smattered with English), but near enough to observe the play of their facial muscles and the corresponding gestures of their dramatic bodies.

Husband and wife? No—he dismissed the idea as it shaped itself. They were too acutely aware of each other, what each said (whatever its import might be) came to the other with too sharp an impact of surprise for habit to have dulled their intercourse. Lovers, then—as he and Sara had once been, for a discreet interval? Kilvert winced at the comparison. He tried, but in vain, to picture Sara Roseneath and himself, in the hour of their rapture, dashing headlong and hatless on board a dirty boat crowded with perspiring work-people, and fighting out the last phase of their amorous conflict between coils of tarry rope and bulging baskets of farm produce. In fact there had been no conflict; he and Sara had ceased their sentimental relations without shedding of blood. But then they had only strolled around the edge of the crater, picking flowers, while these two seemed writhing in its depths.

As Kilvert settled himself on his coil of rope their conversation came to an end. The man walked abruptly away, striding the length of the crowded deck (in his absorption he seemed unaware of the obstacles in his advance), while the woman, propped against her precarious ledge, remained motionless, her eyes fixed, her rough gray head, with the streaks of wavy jet, bowed as under a crushing thought. "They've quarrelled," Kilvert said to himself with a half-envious pang.

The woman sat there for several minutes. Her only motion was to clasp and unclasp her long sunburnt fingers. Kilvert noticed that her hands, which were large for her height, had the same nervous suppleness as the man's; high-strung intellectual hands, as eloquent as her burning brown eyes. As she continued to sit alone their look deepened from feverish fire to a kind of cloudy resignation, as though to say that now the worst was over. "Ah, quarrelled irremediably—" Kilvert thought, disappointed.

Then the man came back. He forced his way impatiently through the heaped-up bags and babies, regained his place at his companion's side, and stood looking down at her, sadly but not resignedly. An unappeased entreaty was in his gaze. Kilvert became aware that the struggle was far from being over, and his own muscles unconsciously braced themselves for the renewal of the conflict. "He won't give up—he *won't* give up!" he exulted inwardly.

The man lowered his head above his companion, and spoke to her in pressing inaudible tones. She listened quietly, without stirring, but Kilvert noticed that her lower lip trembled a little. Was her mouth beautiful? He was not yet sure. It had something of the sinuous strength of her long hands, and the complexity of its curves made it a matchless vehicle for the expression of irony, bitterness and grief. An actress's mouth, perhaps; over-elastic, subtly drawn, capable of being beautiful or ugly as her own emotions were. It struck Kilvert that her whole face, indeed her whole body, was like that: a vehicle, an instrument, a language rather than a plastic fact. Kilvert's interest deepened to excitement as he watched her.

She began to speak, at first very low and gravely; then more eagerly, passionately, passing (as he imagined) from pleading, from tenderness and regret, to the despair of an accepted renouncement. "Ah, don't tempt me—don't begin it all over again!" her eyes and lips seemed to be saying in tortured remonstrance, as his gray head bent above her and their urgent whispers were interwoven. . . .

Kilvert felt that he was beginning to understand the situation. "She's married—unhappily married. That must be it. And everything draws her to this man, who is her predestined mate. . . . But some terrible obstacle lies between them. Her husband, her children, perhaps some obligation of his that he wants to forget, but that she feels compelled, for his own sake, to remind him of, though she does so at the cost of her very life—ah, yes, she's bleeding to death for him! And they've been off, spending a last day together in some quiet place, to talk it all over for the last time; and he won't take her refusal for an answer—and by God, I wouldn't either!" Kilvert inwardly shrieked, kindled to a sudden forgotten vehemence of passion by the mute display of it before him. "When people need each other as desperately as those two do—not mere instinct-driven infants, but a mature experienced man and woman—the gods ought to let them come together, no matter how much it costs, or for how short a time it is! And that's what he's saying to her; by heaven, he's saying: 'I thought I could stand it, but I can't.' . . ."

To Kilvert's surprise his own eyes filled with tears; they came so thick that he had to pull out his handkerchief and wipe them away. What was he mourning—the inevitable break between these two anguished people, or some anguish that he himself had once caught a glimpse of, and missed? There had been that gray-eyed Russian girl, the governess of his sister's children; with her he had very nearly sounded the depths. He remembered one long walk with her in the summer woods, the children scampering ahead. . . . At a turn when they were out of sight, he and she had suddenly kissed and clung to each other. . . . But his sister's children's governess—? Did he mean to marry her? He asked himself that through a long agitated night—recalled the chapter in "Resurrection" where Prince Nekludov paces his room, listening to the drip of the spring thaw in the darkness outside—and was off by the earliest train the next morning, and away to Angkor and Bali the following week. A man can't be too careful—or *can* he? Who knows? He still remembered the shuddering ebb of that night's emotions. . . .

"But what a power emotion is!" he reflected. "I could lift mountains still if I could feel as those two do about anything. I suppose all the people worth remembering—lovers or poets or inventors—have lived at white-heat level, while we crawl along in the temperate zone." Once more he concentrated his attention on the couple facing him. The woman had risen in her turn. She walked away a few steps, and stood leaning against the rail, her gaze fixed on the faint horizon-line that was shaping itself into wavering domes and towers. What did that distant view say to her? Perhaps it symbolized the life she must go back to, the duties, sacrifices, daily wearinesses from which this man was offering her an escape. She knew all that; she saw her fate growing clearer and clearer before her as the boat advanced through the summer twilight; in half an hour more the crossing would be over, and the gang-plank run out to the quay.

The man had not changed his position; he stood where she had left him, as though respecting the secrecy of her distress, or else perhaps too worn out, too empoverished in argument, to resume the conflict. His eyes were fixed on the ground; he looked suddenly years older—a baffled and beaten man. . . .

The woman turned her head first. Kilvert saw her steal a furtive glance at her companion. She detached her hands from the rail, and half moved toward him; then she stiffened herself, resumed her former attitude, and addressed her mournful sunken profile to the contemplation of Venice. . . . But not for long; she looked again; her hands twitched, her face quivered, and suddenly she swept about, rejuvenated, and crossed the space between herself and her companion. He started at her touch on his arm, and looked at her, bewildered, reproachful, while she began to speak low and rapidly, as though all that was left to be said must be crowded into the diminishing minutes before the boat drew alongside the quay. "Ah, how like a woman!" Kilvert groaned, all his compassion transferred to the man. "Now she's going to begin it all over again—just as he'd begun to resign himself to the inevitable!"

Yet he envied the man on whom this intolerable strain was imposed. "How she must love him to torture him so!" he ejaculated. "She looks ten years younger since she's come back to him. Anything better than to spend these last minutes apart from him. . . . Nothing that he may be suffering counts a single instant in comparison with that. . . ." He saw the man's brow darken, his eyebrows jut out almost savagely over his suffering bewildered eyes, and his lips open to utter a word, a single word, that Kilvert could not hear, but of which he traced the passage on the woman's face as if it had been the sting of a whip. She paled under her deep sunburn, her head drooped, she clung to her companion desolately, almost helplessly, and for a minute they neither spoke nor looked at each other. Then Kilvert saw the man's hand steal toward hers and clasp it as it still lay on his arm. He spoke again, more softly, and her head sank lower, but she made no answer. They both looked exhausted with the struggle.

Two men who had been sitting near by got up and began to collect their bags and baskets. One of the couple whom Kilvert was watching pointed out to the other the seats thus vacated, and the two moved over and sat down on the narrow board. Dusk was falling, and Kilvert could no longer see their faces distinctly; but he noticed that the man had slipped his arm about his companion, not so much to embrace as to support her. She smiled a little at his touch, and leaned back, and they sat silent, their worn faces half averted from one another, as though they had reached a point beyond entreaties and arguments. Kilvert watched them in an agony of participation. . . .

Now the boat was crossing the Grand Canal; the dusky

palaces glimmered with lights, lamplit prows flashed out from the side canals, the air was full of cries and guttural hootings. On board the boat the passengers were all afoot, assembling children and possessions, rummaging for tickets, chattering and pushing. Kilvert sat quiet. He knew the boat would first touch near the railway station, where most of the passengers would probably disembark, before it carried him to his own landing-place at the Piazzetta. The man and woman sat motionless also; he concluded with satisfaction that they would probably land at the Piazzetta, and that there he might very likely find some one waiting for him—some friend of Mrs. Roseneath's, or a servant sent to meet him—and might just conceivably discover who his passionate pilgrims were.

But suddenly the man began to speak again, quickly, vehemently, in less guarded tones. He was speaking Italian now, easily and fluently, though it was obvious from his intonation that it was not his native tongue. "You promised—you promised!" Kilvert heard him reiterate, no doubt made reckless by the falling darkness and the hurried movements of the passengers. The woman's lips seemed to shape a "no" in reply; but Kilvert could not be sure. He knew only that she shook her head once or twice, softly, resignedly. Then the two lapsed once more into silence, and the man leaned back and stared ahead of him.

The boat had drawn close to her first landing-stage, and the gang-plank was being run out. The couple sat listlessly watching it, still avoiding each other's eyes. The people who were getting off streamed by them, chattering and jostling each other, lifting children and baskets of fowls over their heads. The couple watched. . . .

And then, suddenly, as the last passengers set foot on the quay, and the whistle for departure sounded, the woman sprang up, forced her way between the sailors who had their hands on the gang-plank, and rushed ashore without a backward glance or gesture. The man, evidently taken by surprise, started to his feet and tried to follow; but a bewildered mother clutching a baby blocked his way, the bell rang, and the gangplank was already being hauled onto the boat. . . . The man drew back baffled, and stood straining his eyes after the fugitive; but she had already vanished in the dispersing throng.

As Kilvert's gaze followed her he felt as if he too were straining his eyes in the pursuit of some rapture just glimpsed and missed. It might have been his own lost destiny mocking him in the flight of this haggard woman stumbling away distraught from her last hope of youth and freedom. Kilvert saw the man she had forsaken raise his hand to his eyes with a vague hopeless gesture, then give his shoulders a shake and stand leaning against the rail, unseeing, unhearing. "It's the end," Kilvert muttered to himself.

The boat was now more than half empty, and as they swung back into the Grand Canal he was tempted to go up to the solitary traveller and say a word to him—perhaps only ask him for a light, or where the boat touched next. But the man's face was too closed, too stricken; Kilvert did not dare intrude on such a secrecy of suffering. At the Piazzetta the man, who had taken up his place near the gang-plank, was among the first to hurry ashore, and in the confusion and the cross-play of lights Kilvert for a moment lost sight of him. But his tall gray head reappeared again above the crowd just as Kilvert himself was greeted by young Harry Breck, Mrs. Roseneath's accomplished private secretary. Kilvert seized the secretary's arm. "Look here! Who's that man over there? The tall fellow with gray hair and reddish beard . . . stalking-cap . . . there, ahead of you," Kilvert gasped incoherently, clutching the astonished Breck, who was directing one of Mrs. Roseneath's gondoliers toward his luggage.

"Tall man—where?" Young Breck, swinging round, lifted himself on his tiptoes to follow the other's gesture.

"There—over there! Don't you see? The man with a stalking-cap—"

"That? I can't be certain at this distance; but it looks like Brand, the 'cellist, don't it? Want to speak to him? No? All right. Anyhow, I'm not so sure. . . ."

They went down the steps to the gondola.

II

"That, would account for their hands," Kilvert suddenly thought, rousing himself to wave away a second offering of *langoustines à la Vénitienne*. He looked down Mrs. Rose-

neath's shining dinner-table, trying to force himself to a real-
isation of the scene; but the women's vivid painted heads, the
men's polished shirt-fronts, the gliding gondoliers in white
duck and gold-fringed sashes, handing silver dishes down the
table, all seemed as remote and unrelated to reality as the
great Tiepolesque fresco which formed the background of the
scene. Before him Kilvert could see only a middle-aged life-
worn man and woman torn with the fulness of human passion. "If he's a musician, so is she, probably," he thought; and
this evocation of their supple dramatic hands presented itself
as a new clue to their identity.

He did not know why he was so anxious to find out who
they were. Indeed, some secret apprehension half held him
back from pressing his inquiries. "Brand the 'cellist—" from
young Breck's tone it would seem that the name was well-
known among musicians. Kilvert racked his memories; but
music and musicians were not prominent in them, and he
could not discover any association with the name of Brand—
or any nationality either, since it might have been at home
anywhere from Edinburgh to Oslo.

Well, all this brooding was really morbid. Was it possible
that he would stoop to gather up gossip about this couple,
even if he succeeded in finding out who they were? No! All he
wanted was to identify them, to be able to call them by name,
and then enshrine them in some secret niche of memory in all
their tragic isolation. "Musicians' hands—that's it," he murmured.

But the problem would not let him rest, and after dinner,
forsaking the groups who were scattering and forming again
down the length of the great frescoed saloon, he found a pretext for joining Breck on the balcony.

"That man I pointed out as I left the boat—you said he was
a musician?"

"When? Oh, as you were leaving the boat? Well, he looked
uncommonly like Julian Brand. You've never heard him? Not
much in that line, are you? Thought not. They gave you a
cigar, I hope?" he added, suddenly remembering his duties.

Kilvert waved that away too. "I'm not particularly musical.
But his head struck me. They were sitting near me on the
boat."

"They? Who?" queried Breck absently, craning his head back toward the saloon to make sure that the *liqueurs* were being handed.

"This man. He was with a woman, very dark, black hair turning gray, splendid eyes—dreadfully badly dressed, and not young, but tingling. Something gypsy-like about her. Who was she, do you suppose? They seemed very intimate."

"Love-making, eh?"

"No. Much more—more *intimate* than that. Hating and loving and despairing all at once," stammered Kilvert, reluctant to betray himself to such ears, yet driven by the irresistible need to find out what he could from this young fool. "They weren't husband and wife, either, you understand."

Breck laughed. "Obviously! You said they were intimate."

"Well, who was she then—the woman? Can you tell me?"

Breck wrinkled his brows retrospectively. He saw so many people in the course of a day, his uncertain frown seemed to plead. "Splendid eyes, eh?" he repeated, as if to gain time.

"Well, burning—"

"Ah, burning," Breck echoed, his eyes on the room. "But I must really . . . Here, Count Dossi's the very man to tell you," he added, hurrying away in obedience to a signal from Mrs. Roseneath.

The small, dry waxen-featured man who replaced him was well-known to Kilvert, and to all cosmopolitan idlers. He was an Anglo-Italian by birth, with a small foothold in Rome, where he spent the winter months, drifting for the rest of the year from one centre of fashion to another, and gathering with impartial eye and indefatigable memory the items of a diary which, he boasted, could not safely be published till fifty years after his death. Count Dossi bent on Kilvert his coldly affable glance. "Who has burning eyes?" he asked. "I came out here in search of a light, but hadn't hoped to find one of that kind." He produced a cigarette, and continued, as he held it to Kilvert's lighter: "There are not so many incandescent orbs left in the world that one shouldn't be able to identify them."

Kilvert shrank from exposing the passionate scene on the boat to Count Dossi's disintegrating scrutiny; yet he could not bear to miss the chance of tracing the two who had given him so strange a cross-section of their souls. He tried to appear indifferent, and slightly ironical. "There are still some. . . ."

"Oh, no doubt. A woman, I suppose?"

Kilvert nodded. "But neither young nor beautiful—by rule, at least."

"Who is beautiful, by rule? A plaster cast at best. But your lady interests me. Who is she? I know a good many people. . . ."

Kilvert, tempted, began to repeat his description of the couple, and Count Dossi, meditatively twisting his cigarette, listened with a face wrinkled with irony. "Ah, that's interesting," he murmured, as the other ended. "Musicians' hands, you say?"

"Well, I thought—"

"You probably thought rightly. I should say Breck's guess was correct. From your description the man was almost certainly Brand, the 'cellist. He was to arrive about this time for a series of concerts with Margaret Aslar. You've heard the glorious Margaret? Yes, it must have been Brand and Aslar. . . ." He pinched his lips in a dry smile. "Very likely she crossed over to Fusina to meet him. . . ."

"To meet him? But I should have thought they'd been together for hours. They were in the thick of a violent discussion when they came on board. . . . They looked haggard, worn out . . . and so absorbed in each other that they hardly knew where they were."

Dossi nodded appreciatively. "No, they wouldn't—they wouldn't! The foolish things. . . ."

"Ah—they care so desperately for each other?" Kilvert murmured.

Dossi lifted his thin eyebrows. "Care—? They care frantically for each other's music; they can't get on without each other—in that respect."

"But when I saw them they were not thinking about anybody's music; they were thinking about each other. They were desperate . . . they . . . they . . ."

"Ah, just so! Fighting like tigers, weren't they?"

"Well, one minute, yes—and the next, back in each other's arms, almost."

"Of course! Can't I see them? They were probably quarrelling about which of their names should come first on the
programme, and have the biggest letters. And Brand's weak;
I back Margaret to come out ahead. . . . You'll see when
the bills are posted up." He chuckled at the picture, and
was turning to re-enter the room when he paused to say:
"But, by the way, they're playing here tomorrow night,
aren't they? Yes; I'm sure our hostess told me this afternoon
that she'd finally captured them. They don't often play in
private houses—Margaret hates it, I believe. But when Mrs.
Roseneath sets her heart on anything she's irresistible." With
a nod and smile he strolled back into the long saloon where
the guests were dividing into groups about the bridge-
tables.

Kilvert continued to lean on the stone balustrade and look
down into the dark secret glitter of the canal. He was fairly
sure that Dossi's identification of the mysterious couple was
correct; but of course his explanation of their quarrel was absurd. A child's quarrel over toys and spangles! That was how
people of the world interpreted the passions of great artists.
Kilvert's heart began to beat excitedly at the thought of seeing and hearing his mysterious couple. And yet—supposing
they turned out to be mere tawdry *cabotins*? Would it not be
better to absent himself from the concert and nurse his
dream? It was odd how Dossi's tone dragged down those
vivid figures to the level of the dolls about Mrs. Roseneath's
bridge-tables.

III

Kilvert had not often known his hostess to be in the field as
early as ten in the morning. But this was a field-day, almost as
important as the day of the fancy ball, since two or three passing royalties (and not in exile either) had suddenly signified
their desire to be present at her musical party that evening;
and Mrs. Roseneath, on such occasions, had the soldier's gift
of being in the saddle at dawn. But when Kilvert—his own
café-au-lait on the balcony barely despatched—was summoned to her room by an agitated maid, he found the mistress even more agitated.

"They've chucked—they've chucked for tonight! The devils —they won't come!" Mrs. Roseneath cried out, waving a pale hand toward a letter lying on her brocaded bedspread.

"But do take a mouthful of tea, madam," the maid intervened, proffering a tray.

"Tea? How can I take tea? Take it away! It's a catastrophe, John—a catastrophe . . . and Breck's such a helpless fool when it comes to anything beyond getting people together for bridge," Mrs. Roseneath lamented, sinking back discouraged among her pillows.

"But who's chucked? The Prince and Princess?"

"Lord, no! They're all coming; the King is too, I mean. And *he's* musical, and has stayed over on purpose. . . . It's Aslar, of course, and Brand. . . . Her note is perfectly insane. She says Brand's disappeared, and she's half crazy, and can't play without him."

"Disappeared—the 'cellist?"

"Oh, for heaven's sake, read the note, and don't just stand there and repeat what I say! Where on earth am I to get other performers for this evening, if you don't help me?"

Kilvert stared back blankly. "I don't know."

"You don't know? But you must know! Oh, John, you must go instantly to see her. You're the only person with brains—the only one who'll know how to talk to such people. If I offered to double the fee, do you suppose—?"

"Oh, no, no!" Kilvert protested indignantly, without knowing why.

"Well, what I'd already agreed to give is colossal," Mrs. Roseneath sighed, "so perhaps it's not that, after all. John, darling, you must go and see her at once! You'll know what to say. She must keep her engagement, she must telegraph, she must send a motor after him; if she can't find *him*, she must get hold of another 'cellist. None of these people will know if it's Brand or not. I'll lie about it if I have to. Oh, John, ring for the gondola! Don't lose an instant . . . say anything you like, use any argument . . . only make her see it's her duty!" Before the end of the sentence he was out of her door, borne on the rush of Mrs. Roseneath's entreaties down the long marble flights to the gondola. . . .

Kilvert was in the mood to like the shabbiness, the dinginess almost, of the little hotel on an obscure canal to which
the gondola carried him. He liked even the slit of untidy garden, in which towels were drying on a sagging rope, the umbrella-stand in imitation of rustic woodwork, the slatternly
girl with a shawl over her head delivering sea-urchins to the
black-wigged landlady. This was the way real people lived, he
thought, glancing at a crumby dining-room glimpsed
through glass doors. He thought he would find a pretext for
moving there the next day from the Palazzo, and very nearly
paused to ask the landlady if she could take him in. But his errand was urgent, and he went on.

The room into which he was shown was small, and rather
bare. A worn cashmere shawl had been thrown over the low
bed in a hasty attempt to convert it into a divan. The centre
front was filled by a grand piano built on a concert-stage
scale, and looking larger than any that Kilvert had ever seen.
Between it and the window stood a woman in a frayed purple
silk dressing-gown, her tumbled grayish hair streaked with jet
tossed back from her drawn dusky face. She had evidently not
noticed Kilvert the previous evening on the boat, for the
glance she turned on him was unrecognising. Obviously she
resented his intrusion. "You come from Mrs. Roseneath,
don't you? About tonight's concert? I said you could come
up in order to get it over sooner. But it's no use whatever—
none! Please go back and tell her so."

She was speaking English now, with a slightly harsh yet rich
intonation, and an accent he could not quite place, but
guessed to be partly Slavonic. He stood looking at her in an
embarrassed silence. He was not without social adroitness, or
experience in exercising it; but he felt as strongly as she evidently did that his presence was an intrusion. "I don't believe
I know how to talk to real people," he reproached himself inwardly.

"Before you send me away," he said at length, "you must
at least let me deliver Mrs. Roseneath's message of sympathy."

Margaret Aslar gave a derisive shrug. "Oh, sympathy—!"

He paused a moment, and then ventured: "Don't you
need it? On the boat yesterday evening I rather thought you
did."

She turned toward him with a quick swing of her whole body. "The boat yesterday evening? You were there?"

"I was sitting close to you. I very nearly had the impertinence to go up to you and tell you I was—sorry."

She received this in a wondering silence. Then she dropped down on the piano-stool, and rested her thin elbows on the closed lid of the instrument, and her drooping head on her hands. After a moment she looked up and signed to him to take the only chair. "Put the music on the floor," she directed. Kilvert obeyed.

"You were right—I need pity, I need sympathy," she broke out, her burning eyes on his.

"I wish I could give you something more—give you real help, I mean."

She continued to gaze at him intently. "Oh, if you could bring him back to me!" she exclaimed, lifting her prayerful hands with the despair of the mourning women in some agonizing Deposition.

"I would if I could—if you'd tell me how," Kilvert murmured.

She shook her head, and sank back into her weary attitude at the piano. "What nonsense I'm talking! He's gone for good, and I'm a desolate woman."

Kilvert had by this time entirely forgotten the object of his visit. All he felt was a burning desire to help this stricken Ariadne.

"Are you sure I couldn't find him and bring him back—if you gave me a clue?"

She sat silent, her face plunged in her long tortured hands. Finally she looked up again to murmur: "No. I said things he can never forgive—"

"But if you tell him that, perhaps he will," suggested Kilvert.

She looked at him questioningly, and then gave a slight laugh. "Ah, you don't know—you don't know either of us!"

"Perhaps I could get to, if you'd help me; if you could tell me, for instance, without breach of confidence, the subject of that painful discussion you were having yesterday—a lovers' quarrel, shall we call it?"

She seemed to catch only the last words, and flung them back at him with a careless sneer. "Lovers' quarrel? Between *us*? Do you take us for children?" She swept her long arms across the piano-lid, as if it were an open keyboard. "Lovers' quarrels are pastry *éclairs*. Brand and I are artists, Mr.——Mr.——"

"Kilvert."

"I've never denied his greatness as an artist—never! And he knows it. No living 'cellist can touch him. I've heard them all, and I know. But, good heavens, if you think that's enough for him!"

"Such praise from you—"

She laughed again. "One would think so! Praise from Margaret Aslar! But no—! You say you saw us yesterday on the boat. I'd gone to Fusina to meet him—really in the friendliest spirit. He'd been off on tour in Poland and Hungary; I hadn't seen him for weeks. And I was so happy, looking forward to our meeting so eagerly. I thought it was such a perfect opportunity for talking over our Venetian programmes; tonight's, and our two big concerts next week. Wouldn't you have thought so too? He arrived half an hour before the boat started, and his first word was: 'Have you settled the programmes?' After that—well, you say you saw us. . . ."

"But he was awfully glad to see you; I saw that, at any rate."

"Oh, yes; awfully glad! He thought that after such a separation I'd be like dough in his hands—accept anything, agree to anything! I had settled the programmes; but when he'd looked them over, he just handed them back to me with that sort of *sotto voce* smile he has, and said: 'Beautiful—perfect. But I thought it was understood that we were to appear together?' "

"Well—wasn't it?" Kilvert interjected, beginning to flounder.

She glanced at him with a shrug. "When Brand smiles like that it means: 'I see you've made out the whole programme to your own advantage. It's really a piano solo from one end to the other'. That's what he means. Of course it isn't, you understand; but the truth is that nowadays he has come to consider me simply as an accompanist, and would like to have our tour regarded as a series of 'cello concerts, so that he's furious when I don't subordinate myself entirely."

Kilvert listened in growing bewilderment. He knew very little about artists, except that they were odd and unaccountable. He would have given all his possessions to be one himself; but he wasn't, and he had never felt his limitations more keenly than at this moment. Still, he argued with himself, fundamentally we're all made of the same stuff, and this splendid fury is simply a woman in love, who's afraid of having lost her lover. He tried to pursue the argument on those lines.

"After all—suppose you were to subordinate yourself, or at least affect to? Offer to let him make out your next few programmes, I mean . . . if you know where he's to be found, I could carry your message. . . ."

"Let him give a 'cello tour with 'Mrs. J. Margaret Aslar at the piano'—in small type, at the bottom of the page? Ah," she cried, swept to her feet by a great rush of Sybilline passion, "*that's* what you think of my playing, is it? I always knew fashionable people could barely distinguish a barrel-organ from a Steinway—but I didn't know they confused the players as well as the instruments."

Kilvert felt suddenly reassured by her unreasonableness. "I wasn't thinking of you as a player—but only as a woman."

"A woman? Any woman, I suppose?"

"A woman in love *is* 'any woman.' A man in love is 'any man.' If you tell your friend that all that matters is your finding him again, he'll put your name back on the programme wherever you want it to be."

Margaret Aslar, leaning back against the piano, stood looking down at him sternly. "Have you *no* respect for art?" she exclaimed.

"Respect for art? But I venerate it—in all its forms!" Kilvert stammered, overwhelmed.

"Well, then—you ought to try to understand its interpreters. We're instruments, you see, Mr.—— Mr.——"

"Kilvert."

"We're the pipes the god plays on—not mere servile eyes or ears, like all the rest of you! And whatever branch of art we're privileged to represent, that we must uphold, we must defend—even against the promptings of our own hearts. Brand has left me because he won't recognise that *my* branch is higher, is more important, than his. In his infatuated obstinacy he won't admit what all the music of all the greatest composers goes to show; that the piano ranks above the 'cello. And yet it's so obvious, isn't it? I could have made my career as a great pianist without him—but where would he as a 'cellist be without me? Ah, let him try—let him try! That's what I've always told him. If he thinks any girl of twenty, because she has long eyelashes, and pretends to swoon whenever he plays his famous Beethoven adagio, can replace an artist who is his equal; but his equal in a higher form of art—" She broke off, and sank down again on the piano-stool. "Our association has made him; but he won't admit it. He won't admit that the 'cello has no life of its own without the piano. Well, let him see how he feels as number four in a string quartet! Because that's what he'll have to come to now."

Kilvert felt himself out of his depth in this tossing sea of technical resentments. He might have smiled at it in advance, as a display of artistic fatuity; but now he divined, under the surface commotion, something nobler, something genuine and integral. "I've never before met a mouthpiece of the gods," he thought, "and I don't believe I know how to talk to them."

And then, with a start, he recalled the humble purpose of his mission, and that he was there, not as the answering mouthpiece of divinity, but only as Mrs. Roseneath's. After all, it was hard on her to have her party wrecked for a whim. He looked at Margaret Aslar with a smile.

"You have a wonderful opportunity of proving your argument to your friend this very evening. Everybody in Venice is coming to hear you at Mrs. Roseneath's. You have simply to give a piano recital to show that you need no one to help you."

She gazed at him in a sort of incredulous wonder, and slowly an answering smile stole over her grave lips. "Ah, he'd see *then*—he'd see!" She seemed to be looking beyond Kilvert's shoulder, at a figure unseen by him, to whom she flung out her ironic challenge. "Let him go off, and do as much himself! Let him try to cram a house to bursting, and get ten recalls, with a stammering baby at the piano!" She put up her hands to her tossed hair. "I've grown gray at this work—and so has he! Twenty years ago we began. And every gray hair is a string in the perfect instruments that time has made of us. That's what a man never sees—never remembers! Ah, just let him try; let him have his lesson now, if he wants to!"

Kilvert sprang up, as if swept to his feet on the waves of her agitation. "You will come then, won't you? And the programme—? Can I go back and say you'll have it ready in an hour or two? I hate to bother you; but, you see, Mrs. Roseneath's in suspense—I must hurry back now with your promise."

"My promise?" Margaret Aslar confronted him with a brow of tragic wonderment. Her face reminded him of a wind-swept plain with cloud-shadows rushing over it. "My promise—to play tonight without Brand? But my poor Mr.—— Mr.——"

"Kilvert."

"Are you serious? Really serious? Do you really suppose that a tree torn up by the roots and flung to the ground can give out the same music as when it stands in the forest by its mate, and the wind rushes through their branches? I couldn't play a note tonight. I must bury my old self first—the self made out of Brand and Margaret Aslar. Tell Mrs. Roseneath I'm sorry—tell her anything you like. Tell her I'm burying a friend; tell her that Brand's dead—and he *is* dead, now that he's lost me. Tell her I must watch by him tonight. . . ."

She stood before Kilvert with lifted arms, in an attitude of sculptural desolation; then she turned away and went and leaned in the window, as unconscious of his presence as if he had already left the room.

Kilvert wanted to speak, to argue, urge, entreat; but a kind of awe, a sense of her inaccessibility, restrained him. What plea of expediency would weigh anything in the scales of such anger and such sorrow? He stood waiting for a while, trying to think of something to say; but no words came, and he slipped out and closed the door on the greatest emotional spectacle he had ever witnessed.

The whirr of wings was still in his ears when he reached the door of the hotel and began to walk along the narrow street leading to the nearest *traghetto*. A few yards from the door he almost stumbled against a man who, turning a corner, stopped abruptly in his path. They looked at each other in surprise, and Kilvert stammered: "You're Mr. Brand?"

The other smiled and nodded. He had the delicately shaded smile of a man who seldom laughs, and its kindly disenchanted curve betrayed a hint of recognition. "Yes. I saw you yesterday on the Fusina boat, didn't I?"

Kilvert glanced up and down the narrow deserted *calle*. He seemed, for the first time in his life, to have his hand on the wheels of destiny, and the contact scorched his palm. He had forgotten all about Mrs. Roseneath and the concert. He was still in the presence of the woman upstairs in the shabby hotel, and his only thought was: "He's come back to her!"

Brand's eyes were resting on him with a glance of amiable curiosity, and he was conscious that, in that narrow lane, they were actually obstructing each other's passage, and that his business was to draw aside, bow and pass on. But something suddenly impelled him to speak. "My name's Kilvert. I've just come from Madame Aslar's."

Brand nodded again; he seemed neither surprised nor put off by the half-confidential tone of the remark.

"Ah? I supposed so," he agreed affably.

"Now, why did he suppose so?" Kilvert wondered; and, feeling that the onus of explaining was on his side, he added, collecting himself: "I'm staying with Mrs. Roseneath, and she sent me as—as an ambassador, to reason with Madame Aslar, to do what I could to persuade her . . ."

Brand looked genuinely surprised. "Reason with her?" he echoed, as though faintly amused at any one's attempting so impossible a task.

"About the concert tonight at Mrs. Roseneath's."

"Oh, the devil! At Mrs. Roseneath's? I'd forgotten all about it! Is Margaret going to play?"

The two men looked at each other a moment, as if attempting to measure the situation; then Kilvert took a plunge. "Of course not. She refused absolutely."

The other gave a low whistle. "Refused? What's up now? Why 'of course'—?"

It was Kilvert's turn to sound his surprise. "But without you—she says she'll never play a note without you!"

The musician answered with a wondering glance. His lips were grave, but the disenchanted smile in the depths of his eyes turned into a faint glimmer of satisfaction. "Play without me? Of course she won't—she *can't*! I'm glad she's admitted it for once." He scrutinised Kilvert with quiet irony. "I suppose our lives have no secrets for you, if you've been talking with Margaret. I came back, of course, because we must get through our Venetian engagements somehow. After that—"

"Oh," Kilvert interrupted passionately, "don't say: 'After that'!"

Brand gave a careless shrug. "After that, I shall come back again; I shall keep on coming back; always for the same reason, I suppose."

"If you could see her as she is now, you'd need no other reason than herself!"

The musician repeated his shrug, this time with a gesture of retrospective weariness. "If only she'd leave me alone about that Polish girl! As if a man couldn't have a chance accompanist without . . . Her fatal mistake is always mixing the eternal with the transient. But every woman does that, I suppose. Oh, well, we're chained to each other by something we love better than ourselves; and she knows it. She knows I'll always come back—I'll always have to." He stood looking at Kilvert as if this odd burst of confidence had suddenly turned them into old friends. "Do you know what programme she's settled on for tonight?" he added wearily, as he turned toward the door of the hotel.

Joy in the House

THE MOMENT the big liner began to move out of harbour Christine Ansley went down to her small inside stateroom and addressed herself, attentively and systematically, to unpacking and arranging her things. Only a week between Havre and New York; but that was no reason why she should not be comfortably settled, have everything within easy reach, "ship-shape," in fact—she saw now the fitness of the term.

She sat down on the narrow berth with a sigh of mingled weariness and satisfaction. The wrench had been dreadful— the last hours really desperate; she was shaken with them still—but the very moment the steamer began to glide out into the open the obsession fell from her, the tumult and the agony seemed to grow unreal, remote, as if they had been part of a sensational film she had sat and gazed at from the stalls. The real woman, her only real self, was here in this cabin, homeward bound, was Mrs. Devons Ansley—ah, thank God, still Mrs. Devons Ansley!—and not the bewildered shattered Christine who, a few hours earlier, had stumbled out of the room in the hotel at Havre, repeating to the man who sat, his face buried in his arms, and neither moved nor spoke any longer: "I can't . . . I mean I must. . . . I promised Devons I'd go back. . . . You *know* I promised!"

That was barely three hours ago. But by this time no doubt Jeff Lithgow was in the train again, on his way back to Paris; and she was here, on this blessed boat, in this dear little cabin of her own, sitting on the narrow berth in which she would sleep undisturbed through the long safe quiet night and on into the next day, for as many hours on end as she chose. A whole week by herself, in which to sleep, and to think things over, and gradually to become Christine Ansley again—oh, yes, forever! The time seemed too short; she wished the steamer were bound across the Pacific at its widest. . . .

She began to unpack, shaking out the garments she had flung into her steamer-trunk that morning, she didn't know how! What a welter of untidiness and confusion she had come out of: things always being pitched into trunks or tumbled out, in the perpetual rush and confusion of their unsettled lives. Poor Jeff! He would never be anything but a roamer . . . With whom would he roam next, she wondered? But that speculation did not detain her long. She wanted to turn her thoughts away from Jeff, not to follow him through his subsequent divagations. . . . She supposed all artists were like that; he said they were. Painters especially. . . . Not that she had ever thought him a great painter—not *really*. . . . His portrait of her, for instance! Why, she must have sat for it sixty times—no, sixty-two; she'd counted. . . . Hours and hours of stiff neck and petrified joints. . . . He had a theory that a painter should always catch his subjects unawares, but there wasn't much unawareness about his practice! She was thankful Devons had never seen that portrait. . . . Of course Devons didn't know much about painting; at least that particular kind of painting. In his own line—as a militant moralist, and an amateur lecturer on the New Psychology—he prided himself on being in the advance guard, an "ultra," as he smilingly boasted; but though he had a smattering of Academic culture, and had once discoursed on Renaissance Painters to the Stokesburg Wednesday Evening Club, his business as an active real-estate agent had prevented his having time to deal with the moderns, and Christine recalled his genial guffaw when he had first encountered a picture of Jeff's at Mabel Breck's: "My Lithgow," Mabel simperingly called it.

"That a Lithgow, is it? Glad to know! I saw at once it wasn't a picture," Dev had guffawed—how it had mortified Christine at the time! Mabel had been obviously annoyed; Mabel liked to be in the "last boat," but not alone there; but Mabel's husband and the others had enjoyed the joke, and been put at their ease by it, for Devons passed for a wit in their set, and Stokesburg, in spite of its thirst for modern culture, was not yet collecting Lithgows. . . .

Jeff had a brilliant talent; Christine had been among the first to recognise it. At least among the first at Stokesburg; for when she went to New York that spring she found that everybody (the "everybody" she wanted to be one of) was talking of him, and wondering whether one oughtn't to get in ahead and buy his pictures. Yes, of course Jeff had talent—but there was something unstable, unreliable in his talent, just as there was in his character . . . whereas Devons . . .

She put up her hands and hid her face in them for a moment. . . . Why this perpetual pendulum swing: Jeff—Devons, Devons—Jeff, backward and forward in her brain? The Jeff affair was over, wound up, wiped out of existence; she was Mrs. Devons Ansley, going back to her husband after a six months' absence. No; no six months, even. Five months and sixteen days. That had been the understanding when she and Devons had parted at the station (so like him to drive her to the station, and see that she was properly settled in the New York train, and had the newspapers, and a box of chocolates!). He had said then, slipping a letter into her hand with her ticket: "Here, my dear; I've put it in writing so that there can be no mistake. Any time within six months, if you want to come back, there'll be joy in the house. Joy in the house!" He had said it emphatically, deliberately, with a drawn smile, and ended on a sort of nervous parody of his large hospitable laugh. "*Within* six months! After that, of course, I shall assume . . . I shall feel obliged to assume . . ." The train was already moving, but his strained grin, his laborious laugh, had followed her. It had been "poor Dev" then—till she saw Jeff's dark eager head working a way toward her through the crowd at the Grand Central station. . . .

Well—she had made a horrible mistake, and she had recognised it in time. Many women make just such mistakes, but to few, even in communities more advanced than Stokesburg, is given the opportunity of wiping out the past and beginning over again. She owed that to Devons; to his really superhuman generosity. It was something she would never forget; she would devote the rest of her life to making up to him for it—to that, and to bringing up their boy to appreciate and revere his father. . . . When she thought of the boy—her baby Christopher—the sense of her iniquity, of her inhumanity, overcame her afresh. She had walked out of the house and left husband and child to fend for themselves, consoling herself with the idea that the same thing happened to lots of children whose parents were "unsuited" to each other, and that they never seemed much the worse for it. And then Christopher's Susan was a perfect nurse, and Mrs. Robbit, Devons's mother (who had remarried, but was again a widow) lived only five minutes away, and was devoted to her son and to the boy, and would manage everything ever so much better than Christine ever had. That had stilled her conscience as she pushed her way through the crowd to join Jeff at the Grand Central . . . but now?

Now she saw that, but for her husband's magnanimity, his loyalty to his given word, she would have been alone and adrift, husbandless and childless—for whatever happened (even if Jeff had been able to persuade his wife to divorce him, which had never been very sure, Madge Lithgow's views being less "advance guard" and more proprietary than Devons's); whatever happened, Christine now knew, she could never have married Jeffrey Lithgow. . . . Anything, anything but that!

"A trial marriage," Devons had called it, stiffening his lips into a benedictory smile on the day when she had wrung his consent from him. "Let's call it that, shall we? A marriage, I'll understand—not an elopement. For, of course, my child, unless your object is marriage—and unless you have a definite understanding—er . . . er . . . pledge—I couldn't possibly let you expose yourself—." A man like Devons, of course, couldn't dream that, to men like Jeff Lithgow, marriage means nothing; that they don't care whether they're married or not, because it makes no practical difference to them—no difference in their way of thinking or living. After all, what's the meaning of "self-realisation," if you're to let your life be conditioned and contracted by somebody else's? To the abstract argument, of course, Devons would have agreed; it was exactly what he was always preaching and proclaiming. "You wouldn't think it a virtue to limp about in a tight shoe, would you? Then, if the domestic shoe pinches—" didn't she know all the figures of speech and all the deductions? Jeff, on the contrary, had never thought about such questions, or worried about his own conduct or anybody else's. Abstract reasoning sent him to sleep, and he was unaware of institutions unless they got in his way and tripped him up. Every faculty was concentrated on the pursuit of his two passions: painting and loving. He said perhaps some time he'd take a day off—from painting, that is—and find out about the rest of life. . . .

With Devons it was just the other way. He was forever taking out his convictions and re-examining and re-formulating them. But he might lecture on "The New Morality" to the end of time, and talk as loudly as he pleased about individual liberty, and living one's life: *his* life was one of bed-room slippers and the evening paper by a clean gas-fire, with his wife stitching across the hearth, and telling him that the baby's first tooth was showing. Only, having proclaimed the doctrine of sentimental liberty so long and loudly, when he was asked to apply his doctrine to his wife's case he had either to admit it was a failure, or to accept the consequences; and he had accepted them.

She remembered the first day she had really listened to Jeff, consented to take his entreaties seriously, his look of genuine surprise when she had questioned: "Yes—but what about your wife?"

"Who—Madge?" (As if he had had several, and wasn't sure which!) "Oh, Madge's all right. She's A-1." That settled it, his easy smile seemed to say.

"But if you feel like that about her—why do you want to leave her?"

He took the end of one of his paint-brushes and ran it through the tawny-brown ripples of Christine's hair. "Because she smells of soap," he said gravely.

"Oh, Jeff—how monstrous!" But how could she help laughing with him when he laughed? "Madge understands—she *knows*," he continued, reassuring her. "Doesn't Ansley *know*?" he added, with sudden insight. And she murmured: "I suppose people can't help knowing when they're out of step. . . ." "Well, what's worrying you, then? Turn your head a fraction of a hair's breadth to the left, will you, darling? There—that's it. . . . For how many æons of time do you suppose the Creator has been storing the light in your hair for me? It may come from some star thirty million light-years away. Especially stored up for Jeff Lithgow!"

"But then, if it comes from as far off as that, the star's dead already; been dead for æons; the Christine star, you know."

At that he had drawn up his tormented eyebrows to meet the dusky-brown wrinkles of his forehead. "*You* dead? Why, you've hardly begun to be alive! You're a lovely buried lady that I've stumbled on in a desert tomb, shrouded in your golden hair; and being a sorcerer I'm breathing life into you. There! You're actually getting rosier with every word. . . ."

"Yes," she laughed. "But those resuscitated ladies never stay alive long. What are you going to do when I crumble on you?"

He threw down his brushes. "Do? Kill myself. I've waited for you too long," he said with a sudden sombreness, and a shiver swept through her that checked her laugh.

"Well—as long as you don't kill *me*!" she bantered back with dry lips.

"*You*? I won't have to. You'll die of losing me," he announced in his calm concentrated voice. "This isn't any ordinary flurry, you understand; it's one of those damned predestined things. . . . Child! You've moved again. Here— do try to look steadily at the left-hand upper corner of that picture-frame. So . . ." He sank back into his absorption with a murmur of deep content.

Yes; she saw it now. That was the kind of thing that had dazzled her—the light-years, and the buried lady, and that calm fatalistic vision: "You'll die of losing me—*Und mein Stamm sind jene Asra* . . ." and all the rest of it.

And then—the reality? Well, it wasn't that he seemed to love her less. Perhaps it was, in part, that the violence, the absoluteness of his love, was too much for her, was more than mortal stature—hers at any rate—could carry. There were days when she simply staggered under the load. And somehow he never seemed to try to share it with her—just left her to bear this prodigious burden of being loved by him as he left her, when they got out at a railway station, to stagger under the burden of their joint bags and wraps, to dive after the umbrellas, capture a porter and hunt for the hotel bus, while he solicitously nursed those sacred objects, his "painting things," and forgot about everything else, herself included.

Not that he wasn't kind; but how could he notice a poor woman carrying too heavy a load when he was miles above the earth, floating overhead in his native medium, in the stratosphere, as he called it? Why wouldn't she come up there with him? he was always asking her. "Don't say you couldn't breathe up there, when your eyes are made of two pieces of it." She had thought that enchanting, she remembered. . . .

But then, one day, when her eyes reminded him of something else, and he was bending over them, as he said, to fish for his lost soul—that day he had drawn back suddenly, and exclaimed, in a voice strident with jealousy: "Who's that other man in your eyes?"

Genuinely bewildered, she lifted them from the letter she had been reading. "The other man?" They filled with tears. "Oh, such a darling man! My little boy. This is from his Nanny—"

"Your little boy?" He seemed really not to know of whom she was speaking.

"My son Christopher. You haven't forgotten, I suppose, that I have a child at home, and must sometimes think of him?"

His own eyes darkened with momentary pity. "Oh, you poor lost mother-bird! But we'll have another child," he declared with sudden conviction, as if he were saying: "Poor child yourself—you've broken your toy, but I'll buy you another. . . ."

And then there had been the other day, less painful but more humiliating, when he had to tell her that the London dealer had returned the picture sent on approval, and that there wasn't money enough left to pay the hotel bill in that horrid place where the woman had been so insolent that they had already decided to leave—the day when they had had to bear her rudeness, and invent things to pacify her, and Jeff had offered to paint a head of her little girl in payment, and the monster had looked at one of his canvases, and said: *"Est-ce que Monsieur se moque de moi?"* Ah, how Christine hated the memory of it, she who had always held her head so high, and marked her passage by such liberalities! Devons, who wasn't always generous, gave big tips in travelling, perhaps because it was an easy way of adding to his own consequence, and because he liked to be blessed by beggars, and have servants rush to open doors for him. "It takes so little to make them happy," he always said, referring to the poor and the dependent; and Christine sometimes wondered how he knew.

She wasn't sure any longer that it took so little to make anybody happy. In her case it seemed to have taken the best of four or five people's lives, and left her so little happy that, with her steamer-trunk half unpacked, and the luncheon gong booming, she could only throw herself down on her berth and weep.

II

"A wireless, ma'am," the steward said, coming up to her on the last day out.

Christine took the message tremblingly; she had to wait a minute before breaking the band. Supposing it should be from Jeff, re-opening the whole question, arguing, pleading, reproaching her again? Or from Devons, to say that after all he had presumed too much on his moral courage in saying she might come back to him, with all Stokesburg maliciously agog for her return? Or the boy?—Ah, if it should be to say that Christopher was ill, was dead—her child whom she had abandoned so light-heartedly, and then, after a few weeks, begun to fret and yearn for with an incessant torment of self-reproach? How could she bear that, how could she bear it? The great tragic folds of her destiny were more than she could ever fill, were cut on a scale too vast for her. "Any answer, ma'am?" asked the hovering steward; and she stiffened herself and opened the telegram.

"In two days more there will be joy in the house. Devons and Christopher," she read, and the happy tears rushed to her eyes.

"Yes—there's an answer." She found her pen, the steward produced a form, and she scribbled: "And in my heart, you darlings." Yes; it was swelling, ripening in her heart, the joy of her return to these two people who were hers, who were waiting for her, to whom, in spite of everything, she was still, sacredly and inalienably, "my wife," "my mother." The steward hurried away, and she leaned back with closed eyes and a meditative heart.

What a relief to be drawn back into her own peaceful circle—to stop thinking about Jeff and the last tormented months, and glide, through the door of that tender welcome, into the safe haven of home! She kept her eyes shut, and tried to feel that home again, to see and hear it. . . .

A house in Crest Avenue—how proud she had been of it when Devons had first brought her there! Proud of the smooth circle of turf before the door, the two cut-leaved maples, the carefully clipped privet hedge, the honeysuckle over the porch. It was in the very best neighborhood, high up, dry, airy, healthy—and with the richest people living close by. Old Mrs. Briscott, and the Barkly Troys, and the young Palmers building their great new house on the ridge just above; Devons had the right to be proud of taking his young wife to such a home. But what she thought of now was not the Briscotts and the Troys and the Palmers—no, not even Mabel Breck and her "last boat," or the other social and topographical amenities of Crest Avenue, but just the space enclosed in her own privet hedge: the garden she and Devons had fussed over, ordered seeds and tools for, the house with its wide friendly gables and the inevitable Colonial porch, the shining order within doors, the sunny neatness of the nursery, the spring bulbs in Chinese bowls on the south window-seat in the drawing-room, her books in their low mahogany book-shelves, Devons's own study, that was as tidy and glossy as a model dairy, and Martha's broad smile and fluted cap on the threshold. Even to see Martha's smile again would be a separate and individual joy! And at last her clothes would be properly mended and pressed, and she would be able to splash about at leisure in the warm bathroom. . . .

She was not in the least ashamed of lingering over these small sensual joys. She had not made enough of them when they were hers, and dwelling on them now helped to shut out something dark and looming on the threshold of her thoughts—the confused sense that life is not a matter of water-tight compartments, that no effort of the will can keep experiences from interpenetrating and colouring each other, and that for all her memories and yearnings she was really a new strange Christine entering upon a new strange life. . . .

As the train reached Stokesburg, she leaned out, hungry for the sight of Christopher. She saw a round pink face, an arm agitating a new straw hat, a large pink hand gesticulating.

"No; the boy's waiting for you at home with his grandmother. I wanted to be alone to greet my wife. Let me take your bag, my darling. So; be careful how you jump." He enveloped her with almost paternal vigilance, receiving her on his broad chest as she stepped down on the platform. He smelt of eau de Cologne and bath salts; something sanitary, crisp and blameless exhaled itself from his whole person. If anything could ever corrupt him, it would not be moth and rust. . . .

She wanted to speak, to answer what he was saying; but her lips were dry. "And Christopher?" Her throat contracted as she tried to ask.

"Bless the boy! He's growing out of all his clothes. Mother says—"

Oh, the relief in her heart! "I suppose Susan's had Mrs. Shetter in to help her with the sewing?" How sweet it was to be saying the old usual things in the old usual way!

"Well, Susan—the fact is, Susan's not here any more. She—"

Susan not here! Susan no longer with Christopher? Christine's heart contracted again, she felt herself suddenly plunged full into the unknown, the disquieting. What had happened, why had her boy been separated from his nurse? But she hardly heard her husband's answer—she was thinking in a tumult: "After all, he was separated from his mother . . ."

"The fact is, Susan was too hide-bound, too old-fashioned. She was afraid of fresh air. She inflicted silly punishments. Mother and I felt that a change was necessary. You'll see what Miss Bilk has done already—"

"Miss Bilk!" Ah, how she was prepared to hate Miss Bilk! And her mother-in-law also, for interfering and introducing new ideas and people behind her back. Christine had always felt, under Mrs. Robbit's blandness and acquiescence, a secret itch to meddle and advise. And of course Devons had been wax in her hands. . . .

And here they were at the white gate, and across the newly clipped privet the house smiled at them from all its glittering windows. On the shiny door-step stood Mrs. Robbit, large and soft and beautifully dressed; and from her arms shot forth a flying figure, shouting: "Daddy—Daddy!" as the car drew up.

Daddy—only Daddy! Christine hung back, her dry eyes devouring the child, her lips twitching. "My son, here's your mother; here's darling mummy, back from her long journey. You know I always said she'd come," Devons admonished him.

Christopher stopped short, glanced at her, and twisted his hand nervously in his father's. She fell on her knees before him. "Chris—my Chris! You haven't forgotten me?"

"I thought you were dead," he said.

"Christopher, I told you every day that your mother had only gone away on a journey," his father rebuked him.

"Yes; but that's what they always say when they're dead," the child rejoined, kicking the gravel, and looking away from his mother. "You won't lock up my wireless, will you?" he asked suddenly. "Not because I thought you were dead?"

The tension was relieved by tears and laughter, and with the boy on his father's shoulder, husband and wife walked up the carefully raked gravel to where Mrs. Robbit smiled and rustled between newly painted tubs of blue hydrangeas. "I wanted you to have your first moments alone with Chris and Devons—my daughter!" Mrs. Robbit murmured, enfolding Christine in an embrace that breathed of hygiene and Christian charity.

Miss Bilk, discretion itself, hung in the background, hiding behind her spectacles. When Christine saw how neutral-tinted she was, and how large the spectacles were, her secret apprehension was relieved. Had she actually felt jealous of Miss Bilk? Was it possible that Jeff had so altered her whole angle of vision, taught her to regard all men and women as carnivora perpetually devouring each other in hate or love? She put an appeased hand in the nursery-governess's, and walked across the threshold with a quiet heart.

"Oh—how lovely!" she exclaimed in the doorway. On the varnished white stair-rail, facing her from a half-way landing, hung a panel on which skilful hands had woven in tight violets and roses:

JOY IN THE HOUSE

She gazed at it with tear-filled eyes. "How lovely of you all," she murmured.

"It was his idea," said Mrs. Robbit, with a fluffy gesture at her son.

"Ah, but mother did all the other flowers herself," the son interposed dutifully; and between the two, the reassured Christopher capering ahead, Christine re-entered her own drawing-room, saw the sunshine on the south window-seat, the hyacinths in the Chinese bowls, and flowers, flowers everywhere, disposed to welcome her.

"Joy in the house," her husband repeated, laying his lips on hers in an almost ritual gesture, while Mrs. Robbit delicately averted her swimming eyes.

"Yes—joy in the house, my daughter!"

"The parenthesis closed—everything between wiped out, obliterated, forgotten," Devons continued with rising eloquence.

Christine looked about her, trying to recognise them all again, and herself among them. "Home—" she murmured, straining every nerve to make it feel so.

"Home, sweet Home!" echoed her mother-in-law archly.

III

In the nursery, she had to admit, Miss Bilk had introduced the reign of reason. The windows were wide open day and night, Chris had his daily sun-bath, his baby gymnastics, his assorted vitamins. And he seemed not to dislike the calm spectacled guardian who had replaced his old impulsive Nanny. After dinner, and a goodnight kiss to her sleeping son, Christine said to her husband: "Yes, the boy looks splendidly. I'm sure Miss Bilk's all right. But it must have nearly killed Susan."

Devons's rosy beatitude was momentarily clouded. "That's just it. She made a dreadful scene—though she knew that scenes were the one thing strictly forbidden. She excited the child so that I had to send her off the same night."

"Oh, poor Susan! What she must have suffered—"

"My dear, she made the child suffer. I overheard her telling him that you'd gone away because you didn't love him. And I will not permit suffering in my house."

Christine startled herself by a sudden laugh. "I wonder how you're going to keep it out?"

"How?" He shone on her admonishingly over his gold-rimmed eyeglasses. "By ignoring it, denying it, saying: 'It won't happen—it can't happen! Not to simple kindly people like us.'" He paused and gave a shy cough. "I said that to myself, nearly six months ago, the day you told me you . . . you wished to travel. . . . Now you see . . ."

Compunction flushed her, and she stood up and went to him. "Oh, you've been splendid—don't think I don't feel it. . . ." She drew a deep breath. "It's lovely to be here—at peace again. . . ."

"Where you belong," he murmured, lifting her hand to his lips.

"Where I belong," she echoed. She was so grateful to him for attempting nothing more than that reverential salute that she had nearly bent to touch his forehead. But something in her resisted, and she went back to her armchair. The gas-fire sparkled between them. He said ceremoniously: "You permit?" as he lit his pipe, and sank back in his armchair with the sigh of happy digestion. You had only to forbid sorrow to look in at the door, or drive it out when it forced its way in disguised as Susan. In both cases the end had justified the means, and he sat placidly among the rebuilt ruins. No wonder he stirred his pipe with a tranquil hand. He smiled at her across the fire.

"You're tired, my dear, after your night in the train?"

"I suppose so . . . yes . . . and coming back. . . ."

He shook a pink finger admonishingly. "Too much emotion. I want you to have only calm happy thoughts. Go up to bed now and have a long quiet sleep."

Ah, how tactful, how thoughtful he was! He was not going to drag her back too soon into the old intimacy. . . . He knew, he must know, how she was entangled in those other memories. They kissed goodnight, stiffly, half fraternally, and he called after her, as she mounted the stairs under the triumphal flower-piece that was already fading: "In the morning Chris and I'll come in to see how you've slept."

What a good thing, she thought the next morning, that in the Stokesburg world every man had an office, and had to go to it. Life was incredibly simplified by not having one's husband about the house all day. With Jeff there was always the anxious problem of the days when he didn't want to paint, and just messed about and disturbed the settled order of things, irritating himself and her. Now she heard the front door open and close at the usual hour, and said to herself that Devons was already on his way down town. She leaned back luxuriously against her pillows, smiling at the bright spring sunlight on her coverlet, the pretty breakfast set which Martha had brought to the bedside (a "surprise" from Mrs. Robbit, the maid told her), and Chris's jolly shouts overhead. Yes, home was sweet on those terms . . . "I've waked from a bad dream," she thought.

When she came down a little later she was surprised to hear her husband's voice in the hall. It had not been to let him out that the front door had opened and closed. She paused on the landing, and saw him standing in the hall, his hat on, his hand on the door-handle, apparently addressing himself to some one who was already on the threshold.

"No, no—no publicity, please! On no account whatever! The matter is *closed*, you can say. Nothing changed: not a cloud on the horizon. My wife's a great traveller—that's all there is to it. Just a private episode with a happy ending—a Happy Ending!" he added, joyously stressing the capitals. The door shut on the invisible visitor and she saw Devons walk humming toward the umbrella-stand, select another stick, tap the barometer on the wall, and go out in his turn. "A reporter," Christine thought, wincing under the consciousness that it was to spy out her arrival that the man had come, and thankful that he had not waylaid her in the hall. "Devons always knew how to deal with them," she concluded, with a wife's comfortable dismissal of difficulties she need not cope with.

The house was exquisitely calm and orderly. She liked the idea of resuming her household duties, talking over the marketing with the cook, discussing a new furniture polish with Martha. It was soothing to move from one tidy room to the other, noting that ash-trays and paper-baskets had been emptied, cushions shaken up, scattered newspapers banished. Did the rooms look a trifle too tidy, had their personality been tidied away with the rest? She recalled with a shudder that chaotic room at the Havre hotel, and her struggle to sort out her things from Jeff's, in the sordid overnight confusion, while he sat at the table with his face buried.

For a moment, the evening before, she had wanted to talk to Devons of what was in her mind, to establish some sort of understanding with him; but how could she, when he declared that nothing was changed, spoke of her six months' absence as caused by a commendable desire for sight-seeing, tidied away all her emotion, and all reality, as the maid swept away pipe-ashes and stale newspapers? And now she saw that it was better so; that any return to the past would only stir up evil sediments, that the "nothing has happened" attitude was the safest, the wisest—and the easiest. She must just put away her anxious introspections, and fall in with her husband's plan. After all, she owed him that. "But I wish I could forget about Susan. He wasn't kind to Susan," she thought as she sat down at her writing-table.

She caught the ring of the front door bell, and Martha crossing the hall. Her mother-in-law, she supposed. She heard a woman's voice, and rose to welcome Mrs. Robbit. But the maid met her on the threshold, signing to her mysteriously. "There's a lady; she won't come in."

"Won't come in?"

"No. She says she wants to speak to you outside."

Christine walked buoyantly across the room. Its brightness and order struck her again; the flowers filled the air with summer. She crossed the hall, and in the open doorway saw a small slight woman standing. Christine's heart stood still. "Mrs. Lithgow!" she faltered.

Mrs. Lithgow turned on her a sharp birdlike face, drawn and dusky under graying hair. She was said to be older than her husband, and she looked so now.

"I wouldn't send in my name, because I knew if I did you'd tell the maid to say you were out." She spoke quickly, in a staccato voice which had something of Jeff's stridency.

"Say I was out—but why?" Christine stood looking at her shyly, kindly. There had been a day when the meeting with Jeff's wife would have filled her with anguish and terror; but now that the Jeff episode was happily over—obliterated, wiped out, as Devons said—what could she be to Mrs. Lithgow but a messenger of peace? "Why shouldn't I see you?" she repeated with a smile.

Mrs. Lithgow stood in the middle of the hall. Suddenly she looked up and her eyes rested on the withered "Joy in the House" that confronted her. "Well—because of *that*!" she said with a sharp laugh.

Christine coloured up. How indelicate—how like Jeff! she thought. The shock of the sneer made her feel how deeply she herself had already been reabsorbed into the pacifying atmosphere of Crest Avenue. "Do come in," she said, ignoring the challenge.

Mrs. Lithgow followed her into the drawing-room and Christine closed the door. Her visitor stood still, looking about her as she had looked about the hall. "Flowers everywhere, joy everywhere," she said, with the same low rasping laugh.

Christine flushed again, again felt herself more deeply committed to the Crest Avenue attitude. "Won't you sit down?" she suggested courteously.

The other did not seem to hear. "And not one petal on his grave!" she burst out with a sudden hysterical cry.

Christine gave a start of alarm. Was the woman off her balance—or only unconsciously imitating Jeff's crazy ravings? After a moment Christine's apprehension gave way to pity—she felt that she must quiet and reassure the poor creature. Perhaps Mrs. Lithgow, who was presumably not kept informed of the course of her husband's amatory adventures, actually thought that Christine meant to rejoin him. Perhaps she had come to warn her rival that she would never under any circumstances consent to a divorce.

"Mrs. Lithgow," Christine began, "I know you must think badly of me. I don't mean to defend myself. But perhaps you don't know that I've fully realised the wrong I've done, and that I've parted definitely from Jeff . . ."

Mrs. Lithgow, sitting rigid in the opposite chair, emitted one of her fierce little ejaculations. "Not know? Oh, yes: I know. Look at this." She drew a telegram out of her bag, and handed it to Christine, who unfolded it and read: "I thought I could stand her leaving me but I can't. Goodbye."

"You see he kept me informed of your slightest movements," said Mrs. Lithgow with a kind of saturnine satisfaction.

Christine sat staring in silence at the message. She felt faint and confused. Why was the poor woman showing her those pitiful words, so obviously meant for no other eyes? She was seized with an agony of pity and remorse. "But it's all over, it's all over," she murmured penitently, propitiatingly.

"All over—yes! I was starting for Havre when I got that cable three days ago. But the other message caught me on my way to the train."

"The other message?"

"Well, the one that said it was all over. He was buried yesterday. The Consul was there. It was the Consul who cabled me not to come—it was just as well; for I'd have had to borrow the money, and there are the children to think of. He hardly ever sent me any money," added Mrs. Lithgow dispassionately. Her hysterical excitement had subsided with the communication of what she had come to say, and she spoke in a low monotonous voice like an absent-minded child haltingly reciting a lesson.

Christine stood before her, the telegram in her shaking hands. Mrs. Lithgow's words were still remote and unreal to her: they sounded like the ticking out of a message on a keyboard—a message that would have to be decoded. . . . "Jeff—Jeff? You mean—you don't mean he's dead?" she gasped.

Mrs. Lithgow looked at her in astonishment. "You didn't know—you really didn't know?"

"Know? How could you suppose . . . how could I imagine . . . ?"

"How could you imagine you'd—killed him?"

"Ah, no! No! Not that—don't say that!"

"As if you'd held the revolver," said Mrs. Lithgow implacably.

"Ah, no—no, no!"

"He held out for two days . . . he tried to pull himself together. I thought you must have seen it in one of those papers they print on the steamer."

Christine shook her head. "I never looked at them."

"And you actually mean to say your husband didn't tell you?" Again Christine made a shuddering gesture of negation.

"Well," said Mrs. Lithgow, with her little acrid laugh, "now you know why he hung up that 'Joy In The House' for your arrival."

"Oh, don't say that—don't be so inhuman!"

"Well—don't he read the papers either?"

"He couldn't have . . . seen this . . ."

"He must have been blind, then. There's been nothing else in the papers. My husband was famous," said Mrs. Lithgow with a sudden bitter pride.

Christine had dropped down sobbing into a chair. "Oh, spare me—spare me!" she cried out, hiding her face.

"I don't know why I should," she heard Mrs. Lithgow say behind her. Christine struggled to her feet, and the two women stood looking at each other in silence.

"There's no joy in the house for *me*," said Mrs. Lithgow drily.

"Oh, don't—don't speak of that again! That silly thing . . ."

"My husband's epitaph."

"How can you speak to me in that way?" Christine struggled to control herself, to fight down the humiliation and the horror. "It wasn't my fault—I mean that he . . . I was not the only one. . . . He was always imagining . . ."

"He was always looking for the woman? Yes; artists are like that, I believe. But he was sure he'd found her when he found you. He never hid it from me. He told you so, didn't he? He told you he couldn't live without you? Only I suppose you didn't believe him. . . ."

Christine sank down again with covered face. Only Mrs. Lithgow's last words had reached her. "You didn't believe him. . . ." But hadn't she, in the inmost depths of herself, believed him? Hadn't she felt, during those last agonizing hours in the hotel at Havre, that what he told her was the truth, hadn't she known that his life was actually falling in ruins, hadn't her only care been to escape before the ruins fell on her and destroyed her too? Her husband had said the night before that she had come back to the place where she belonged; but if human responsibility counted for anything, wasn't her place rather in that sordid hotel room where a man sat with buried face because he could not bear to see the door close on her forever?

"Oh, what can I do—what can I do?" broke from her in her desolate misery.

Mrs. Lithgow took the outcry as addressed to herself. "Do? For me, do you mean? I forgot—it was what I came for. About his pictures . . . I have to think about that already. The lawyers say I must. . . . Do you know where they are, what he'd done with them? Had he given you any to bring home?" She hung her head, turning sallow under her duskiness. "They say his dying in this terrible way will . . . will help the sale. . . . I have to think of the children. I'm beyond minding anything for myself. . . ."

Christine looked at her vacantly. She was thinking: "I tried to escape from the ruins, and here they are crashing about me." At first she could not recall anything about the pictures; then her memory cleared, and gave her back the address of a painter in Paris with whom Jeff had told her that he had left some of his things, in the hope that the painter might sell them. He had been worried, she remembered, because there was no money to send home for the children; he had hoped his friend would contrive to raise a few hundred francs on the pictures. She faltered out the address, and Mrs. Lithgow noted it down carefully on the back of her husband's farewell cable. She was beyond minding even that, Christine supposed. Mrs. Lithgow pushed the cable back into her shabby bag.

"Well," she said, "I suppose you and I haven't got anything else to say to each other."

It was on Christine's lips to break out: "Only that I know now how I loved him—" but she dared not. She moved a few steps nearer to Mrs. Lithgow, and held out her hands beseechingly. But the widow did not seem to see them. "Goodbye," she said, and walked rigidly across the hall and out of the door.

Christine followed her half way and then, as the door closed, turned back and looked up at the "Joy in the House" that still dangled inanely from the stair-rail. She was sure now that her husband had known of Jeff Lithgow's death. How could he not have known of it? Even if he had not been the most careful and conscientious of newspaper readers, the house must have been besieged by reporters. Everybody in Stokesburg knew that she and Lithgow had gone off together; though they had slipped on board the steamer unnoticed the papers had rung with their adventure for days afterward. And of course the man she had caught Devons amiably banishing that morning was a journalist who had come to see how she had taken the news of the suicide. . . .

Yes; they had all known, and had all concealed it from her; her husband, her mother-in-law, Miss Bilk; even Martha and the cook had known. It had been Devons's order that there should not be a cloud on the horizon; and there had not been one. She sat down on a chair in the white shiny hall, with its spick-and-span Chinese rug, the brass umbrella-stand, the etchings in their neat ebony mouldings. She would always see Mrs. Lithgow now, a blot on the threshold, a black restless ghost in the pretty drawing-room. Yes; Devons had known, and it had made no difference to him. His serenity and his good-humour were not assumed. He would probably say: Why should Lithgow's death affect him? It was the providential solving of a problem. He wished the poor fellow no ill; but it was certainly simpler to have him out of the way. . . .

Christine sprang up with a spurt of energy. She must get away, get away at once from this stifling atmosphere of tolerance and benevolence, of smoothing over and ignoring and dissembling. Anywhere out into the live world, where men and women struggled and loved and hated, and quarrelled and came together again with redoubled passion. . . . But the hand which had opened that world to her was dead, was stiff in the coffin already. "He was buried yesterday," she muttered. . . .

Martha came out into the hall to carry a vase of fresh flowers into the drawing-room. Christine stood up with weary limbs. "You'd better take that down—the flowers are dead," she said, pointing to the inscription dangling from the stairs. Martha looked surprised and a little grieved. "Oh, ma'am— do you think Mr. Ansley would like you to? He worked over it so hard himself, him and Miss Bilk and me. And Mr. Chris helped us too. . . ."

"Take it down," Christine commanded sternly.

"But there's the boy—" she thought; and walked slowly up the stairs to find her son.

Charm Incorporated

JIM! I'm afraid. . . I'm dreadfully afraid. . ."

James Targatt's wife knelt by his armchair, the dark hair flung off her forehead, her dark eyes large with tears as they yearned up at him through those incredibly long lashes.

"Afraid? Why—what's the matter?" he retorted, annoyed at being disturbed in the slow process of digesting the dinner he had just eaten at Nadeja's last new restaurant—a Ukrainian one this time. For they went to a different restaurant every night, usually, at Nadeja's instigation, hunting out the most exotic that New York at the high tide of its prosperity had to offer. "That sturgeon stewed in cream—" he thought wearily. "Well, what is it?"

"It's Boris, darling. I'm afraid Boris is going to marry a film-star. That Halma Hoboe, you know. . . She's the greatest of them all. . ." By this time the tears were running down Nadeja's cheeks. Targatt averted his mind from the sturgeon long enough to wonder if he would ever begin to understand his wife, much less his wife's family.

"Halma Hoboe? Well, why on earth shouldn't he? Has she got her divorce from the last man all right?"

"Yes, of course." Nadeja was still weeping. "But I thought perhaps you'd mind Boris's leaving us. He will have to stay out at Hollywood now, he says. And I shall miss my brother so dreadfully. Hollywood's very far from New York—no? We shall all miss Boris, shan't we, James?"

"Yes, yes. Of course. Great boy, Boris! Funny, to be related to a movie-star. 'My sister-in-law, Halma Hoboe'. Well, as long as he couldn't succeed on the screen himself—" said Targatt, suddenly sounding a latent relief, which came to the surface a moment later. "*She'll* have to pay his bills now," he muttered, too low for his wife to hear. He reached out for a second cigar, let his head sink back comfortably against the chair-cushions, and thought to himself: "Well, perhaps the luck's turning. . ." For it was the first time, in the eight years of his marriage to Nadeja, that any information imparted to

653

him concerning her family had not immediately led up to his having to draw another cheque.

II

James Targatt had always been on his guard against any form of sentimental weakness; yet now, as he looked back on his life, he began to wonder if the one occasion on which he had been false to this principle might not turn out to be his best stroke of business.

He had not had much difficulty in guarding himself against marriage. He had never felt an abstract yearning for father-hood, or believed that to marry an old-fashioned affectionate girl, who hated society, and wanted to stay at home and darn and scrub, would really help an ambitious man in his career. He thought it was probably cheaper in the end to have your darning and scrubbing done for you by professionals, even if they came from one of those extortionate valeting establish-ments that used, before the depression, to charge a dollar a minute for such services. And eventually he found a stranded German widow who came to him on starvation wages, fed him well and inexpensively, and kept the flat looking as fresh and shiny as a racing-yacht. So there was no earthly obligation for him to marry; and when he suddenly did so, no question of expediency had entered into the arrangement.

He supposed afterward that what had happened to him was what people called falling in love. He had never allowed for that either, and even now he was not sure if it was the right name for the knock-down blow dealt to him by his first sight of Nadeja. Her name told you her part of the story clearly enough. She came straight out of that struggling mass of in-distinguishable human misery that Targatt called "Wardrift". One day—he still wondered how, for he was always fiercely on his guard against such intrusions—she had forced her way into his office, and tried to sell him (of all things!) a picture painted by her brother Serge. They were all starving, she said; and very likely it was true. But that had not greatly moved him. He had heard the same statement made too often by too many people, and it was too painfully connected in his mind with a dreaded and rapidly increasing form of highway robbery called "Appeals". Besides, Targatt's imagination was not particularly active, and as he was always sure of a good meal himself, it never much disturbed him to be told that others were not. So he couldn't to this day have told you how it came about that he bought Serge's picture on the spot, and married Nadeja a few weeks afterward. He had been knocked on the head—sandbagged; a regular hold-up. That was the only way to describe it.

Nadeja made no attempt to darn or scrub for him—which was perhaps just as well, as he liked his comforts. On the contrary, she made friends at once with the German widow, and burdened that industrious woman with the additional care of her own wardrobe, which was negligible before her marriage, but increased rapidly after she became Mrs. Targatt. There was a second servant's room above the flat, and Targatt rather reluctantly proposed that they should get in a girl to help Hilda; but Nadeja said, no, she didn't believe Hilda would care for that; and the room would do so nicely for Paul, her younger brother, the one who was studying to be a violinist.

Targatt hated music, and suffered acutely (for a New Yorker) from persistently recurring noises; but Paul, a nice boy, also with long-lashed eyes, moved into the room next to Hilda's, and practised the violin all day and most of the night. The room was directly over that which Targatt now shared with Nadeja—and of which all but the space occupied by his shaving-stand had by this time become her exclusive property. But he bore with Paul's noise, and it was Hilda who struck. She said she loved music that gave her *Heimweh*, but this kind only kept her awake; and to Targatt's horror she announced her intention of leaving at the end of the month.

It was the biggest blow he had ever had since he had once—and once only—been on the wrong side of the market. He had no time to hunt for another servant, and was sure Nadeja would not know how to find one. Nadeja, when he broke the news to her, acquiesced in this view of her incapacity. "But why do we want a servant? I could never see," she said. "And Hilda's room would do very nicely for my sister Olga, who is learning to be a singer. She and Paul could practise together—"

"Oh, Lord," Targatt interjected.

"And we could all go out to restaurants; a different one every night; it's much more fun, isn't it? And there are people who come in and clean—no? Hilda was a robber—I didn't want to tell you, but. . ."

Within a week the young Olga, whose eyelashes were even longer than Paul's, was settled in the second servant's room, and within a month Targatt had installed a grand piano in his own drawing-room (where it took up all the space left by Nadeja's divan), so that Nadeja could accompany Olga when Paul was not available.

III

Targatt had never, till that moment, thought much about Nadeja's family. He understood that his father-in-law had been a Court dignitary of high standing, with immense landed estates, and armies of slaves—no, he believed they didn't have slaves, or serfs, or whatever they called them, any longer in those outlandish countries east or south of Russia. Targatt was not strong on geography. He did not own an atlas, and had never yet had time to go to the Public Library and look up his father-in-law's native heath. In fact, he had never had time to read, or to think consecutively on any subject but money-making; he knew only that old man Kouradjine had been a big swell in some country in which the Bolsheviks had confiscated everybody's property, and where the women (and the young men too) apparently all had long eyelashes. But that was all part of a vanished fairy-tale; at present the old man was only Number So-much on one Near East Relief list, while Paul and Olga and the rest of them (Targatt wasn't sure even yet how many there were) figured on similar lists, though on a more modest scale, since they were supposedly capable of earning their own living. But were they capable of it, and was there any living for them to earn? That was what Targatt in the course of time began to ask himself.

Targatt was not a particularly sociable man; but in his bachelor days he had fancied inviting a friend to dine now and then, chiefly to have the shine on his mahogany table marvelled at, and Hilda's *Wiener-schnitzel* praised. This was all over now. His meals were all taken in restaurants—a different one each time; and they were usually shared with Paul, Olga, Serge (the painter) and the divorced sister, Katinka, who had three children and a refugee lover, Dmitri.

At first this state of affairs was very uncomfortable, and even painful, for Targatt; but since it seemed inevitable he adjusted himself to it, and buried his private cares in an increased business activity.

His activity was, in fact, tripled by the fact that it was no longer restricted to his own personal affairs, but came more and more to include such efforts as organizing an exhibition of Serge's pictures, finding the funds for Paul's violin tuition, trying to make it worth somebody's while to engage Olga for a concert tour, pushing Katinka into a saleswoman's job at a fashionable dress-maker's, and persuading a friend in a bank to recommend Dmitri as interpreter to foreign clients. All this was difficult enough, and if Targatt had not been sustained by Nadeja's dogged optimism his courage might have failed him; but the crowning problem was how to deal with the youngest brother, Boris, who was just seventeen, and had the longest eyelashes of all. Boris was too old to be sent to school, too young to be put into a banker's or broker's office, and too smilingly irresponsible to hold the job for twenty-four hours if it had been offered to him. Targatt, for three years after his marriage, had had only the vaguest idea of Boris's existence, for he was not among the first American consignment of the family. But suddenly he drifted in alone, from Odessa or Athens, and joined the rest of the party at the restaurant. By this time the Near East Relief Funds were mostly being wound up, and in spite of all Targatt's efforts it was impossible to get financial aid for Boris, so for the first months he just lolled in a pleasant aimless way on Nadeja's divan; and as he was very particular about the quality of his cigarettes, and consumed a large supply daily, Targatt for the first time began to regard one of Nadeja's family with a certain faint hostility.

Boris might have been less of a trial if, by the time he came, Targatt had been able to get the rest of the family on their legs; but, however often he repeated this attempt, they invariably toppled over on him. Serge could not sell his pictures, Paul could not get an engagement in an orchestra, Olga had given up singing for dancing, so that her tuition had to begin all over again; and to think of Dmitri and Katinka, and Katinka's three children, was not conducive to repose at the end of a hard day in Wall Street.

Yet in spite of everything Targatt had never really been able to remain angry for more than a few moments with any member of the Kouradjine group. For some years this did not particularly strike him; he was given neither to self-analysis nor to the dissection of others, except where business dealings were involved. He had been taught, almost in the nursery, to discern, and deal with, the motives determining a given course in business; but he knew no more of human nature's other mainsprings than if the nursery were still his habitat. He was vaguely conscious that Nadeja was aware of this, and that it caused her a faint amusement. Once, when they had been dining with one of his business friends, and the latter's wife, an ogling bore, had led the talk to the shop-worn question of how far mothers ought to enlighten their little girls on—well, you know. . . Just *how much* ought they to be taught? That was the delicate point, Mrs. Targatt, wasn't it?—Nadeja, thus cornered, had met the question with a gaze of genuine bewilderment. "Taught? Do they have to be *taught*? I think it is Nature who will tell them—no? But myself I should first teach dressmaking and cooking," she said with her shadowy smile. And now, reviewing the Kouradjine case, Targatt suddenly thought: "But that's it! Nature *does* teach the Kouradjines. It's a gift like a tenor voice. The thing is to know how to make the best use of it—" and he fell to musing on this newly discovered attribute. It was—what? Charm? Heaven forbid! The very word made his flesh creep with memories of weary picnics and wearier dinners where, with pink food in fluted papers, the discussion of "What is Charm?" had formed the staple diet. "I'd run a mile from a woman with charm; and so would most men," Targatt thought with a retrospective shudder. And he tried, for the first time, to make a conscious inventory of Nadeja's attributes.

She was not beautiful; he was certain of that. He was not good at seeing people, really seeing them, even when they were before his eyes, much less at visualizing them in absence. When Nadeja was away all he could ever evoke of her was a pleasant blur. But he wasn't such a blind bat as not to know when a woman was beautiful. Beauty, however, was made to look at, not to live with; he had never wanted to marry a beautiful woman. And Nadeja wasn't clever, either; not in talk, that is. (And that, he mused, was certainly one of her qualities.) With regard to the other social gifts, so-called: cards, for instance? Well, he knew she and Katinka were not above fishing out an old pack and telling their fortunes, when they thought he wasn't noticing; but anything as scientific as bridge frightened her, and she had the good sense not to try to learn. So much for society; and as for the home—well, she could hardly be called a good housekeeper, he supposed. But remembering his mother, who had been accounted a paragon in that line, he gave thanks for this deficiency of Nadeja's also. Finally he said to himself: "I seem to like her for all the things she is *not*." This was not satisfactory; but he could do no better. "Well, somehow, she fits into the cracks," he concluded; and inadequate as this also sounded, he felt it might turn out to be a clue to the Kouradjines. Yes, they certainly fitted in; squeezing you a little, overlapping you a good deal, but never—and there was the point—sticking into you like the proverbial thorn, or crowding you uncomfortably, or for any reason making you wish they weren't there.

This fact, of which he had been dimly conscious from the first, arrested his attention now because he had a sudden glimpse of its business possibilities. Little Boris had only had to borrow a hundred dollars of him for the trip to Hollywood, and behold little Boris was already affianced to the world's leading movie-star! In the light of this surprising event Targatt suddenly recalled that Katinka, not long before, had asked him if he wouldn't give Dmitri, who had not been a success at the bank, a letter recommending him for some sort of employment in the office of a widowed millionaire who was the highest light on Targatt's business horizon. Targatt had received the suggestion without enthusiasm. "Your sister's crazy," he said to Nadeja. "How can I recommend that fellow to a man like Bellamy? Has he ever had any business training?"

"Well, we know Mr. Bellamy's looking for a book-keeper, because he asked you if you knew of one," said Nadeja.

"Yes; but what are Dmitri's qualifications? Does he know anything whatever about book-keeping?"

"No; not yet. But he says perhaps he could buy a little book about it."

"Oh, Lord—" Targatt groaned.

"Even so, you don't think you could recommend him, darling?"

"No; I couldn't, I'm afraid."

Nadeja did not insist; she never insisted. "I've found out a new restaurant, where they make much better blinys. Shall I tell them all to meet us there tonight at half-past eight?" she suggested.

Now, in the light of Boris's news, Targatt began to think this conversation over. Dmitri was an irredeemable fool; but Katinka—what about giving the letter for old Bellamy to Katinka? Targatt didn't see exactly how he could word it; but he had an idea that Nadeja would tell him. Those were the ways in which she was really clever. A few days later he asked: "Has Dmitri got a job yet?"

She looked at him in surprise. "No; as you couldn't recommend him he didn't buy the book."

"Oh, damn the book. . . See here, Nadeja; supposing I were to give Katinka a letter for old Bellamy?"

He had made the suggestion with some embarrassment, half expecting that he would have to explain. But not to Nadeja. "Oh, darling, you always think of the right thing," she answered, kissing him; and as he had foreseen she told him just how to word the letter.

"And I will lend her my silver fox to wear," she added. Certainly the social education of the Kouradjines had been far more comprehensive than Targatt's.

Katinka went to see Mr. Bellamy, and when she returned she reported favourably on the visit. Nothing was as yet decided about Dmitri, as she had been obliged to confess that he had had no training as an accountant; but Mr. Bellamy had been very kind, and had invited her to come to his house some afternoon to see his pictures.

From this visit also Katinka came back well-pleased, though she seemed not to have accomplished anything further with regard to Dmitri. She had, however, been invited by Mr.

Bellamy to dine and go to a play; and a few weeks afterward she said to Targatt and Nadeja: "I think I will live with Mr. Bellamy. He has an empty flat that I could have, and he would furnish it beautifully."

Though Targatt prided himself on an unprejudiced mind he winced slightly at this suggestion. It seemed cruel to Dmitri, and decidedly uncomfortable as far as Targatt and Nadeja were concerned.

"But, Katinka, if Bellamy's so gone on you, he ought to marry you," he said severely.

Katinka nodded her assent. "Certainly he ought. And I think he will, after I have lived with him a few months."

This upset every single theory of Targatt's with regard to his own sex. "But, my poor girl—if you go and live with a man first like . . . like any woman he could have for money, why on earth should he want to marry you afterward?"

Katinka looked at him calmly. Her eyelashes were not as long as Nadeja's, but her eyes were as full of wisdom. "Habit," she said simply; and in an instant Targatt's conventional world was in fragments at his feet. Who knew better than he did that if you once had the Kouradjine habit you couldn't be cured of it? He said nothing more, and sat back to watch what happened to Mr. Bellamy.

IV

Mr. Bellamy did not offer Dmitri a position as book-keeper; but soon after his marriage to Katinka he took him into his house as social secretary. Targatt had a first movement of surprise and disapproval, but he saw that Nadeja did not share it. "That's very nice," she said. "I was sure Katinka would not desert Dmitri. And Mr. Bellamy is so generous. He is going to adopt Katinka's three children."

But it must not be thought that the fortunes of all the Kouradjines ran as smoothly. For a brief moment Targatt had imagined that the infatuated Bellamy was going to assume the charge of the whole tribe; but Wall Street was beginning to be uneasy, and Mr. Bellamy restricted his hospitality to Katinka's children and Dmitri, and, like many of the very rich, manifested no interest in those whose misfortunes did not immediately interfere with his own comfort. Thus vanished even the dream of a shared responsibility, and Targatt saw himself facing a business outlook decidedly less dazzling, and with a still considerable number of Kouradjines to provide for. Olga, in particular, was a cause of some anxiety. She was less adaptable, less suited to fitting into cracks, than the others, and her various experiments in song and dance had all broken down for lack of perseverance. But she was (at least so Nadeja thought) by far the best-looking of the family; and finally Targatt decided to pay for her journey to Hollywood, in the hope that Boris would put her in the way of becoming a screen star. This suggestion, however, was met by a telegram from Boris ominously dated from Reno: "Don't send Olga am divorcing Halma."

For the first time since his marriage Targatt felt really discouraged. Were there perhaps too many Kouradjines, and might the Kouradjine habit after all be beginning to wear thin? The family were all greatly perturbed by Boris's news, and when—after the brief interval required to institute and complete divorce proceedings against his film star—Boris left Reno and turned up in New York, his air of unperturbed good-humour was felt to be unsuitable to the occasion. Nadeja, always hopeful, interpreted it as meaning that he was going to marry another and even richer star; but Boris said God forbid, and no more Hollywood for him. Katinka and Bellamy did not invite him to come and stay, and the upshot of it was that his bed was made up on the Targatts' drawing-room divan, while he shared the bathroom with Targatt and Nadeja.

Things dragged on in this way for some weeks, till one day Nadeja came privately to her husband. "He has got three millions," she whispered with wide eyes. "Only yesterday was he sure. The cheque has come. Do you think, darling, she ought to have allowed him more?"

Targatt did not think so; he was inarticulate over Boris's achievement. "What's he going to do with it?" he gasped.

"Well, I think first he will invest it, and then he will go to the Lido. There is a young girl there, I believe, that he is in love with. I knew Boris would not divorce for nothing. He is going there to meet her."

Targatt could not disguise an impulse of indignation. Before investing his millions, was Boris not going to do anything for his family? Nadeja said she had thought of that too; but Boris said he had invested the money that morning, and of course there would be no interest coming in till the next quarter. And meanwhile he was so much in love that he had taken his passage for the following day on the *Berengaria*. Targatt thought that only natural, didn't he?

Targatt swallowed his ire, and said, yes, he supposed it was natural enough. After all, if the boy had found a young girl he could really love and respect, and if he had the money to marry her and settle down, no one could blame him for rushing off to press his suit. And Boris rushed.

But meanwhile the elimination of two Kouradjines had not had the hoped-for effect of reducing the total number of the tribe. On the contrary, that total had risen; for suddenly three new members had appeared. One was an elderly and completely ruined Princess (a distant cousin, Nadeja explained) with whom old Kouradjine had decided to contract a tardy alliance, now that the rest of the family were provided for. ("He could do no less," Katinka and Nadeja mysteriously agreed.) And the other, and more sensational, newcomers were two beautiful young creatures, known respectively to the tribe as Nick and Mouna, but whose difficulties at the passport office made it seem that there were legal doubts as to their remaining names. These difficulties, through Targatt's efforts, were finally overcome, and snatched from the jaws of Ellis Island, Nick and Mouna joyfully joined the party at another new restaurant, "The Transcaucasian", which Nadeja had recently discovered.

Targatt's immensely enlarged experience of human affairs left him in little doubt as to the parentage of Nick and Mouna, and when Nadeja whispered to him one night (through the tumult of Boris's late bath next door): "You see, poor Papa felt he could not longer fail to provide for them," Targatt did not dream of asking why.

But he now had no less than seven Kouradjines more or less dependent on him, and the next night he sat up late and did some figuring and thinking. Even to Nadeja he could not explain in blunt language the result of this vigil; but he said to her the following day: "What's become of that flat of Bellamy's that Katinka lived in before—"

"Why, he gave the lease to Katinka as a wedding-present; but it seems that people are no more as rich as they were, and as it's such a very handsome flat, and the rent is high, the tenants can no longer afford to keep it—"

"Well," said Targatt with sudden resolution, "tell your sister if she'll make a twenty-five per cent cut on the rent I'll take over the balance of the lease."

Nadeja gasped. "Oh, James, you are an angel! But what do you think you could then do with it?"

Targatt threw back his shoulders. "Live in it," he recklessly declared.

v

It was the first time (except when he had married Nadeja) that he had ever been reckless; and there was no denying that he enjoyed the sensation. But he had not acted wholly for the sake of enjoyment; he had an ulterior idea. What that idea was he did not choose to communicate to any one at present. He merely asked Katinka, who, under the tuition of Mr. Bellamy's experienced butler, had developed some rudimentary ideas of house-keeping, to provide Nadeja with proper servants, and try to teach her how to use them; and he then announced to Nadeja that he had made up his mind to do a little entertaining. He and Nadeja had already made a few fashionable acquaintances at the Bellamys', and these they proceeded to invite to the new flat, and to feed with exotic food, and stimulate with abstruse cocktails. At these dinners Targatt's new friends met the younger and lovelier of the Kouradjines: Paul, Olga, Nick and Mouna, and they always went away charmed with the encounter.

Considerable expense was involved by this new way of life; and still more when Nadeja, at Targatt's instigation, invited Olga, Nick and Mouna to come and live with them. Nadeja was overcome with gratitude at this suggestion; but her gratitude, like all her other emotions, was so exquisitely modulated that it fell on Targatt like the gentle dew from heaven, merely fostering in him a new growth of tenderness. But still

Targatt did not explain himself. He had his idea, and knowing that Nadeja would not bother him with questions he sat back quietly and waited, though Wall Street was growing more and more unsettled, and there had been no further news of Boris, and Paul and Olga were still without a job.

The Targatts' little dinners, and Nadeja's exclusive cocktail parties, began to be the rage in a set far above the Bellamys'. There were almost always one or two charming young Kouradjines present; but they were now so sought after in smartest Park Avenue and gayest Long Island that Targatt and Nadeja had to make sure of securing their presence beforehand, so there was never any danger of there being too many on the floor at once.

On the contrary, there were occasions when they all simultaneously failed to appear; and on one of these evenings, Targatt, conscious that the party had not "come off", was about to vent his irritation against the absent Serge, when Nadeja said gently: "I'm sorry Serge didn't tell you. But I think he was married today to Mrs. Leeper."

"Mrs. Leeper? Not the Dazzle Tooth-Paste woman he met at the Bellamys', who wanted him to decorate her ball-room?"

"Yes; but I think she did not after all want him to decorate her ball-room. And so she has married him instead."

A year earlier Targatt would have had no word but an uncomprehending groan. But since then his education had proceeded by leaps and bounds, and now he simply said: "I see—" and turned back to his breakfast with a secret smile. He had received Serge's tailor's bill the day before, and had been rehearsing half the night what he was going to say to Serge when they met. But now he merely remarked: "That woman has a two million dollar income," and thought to himself that the experiment with the flat was turning out better than he could have imagined. If Serge could be disposed of so easily there was no cause to despair of Paul or Olga. "Hasn't Mrs. Leeper a nephew?" he asked Nadeja; who, as if she had read his thought, replied regretfully: "Yes; but I'm afraid he's married."

"Oh, well—send Boris to talk to him!" Targatt jeered; and Nadeja, who never laughed, smiled a little and replied: "Boris too will soon be married." She handed her husband the morning papers, which he had not yet had time to examine, and he read, in glowing headlines, the announcement of the marriage in London of Prince Boris Kouradjine, son of Prince Peter Kouradjine, hereditary sovereign of Daghestan, and Chamberlain at the court of his late Imperial Majesty the Czar Nicholas, to Miss Mamie Guggins of Rapid Rise, Oklahoma. "Boris has a little exaggerated our father's rank," Nadeja commented; but Targatt said thoughtfully: "No one can exaggerate the Guggins fortune." And Nadeja gave a quiet sigh.

It must not be supposed that this rise in the fortunes of the Kouradjines was of any direct benefit to Targatt. He had never expected that, or even hoped it. No Kouradjine had ever suggested making any return for the sums expended by Targatt in vainly educating and profitably dressing his irresistible in-laws; nor had Targatt's staggering restaurant bills been reduced by any offer of participation. Only the old Princess (as it was convenient, with so many young ones about, to call her when she was out of hearing) had said tearfully, on her wedding-day: "Believe me, my good James, what you have done for us all will not be forgotten when we return to Daghestan." And she spoke with such genuine emotion, the tears were so softening to her tired magnificent eyes, that Targatt, at the moment, felt himself repaid.

Other and more substantial returns he did draw from his alliance with the Kouradjines; and it was the prospect of these which had governed his conduct. From the day when it had occurred to him to send Katinka to intercede with Mr. Bellamy, Targatt had never once swerved from his purpose. And slowly but surely he was beginning to reap his reward.

Mr. Bellamy, for instance, had not seen his way to providing for the younger Kouradjines; but he was ready enough to let Targatt in on the ground floor of one of those lucrative deals usually reserved for the already wealthy. Mrs. Leeper, in her turn, gave him the chance to buy a big block of Dazzle Tooth-Paste shares on exceptional terms; and as fashion and finance became aware of the younger Kouradjines, and fell under their spell, Targatt's opportunities for making quick turnovers became almost limitless. And now a pleasant glow stole down his spine at the thought that all previous Kouradjine alliances paled before the staggering wealth of Boris's bride. "Boris really does owe me a good turn," he mused; but he had no expectation that it would be done with Boris's knowledge. The new Princess Boris was indeed induced to hand over her discarded wardrobe to Olga and Mouna, and Boris presented cigarette cases to his brothers and brother-in-law; but here his prodigalities ended. Targatt, however, was not troubled; for years he had longed to meet the great Mr. Guggins, and here he was, actually related to that gentleman's only child!

Mr. Guggins, when under the influence of domestic happiness or alcohol, was almost as emotional as the Kouradjines. On his return to New York, after the parting from his only child, he was met on the dock by Targatt and Nadeja, who suggested his coming to dine that night at a jolly new restaurant with all the other Kouradjines; and Mrs. Guggins was so much drawn to the old Princess, to whom she confided how difficult it was to get reliable window-washers at Rapid Rise, that the next day Targatt, as he would have put it, had the old man in his pocket. Mr. Guggins stayed a week in New York, and when he departed Targatt knew enough about the Guggins industries to make some very useful reinvestments; and Mrs. Guggins carried off Olga as her social secretary.

VI

Stimulated by these successive achievements Targatt's tardily developed imagination was growing like an Indian juggler's tree. He no longer saw any limits to what might be done with the Kouradjines. He had already found a post for the old Prince as New York representative of a leading firm of Paris picture-dealers, Paul and Nick were professional dancers at fashionable night-clubs, and for the moment only Mouna, the lovely but difficult, remained on Targatt's mind and his pay-roll.

It was the first time in his life that Targatt had tasted the fruits of ease, and he found them surprisingly palatable. He was no longer young, it took him more time than of old to get around a golf-course, and he occasionally caught himself

telling his good stories twice over to the same listener. But life
was at once exciting and peaceful, and he had to own that his
interests had been immensely enlarged. All that, of course, he
owed in the first instance to Nadeja. Poor Nadeja—she was
not as young as she had been, either. She was still slender and
supple, but there were little lines in the corners of her eyes,
and a certain droop of the mouth. Others might not notice
these symptoms, Targatt thought; but they had not escaped
him. For Targatt, once so unseeing in the presence of beauty,
had now become an adept in appraising human flesh-and-
blood, and smiled knowingly when his new friends commended Mouna's young charms, or inclined the balance in
favour of the more finished Olga. There was nothing any one
could tell him now about the relative "values" of the
Kouradjines: he had them tabulated as if they were vintage
wines, and it was a comfort to him to reflect that Nadeja was,
after all, the one whose market value was least considerable. It
was sheer luck—a part of his miraculous Kouradjine luck—
that his choice had fallen on the one Kouradjine about whom
there was never likely to be the least fuss or scandal; and after
an exciting day in Wall Street, or a fatiguing struggle to extri-
cate Paul or Mouna from some fresh scrape, he would sink
back with satisfaction into his own unruffled domesticity.

There came a day, however, when he began to feel that the
contrast between his wife and her sisters was too much to
Nadeja's disadvantage. Was it because the others had smarter
clothes—or, like Katinka, finer jewels? Poor Nadeja, he reflected, had never had any jewels since her engagement ring;
and that was a shabby affair. Was it possible, Targatt conjectured, that as middle age approached she was growing dowdy,
and needed the adventitious enhancements of dress-maker
and beauty doctor? Half sheepishly he suggested that she
oughtn't to let herself be outdone by Katinka, who was two
or three years her senior; and he reinforced the suggestion by
a diamond chain from Cartier's and a good-humoured hint
that she might try Mrs. Bellamy's dress-maker.

Nadeja received the jewel with due raptures, and appeared
at their next dinner in a gown which was favourably noticed
by every one present. Katinka said: "Well, at last poor Nadeja
is really *dressed*," and Mouna sulked visibly, and remarked to

her brother-in-law: "If you want the right people to ask me about you might let me get a few clothes at Nadeja's place."

All this was as it should be, and Targatt's satisfaction increased as he watched his wife's returning bloom. It seemed funny to him that, even on a sensible woman like Nadeja, clothes and jewels should act as a tonic; but then the Kouradjines *were* funny, and heaven knew Targatt had no reason to begrudge them any of their little fancies—especially now that Olga's engagement to Mrs. Guggins' brother (representative of the Guggins interests in London and Paris) had been officially announced. When the news came, Targatt gave his wife a pair of emerald ear-rings, and suggested that they should take their summer holiday in Paris.

It was the same winter that New York was thrown into a flutter by the announcement that the famous portrait painter, Axel Svengaart, was coming over to "do" a chosen half-dozen sitters. Svengaart had never been to New York before, had always sworn that anybody who wanted to be painted by him must come to his studio at Oslo; but it suddenly struck him that the American background might give a fresh quality to his work, and after painting one lady getting out of her car in front of her husband's motor-works, and Mrs. Guggins against the background of a spouting oil-well at Rapid Rise, he appeared in New York to organise a show of these sensational canvases. New York was ringing with the originality and audacity of this new experiment. After expecting to be "done" in the traditional setting of the Gothic library or the Quattro Cento *salon*, it was incredibly exciting to be portrayed literally surrounded by the acknowledged sources of one's wealth; and the wife of a fabulously rich plumber was nearly persuaded to be done stepping out of her bath, in a luxury bathroom fitted with the latest ablutionary appliances.

Fresh from these achievements, Axel Svengaart carried his Viking head and Parisian monocle from one New York drawing-room to another, gazing, appraising—even, though rarely, praising—but absolutely refusing to take another order, or to postpone by a single day the date of his sailing. "I've got it all here," he said, touching first his brow and then his pocket; and the dealer who acted as his impresario let it be understood that even the most exaggerated offers would be rejected.

Targatt had, of course, met the great man. In old days he would have been uncomfortably awed by the encounter; but now he could joke easily about the Gugginses, and even ask Svengaart if he had not been struck by his sister-in-law, who was Mrs. Guggins's social secretary, and was about to marry Mr. Guggins's Paris representative.

"Ah—the lovely Kouradjine; yes. She made us some delicious blinys," Svengaart nodded approvingly; but Targatt saw with surprise that as a painter he was uninterested in Olga's plastic possibilities.

"Ah, well, I suppose you've had enough of us—I hear you're off this week."

The painter dropped his monocle. "Yes, I've had enough." It was after dinner, at the Bellamys', and abruptly he seated himself on the sofa at Targatt's side. "I don't like your frozen food," he pursued. "There's only one thing that would make me put off my sailing." He readjusted his monocle and looked straight at Targatt. "If you'll give me the chance to paint Mrs. Targatt—oh, for that I'd wait another month."

Targatt stared at him, too surprised to answer. Nadeja—the great man wanted to paint Nadeja! The idea aroused so many conflicting considerations that his reply, when it came, was a stammer. "Why, really . . . this is a surprise . . . a great honour, of course. . ." A vision of Svengaart's price for a mere head thrust itself hideously before his eyes. Svengaart, seeing him as it were encircled by millionaires, probably took him for a very rich man—was perhaps manoeuvring to extract an extra big offer from him. For what other inducement could there be to paint Nadeja? Targatt turned the question with a joke. "I suspect you're confusing me with my brother-in-law Bellamy. He ought to have persuaded you to paint his wife. But I'm afraid my means wouldn't allow . . ."

The other interrupted him with an irritated gesture. "Please—my dear sir. I can never be 'persuaded' to do a portrait. And in the case of Mrs. Targatt I had no idea of selling you her picture. If I paint her, it would be for myself."

Targatt's stare widened. "For yourself? You mean—you'd paint the picture just to keep it?" He gave an embarrassed laugh. "Nadeja would be enormously flattered, of course. But, between ourselves, would you mind telling me why you want to do her?"

Svengaart stood up with a faint laugh. "Because she's the only really paintable woman I've seen here. The lines are incomparable for a full-length. And I can't tell you how I should enjoy the change."

Targatt continued to stare. Murmurs of appreciation issued from his parched lips. He remembered now that Svengaart's charge for a three-quarter-length was fifteen thousand dollars. And he wanted to do Nadeja full length for nothing! Only— Targatt reminded himself—the brute wanted to keep the picture. So where was the good? It would only make Nadeja needlessly conspicuous; and to give all those sittings for nothing. . . Well, it looked like sharp practice, somehow. . .

"Of course, as I say, my wife would be immensely flattered; only she's very busy—her family, social obligations and so on; I really can't say. . ."

Svengaart smiled. "In the course of a portrait I usually make a good many studies; some almost as finished as the final picture. If Mrs. Targatt cared to accept one—"

Targatt flushed to the roots of his thinning hair. A Svengaart study over the drawing-room mantelpiece! ("Yes— nice thing of Nadeja, isn't it? You'd know a Svengaart anywhere. . . It was his own idea; he insisted on doing her. . .")

Nadeja was just lifting a pile of music from the top of the grand piano. She was going to accompany Mouna, who had taken to singing. As she stood with lifted arms, profiled against the faint hues of the tapestried wall, the painter exclaimed: "There—there! I have it! Don't you see now why I want to do her?"

But Targatt, for the moment, could not speak. Secretly he thought Nadeja looked much as usual—only perhaps a little more tired; she had complained of a headache that morning. But his courage rose to the occasion. "Ah, my wife's famous 'lines', eh? Well, well, I can't promise—you'd better come over and try to persuade her yourself."

He was so dizzy with it that as he led Svengaart toward the piano the Bellamys' parquet floor felt like glass under his unsteady feet.

VII

Targatt's rapture was acute but short-lived. Nadeja "done" by Axel Svengaart—he had measured the extent of it in a flash. He had stood aside and watched her with a deep smile of satisfaction while the light of wonder rose in her eyes; when she turned them on him for approval he had nodded his assent. Of course she must sit to the great man, his glance signalled back. He saw that Svengaart was amused at her having to ask her husband's permission; but this only intensified Targatt's satisfaction. They'd see, damn it, if his wife could be ordered about like a professional model! Perhaps the best moment was when, the next day, she said timidly: "But, Jim, have you thought about the price?" and he answered, his hands in his pockets, an easy smile on his lips: "There's no price to think about. He's doing you for the sake of your beautiful 'lines'. And we're to have a replica, free gratis. Did you know you had beautiful lines, old Nad?"

She looked at him gravely for a moment. "I hadn't thought about them for a long time," she said.

Targatt laughed and tapped her on the shoulder. What a child she was! But afterward it struck him that she had not been particularly surprised by the painter's request. Perhaps she had always known she was paintable, as Svengaart called it. Perhaps—and here he felt a little chill run over him—perhaps Svengaart had spoken to her already, had come to an understanding with her before making his request to Targatt. The idea made Targatt surprisingly uncomfortable, and he reflected that it was the first occasion in their married life when he had suspected Nadeja of even the most innocent duplicity. And this, if it were true, could hardly be regarded as wholly innocent. . .

Targatt shook the thought off impatiently. He was behaving like the fellow in "Pagliacci". Really this associating with foreigners might end in turning a plain business man into an opera-singer! It was the day of the first sitting, and as he started for his office he called back gaily to Nadeja: "Well, so long! And don't let that fellow turn your head."

He could not get much out of Nadeja about the sittings. It was not that she seemed secretive; but she was never very good at reporting small talk, and things that happened outside of the family circle, even if they happened to herself, always seemed of secondary interest to her. And meanwhile the sittings went on and on. In spite of his free style Svengaart was a slow worker; and he seemed to find Nadeja a difficult subject. Targatt began to brood over the situation: some people thought the fellow handsome, in the lean grey-hound style; and he had an easy cosmopolitan way—the European manner. It was what Nadeja was used to; would she suddenly feel that she had missed something during all these years? Targatt turned cold at the thought. It had never before occurred to him what a humdrum figure he was. The contemplation of his face in the shaving-glass became so distasteful to him that he averted his eyes, and nearly cut his throat in consequence. Nothing of the grey-hound style about him—or the Viking either.

Slowly, as these thoughts revolved in his mind, he began to feel that he, who had had everything from Nadeja, had given her little or nothing in return. What he had done for her people weighed as nothing in this revaluation of their past. The point was: what sort of a life had he given Nadeja? And the answer: No life at all! She had spent her best years looking after other people; he could not remember that she had ever asserted a claim or resented an oversight. And yet she was neither dull nor insipid: she was simply Nadeja—a creature endlessly tolerant, totally unprejudiced, sublimely generous and unselfish.

Well—it would be funny, Targatt thought, with a twist of almost physical pain, if nobody else had been struck by such unusual qualities. If it had taken him over ten years to find them out, others might have been less blind. He had never noticed her "lines", for instance; yet that painter fellow, the moment he'd clapped eyes on her—!

Targatt sat in his study, twisting about restlessly in his chair. Where *was* Nadeja, he wondered? The winter dusk had fallen, and painters do not work without daylight. The day's sitting must be over—and yet she had not come back. Usually she was always there to greet him on his return from the office. She had taught him to enjoy his afternoon tea, with a tiny caviar sandwich and a slice of lemon, and the samovar was already murmuring by the fire. When she went to see any of her family she always called up to say if she would be late; but the maid said there had been no message from her.

Targatt got up and walked the floor impatiently; then he sat down again, lit a cigarette, and threw it away. Nadeja, he remembered, had not been in the least shocked when Katinka had decided to live with Mr. Bellamy; she had merely wondered if the step were expedient, and had finally agreed with Katinka that it was. Nor had Boris's matrimonial manoeuvres seemed to offend her. She was entirely destitute of moral indignation; this painful reality was now borne in on Targatt for the first time. Cruelty shocked her; but otherwise she seemed to think that people should do as they pleased. Yet, all the while, had she ever done what *she* pleased? There was the torturing enigma! She seemed to allow such latitude to others, yet to ask so little for herself.

Well, but didn't the psychologist fellows say that there was an hour in every woman's life—every self-sacrificing woman's—when the claims of her suppressed self suddenly asserted themselves, body and soul, and she forgot everything else, all her duties, ties, responsibilities? Targatt broke off with a bitter laugh. What did "duties, ties, responsibilities" mean to Nadeja? No more than to any of the other Kouradjines. Their vocabulary had no parallels with his. He felt a sudden overwhelming loneliness, as if all these years he had been married to a changeling, an opalescent creature swimming up out of the sea. . .

No, she couldn't be at the studio any longer; or if she were, it wasn't to sit for her portrait. Curse the portrait, he thought—why had he ever consented to her sitting to Svengaart? Sheer cupidity; the snobbish ambition to own a Svengaart, the glee of getting one for nothing. The more he proceeded with this self-investigation the less he cared for the figure he cut. But however poor a part he had played so far, he wasn't going to add to it the rôle of the duped husband. . .

"Damn it, I'll go round there myself and see," he muttered, squaring his shoulders, and walking resolutely across the room to the door. But as he reached the entrance-hall the faint click of a latchkey greeted him; and sweeter music he had never heard. Nadeja stood in the doorway, pale but smiling. "Jim—you were not going out again?"

He gave a sheepish laugh. "Do you know what time it is? I was getting scared."

"Scared for me?" She smiled again. "Dear me, yes! It's nearly dinner-time, isn't it?"

He followed her into the drawing-room and shut the door. He felt like a husband in an old-fashioned problem play; and in a moment he had spoken like one. "Nad, where've you come from?" he broke out abruptly.

"Why, the studio. It was my last sitting."

"People don't sit for their portraits in the dark."

He saw a faint surprise in her eyes as she bent to the samovar. "No; I was not sitting all the time. Not for the last hour or more, I suppose."

She spoke as quietly as usual, yet he thought he caught a tremor of resentment in her voice. Against himself—or against the painter? But how he was letting his imagination run away with him! He sat down in his accustomed armchair, took the cup of tea she held out. He was determined to behave like a reasonable being, yet never had reason appeared to him so unrelated to reality. "Ah, well—I suppose you two had a lot of things to talk about. You rather fancy Svengaart, don't you?"

"Oh, yes; I like him very much. Do you know," she asked earnestly, "how much he has made during his visit to America? It was of course in confidence that he told me. Two hundred thousand dollars. And he was rich before."

She spoke so solemnly that Targatt burst into a vague laugh. "Well, what of it? I don't know that it showed much taste to brag to you about the way he skins his sitters. But it shows he didn't make much of a sacrifice in painting you for nothing," he said irritably.

"No; I said to him he might have done you too."

"*Me?*" Targatt's laugh redoubled. "Well, what did he say to that?"

"Oh, he laughed as you are now laughing," Nadeja rejoined. "But he says he will never marry—never."

Targatt put down his cup with a rattle. "*Never marry?*

What the devil are you talking about? Who cares whether he marries, anyhow?" he gasped with a dry throat.

"I do," said Nadeja.

There was a silence. Nadeja was lifting her tea-cup to her lips, and something in the calm free movement reminded him of Svengaart's outburst when he had seen her lift the pile of music. For the first time in his life Targatt seemed to himself to be looking at her; and he wondered if it would also be the last. He cleared his throat and tried to speak, to say something immense, magnanimous. "Well, if—"

"No; it's useless. He will hear nothing. I said to him: 'You will never anywhere find such a *plastik* as Mouna's' . . ."

"Mouna's?"

She turned to him with a slight shrug. "Oh, my poor Jim, are you quite blind? Haven't you seen how we have all been trying to make him want to marry Mouna? It will be almost my first failure, I think," she concluded with a half-apologetic sigh.

Targatt rested his chin on his hands and looked up at her. She looked tired, certainly, and older; too tired and old for any one still well under forty. And Mouna—why in God's name should she be persecuting this man to marry Mouna? It was indecent, it was shocking, it was unbelievable. . . Yet not for a moment did he doubt the truth of what she said.

"Mouna?" he could only repeat stupidly.

"Well, you see, darling, we're all a little anxious about Mouna. And I was so glad when Svengaart asked to paint me, because I thought: 'Now's my opportunity.' But no, it was not to be."

Targatt drew a deep breath. He seemed to be inhaling some life-giving element, and it was with the most superficial severity that he said: "I don't fancy this idea of your throwing your sister at men's heads."

"No, it was no use," Nadeja sighed, with her usual complete unawareness of any moral rebuke in his comment.

Targatt stood up uneasily. "He wouldn't have her at any price?"

She shook her head sadly. "Foolish man!"

Targatt went up to her and took her abruptly by the wrist.

"Look at me, Nadeja—straight. Did he refuse her because he wanted *you*?"

She gave her light lift of the shoulders, and the rare colour flitted across her pale cheeks. "Isn't it always the way of men? What they can't get—"

"Ah; so he's been making love to you all this time, has he?"

"But of course not, James. What he wished was to marry me. That is something quite different, is it not?"

"Yes. I see."

Targatt had released her wrist and turned away. He walked once or twice up and down the length of the room, no more knowing where he was than a man dropped blindfold onto a new planet. He knew what he wanted to do and to say; the words he had made up his mind to speak stood out in letters of fire against the choking blackness. "You must feel yourself free—." Five words, and so easy to speak! "Perfectly free— perfectly free," a voice kept crying within him. It was the least he could do, if he were ever to hold up his head again; but when he opened his mouth to speak not a sound came. At last he halted before Nadeja again, his face working like a frightened child's.

"Nad—what would you like best in the world to do? If you'll tell me I—I want you to do it!" he stammered. And with hands of ice he waited.

Nadeja looked at him with a slowly growing surprise. She had turned very pale again.

"Even if," he continued, half choking, "you understand, Nad, even if—"

She continued to look at him in her grave maternal way. "Is this true, what you are now saying?" she asked very low. Targatt nodded.

A little smile wavered over her lips. "Well, darling, if only I could have got Mouna safely married, I should have said: Don't you think that now at last we could afford to have a baby?"

Pomegranate Seed

CHARLOTTE ASHBY paused on her doorstep. Dark had descended on the brilliancy of the March afternoon, and the grinding rasping street life of the city was at its highest. She turned her back on it, standing for a moment in the old-fashioned, marble-flagged vestibule before she inserted her key in the lock. The sash curtains drawn across the panes of the inner door softened the light within to a warm blur through which no details showed. It was the hour when, in the first months of her marriage to Kenneth Ashby, she had most liked to return to that quiet house in a street long since deserted by business and fashion. The contrast between the soulless roar of New York, its devouring blaze of lights, the oppression of its congested traffic, congested houses, lives, minds and this veiled sanctuary she called home, always stirred her profoundly. In the very heart of the hurricane she had found her tiny islet—or thought she had. And now, in the last months, everything was changed, and she always wavered on the doorstep and had to force herself to enter.

While she stood there she called up the scene within: the hall hung with old prints, the ladderlike stairs, and on the left her husband's long shabby library, full of books and pipes and worn armchairs inviting to meditation. How she had loved that room! Then, upstairs, her own drawing-room, in which, since the death of Kenneth's first wife, neither furniture nor hangings had been changed, because there had never been money enough, but which Charlotte had made her own by moving furniture about and adding more books, another lamp, a table for the new reviews. Even on the occasion of her only visit to the first Mrs. Ashby—a distant, self-centred woman, whom she had known very slightly—she had looked about her with an innocent envy, feeling it to be exactly the drawing-room she would have liked for herself; and now for more than a year it had been hers to deal with as she chose—the room to which she hastened back at dusk on winter days, where she sat reading by the fire, or answering notes at the pleasant roomy desk, or going over her stepchildren's copy books, till she heard her husband's step.

Sometimes friends dropped in; sometimes—oftener—she was alone; and she liked that best, since it was another way of being with Kenneth, thinking over what he had said when they parted in the morning, imagining what he would say when he sprang up the stairs, found her by herself and caught her to him.

Now, instead of this, she thought of one thing only—the letter she might or might not find on the hall table. Until she had made sure whether or not it was there, her mind had no room for anything else. The letter was always the same—a square grayish envelope with "Kenneth Ashby, Esquire.," written on it in bold but faint characters. From the first it had struck Charlotte as peculiar that anyone who wrote such a firm hand should trace the letters so lightly; the address was always written as though there were not enough ink in the pen, or the writer's wrist were too weak to bear upon it. Another curious thing was that, in spite of its masculine curves, the writing was so visibly feminine. Some hands are sexless, some masculine, at first glance; the writing on the gray envelope, for all its strength and assurance, was without doubt a woman's. The envelope never bore anything but the recipient's name; no stamp, no address. The letter was presumably delivered by hand—but by whose? No doubt it was slipped into the letter box, whence the parlour maid, when she closed the shutters and lit the lights, probably extracted it. At any rate, it was always in the evening, after dark, that Charlotte saw it lying there. She thought of the letter in the singular, as "it", because, though there had been several since her marriage—seven, to be exact—they were so alike in appearance that they had become merged in one another in her mind, become one letter, become "it".

The first had come the day after their return from their honeymoon—a journey prolonged to the West Indies, from which they had returned to New York after an absence of more than two months. Re-entering the house with her husband, late on that first evening—they had dined at his mother's—she had seen, alone on the hall table, the gray envelope. Her eye fell on it before Kenneth's, and her first thought was: "Why, I've seen that writing before;" but where she could not recall. The memory was just definite enough for her to identify the script whenever it looked up at her faintly from the same pale envelope; but on that first day she would have thought no more of the letter if, when her husband's glance lit on it, she had not chanced to be looking at him. It all happened in a flash—his seeing the letter, putting out his hand for it, raising it to his short-sighted eyes to decipher the faint writing, and then abruptly withdrawing the arm he had slipped through Charlotte's, and moving away to the hanging light, his back turned to her. She had waited—waited for a sound, an exclamation; waited for him to open the letter; but he had slipped it into his pocket without a word and followed her into the library. And there they had sat down by the fire and lit their cigarettes, and he had remained silent, his head thrown back broodingly against the armchair, his eyes fixed on the hearth, and presently had passed his hand over his forehead and said: "Wasn't it unusually hot at my mother's tonight? I've got a splitting head. Mind if I take myself off to bed?"

That was the first time. Since then Charlotte had never been present when he had received the letter. It usually came before he got home from his office, and she had to go upstairs and leave it lying there. But even if she had not seen it, she would have known it had come by the change in his face when he joined her—which, on those evenings, he seldom did before they met for dinner. Evidently, whatever the letter contained, he wanted to be by himself to deal with it; and when he reappeared he looked years older, looked emptied of life and courage, and hardly conscious of her presence. Sometimes he was silent for the rest of the evening; and if he spoke, it was usually to hint some criticism of her household arrangements, suggest some change in the domestic administration, to ask, a little nervously, if she didn't think Joyce's nursery governess was rather young and flighty, or if she herself always saw to it that Peter—whose throat was delicate—was properly wrapped up when he went to school. At such times Charlotte would remember the friendly warnings she had received when she became engaged to Kenneth Ashby: "Marrying a heartbroken widower! Isn't that rather risky?

You know Elsie Ashby absolutely dominated him"; and how she had jokingly replied: "He may be glad of a little liberty for a change." And in this respect she had been right. She had needed no one to tell her, during the first months, that her husband was perfectly happy with her. When they came back from their protracted honeymoon the same friends said: "What have you done to Kenneth? He looks twenty years younger"; and this time she answered with careless joy: "I suppose I've got him out of his groove."

But what she noticed after the gray letters began to come was not so much his nervous tentative faultfinding—which always seemed to be uttered against his will—as the look in his eyes when he joined her after receiving one of the letters. The look was not unloving, not even indifferent; it was the look of a man who had been so far away from ordinary events that when he returns to familiar things they seem strange. She minded that more than the faultfinding.

Though she had been sure from the first that the handwriting on the gray envelope was a woman's, it was long before she associated the mysterious letters with any sentimental secret. She was too sure of her husband's love, too confident of filling his life, for such an idea to occur to her. It seemed far more likely that the letters—which certainly did not appear to cause him any sentimental pleasure—were addressed to the busy lawyer than to the private person. Probably they were from some tiresome client—women, he had often told her, were nearly always tiresome as clients—who did not want her letters opened by his secretary and therefore had them carried to his house. Yes; but in that case the unknown female must be unusually troublesome, judging from the effect her letters produced. Then again, though his professional discretion was exemplary, it was odd that he had never uttered an impatient comment, never remarked to Charlotte, in a moment of expansion, that there was a nuisance of a woman who kept badgering him about a case that had gone against her. He had made more than one semi-confidence of the kind—of course without giving names or details; but concerning this mysterious correspondent his lips were sealed.

There was another possibility: what is euphemistically called an "old entanglement". Charlotte Ashby was a sophisticated woman. She had few illusions about the intricacies of the human heart; she knew that there were often old entanglements. But when she had married Kenneth Ashby, her friends, instead of hinting at such a possibility, had said: "You've got your work cut out for you. Marrying a Don Juan is a sinecure to it. Kenneth's never looked at another woman since he first saw Elsie Corder. During all the years of their marriage he was more like an unhappy lover than a comfortably contented husband. He'll never let you move an armchair or change the place of a lamp; and whatever you venture to do, he'll mentally compare with what Elsie would have done in your place."

Except for an occasional nervous mistrust as to her ability to manage the children—a mistrust gradually dispelled by her good humour and the children's obvious fondness for her—none of these forebodings had come true. The desolate widower, of whom his nearest friends said that only his absorbing professional interests had kept him from suicide after his first wife's death, had fallen in love, two years later, with Charlotte Gorse, and after an impetuous wooing had married her and carried her off on a tropical honeymoon. And ever since he had been as tender and loverlike as during those first radiant weeks. Before asking her to marry him he had spoken to her frankly of his great love for his first wife and his despair after her sudden death; but even then he had assumed no stricken attitude, or implied that life offered no possibility of renewal. He had been perfectly simple and natural, and had confessed to Charlotte that from the beginning he had hoped the future held new gifts for him. And when, after their marriage, they returned to the house where his twelve years with his first wife had been spent, he had told Charlotte at once that he was sorry he couldn't afford to do the place over for her, but that he knew every woman had her own views about furniture and all sorts of household arrangements a man would never notice, and had begged her to make any changes she saw fit without bothering to consult him. As a result, she made as few as possible; but his way of beginning their new life in the old setting was so frank and unembarrassed that it put her immediately at her ease, and she was almost sorry to find that the portrait of Elsie Ashby, which used to hang over the desk in his library, had been transferred in their absence to the children's nursery. Knowing herself to be the indirect cause of this banishment, she spoke of it to her husband; but he answered: "Oh, I thought they ought to grow up with her looking down on them." The answer moved Charlotte, and satisfied her; and as time went by she had to confess that she felt more at home in her house, more at ease and in confidence with her husband, since that long coldly beautiful face on the library wall no longer followed her with guarded eyes. It was as if Kenneth's love had penetrated to the secret she hardly acknowledged to her own heart—her passionate need to feel herself the sovereign even of his past.

With all this stored-up happiness to sustain her, it was curious that she had lately found herself yielding to a nervous apprehension. But there the apprehension was; and on this particular afternoon—perhaps because she was more tired than usual, or because of the trouble of finding a new cook or, for some other ridiculously trivial reason, moral or physical—she found herself unable to react against the feeling. Latchkey in hand, she looked back down the silent street to the whirl and illumination of the great thoroughfare beyond, and up at the sky already aflare with the city's nocturnal life. "Outside there," she thought, "sky-scrapers, advertisements, telephones, wireless, aeroplanes, movies, motors, and all the rest of the twentieth century; and on the other side of the door something I can't explain, can't relate to them. Something as old as the world, as mysterious as life. . . Nonsense! What am I worrying about? There hasn't been a letter for three months now—not since the day we came back from the country after Christmas. . . Queer that they always seem to come after our holidays! . . . Why should I imagine there's going to be one tonight!"

No reason why, but that was the worst of it—one of the worsts!—that there were days when she would stand there cold and shivering with the premonition of something inexplicable, intolerable, to be faced on the other side of the curtained panes; and when she opened the door and went in, there would be nothing; and on other days when she felt the same premonitory chill, it was justified by the sight of the gray envelope. So that ever since the last had come she had taken to feeling cold and premonitory every evening, because she never opened the door without thinking the letter might be there.

Well, she'd had enough of it; that was certain. She couldn't go on like that. If her husband turned white and had a headache on the days when the letter came, he seemed to recover afterward; but she couldn't. With her the strain had become chronic, and the reason was not far to seek. Her husband knew from whom the letter came and what was in it; he was prepared beforehand for whatever he had to deal with, and master of the situation, however bad; whereas she was shut out in the dark with her conjectures.

"I can't stand it! I can't stand it another day!" she exclaimed aloud, as she put her key in the lock. She turned the key and went in; and there, on the table, lay the letter.

II

She was almost glad of the sight. It seemed to justify everything, to put a seal of definiteness on the whole blurred business. A letter for her husband; a letter from a woman—no doubt another vulgar case of "old entanglement". What a fool she had been ever to doubt it, to rack her brains for less obvious explanations! She took up the envelope with a steady contemptuous hand, looked closely at the faint letters, held it against the light and just discerned the outline of the folded sheet within. She knew that now she would have no peace till she found out what was written on that sheet.

Her husband had not come in; he seldom got back from his office before half-past six or seven, and it was not yet six. She would have time to take the letter up to the drawing-room, hold it over the tea-kettle which at that hour always simmered by the fire in expectation of her return, solve the mystery and replace the letter where she had found it. No one would be the wiser, and her gnawing uncertainty would be over. The alternative, of course, was to question her husband; but to do that seemed even more difficult. She weighed the letter between thumb and finger, looked at it again under the light, started up the stairs with the envelope—and came down again and laid it on the table.

"No, I evidently can't," she said, disappointed.

What should she do, then? She couldn't go up alone to that warm welcoming room, pour out her tea, look over her correspondence, glance at a book or review—not with that letter lying below and the knowledge that in a little while her husband would come in, open it and turn into the library alone, as he always did on the days when the gray envelope came.

Suddenly she decided. She would wait in the library and see for herself; see what happened between him and the letter when they thought themselves unobserved. She wondered the idea had never occurred to her before. By leaving the door ajar, and sitting in the corner behind it, she could watch him unseen. . . Well, then, she would watch him! She drew a chair into the corner, sat down, her eyes on the crack, and waited.

As far as she could remember, it was the first time she had ever tried to surprise another person's secret, but she was conscious of no compunction. She simply felt as if she were fighting her way through a stifling fog that she must at all costs get out of.

At length she heard Kenneth's latchkey and jumped up. The impulse to rush out and meet him had nearly made her forget why she was there; but she remembered in time and sat down again. From her post she covered the whole range of his movements—saw him enter the hall, draw the key from the door and take off his hat and overcoat. Then he turned to throw his gloves on the hall table, and at that moment he saw the envelope. The light was full on his face, and what Charlotte first noted there was a look of surprise. Evidently he had not expected the letter—had not thought of the possibility of its being there that day. But though he had not expected it, now that he saw it he knew well enough what it contained. He did not open it immediately, but stood motionless, the colour slowly ebbing from his face. Apparently he could not make up his mind to touch it; but at length he put out his hand, opened the envelope, and moved with it to the light. In doing so he turned his back on Charlotte, and she saw only his bent head and slightly stooping shoulders. Apparently all the writing was on one page, for he did not turn the sheet but continued to stare at it for so long that he must have reread it a dozen times—or so it seemed to the woman breathlessly watching him. At length she saw him move; he raised the letter still closer to his eyes, as though he had not fully deciphered it. Then he lowered his head, and she saw his lips touch the sheet.

"Kenneth!" she exclaimed, and went out into the hall.

The letter clutched in his hand, her husband turned and looked at her. "Where were you?" he said, in a low bewildered voice, like a man waked out of his sleep.

"In the library, waiting for you." She tried to steady her voice: "What's the matter! What's in that letter? You look ghastly."

Her agitation seemed to calm him, and he instantly put the envelope into his pocket with a slight laugh. "Ghastly? I'm sorry. I've had a hard day in the office—one or two complicated cases. I look dog-tired, I suppose."

"You didn't look tired when you came in. It was only when you opened that letter—"

He had followed her into the library, and they stood gazing at each other. Charlotte noticed how quickly he had regained his self-control; his profession had trained him to rapid mastery of face and voice. She saw at once that she would be at a disadvantage in any attempt to surprise his secret, but at the same moment she lost all desire to manoeuvre, to trick him into betraying anything he wanted to conceal. Her wish was still to penetrate the mystery, but only that she might help him to bear the burden it implied. "Even if it *is* another woman," she thought.

"Kenneth," she said, her heart beating excitedly, "I waited here on purpose to see you come in. I wanted to watch you while you opened that letter."

His face, which had paled, turned to dark red; then it paled again. "That letter? Why especially that letter?"

"Because I've noticed that whenever one of those letters comes it seems to have such a strange effect on you."

A line of anger she had never seen before came out between his eyes, and she said to herself: "The upper part of his face is too narrow; this is the first time I ever noticed it."

She heard him continue, in the cool and faintly ironic tone of the prosecuting lawyer making a point: "Ah; so you're in the habit of watching people open their letters when they don't know you're there?"

"Not in the habit. I never did such a thing before. But I had to find out what she writes to you, at regular intervals, in those gray envelopes."

He weighed this for a moment; then: "The intervals have not been regular," he said.

"Oh, I daresay you've kept a better account of the dates than I have," she retorted, her magnanimity vanishing at his tone. "All I know is that every time that woman writes to you—"

"Why do you assume it's a woman?"

"It's a woman's writing. Do you deny it?"

He smiled. "No, I don't deny it. I asked only because the writing is generally supposed to look more like a man's."

Charlotte passed this over impatiently. "And this woman—what does she write to you about?"

Again he seemed to consider a moment. "About business."

"Legal business?"

"In a way, yes. Business in general."

"You look after her affairs for her?"

"Yes."

"You've looked after them for a long time?"

"Yes. A very long time."

"Kenneth, dearest, won't you tell me who she is?"

"No. I can't." He paused, and brought out, as if with a certain hesitation: "Professional secrecy."

The blood rushed from Charlotte's heart to her temples. "Don't say that—don't!"

"Why not?"

"Because I saw you kiss the letter."

The effect of the words was so disconcerting that she instantly repented having spoken them. Her husband, who had submitted to her cross-questioning with a sort of contemptuous composure, as though he were humouring an unreasonable child, turned on her a face of terror and distress. For a minute he seemed unable to speak; then, collecting himself with an effort, he stammered out: "The writing is very faint; you must have seen me holding the letter close to my eyes to try to decipher it."

"No; I saw you kissing it." He was silent. "Didn't I see you kissing it?"

He sank back into indifference. "Perhaps."

"Kenneth! You stand there and say that—to me?"

"What possible difference can it make to you? The letter is on business, as I told you. Do you suppose I'd lie about it? The writer is a very old friend whom I haven't seen for a long time."

"Men don't kiss business letters, even from women who are very old friends, unless they have been their lovers, and still regret them."

He shrugged his shoulders slightly and turned away, as if he considered the discussion at an end and were faintly disgusted at the turn it had taken.

"Kenneth!" Charlotte moved toward him and caught hold of his arm.

He paused with a look of weariness and laid his hand over hers. "Won't you believe me?" he asked gently.

"How can I? I've watched these letters come to you—for months now they've been coming. Ever since we came back from the West Indies—one of them greeted me the very day we arrived. And after each one of them I see their mysterious effect on you, I see you disturbed, unhappy, as if someone were trying to estrange you from me."

"No, dear; not that. Never!"

She drew back and looked at him with passionate entreaty. "Well, then, prove it to me, darling. It's so easy!"

He forced a smile. "It's not easy to prove anything to a woman who's once taken an idea into her head."

"You've only got to show me the letter."

His hand slipped from hers and he drew back and shook his head.

"You won't?"

"I can't."

"Then the woman who wrote it is your mistress."

"No, dear. No."

"Not now, perhaps. I suppose she's trying to get you back, and you're struggling, out of pity for me. My poor Kenneth!"

"I swear to you she never was my mistress."

Charlotte felt the tears rushing to her eyes. "Ah, that's

worse, then—that's hopeless! The prudent ones are the kind that keep their hold on a man. We all know that." She lifted her hands and hid her face in them.

Her husband remained silent; he offered neither consolation nor denial, and at length, wiping away her tears, she raised her eyes almost timidly to his.

"Kenneth, think! We've been married such a short time. Imagine what you're making me suffer. You say you can't show me this letter. You refuse even to explain it."

"I've told you the letter is on business. I will swear to that too."

"A man will swear to anything to screen a woman. If you want me to believe you, at least tell me her name. If you'll do that, I promise you I won't ask to see the letter."

There was a long interval of suspense, during which she felt her heart beating against her ribs in quick admonitory knocks, as if warning her of the danger she was incurring.

"I can't," he said at length.

"Not even her name?"

"No."

"You can't tell me anything more?"

"No."

Again a pause; this time they seemed both to have reached the end of their arguments and to be helplessly facing each other across a baffling waste of incomprehension.

Charlotte stood breathing rapidly, her hands against her breast. She felt as if she had run a hard race and missed the goal. She had meant to move her husband and had succeeded only in irritating him; and this error of reckoning seemed to change him into a stranger, a mysterious incomprehensible being whom no argument or entreaty of hers could reach. The curious thing was that she was aware in him of no hostility or even impatience, but only of a remoteness, an inaccessibility, far more difficult to overcome. She felt herself excluded, ignored, blotted out of his life. But after a moment or two, looking at him more calmly, she saw that he was suffering as much as she was. His distant guarded face was drawn with pain; the coming of the gray envelope, though it always cast a shadow, had never marked him as deeply as this discussion with his wife.

Charlotte took heart; perhaps, after all, she had not spent her last shaft. She drew nearer and once more laid her hand on his arm. "Poor Kenneth! If you knew how sorry I am for you—"

She thought he winced slightly at this expression of sympathy, but he took her hand and pressed it.

"I can think of nothing worse than to be incapable of loving long," she continued; "to feel the beauty of a great love and to be too unstable to bear its burden."

He turned on her a look of wistful reproach. "Oh, don't say that of me. Unstable!"

She felt herself at last on the right tack, and her voice trembled with excitement as she went on: "Then what about me and this other woman? Haven't you already forgotten Elsie twice within a year?"

She seldom pronounced his first wife's name; it did not come naturally to her tongue. She flung it out now as if she were flinging some dangerous explosive into the open space between them, and drew back a step, waiting to hear the mine go off.

Her husband did not move; his expression grew sadder, but showed no resentment. "I have never forgotten Elsie," he said.

Charlotte could not repress a faint laugh. "Then, you poor dear, between the three of us—"

"There are not—" he began; and then broke off and put his hand to his forehead.

"Not what?"

"I'm sorry; I don't believe I know what I'm saying. I've got a blinding headache." He looked wan and furrowed enough for the statement to be true, but she was exasperated by his evasion.

"Ah, yes; the gray-envelope headache!"

She saw the surprise in his eyes. "I'd forgotten how closely I've been watched," he said coldly. "If you'll excuse me, I think I'll go up and try an hour in the dark, to see if I can get rid of this neuralgia."

She wavered; then she said, with desperate resolution: "I'm sorry your head aches. But before you go I want to say that sooner or later this question must be settled between us.

Someone is trying to separate us, and I don't care what it costs me to find out who it is." She looked him steadily in the eyes. "If it costs me your love, I don't care! If I can't have your confidence I don't want anything from you."

He still looked at her wistfully. "Give me time."

"Time for what? It's only a word to say."

"Time to show you that you haven't lost my love or my confidence."

"Well, I'm waiting."

He turned toward the door, and then glanced back hesitatingly. "Oh, do wait, my love," he said, and went out of the room.

She heard his tired step on the stairs and the closing of his bedroom door above. Then she dropped into a chair and buried her face in her folded arms. Her first movement was one of compunction; she seemed to herself to have been hard, unhuman, unimaginative. "Think of telling him that I didn't care if my insistence cost me his love! The lying rubbish!" She started up to follow him and unsay the meaningless words. But she was checked by a reflection. He had had his way, after all; he had eluded all attacks on his secret, and now he was shut up alone in his room, reading that other woman's letter.

III

She was still reflecting on this when the surprised parlourmaid came in and found her. No, Charlotte said, she wasn't going to dress for dinner; Mr. Ashby didn't want to dine. He was very tired and had gone up to his room to rest; later she would have something brought on a tray to the drawing-room. She mounted the stairs to her bedroom. Her dinner dress was lying on the bed, and at the sight the quiet routine of her daily life took hold of her and she began to feel as if the strange talk she had just had with her husband must have taken place in another world, between two beings who were not Charlotte Gorse and Kenneth Ashby, but phantoms projected by her fevered imagination. She recalled the year since her marriage—her husband's constant devotion; his persistent, almost too insistent tenderness; the feeling he had given her at times of being too eagerly dependent on her, too

searchingly close to her, as if there were not air enough between her soul and his. It seemed preposterous, as she recalled all this, that a few moments ago she should have been
accusing him of an intrigue with another woman! But, then,
what—

Again she was moved by the impulse to go up to him, beg
his pardon and try to laugh away the misunderstanding. But
she was restrained by the fear of forcing herself upon his privacy. He was troubled and unhappy, oppressed by some grief
or fear; and he had shown her that he wanted to fight out his
battle alone. It would be wiser, as well as more generous, to
respect his wish. Only, how strange, how unbearable, to be
there, in the next room to his, and feel herself at the other
end of the world! In her nervous agitation she almost regretted not having had the courage to open the letter and put it
back on the hall table before he came in. At least she would
have known what his secret was, and the bogy might have
been laid. For she was beginning now to think of the mystery
as something conscious, malevolent: a secret persecution before which he quailed, yet from which he could not free himself. Once or twice in his evasive eyes she thought she had
detected a desire for help, an impulse of confession, instantly
restrained and suppressed. It was as if he felt she could have
helped him if she had known, and yet had been unable to tell
her!

There flashed through her mind the idea of going to his
mother. She was very fond of old Mrs. Ashby, a firm-fleshed
clear-eyed old lady, with an astringent bluntness of speech
which responded to the forthright and simple in Charlotte's
own nature. There had been a tacit bond between them ever
since the day when Mrs. Ashby senior, coming to lunch for
the first time with her new daughter-in-law, had been received
by Charlotte downstairs in the library, and glancing up at the
empty wall above her son's desk, had remarked laconically:
"Elsie gone, eh?" adding, at Charlotte's murmured explanation: "Nonsense. Don't have her back. Two's company."
Charlotte, at this reading of her thoughts, could hardly refrain from exchanging a smile of complicity with her mother-
in-law; and it seemed to her now that Mrs. Ashby's almost
uncanny directness might pierce to the core of this new mys-

tery. But here again she hesitated, for the idea almost suggested a betrayal. What right had she to call in any one, even so close a relation, to surprise a secret which her husband was trying to keep from her? "Perhaps, by and by, he'll talk to his mother of his own accord," she thought, and then ended: "But what does it matter? He and I must settle it between us."

She was still brooding over the problem when there was a knock on the door and her husband came in. He was dressed for dinner and seemed surprised to see her sitting there, with her evening dress lying unheeded on the bed.

"Aren't you coming down?"

"I thought you were not well and had gone to bed," she faltered.

He forced a smile. "I'm not particularly well, but we'd better go down." His face, though still drawn, looked calmer than when he had fled upstairs an hour earlier.

"There it is; he knows what's in the letter and has fought his battle out again, whatever it is," she reflected, "while I'm still in darkness." She rang and gave a hurried order that dinner should be served as soon as possible—just a short meal, whatever could be got ready quickly, as both she and Mr. Ashby were rather tired and not very hungry.

Dinner was announced, and they sat down to it. At first neither seemed able to find a word to say; then Ashby began to make conversation with an assumption of ease that was more oppressive than his silence. "How tired he is! How terribly overtired!" Charlotte said to herself, pursuing her own thoughts while he rambled on about municipal politics, aviation, an exhibition of modern French painting, the health of an old aunt and the installing of the automatic telephone. "Good heavens, how tired he is!"

When they dined alone they usually went into the library after dinner, and Charlotte curled herself up on the divan with her knitting while he settled down in his armchair under the lamp and lit a pipe. But this evening, by tacit agreement, they avoided the room in which their strange talk had taken place, and went up to Charlotte's drawing-room.

They sat down near the fire, and Charlotte said: "Your pipe?" after he had put down his hardly tasted coffee.

He shook his head. "No, not tonight."

"You must go to bed early; you look terribly tired. I'm sure they overwork you at the office."

"I suppose we all overwork at times."

She rose and stood before him with sudden resolution. "Well, I'm not going to have you use up your strength slaving in that way. It's absurd. I can see you're ill." She bent over him and laid her hand on his forehead. "My poor old Kenneth. Prepare to be taken away soon on a long holiday."

He looked up at her, startled. "A holiday?"

"Certainly. Didn't you know I was going to carry you off at Easter? We're going to start in a fortnight on a month's voyage to somewhere or other. On any one of the big cruising steamers." She paused and bent closer, touching his forehead with her lips. "I'm tired, too, Kenneth."

He seemed to pay no heed to her last words, but sat, his hands on his knees, his head drawn back a little from her caress, and looked up at her with a stare of apprehension. "Again? My dear, we can't; I can't possibly go away."

"I don't know why you say 'again', Kenneth; we haven't taken a real holiday this year."

"At Christmas we spent a week with the children in the country."

"Yes, but this time I mean away from the children, from servants, from the house. From everything that's familiar and fatiguing. Your mother will love to have Joyce and Peter with her."

He frowned and slowly shook his head. "No, dear; I can't leave them with my mother."

"Why, Kenneth, how absurd! She adores them. You didn't hesitate to leave them with her for over two months when we went to the West Indies."

He drew a deep breath and stood up uneasily. "That was different."

"Different? Why?"

"I mean, at that time I didn't realize"— He broke off as if to choose his words and then went on: "My mother adores the children, as you say. But she isn't always very judicious. Grandmothers always spoil children. And she sometimes talks before them without thinking." He turned to his wife with an almost pitiful gesture of entreaty. "Don't ask me to, dear."

Charlotte mused. It was true that the elder Mrs. Ashby had a fearless tongue, but she was the last woman in the world to say or hint anything before her grandchildren at which the most scrupulous parent could take offense. Charlotte looked at her husband in perplexity.

"I don't understand."

He continued to turn on her the same troubled and entreating gaze. "Don't try to," he muttered.

"Not try to?"

"Not now—not yet." He put up his hands and pressed them against his temples. "Can't you see that there's no use in insisting? I can't go away, no matter how much I might want to."

Charlotte still scrutinized him gravely. "The question is, *do* you want to?"

He returned her gaze for a moment; then his lips began to tremble, and he said, hardly above his breath: "I want—anything you want."

"And yet—"

"Don't ask me. I can't leave—I can't!"

"You mean that you can't go away out of reach of those letters!"

Her husband had been standing before her in an uneasy half-hesitating attitude; now he turned abruptly away and walked once or twice up and down the length of the room, his head bent, his eyes fixed on the carpet.

Charlotte felt her resentfulness rising with her fears. "It's that," she persisted. "Why not admit it? You can't live without them."

He continued his troubled pacing of the room; then he stopped short, dropped into a chair and covered his face with his hands. From the shaking of his shoulders, Charlotte saw that he was weeping. She had never seen a man cry, except her father after her mother's death, when she was a little girl; and she remembered still how the sight had frightened her. She was frightened now; she felt that her husband was being dragged away from her into some mysterious bondage, and that she must use up her last atom of strength in the struggle for his freedom, and for hers.

"Kenneth—Kenneth!" she pleaded, kneeling down beside him. "Won't you listen to me? Won't you try to see what I'm suffering? I'm not unreasonable, darling; really not. I don't suppose I should ever have noticed the letters if it hadn't been for their effect on you. It's not my way to pry into other people's affairs; and even if the effect had been different—yes, yes; listen to me—if I'd seen that the letters made you happy, that you were watching eagerly for them, counting the days between their coming, that you wanted them, that they gave you something I haven't known how to give—why, Kenneth, I don't say I shouldn't have suffered from that, too; but it would have been in a different way, and I should have had the courage to hide what I felt, and the hope that some day you'd come to feel about me as you did about the writer of the letters. But what I can't bear is to see how you dread them, how they make you suffer, and yet how you can't live without them and won't go away lest you should miss one during your absence. Or perhaps," she added, her voice breaking into a cry of accusation—"perhaps it's because she's actually forbidden you to leave. Kenneth, you must answer me! Is that the reason? Is it because she's forbidden you that you won't go away with me?"

She continued to kneel at his side, and raising her hands, she drew his gently down. She was ashamed of her persistence, ashamed of uncovering that baffled disordered face, yet resolved that no such scruples should arrest her. His eyes were lowered, the muscles of his face quivered; she was making him suffer even more than she suffered herself. Yet this no longer restrained her.

"Kenneth, is it that? She won't let us go away together?"

Still he did not speak or turn his eyes to her; and a sense of defeat swept over her. After all, she thought, the struggle was a losing one. "You needn't answer. I see I'm right," she said.

Suddenly, as she rose, he turned and drew her down again. His hands caught hers and pressed them so tightly that she felt her rings cutting into her flesh. There was something frightened, convulsive in his hold; it was the clutch of a man who felt himself slipping over a precipice. He was staring up at her now as if salvation lay in the face she bent above him. "Of course we'll go away together. We'll go wherever you want," he said in a low confused voice; and putting his arm about her, he drew her close and pressed his lips on hers.

IV

Charlotte had said to herself: "I shall sleep tonight," but instead she sat before her fire into the small hours, listening for any sound that came from her husband's room. But he, at any rate, seemed to be resting after the tumult of the evening. Once or twice she stole to the door and in the faint light that came in from the street through his open window she saw him stretched out in heavy sleep—the sleep of weakness and exhaustion. "He's ill," she thought—"he's undoubtedly ill. And it's not overwork; it's this mysterious persecution."

She drew a breath of relief. She had fought through the weary fight and the victory was hers—at least for the moment. If only they could have started at once—started for anywhere! She knew it would be useless to ask him to leave before the holidays; and meanwhile the secret influence—as to which she was still so completely in the dark—would continue to work against her, and she would have to renew the struggle day after day till they started on their journey. But after that everything would be different. If once she could get her husband away under other skies, and all to herself, she never doubted her power to release him from the evil spell he was under. Lulled to quiet by the thought, she too slept at last.

When she woke, it was long past her usual hour, and she sat up in bed surprised and vexed at having overslept herself. She always liked to be down to share her husband's breakfast by the library fire; but a glance at the clock made it clear that he must have started long since for his office. To make sure, she jumped out of bed and went into his room; but it was empty. No doubt he had looked in on her before leaving, seen that she still slept, and gone downstairs without disturbing her; and their relations were sufficiently loverlike for her to regret having missed their morning hour.

She rang and asked if Mr. Ashby had already gone. Yes,

nearly an hour ago, the maid said. He had given orders that
Mrs. Ashby should not be waked and that the children should
not come to her till she sent for them. . . Yes, he had gone
up to the nursery himself to give the order. All this sounded
usual enough; and Charlotte hardly knew why she asked:
"And did Mr. Ashby leave no other message?"

Yes, the maid said, he did; she was so sorry she'd forgotten.
He'd told her, just as he was leaving, to say to Mrs. Ashby
that he was going to see about their passages, and would she
please be ready to sail tomorrow?

Charlotte echoed the woman's "Tomorrow," and sat staring at her incredulously. "Tomorrow—you're sure he said to
sail tomorrow?"

"Oh, ever so sure, ma'am. I don't know how I could have
forgotten to mention it."

"Well, it doesn't matter. Draw my bath, please." Charlotte
sprang up, dashed through her dressing, and caught herself
singing at her image in the glass as she sat brushing her hair.
It made her feel young again to have scored such a victory.
The other woman vanished to a speck on the horizon, as this
one, who ruled the foreground, smiled back at the reflection
of her lips and eyes. He loved her, then—he loved her as passionately as ever. He had divined what she had suffered, had
understood that their happiness depended on their getting
away at once, and finding each other again after yesterday's
desperate groping in the fog. The nature of the influence that
had come between them did not much matter to Charlotte
now; she had faced the phantom and dispelled it. "Courage—
that's the secret! If only people who are in love weren't always
so afraid of risking their happiness by looking it in the eyes."
As she brushed back her light abundant hair it waved electri-
cally above her head, like the palms of victory. Ah, well, some
women knew how to manage men, and some didn't—and
only the fair—she gaily paraphrased—deserve the brave!
Certainly she was looking very pretty.

The morning danced along like a cockleshell on a bright
sea—such a sea as they would soon be speeding over. She ordered a particularly good dinner, saw the children off to their
classes, had her trunks brought down, consulted with the
maid about getting out summer clothes—for of course they

would be heading for heat and sunshine—and wondered if she oughtn't to take Kenneth's flannel suits out of camphor. "But how absurd," she reflected, "that I don't yet know where we're going!" She looked at the clock, saw that it was close on noon, and decided to call him up at his office. There was a slight delay; then she heard his secretary's voice saying that Mr. Ashby had looked in for a moment early, and left again almost immediately. . . Oh, very well; Charlotte would ring up later. How soon was he likely to be back? The secretary answered that she couldn't tell; all they knew in the office was that when he left he had said he was in a hurry because he had to go out of town.

Out of town! Charlotte hung up the receiver and sat blankly gazing into new darkness. Why had he gone out of town? And where had he gone? And of all days, why should he have chosen the eve of their suddenly planned departure? She felt a faint shiver of apprehension. Of course he had gone to see that woman—no doubt to get her permission to leave. He was as completely in bondage as that; and Charlotte had been fatuous enough to see the palms of victory on her forehead. She burst into a laugh and, walking across the room, sat down again before her mirror. What a different face she saw! The smile on her pale lips seemed to mock the rosy vision of the other Charlotte. But gradually her colour crept back. After all, she had a right to claim the victory, since her husband was doing what she wanted, not what the other woman exacted of him. It was natural enough, in view of his abrupt decision to leave the next day, that he should have arrangements to make, business matters to wind up; it was not even necessary to suppose that his mysterious trip was a visit to the writer of the letters. He might simply have gone to see a client who lived out of town. Of course they would not tell Charlotte at the office; the secretary had hesitated before imparting even such meagre information as the fact of Mr. Ashby's absence. Meanwhile she would go on with her joyful preparations, content to learn later in the day to what particular island of the blest she was to be carried.

The hours wore on, or rather were swept forward on a rush of eager preparations. At last the entrance of the maid who came to draw the curtains roused Charlotte from her labours, and she saw to her surprise that the clock marked five. And she did not yet know where they were going the next day! She rang up her husband's office and was told that Mr. Ashby had not been there since the early morning. She asked for his partner, but the partner could add nothing to her information, for he himself, his suburban train having been behind time, had reached the office after Ashby had come and gone. Charlotte stood perplexed; then she decided to telephone to her mother-in-law. Of course Kenneth, on the eve of a month's absence, must have gone to see his mother. The mere fact that the children—in spite of his vague objections—would certainly have to be left with old Mrs. Ashby, made it obvious that he would have all sorts of matters to decide with her. At another time Charlotte might have felt a little hurt at being excluded from their conference, but nothing mattered now but that she had won the day, that her husband was still hers and not another woman's. Gaily she called up Mrs. Ashby, heard her friendly voice, and began: "Well, did Kenneth's news surprise you? What do you think of our elopement?"

Almost instantly, before Mrs. Ashby could answer, Charlotte knew what her reply would be. Mrs. Ashby had not seen her son, she had had no word from him and did not know what her daughter-in-law meant. Charlotte stood silent in the intensity of her surprise. "But then, where *has* he been?" she thought. Then, recovering herself, she explained their sudden decision to Mrs. Ashby, and in doing so, gradually regained her own self-confidence, her conviction that nothing could ever again come between Kenneth and herself. Mrs. Ashby took the news calmly and approvingly. She, too, had thought that Kenneth looked worried and overtired, and she agreed with her daughter-in-law that in such cases change was the surest remedy. "I'm always so glad when he gets away. Elsie hated travelling; she was always finding pretexts to prevent his going anywhere. With you, thank goodness, it's different." Nor was Mrs. Ashby surprised at his not having had time to let her know of his departure. He must have been in a rush from the moment the decision was taken; but no doubt he'd drop in before dinner. Five minutes' talk was really all they needed. "I hope you'll gradually cure Kenneth of his mania for going over and over a question that could be settled in a dozen words. He never used to be like that, and if he carried the habit into his professional work he'd soon lose all his clients. . . Yes, do come in for a minute, dear, if you have time; no doubt he'll turn up while you're here." The tonic ring of Mrs. Ashby's voice echoed on reassuringly in the silent room while Charlotte continued her preparations.

Toward seven the telephone rang, and she darted to it. Now she would know! But it was only from the conscientious secretary, to say that Mr. Ashby hadn't been back, or sent any word, and before the office closed she thought she ought to let Mrs. Ashby know. "Oh, that's all right. Thanks a lot!" Charlotte called out cheerfully, and hung up the receiver with a trembling hand. But perhaps by this time, she reflected, he was at his mother's. She shut her drawers and cupboards, put on her hat and coat and called up to the nursery that she was going out for a minute to see the children's grandmother.

Mrs. Ashby lived near by, and during her brief walk through the cold spring dusk Charlotte imagined that every advancing figure was her husband's. But she did not meet him on the way, and when she entered the house she found her mother-in-law alone. Kenneth had neither telephoned nor come. Old Mrs. Ashby sat by her bright fire, her knitting needles flashing steadily through her active old hands, and her mere bodily presence gave reassurance to Charlotte. Yes, it was certainly odd that Kenneth had gone off for the whole day without letting any of them know; but, after all, it was to be expected. A busy lawyer held so many threads in his hands that any sudden change of plan would oblige him to make all sorts of unforeseen arrangements and adjustments. He might have gone to see some client in the suburbs and been detained there; his mother remembered his telling her that he had charge of the legal business of a queer old recluse somewhere in New Jersey, who was immensely rich but too mean to have a telephone. Very likely Kenneth had been stranded there.

But Charlotte felt her nervousness gaining on her. When Mrs. Ashby asked her at what hour they were sailing the next day and she had to say she didn't know—that Kenneth had simply sent her word he was going to take their passages—the uttering of the words again brought home to her the strangeness of the situation. Even Mrs. Ashby conceded that it was odd; but she immediately added that it only showed what a rush he was in.

"But, mother, it's nearly eight o'clock! He must realize that I've got to know when we're starting tomorrow."

"Oh, the boat probably doesn't sail till evening. Sometimes they have to wait till midnight for the tide. Kenneth's probably counting on that. After all, he has a level head."

Charlotte stood up. "It's not that. Something has happened to him."

Mrs. Ashby took off her spectacles and rolled up her knitting. "If you begin to let yourself imagine things—"

"Aren't you in the least anxious?"

"I never am till I have to be. I wish you'd ring for dinner, my dear. You'll stay and dine? He's sure to drop in here on his way home."

Charlotte called up her own house. No, the maid said, Mr. Ashby hadn't come in and hadn't telephoned. She would tell him as soon as he came that Mrs. Ashby was dining at his mother's. Charlotte followed her mother-in-law into the dining-room and sat with parched throat before her empty plate, while Mrs. Ashby dealt calmly and efficiently with a short but carefully prepared repast. "You'd better eat something, child, or you'll be as bad as Kenneth. . . Yes, a little more asparagus, please, Jane."

She insisted on Charlotte's drinking a glass of sherry and nibbling a bit of toast; then they returned to the drawing-room, where the fire had been made up, and the cushions in Mrs. Ashby's armchair shaken out and smoothed. How safe and familiar it all looked; and out there, somewhere in the uncertainty and mystery of the night, lurked the answer to the two women's conjectures, like an indistinguishable figure prowling on the threshold.

At last Charlotte got up and said: "I'd better go back. At this hour Kenneth will certainly go straight home."

Mrs. Ashby smiled indulgently. "It's not very late, my dear. It doesn't take two sparrows long to dine."

"It's after nine." Charlotte bent down to kiss her. "The fact is, I can't keep still."

Mrs. Ashby pushed aside her work and rested her two hands on the arms of her chair. "I'm going with you," she said, helping herself up.

Charlotte protested that it was too late, that it was not necessary, that she would call up as soon as Kenneth came in, but Mrs. Ashby had already rung for her maid. She was slightly lame, and stood resting on her stick while her wraps were brought. "If Mr. Kenneth turns up, tell him he'll find me at his own house," she instructed the maid as the two women got into the taxi which had been summoned. During the short drive Charlotte gave thanks that she was not returning home alone. There was something warm and substantial in the mere fact of Mrs. Ashby's nearness, something that corresponded with the clearness of her eyes and the texture of her fresh firm complexion. As the taxi drew up she laid her hand encouragingly on Charlotte's. "You'll see; there'll be a message."

The door opened at Charlotte's ring and the two entered. Charlotte's heart beat excitedly; the stimulus of her mother-in-law's confidence was beginning to flow through her veins.

"You'll see—you'll see," Mrs. Ashby repeated.

The maid who opened the door said no, Mr. Ashby had not come in, and there had been no message from him.

"You're sure the telephone's not out of order?" his mother suggested; and the maid said, well, it certainly wasn't half an hour ago; but she'd just go and ring up to make sure. She disappeared, and Charlotte turned to take off her hat and cloak. As she did so her eyes lit on the hall table, and there lay a gray envelope, her husband's name faintly traced on it. "Oh!" she cried out, suddenly aware that for the first time in months she had entered her house without wondering if one of the gray letters would be there.

"What is it, my dear?" Mrs. Ashby asked with a glance of surprise.

Charlotte did not answer. She took up the envelope and stood staring at it as if she could force her gaze to penetrate to what was within. Then an idea occurred to her. She turned and held out the envelope to her mother-in-law.

"Do you know that writing?" she asked.

Mrs. Ashby took the letter. She had to feel with her other hand for her eyeglasses, and when she had adjusted them she lifted the envelope to the light. "Why!" she exclaimed; and then stopped. Charlotte noticed that the letter shook in her usually firm hand. "But this is addressed to Kenneth," Mrs. Ashby said at length, in a low voice. Her tone seemed to imply that she felt her daughter-in-law's question to be slightly indiscreet.

"Yes, but no matter," Charlotte spoke with sudden decision. "I want to know—do you know the writing?"

Mrs. Ashby handed back the letter. "No," she said distinctly.

The two women had turned into the library. Charlotte switched on the electric light and shut the door. She still held the envelope in her hand.

"I'm going to open it," she announced.

She caught her mother-in-law's startled glance. "But, dearest—a letter not addressed to you? My dear, you can't!"

"As if I cared about that—now!" She continued to look intently at Mrs. Ashby. "This letter may tell me where Kenneth is."

Mrs. Ashby's glossy bloom was effaced by a quick pallor; her firm cheeks seemed to shrink and wither. "Why should it? What makes you believe— It can't possibly—"

Charlotte held her eyes steadily on that altered face. "Ah, then you *do* know the writing?" she flashed back.

"Know the writing? How should I? With all my son's correspondents. . . What I do know is—" Mrs. Ashby broke off and looked at her daughter-in-law entreatingly, almost timidly.

Charlotte caught her by the wrist. "Mother! What do you know? Tell me! You must!"

"That I don't believe any good ever came of a woman's opening her husband's letters behind his back."

The words sounded to Charlotte's irritated ears as flat as a phrase culled from a book of moral axioms. She laughed impatiently and dropped her mother-in-law's wrist. "Is that all? No good can come of this letter, opened or unopened. I know that well enough. But whatever ill comes, I mean to find out what's in it." Her hands had been trembling as they held the envelope, but now they grew firm, and her voice also. She still gazed intently at Mrs. Ashby. "This is the ninth letter addressed in the same hand that has come for Kenneth since we've been married. Always these same gray envelopes. I've kept count of them because after each one he has been like a man who has had some dreadful shock. It takes him hours to shake off their effect. I've told him so. I've told him I must know from whom they come, because I can see they're killing him. He won't answer my questions; he says he can't tell me anything about the letters; but last night he promised to go away with me—to get away from them."

Mrs. Ashby, with shaking steps, had gone to one of the armchairs and sat down in it, her head drooping forward on her breast. "Ah," she murmured.

"So now you understand—"

"Did he tell you it was to get away from them?"

"He said, to get away—to get away. He was sobbing so that he could hardly speak. But I told him I knew that was why."

"And what did he say?"

"He took me in his arms and said he'd go wherever I wanted."

"Ah, thank God!" said Mrs. Ashby. There was a silence, during which she continued to sit with bowed head, and eyes averted from her daughter-in-law. At last she looked up and spoke. "Are you sure there have been as many as nine?"

"Perfectly. This is the ninth. I've kept count."

"And he has absolutely refused to explain?"

"Absolutely."

Mrs. Ashby spoke through pale contracted lips. "When did they begin to come? Do you remember?"

Charlotte laughed again. "Remember? The first one came the night we got back from our honeymoon."

"All that time?" Mrs. Ashby lifted her head and spoke with sudden energy. "Then— Yes, open it."

The words were so unexpected that Charlotte felt the blood in her temples, and her hands began to tremble again. She tried to slip her finger under the flap of the envelope, but it was so tightly stuck that she had to hunt on her husband's writing table for his ivory letter-opener. As she pushed about the familiar objects his own hands had so lately touched, they sent through her the icy chill emanating from the little personal effects of someone newly dead. In the deep silence of the room the tearing of the paper as she slit the envelope sounded like a human cry. She drew out the sheet and carried it to the lamp.

"Well?" Mrs. Ashby asked below her breath.

Charlotte did not move or answer. She was bending over the page with wrinkled brows, holding it nearer and nearer to the light. Her sight must be blurred, or else dazzled by the reflection of the lamplight on the smooth surface of the paper, for, strain her eyes as she would, she could discern only a few faint strokes, so faint and faltering as to be nearly undecipherable.

"I can't make it out," she said.

"What do you mean, dear?"

"The writing's too indistinct. . . Wait."

She went back to the table and, sitting down close to Kenneth's reading lamp, slipped the letter under a magnifying glass. All this time she was aware that her mother-in-law was watching her intently.

"Well?" Mrs. Ashby breathed.

"Well, it's no clearer. I can't read it."

"You mean the paper is an absolute blank?"

"No, not quite. There is writing on it. I can make out something like 'mine'—oh, and 'come'. It might be 'come'."

Mrs. Ashby stood up abruptly. Her face was even paler than before. She advanced to the table and, resting her two hands on it, drew a deep breath. "Let me see," she said, as if forcing herself to a hateful effort.

Charlotte felt the contagion of her whiteness. "She knows," she thought. She pushed the letter across the table. Her mother-in-law lowered her head over it in silence, but without touching it with her pale wrinkled hands.

Charlotte stood watching her as she herself, when she had tried to read the letter, had been watched by Mrs. Ashby. The latter fumbled for her glasses, held them to her eyes, and bent still closer to the outspread page, in order, as it seemed, to avoid touching it. The light of the lamp fell directly on her old face, and Charlotte reflected what depths of the unknown may lurk under the clearest and most candid lineaments. She had never seen her mother-in-law's features express any but simple and sound emotions—cordiality, amusement, a kindly sympathy; now and again a flash of wholesome anger. Now they seemed to wear a look of fear and hatred, of incredulous dismay and almost cringing defiance. It was as if the spirits warring within her had distorted her face to their own like-ness. At length she raised her head. "I can't—I can't," she said in a voice of childish distress.

"You can't make it out either?"

She shook her head, and Charlotte saw two tears roll down her cheeks.

"Familiar as the writing is to you?" Charlotte insisted with twitching lips.

Mrs. Ashby did not take up the challenge. "I can make out nothing—nothing."

"But you do know the writing?"

Mrs. Ashby lifted her head timidly; her anxious eyes stole with a glance of apprehension around the quiet familiar room. "How can I tell? I was startled at first. . ."

"Startled by the resemblance?"

"Well, I thought—"

"You'd better say it out, mother! You knew at once it was *her* writing?"

"Oh, wait, my dear—wait."

"Wait for what?"

Mrs. Ashby looked up; her eyes, travelling slowly past Charlotte, were lifted to the blank wall behind her son's writ-ing table.

Charlotte, following the glance, burst into a shrill laugh of accusation. "I needn't wait any longer! You've answered me now! You're looking straight at the wall where her picture used to hang!"

Mrs. Ashby lifted her hand with a murmur of warning. "Sh-h."

"Oh, you needn't imagine that anything can ever frighten me again!" Charlotte cried.

Her mother-in-law still leaned against the table. Her lips

moved plaintively. "But we're going mad—we're both going mad. We both know such things are impossible."

Her daughter-in-law looked at her with a pitying stare. "I've known for a long time now that everything was possible."

"Even this?"

"Yes, exactly this."

"But this letter—after all, there's nothing in this letter—"

"Perhaps there would be to him. How can I tell? I remember his saying to me once that if you were used to a handwriting the faintest stroke of it became legible. Now I see what he meant. He *was* used to it."

"But the few strokes that I can make out are so pale. No one could possibly read that letter."

Charlotte laughed again. "I suppose everything's pale about a ghost," she said stridently.

"Oh, my child—my child—don't say it!"

"Why shouldn't I say it, when even the bare walls cry it out? What difference does it make if her letters are illegible to you and me? If even you can see her face on that blank wall, why shouldn't he read her writing on this blank paper? Don't you see that she's everywhere in this house, and the closer to him because to everyone else she's become invisible?" Charlotte dropped into a chair and covered her face with her hands. A turmoil of sobbing shook her from head to foot. At length a touch on her shoulder made her look up, and she saw her mother-in-law bending over her. Mrs. Ashby's face seemed to have grown still smaller and more wasted, but it had resumed its usual quiet look. Through all her tossing anguish, Charlotte felt the impact of that resolute spirit.

"Tomorrow—tomorrow. You'll see. There'll be some explanation tomorrow."

Charlotte cut her short. "An explanation? Who's going to give it, I wonder?"

Mrs. Ashby drew back and straightened herself heroically. "Kenneth himself will," she cried out in a strong voice. Charlotte said nothing, and the old woman went on: "But meanwhile we must act; we must notify the police. Now, without a moment's delay. We must do everything—everything."

Charlotte stood up slowly and stiffly; her joints felt as cramped as an old woman's. "Exactly as if we thought it could do any good to do anything?"

Resolutely Mrs. Ashby cried: "Yes!" and Charlotte went up to the telephone and unhooked the receiver.

Confession

THIS is the way it began; stupidly, trivially, out of nothing, as fatal things do.

I was sitting at the corner table in the hotel restaurant; I mean the left-hand corner as you enter from the hall. . . As if that mattered! A table in that angle, with a view over the mountains, was too good for an unaccompanied traveller, and I had it only because the head-waiter was a good-natured fellow who . . . As if that mattered, either! Why can't I come to the point?

The point is that, entering the restaurant that day with the doubtful step of the newly-arrived, she was given the table next to me. Colossal Event—eh? But if you've ever known what it is, after a winter of semi-invalidism on the Nile, to be told that, before you're fit to go back and take up your job in New York—before that little leak in your lung is patched up tight—you've got to undergo another three or four months of convalescence on top of an Alp; if you've dragged through all those stages of recovery, first among one pack of hotel idlers, then among another, you'll know what small incidents can become Colossal Events against the empty horizon of your idleness.

Not that a New York banker's office (even before the depression) commanded a very wide horizon, as I understand horizons; but before arguing that point with me, wait and see what it's like to look out day after day on a dead-level of in-occupation, and you'll know what a towering affair it may become to have your temperature go up a point, or a woman you haven't seen before stroll into the dining-room, and sit down at the table next to yours.

But what magnified this very ordinary incident for me was the immediate sense of something out of the ordinary in the woman herself. Beauty? No; not even. (I say "even" because there are far deadlier weapons, as we all know.) No, she was not beautiful; she was not particularly young; and though she carried herself well, and was well dressed (though over-expensively, I thought), there was nothing in that to single her out in a fashionable crowd.

What then? Well, what struck me first in her was a shy but intense curiosity about everything in that assemblage of commonplace and shop-worn people. Here was a woman, evidently well-bred and well-off, to whom a fashionable hotel restaurant in the Engadine during the summer was apparently a sight so unusual, and composed of elements so novel and inexplicable, that she could hardly remember to eat in the subdued excitement of watching all that was going on about her.

As to her own appearance, it obviously did not preoccupy her—or figured only as an element of her general and rather graceful timidity. She was so busy observing all the dull commonplace people about her that it had presumably never occurred to her that she, who was neither dull nor commonplace, might be herself the subject of observation. (Already I found myself resenting any too protracted stare from the other tables.)

Well, to come down to particulars: she was middling tall, slight, almost thin; pale, with a long somewhat narrow face and dark hair; and her wide blue-gray eyes were so light and clear that her hair and complexion seemed dusky in contrast. A melancholy mouth, which lit up suddenly when she smiled—but her smiles were rare. Dress, sober, costly, severely "lady-like"; her whole appearance, shall I say a trifle old-fashioned—or perhaps merely provincial? But certainly it was not only her dress which singled her out from the standardized beauties at the other tables. Perhaps it was the fact that her air of social inexperience was combined with a look, about the mouth and eyes, of having had more experience, of some other sort, than any woman in the room.

But of what sort? That was what baffled me. I could only sum it up by saying to myself that she was different; which, of course, is what every man feels about the woman he is about to fall in love with, no matter how painfully usual she may appear to others. But I had no idea that I was going to fall in love with the lady at the next table, and when I defined her as "different" I did not mean it subjectively, did not mean different to *me*, but in herself, mysteriously, and independently of the particular impression she made on me. In short, she appeared, in spite of her dress and bearing, to be a little uncertain and ill at ease in the ordinary social scene, but at home and sure of herself elsewhere. Where?

I was still asking myself this when she was joined by a companion. One of the things one learns in travelling is to find out about people by studying their associates; and I wished that the lady who interested me had not furnished me with this particular kind of clue. The woman who joined her was probably of about her own age; but that seemed to be the only point of resemblance between them. The newcomer was stout, with mahogany-dyed hair, and small eyes set too close to a coarse nose. Her complexion, through a careless powdering, was flushed, and netted with little red veins, and her chin sloped back under a vulgar mouth to a heavy white throat. I had hoped she was only a chance acquaintance of the dark lady's; but she took her seat without speaking, and began to study the menu without as much as a glance at her companion. They were fellow-travellers, then; and though the newcomer was as richly dressed as the other, and I judged more fashionably, I detected at once that she was a subordinate, probably a paid one, and that she sought to conceal it by an exaggerated assumption of equality. But how could the one woman have chosen the other as a companion? It disturbed my mental picture of the dark lady to have to fit into it what was evidently no chance association.

"Have you ordered my beer?" the last comer asked, drawing off her long gloves from thick red fingers crammed with rings (the dark lady wore none, I had noticed.)

"No, I haven't," said the other.

Her tone somehow suggested: "Why should I? Can't you ask for what you want yourself?" But a moment later she had signed to the head-waiter, and said, in a low tone: "Miss Wilpert's Pilsener, please—as usual."

"Yes; *as usual*. Only nobody ever remembers it! I used to be a lot better served when I had to wait on myself."

The dark lady gave a faint laugh of protest.

Miss Wilpert, after a critical glance at the dish presented to her, transferred a copious portion to her plate, and squared herself before it. I could almost imagine a napkin tucked into the neck of her dress, below the crease in her heavy white throat.

"There were three women ahead of me at the hairdresser's," she grumbled.

The dark lady glanced at her absently. "It doesn't matter."

"What doesn't matter?" snapped her companion. "That I should be kept there two hours, and have to wait till two o'clock for my lunch?"

"I meant that your being late didn't matter to me."

"I daresay not," retorted Miss Wilpert. She poured down a draught of Pilsener, and set the empty glass beside her plate. "So you're in the 'nothing matters' mood again, are you?" she said, looking critically at her companion.

The latter smiled faintly. "Yes."

"Well, then—what are we staying here for? You needn't sacrifice yourself for me, you know."

A lady, finishing her lunch, crossed the room, and in passing out stopped to speak to my neighbour. "Oh, Mrs. Ingram" (so her name was Ingram), "can't we persuade you to join us at bridge when you've had your coffee?"

Mrs. Ingram smiled, but shook her head. "Thank you so much. But you know I don't play cards."

"Principles!" jerked out Miss Wilpert, wiping her rouged lips after a second glass of Pilsener. She waved her fat hand toward the retreating lady. "I'll join up with you in half an hour," she cried in a penetrating tone.

"Oh, do," said the lady with an indifferent nod.

I had finished my lunch, drunk my coffee, and smoked more than my strict ration of cigarettes. There was no other excuse for lingering, and I got up and walked out of the restaurant. My friend Antoine, the head-waiter, was standing near the door, and in passing I let my lips shape the inaudible question: "The lady at the next table?"

Antoine knew every one, and also every one's history. I wondered why he hesitated for a moment before replying: "Ah—Mrs. Ingram? Yes. From California."

"Er—regular visitor?"

"No. I think on her first trip to Europe."

"Ah. Then the other lady's showing her about?"

Antoine gave a shrug. "I think not. She seems also new."

"I like the table you've given me, Antoine," I remarked; and he nodded compliantly.

I was surprised, therefore, that when I came down to dinner that evening I had been assigned to another seat, on the farther side of the restaurant. I asked for Antoine, but it was his evening off, and the understudy who replaced him could only say that I had been moved by Antoine's express orders. "Perhaps it was on account of the draught, sir."

"Draught be blowed! Can't I be given back my table?"

He was very sorry, but, as I could see, the table had been allotted to an infirm old lady, whom it would be difficult, and indeed impossible, to disturb.

"Very well, then. At lunch tomorrow I shall expect to have it back," I said severely.

In looking back over the convalescent life, it is hard to recall the exaggerated importance every trifle assumes when there are only trifles to occupy one. I was furious at having had my place changed; and still more so when, the next day at lunch, Antoine, as a matter of course, conducted me to the table I had indignantly rejected the night before.

"What does this mean? I told you I wanted to go back to that corner table—"

Not a muscle moved in his non-committal yet all-communicating face. "So sorry, sir."

"Sorry? Why, you promised me—"

"What can I do? Those ladies have our most expensive suite; and they're here for the season."

"Well, what's the matter with the ladies? I've no objection to them. They're my compatriots."

Antoine gave me a spectral smile. "That appears to be the reason, sir."

"The reason? They've given you a reason for asking to have me moved?"

"The big red one did. The other, Mrs. Ingram, as you can see, is quite different—though both are a little odd," he added thoughtfully.

"Well—the big red one?"

"The *dame de compagnie*. You must excuse me, sir; but she says she doesn't like Americans. And as the management are anxious to oblige Mrs. Ingram—"

I gave a haughty laugh. "I see. Whereas a humble lodger like myself— But there are other hotels at Mont Soleil, you may remind the management from me."

"Oh, Monsieur, Monsieur—you can't be so severe on a lady's whim," Antoine murmured reprovingly.

Of course I couldn't. Antoine's advice was always educational. I shrugged, and accepting my banishment, looked about for another interesting neighbour to watch instead of Mrs. Ingram. But I found that no one else interested me. . .

II

"Don't you think you might tell me now," I said to Mrs. Ingram a few days later, "why your friend insisted on banishing me to the farther end of the restaurant?"

I need hardly say that, in spite of Miss Wilpert's prejudice against her compatriots, she had not been able to prevent my making the acquaintance of Mrs. Ingram. I forget how it came about—the pretext of a dropped letter, a deck chair to be moved out of the sun, or one of the hundred devices which bring two people together when they are living idle lives under the same roof. I had not gained my end without difficulty, however, for the ill-assorted pair were almost always together. But luckily Miss Wilpert played bridge, and Mrs. Ingram did not, and before long I had learned to profit by this opportunity, and in the course of time to make the fullest use of it.

Yet after a fortnight I had to own that I did not know much more about Mrs. Ingram than when I had first seen her. She was younger than I had thought, probably not over thirty-two or three; she was wealthy; she was shy; she came from California, or at any rate had lived there. For the last two years or more she appeared to have travelled, encircling the globe, and making long stays in places as far apart as Ceylon, Teneriffe, Rio and Cairo. She seemed, on the whole, to have enjoyed these wanderings. She asked me many questions about the countries she had visited, and I saw that she belonged to the class of intelligent but untaught travellers who can learn more by verbal explanations than from books. Unprepared as she was for the sights awaiting her, she had necessarily observed little, and understood less; but she had been struck by the more conspicuous features of the journey, and the Taj, the Parthenon and the Pyramids had not escaped her. On the subject of her travels she was at least superficially communicative; and as she never alluded to husband or child, or to any other friend or relative, I was driven to conclude that Miss Wilpert had been her only companion. This deepened the mystery, and made me feel that I knew no more of her real self than on the day when I had first seen her; but, perhaps partly for that reason, I found her increasingly interesting. It was clear that she shrank from strangers, but I could not help seeing that with me she was happy and at ease, and as ready as I was to profit by our opportunities of being together. It was only when Miss Wilpert appeared that her old shyness returned, and I suspected that she was reluctant to let her companion see what good friends we had become.

I had put my indiscreet question about Miss Wilpert somewhat abruptly, in the hope of startling Mrs. Ingram out of her usual reserve; and I saw by the quick rise of colour under her pale skin that I had nearly succeeded. But after a moment she replied, with a smile: "I can't believe Cassie ever said anything so silly."

"You can't? Then I wish you'd ask her; and if it was just an invention of that head-waiter's I'll make him give me back my table before he's a day older."

Mrs. Ingram still smiled. "I hope you won't make a fuss about such a trifle. Perhaps Cassie did say something foolish. She's not used to travelling, and sometimes takes odd notions."

The ambiguity of the answer was obviously meant to warn me off; but having risked one question I was determined to risk another. "Miss Wilpert's a very old friend, I suppose?"

"Yes; very," said Mrs. Ingram non-committally.

"And was she always with you when you were at home?"

My question seemed to find her unprepared. "At home—?"

"I mean, where you lived. California, wasn't it?"

She looked relieved. "Oh, yes; Cassie Wilpert was with me in California."

"But there she must have had to associate with her compatriots?"

"Yes; that's one reason why she was so glad when I decided to travel," said Mrs. Ingram with a faint touch of irony, and then added: "Poor Cassie was very unhappy at one time; there were people who were unkind to her. That accounts for her prejudices, I suppose."

"I'm sorry I'm one of them. What can I do to make up to her?"

I fancied I saw a slight look of alarm in Mrs. Ingram's eyes. "Oh, you'd much better leave her alone."

"But she's always with you; and I don't want to leave you alone."

Mrs. Ingram smiled, and then sighed. "We shall be going soon now."

"And then Miss Wilpert will be rid of me?"

Mrs. Ingram looked at me quickly; her eyes were plaintive, almost entreating. "I shall never leave her; she's been like a— a sister to me," she murmured, answering a question I had not put.

The word startled me; and I noticed that Mrs. Ingram had hesitated a moment before pronouncing it. A sister to her— that coarse red-handed woman? The words sounded as if they had been spoken by rote. I saw at once that they did not express the speaker's real feeling, and that, whatever that was, she did not mean to let me find it out.

Some of the bridge-players with whom Miss Wilpert consorted were coming toward us, and I stood up to leave. "Don't let Miss Wilpert carry you off on my account. I promise you I'll keep out of her way," I said, laughing.

Mrs. Ingram straightened herself almost imperiously. "I'm not at Miss Wilpert's orders; she can't take me away from any place I choose to stay in," she said; but a moment later, lowering her voice, she breathed to me quickly: "Go now; I see her coming."

III

I don't mind telling you that I was not altogether happy about my attitude toward Mrs. Ingram. I'm not given to prying into other people's secrets; yet I had not scrupled to try to trap her into revealing hers. For that there was a secret I was now convinced; and I excused myself for trying to get to the bottom of it by the fact that I was sure I should find Miss Wilpert there, and that the idea was abhorrent to me. The relation between the two women, I had by now discovered, was one of mutual animosity; not the kind of animosity which may be the disguise of more complicated sentiments, but the simple incompatibility that was bound to exist between two women so different in class and character. Miss Wilpert was a coarse, uneducated woman, with, as far as I could see, no redeeming qualities, moral or mental, to bridge the distance between herself and her companion; and the mystery was that any past tie or obligation, however strong, should have made Mrs. Ingram tolerate her.

I knew how easily rich and idle women may become dependent on some vulgar tyrannical house-keeper or companion who renders them services and saves them trouble; but I saw at once that this theory did not explain the situation. On the contrary, it was Miss Wilpert who was dependent on Mrs. Ingram, who looked to her as guide, interpreter, and manager of their strange association. Miss Wilpert possessed no language but her own, and of that only a local vernacular which made it difficult to explain her wants (and they were many) even to the polyglot servants of a Swiss hotel. Mrs. Ingram spoke a carefully acquired if laborious French, and was conscientiously preparing for a winter in Naples by taking a daily lesson in Italian; and I noticed that whenever an order was to be given, an excursion planned, or any slight change effected in the day's arrangements, Miss Wilpert, suddenly embarrassed and helpless, always waited for Mrs. Ingram to interpret for her. It was obvious, therefore, that she was a burden and not a help to her employer, and that I must look deeper to discover the nature of their bond.

Mrs. Ingram, guide-book in hand, appealed to me one day about their autumn plans. "I think we shall be leaving next week; and they say here we ought not to miss the Italian lakes."

"Leaving next week? But why? The lakes are not at their best till after the middle of September. You'll find them very stuffy after this high air."

Mrs. Ingram sighed. "Cassie's tired of it here. She says she doesn't like the people."

I looked at her, and then ventured with a smile: "Don't you mean that she doesn't like me?"

"I don't see why you think that—"

"Well, I daresay it sounds rather fatuous. But you *do* know why I think it; and you think it yourself." I hesitated a moment, and then went on, lowering my voice: "Since you attach such importance to Miss Wilpert's opinions, it's natural I should want to know why she dislikes seeing me with you."

Mrs. Ingram looked at me helplessly. "Well, if she doesn't like you—"

"Yes; but in reality I don't think it's me she dislikes, but the fact of my being with you."

She looked disturbed at this. "But if she dislikes you, it's natural she shouldn't want you to be with me."

"And do her likes and dislikes regulate all your friendships?"

"Friendships? I've so few; I know hardly any one," said Mrs. Ingram, looking away.

"You'd have as many as you chose if she'd let you," I broke out angrily.

She drew herself up with the air of dignity she could assume on occasion. "I don't know why you find so much pleasure in saying disagreeable things to me about my—my friend."

The answer rushed to my lips: "Why did she begin by saying disagreeable things about me?"—but just in time I saw that I was on the brink of a futile wrangle with the woman whom, at that moment, I was the most anxious not to displease. How anxious, indeed, I now saw for the first time, in the light of my own anger. For what on earth did I care for the disapproval of a creature like Miss Wilpert, except as it interfered with my growing wish to stand well with Kate Ingram? The answer I did make sprang to my lips before I could repress it. "Because—you must know by this time. Because I can't bear that anything or any one should come between us."

"Between us—?"

I pressed on, hardly knowing what I was saying. "Because

nothing matters to me as much as what you feel about me. In fact, nothing else matters at all."

The words had rushed out, lighting up the depths of my feeling as much to myself as to Mrs. Ingram. Only then did I remember how little I knew of the woman to whom they were addressed—not even her maiden name, nor as much as one fact of her past history. I did not even know if she were married, widowed or divorced. All I did know was that I had fallen in love with her—and had told her so.

She sat motionless, without a word. But suddenly her eyes filled, and I saw that her lips were trembling too much for her to speak.

"Kate—" I entreated; but she drew back, shaking her head. "No—"

"Why 'no'? Because I've made you angry—?"

She shook her head again. "I feel that you're a true friend—"

"I want you to feel much more than that."

"It's all I can ever feel—for any one. I shall never—never . . ." She broke down, and sat struggling with her tears.

"Do you say that because you're not free?"

"Oh, no—oh, no—"

"Then is it because you don't like me? Tell me that, and I won't trouble you again."

We were sitting alone in a deserted corner of the lounge. The diners had scattered to the wide verandahs, the card-room or the bar. Miss Wilpert was safely engaged with a party of bridge-players in the farthest room of the suite, and I had imagined that at last I should be able to have my talk out with Mrs. Ingram. I had hardly meant it to take so grave a turn; but now that I had spoken I knew my choice was made.

"If you tell me you don't like me, I won't trouble you any more," I repeated, trying to keep her eyes on mine. Her lids quivered, and she looked down at her uneasy hands. I had often noticed that her hands were the only unquiet things about her, and now she sat clasping and unclasping them without ceasing.

"I can't tell you that I don't like you," she said, very low. I leaned over to capture those restless fingers, and quiet them in mine; but at the same moment she gave a start, and I saw that she was not looking at me, but over my shoulder at some one who must have crossed the lounge behind me. I turned and saw a man I had not noticed before in the hotel, but whose short square-shouldered figure struck me as vaguely familiar.

"Is that some one you know?" I asked, surprised by the look in her face.

"N-no. I thought it was. . . I must have been mistaken . . ." I saw that she was struggling to recover her self-control, and I looked again at the newcomer, who had stopped on his way to the bar to speak to one of the hall-porters.

"Why, I believe it's Jimmy Shreve—Shreve of the New York *Evening Star*," I said. "It looks like him. Do you know him?"

"No."

"Then, please—won't you answer the question I was just asking you?"

She had grown very pale, and was twisting her long fingers distressfully. "Oh, not now; not now. . ."

"Why not now? After what you've told me, do you suppose I'm going to be put off without a reason?"

"There's my reason!" she exclaimed with a nervous laugh. I looked around, and saw Miss Wilpert approaching. She looked unusually large and flushed, and her elaborate evening dress showed a displeasing expanse of too-white skin.

"Ah, that's your reason? I thought so!" I broke out bitterly.

One of Mrs. Ingram's quick blushes overswept her. "I didn't mean that—you've no right to say so. I only meant that I'd promised to go with her. . ."

Miss Wilpert was already towering over us, loud-breathing and crimson. I suspected that in the intervals of bridge she had more than once sought refreshment at the bar. "Well, so this is where you've hidden yourself away, is it? I've hunted for you all over the place; but I didn't suppose you'd choose a dark corner under the stairs. I presume you've forgotten that you asked them to reserve seats for us for those Javanese dances. They won't keep our places much longer; the ball-room's packed already."

I sat still, almost holding my breath, and watched the two

women. I guessed that a crucial point in the struggle between them had been reached, and that a word from me might wreck my chances. Mrs. Ingram's colour faded quickly, as it always did, but she forced a nervous smile. "I'd no idea it was so late."

"Well, if your watch has stopped, there's the hall clock right in front of you," said Miss Wilpert, with quick panting breaths between the words. She waited a moment. "Are you coming?"

Mrs. Ingram leaned back in her deep armchair. "Well, no— I don't believe I am."

"You're *not*?"

"No. I think I like it better here."

"But you must be crazy! You asked that Italian Countess to keep us two seats next to hers—"

"Well, you can go and ask her to excuse me—say I'm tired. The ball-room's always so hot."

"Land's sake! How'm I going to tell her all that in Italian? You know she don't speak a word of English. She'll think it's pretty funny if you don't come; and so will the others. You always say you hate to have people talk about you; and yet here you sit, stowed away in this dark corner, like a school-girl with her boy friend at a Commencement dance—"

Mrs. Ingram stood up quickly. "Cassie, I'm afraid you must have been losing at bridge. I never heard you talk so foolishly. But of course I'll come if you think the Countess expects us." She turned to me with a little smile, and suddenly, shyly, held out her hand. "You'll tell me the rest tomorrow morning," she said, looking straight at me for an instant; then she turned and followed Cassie Wilpert.

I stood watching them with a thumping heart. I didn't know what held these women together, but I felt that in the last few minutes a link of the chain between them had been loosened, and I could hardly wait to see it snap.

I was still standing there when the man who had attracted Mrs. Ingram's notice came out of the bar, and walked toward me; and I saw that it was in fact my old acquaintance Jimmy Shreve, the bright particular ornament of the *Evening Star*. We had not met for a year or more, and his surprise at the encounter was as great as mine. "Funny, coming across you in this jazz crowd. I'm here to get away from my newspaper; but what has brought you?"

I explained that I had been ill the previous year, and, by the doctor's orders, was working out in the Alps the last months of my convalescence; and he listened with the absent-minded sympathy which one's friends give to one's ailments, particularly when they are on the mend.

"Well—well—too bad you've had such a mean time. Glad you're out of it now, anyway," he muttered, snapping a reluctant cigarette-lighter, and finally having recourse to mine. As he bent over it he said suddenly: "Well, what about Kate Spain?"

I looked at him in bewilderment. For a moment the question was so unintelligible that I wondered if he too were a sufferer, and had been sent to the heights for medical reasons; but his sharp little professional eyes burned with a steady spark of curiosity as he took a close-up of me across the lighter. And then I understood; at least I understood the allusion, though its relevance escaped me.

"Kate Spain? Oh, you mean that murder trial at Cayuga? You got me a card for it, didn't you? But I wasn't able to go."

"I remember. But you've made up for it since, I see." He continued to twinkle at me meaningly; but I was still groping. "What do you think of her?" he repeated.

"Think of her? Why on earth should I think of her at all?"

He drew back and squared his sturdy shoulders in evident enjoyment. "Why, because you've been talking to her as hard as you could for the last two hours," he chuckled.

I stood looking at him blankly. Again it occurred to me that under his tight journalistic mask something had loosened and gone adrift. But I looked at the steadiness of the stumpy fingers which held his cigarette. The man had himself under perfect control.

"Kate Spain?" I said, collecting myself. "Does that lady I was talking to really look to you like a murderess?"

Shreve made a dubious gesture. "I'm not so sure what murderesses look like. But, as it happens, Kate Spain was acquitted."

"So she was. Still, I don't think I'll tell Mrs. Ingram that she looks like her."

Shreve smiled incredulously. "Mrs. Ingram? Is that what you call her?"

"It's her name. I was with Mrs. Ingram, of California."

"No, you weren't. You were with Kate Spain. She knows me well enough—ask her. I met her face to face just now, going into the ball-room. She was with a red-headed Jezebel that I don't know."

"Ah, you don't know the red-headed lady? Well, that shows you're mistaken. For Miss Cassie Wilpert has lived with Mrs. Ingram as her companion for several years. They're inseparable."

Shreve tossed away his cigarette and stood staring at me. "Cassie Wilpert? Is that what that great dressed-up prize-fighter with all the jewelry calls herself? Why, see here, Severance, Cassie was the servant girl's name, sure enough: Cassie—don't you remember? It was her evidence that got Kate Spain off. But at the trial she was a thin haggard Irish girl in dirty calico. To be sure, I suppose old Ezra Spain starved his servant as thoroughly as he starved his daughter. You remember Cassie's description of the daily fare: Sunday, boiled mutton; Monday, cold mutton; Tuesday, mutton hash; Wednesday, mutton stew—and I forget what day the dog got the mutton bone. Why, it was Cassie who knocked the prosecution all to pieces. At first it was doubtful how the case would go; but she testified that she and Kate Spain were out shopping together when the old man was murdered; and the prosecution was never able to shake her evidence."

Remember it? Of course I remembered every detail of it, with a precision which startled me, considering I had never, to my knowledge, given the Kate Spain trial a thought since the talk about it had died out with the woman's acquittal. Now it all came back to me, every scrap of evidence, all the sordid and sinister gossip let loose by the trial: the tale of Ezra Spain, the wealthy miser and tyrant, of whom no one in his native town had a good word to say, who was reported to have let his wife die of neglect because he would not send for a doctor till it was too late, and who had been too mean to supply her with food and medicines, or to provide a trained nurse for her. After his wife's death his daughter had continued to live with him, brow-beaten and starved in her turn, and apparently lacking the courage to cast herself penniless and inexperienced upon the world. It had been almost with a sense of relief that Cayuga had learned of the old man's murder by a wandering tramp who had found him alone in the house, and had killed him in his sleep, and got away with what little money there was. Now at last, people said, that poor persecuted daughter with the wistful eyes and the frightened smile would be free, would be rich, would be able to come out of her prison, and marry and enjoy her life, instead of wasting and dying as her mother had died. And then came the incredible rumour that, instead of coming out of prison—the prison of her father's house—she was to go into another, the kind one entered in hand-cuffs, between two jailers: was to go there accused of her father's murder.

"I've got it now! Cassie Donovan—that was the servant's name," Shreve suddenly exclaimed. "Don't you remember?"

"No, I don't. But this woman's name, as I've told you, isn't Donovan—it's Wilpert, Miss Wilpert."

"Her new name, you mean? Yes. And Kate Spain's new name, you say, is Mrs. Ingram. Can't you see that the first thing they'd do, when they left Cayuga, would be to change their names?"

"Why should they, when nothing was proved against them? And you say yourself you didn't recognize Miss Wilpert," I insisted, struggling to maintain my incredulity.

"No; I didn't remember that she might have got fat and dyed her hair. I guess they do themselves like fighting cocks now, to make up for past privations. They say the old man cut up even fatter than people expected. But prosperity hasn't changed Kate Spain. I knew her at once; I'd have known her anywhere. And she knew me."

"She didn't know you," I broke out; "she said she was mistaken."

Shreve pounced on this in a flash. "Ah—so at first she thought she did?" He laughed. "I don't wonder she said afterward she was mistaken. I don't dye my hair yet, but I'm afraid I've put on nearly as much weight as Cassie Donovan." He paused again, and then added: "All the same, Severance, she did know me."

I looked at the little journalist and laughed back at him.

"What are you laughing at?"

"At you. At such a perfect case of professional deformation. Wherever you go you're bound to spot a criminal; but I should have thought even Mont Soleil could have produced a likelier specimen than my friend Mrs. Ingram."

He looked a little startled at my tone. "Oh, see here; if she's such a friend I'm sorry I said anything."

I rose to heights of tolerance. "Nothing you can say can harm her, my dear fellow."

"Harm her? Why on earth should it? I don't want to harm her."

"Then don't go about spreading such ridiculous gossip. I don't suppose any one cares to be mistaken for a woman who's been tried for her life; and if I were a relation of Mrs. Ingram's I'm bound to tell you I should feel obliged to put a stop to your talk."

He stared in surprise, and I thought he was going to retort in the same tone; but he was a fair-minded little fellow, and after a moment I could see he'd understood. "All right, Severance; of course I don't want to do anything that'll bother her. . ."

"Then don't go on talking as if you still thought she was Kate Spain."

He gave a hopeless shrug. "All right. I won't. Only she *is*, you know; what'll you bet on it, old man?"

"Good night," I said with a nod, and turned away. It was obviously a fixed idea with him; and what harm could such a crank do to me, much less to a woman like Mrs. Ingram?

As I left him he called after me: "If she ain't, who is she? Tell me that, and I'll believe you."

I walked away without answering.

IV

I went up to bed laughing inwardly at poor Jimmy Shreve. His craving for the sensational had certainly deformed his critical faculty. How it would amuse Mrs. Ingram to hear that he had identified her with the wretched Kate Spain! Well, she should hear it; we'd laugh over it together the next day. For she had said, in bidding me goodnight: "You'll tell me the rest in the morning." And that meant—could only mean—that she was going to listen to me, and if she were going to listen, she must be going to answer as I wished her to. . .

Those were my thoughts as I went up to my room. They were scarcely less confident while I was undressing. I had the hope, the promise almost, of what, at the moment, I most wished for—the only thing I wished for, in fact. I was amazed at the intensity with which I wished it. From the first I had tried to explain away my passion by regarding it as the idle man's tendency to fall into sentimental traps; but I had always known that what I felt was not of that nature. This quiet woman with the wide pale eyes and melancholy mouth had taken possession of me; she seemed always to have inhabited my mind and heart; and as I lay down to sleep I tried to analyze what it was in her that made her seem already a part of me.

But as soon as my light was out I knew I was going to lie awake all night; and all sorts of unsought problems instantly crowded out my sentimental musings. I had laughed at Shreve's inept question: "If she ain't Kate Spain, who is she?" But now an insistent voice within me echoed: Who is she? What, in short, did I know of her? Not one single fact which would have permitted me to disprove his preposterous assertion. Who was she? Was she married, unmarried, divorced, a widow? Had she children, parents, relations distant or near? Where had she lived before going to California, and when had she gone there? I knew neither her birthplace, nor her maiden name, or indeed any fact about her except the all-dominating fact of herself.

In rehearsing our many talks with the pitiless lucidity of sleeplessness I saw that she had the rare gift of being a perfect listener; the kind whose silence supplies the inaudible questions and answers most qualified to draw one on. And I had been drawn on; ridiculously, fatuously, drawn on. She was in possession of all the chief facts of my modest history. She knew who I was, where I came from, who were my friends, my family, my antecedents; she was fully informed as to my plans, my hopes, my preferences, my tastes and hobbies. I had even confided to her my passion for Brahms and for book-collecting, and my dislike for the wireless, and for one of my brothers-in-law. And in return for these confidences she had given me—what? An understanding smile, and the occasional murmur: "Oh, do you feel that too? I've always felt it."

Such was the actual extent of my acquaintance with Mrs. Ingram; and I perceived that, though I had laughed at Jimmy Shreve's inept assertion, I should have been utterly unable to disprove it. I did not know who Mrs. Ingram was, or even one single fact about her.

From that point to supposing that she could be Kate Spain was obviously a long way. She might be—well, let's say almost anything; but not a woman accused of murder, and acquitted only because the circumstantial evidence was insufficient to hang her. I dismissed the grotesque supposition at once; there were problems enough to keep me awake without that.

When I said that I knew nothing of Mrs. Ingram I was mistaken. I knew one fact about her; that she could put up with Cassie Wilpert. It was only a clue, but I had felt from the first that it was a vital one. What conceivable interest or obligation could make a woman like Mrs. Ingram endure such an intimacy? If I knew that, I should know all I cared to know about her; not only about her outward circumstances but her inmost self.

Hitherto, in indulging my feeling for her, I had been disposed to slip past the awkward obstacle of Cassie Wilpert; but now I was resolved to face it. I meant to ask Kate Ingram to marry me. If she refused, her private affairs were obviously no business of mine; but if she accepted I meant to have the Wilpert question out with her at once.

It seemed a long time before daylight came; and then there were more hours to be passed before I could reasonably present myself to Mrs. Ingram. But at nine I sent a line to ask when she would see me; and a few minutes later my note was returned to me by the floor-waiter.

"But this isn't an answer; it's my own note," I exclaimed.

Yes; it was my own note. He had brought it back because the lady had already left the hotel.

"Left? Gone out, you mean?"

"No; left with all her luggage. The two ladies went an hour ago."

In a few minutes I was dressed and had hurried down to

the concierge. It was a mistake, I was sure; of course Mrs. Ingram had not left. The floor-waiter, whom I had long since classed as an idiot, had simply gone to the wrong door. But no; the concierge shook his head. It was not a mistake. Mrs. Ingram and Miss Wilpert had gone away suddenly that morning by motor. The chauffeur's orders were to take them to Italy; to Baveno or Stresa, he thought; but he wasn't sure, and the ladies had left no address. The hotel servants said they had been up all night packing. The heavy luggage was to be sent to Milan; the concierge had orders to direct it to the station. That was all the information he could give—and I thought he looked at me queerly as he gave it.

V

I did not see Jimmy Shreve again before leaving Mont Soleil that day; indeed I exercised all my ingenuity in keeping out of his way. If I were to ask any further explanations, it was of Mrs. Ingram that I meant to ask them. Either she was Kate Spain, or she was not; and either way, she was the woman to whom I had declared my love. I should have thought nothing of Shreve's insinuations if I had not recalled Mrs. Ingram's start when she first saw him. She herself had owned that she had taken him for some one she knew; but even this would not have meant much if she and her companion had not disappeared from the hotel a few hours later, without leaving a message for me, or an address with the hall-porter.

I did not for a moment suppose that this disappearance was connected with my talk of the previous evening with Mrs. Ingram. She herself had expressed the wish to prolong that talk when Miss Wilpert interrupted it; and failing that, she had spontaneously suggested that we should meet again the next morning. It would have been less painful to think that she had fled before the ardour of my wooing than before the dread of what Shreve might reveal about her; but I knew the latter reason was the more likely.

The discovery stunned me. It took me some hours to get beyond the incredible idea that this woman, whose ways were so gentle, with whose whole nature I felt myself in such delightful harmony, had stood her trial as a murderess—and the murderess of her own father. But the more I revolved this possibility the less I believed in it. There might have been other—and perhaps not very creditable—reasons for her abrupt flight; but that she should be flying because she knew that Shreve had recognized her seemed, on further thought, impossible.

Then I began to look at the question from another angle. Supposing she *were* Kate Spain? Well, her father had been assassinated by a passing tramp; so the jury had decided. Probably suspicion would never have rested on her if it had not been notorious in Cayuga that the old man was a selfish miser, who for years had made his daughter's life intolerable. To those who knew the circumstances it had seemed conceivable, seemed almost natural, that the poor creature should finally turn against him. Yet she had had no difficulty in proving her innocence; it was clearly established that she was out of the house when the crime was committed. Her having been suspected, and tried, was simply one of those horrible blunders of which innocent persons have so often been the victims. Do what she would to live it down, her name would always remain associated with that sordid tragedy; and wasn't it natural that she should flee from any reminder of it, any suspicion that she had been recognized, and her identity proclaimed by a scandal-mongering journalist? If she were Kate Spain, the dread of having the fact made known to every one in that crowded hotel was enough to drive her out of it. But if her departure had another cause, in no way connected with Shreve's arrival, might it not have been inspired by a sudden whim of Cassie Wilpert's? Mrs. Ingram had told me that Cassie was bored and wanted to get away; and it was all too clear that, however loudly she proclaimed her independence, she always ended by obeying Miss Wilpert.

It was a melancholy alternative. Poor woman—poor woman either way, I thought. And by the time I had reached this conclusion, I was in the train which was hurrying me to Milan. Whatever happened I must see her, and hear from her own lips what she was flying from.

I hadn't much hope of running down the fugitives at Stresa or Baveno. It was not likely that they would go to either of the places they had mentioned to the concierge; but I went to both the next morning, and carried out a minute inspection of all the hotel lists. As I had foreseen, the travellers were not to be found, and I was at a loss to know where to turn next. I knew, however, that the luggage the ladies had sent to Milan was not likely to arrive till the next day, and concluded that they would probably wait for it in the neighbourhood; and suddenly I remembered that I had once advised Mrs. Ingram—who was complaining that she was growing tired of fashionable hotels—to try a little *pension* on the lake of Orta, where she would be miles away from "palaces", and from the kind of people who frequent them. It was not likely that she would have remembered this place; but I had put a pencil stroke beside the name in her guide-book, and that might recall it to her. Orta, at any rate, was not far off; and I decided to hire a car at Stresa, and go there before carrying on my journey.

VI

I don't suppose I shall ever get out of my eyes the memory of the public sitting-room in the *pension* at Orta. It was there that I waited for Mrs. Ingram to come down, wondering if she would, and what we should say to each other when she did.

There were three windows in a row, with clean heavily starched Nottingham lace curtains carefully draped to exclude the best part of the matchless view over lake and mountains. To make up for this privation the opposite wall was adorned with a huge oil-painting of a Swiss water-fall. In the middle of the room was a table of sham ebony, with ivory inlays, most of which had long since worked out of their grooves, and on the table the usual dusty collection of tourist magazines, fashion papers, and tattered copies of *Zion's Weekly* and the *Christian Science Monitor*.

What is the human mind made of, that mine, at such a moment, should have minutely and indelibly registered these depressing details? I even remember smiling at the thought of the impression my favourite *pension* must have made on travellers who had just moved out of the most expensive suite in the Mont Soleil Palace.

And then Mrs. Ingram came in.

My first impression was that something about her dress or the arrangement of her hair had changed her. Then I saw that two dabs of rouge had been unskilfully applied to her pale cheeks, and a cloud of powder dashed over the dark semicircles under her eyes. She must have undergone some terrible moral strain since our parting to feel the need of such a disguise.

"I thought I should find you here," I said.

She let me take her two hands, but at first she could not speak. Then she said, in an altered voice: "You must have wondered—"

"Yes; I wondered."

"It was Cassie who suddenly decided—"

"I supposed so."

She looked at me beseechingly. "But she was right, you know."

"Right—about what?"

Her rouged lips began to tremble, and she drew her hands out of mine.

"Before you say anything else," I interrupted, "there's one thing you must let me say. I want you to marry me."

I had not meant to bring it out so abruptly; but something in her pitiful attempt to conceal her distress had drawn me closer to her, drawn me past all doubts and distrusts, all thought of evasion or delay.

She looked at me, still without speaking, and two tears ran over her lids, and streaked the untidy powder on her cheeks.

"No—no—no!" she exclaimed, lifting her thin hand and pressing it against my lips. I drew it down and held it fast.

"Why not? You knew I was going to ask you, the day before yesterday, and when we were interrupted you promised to hear me the next morning. You yourself said: 'tomorrow morning'."

"Yes; but I didn't know then—"

"You didn't know—?"

I was still holding her, and my eyes were fixed on hers. She gave me back my look, deeply and desperately. Then she freed herself.

"Let me go. I'm Kate Spain," she said.

We stood facing each other without speaking. Then I gave a laugh, and answered, in a voice that sounded to me as though I were shouting: "Well, I want to marry you, Kate Spain."

She shrank back, her hands clasped across her breast. "You knew already? That man told you?"

"Who—Jimmy Shreve? What does it matter if he did? Was that the reason you ran away from me?" She nodded.

"And you thought I wouldn't find you?"

"I thought you wouldn't try."

"You thought that, having told you one day that I loved you, I'd let you go out of my life the next?"

She gave me another long look. "You—you're generous. I'm grateful. But you can't marry Kate Spain," she said, with a little smile like the grimace on a dying face.

I had no doubt in my own mind that I could; the first sight of her had carried that conviction home, and I answered: "Can't I, though? That's what we'll see."

"You don't know what my life is. How would you like, wherever you went, to have some one suddenly whisper behind you: 'Look. That's Kate Spain'?"

I looked at her, and for a moment found no answer. My first impulse of passionate pity had swept me past the shock of her confession; as long as she was herself, I seemed to feel, it mattered nothing to me that she was also Kate Spain. But her last words called up a sudden vision of the life she must have led since her acquittal; the life I was asking to share with her. I recalled my helpless wrath when Shreve had told me who she was; and now I seemed to hear the ugly whisper—"Kate Spain, Kate Spain"—following us from place to place, from house to house; following my wife and me.

She took my hesitation for an answer. "You hadn't thought of that, had you? But I think of nothing else, day and night. For three years now I've been running away from the sound of my name. I tried California first; it was at the other end of the country, and some of my mother's relations lived there. They were kind to me, everybody was kind; but wherever I went I heard my name: Kate Spain—Kate Spain! I couldn't go to church, or to the theatre, or into a shop to buy a spool of thread, without hearing it. What was the use of calling

myself Mrs. Ingram, when, wherever I went, I heard Kate
Spain? The very school-children knew who I was, and rushed
out to see me when I passed, I used to get letters from people who collected autographs, and wanted my signature: 'Kate
Spain, you know.' And when I tried shutting myself up, people said: 'What's she afraid of? Has she got something to hide,
after all?' and I saw that it made my cousins uncomfortable,
and shy with me, because I couldn't lead a normal life like
theirs. . . After a year I couldn't stand it, and so we came
away, and went round the world. . . But wherever we go it
begins again: and I know now I can never get away from it."
She broke down, and hid her face for a moment. Then she
looked up at me and said: "And so you must go away, you
see."

I continued to look at her without speaking: I wanted the
full strength of my will to go out to her in my answer. "I see,
on the contrary, that I must stay."

She gave me a startled glance. "No—no."

"Yes, yes. Because all you say is a nervous dream; natural
enough, after what you've been through, but quite unrelated
to reality. You say you've thought of nothing else, day and
night; but why think of it at all—in that way? Your real name
is Kate Spain. Well—what of it? Why try to disguise it? You've
never done anything to disgrace it. You've suffered through
it, but never been abased. If you want to get rid of it there's
a much simpler way; and that is to take mine instead. But
meanwhile, if people ask you if you're Kate Spain, try saying
yes, you are, instead of running away from them."

She listened with bent head and interlocked hands, and I
saw a softness creep about her lips. But after I had ceased she
looked up at me sadly. "You've never been tried for your life,"
she said.

The words struck to the roots of my optimism. I remembered in a flash that when I had first seen her I had thought
there was a look about her mouth and eyes unlike that of any
other woman I had known; as if she had had a different experience from theirs. Now I knew what that experience was:
the black shadow of the criminal court, and the long lonely
fight to save her neck. And I'd been trying to talk reason to a
woman who'd been through that!

"My poor girl—my poor child!" I held out my arms, and she fell into them and wept out her agony. There were no more words to be said; no words could help her. Only the sense of human nearness, human pity, of a man's arms about her, and his heart against hers, could draw her out of her icy hell into the common warmth of day.

Perhaps it was the thought of that healing warmth which made me suddenly want to take her away from the Nottingham lace curtains and the Swiss water-fall. For a while we sat silent, and I held her close; then I said: "Come out for a walk with me. There are beautiful walks close by, up through the beechwoods."

She looked at me with a timid smile. I knew now that she would do all I told her to; but before we started out I must rid my mind of another load. "I want to have you all to my-self for the rest of the day. Where's Miss Wilpert?" I asked.

Miss Wilpert was away in Milan, she said, and would not be back till late. She had gone to see about passport visas and passages on a cruising liner which was sailing from Genoa to the Ægean in a few days. The ladies thought of taking the cruise. I made no answer, and we walked out through the *pension* garden, and mounted the path to the beechwoods.

We wandered on for a long time, saying hardly anything to each other; then we sat down on the mossy steps of one of the little pilgrimage chapels among the trees. It is a place full of sweet solitude, and gradually it laid its quieting touch on the tormented creature at my side.

As we sat there the day slipped down the sky, and we watched, through the great branches, the lake turning golden and then fading, and the moon rising above the mountains. I put my hand on hers. "And now let's make some plans," I said.

I saw the apprehensive look come back to her eyes. "Plans—oh, why, today?"

"Isn't it natural that two people who've decided to live to-gether should want to talk over their future? When are we going to be married—to begin with?"

She hesitated for a long time, clasping and unclasping her unhappy hands. She had passed the stage of resistance, and I was almost sure she would not return to it again. I waited, and at length she said, looking away from me: "But you don't like Cassie."

The words were a shock, though I suppose I must have expected them. On the whole, I was glad they had been spoken; I had not known how to bring the subject up, and it was better she should do it for me.

"Let's say, dear, that Cassie and I don't like each other. Isn't that nearer the truth?"

"Well, perhaps; but—"

"Well, that being so, Cassie will certainly be quite as anxious to strike out for herself as I shall be to—"

She interrupted me with a sudden exclamation. "No, no! She'll never leave me—never."

"Never leave you? Not when you're my wife?"

She hung her head, and began her miserable finger-weaving again. "No; not even if she lets me—"

"Lets you—?"

"Marry you," she said in a whisper.

I mastered her hands, and forced her to turn around to me. "Kate—look at me; straight at me. Shall I tell you something? Your worst enemy's not Kate Spain; it's Cassie Wilpert."

She freed herself from my hold and drew back. "My worst enemy? Cassie—she's been my only friend!"

"At the time of the trial, yes. I understand that; I understand your boundless gratitude for the help she gave you. I think I feel about that as you'd want me to. But there are other ways of showing your gratitude than by sharing the rest of your life with her."

She listened, drooping again. "I've tried every other way," she said at length, below her breath.

"What other ways?"

"Oh, everything. I'm rich you know, now," she interrupted herself, her colour rising. "I offered her the house at Cayuga—it's a good house; they say it's very valuable. She could have sold it if she didn't want to live there. And of course I would have continued the allowance I'm giving her—I would have doubled it. But what she wanted was to stay with me; the new life she was leading amused her. She was a poor servant-girl, you know; and she had a dreadful time when—when my father was alive. She was our only help. . . I suppose you read about it all . . . and even then she was good to me. . . She dared to speak to him as I didn't. . . And then, at the trial. . . The trial lasted a whole month; and it was a month with thirty-one days. . . Oh, don't make me go back to it—for God's sake don't!" she burst out, sobbing.

It was impossible to carry on the discussion. All I thought of was to comfort her. I helped her to her feet, whispering to her as if she had been a frightened child, and putting my arm about her to guide her down the path. She leaned on me, pressing her arm against mine. At length she said: "You see it can't be; I always told you it could never be."

"I see more and more that it must be; but we won't talk about that now," I answered.

We dined quietly in a corner of the *pension* dining-room, which was filled by a colony of British old maids and retired army officers and civil servants—all so remote from the world of the "Ezra Spain case" that, if Shreve had been there to proclaim Mrs. Ingram's identity, the hated syllables would have waked no echo. I pointed this out to Mrs. Ingram, and reminded her that in a few years all memory of the trial would have died out, even in her own country, and she would be able to come and go unobserved and undisturbed. She shook her head and murmured: "Cassie doesn't think so"; but when I suggested that Miss Wilpert might have her own reasons for cultivating this illusion, she did not take up the remark, and let me turn to pleasanter topics.

After dinner it was warm enough to wander down to the shore in the moonlight, and there, sitting in the little square along the lakeside, she seemed at last to cast off her haunting torment, and abandon herself to the strange new sense of happiness and safety. But presently the church bell rang the hour, and she started up, insisting that we must get back to the *pension* before Miss Wilpert's arrival. She would be there soon now, and Mrs. Ingram did not wish her to know of my presence till the next day.

I agreed to this, but stipulated that the next morning the news of our approaching marriage should be broken to Miss Wilpert, and that as soon as possible afterward I should be

told of the result. I wanted to make sure of seeing Kate the
moment her talk with Miss Wilpert was over, so that I could
explain away—and above all, laugh away—the inevitable
threats and menaces before they grew to giants in her tormented imagination. She promised to meet me between
eleven and twelve in the deserted writing-room, which we
were fairly sure of having to ourselves at that hour; and from
there I could take her up the hillside to have our talk out
undisturbed.

VII

I did not get much sleep that night, and the next morning before the *pension* was up I went out for a short row on
the lake. The exercise braced my nerves, and when I got
back I was prepared to face with composure whatever further
disturbances were in store. I did not think they would be as
bad as they appeared to my poor friend's distracted mind,
and was convinced that if I could keep a firm hold on her
will the worst would soon be over. It was not much past
nine, and I was just finishing the *café au lait* I had ordered
on returning from my row, when there was a knock at my
door. It was not the casual knock of a tired servant coming
to remove a tray, but a sharp nervous rap immediately followed by a second; and, before I could answer, the door
opened and Miss Wilpert appeared. She came directly in,
shut the door behind her, and stood looking at me with a
flushed and lowering stare. But it was a look I was fairly used
to seeing when her face was turned to mine, and my first
thought was one of relief. If there was a scene ahead, it was
best that I should bear the brunt of it; I was not half so
much afraid of Miss Wilpert as of the Miss Wilpert of Kate's
imagination.

I stood up and pushed forward my only armchair. "Do you
want to see me, Miss Wilpert? Do sit down."

My visitor ignored the suggestion. "Want to see you? God
knows I don't. . . I wish we'd never laid eyes on you, either
of us," she retorted in a thick passionate voice. If the hour
had not been so early I should have suspected her of having
already fortified herself for the encounter.

"Then, if you won't sit down, and don't want to see me—" I began affably; but she interrupted me.

"I don't *want* to see you; but I've got to. You don't suppose I'd be here if I didn't have something to say to you?"

"Then you'd better sit down, after all."

She shook her head, and remained leaning in the window-jamb, one elbow propped on the sill. "What I want to know is: what business has a dandified gentleman like you to go round worming women's secrets out of them?"

Now we were coming to the point. "If I've laid myself open to the charge," I said quietly, "at least it's not because I've tried to worm out yours."

The retort took her by surprise. Her flush darkened, and she fixed her small suspicious eyes on mine.

"*My* secrets?" she flamed out. "What do you know about my secrets?" She pulled herself together with a nervous laugh. "What an old fool I am! You're only trying to get out of answering my question. What I want to know is what call you have to pry into my friend's private affairs?"

I hesitated, struggling again with my anger. "If I've pried into them, as you call it, I did so, as you probably know, only after I'd asked Mrs. Ingram to be my wife."

Miss Wilpert's laugh became an angry whinny. "Exactly! If indeed you didn't ask her to be your wife to get her secret out of her. She's so unsuspicious that the idea never crossed her mind till I told her what I thought of the trick you'd played on her."

"Ah, you suggested it was a trick? And how did she take the suggestion?"

Miss Wilpert stood for a moment without speaking; then she came up to the table and brought her red fist down on it with a bang. "I tell you she'll never marry you!" she shouted.

I was on the verge of shouting back at her; but I controlled myself, conscious that we had reached the danger-point in our struggle. I said nothing, and waited.

"Don't you hear what I say?" she challenged me.

"Yes; but I refuse to take what you say from any one but Mrs. Ingram." My composure seemed to steady Miss Wilpert. She looked at me dubiously, and then dropped into the chair

I had pushed forward. "You mean you want her to tell you herself?"

"Yes." I sat down also, and again waited.

Miss Wilpert drew a crumpled handkerchief across her lips. "Well, I can get her to tell you—easy enough. She'll do anything I tell her. Only I thought you'd want to act like a gentleman, and spare her another painful scene—"

"Not if she's unwilling to spare me one."

Miss Wilpert considered this with a puzzled stare. "She'll tell you just what I'm telling you—you can take my word for that."

"I don't want anybody's word but hers."

"If you think such a lot of her I'd have thought you'd rather have gone away quietly, instead of tormenting her any more." Still I was silent, and she pulled her chair up to the table, and stretched her thick arms across it. "See here, Mr. Severance—now you listen to me."

"I'm listening."

"You know I love Kate so that I wouldn't harm a hair of her head," she whimpered. I made no comment, and she went on, in a voice grown oddly low and unsteady: "But I don't want to quarrel with you. What's the use?"

"None whatever. I'm glad you realize it."

"Well, then, let's you and me talk it over like old friends. Kate can't marry you, Mr. Severance. Is that plain? She can't marry you, and she can't marry anybody else. All I want is to spare her more scenes. Won't you take my word for it, and just slip off quietly if I promise you I'll make it all right, so she'll bear you no ill-will?"

I listened to this extraordinary proposal as composedly as I could; but it was impossible to repress a slight laugh. Miss Wilpert took my laugh for an answer, and her discoloured face crimsoned furiously. "Well?"

"Nonsense, Miss Wilpert. Of course I won't take your orders to go away."

She rested her elbows on the table, and her chin on her crossed hands. I saw she was making an immense effort to control herself. "See here, young man, now you listen. . ."

Still I sat silent, and she sat looking at me, her thick lower lip groping queerly, as if it were feeling for words she could not find.

"I tell you—" she stammered.

I stood up. "If vague threats are all you have to tell me, perhaps we'd better bring our talk to an end."

She rose also. "To an end? Any minute, if you'll agree to go away."

"Can't you see that such arguments are wasted on me?"

"You mean to see her?"

"Of course I do—at once, if you'll excuse me."

She drew back unsteadily, and put herself between me and the door. "You're going to her now? But I tell you you can't! You'll half kill her. Is that what you're after?"

"What I'm after, first of all, is to put an end to this use-less talk," I said, moving toward the door. She flung herself heavily backward, and stood against it, stretching out her two arms to block my way. "She can't marry—she can't marry you!" she screamed.

I stood silent, my hands in my pockets. "You—you don't believe me?" she repeated.

"I've nothing more to say to you, Miss Wilpert."

"Ah, you've nothing more to say to me? Is that the tune? Then I'll tell you that I've something more to say to you; and you're not going out of this room till you've heard it. And you'll wish you were dead when you have."

"If it's anything about Mrs. Ingram, I refuse to hear it; and if you force me to, it will be exactly as if you were speaking to a man who's stone deaf. So you'd better ask yourself if it's worth while."

She leaned against the door, her heavy head dropped queerly forward. "Worth while—worth while? It'll be worth your while not to hear it—I'll give you a last chance," she said.

"I should be much obliged if you'd leave my room, Miss Wilpert."

" 'Much obliged'?" she simpered, mimicking me. "You'd be much obliged, would you? Hear him, girls—ain't he styl-ish? Well, I'm going to leave your room in a minute, young gentleman; but not till you've heard your death-sentence."

I smiled. "I shan't hear it, you know. I shall be stone deaf."

She gave a little screaming laugh, and her arms dropped to her sides. "Stone deaf, he says. And to the day of his death he'll never get out of his ears what I'm going to tell him. . ." She moved forward again, lurching a little; she seemed to be trying to take the few steps back to the table, and I noticed that she had left her hand-bag on it. I took it up. "You want your bag?"

"My bag?" Her jaw fell slightly, and began to tremble again. "Yes, yes . . . my bag . . . give it to me. Then you'll know all about Kate Spain. . ." She got as far as the armchair, dropped into it sideways, and sat with hanging head, and arms lolling at her sides. She seemed to have forgotten about the bag, though I had put it beside her.

I stared at her, horrified. Was she as drunk as all that—or was she ill, and desperately ill? I felt cold about the heart, and went up, and took hold of her. "Miss Wilpert—won't you get up? Aren't you well?"

Her swollen lips formed a thin laugh, and I saw a thread of foam in their corners. "Kate Spain. . . I'll tell you. . ." Her head sank down onto her creased white throat. Her arms hung lifeless; she neither spoke nor moved.

VIII

After the first moment of distress and bewilderment, and the two or three agitated hours spent in consultations, telephonings, engaging of nurses, and enquiring about nursing homes, I was at last able to have a few words with Mrs. Ingram.

Miss Wilpert's case was clear enough; a stroke produced by sudden excitement, which would certainly—as the doctors summoned from Milan advised us—result in softening of the brain, probably followed by death in a few weeks. The direct cause had been the poor woman's fit of rage against me; but the doctors told me privately that in her deteriorated condition any shock might have brought about the same result. Continual over-indulgence in food and drink—in drink especially—had made her, physiologically, an old woman before her time; all her organs were worn out, and the best that could be hoped was that the bodily resistance which some-times develops when the mind fails would not keep her too long from dying.

I had to break this as gently as I could to Mrs. Ingram, and at the same time to defend myself against the painful infer-ences she might draw from the way in which the attack had happened. She knew—as the whole horrified *pension* knew—that Miss Wilpert had been taken suddenly ill in my room; and any one living on the same floor must have been aware that an angry discussion had preceded the attack. But Kate Ingram knew more; she, and she alone, knew why Cassie Wilpert had gone to my room, and when I found myself alone with her I instantly read that knowledge in her face. This being so, I thought it better to make no pretence.

"You saw Miss Wilpert, I suppose, before she came to me?" I asked.

She made a faint assenting motion; I saw that she was too shaken to speak.

"And she told you, probably, that she was going to tell me I must not marry you."

"Yes—she told me."

I sat down beside her and took her hand. "I don't know what she meant," I went on, "or how she intended to prevent it; for before she could say anything more—"

Kate Ingram turned to me quickly. I could see the life rush-ing back to her stricken face. "You mean—she didn't say any-thing more?"

"She had no time to."

"Not a word more?"

"Nothing—"

Mrs. Ingram gave me one long look; then her head sank between her hands. I sat beside her in silence, and at last she dropped her hands and looked up again. "You've been very good to me," she said.

"Then, my dear, you must be good too. I want you to go to your room at once and take a long rest. Everything is arranged; the nurse has come. Early tomorrow morning the ambulance will be here. You can trust me to see that things are looked after."

Her eyes rested on me, as if she were trying to grope for

the thoughts beyond this screen of words. "You're sure she said nothing more?" she repeated.

"On my honour, nothing."

She got up and went obediently to her room.

It was perfectly clear to me that Mrs. Ingram's docility during those first grim days was due chiefly to the fact of her own helplessness. Little of the practical experience of every-day life had come into her melancholy existence, and I was not surprised that, in a strange country and among unfamiliar faces, she should turn to me for support. The shock of what had occurred, and God knows what secret dread behind it, had prostrated the poor creature, and the painful details still to be dealt with made my nearness a necessity. But, as far as our personal relations were concerned, I knew that sooner or later an emotional reaction would come.

For the moment it was kept off by other cares. Mrs. Ingram turned to me as to an old friend, and I was careful to make no other claim on her. She was installed at the nursing-home in Milan to which her companion had been transported; and I saw her there two or three times daily. Happily for the sick woman, the end was near; she never regained consciousness, and before the month was out she was dead. Her life ended without a struggle, and Mrs. Ingram was spared the sight of protracted suffering; but the shock of the separation was inevitable. I knew she did not love Cassie Wilpert, and I measured her profound isolation when I saw that the death of this woman left her virtually alone.

When we returned from the funeral I drove her back to the hotel where she had engaged rooms, and she asked me to come to see her there the next afternoon.

At Orta, after Cassie Wilpert's sudden seizure, and before the arrival of the doctors, I had handed her bag over to Mrs. Ingram, and had said: "You'd better lock it up. If she gets worse the police might ask for it."

She turned ashy pale. "The police—?"

"Oh, you know there are endless formalities of that kind in all Latin countries. I should advise you to look through the bag yourself, and see if there's anything in it she might prefer not to have you keep. If there is, you'd better destroy it."

I knew at the time that she had guessed I was referring to

some particular paper; but she took the bag from me without speaking. And now, when I came to the hotel at her summons, I wondered whether she would allude to the matter, whether in the interval it had passed out of her mind, or whether she had decided to say nothing. There was no doubt that the bag had contained something which Miss Wilpert was determined that I should see; but, after all, it might have been only a newspaper report of the Spain trial. The unhappy creature's brain was already so confused that she might have attached importance to some document that had no real significance. I hoped it was so, for my one desire was to put out of my mind the memory of Cassie Wilpert, and of what her association with Mrs. Ingram had meant.

At the hotel I was asked to come up to Mrs. Ingram's private sitting-room. She kept me waiting for a little while, and when she appeared she looked so frail and ill in her black dress that I feared she might be on the verge of a nervous break-down.

"You look too tired to see any one today. You ought to go straight to bed and let me send for the doctor," I said.

"No—no." She shook her head, and signed to me to sit down. "It's only . . . the strangeness of everything. I'm not used to being alone. I think I'd better go away from here to-morrow," she began excitedly.

"I think you had, dear. I'll make any arrangements you like, if you'll tell me where you want to go. And I'll come and join you, and arrange as soon as possible about our marriage. Such matters can be managed fairly quickly in France."

"In France?" she echoed absently, with a little smile.

"Or wherever else you like. We might go to Rome."

She continued to smile; a strained mournful smile, which began to frighten me. Then she spoke. "I shall never forget what you've been to me. But we must say goodbye now. I can't marry you. Cassie did what was right—she only wanted to spare me the pain of telling you."

I looked at her steadily. "When you say you can't marry me," I asked, "do you mean that you're already married, and can't free yourself?"

She seemed surprised. "Oh, no. I'm not married—I was never married."

"Then, my dear—"

She raised one hand to silence me; with the other she opened her little black hand-bag and drew out a sealed envelope. "This is the reason. It's what she meant to show you—"

I broke in at once: "I don't want to see anything she meant to show me. I told her so then, and I tell you so now. Whatever is in that envelope, I refuse to look at it."

Mrs. Ingram gave me a startled glance. "No, no. You must read it. Don't force me to tell you—that would be worse. . ."

I jumped up and stood looking down into her anguished face. Even if I hadn't loved her, I should have pitied her then beyond all mortal pity.

"Kate," I said, bending over her, and putting my hand on her icy-cold one, "when I asked you to marry me I buried all such questions, and I'm not going to dig them up again to-day—or any other day. The past's the past. It's at an end for us both, and tomorrow I mean to marry you, and begin our future."

She smiled again, strangely, I thought, and then suddenly began to cry. Then she flung her arms about my neck, and pressed herself against me. "Say goodbye to me now—say goodbye to Kate Spain," she whispered.

"Goodbye to Kate Spain, yes; but not to Kate Severance."

"There'll never be a Kate Severance. There never can be. Oh, won't you understand—won't you spare me? Cassie was right; she tried to do her duty when she saw I couldn't do it. . ."

She broke into terrible sobs, and I pressed my lips against hers to silence her. She let me hold her for a while, and when she drew back from me I saw that the battle was half won. But she stretched out her hand toward the envelope. "You must read it—"

I shook my head. "I won't read it. But I'll take it and keep it. Will that satisfy you, Kate Severance?" I asked. For it had suddenly occurred to me that, if I tore the paper up before her, I should only force her, in her present mood, to the more cruel alternative of telling me what it contained.

I saw at once that my suggestion quieted her. "You will take it, then? You'll read it tonight? You'll promise me?"

"No, my dear. All I promise you is to take it with me, and not to destroy it."

She took a long sobbing breath, and drew me to her again. "It's as if you'd read it already, isn't it?" she said below her breath.

"It's as if it had never existed—because it never will exist for me." I held her fast, and kissed her again. And when I left her I carried the sealed envelope away with me.

IX

All that happened seven years ago; and the envelope lies before me now, still sealed. Why should I have opened it?

As I carried it home that night at Milan, as I drew it out of my pocket and locked it away among my papers, it was as transparent as glass to me. I had no need to open it. Already it had given me the measure of the woman who, deliberately, determinedly, had thrust it into my hands. Even as she was in the act of doing so, I had understood that with Cassie Wilpert's death the one danger she had to fear had been removed; and that, knowing herself at last free, at last safe, she had voluntarily placed her fate in my keeping.

"Greater love hath no man—certainly no woman," I thought. Cassie Wilpert, and Cassie Wilpert alone, held Kate Spain's secret—the secret which would doubtless have destroyed her in the eyes of the world, as it was meant to destroy her in mine. And that secret, when it had been safely buried with Cassie Wilpert, Kate Spain had deliberately dug up again, and put into my hands.

It took her some time to understand the use I meant to make of it. She did not dream, at first, that it had given me a complete insight into her character, and that that was all I wanted of it. Weeks of patient waiting, of quiet reasoning, of obstinate insistence, were required to persuade her that I was determined to judge her, not by her past, whatever it might have been, but by what she had unconsciously revealed of herself since I had known her and loved her.

"You can't marry me—you know why you can't marry me," she had gone on endlessly repeating; till one day I had turned on her, and declared abruptly: "Whatever happens, this is to be our last talk on the subject. I will never return to it again, or let you return to it. But I swear one thing to you now; if you know how your father died, and have kept silence to shield some one—to shield I don't care who—" I looked straight into her eyes as I said this—"if this is your reason for thinking you ought not to marry me, then I tell you now that it weighs nothing with me, and never will."

She gave me back my look, long and deeply; then she bent and kissed my hands. That was all.

I had hazarded a great deal in saying what I did; and I knew the risk I was taking. It was easy to answer for the present; but how could I tell what the future, our strange incalculable future together, might bring? It was that which she dreaded, I knew; not for herself, but for me. But I was ready to risk it, and a few weeks after that final talk—for final I insisted on its being—I gained my point, and we were married.

We were married; and for five years we lived our strange perilous dream of happiness. That fresh unfading happiness which now and then mocks the lot of poor mortals; but not often—and never for long.

At the end of five years my wife died; and since then I have lived alone among memories so made of light and darkness that sometimes I am blind with remembered joy, and sometimes numb under present sorrow. I don't know yet which will end by winning the day with me; but in my uncertainty I am putting old things in order—and there on my desk lies the paper I have never read, and beside it the candle with which I shall presently burn it.

Roman Fever

F ROM the table at which they had been lunching two
American ladies of ripe but well-cared-for middle age
moved across the lofty terrace of the Roman restaurant and,
leaning on its parapet, looked first at each other, and then
down on the outspread glories of the Palatine and the Forum,
with the same expression of vague but benevolent approval.

As they leaned there a girlish voice echoed up gaily from
the stairs leading to the court below. "Well, come along,
then," it cried, not to them but to an invisible companion,
"and let's leave the young things to their knitting"; and a
voice as fresh laughed back: "Oh, look here, Babs, not actually *knitting*—" "Well, I mean figuratively," rejoined the first.
"After all, we haven't left our poor parents much else to
do. . ." and at that point the turn of the stairs engulfed the
dialogue.

The two ladies looked at each other again, this time with a
tinge of smiling embarrassment, and the smaller and paler one
shook her head and coloured slightly.

"Barbara!" she murmured, sending an unheard rebuke after the mocking voice in the stairway.

The other lady, who was fuller, and higher in colour, with
a small determined nose supported by vigorous black eyebrows, gave a good-humoured laugh. "That's what our
daughters think of us!"

Her companion replied by a deprecating gesture. "Not of
us individually. We must remember that. It's just the collective modern idea of Mothers. And you see—" Half guiltily
she drew from her handsomely mounted black hand-bag a
twist of crimson silk run through by two fine knitting needles.
"One never knows," she murmured. "The new system has
certainly given us a good deal of time to kill; and sometimes
I get tired just looking—even at this." Her gesture was now
addressed to the stupendous scene at their feet.

The dark lady laughed again, and they both relapsed upon
the view, contemplating it in silence, with a sort of diffused
serenity which might have been borrowed from the spring

effulgence of the Roman skies. The luncheon-hour was long past, and the two had their end of the vast terrace to themselves. At its opposite extremity a few groups, detained by a lingering look at the outspread city, were gathering up guide-books and fumbling for tips. The last of them scattered, and the two ladies were alone on the air-washed height.

"Well, I don't see why we shouldn't just stay here," said Mrs. Slade, the lady of the high colour and energetic brows. Two derelict basket-chairs stood near, and she pushed them into the angle of the parapet, and settled herself in one, her gaze upon the Palatine. "After all, it's still the most beautiful view in the world."

"It always will be, to me," assented her friend Mrs. Ansley, with so slight a stress on the "me" that Mrs. Slade, though she noticed it, wondered if it were not merely accidental, like the random underlinings of old-fashioned letter-writers.

"Grace Ansley was always old-fashioned," she thought; and added aloud, with a retrospective smile: "It's a view we've both been familiar with for a good many years. When we first met here we were younger than our girls are now. You remember?"

"Oh, yes, I remember," murmured Mrs. Ansley, with the same undefinable stress.— "There's that head-waiter wondering," she interpolated. She was evidently far less sure than her companion of herself and of her rights in the world.

"I'll cure him of wondering," said Mrs. Slade, stretching her hand toward a bag as discreetly opulent-looking as Mrs. Ansley's. Signing to the head-waiter, she explained that she and her friend were old lovers of Rome, and would like to spend the end of the afternoon looking down on the view— that is, if it did not disturb the service? The head-waiter, bowing over her gratuity, assured her that the ladies were most welcome, and would be still more so if they would condescend to remain for dinner. A full moon night, they would remember. . .

Mrs. Slade's black brows drew together, as though references to the moon were out-of-place and even unwelcome. But she smiled away her frown as the head-waiter retreated. "Well, why not? We might do worse. There's no knowing, I suppose, when the girls will be back. Do you even know back from *where*? I don't!"

Mrs. Ansley again coloured slightly. "I think those young Italian aviators we met at the Embassy invited them to fly to Tarquinia for tea. I suppose they'll want to wait and fly back by moonlight."

"Moonlight—moonlight! What a part it still plays. Do you suppose they're as sentimental as we were?"

"I've come to the conclusion that I don't in the least know what they are," said Mrs. Ansley. "And perhaps we didn't know much more about each other."

"No; perhaps we didn't."

Her friend gave her a shy glance. "I never should have supposed you were sentimental, Alida."

"Well, perhaps I wasn't." Mrs. Slade drew her lids together in retrospect; and for a few moments the two ladies, who had been intimate since childhood, reflected how little they knew each other. Each one, of course, had a label ready to attach to the other's name; Mrs. Delphin Slade, for instance, would have told herself, or any one who asked her, that Mrs. Horace Ansley, twenty-five years ago, had been exquisitely lovely— no, you wouldn't believe it, would you? . . . though, of course, still charming, distinguished. . . Well, as a girl she had been exquisite; far more beautiful than her daughter Barbara, though certainly Babs, according to the new standards at any rate, was more effective—had more *edge*, as they say. Funny where she got it, with those two nullities as parents. Yes; Horace Ansley was—well, just the duplicate of his wife. Museum specimens of old New York. Good-looking, irreproachable, exemplary. Mrs. Slade and Mrs. Ansley had lived opposite each other—actually as well as figuratively—for years. When the drawing-room curtains in No. 20 East 73rd Street were renewed, No. 23, across the way, was always aware of it. And of all the movings, buyings, travels, anniversaries, illnesses—the tame chronicle of an estimable pair. Little of it escaped Mrs. Slade. But she had grown bored with it by the time her husband made his big *coup* in Wall Street, and when they bought in upper Park Avenue had already begun to think: "I'd rather live opposite a speak-easy for a change; at least one might see it raided." The idea of seeing Grace raided was so amusing that (before the move) she launched it at a woman's lunch. It made a hit, and went the rounds—she sometimes wondered if it had crossed the street, and reached Mrs. Ansley. She hoped not, but didn't much mind. Those were the days when respectability was at a discount, and it did the irreproachable no harm to laugh at them a little.

A few years later, and not many months apart, both ladies lost their husbands. There was an appropriate exchange of wreaths and condolences, and a brief renewal of intimacy in the half-shadow of their mourning; and now, after another interval, they had run across each other in Rome, at the same hotel, each of them the modest appendage of a salient daughter. The similarity of their lot had again drawn them together, lending itself to mild jokes, and the mutual confession that, if in old days it must have been tiring to "keep up" with daughters, it was now, at times, a little dull not to.

No doubt, Mrs. Slade reflected, she felt her unemployment more than poor Grace ever would. It was a big drop from being the wife of Delphin Slade to being his widow. She had always regarded herself (with a certain conjugal pride) as his equal in social gifts, as contributing her full share to the making of the exceptional couple they were; but the difference after his death was irremediable. As the wife of the famous corporation lawyer, always with an international case or two on hand, every day brought its exciting and unexpected obligation: the impromptu entertaining of eminent colleagues from abroad, the hurried dashes on legal business to London, Paris or Rome, where the entertaining was so handsomely reciprocated; the amusement of hearing in her wake: "What, that handsome woman with the good clothes and the eyes is Mrs. Slade—*the* Slade's wife? Really? Generally the wives of celebrities are such frumps."

Yes; being *the* Slade's widow was a dullish business after that. In living up to such a husband all her faculties had been engaged; now she had only her daughter to live up to, for the son who seemed to have inherited his father's gifts had died suddenly in boyhood. She had fought through that agony because her husband was there, to be helped and to help; now, after the father's death, the thought of the boy had become unbearable. There was nothing left but to mother her daughter; and dear Jenny was such a perfect daughter that she needed no excessive mothering. "Now with Babs Ansley I don't know that I *should* be so quiet," Mrs. Slade sometimes half-enviously reflected; but Jenny, who was younger than her brilliant friend, was that rare accident, an extremely pretty girl who somehow made youth and prettiness seem as safe as their absence. It was all perplexing—and to Mrs. Slade a little boring. She wished that Jenny would fall in love—with the wrong man, even; that she might have to be watched, out-manoeuvred, rescued. And instead, it was Jenny who watched her mother, kept her out of draughts, made sure that she had taken her tonic. . .

Mrs. Ansley was much less articulate than her friend, and her mental portrait of Mrs. Slade was slighter, and drawn with fainter touches. "Alida Slade's awfully brilliant; but not as brilliant as she thinks," would have summed it up; though she would have added, for the enlightenment of strangers, that Mrs. Slade had been an extremely dashing girl; much more so than her daughter, who was pretty, of course, and clever in a way, but had none of her mother's—well, "vividness", some one had once called it. Mrs. Ansley would take up current words like this, and cite them in quotation marks, as unheard-of audacities. No; Jenny was not like her mother. Sometimes Mrs. Ansley thought Alida Slade was disappointed; on the whole she had had a sad life. Full of failures and mistakes; Mrs. Ansley had always been rather sorry for her. . .

So these two ladies visualized each other, each through the wrong end of her little telescope.

II

For a long time they continued to sit side by side without speaking. It seemed as though, to both, there was a relief in laying down their somewhat futile activities in the presence of the vast Memento Mori which faced them. Mrs. Slade sat quite still, her eyes fixed on the golden slope of the Palace of the Cæsars, and after a while Mrs. Ansley ceased to fidget with her bag, and she too sank into meditation. Like many intimate friends, the two ladies had never before had occasion to be silent together, and Mrs. Ansley was slightly embarrassed by what seemed, after so many years, a new stage in their intimacy, and one with which she did not yet know how to deal.

Suddenly the air was full of that deep clangour of bells which periodically covers Rome with a roof of silver. Mrs. Slade glanced at her wrist-watch. "Five o'clock already," she said, as though surprised.

Mrs. Ansley suggested interrogatively: "There's bridge at the Embassy at five." For a long time Mrs. Slade did not answer. She appeared to be lost in contemplation, and Mrs. Ansley thought the remark had escaped her. But after a while she said, as if speaking out of a dream: "Bridge, did you say? Not unless you want to. . . But I don't think I will, you know."

"Oh, no," Mrs. Ansley hastened to assure her. "I don't care to at all. It's so lovely here; and so full of old memories, as you say." She settled herself in her chair, and almost furtively drew forth her knitting. Mrs. Slade took sideway note of this activity, but her own beautifully cared-for hands remained motionless on her knee.

"I was just thinking," she said slowly, "what different things Rome stands for to each generation of travellers. To our grandmothers, Roman fever; to our mothers, sentimental dangers—how we used to be guarded!—to our daughters, no more dangers than the middle of Main Street. They don't know it—but how much they're missing!"

The long golden light was beginning to pale, and Mrs. Ansley lifted her knitting a little closer to her eyes. "Yes; how we were guarded!"

"I always used to think," Mrs. Slade continued, "that our mothers had a much more difficult job than our grandmothers. When Roman fever stalked the streets it must have been comparatively easy to gather in the girls at the danger hour; but when you and I were young, with such beauty calling us, and the spice of disobedience thrown in, and no worse risk than catching cold during the cool hour after sunset, the mothers used to be put to it to keep us in—didn't they?"

She turned again toward Mrs. Ansley, but the latter had reached a delicate point in her knitting. "One, two, three—slip two; yes, they must have been," she assented, without looking up.

Mrs. Slade's eyes rested on her with a deepened attention. "She can knit—in the face of *this*! How like her. . ."

Mrs. Slade leaned back, brooding, her eyes ranging from the ruins which faced her to the long green hollow of the Forum, the fading glow of the church fronts beyond it, and the outlying immensity of the Colosseum. Suddenly she thought: "It's all very well to say that our girls have done away with sentiment and moonlight. But if Babs Ansley isn't out to catch that young aviator—the one who's a Marchese—then I don't know anything. And Jenny has no chance beside her. I know that too. I wonder if that's why Grace Ansley likes the two girls to go everywhere together? My poor Jenny as a foil—!" Mrs Slade gave a hardly audible laugh, and at the sound Mrs. Ansley dropped her knitting.

"Yes—?"

"I—oh, nothing. I was only thinking how your Babs carries everything before her. That Campolieri boy is one of the best matches in Rome. Don't look so innocent, my dear—you know he is. And I was wondering, ever so respectfully, you understand . . . wondering how two such exemplary characters as you and Horace had managed to produce anything quite so dynamic." Mrs. Slade laughed again, with a touch of asperity.

Mrs. Ansley's hands lay inert across her needles. She looked straight out at the great accumulated wreckage of passion and splendour at her feet. But her small profile was almost expressionless. At length she said: "I think you overrate Babs, my dear."

Mrs. Slade's tone grew easier. "No; I don't. I appreciate her. And perhaps envy you. Oh, my girl's perfect; if I were a chronic invalid I'd—well, I think I'd rather be in Jenny's hands. There must be times . . . but there! I always wanted a brilliant daughter . . . and never quite understood why I got an angel instead."

Mrs. Ansley echoed her laugh in a faint murmur. "Babs is an angel too."

"Of course—of course! But she's got rainbow wings. Well, they're wandering by the sea with their young men; and here we sit . . . and it all brings back the past a little too acutely."

Mrs. Ansley had resumed her knitting. One might almost

have imagined (if one had known her less well, Mrs. Slade reflected) that, for her also, too many memories rose from the lengthening shadows of those august ruins. But no; she was simply absorbed in her work. What was there for her to worry about? She knew that Babs would almost certainly come back engaged to the extremely eligible Campolieri. "And she'll sell the New York house, and settle down near them in Rome, and never be in their way . . . she's much too tactful. But she'll have an excellent cook, and just the right people in for bridge and cocktails . . . and a perfectly peaceful old age among her grandchildren."

Mrs. Slade broke off this prophetic flight with a recoil of self-disgust. There was no one of whom she had less right to think unkindly than of Grace Ansley. Would she never cure herself of envying her? Perhaps she had begun too long ago.

She stood up and leaned against the parapet, filling her troubled eyes with the tranquillizing magic of the hour. But instead of tranquillizing her the sight seemed to increase her exasperation. Her gaze turned toward the Colosseum. Already its golden flank was drowned in purple shadow, and above it the sky curved crystal clear, without light or colour. It was the moment when afternoon and evening hang balanced in mid-heaven.

Mrs. Slade turned back and laid her hand on her friend's arm. The gesture was so abrupt that Mrs. Ansley looked up, startled.

"The sun's set. You're not afraid, my dear?"

"Afraid—?"

"Of Roman fever or pneumonia? I remember how ill you were that winter. As a girl you had a very delicate throat, hadn't you?"

"Oh, we're all right up here. Down below, in the Forum, it does get deathly cold, all of a sudden . . . but not here."

"Ah, of course you know because you had to be so careful." Mrs Slade turned back to the parapet. She thought: "I must make one more effort not to hate her." Aloud she said: "Whenever I look at the Forum from up here, I remember that story about a great-aunt of yours, wasn't she? A dreadfully wicked great-aunt?"

"Oh, yes; Great-aunt Harriet. The one who was supposed to have sent her young sister out to the Forum after sunset to gather a night-blooming flower for her album. All our great-aunts and grandmothers used to have albums of dried flowers."

Mrs. Slade nodded. "But she really sent her because they were in love with the same man—"

"Well, that was the family tradition. They said Aunt Harriet confessed it years afterward. At any rate, the poor little sister caught the fever and died. Mother used to frighten us with the story when we were children."

"And you frightened *me* with it, that winter when you and I were here as girls. The winter I was engaged to Delphin."

Mrs. Ansley gave a faint laugh. "Oh, did I? Really frightened you? I don't believe you're easily frightened."

"Not often; but I was then. I was easily frightened because I was too happy. I wonder if you know what that means?"

"I—yes . . ." Mrs. Ansley faltered.

"Well, I suppose that was why the story of your wicked aunt made such an impression on me. And I thought: 'There's no more Roman fever, but the Forum is deathly cold after sunset—especially after a hot day. And the Colosseum's even colder and damper'."

"The Colosseum—?"

"Yes. It wasn't easy to get in, after the gates were locked for the night. Far from easy. Still, in those days it could be managed; it *was* managed, often. Lovers met there who couldn't meet elsewhere. You knew that?"

"I—I daresay. I don't remember."

"You don't remember? You don't remember going to visit some ruins or other one evening, just after dark, and catching a bad chill? You were supposed to have gone to see the moon rise. People always said that expedition was what caused your illness."

There was a moment's silence; then Mrs. Ansley rejoined: "Did they? It was all so long ago."

"Yes. And you got well again—so it didn't matter. But I suppose it struck your friends—the reason given for your illness, I mean—because everybody knew you were so prudent on account of your throat, and your mother took such care of you. . . You *had* been out late sight-seeing, hadn't you, that night?"

"Perhaps I had. The most prudent girls aren't always prudent. What made you think of it now?"

Mrs. Slade seemed to have no answer ready. But after a moment she broke out: "Because I simply can't bear it any longer—!"

Mrs. Ansley lifted her head quickly. Her eyes were wide and very pale. "Can't bear what?"

"Why—your not knowing that I've always known why you went."

"Why I went—?"

"Yes. You think I'm bluffing, don't you? Well, you went to meet the man I was engaged to—and I can repeat every word of the letter that took you there."

While Mrs. Slade spoke Mrs. Ansley had risen unsteadily to her feet. Her bag, her knitting and gloves, slid in a panic-stricken heap to the ground. She looked at Mrs. Slade as though she were looking at a ghost.

"No, no—don't," she faltered out.

"Why not? Listen, if you don't believe me. 'My one darling, things can't go on like this. I must see you alone. Come to the Colosseum immediately after dark tomorrow. There will be somebody to let you in. No one whom you need fear will suspect'—but perhaps you've forgotten what the letter said?"

Mrs. Ansley met the challenge with an unexpected composure. Steadying herself against the chair she looked at her friend, and replied: "No; I know it by heart too."

"And the signature? 'Only *your* D.S.' Was that it? I'm right, am I? That was the letter that took you out that evening after dark?"

Mrs. Ansley was still looking at her. It seemed to Mrs. Slade that a slow struggle was going on behind the voluntarily controlled mask of her small quiet face. "I shouldn't have thought she had herself so well in hand," Mrs. Slade reflected, almost resentfully. But at this moment Mrs. Ansley spoke. "I don't know how you knew. I burnt that letter at once."

"Yes; you would, naturally—you're so prudent!" The sneer

was open now. "And if you burnt the letter you're wondering how on earth I know what was in it. That's it, isn't it?"

Mrs. Slade waited, but Mrs. Ansley did not speak.

"Well, my dear, I know what was in that letter because I wrote it!"

"You wrote it?"

"Yes."

The two women stood for a minute staring at each other in the last golden light. Then Mrs. Ansley dropped back into her chair. "Oh," she murmured, and covered her face with her hands.

Mrs. Slade waited nervously for another word or movement. None came, and at length she broke out: "I horrify you."

Mrs. Ansley's hands dropped to her knee. The face they uncovered was streaked with tears. "I wasn't thinking of you. I was thinking—it was the only letter I ever had from him!"

"And I wrote it. Yes; I wrote it! But I was the girl he was engaged to. Did you happen to remember that?"

Mrs. Ansley's head drooped again. "I'm not trying to excuse myself. . . I remembered. . ."

"And still you went?"

"Still I went."

Mrs. Slade stood looking down on the small bowed figure at her side. The flame of her wrath had already sunk, and she wondered why she had ever thought there would be any satisfaction in inflicting so purposeless a wound on her friend. But she had to justify herself.

"You do understand? I'd found out—and I hated you, hated you. I knew you were in love with Delphin—and I was afraid; afraid of you, of your quiet ways, your sweetness . . . your . . . well, I wanted you out of the way, that's all. Just for a few weeks; just till I was sure of him. So in a blind fury I wrote that letter. . . I don't know why I'm telling you now."

"I suppose," said Mrs. Ansley slowly, "it's because you've always gone on hating me."

"Perhaps. Or because I wanted to get the whole thing off my mind." She paused. "I'm glad you destroyed the letter. Of course I never thought you'd die."

Mrs. Ansley relapsed into silence, and Mrs. Slade, leaning

above her, was conscious of a strange sense of isolation, of being cut off from the warm current of human communion. "You think me a monster!"

"I don't know. . . . It was the only letter I had, and you say he didn't write it?"

"Ah, how you care for him still!"

"I cared for that memory," said Mrs. Ansley.

Mrs. Slade continued to look down on her. She seemed physically reduced by the blow—as if, when she got up, the wind might scatter her like a puff of dust. Mrs. Slade's jealousy suddenly leapt up again at the sight. All these years the woman had been living on that letter. How she must have loved him, to treasure the mere memory of its ashes! The letter of the man her friend was engaged to. Wasn't it she who was the monster?

"You tried your best to get him away from me, didn't you? But you failed; and I kept him. That's all."

"Yes. That's all."

"I wish now I hadn't told you. I'd no idea you'd feel about it as you do; I thought you'd be amused. It all happened so long ago, as you say; and you must do me the justice to remember that I had no reason to think you'd ever taken it seriously. How could I, when you were married to Horace Ansley two months afterward? As soon as you could get out of bed your mother rushed you off to Florence and married you. People were rather surprised—they wondered at its being done so quickly; but I thought I knew. I had an idea you did it out of *pique*—to be able to say you'd got ahead of Delphin and me. Girls have such silly reasons for doing the most serious things. And your marrying so soon convinced me that you'd never really cared."

"Yes. I suppose it would," Mrs. Ansley assented.

The clear heaven overhead was emptied of all its gold. Dusk spread over it, abruptly darkening the Seven Hills. Here and there lights began to twinkle through the foliage at their feet. Steps were coming and going on the deserted terrace—waiters looking out of the doorway at the head of the stairs, then reappearing with trays and napkins and flasks of wine. Tables were moved, chairs straightened. A feeble string of electric lights flickered out. Some vases of faded flowers were carried away, and brought back replenished. A stout lady in a dust-coat suddenly appeared, asking in broken Italian if any one had seen the elastic band which held together her tattered Baedeker. She poked with her stick under the table at which she had lunched, the waiters assisting.

The corner where Mrs. Slade and Mrs. Ansley sat was still shadowy and deserted. For a long time neither of them spoke. At length Mrs. Slade began again: "I suppose I did it as a sort of joke—"

"A joke?"

"Well, girls are ferocious sometimes, you know. Girls in love especially. And I remember laughing to myself all that evening at the idea that you were waiting around there in the dark, dodging out of sight, listening for every sound, trying to get in—. Of course I was upset when I heard you were so ill afterward."

Mrs. Ansley had not moved for a long time. But now she turned slowly toward her companion. "But I didn't wait. He'd arranged everything. He was there. We were let in at once," she said.

Mrs. Slade sprang up from her leaning position. "Delphin there? They let you in?— Ah, now you're lying!" she burst out with violence.

Mrs. Ansley's voice grew clearer, and full of surprise. "But of course he was there. Naturally he came—"

"Came? How did he know he'd find you there? You must be raving!"

Mrs. Ansley hesitated, as though reflecting. "But I answered the letter. I told him I'd be there. So he came."

Mrs. Slade flung her hands up to her face. "Oh, God—you answered! I never thought of your answering. . ."

"It's odd you never thought of it, if you wrote the letter."

"Yes. I was blind with rage."

Mrs. Ansley rose, and drew her fur scarf about her. "It is cold here. We'd better go. . . I'm sorry for you," she said, as she clasped the fur about her throat.

The unexpected words sent a pang through Mrs. Slade. "Yes; we'd better go." She gathered up her bag and cloak. "I don't know why you should be sorry for me," she muttered.

Mrs. Ansley stood looking away from her toward the dusky

secret mass of the Colosseum. "Well—because I didn't have to wait that night."

Mrs. Slade gave an unquiet laugh. "Yes; I was beaten there. But I oughtn't to begrudge it to you, I suppose. At the end of all these years. After all, I had everything; I had him for twenty-five years. And you had nothing but that one letter that he didn't write."

Mrs. Ansley was again silent. At length she turned toward the door of the terrace. She took a step, and turned back, facing her companion.

"I had Barbara," she said, and began to move ahead of Mrs. Slade toward the stairway.

The Looking-Glass

M RS. ATTLEE had never been able to understand why there was any harm in giving people a little encouragement when they needed it.

Sitting back in her comfortable armchair by the fire, her working-days over, and her muscular masseuse's hands lying swollen and powerless on her knee, she was at leisure to turn the problem over, and ponder it as there had never been time to do before.

Mrs. Attlee was so infirm now that, when her widowed daughter-in-law was away for the day, her granddaughter Moyra Attlee had to stay with her until the kitchen-girl had prepared the cold supper, and could come in and sit in the parlour.

"You'd be surprised, you know, my dear, to find how discouraged the grand people get, in those big houses with all the help, and the silver dinner plates, and a bell always handy if the fire wants poking, or the pet dog asks for a drink. . . And what'd a masseuse be good for, if she didn't jolly up their minds a little along with their muscles?—as Dr. Welbridge used to say to me many a time, when he'd given me a difficult patient. And he always gave me the most difficult," she added proudly.

She paused, aware (for even now little escaped her) that Moyra had ceased to listen, but accepting the fact resignedly, as she did most things in the slow decline of her days.

"It's a fine afternoon," she reflected, "and likely she's fidgety because there's a new movie on; or that young fellow's fixed it up to get back earlier from New York. . ."

She relapsed into silence, following her thoughts; but presently, as happens with old people, they came to the surface again.

"And I hope I'm a good Catholic, as I said to Father Divott the other day, and at peace with heaven, if ever I was took suddenly—but no matter what happens I've got to risk my punishment for the wrong I did to Mrs. Clingsland, because as long as I've never repented it there's no use telling Father Divott about it. Is there?"

Mrs. Attlee heaved an introspective sigh. Like many humble persons of her kind and creed, she had a vague idea that a sin unrevealed was, as far as the consequences went, a sin uncommitted; and this conviction had often helped her in the difficult task of reconciling doctrine and practice.

II

Moyra Attlee interrupted her listless stare down the empty Sunday street of the New Jersey suburb, and turned an astonished glance on her grandmother.

"Mrs. Clingsland? A wrong you did to Mrs. Clingsland?"

Hitherto she had lent an inattentive ear to her grandmother's ramblings; the talk of old people seemed to be a language hardly worth learning. But it was not always so with Mrs. Attlee's. Her activities among the rich had ceased before the first symptoms of the financial depression; but her tenacious memory was stored with pictures of the luxurious days of which her granddaughter's generation, even in a wider world, knew only by hearsay. Mrs. Attlee had a gift for evoking in a few words scenes of half-understood opulence and leisure, like a guide leading a stranger through the gallery of a palace in the twilight, and now and then lifting a lamp to a shimmering Rembrandt or a jewelled Rubens; and it was particularly when she mentioned Mrs. Clingsland that Moyra caught these dazzling glimpses. Mrs. Clingsland had always been something more than a name to the Attlee family. They knew (though they did not know why) that it was through her help that Grandmother Attlee had been able, years ago, to buy the little house at Montclair, with a patch of garden behind it, where, all through the depression, she had held out, thanks to fortunate investments made on the advice of Mrs. Clingsland's great friend, the banker.

"She had so many friends, and they were all high-up people, you understand. Many's the time she'd say to me: 'Cora' (think of the loveliness of her calling me Cora), 'Cora, I'm going to buy some Golden Flyer shares on Mr. Stoner's advice; Mr. Stoner of the National Union Bank, you know. He's getting me in on the ground floor, as they say, and if you want to step in with me, why come along. There's nothing too good for you, in my opinion,' she used to say. And, as it turned out, those shares have kept their head above water all through the bad years, and now I think they'll see me through, and be there when I'm gone, to help out you children."

Today Moyra Attlee heard the revered name with a new interest. The phrase: "The wrong I did to Mrs. Clingsland," had struck through her listlessness, rousing her to sudden curiosity. What could her grandmother mean by saying she had done a wrong to the benefactress whose bounties she was never tired of recording? Moyra believed her grandmother to be a very good woman—certainly she had been wonderfully generous in all her dealings with her children and grandchildren; and it seemed incredible that, if there had been one grave lapse in her life, it should have taken the form of an injury to Mrs. Clingsland. True, whatever the lapse was, she seemed to have made peace with herself about it; yet it was clear that its being unconfessed lurked disquietingly in the back of her mind.

"How can you say you ever did harm to a friend like Mrs. Clingsland, Gran?"

Mrs. Attlee's eyes grew sharp behind her spectacles, and she fixed them half distrustfully on the girl's face. But in a moment she seemed to recover herself. "Not harm, I don't say; I'll never think I harmed her. Bless you, it wasn't to harm her I'd ever have lifted a finger. All I wanted was to help. But when you try to help too many people at once, the devil sometimes takes note of it. You see, there's quotas nowadays for everything, doing good included, my darling."

Moyra made an impatient movement. She did not care to hear her grandmother philosophize. "Well—but you said you did a wrong to Mrs. Clingsland."

Mrs. Attlee's sharp eyes seemed to draw back behind a mist of age. She sat silent, her hands lying heavily over one another in their tragic uselessness.

"What would *you* have done, I wonder," she began suddenly, "if you'd ha' come in on her that morning, and seen her laying in her lovely great bed, with the lace a yard deep on the sheets, and her face buried in the pillows, so I knew she was crying? Would you have opened your bag same as usual, and got out your cocoanut cream and talcum powder, and the nail polishers, and all the rest of it, and waited there like a statue till she turned over to you; or'd you have gone up to her, and turned her softly round, like you would a baby, and said to her: 'Now, my dear, I guess you can tell Cora Attlee what's the trouble'? Well, that's what I did, anyhow; and there she was, with her face streaming with tears, and looking like a martyred saint on an altar, and when I said to her: 'Come, now, you tell me, and it'll help you,' she just sobbed out: 'Nothing can ever help me, now I've lost it'."

" 'Lost what?' I said, thinking first of her boy, the Lord help me, though I'd heard him whistling on the stairs as I went up; but she said: 'My beauty, Cora—I saw it suddenly slipping out of the door from me this morning'. . . Well, at that I had to laugh, and half angrily too. 'Your beauty,' I said to her, 'and is that all? And me that thought it was your husband, or your son—or your fortune even. If it's only your beauty, can't I give it back to you with these hands of mine? But what are you saying to me about beauty, with that seraph's face looking up at me this minute?' I said to her, for she angered me as if she'd been blaspheming."

"Well, was it true?" Moyra broke in, impatient and yet curious.

"True that she'd lost her beauty?" Mrs. Attlee paused to consider. "Do you know how it is, sometimes when you're doing a bit of fine darning, sitting by the window in the afternoon; and one minute it's full daylight, and your needle seems to find the way of itself; and the next minute you say: 'Is it my eyes?' because the work seems blurred; and presently you see it's the daylight going, stealing away, soft-like, from your corner, though there's plenty left overhead. Well—it was that way with her. . ."

But Moyra had never done fine darning, or strained her eyes in fading light, and she intervened again, more impatiently: "Well, what did she do?"

Mrs. Attlee once more reflected. "Why, she made me tell her every morning that it wasn't true; and every morning she believed me a little less. And she asked everybody in the house, beginning with her husband, poor man—him so bewildered when you asked him anything outside of his business, or his club or his horses, and never noticing any difference in her looks since the day he'd led her home as his bride, twenty years before, maybe. . .

"But there—nothing he could have said, if he'd had the wit to say it, would have made any difference. From the day she saw the first little line around her eyes she thought of herself as an old woman, and the thought never left her for more than a few minutes at a time. Oh, when she was dressed up, and laughing, and receiving company; then I don't say the faith in her beauty wouldn't come back to her, and go to her head like champagne; but it wore off quicker than champagne, and I've seen her run upstairs with the foot of a girl, and then, before she'd tossed off her finery, sit down in a heap in front of one of her big looking-glasses—it was looking-glasses everywhere in her room—and stare and stare till the tears ran down over her powder."

"Oh, well, I suppose it's always hateful growing old," said Moyra, her indifference returning.

Mrs. Attlee smiled retrospectively. "How can I say that, when my own old age has been made so peaceful by all her goodness to me?"

Moyra stood up with a shrug. "And yet you tell me you acted wrong to her. How am I to know what you mean?"

Her grandmother made no answer. She closed her eyes, and leaned her head against the little cushion behind her neck. Her lips seemed to murmur, but no words came. Moyra reflected that she was probably falling asleep, and that when she woke she would not remember what she had been about to reveal.

"It's not much fun sitting here all this time, if you can't even keep awake long enough to tell me what you mean about Mrs. Clingsland," she grumbled.

Mrs. Attlee roused herself with a start.

III

Well (she began) you know what happened in the war—I mean, the way all the fine ladies, and the poor shabby ones too, took to running to the mediums and the *clair-voyants*, or whatever the stylish folk call 'em. The women had to have news of their men; and they were made to pay high enough for it. . . Oh, the stories I used to hear—and the price paid wasn't only money, either! There was a fair lot of swindlers and blackmailers in the business, there was. I'd sooner have trusted a gypsy at a fair. . . But the women just *had* to go to them.

Well, my dear, I'd always had a way of seeing things; from the cradle, even. I don't mean reading the tea-leaves, or dealing the cards; that's for the kitchen. No, no; I mean, feeling there's things about you, behind you, whispering over your shoulder. . . Once my mother, on the Connemara hills, saw the leprechauns at dusk; and she said they smelt fine and high, too. . . Well, when I used to go from one grand house to another, to give my massage and face-treatment, I got more and more sorry for those poor wretches that the sooth-saying swindlers were dragging the money out of for a pack of lies; and one day I couldn't stand it any longer, and though I knew the Church was against it, when I saw one lady nearly crazy, because for months she'd had no news of her boy at the front, I said to her: "If you'll come over to my place tomorrow, I might have a word for you." And the wonder of it was that I *had*! For that night I dreamt a message came saying there was good news for her, and the next day, sure enough, she had a cable, telling her her son had escaped from a German camp. . .

After that the ladies came in flocks—in flocks fairly. . . You're too young to remember, child; but your mother could tell you. Only she wouldn't, because after a bit the priest got wind of it, and then it had to stop . . . so she won't even talk of it any more. But I always said: How could I help it? For I *did* see things, and hear things, at that time. . . And of course the ladies were supposed to come just for the face-treatment . . . and was I to blame if I kept hearing those messages for them, poor souls, or seeing things they wanted me to see?

It's no matter now, for I made it all straight with Father Divott years ago; and now nobody comes after me any more, as you can see for yourself. And all I ask is to be left alone in my chair. . .

But with Mrs. Clingsland—well, that was different. To begin with, she was the patient I liked best. There was nothing she wouldn't do for you, if ever for a minute you could get her to stop thinking of herself . . . and that's saying a good deal, for a rich lady. Money's an armour, you see; and there's few cracks in it. But Mrs. Clingsland was a loving nature, if only anybody'd shown her how to love. . . Oh, dear, and wouldn't she have been surprised if you'd told her that! Her that thought she was living up to her chin in love and love-making. But as soon as the lines began to come about her eyes, she didn't believe in it any more. And she had to be always hunting for new people to tell her she was as beautiful as ever; because she wore the others out, forever asking them: "Don't you think I'm beginning to go off a little?"—till finally fewer and fewer came to the house, and as far as a poor masseuse like me can judge, I didn't much fancy the looks of those that did; and I saw Mr. Clingsland didn't either.

But there was the children, you'll say. I know, I know! And she did love her children in a way; only it wasn't their way. The girl, who was a good bit the eldest, took after her father: a plain face and plain words. Dogs and horses and athletics. With her mother she was cold and scared; so her mother was cold and scared with her. The boy was delicate when he was little, so she could curl him up, and put him into black velvet pants, like that boy in the book—little Lord Something. But when his long legs grew out of the pants, and they sent him to school, she said he wasn't her own little coodly baby any more; and it riles a growing boy to hear himself talked about like that.

She had good friends left, of course; mostly elderly ladies they were, of her own age (for she *was* elderly now; the change had come), who used to drop in often for a gossip; but, bless your heart, they weren't much help, for what she wanted, and couldn't do without, was the gaze of men struck dumb by her beauty. And that was what she couldn't get any longer, except she paid for it. And even so—!

For, you see, she was too quick and clever to be humbugged long by the kind that tried to get things out of her. How she used to laugh at the old double-chinners trotting round to the night-clubs with their boy friends! She laughed at old ladies in love; and yet she couldn't bear to be out of love, though she knew she was getting to be an old lady herself.

Well, I remember one day another patient of mine, who'd never had much looks beyond what you can buy in Fifth Avenue, laughing at me about Mrs. Clingsland, about her dread of old age, and her craze for admiration—and as I listened, I suddenly thought: "Why, we don't either of us know anything about what a beautiful woman suffers when she loses her beauty. For you and me, and thousands like us, beginning to grow old is like going from a bright warm room to one a little less warm and bright; but to a beauty like Mrs. Clingsland it's like being pushed out of an illuminated ballroom, all flowers and chandeliers, into the winter night and the snow." And I had to bite the words back, not to say them to my patient. . .

IV

Mrs. Clingsland brightened up a little when her own son grew up and went to college. She used to go over and see him now and again; or he'd come home for the holidays. And he used to take her out for lunch, or to dance at those cabaret places; and when the head-waiters took her for his sweetheart she'd talk about it for a week. But one day a hall porter said: "Better hurry up, mister. There's your mother waiting for you over there, looking clean fagged out"; and after that she didn't go round with him so much.

For a time she used to get some comfort out of telling me about her early triumphs; and I used to listen patiently, because I knew it was safer for her to talk to me than to the flatterers who were beginning to get round her.

You mustn't think of her, though, as an unkind woman. She was friendly to her husband, and friendly to her children; but they meant less and less to her. What she wanted was a looking-glass to stare into; and when her own people took enough notice of her to serve as looking-glasses, which wasn't often, she didn't much fancy what she saw there. I think this was about the worst time of her life. She lost a tooth; she began to dye her hair; she went into retirement to have her face lifted, and then got frightened, and came out again looking like a ghost, with a pouch under one eye, where they'd begun the treatment. . .

I began to be really worried about her then. She got sour and bitter toward everybody, and I seemed to be the only person she could talk out to. She used to keep me by her for hours, always paying for the appointments she made me miss, and going over the same thing again and again; how when she was young and came into a ball-room, or a restaurant or a theatre, everybody stopped what they were doing to turn and look at her—even the actors on the stage did, she said; and it was the truth, I daresay. But that was over. . .

Well, what could I say to her? She'd heard it all often enough. But there were people prowling about in the background that I didn't like the look of; people, you understand, who live on weak women that can't grow old. One day she showed me a love-letter. She said she didn't know the man who'd sent it; but she knew about him. He was a Count Somebody; a foreigner. He'd had adventures. Trouble in his own country, I guess. . . She laughed and tore the letter up. Another came from him, and I saw that too—but I didn't see her tear it up.

"Oh, I know what he's after," she said. "Those kind of men are always looking out for silly old women with money. . . Ah," says she, "it was different in old times. I remember one day I'd gone into a florist's to buy some violets, and I saw a young fellow there; well, maybe he was a little younger than me—but I looked like a girl still. And when he saw me he just stopped short with what he was saying to the florist, and his face turned so white I thought he was going to faint. I bought my violets; and as I went out a violet dropped from the bunch, and I saw him stoop and pick it up, and hide it away as if it had been money he'd stolen. . . Well," she says, "a few days after that I met him at a dinner, and it turned out he was the son of a friend of mine, a woman older than myself, who'd married abroad. He'd been brought up in England, and had just come to New York to take up a job there. . ."

She lay back with her eyes closed, and a quiet smile on her poor tormented face. "I didn't know it then, but I suppose

that was the only time I've ever been in love. . ." For a while
she didn't say anything more, and I noticed the tears beginning to roll down her cheeks. "Tell me about it, now do, you
poor soul," I says; for I thought, this is better for her than fan-
dangoing with that oily Count whose letter she hasn't torn up.

"There's so little to tell," she said. "We met only four or
five times—and then Harry went down on the *Titanic*."

"Mercy," says I, "and was it all those years ago?"

"The years don't make any difference, Cora," she says.
"The way he looked at me I know no one ever worshipped
me as he did."

"And did he tell you so?" I went on, humouring her;
though I felt kind of guilty toward her husband.

"Some things don't have to be told," says she, with the
smile of a bride. "If only he hadn't died, Cora. . . It's the
sorrowing for him that's made me old before my time."
(Before her time! And her well over fifty.)

Well, a day or two after that I got a shock. Coming out of
Mrs. Clingsland's front door as I was going into it I met a
woman I'd know among a million if I was to meet her again
in hell—where I will, I know, if I don't mind my steps. . .
You see, Moyra, though I broke years ago with all that crys-
tal-reading, and table-rapping, and what the Church forbids,
I was mixed up in it for a time (till Father Divott ordered me
to stop), and I knew, by sight at any rate, most of the big
mediums and their touts. And this woman on the doorstep
was a tout, one of the worst and most notorious in New York;
I knew cases where she'd sucked people dry selling them the
news they wanted, like she was selling them a forbidden drug.
And all of a sudden it came to me that I'd heard it said that
she kept a foreign Count, who was sucking *her* dry—and I
gave one jump home to my own place, and sat down there to
think it over.

I saw well enough what was going to happen. Either she'd
persuade my poor lady that the Count was mad over her
beauty, and get a hold over her that way; or else—and this
was worse—she'd make Mrs. Clingsland talk, and get at the
story of the poor young man called Harry, who was drowned,
and bring her messages from him; and that might go on forever, and bring in more money than the Count. . .

Well, Moyra, could I help it? I was so sorry for her, you see.
I could see she was sick and fading away, and her will weaker
than it used to be; and if I was to save her from those gang-
sters I had to do it right away, and make it straight with my
conscience afterward—if I could. . .

V

I don't believe I ever did such hard thinking as I did that
night. For what was I after doing? Something that was against
my Church and against my own principles; and if ever I got
found out, it was all up with me—me, with my thirty years'
name of being the best masseuse in New York, and none hon-
ester, nor more respectable!

Well, then, I says to myself, what'll happen if that woman
gets hold of Mrs. Clingsland? Why, one way or another, she'll
bleed her white, and then leave her without help or comfort.
I'd seen households where that had happened, and I wasn't
going to let it happen to my poor lady. What I was after was
to make her believe in herself again, so that she'd be in a
kindlier mind toward others . . . and by the next day I'd
thought my plan out, and set it going.

It wasn't so easy, neither; and I sometimes wonder at my
nerve. I'd figured it out that the other woman would have to
work the stunt of the young man who was drowned, because
I was pretty sure Mrs. Clingsland, at the last minute, would
shy away from the Count. Well, then, thinks I, I'll work the
same stunt myself—but how?

You see, dearie, those big people, when they talk and write
to each other, they use lovely words we ain't used to; and I
was afraid if I began to bring messages to her, I'd word them
wrong, and she'd suspect something. I knew I could work it
the first day or the second; but after that I wasn't so sure. But
there was no time to lose, and when I went back to her next
morning I said: "A queer thing happened to me last night. I
guess it was the way you spoke to me about that gentleman—
the one on the *Titanic.* Making me see him as clear as if he
was in the room with us—" and at that I had her sitting up in
bed with her great eyes burning into me like gimlets. "Oh,
Cora, perhaps he *is*! Oh, tell me quickly what happened!"

"Well, when I was laying in my bed last night something came to me from him. I knew at once it was from him; it was a word he was telling me to bring you. . ."

I had to wait then, she was crying so hard, before she could listen to me again; and when I went on she hung on to me, saving the word, as if I'd been her Saviour. The poor woman!

The message I'd hit on for that first day was easy enough. I said he'd told me to tell her he'd always loved her. It went down her throat like honey, and she just lay there and tasted it. But after a while she lifted up her head. "Then why didn't he tell me so?" says she.

"Ah," says I, "I'll have to try to reach him again, and ask him that." And that day she fairly drove me off on my other jobs, for fear I'd be late getting home, and too tired to hear him if he came again. "And he *will* come, Cora; I know he will! And you must be ready for him, and write down everything. I want every word written down the minute he says it, for fear you'll forget a single one."

Well, that was a new difficulty. Writing wasn't ever my strong point; and when it came to finding the words for a young gentleman in love who'd gone down on the *Titanic*, you might as well have asked me to write a Chinese dictionary. Not that I couldn't imagine how he'd have felt; but I didn't for Mary's grace know how to say it for him.

But it's wonderful, as Father Divott says, how Providence sometimes seems to be listening behind the door. That night when I got home I found a message from a patient, asking me to go to see a poor young fellow she'd befriended when she was better off—he'd been her children's tutor, I believe—who was down and out, and dying in a miserable rooming-house down here at Montclair. Well, I went; and I saw at once why he hadn't kept this job, or any other job. Poor fellow, it was the drink; and now he was dying of it. It was a pretty bad story, but there's only a bit of it belongs to what I'm telling you.

He was a highly educated gentleman, and as quick as a flash; and before I'd half explained, he told me what to say, and wrote out the message for me. I remember it now. "He was so blinded by your beauty that he couldn't speak—and when he saw you the next time, at that dinner, in your bare shoulders and your pearls, he felt farther away from you than ever. And he walked the streets till morning, and then went home, and wrote you a letter; but he didn't dare to send it after all."

This time Mrs. Clingsland swallowed it down like champagne. Blinded by her beauty; struck dumb by love of her! Oh, but that's what she'd been thirsting and hungering for all these years. Only, once it had begun, she had to have more of it, and always more . . . and my job didn't get any easier.

Luckily, though, I had that young fellow to help me; and after a while, when I'd given him a hint of what it was all about, he got as much interested as I was, and began to fret for me the days I didn't come.

But, my, what questions she asked. "Tell him, if it's true that I took his breath away that first evening at dinner, to describe to you how I was dressed. They must remember things like that even in the other world, don't you think so? And you say he noticed my pearls?"

Luckily she'd described that dress to me so often that I had no difficulty about telling the young man what to say—and so it went on, and it went on, and one way or another I managed each time to have an answer that satisfied her. But one day, after Harry'd sent her a particularly lovely message from the Over There (as those people call it) she burst into tears and cried out: "Oh, why did he never say things like that to me when we were together?"

That was a poser, as they say; I couldn't imagine why he hadn't. Of course I knew it was all wrong and immoral, anyway; but, poor thing, I don't see who it can hurt to help the love-making between a sick woman and a ghost. And I'd taken care to say a Novena against Father Divott finding me out.

Well, I told the poor young man what she wanted to know, and he said: "Oh, you can tell her an evil influence came between them. Some one who was jealous, and worked against him—here, give me a pencil, and I'll write it out . . ." and he pushed out his hot twitching hand for the paper.

That message fairly made her face burn with joy. "I knew it—I always knew it!" She flung her thin arms about me, and kissed me. "Tell me again, Cora, how he said I looked the first day he saw me. . ."

"Why, you must have looked as you look now," says I to her, "for there's twenty years fallen from your face." And so there was.

What helped me to keep on was that she'd grown so much gentler and quieter. Less impatient with the people who waited on her, more understanding with the daughter and Mr. Clingsland. There was a different atmosphere in the house. And sometimes she'd say: "Cora, there must be poor souls in trouble, with nobody to hold out a hand to them; and I want you to come to me when you run across anybody like that." So I used to keep that poor young fellow well looked after, and cheered up with little dainties. And you'll never make me believe there was anything wrong in that—or in letting Mrs. Clingsland help me out with the new roof on this house, either.

But there was a day when I found her sitting up in bed when I came in, with two red spots on her thin cheeks. And all the peace had gone out of her poor face. "Why, Mrs. Clingsland, my dear, what's the matter?" But I could see well enough what it was. Somebody'd been undermining her belief in spirit-communications, or whatever they call them, and she'd been crying herself into a fever, thinking I'd made up all I'd told her. "How do I know you're a medium, anyhow," she flung out at me with pitiful furious eyes, "and not taking advantage of me with all this stuff every morning?"

Well, the queer thing was that I took offense at that, not because I was afraid of being found out, but because—heaven help us!—I'd somehow come to believe in that young man Harry and his love-making, and it made me angry to be treated as a fraud. But I kept my temper and my tongue, and went on with the massage as if I hadn't heard her; and she was ashamed to say any more to me. The quarrel between us lasted a week; and then one day, poor soul, she said, whimpering like a drug-taker: "Cora, I can't get on without the messages you bring me. The ones I get through other people don't sound like Harry—and yours do."

I was so sorry for her then that I had hard work not to cry with her; but I kept my head, and answered quietly: "Mrs.

Clingsland, I've been going against my Church, and risking my immortal soul, to get those messages through to you; and if you've found others that can help you, so much the better for me, and I'll go and make my peace with Heaven this very evening," I said.

"But the other messages don't help me, and I don't want to disbelieve in you," she sobbed out. "Only lying awake all night and turning things over, I get so miserable. I shall die if you can't prove to me that it's really Harry speaking to you."

I began to pack up my things. "I can't prove that, I'm afraid," I says in a cold voice, turning away my head so she wouldn't see the tears running down my cheeks.

"Oh, but you must, Cora, or I shall die!" she entreated me; and she looked as if she would, the poor soul.

"How can I prove it to you?" I answered. For all my pity for her, I still resented the way she'd spoken; and I thought how glad I'd be to get the whole business off my soul that very night in the confessional.

She opened her great eyes and looked up at me; and I seemed to see the wraith of her young beauty looking out of them. "There's only one way," she whispered.

"Well," I said, still offended, "what's the way?"

"You must ask him to repeat to you that letter he wrote, and didn't dare send to me. I'll know instantly then if you're in communication with him, and if you are I'll never doubt you any more."

Well, I sat down and gave a laugh. "You think it's as easy as that to talk with the dead, do you?"

"I think he'll know I'm dying too, and have pity on me, and do as I ask." I said nothing more, but packed up my things and went away.

VI

That letter seemed to me a mountain in my path; and the poor young man, when I told him, thought so too. "Ah, that's too difficult," he said. But he told me he'd think it over, and do his best—and I was to come back the next day if I could. "If only I knew more about her—or about *him*. It's damn difficult, making love for a dead man to a woman you've never seen," says he with his little cracked laugh. I couldn't deny that it was; but I knew he'd do what he could, and I could see that the difficulty of it somehow spurred him on, while me it only cast down.

So I went back to his room the next evening; and as I climbed the stairs I felt one of those sudden warnings that sometimes used to take me by the throat.

"It's as cold as ice on these stairs," I thought, "and I'll wager there's no one made up the fire in his room since morning." But it wasn't really the cold I was afraid of; I could tell there was worse than that waiting for me.

I pushed open the door and went in. "Well," says I, as cheerful as I could, "I've got a pint of champagne and a thermos of hot soup for you; but before you get them you've got to tell me—"

He laid there in his bed as if he didn't see me, though his eyes were open; and when I spoke to him he didn't answer. I tried to laugh. "Mercy!" I says, "are you so sleepy you can't even look round to see the champagne? Hasn't that slut of a woman been in to 'tend to the stove for you? The room's as cold as death—" I says, and at the word I stopped short. He neither moved nor spoke; and I felt that the cold came from him, and not from the empty stove. I took hold of his hand, and held the cracked looking-glass to his lips; and I knew he was gone to his Maker. I drew his lids down, and fell on my knees beside the bed. "You shan't go without a prayer, you poor fellow," I whispered to him, pulling out my beads.

But though my heart was full of mourning I dursn't pray for long, for I knew I ought to call the people of the house. So I just muttered a prayer for the dead, and then got to my feet again. But before calling in anybody I took a quick look around; for I said to myself it would be better not to leave about any of those bits he'd written down for me. In the shock of finding the poor young man gone I'd clean forgotten all about the letter; but I looked among his few books and papers for anything about the spirit messages, and found nothing. After that I turned back for a last look at him, and a last blessing; and then it was, fallen on the floor and half under the bed, I saw a sheet of paper scribbled over in pencil in his weak writing. I picked it up, and, holy Mother, it was the letter! I hid it away quick in my bag, and I stooped down and kissed him. And then I called the people in.

Well, I mourned the poor young man like a son, and I had a busy day arranging things, and settling about the funeral with the lady that used to befriend him. And with all there was to do I never went near Mrs. Clingsland nor so much as thought of her, that day or the next; and the day after that there was a frantic message, asking what had happened, and saying she was very ill, and I was to come quick, no matter how much else I had to do.

I didn't more than half believe in the illness; I've been about too long among the rich not to be pretty well used to their scares and fusses. But I knew Mrs. Clingsland was just pining to find out if I'd got the letter, and that my only chance of keeping my hold over her was to have it ready in my bag when I went back. And if I didn't keep my hold over her, I knew what slimy hands were waiting in the dark to pull her down.

Well, the labour I had copying out that letter was so great that I didn't hardly notice what was in it; and if I thought about it at all, it was only to wonder if it wasn't worded too plain-like, and if there oughtn't to have been more long words in it, coming from a gentleman to his lady. So with one thing and another I wasn't any too easy in my mind when I appeared again at Mrs. Clingsland's; and if ever I wished myself out of a dangerous job, my dear, I can tell you that was the day. . .

I went up to her room, the poor lady, and found her in bed, and tossing about, her eyes blazing, and her face full of all the wrinkles I'd worked so hard to rub out of it; and the sight of her softened my heart. After all, I thought, these people don't know what real trouble is; but they've manufactured something so like it that it's about as bad as the genuine thing.

"Well," she said in a fever, "well, Cora—the letter? Have you brought me the letter?"

I pulled it out of my bag, and handed it to her; and then I sat down and waited, my heart in my boots. I waited a long time, looking away from her; you couldn't stare at a lady who was reading a message from her sweetheart, could you?

I waited a long time; she must have read the letter very slowly, and then re-read it. Once she sighed, ever so softly; and once she said: "Oh, Harry, no, no—how foolish" . . . and laughed a little under her breath. Then she was still again for so long that at last I turned my head and took a stealthy look at her. And there she lay on her pillows, the hair waving over them, the letter clasped tight in her hands, and her face smoothed out the way it was years before, when I first knew her. Yes—those few words had done more for her than all my labour.

"Well—?" said I, smiling a little at her.

"Oh, Cora—now at last he's spoken to me, really spoken." And the tears were running down her young cheeks.

I couldn't hardly keep back my own, the heart was so light in me. "And now you'll believe in me, I hope, ma'am, won't you?"

"I was mad ever to doubt you, Cora. . ." She lifted the letter to her breast, and slipped it in among her laces. "How did you manage to get it, you darling, you?"

Dear me, thinks I, and what if she asks me to get her another one like it, and then another? I waited a moment, and then I spoke very gravely. "It's not an easy thing, ma'am, coaxing a letter like that from the dead." And suddenly, with a start, I saw that I'd spoken the truth. It *was* from the dead that I'd got it.

"No, Cora; I can well believe it. But this is a treasure I can live on for years. Only you must tell me how I can repay you. . . In a hundred years I could never do enough for you," she says.

Well, that word went to my heart; but for a minute I didn't know how to answer. For it was true I'd risked my soul, and that was something she couldn't pay me for; but then maybe I'd saved hers, in getting her away from those foul people, so the whole business was more of a puzzle to me than ever. But then I had a thought that made me easier.

"Well, ma'am, the day before yesterday I was with a young man about the age of—of your Harry; a poor young man, without health or hope, lying sick in a mean rooming-house. I used to go there and see him sometimes—"

Mrs. Clingsland sat up in bed in a flutter of pity. "Oh,

Cora, how dreadful! Why did you never tell me? You must hire a better room for him at once. Has he a doctor? Has he a nurse? Quick—give me my cheque-book!"

"Thank you, ma'am. But he don't need no nurse nor no doctor; and he's in a room underground by now. All I wanted to ask you for," said I at length, though I knew I might have got a king's ransom from her, "is money enough to have a few masses said for his soul—because maybe there's no one else to do it."

I had hard work making her believe there was no end to the masses you could say for a hundred dollars; but somehow it's comforted me ever since that I took no more from her that day. I saw to it that Father Divott said the masses and got a good bit of the money; so he was a sort of accomplice too, though he never knew it.

Duration

THE PASSAGE in his sister's letter most perplexing to Henly Warbeck was that in which she expressed her satisfaction that the date of his sailing from Lima would land him in Boston in good time for cousin Martha Little's birthday.

Puzzle as he would, the returning Bostonian could get no light on it. "Why," he thought, after a third re-reading, "I didn't suppose Martha Little had ever *had* a birthday since the first one!"

Nothing on the fairly flat horizon of Henly Warbeck's youth had been more lacking in relief than the figure of his father's spinster cousin, Martha Little; and now, returning home after many years in distant and exotic lands (during which, however, contact by correspondence had never been long interrupted), Warbeck could not imagine what change in either Martha Little's character or in that of Boston could have thrust her into even momentary prominence.

Even in his own large family connection, where, to his impatient youth, insignificance seemed endemic, Martha Little had always been the most effaced, contourless, colourless. Nor had any accidental advantage ever lifted her out of her congenital twilight: neither money, nor a bad temper, nor a knack with her clothes, nor any of those happy hazards— chance meetings with interesting people, the whim of a rich relation, the luck of ministering in a street accident to somebody with money to bequeath—which occasionally raise the most mediocre above their level. As far as Warbeck knew, Martha Little's insignificance had been unbroken, and accepted from the outset, by herself and all the family, as the medium she was fated to live in: as a person with weak eyes has to live with the blinds down, and be groped for by stumbling visitors.

The result had been that visitors were few; that Martha was more and more forgotten, or remembered only when she could temporarily replace a nursery governess on holiday, or "amuse" some fidgety child getting over an infantile malady.

Then the family took it for granted that she would step into the breach; but when the governess came back, or the child recovered, she disappeared, and was again immediately forgotten.

Once only, as far as Warbeck knew, had she over-stepped the line thus drawn for her; but that was so long ago that the occasion had already become a legend in his boyhood. It was when old Mrs. Warbeck, Henly's grandmother, gave the famous ball at which her eldest granddaughter came out; the ball discussed for weeks beforehand and months afterward from Chestnut Street to Bay State Road, not because there was anything exceptional about it (save perhaps its massive "handsomeness"), but simply because old Mrs. Warbeck had never given a ball before, and Boston had never supposed she ever would give one, and there had been hardly three months' time in which to get used to the idea that she was really going to—at last!

All this, naturally, had been agitating, not to say upsetting, to Beacon Street and Commonwealth Avenue, and absorbing to the whole immense Warbeck connection; the innumerable Pepperels, Sturlisses and Syngletons, the Graysons, Wrigglesworths and Perches—even to those remote and negligible Littles whose name gave so accurate a measure of their tribal standing. And to that ball there had been a question of asking, not of course *all* the Littles—that would have been really out of proportion—but two or three younger specimens of the tribe, whom circumstances had happened to bring into closer contact with the Warbeck group.

"And then," one of the married daughters had suggested toward the end of the consultation, "there's Martha Little—"

"*Martha?*" old Mrs. Warbeck echoed, incredulous and ironic, as much as to say: "The name's a slip of the tongue, of course; but whom *did* you mean, my dear, when you said 'Martha'?"

But the married daughter had continued, though more doubtfully: "Well, mother, Martha does sometimes help us out of our difficulties. Last winter, you remember, when Maggie's baby had the chickenpox . . . and then, taking Sara's Charlotte three times a week to her drawing-class . . .

and you know, as you invite her to stay with you at Milton every summer when we're at the seaside. . ."

"Ah, you regard that as helping you out of a difficulty?" Mrs. Warbeck drily interposed.

"No, mother, not a difficulty, of course. But it does make us feel so *safe* to know that Martha's with you. And when she hears of the ball she might expect—"

"Expect to *come*?" questioned Mrs. Warbeck.

"Oh, no—how absurd! Only to be invited . . ." the daughters chorussed in reply.

"She'd like to show the invitation at her boarding-house. . ."

"She hasn't many pleasures, poor thing. . ."

"Well, but," the old lady insisted, sticking to her point, "if I did invite her, would she come?"

"To a ball? What an idea!" Martha Little at a ball! Daughters and daughters-in-law laughed. It was really too absurd. But they all had their little debts to settle with Martha Little, and the opportunity was too good to be missed. On the strength of their joint assurances that no risk could possibly be incurred, old Mrs. Warbeck sent the invitation.

The night of the ball came; and so did Martha Little. She was among the first to arrive, and she stayed till the last candle was blown out. The entertainment remained for many years memorable in the annals of Beacon Street, and also in the Warbeck family history, since it was the occasion of Sara's eldest engaging herself to the second of Jake Wrigglesworth's boys (now, Warbeck reflected, himself a grizzled grandparent), and of Phil Syngleton's falling in love with the second Grayson girl; but beyond and above these events towered the formidable fact of Martha Little's one glaring indelicacy. Like Mrs. Warbeck's ball, it was never repeated. Martha retired once more into the twilight in which she belonged, emerging from it, as of old, only when some service was to be rendered somewhere in the many-branched family connection. But the episode of the ball remained fresh in every memory. Martha Little had been invited—*and she had come!* Henly Warbeck, as a little boy, had often heard his aunts describe her appearance: the prim black silk, the antiquated seed-pearls and lace mittens, the obvious "front", more tightly crimped than usual;

how she had pranced up the illuminated stairs, an absurd velvet reticule over her wrist, greeted her mighty kinswoman on the landing, and complacently mingled with the jewelled and feathered throng under the wax candles of the many chandeliers, while Mrs. Warbeck muttered to her daughters in a withering aside: *"I never should have thought it of Martha Little!"*

The escapade had done Martha Little more harm than good. The following summer Mrs. Warbeck had chosen one of her own granddaughters to keep her company at Milton when the family went to the seaside. It was hoped that this would make Martha realize her fatal error; and it did. And though the following year, at the urgent suggestion of the granddaughter chosen to replace her, she was received back into grace, and had what she called her "lovely summer outing" at Milton, there was certainly a shade of difference in her subsequent treatment. The younger granddaughters especially resented the fact that old Mrs. Warbeck had decided never to give another ball; and the old lady was fond of repeating (before Martha Little) that no, really, she couldn't; the family connection was *too large*—she hadn't room for them all. When the girls wanted to dance, their mothers must hire a public room; at her age Mrs. Warbeck couldn't be subjected to the fatigue, and the—the over-crowding.

Martha Little took the hint. As the grand-children grew up and married, her services were probably less often required, and by the time that Henly Warbeck had graduated from the Harvard Law School, and begun his life of distant wanderings, she had vanished into a still deeper twilight. Only once or twice, when some member of the tribe had run across Henly abroad, had Martha's name been mentioned. "Oh, she's as dull as Martha Little," one contemptuous cousin had said of somebody; and the last mention of her had been when Warbeck's sister, Mrs. Pepperel—the one to whom he was now returning—had mentioned, years ago, that a remote Grayson cousin, of the Frostingham branch, had bequeathed to Martha his little house at Frostingham—"so that now she's off our minds." And out of our memories, the speaker might have added; for though Frostingham is only a few miles from Boston it was not likely that many visitors would find their way to Martha Little's door.

No; the allusion in this letter of Mrs. Pepperel's remained cryptic to the returning traveller. As the train approached Boston, he pulled it from his pocket, and re-read it again. "Luckily you'll get here in good time for Martha Little's birthday," Mrs. Pepperel said.

The train was slowing down. "Frosting*ham*," the conductor shouted, stressing the last syllable in the old Boston way. "Thank heaven," Warbeck thought, "nothing ever really changes in Boston!"

A newsboy came through the Pullman with the evening papers. Warbeck unfolded one and read on the first page: "Frostingham preparing to celebrate Miss Martha Little's hundredth birthday." And underneath: "Frostingham's most distinguished centenarian chats with representative of *Transcript*." But the train was slowing down again—and here was Boston. Warbeck thrust the paper into his suit-case, bewildered yet half-understanding. Where else in the world but in Boston would the fact of having lived to be a hundred lift even a Martha Little into the lime-light? Ah, no; Boston forgot nothing, altered nothing. With a swelling heart the penitent exile sprang out, and was folded to the breasts of a long line of Warbecks and Pepperels, all of whom congratulated him on having arrived from the ends of the earth in time for Martha Little's birthday.

II

That night after dinner, Warbeck leaned back at ease in the pleasant dining-room of the old Pepperel house in Chestnut Street. The Copley portraits looked down familiarly from the walls, the old Pepperel Madeira circulated about the table. (In New York, thought Warbeck, Copleys and Madeiras, if there had been any, would both have been sold long since.)

The atmosphere was warm to the returning wanderer. It was pleasant to see about him the animated replicas of the Copleys on the walls, and to listen again to the local intonations, with the funny stress on the last syllable. His unmarried Pepperel nieces were fresh and good-looking; and the youngest, Lyddy, judging from her photograph, conspicuously handsome. But Lyddy was not there. Cousin Martha,

Mrs. Pepperel explained with a certain pride, was so fond of
Lyddy that the girl had to be constantly with her; and since
the preparations for the hundredth birthday had begun,
Lyddy had been virtually a prisoner at Frostingham. "Martha
wouldn't even let her off to come and dine with you tonight;
she says she's too nervous and excited to be left without
Lyddy. Lyddy is my most self-sacrificing child," Mrs. Pepperel
added complacently. One of the younger daughters laughed.

"Cousin Martha says she's going to leave Lyddy her seed-
pearls!"

"Priscilla—!" her mother rebuked her.

"Well, mother, they *are* beauties."

"I should say they were," Mrs. Pepperel bridled. "The old
Wrigglesworth seed-pearls—simply priceless. Martha's been
offered anything for them! All I can say is, if my child gets
them, she's deserved it."

Warbeck reflected. "Were they the funny old ornaments
that everybody laughed at when Martha wore them at
Grandma Warbeck's famous ball?"

His sister wrinkled her brows. "That wonderful ball of
Grandma's? Did Martha wear them there, I wonder—all
those centuries ago? I suppose then that nobody appreciated
them," she murmured.

Warbeck felt as if he were in a dream in which everything
happens upside-down. He was listening to his sister's familiar
kind of family anecdote, told in familiar words and in a familiar setting; but the Family Tyrant, once named with mingled
awe and pride, was no longer the all-powerful Grandma
Warbeck of his childhood, but her effaced imperceptible victim, Martha Little. Warbeck listened sympathetically, yet he
felt an underlying constraint. His sister obviously thought he
lacked interest in the Frostingham celebrations, and even her
husband, whose mental processes were so slow and subter-
ranean that they never altered his motionless countenance,
was heard to mutter: "Well, I don't suppose many families
can produce a brace of centenarians in one year."

"A brace—?" Warbeck laughed, while the nieces giggled,
and their mother looked suddenly grave.

"You know, Grayson, I've never approved of the Perches
forcing themselves in." She turned to Warbeck. "You've been

away so long that you won't understand; but I do think it shows a lack of delicacy in the Perches."

"Why, what have they done?" Warbeck asked; while the nieces' giggles grew uncontrollable.

"Dragged an old Perch great-uncle out of goodness knows where, on the pretext that *he's* a hundred too. Of course we never heard a word of it till your aunts and I decided to do something appropriate about Martha Little. And how do we know he *is* a hundred?"

"Sara!" her husband interjected.

"Well, I think we ought to have asked for an affidavit before a notary. Crowding in at the eleventh hour! Why, Syngleton Perch doesn't even live in Massachusetts. Why don't they have *their* centenary in Rhode Island? Because they know nobody'd go to it—that's why!"

"Sara, the excitement's been too much for you," said Mr. Pepperel judicially.

"Well, I believe it will be, if this sort of thing goes on. Girls, are you sure there are programmes enough? Come— we'd better go up to the drawing-room and go over the list again." She turned affectionately to her brother. "It'll make all the difference to Martha, your being here. She was so excited when she heard you were coming. You've got to sit on the platform next to her—or next but one. Of course she must be between the Senator and the Bishop. Syngleton Perch wanted to crowd into the third place; but it's yours, Martha says; and of course when Martha says a thing, that settles it!"

"Medes and Persians," muttered Mr. Pepperel, with a wink which did not displace his features; but his wife interposed: "Grayson, you know I hate your saying disrespectful things about Martha!"

Warbeck went to bed full of plans for the next day: old friends to be looked up, the Museums to be seen, and a tramp out on the Mill Dam, down the throat of a rousing Boston east wind. But these invigorating plans were shattered by an early message from Frostingham. Cousin Martha Little expected Warbeck to come and see her; he was to lunch early and be at Frostingham at two sharp. And he must not fail to be punctual, for before her afternoon nap cousin Martha was to have a last fitting of her dress for the ceremony.

"You'd think it was her wedding dress!" Warbeck ventured jocosely; but Mrs. Pepperel received the remark without a smile. "Martha is *very* wonderful," she murmured; and her brother acquiesced: "She must be."

At two sharp his car drew up before the little old Grayson house. On the way out to Frostingham the morning papers had shown him photographs of its pilastered front, and a small figure leaning on a stick between the elaborate door-lights. "Two Relics of a Historic Past," the headline ran.

Warbeck, guided by the radiant Lyddy, was led into a small square parlour furnished with the traditional Copleys and mahogany. He perceived that old Grayson's dingy little house had been an unsuspected treasury of family relics; and enthroned among them sat the supreme relic, the Crown Jewel of the clan.

"You don't recognize your cousin Martha!" shrilled a small reedy voice, and a mummied hand shot out of its lace ruffles with a slight upward tilt which Warbeck took as hint to salute it. The hand tasted like an old brown glove that had been kept in a sandal-wood box.

"Of course I know you, cousin Martha. You're not changed the least little bit!"

She lifted from her ruffles a small mottled face like a fruit just changing into a seed-pod. Her expression was obviously resentful. "Not changed? Then you haven't noticed the new way I do my hair?"

The challenge disconcerted Warbeck. "Well, you know, it's a long time since we met—going on for thirty years," he bantered.

"Thirty years?" She wrinkled her brows. "When I was as young as that I suppose I still wore a pompadour!"

When she was as young—as seventy! Warbeck felt like a gawky school-boy. He was at a loss what to say next; but the radiant Lyddy gave him his clue. "Cousin Martha was so delighted when she heard you were coming all the way from Peru on purpose for her Birthday." Her eyes met his with such a look of liquid candour that he saw she believed in the legend herself.

"Well, I don't suppose many of the family have come from farther off than I have," he boasted hypocritically.

Miss Little tilted up her chin again. "Did you fly?" she snapped; and without waiting for his answer: "I'm going to fly this summer. I wanted to go up before my birthday; it would have looked well in the papers. But the weather's been too unsettled."

It would have looked well in the papers! Warbeck listened to her, stupefied. Was it the old Martha Little speaking? There was something changed in Boston, after all. But she began to glance nervously toward the door. "Lyddy, I think I heard the bell."

"I'll go and see, cousin Martha."

Miss Little sank back into her cushions with a satisfied smile. "These reporters—!"

"Ah—you think it's an interview?"

She pursed up her unsteady slit of a mouth. "As if I hadn't told them everything already! It's all coming out in the papers tomorrow. Haven't touched wine or black coffee for forty years. . . Light massage every morning; very light supper at six. . . I cleaned out the canary's cage myself every day till last December. . . Oh, and I *love* my Sunday sermon on the wireless. . . But they won't leave a poor old woman in peace. 'Miss Little, won't you give us your views on President Coolidge—or on companionate marriage?' I suppose this one wants to force himself in for the rehearsal."

"The rehearsal?"

She pursed up her mouth again. "Sara Pepperel didn't tell you? Such featherheads, all those Pepperels! Even Lyddy— though she's a good child. . . I'm to try on my dress at three; and after that, just a little informal preparation for the ceremony. The Frostingham selectmen are to present me with a cane . . . a gold-headed cane with an inscription . . . *Lyddy!*" Her thread of a voice rose in a sudden angry pipe.

Lyddy thrust in a flushed and anxious face. "Oh, cousin Martha—"

"Well, *is* it a reporter? What paper? Tell him, if he'll promise to sit perfectly quiet. . ."

"It's not a reporter, cousin Martha. It's—it's cousin Syngleton Perch. He says he wants to pay you his respects:

and he thinks he ought to take part in the rehearsal. Now please don't excite yourself, cousin Martha!"

"Excite myself, child? Syngleton Perch can't steal my birthday, can he? If he chooses to assist at it—after all, the Perches are our own people; his mother was a Wrigglesworth." Miss Little drew herself up by the arms of her chair. "Show your cousin Syngleton in, my dear."

On the threshold a middle-aged motherly voice said, rather loudly: "This way, uncle Syngleton. You won't take my arm? Well, then put your stick *there*; so—this way; careful . . ." and there tottered in, projected forward by a series of jaunty jerks, and the arm of his unseen guide, a small old gentleman in a short pea-jacket, with a round withered head buried in layers of woollen scarf, and eyes hidden behind a huge pair of black spectacles.

"Where's my old friend Martha Little? Now, then, Marty, don't you try and hide yourself away from young Syngleton. Ah, there she is! *I* see her!" cousin Syngleton rattled out in a succession of parrot-like ejaculations, as his elderly Antigone and the young Lyddy steered him cautiously toward Miss Little's throne.

From it she critically observed the approach of the rival centenarian; and as he reached her side, and stretched out his smartly-gloved hand, she dropped hers into it with a faint laugh. "Well, you really *are* a hundred, Syngleton Perch; there's no doubt about that," she said in her high chirp. "And I wonder whether you haven't postponed your anniversary a year or two?" she added with a caustic touch, and a tilt of her chin toward Warbeck.

III

Transporting centenarians from one floor to another was no doubt a delicate business, for the vigilant Lyddy had staged the trying-on of the ceremonial dress in the dining-room, where the rehearsal was also to take place. Miss Little withdrew, and cousin Syngleton Perch's watchful relative, having installed him in an armchair facing Warbeck's as carefully as if she had been balancing a basket of eggs on a picket fence, slipped off with an apologetic smile to assist at the trying-on. "I know you'll take care of him, cousin Henly," she murmured in a last appeal; and added, bending to Warbeck's ear: "Please remember he's a little deaf; and don't let him get too excited talking about his love-affairs."

Uncle Syngleton, wedged in tightly with cushions, and sustained by a footstool, peered doubtfully at Warbeck as the latter held out his cigarette-case. "Tobacco? Well . . . look here, young man, what paper do you represent?" he asked, his knotty old hand yearningly poised above the coveted cigarette.

Warbeck explained in a loud voice that he was not a journalist, but a member of the family; but Mr. Perch shook his head incredulously. "That's what they all say; worming themselves in everywhere. Plain truth is, I never saw you before, nor you me. But see here; we may have to wait an hour while that young charmer gets into her party togs, and I don't know's I can hold out that long without a puff of tobacco." He shot a wrinkled smile at Warbeck. "Time was when I'd'a been in there myself, assisting at the dish-abille." (He pronounced the first syllable *dish*.) A look of caution replaced his confidential smirk. "Well, young man, I suppose what you want is my receipt for keeping hale and hearty up to the century line. But there's nothing new about it: it's just the golden rule of good behaviour that our mothers taught us in the nursery. No wine, no tobacco, no wom—. Well," he broke off, with a yearning smile at the cigarette-case, "I don't mind if I do. Got a light, young gentleman? Though if I *was* to assist at an undressing, I don't say," he added meditatively, "that it'd be Martha Little's I'd choose. I remember her when she warn't over thirty—too much like a hygienic cigarette even then, for my fancy. De-nicotinized, I call her. Well, I like the unexpurgated style better." He held out his twitching hand to Warbeck's lighter, and inserted a cigarette between his purplish lips. "Some punch in that! Only don't you give me away, will you? Not in the papers, I mean. Remember old Syngleton Perch's slogan: 'Live straight and you'll live long. No wine, no tobacco, no wom—'." Again he broke off, and thumped his crumpled fist excitedly against the chair-arm. "Damn it, sir, I never *can* finish that lie, somehow! Old Syngleton a vestal? Not if I know anything about him!"

*

The door opened, and Lyddy and the motherly Antigone showed their flushed faces. "Now then, uncle Syngleton—all ready!"

They were too much engrossed to notice Warbeck, but he saw that his help was welcome, for extricating Syngleton from his armchair was like hooking up a broken cork which, at each prod, slips down farther into the neck of the bottle. Once on his legs he goose-stepped valiantly forward; but until he had been balanced on them he tended to fold up at the very moment when his supporters thought they could prudently release him.

The transit accomplished, Warbeck found himself in a room from which the dining-table had been removed to make way for an improvised platform supporting a row of armchairs. In the central armchair Martha Little, small and hieratic, sat enthroned. About her billowed the rich folds of a silvery shot-silk, and the Wrigglesworth seed-pearls hung over her hollow chest and depended from her dusky withered ears. A row of people sat facing her, at the opposite end of the room, and Warbeck noticed that two or three already had their pens in leash above open notebooks. A strange young woman of fashionable silhouette was stooping over the shot-silk draperies and ruffling them with a professional touch. "Isn't she too old-world for anything? Just the Martha Washington note: isn't it lovely, with her pearls? Please note: *The Wrigglesworth pearls*, Miss Lusky," she recommended to a zealous reportress with suspended pen.

"Now, whatever you do, don't shake me!" snapped the shot-silk divinity, as Syngleton and his supporters neared the platform. ("It's the powder in her hair she's nervous about," Lyddy whispered to Warbeck.)

The business of raising the co-divinity to her side was at once ticklish and laborious, for Mr. Perch resented feminine assistance in the presence of strange men, and Warbeck, even with the bungling support of one of the journalists, found it difficult to get his centenarian relative hoisted to the platform. Any attempt to lift him caused his legs to shoot upward, and to steady and direct this levitating tendency required an experience in which both assistants were lacking.

"*There!*" his household Antigone intervened, seizing one

ankle while Lyddy clutched the other; and thus ballasted
Syngleton Perch recovered his powers of self-direction and
made for the armchair on Miss Little's right. At his approach
she uttered a shrill cry and tried to raise herself from her seat.

"No, no! This is the Bishop's!" she protested, defending
the chair with her mittened hand.

"Oh, my—there go all the folds of her skirt," wailed the
dress-maker from the background.

Syngleton Perch stood on the platform and his bullet head
grew purple. "Can't stand—got to sit down or keep going,"
he snapped.

Martha Little subsided majestically among her disordered
folds. "Well—keep going!" she decreed.

"Oh, cousin Martha," Lyddy murmured.

"Well, what of cousin Martha? It's *my* rehearsal, isn't it?"
the lady retorted, like a child whimpering for a toy.

"Cousin Martha—cousin *Martha*!" Lyddy whispered,
while Syngleton, with flickering legs, protested: "Don't I belong anywhere in this show?" and Warbeck caught Lyddy's
warning murmur: "Don't forget, cousin Martha, *his mother
was a Wrigglesworth!*"

As if by magic Miss Little's exasperation gave way to a resigned grimace. "*He* says so," she muttered sulkily; but the
appeal to the great ancestral name had not been vain, and
she suffered her rival to be established in the armchair just
beyond the Bishop's, while his guide, hovering over his
shoulder, announced to the journalists: "Mr. Syngleton
Perch, of South Perch, Rhode Island, whose hundredth birthday will be celebrated with that of his cousin Miss Little tomorrow—"

"H'm—*tomorrow!*" Miss Little suddenly exclaimed, again
attempting to rise from her throne; while Syngleton's staccato
began to unroll the automatic phrase: "I suppose you young
men all want to know my receipt for keeping hale and hearty
up to the century line. Well, there's nothing new about it: it's
just the golden rule . . . the . . . what the devil's *that?*" he
broke off with a jerk of his chin toward the door.

Warbeck saw that an object had been handed into the room
by a maid, and was being passed from hand to hand up to the
platform. "Oh," Lyddy exclaimed breathlessly, "of course!

It's the ebony cane! The Selectmen have sent it up for cousin Martha to try today, so that she'll be sure it was just right for her to lean on when she walks out of the Town Hall to-morrow after the ceremony. Look what a beauty it is—you'll let these gentlemen look at it, won't you, cousin Martha?"

"If they can look at me I suppose they can look at my cane," said Miss Little imperially, while the commemorative stick was passed about the room amid admiring exclamations, and attempts to decipher its laudatory inscription. " 'Offered to Frostingham's most beloved and distinguished citizen, Martha Wrigglesworth Little, in commemoration of the hundredth anniversary of her birth, by her friends the Mayor and Selectmen' . . . very suitable, very interesting," an elderly cousin read aloud with proper emotion, while Mr. Perch was heard to enquire anxiously: "Isn't there anything about me on that cane?" and his companion reassured him: "Of course South Perch means to offer you one of your very own when we go home."

Finally the coveted object was restored to Miss Little, who, straightening herself with a supreme effort, sat resting both hands on the gold crutch while Lyddy hailed the approach of imaginary dignitaries with the successive announcements: "The Bishop—the Mayor. . . But, no, they'd better be seated before you arrive, hadn't they, cousin Martha? And exactly *when* is the cane to be presented? Oh, well, we'll settle all the details to-morrow . . . the main thing now is the stepping down from the platform and walking out of the Hall, isn't it? Miss Lusky, careful, please. . . Gentlemen, will you all move your chairs back? . . . Uncle Henly," she appealed to Warbeck, "perhaps you'll be kind enough to act as Mayor, and give your arm to cousin Martha? Ready, cousin Martha? So—"

But as she was about to raise Miss Little from her seat, and hook her securely onto Warbeck's arm, a cry between a sob and an expletive burst from the purple lips of cousin Syngleton.

"Why can't *I* be the Mayor—ain't I got any rights in this damned show?" he burst out passionately, his legs jerking upward as he attempted to raise himself on his elbows.

His Antigone intervened with a reproachful murmur.

"Why, uncle Syngleton, what in the world are you thinking of? You can't act as anybody but *yourself* tomorrow! But I'm going to be the Bishop now, and give you my arm—there, like this. . ."

Miss Little, who had just gained her feet, pressed heavily on Warbeck's arm in her effort to jerk around toward Mr. Perch. "Oh, he's going to take the Bishop's arm, is he? Well, the Bishop had better look out, or he'll take his seat too," she chuckled ironically.

Cousin Syngleton turned a deeper purple. "Oh, I'll take his seat too, will I? Well, why not? Isn't this my anniversary as much as it is yours, Martha Little? I suppose you think I'd better follow after you and carry your train, eh?"

Miss Little drew herself up to a height that seemed to over-shadow every one around her. Warbeck felt her shaking on his arm like a withered leaf, but her lips were dangerously merry.

"No; I think you'd better push the Mayor out of the way and give *me* your arm, Syngleton Perch," she flung back gaily.

"Well, why not?" Mr. Perch rejoined, his innocent smile meeting her perfidious one; and some one among the look-ers-on was imprudent enough to exclaim: "Oh, wouldn't that be too lovely!"

"Oh, uncle Syngleton," Lyddy appealed to him—"do you really suppose you *could*?"

"Could—could—could, young woman? Who says I can't, I'd like to know?" uncle Syngleton sputtered, his arms and legs gyrating vehemently toward Miss Little, who now stood quite still on Warbeck's arm, the cane sustaining her, and her fixed smile seeming to invite her rival's approach.

"An interesting experiment," Warbeck heard some one mutter in the background, and Miss Little's head turned in the direction of the speaker. "This is only a rehearsal," she declared incisively.

She remained motionless and untrembling while the Antigone and Lyddy guided cousin Syngleton precariously toward her; but just as Warbeck thought she was about to de-tach her hand from his arm, and transfer her frail weight to Mr. Perch's, she made an unexpected movement. Its immedi-ate result—Warbeck could never say how—was to shoot for-ward the famous ebony stick which her abrupt gesture (was it unconsciously?) drove directly into the path of uncle Syngleton. In another instant—but one instant too late for rescue—Warbeck saw the stick entangled in the old man's wavering feet, and beheld him shoot wildly upward, and then fall over with a crash. Every one in the room gathered about with agitated questions and exclamations, struggling to lift him to his feet; only Miss Little continued to stand apart, her countenance unmoved, her aged fingers still imbedded in Warbeck's arm.

The old man, prone and purple, was being cautiously lifted down from the platform, while the bewildered spectators parted, awe-struck, to make way for his frightened bearers. Warbeck followed their movements with alarm; then he turned anxiously toward the frail figure on his arm. How would she bear the shock, he asked himself, with a leap of the imagination which seemed to lay her also prone at his feet. But she stood upright, unmoved, and Warbeck met her resolute eyes with a start, and saw in their depths a century of slow revenge.

"Oh, cousin Martha—cousin *Martha*," he breathed, in a whisper of mingled terror and admiration. . .

"Well, what? I told you it was only a rehearsal," said Martha Little, with her ancient smile.

All Souls'

QUEER and inexplicable as the business was, on the surface it appeared fairly simple—at the time, at least; but with the passing of years, and owing to there not having been a single witness of what happened except Sara Clayburn herself, the stories about it have become so exaggerated, and often so ridiculously inaccurate, that it seems necessary that some one connected with the affair, though not actually present—I repeat that when it happened my cousin was (or thought she was) quite alone in her house—should record the few facts actually known.

In those days I was often at Whitegates (as the place had always been called)—I was there, in fact, not long before, and almost immediately after, the strange happenings of those thirty-six hours. Jim Clayburn and his widow were both my cousins, and because of that, and of my intimacy with them, both families think I am more likely than anybody else to be able to get at the facts, as far as they can be called facts, and as anybody can get at them. So I have written down, as clearly as I could, the gist of the various talks I had with cousin Sara, when she could be got to talk—it wasn't often—about what occurred during that mysterious week-end.

I read the other day in a book by a fashionable essayist that ghosts went out when electric light came in. What nonsense! The writer, though he is fond of dabbling, in a literary way, in the supernatural, hasn't even reached the threshold of his subject. As between turreted castles patrolled by headless victims with clanking chains, and the comfortable suburban house with a refrigerator and central heating where you feel, as soon as you're in it, *that there's something wrong*, give me the latter for sending a chill down the spine! And, by the way, haven't you noticed that it's generally not the high-strung and imaginative who see ghosts, but the calm matter-of-fact people who don't believe in them, and are sure they wouldn't mind if they did see one? Well, that was the case with Sara Clayburn and her house. The house, in spite of its age—it was built, I believe, about 1780—was open, airy, high-ceilinged, with electricity, central heating and all the modern appliances; and its mistress was—well, very much like her house. And, anyhow, this isn't exactly a ghost-story, and I've dragged in the analogy only as a way of showing you what kind of woman my cousin was, and how unlikely it would have seemed that what happened at Whitegates should have happened just there—or to her.

When Jim Clayburn died the family all thought that, as the couple had no children, his widow would give up Whitegates and move either to New York or Boston—for being of good Colonial stock, with many relatives and friends, she would have found a place ready for her in either. But Sally Clayburn seldom did what other people expected, and in this case she did exactly the contrary: she stayed at Whitegates.

"What, turn my back on the old house—tear up all the family roots, and go and hang myself up in a bird-cage flat in one of those new sky-scrapers in Lexington Avenue, with a bunch of chickweed and a cuttle-fish to replace my good Connecticut mutton? No, thank you. Here I belong, and here I stay till my executors hand the place over to Jim's next of kin—that stupid fat Presley boy. . . Well, don't let's talk about him. But I tell you what—I'll keep him out of here as long as I can." And she did—for being still in the early fifties when her husband died, and a muscular, resolute figure of a woman, she was more than a match for the fat Presley boy, and attended his funeral a few years ago, in correct mourning, with a faint smile under her veil.

Whitegates was a pleasant hospitable-looking house, on a height overlooking the stately windings of the Connecticut river; but it was five or six miles from Norrington, the nearest town, and its situation would certainly have seemed remote and lonely to modern servants. Luckily, however, Sara Clayburn had inherited from her mother-in-law two or three old stand-bys who seemed as much a part of the family tradition as the roof they lived under; and I never heard of her having any trouble in her domestic arrangements.

The house, in Colonial days, had been four-square, with four spacious rooms on the ground-floor, an oak-floored hall dividing them, the usual kitchen-extension at the back, and a good attic under the roof. But Jim's grand-parents, when interest in the "Colonial" began to revive, in the early 'eighties, had added two wings, at right angles to the south front, so that the old "circle" before the front door became a grassy court, enclosed on three sides, with a big elm in the middle. Thus the house was turned into a roomy dwelling, in which the last three generations of Clayburns had exercised a large hospitality; but the architect had respected the character of the old house, and the enlargement made it more comfortable without lessening its simplicity. There was a lot of land about it, and Jim Clayburn, like his fathers before him, farmed it, not without profit, and played a considerable and respected part in state politics. The Clayburns were always spoken of as a "good influence" in the county, and the townspeople were glad when they learned that Sara did not mean to desert the place—"though it must be lonesome, winters, living all alone up there atop of that hill", they remarked as the days shortened, and the first snow began to pile up under the quadruple row of elms along the common.

Well, if I've given you a sufficiently clear idea of Whitegates and the Clayburns—who shared with their old house a sort of reassuring orderliness and dignity—I'll efface myself, and tell the tale, not in my cousin's words, for they were too confused and fragmentary, but as I built it up gradually out of her half-avowals and nervous reticences. If the thing happened at all—and I must leave you to judge of that—I think it must have happened in this way. . .

I

The morning had been bitter, with a driving sleet—though it was only the last day of October—but after lunch a watery sun showed for a while through banked-up woolly clouds, and tempted Sara Clayburn out. She was an energetic walker, and given, at that season, to tramping three or four miles along the valley road, and coming back by way of Shaker's wood. She had made her usual round, and was following the main drive to the house when she overtook a plainly dressed woman walking in the same direction. If the scene had not

been so lonely—the way to Whitegates at the end of an autumn day was not a frequented one—Mrs. Clayburn might
not have paid any attention to the woman, for she was in no
way noticeable; but when she caught up with the intruder my
cousin was surprised to find that she was a stranger—for the
mistress of Whitegates prided herself on knowing, at least by
sight, most of her country neighbours. It was almost dark,
and the woman's face was hardly visible; but Mrs. Clayburn
told me she recalled her as middle-aged, plain and rather pale.

Mrs. Clayburn greeted her, and then added: "You're going
to the house?"

"Yes, ma'am," the woman answered, in a voice that the
Connecticut valley in old days would have called "foreign",
but that would have been unnoticed by ears used to the modern multiplicity of tongues. "No, I couldn't say where she
came from," Sara always said. "What struck me as queer was
that I didn't know her."

She asked the woman, politely, what she wanted, and the
woman answered: "Only to see one of the girls." The answer
was natural enough, and Mrs. Clayburn nodded and turned
off from the drive to the lower part of the gardens, so that she
saw no more of the visitor then or afterward. And, in fact, a
half hour later something happened which put the stranger
entirely out of her mind. The brisk and light-footed Mrs.
Clayburn, as she approached the house, slipped on a frozen
puddle, turned her ankle and lay suddenly helpless.

Price, the butler, and Agnes, the dour old Scottish maid
whom Sara had inherited from her mother-in-law, of course
knew exactly what to do. In no time they had their mistress
stretched out on a lounge, and Dr. Selgrove had been called
up from Norrington. When he arrived, he ordered Mrs.
Clayburn to bed, did the necessary examining and bandaging,
and shook his head over her ankle, which he feared was frac-
tured. He thought, however, that if she would swear not to
get up, or even shift the position of her leg, he could spare
her the discomfort of putting it in plaster. Mrs. Clayburn
agreed, the more promptly as the doctor warned her that any
rash movement would prolong her immobility. Her quick
imperious nature made the prospect trying, and she was

annoyed with herself for having been so clumsy. But the mischief was done, and she immediately thought what an opportunity she would have for going over her accounts and catching up with her correspondence. So she settled down resignedly in her bed.

"And you won't miss much, you know, if you have to stay there a few days. It's beginning to snow, and it looks as if we were in for a good spell of it," the doctor remarked, glancing through the window as he gathered up his implements. "Well, we don't often get snow here as early as this; but winter's got to begin sometime," he concluded philosophically. At the door he stopped to add: "You don't want me to send up a nurse from Norrington? Not to nurse you, you know; there's nothing much to do till I see you again. But this is a pretty lonely place when the snow begins, and I thought maybe—"

Sara Clayburn laughed. "Lonely? With my old servants? You forget how many winters I've spent here alone with them. Two of them were with me in my mother-in-law's time."

"That's so," Dr. Selgrove agreed. "You're a good deal luckier than most people, that way. Well, let me see; this is Saturday. We'll have to let the inflammation go down before we can X-ray you. Monday morning, first thing, I'll be here with the X-ray man. If you want me sooner, call me up." And he was gone.

II

The foot, at first, had not been very painful; but toward the small hours Mrs. Clayburn began to suffer. She was a bad patient, like most healthy and active people. Not being used to pain she did not know how to bear it; and the hours of wakefulness and immobility seemed endless. Agnes, before leaving her, had made everything as comfortable as possible. She had put a jug of lemonade within reach, and had even (Mrs. Clayburn thought it odd afterward) insisted on bringing in a tray with sandwiches and a thermos of tea. "In case you're hungry in the night, madam."

"Thank you; but I'm never hungry in the night. And I certainly shan't be tonight—only thirsty. I think I'm feverish."

"Well, there's the lemonade, madam."

"That will do. Take the other things away, please." (Sara had always hated the sight of unwanted food "messing about" in her room.)

"Very well, madam. Only you might—"

"Please take it away," Mrs. Clayburn repeated irritably.

"Very good, madam." But as Agnes went out, her mistress heard her set the tray down softly on a table behind the screen which shut off the door.

"Obstinate old goose!" she thought, rather touched by the old woman's insistence.

Sleep, once it had gone, would not return, and the long black hours moved more and more slowly. How late the dawn came in November! "If only I could move my leg," she grumbled.

She lay still and strained her ears for the first steps of the servants. Whitegates was an early house, its mistress setting the example; it would surely not be long now before one of the women came. She was tempted to ring for Agnes, but refrained. The woman had been up late, and this was Sunday morning, when the household was always allowed a little extra time. Mrs. Clayburn reflected restlessly: "I was a fool not to let her leave the tea beside the bed, as she wanted to. I wonder if I could get up and get it?" But she remembered the doctor's warning, and dared not move. Anything rather than risk prolonging her imprisonment. . .

Ah, there was the stable-clock striking. How loud it sounded in the snowy stillness! One—two—three—four—five. . .

What? Only five? Three hours and a quarter more before she could hope to hear the door-handle turned. . . After a while she dozed off again, uncomfortably.

Another sound aroused her. Again the stable-clock. She listened. But the room was still in deep darkness, and only six strokes fell. . . She thought of reciting something to put her to sleep; but she seldom read poetry, and being naturally a good sleeper, she could not remember any of the usual devices against insomnia. The whole of her leg felt like lead now. The bandages had grown terribly tight—her ankle must have swollen. . . She lay staring at the dark windows, watching for the first glimmer of dawn. At last she saw a pale filter of day-light through the shutters. One by one the objects between the bed and the window recovered first their outline, then their bulk, and seemed to be stealthily re-grouping them-selves, after goodness knows what secret displacements during the night. Who that has lived in an old house could possibly believe that the furniture in it stays still all night? Mrs. Clayburn almost fancied she saw one little slender-legged table slipping hastily back into its place.

"It knows Agnes is coming, and it's afraid," she thought whimsically. Her bad night must have made her imaginative, for such nonsense as that about the furniture had never oc-curred to her before. . . .

At length, after hours more, as it seemed, the stable-clock struck eight. Only another quarter of an hour. She watched the hand moving slowly across the face of the little clock be-side her bed. . . Ten minutes . . . five . . . only five! Agnes was as punctual as destiny . . . in two minutes now she would come. The two minutes passed, and she did not come. Poor Agnes—she had looked pale and tired the night before. She had overslept herself, no doubt—or perhaps she felt ill, and would send the housemaid to replace her. Mrs. Clayburn waited.

She waited half an hour; then she reached up to the bell at the head of the bed. Poor old Agnes—her mistress felt guilty about waking her. But Agnes did not appear—and after a considerable interval Mrs. Clayburn, now with a certain im-patience, rang again. She rang once; twice; three times—but still no one came.

Once more she waited; then she said to herself: "There must be something wrong with the electricity." Well—she could find out by switching on the bed-lamp at her elbow (how admirably the room was equipped with every practical appliance!). She switched it on—but no light came. Electric current cut off; and it was Sunday, and nothing could be done about it till the next morning. Unless it turned out to be just a burnt-out fuse, which Price could remedy. Well, in a mo-ment now some one would surely come to her door.

It was nine o'clock before she admitted to herself that something uncommonly strange must have happened in the house. She began to feel a nervous apprehension; but she was not the woman to encourage it. If only she had had the telephone put in her room, instead of out on the landing! She measured mentally the distance to be travelled, remembered Dr. Selgrove's admonition, and wondered if her broken ankle would carry her there. She dreaded the prospect of being put in plaster, but she had to get to the telephone, whatever happened.

She wrapped herself in her dressing-gown, found a walking stick, and resting heavily on it, dragged herself to the door. In her bedroom the careful Agnes had closed and fastened the shutters, so that it was not much lighter there than at dawn; but outside in the corridor the cold whiteness of the snowy morning seemed almost reassuring. Mysterious things—dreadful things—were associated with darkness; and here was the wholesome prosaic daylight come again to banish them. Mrs. Clayburn looked about her and listened. Silence. A deep nocturnal silence in that day-lit house, in which five people were presumably coming and going about their work. It was certainly strange. . . She looked out of the window, hoping to see some one crossing the court or coming along the drive. But no one was in sight, and the snow seemed to have the place to itself: a quiet steady snow. It was still falling, with a business-like regularity, muffling the outer world in layers on layers of thick white velvet, and intensifying the silence within. A noiseless world—were people so sure that absence of noise was what they wanted? Let them first try a lonely country-house in a November snow-storm!

She dragged herself along the passage to the telephone. When she unhooked the receiver she noticed that her hand trembled.

She rang up the pantry—no answer. She rang again. Silence—more silence! It seemed to be piling itself up like the snow on the roof and in the gutters. Silence. How many people that she knew had any idea what silence was—and how loud it sounded when you really listened to it?

Again she waited; then she rang up "Central". No answer. She tried three times. After that she tried the pantry again. . . The telephone was cut off, then; like the electric current. Who was at work downstairs, isolating her thus from the world? Her heart began to hammer. Luckily there was a chair near the telephone, and she sat down to recover her strength—or was it her courage?

Agnes and the housemaid slept in the nearest wing. She would certainly get as far as that when she had pulled herself together. Had she the courage—? Yes; of course she had. She had always been regarded as a plucky woman; and had so regarded herself. But this silence—

It occurred to her that by looking from the window of a neighbouring bathroom she could see the kitchen chimney. There ought to be smoke coming from it at that hour; and if there were she thought she would be less afraid to go on. She got as far as the bathroom and looking through the window saw that no smoke came from the chimney. Her sense of loneliness grew more acute. Whatever had happened below stairs must have happened before the morning's work had begun. The cook had not had time to light the fire, the other servants had not yet begun their round. She sank down on the nearest chair, struggling against her fears. What next would she discover if she carried on her investigations?

The pain in her ankle made progress difficult; but she was aware of it now only as an obstacle to haste. No matter what it cost her in physical suffering, she must find out what was happening below stairs—or had happened. But first she would go to the maid's room. And if that were empty—well, somehow she would have to get herself downstairs.

She limped along the passage, and on the way steadied herself by resting her hand on a radiator. It was stone-cold. Yet in that well-ordered house in winter the central heating, though damped down at night, was never allowed to go out, and by eight in the morning a mellow warmth pervaded the rooms. The icy chill of the pipes startled her. It was the chauffeur who looked after the heating—so he too was involved in the mystery, whatever it was, as well as the house-servants. But this only deepened the problem.

III

At Agnes's door Mrs. Clayburn paused and knocked. She expected no answer, and there was none. She opened the door and went in. The room was dark and very cold. She went to the window and flung back the shutters; then she looked slowly around, vaguely apprehensive of what she might see. The room was empty; but what frightened her was not so much its emptiness as its air of scrupulous and undisturbed order. There was no sign of any one having lately dressed in it—or undressed the night before. And the bed had not been slept in.

Mrs. Clayburn leaned against the wall for a moment; then she crossed the floor and opened the cupboard. That was where Agnes kept her dresses; and the dresses were there, neatly hanging in a row. On the shelf above were Agnes's few and unfashionable hats, re-arrangements of her mistress's old ones. Mrs. Clayburn, who knew them all, looked at the shelf, and saw that one was missing. And so was also the warm winter coat she had given to Agnes the previous winter.

The woman was out, then; had gone out, no doubt, the night before, since the bed was unslept in, the dressing and washing appliances untouched. Agnes, who never set foot out of the house after dark, who despised the movies as much as she did the wireless, and could never be persuaded that a little innocent amusement was a necessary element in life, had deserted the house on a snowy winter night, while her mistress lay upstairs, suffering and helpless! Why had she gone, and where had she gone? When she was undressing Mrs. Clayburn the night before, taking her orders, trying to make her more comfortable, was she already planning this mysterious nocturnal escape? Or had something—the mysterious and dreadful Something for the clue of which Mrs. Clayburn was still groping—occurred later in the evening, sending the maid downstairs and out of doors into the bitter night? Perhaps one of the men at the garage—where the chauffeur and gardener lived—had been suddenly taken ill, and some one had run up to the house for Agnes. Yes—that must be the explanation. . . Yet how much it left unexplained.

Next to Agnes's room was the linen-room; beyond that was the housemaid's door. Mrs. Clayburn went to it and knocked. "Mary!" No one answered, and she went in. The room was in the same immaculate order as her maid's, and here too the bed was unslept in, and there were no signs of dressing or

undressing. The two women had no doubt gone out together—gone where?

More and more the cold unanswering silence of the house
weighed down on Mrs. Clayburn. She had never thought of
it as a big house, but now, in this snowy winter light, it
seemed immense, and full of ominous corners around which
one dared not look.

Beyond the housemaid's room were the back-stairs. It was
the nearest way down, and every step that Mrs. Clayburn
took was increasingly painful; but she decided to walk slowly
back, the whole length of the passage, and go down by the
front stairs. She did not know why she did this; but she felt
that at the moment she was past reasoning, and had better
obey her instinct.

More than once she had explored the ground-floor alone in
the small hours, in search of unwonted midnight noises; but
now it was not the idea of noises that frightened her, but that
inexorable and hostile silence, the sense that the house had
retained in full daylight its nocturnal mystery, and was watching her as she was watching it; that in entering those empty
orderly rooms she might be disturbing some unseen confabu-
lation on which beings of flesh-and-blood had better not intrude.

The broad oak stairs were beautifully polished, and so slippery that she had to cling to the rail and let herself down
tread by tread. And as she descended, the silence descended
with her—heavier, denser, more absolute. She seemed to feel
its steps just behind her, softly keeping time with hers. It had
a quality she had never been aware of in any other silence, as
though it were not merely an absence of sound, a thin barrier
between the ear and the surging murmur of life just beyond,
but an impenetrable substance made out of the world-wide
cessation of all life and all movement.

Yes, that was what laid a chill on her: the feeling that there
was no limit to this silence, no outer margin, nothing beyond
it. By this time she had reached the foot of the stairs and was
limping across the hall to the drawing-room. Whatever she
found there, she was sure, would be mute and lifeless; but
what would it be? The bodies of her dead servants, mown
down by some homicidal maniac? And what if it were her

turn next—if he were waiting for her behind the heavy curtains of the room she was about to enter? Well, she must find
out—she must face whatever lay in wait. Not impelled by
bravery—the last drop of courage had oozed out of her—but
because anything, anything was better than to remain shut up
in that snow-bound house without knowing whether she was
alone in it or not. "I must find that out, I must find that out,"
she repeated to herself in a sort of meaningless sing-song.

The cold outer light flooded the drawing-room. The shutters had not been closed, nor the curtains drawn. She looked
about her. The room was empty, and every chair in its usual
place. Her armchair was pushed up by the chimney, and the
cold hearth was piled with the ashes of the fire at which she
had warmed herself before starting on her ill-fated walk. Even
her empty coffee cup stood on a table near the armchair. It
was evident that the servants had not been in the room since
she had left it the day before after luncheon. And suddenly
the conviction entered into her that, as she found the drawing-room, so she would find the rest of the house: cold, orderly—and empty. She would find nothing, she would find no
one. She no longer felt any dread of ordinary human dangers
lurking in those dumb spaces ahead of her. She knew she was
utterly alone under her own roof. She sat down to rest her
aching ankle, and looked slowly about her.

There were the other rooms to be visited, and she was determined to go through them all—but she knew in advance
that they would give no answer to her question. She knew it,
seemingly, from the quality of the silence which enveloped
her. There was no break, no thinnest crack in it anywhere. It
had the cold continuity of the snow which was still falling
steadily outside.

She had no idea how long she waited before nerving herself to continue her inspection. She no longer felt the pain in
her ankle, but was only conscious that she must not bear her
weight on it, and therefore moved very slowly, supporting
herself on each piece of furniture in her path. On the ground-
floor no shutter had been closed, no curtain drawn, and she
progressed without difficulty from room to room: the library,
her morning-room, the dining-room. In each of them, every
piece of furniture was in its usual place. In the dining-room,

the table had been laid for her dinner of the previous evening, and the candelabra, with candles unlit, stood reflected in the dark mahogany. She was not the kind of woman to nibble a poached egg on a tray when she was alone, but always came down to the dining-room, and had what she called a civilized meal.

The back premises remained to be visited. From the dining-room she entered the pantry, and there too everything was in irreproachable order. She opened the door and looked down the back passage with its neat linoleum floor-covering. The deep silence accompanied her; she still felt it moving watchfully at her side, as though she were its prisoner and it might throw itself upon her if she attempted to escape. She limped on toward the kitchen. That of course would be empty too, and immaculate. But she must see it.

She leaned a minute in the embrasure of a window in the passage. "It's like the Mary Celeste—a Mary Celeste on *terra firma*," she thought, recalling the unsolved sea-mystery of her childhood. "No one ever knew what happened on board the Mary Celeste. And perhaps no one will ever know what has happened here. Even I shan't know."

At the thought her latent fear seemed to take on a new quality. It was like an icy liquid running through every vein, and lying in a pool about her heart. She understood now that she had never before known what fear was, and that most of the people she had met had probably never known either. For this sensation was something quite different. . .

It absorbed her so completely that she was not aware how long she remained leaning there. But suddenly a new impulse pushed her forward, and she walked on toward the scullery. She went there first because there was a service-slide in the wall, through which she might peep into the kitchen without being seen; and some indefinable instinct told her that the kitchen held the clue to the mystery. She still felt strongly that whatever had happened in the house must have its source and centre in the kitchen.

In the scullery, as she had expected, everything was clean and tidy. Whatever had happened, no one in the house appeared to have been taken by surprise; there was nowhere any sign of confusion or disorder. "It looks as if they'd known beforehand, and put everything straight," she thought. She glanced at the wall facing the door, and saw that the slide was open. And then, as she was approaching it, the silence was broken. A voice was speaking in the kitchen— a man's voice, low but emphatic, and which she had never heard before.

She stood still, cold with fear. But this fear was again a different one. Her previous terrors had been speculative, conjectural, a ghostly emanation of the surrounding silence. This was a plain every-day dread of evil-doers. Oh, God, why had she not remembered her husband's revolver, which ever since his death had lain in a drawer in her room?

She turned to retreat across the smooth slippery floor but half-way her stick slipped from her, and crashed down on the tiles. The noise seemed to echo on and on through the emptiness, and she stood still, aghast. Now that she had betrayed her presence, flight was useless. Whoever was beyond the kitchen door would be upon her in a second. . .

But to her astonishment the voice went on speaking. It was as though neither the speaker nor his listeners had heard her. The invisible stranger spoke so low that she could not make out what he was saying, but the tone was passionately earnest, almost threatening. The next moment she realized that he was speaking in a foreign language, a language unknown to her. Once more her terror was surmounted by the urgent desire to know what was going on, so close to her yet unseen. She crept to the slide, peered cautiously through into the kitchen, and saw that it was as orderly and empty as the other rooms. But in the middle of the carefully scoured table stood a portable wireless, and the voice she heard came out of it. . .

She must have fainted then, she supposed; at any rate she felt so weak and dizzy that her memory of what next happened remained indistinct. But in the course of time she groped her way back to the pantry, and there found a bottle of spirits—brandy or whisky, she could not remember which. She found a glass, poured herself a stiff drink, and while it was flushing through her veins, managed, she never knew with how many shuddering delays, to drag herself through the deserted ground-floor, up the stairs, and down the corridor to her own room. There, apparently, she fell across the threshold, again unconscious. . .

When she came to, she remembered, her first care had been to lock herself in; then to recover her husband's revolver. It was not loaded, but she found some cartridges, and succeeded in loading it. Then she remembered that Agnes, on leaving her the evening before, had refused to carry away the tray with the tea and sandwiches, and she fell on them with a sudden hunger. She recalled also noticing that a flask of brandy had been put beside the thermos, and being vaguely surprised. Agnes's departure, then, had been deliberately planned, and she had known that her mistress, who never touched spirits, might have need of a stimulant before she returned. Mrs. Clayburn poured some of the brandy into her tea, and swallowed it greedily.

After that (she told me later) she remembered that she had managed to start a fire in her grate, and after warming herself, had got back into her bed, piling on it all the coverings she could find. The afternoon passed in a haze of pain, out of which there emerged now and then a dim shape of fear—the fear that she might lie there alone and untended till she died of cold, and of the terror of her solitude. For she was sure by this time that the house was empty—completely empty, from garret to cellar. She knew it was so, she could not tell why; but again she felt that it must be because of the peculiar quality of the silence—the silence which had dogged her steps wherever she went, and was now folded down on her like a pall. She was sure that the nearness of any other human being, however dumb and secret, would have made a faint crack in the texture of that silence, flawed it as a sheet of glass is flawed by a pebble thrown against it. . .

IV

"Is that easier?" the doctor asked, lifting himself from bending over her ankle. He shook his head disapprovingly. "Looks to me as if you'd disobeyed orders—eh? Been moving about, haven't you? And I guess Dr. Selgrove told you to keep quiet till he saw you again, didn't he?"

The speaker was a stranger, whom Mrs. Clayburn knew

only by name. Her own doctor had been called away that morning to the bedside of an old patient in Baltimore, and had asked this young man, who was beginning to be known at Norrington, to replace him. The newcomer was shy, and somewhat familiar, as the shy often are, and Mrs. Clayburn decided that she did not much like him. But before she could convey this by the tone of her reply (and she was past-mistress of the shades of disapproval) she heard Agnes speaking—yes, Agnes, the same, the usual Agnes, standing behind the doctor, neat and stern-looking as ever. "Mrs. Clayburn must have got up and walked about in the night instead of ringing for me, as she'd ought to," Agnes intervened severely.

This was too much! In spite of the pain, which was now exquisite, Mrs. Clayburn laughed. "Ringing for you? How could I, with the electricity cut off?"

"The electricity cut off?" Agnes's surprise was masterly. "Why, when was it cut off?" She pressed her finger on the bell beside the bed, and the call tinkled through the quiet room. "I tried that bell before I left you last night, madam, because if there'd been anything wrong with it I'd have come and slept in the dressing-room sooner than leave you here alone."

Mrs. Clayburn lay speechless, staring up at her. "Last night? But last night I was all alone in the house."

Agnes's firm features did not alter. She folded her hands resignedly across her trim apron. "Perhaps the pain's made you a little confused, madam." She looked at the doctor, who nodded.

"The pain in your foot must have been pretty bad," he said.

"It was," Mrs. Clayburn replied. "But it was nothing to the horror of being left alone in this empty house since the day before yesterday, with the heat and the electricity cut off, and the telephone not working."

The doctor was looking at her in evident wonder. Agnes's sallow face flushed slightly, but only as if in indignation at an unjust charge. "But, madam, I made up your fire with my own hands last night—and look, it's smouldering still. I was getting ready to start it again just now, when the doctor came."

"That's so. She was down on her knees before it," the doctor corroborated.

Again Mrs. Clayburn laughed. Ingeniously as the tissue of lies was being woven about her, she felt she could still break through it. "I made up the fire myself yesterday—there was no one else to do it," she said, addressing the doctor, but keeping her eyes on her maid. "I got up twice to put on more coal, because the house was like a sepulchre. The central heating must have been out since Saturday afternoon."

At this incredible statement Agnes's face expressed only a polite distress; but the new doctor was evidently embarrassed at being drawn into an unintelligible controversy with which he had no time to deal. He said he had brought the X-ray photographer with him, but that the ankle was too much swollen to be photographed at present. He asked Mrs. Clayburn to excuse his haste, as he had all Dr. Selgrove's patients to visit besides his own, and promised to come back that evening to decide whether she could be X-rayed then, and whether, as he evidently feared, the ankle would have to be put in plaster. Then, handing his prescriptions to Agnes, he departed.

Mrs. Clayburn spent a feverish and suffering day. She did not feel well enough to carry on the discussion with Agnes; she did not ask to see the other servants. She grew drowsy, and understood that her mind was confused with fever. Agnes and the housemaid waited on her as attentively as usual, and by the time the doctor returned in the evening her temperature had fallen; but she decided not to speak of what was on her mind until Dr. Selgrove reappeared. He was to be back the following evening, and the new doctor preferred to wait for him before deciding to put the ankle in plaster—though he feared this was now inevitable.

V

That afternoon Mrs. Clayburn had me summoned by telephone, and I arrived at Whitegates the following day. My cousin, who looked pale and nervous, merely pointed to her foot, which had been put in plaster, and thanked me for coming to keep her company. She explained that Dr. Selgrove had been taken suddenly ill in Baltimore, and would not be back for several days, but that the young man who replaced him seemed fairly competent. She made no allusion to the strange incidents I have set down, but I felt at once that she had received a shock which her accident, however painful, could not explain.

Finally, one evening, she told me the story of her strange week-end, as it had presented itself to her unusually clear and accurate mind, and as I have recorded it above. She did not tell me this till several weeks after my arrival; but she was still upstairs at the time, and obliged to divide her days between her bed and a lounge. During those endless intervening weeks, she told me, she had thought the whole matter over: and though the events of the mysterious thirty-six hours were still vivid to her, they had already lost something of their haunting terror, and she had finally decided not to re-open the question with Agnes, or to touch on it in speaking to the other servants. Dr. Selgrove's illness had been not only serious but prolonged. He had not yet returned, and it was reported that as soon as he was well enough he would go on a West Indian cruise, and not resume his practice at Norrington till the spring. Dr. Selgrove, as my cousin was perfectly aware, was the only person who could prove that thirty-six hours had elapsed between his visit and that of his successor; and the latter, a shy young man, burdened by the heavy additional practice suddenly thrown on his shoulders, told me (when I risked a little private talk with him) that in the haste of Dr. Selgrove's departure the only instructions he had given about Mrs. Clayburn were summed up in the brief memorandum: "Broken ankle. Have X-rayed."

Knowing my cousin's authoritative character, I was surprised at her decision not to speak to the servants of what had happened; but on thinking it over I concluded she was right. They were all exactly as they had been before that unexplained episode: efficient, devoted, respectful and respectable. She was dependent on them and felt at home with them, and she evidently preferred to put the whole matter out of her mind, as far as she could. She was absolutely certain that something strange had happened in her house, and I was more than ever convinced that she had received a shock which the accident of a broken ankle was not sufficient to account for; but in the end I agreed that nothing was to be gained by cross-questioning the servants or the new doctor.

I was at Whitegates off and on that winter and during the following summer, and when I went home to New York for good early in October I left my cousin in her old health and spirits. Dr. Selgrove had been ordered to Switzerland for the summer, and this further postponement of his return to his practice seemed to have put the happenings of the strange week-end out of her mind. Her life was going on as peacefully and normally as usual, and I left her without anxiety, and indeed without a thought of the mystery, which was now nearly a year old.

I was living then in a small flat in New York by myself, and I had hardly settled into it when, very late one evening—on the last day of October—I heard my bell ring. As it was my maid's evening out, and I was alone, I went to the door myself, and on the threshold, to my amazement, I saw Sara Clayburn. She was wrapped in a fur cloak, with a hat drawn down over her forehead, and a face so pale and haggard that I saw something dreadful must have happened to her. "Sara," I gasped, not knowing what I was saying, "where in the world have you come from at this hour?"

"From Whitegates. I missed the last train and came by car." She came in and sat down on the bench near the door. I saw that she could hardly stand, and sat down beside her, putting my arm about her. "For heaven's sake, tell me what's happened."

She looked at me without seeming to see me. "I telephoned to Nixon's and hired a car. It took me five hours and a quarter to get here." She looked about her. "Can you take me in for the night? I've left my luggage downstairs."

"For as many nights as you like. But you look so ill—"

She shook her head. "No; I'm not ill. I'm only frightened—deathly frightened," she repeated in a whisper.

Her voice was so strange, and the hands I was pressing between mine were so cold, that I drew her to her feet and led her straight to my little guest-room. My flat was in an old-fashioned building, not many stories high, and I was on more human terms with the staff than is possible in one of the modern Babels. I telephoned down to have my cousin's bags brought up, and meanwhile I filled a hot water bottle, warmed the bed, and got her into it as quickly as I could. I had never seen her as unquestioning and submissive, and that alarmed me even more than her pallor. She was not the woman to let herself be undressed and put to bed like a baby; but she submitted without a word, as though aware that she had reached the end of her tether.

"It's good to be here," she said in a quieter tone, as I tucked her up and smoothed the pillows. "Don't leave me yet, will you—not just yet."

"I'm not going to leave you for more than a minute—just to get you a cup of tea," I reassured her; and she lay still. I left the door open, so that she could hear me stirring about in the little pantry across the passage, and when I brought her the tea she swallowed it gratefully, and a little colour came into her face. I sat with her in silence for some time, but at last she began: "You see it's exactly a year—"

I should have preferred to have her put off till the next morning whatever she had to tell me; but I saw from her burning eyes that she was determined to rid her mind of what was burdening it, and that until she had done so it would be useless to proffer the sleeping-draught I had ready.

"A year since what?" I asked stupidly, not yet associating her precipitate arrival with the mysterious occurrences of the previous year at Whitegates.

She looked at me in surprise. "A year since I met that woman. Don't you remember—the strange woman who was coming up the drive the afternoon when I broke my ankle? I didn't think of it at the time, but it was on All Souls' eve that I met her."

Yes, I said, I remembered that it was.

"Well—and this is All Souls' eve, isn't it? I'm not as good as you are on Church dates, but I thought it was."

"Yes. This is All Souls' eve."

"I thought so. . . Well, this afternoon I went out for my usual walk. I'd been writing letters, and paying bills, and didn't start till late; not till it was nearly dusk. But it was a lovely clear evening. And as I got near the gate, there was the woman coming in—the same woman . . . going toward the house. . ."

I pressed my cousin's hand, which was hot and feverish now. "If it was dusk, could you be perfectly sure it was the same woman?" I asked.

"Oh, perfectly sure; the evening was so clear. I knew her and she knew me; and I could see she was angry at meeting me. I stopped her and asked: 'Where are you going?' just as I had asked her last year. And she said, in the same queer half-foreign voice: 'Only to see one of the girls', as she had before. Then I felt angry all of a sudden, and I said: 'You shan't set foot in my house again. Do you hear me? I order you to leave.' And she laughed; yes, she laughed—very low, but distinctly. By that time it had got quite dark, as if a sudden storm was sweeping up over the sky, so that though she was so near me I could hardly see her. We were standing by the clump of hemlocks at the turn of the drive, and as I went up to her, furious at her impertinence, she passed behind the hemlocks, and when I followed her she wasn't there. . . No; I swear to you she wasn't there. . . And in the darkness I hurried back to the house, afraid that she would slip by me and get there first. And the queer thing was that as I reached the door the black cloud vanished, and there was the transparent twilight again. In the house everything seemed as usual, and the servants were busy about their work; but I couldn't get it out of my head that the woman, under the shadow of that cloud, had somehow got there before me." She paused for breath, and began again: "In the hall I stopped at the telephone and rang up Nixon, and told him to send me a car at once to go to New York, with a man he knew to drive me. And Nixon came with the car himself. . ."

Her head sank back on the pillow, and she looked at me like a frightened child. "It was good of Nixon," she said.

"Yes; it was very good of him. But when they saw you leaving—the servants I mean. . ."

"Yes. Well, when I got upstairs to my room I rang for Agnes. She came, looking just as cool and quiet as usual. And when I told her I was starting for New York in half an hour—I said it was on account of a sudden business call—well, then her presence of mind failed her for the first time. She forgot to look surprised, she even forgot to make an objection—and you know what an objector Agnes is. And as I watched her I could see a little secret spark of relief in her eyes, though she was so on her guard. And she just said: 'Very well, madam', and asked me what I wanted to take with me. Just as if I were in the habit of dashing off to New York after dark on an autumn night to meet a business engagement! No, she made a mistake not to show any surprise—and not even to ask me why I didn't take my own car. And her losing her head in that way frightened me more than anything else. For I saw she was so thankful I was going that she hardly dared speak, for fear she should betray herself, or I should change my mind."

After that Mrs. Clayburn lay a long while silent, breathing less unrestfully; and at last she closed her eyes, as though she felt more at ease now that she had spoken, and wanted to sleep. As I got up quietly to leave her, she turned her head a little and murmured: "I shall never go back to Whitegates again." Then she shut her eyes, and I saw that she was falling asleep.

I have set down above, I hope without omitting anything essential, the record of my cousin's strange experience as she told it to me. Of what happened at Whitegates that is all I can personally vouch for. The rest—and of course there is a rest—is pure conjecture, and I give it only as such.

My cousin's maid, Agnes, was from the isle of Skye, and the Hebrides, as everyone knows, are full of the supernatural—whether in the shape of ghostly presences, or the almost ghostlier sense of unseen watchers peopling the long nights of those stormy solitudes. My cousin, at any rate, always regarded Agnes as the—perhaps unconscious, at any rate irresponsible—channel through which communications from the other side of the veil reached the submissive household at Whitegates. Though Agnes had been with Mrs. Clayburn for a long time without any peculiar incident revealing this affinity with the unknown forces, the power to communicate with them may all the while have been latent in the woman, only awaiting a kindred touch; and that touch may have been given by the unknown visitor whom my cousin, two years in succession, had met coming up the drive at Whitegates on the eve of All Souls'. Certainly the date bears out my hypothesis; for I suppose that, even in this unimaginative age, a few people still remember that All Souls' eve is the night when the dead can walk—and when, by the same token, other spirits, piteous or malevolent, are also freed from the restrictions which secure the earth to the living on the other days of the year.

If the recurrence of this date is more than a coincidence— and for my part I think it is—then I take it that the strange woman who twice came up the drive at Whitegates on All Souls' eve was either a "fetch", or else, more probably, and more alarmingly, a living woman inhabited by a witch. The history of witchcraft, as is well known, abounds in such cases, and such a messenger might well have been delegated by the powers who rule in these matters to summon Agnes and her fellow-servants to a midnight "Coven" in some neighbouring solitude. To learn what happens at Covens, and the reason of the irresistible fascination they exercise over the timorous and superstitious, one need only address oneself to the immense body of literature dealing with these mysterious rites. Anyone who has once felt the faintest curiosity to assist at a Coven apparently soon finds the curiosity increase to desire, the desire to an uncontrollable longing, which, when the opportunity presents itself, breaks down all inhibitions; for those who have once taken part in a Coven will move heaven and earth to take part again.

Such is my—conjectural—explanation of the strange happenings at Whitegates. My cousin always said she could not believe that incidents which might fit into the desolate landscape of the Hebrides could occur in the cheerful and populous Connecticut valley; but if she did not believe, she at least feared—such moral paradoxes are not uncommon—and though she insisted that there must be some natural explanation of the mystery, she never returned to investigate it.

"No, no," she said with a little shiver, whenever I touched on the subject of her going back to Whitegates, "I don't want ever to risk seeing that woman again. . ." And she never went back.

CHRONOLOGY

NOTE ON THE TEXTS

NOTES

Chronology

1862   Born January 24 at 14 West 23rd Street, New York City, and baptized Edith Newbold Jones; third and last child of George Frederic Jones and Lucretia Stevens Rhinelander (brothers are Frederic, b. 1846, and Henry, b. 1850). Parents belong to long-established, socially prominent New York families. Father's income based on Manhattan land-holdings.

1865   Receives gift of spitz puppy, beginning a lifelong passion for small dogs.

1866   Post–Civil War depression in real estate market causes family to move to Europe for prolonged residence. Sails to England in November with parents, nurse Hannah Doyle ("Doyley"), and brother Henry, who begins law studies at Trinity Hall College, Cambridge.

1867   Family spends year in Rome.

1868   Family travels through Spain and settles in Paris. Taught to read by father; recites Tennyson for visiting maternal grandmother. Begins "making up," inventing stories using parents and their friends as characters.

1870–71   Stays at Wildbad, a spa in Württemberg, while mother takes water cure. Studies New Testament in German, takes walks in Black Forest. Suffers severe attack of typhoid fever (later remembers convalescence as beginning of recurrent apprehension of "some dark undefinable menace forever dogging my steps, lurking and threatening"). Family settles in Florence at end of 1870.

1872–75   Family returns to the United States, dividing year between three-story brownstone on West 23rd Street, New York, and Pencraig, their summer home in Newport, Rhode Island. At Pencraig rides pony, swims in cove, watches archery contests, visits neighboring family of astronomer Lewis Rutherfurd. Studies French, medieval and romantic German poetry with Rutherfurd family governess, Anna Bahlmann (who later becomes her governess). Begins lifelong friendship with sister-in-law Mary Cadwalader Jones, wife (later divorced) of brother Frederic. In father's eight-hundred-volume New York library finds histories (including Plutarch, Macaulay, Carlyle, Parkman), diaries and correspondence (Pepys, Cowper, Madame de Sévigné), criticism (Sainte-Beuve), art history and archaeology (Ruskin, Schliemann), poetry (Homer and Dante in translation, most English poets, some French), and a few novels (Scott, Irving). Mother forbids the reading of contemporary fiction. Later remembers reading as "a secret ecstasy of communion." Summer 1875, forms close friendship with Emelyn, daughter of Edward Abiel Washburn, rector of Calvary Church, New York.

1876–77   Begins *Fast and Loose*, 30,000-word novella about trials of ill-starred young lovers, autumn 1876. Keeps enterprise secret from everyone except Emelyn Washburn. Finished January 1877, manuscript includes mock hostile reviews ("every character is a failure, the plot a vacuum").

1878–79   *Verses*, volume of twenty-nine poems, printed in Newport, arranged and paid for by mother. Summer 1879, Newport neighbor Allen Thorndike Rice shows some of the poems to Henry Wadsworth Longfellow and then sends them to William Dean Howells. Howells publishes one in *Atlantic Monthly*. Makes social debut.

1880–81   Two poems appear in the New York *World*. Courted in New York, Newport, and Bar Harbor, Maine, by Henry Leyden Stevens, twenty-one-year-old son of prominent social figure, Mrs. Paran Stevens. November 1880, goes to southern France with mother and ailing father. Henry Stevens joins them September 1881.

1882   Father, age sixty-one, dies in Cannes in March. Inherits over $20,000 in trust fund. August, engagement to Henry Stevens announced in Newport, with marriage scheduled for autumn. Engagement is broken off, apparently at insistence of Mrs. Stevens. Travels with mother to Paris.

1883   Spends summer at Bar Harbor. Meets Walter Van Rensselaer Berry, twenty-four-year-old Harvard graduate studying for admission to the District of Columbia bar.

They become close, but Berry leaves without proposing marriage. In August, Edward Robbins ("Teddy") Wharton, friend of brother Henry, arrives in Bar Harbor and begins courtship. A thirty-three-year-old Harvard graduate interested mainly in camping, hunting, fishing, and riding, he lives with his family in Boston and receives a $2,000 annuity from them.

1884   Hires Catherine Gross, Alsatian immigrant, as personal attendant (she will be Wharton's companion and housekeeper for over four decades).

1885–88   Marries Edward Wharton April 29, 1885, at Trinity Chapel, New York City. Henry Stevens dies of tuberculosis, July 18, 1885. Whartons move into Pencraig Cottage, small house on mother's Newport estate, leaving every February for four months of European travel, mostly in Italy. Introduced by Egerton Winthrop, wealthy New York art collector and their occasional traveling companion, to contemporary French literature and works of Darwin, Huxley, Spencer, Haeckel, and other writers on evolution. Whartons spend a year's income (about $10,000) on four-month Aegean cruise, 1888. Learns in Athens that she has inherited $120,000 from reclusive New York cousin Joshua Jones.

1889   Rents small house on Madison Avenue, New York City. Four poems accepted for publication by *Scribner's Magazine*, *Harper's Monthly*, and *Century Illustrated Monthly Magazine*.

1890–92   Suffers intermittently from inexplicable nausea and fatigue. Short story, "Mrs. Manstey's View," accepted by *Scribner's* May 1890, published July 1891. Purchases narrow house on Fourth Avenue near 78th Street (eventually 884 Park Avenue) for $19,670 in November 1891. (A few years later acquires its adjoining twin at 882 Park for the household staff to live in.) Works on long short story, "Bunner Sisters." It is rejected by *Scribner's*, December 1892.

1893   Buys Land's End, Newport estate overlooking the Atlantic, for $80,000 in March. Works with Boston architect Ogden Codman on decoration of its interior. French novelist Paul Bourget and his wife are guests. Three stories, "That Good May Come," "The Fulness of Life," and "The Lamp of Psyche," accepted by *Scribner's*, whose editor, Edward Burlingame, proposes a short-story volume for Charles Scribner's Sons. Wharton agrees, suggesting inclusion of "Bunner Sisters." Sails for Europe in December.

1894–95 Burlingame rejects "Something Exquisite" (later revised and published as "Friends"). Writes to him from Florence, expressing gratitude for his criticism and doubt about her own abilities. Travels through Tuscany. Visits Violet Paget ("Vernon Lee"), English novelist and historian of eighteenth-century Italy. After research at monastery of San Vivaldo and in Florence museums, identifies group of terra-cotta sculptures, previously thought to date from the seventeenth century, as work of the late fifteenth–early sixteenth century school of the Robbias. Writes article for *Scribner's* on her findings and surrounding Tuscan landscape. Notifies Burlingame in July 1894 that short-story volume will need another six months to prepare. Suffering from intense exhaustion, nausea, and melancholia, breaks off correspondence with Burlingame for sixteen months. Mother moves to Paris (brothers Frederic and Henry both live in Europe); meetings and correspondence with her become infrequent. Writes "The Valley of Childish Things, and Other Emblems," collection of ten short fables, and sends it in December 1895 to Burlingame, who rejects it.

1896–97 Writes, with architect Ogden Codman, *The Decoration of Houses*, study of interior arrangements and furnishings in upper-class city homes. Shows incomplete manuscript to Burlingame, who gives it to William Brownell, senior editor at Scribner's. Summer 1897, resumes friendship with Walter Berry, who stays for a month at Land's End, assisting Wharton in the revision of *The Decoration of Houses* (Codman is incapacitated by sunstroke). Wharton persuades Brownell to increase the number of halftone plates and makes extensive recommendations concerning the book's design. Published by Scribner's December 1897; sales are unexpectedly good.

1898 Writes and revises seven stories between March and July, despite recurring illness. In letter to Burlingame, discusses her earliest stories: "I regard them as the excesses of youth. They were all written 'at the top of my voice,' & The Fulness of Life is one long shriek—I may not write any better, but at least I hope that I write in a lower key . . ." Suffers mental and physical breakdown in August. Goes to Philadelphia in October to take the "rest cure" invented by Dr. S. Weir Mitchell and is treated as an outpatient under Mitchell's supervision. Therapy involves massage, electrical stimulation of the muscles, abundant eating, and near total isolation.

1899   January, settles with Edward for four-month stay in house at 1329 K Street in Washington, found for them by Walter Berry, who becomes close literary adviser and supporter. *The Greater Inclination*, long-delayed collection of short stories, published by Scribner's in March to enthusiastic reviews; sales exceed 3,000 copies. Protests to Scribner's that book has been insufficiently advertised. Begins extensive correspondence with Sara Norton, daughter of Harvard professor Charles Eliot Norton. Summer, travels in Europe, joined by the Bourgets in Switzerland; tours northern Italy with them, through Bergamo and Val Camonica. Returns to Land's End in September. Seeking escape from Newport climate, visits Lenox, Massachusetts, in fall.

1900   Novella, *The Touchstone* (in England, *A Gift from the Grave*), appears in the March and April *Scribner's*; published by Scribner's in April, selling 5,000 copies by year's end. Travels in England, Paris, and northern Italy, again accompanied by the Bourgets. Spends summer and fall at inn in Lenox while Edward goes on yachting trip. Begins concerted work on novel *The Valley of Decision*. Sends Henry James copy of "The Line of Least Resistance"; he responds with praise and detailed criticism, encouraging further effort. Wharton removes story from volume being prepared.

1901   February to June, negotiates purchase for $40,600 of 113-acre Lenox property extending into the village of Lee. After breaking with Codman over his fee, hires architect Francis V. L. Hoppin to design house modeled on Christopher Wren's Belton House in Lincolnshire, England.

Oversees landscaping and gardening. *Crucial Instances*, second volume of stories, published by Scribner's in April. Mother dies in Paris, age seventy-six, on June 28. Her will leaves large sums outright to Frederic and Henry but creates a trust fund for Wharton's share of the remainder of the estate. Trust eventually amounts to $90,000; total annual income from parents' and Joshua Jones's trusts is about $22,000. Wharton visits London and Paris and persuades her brothers to make husband Edward co-trustee with brother Henry. Works on play *The Man of Genius* (never finished) and on dramatization of Prosper Mérimée's *Manon Lescaut* (never produced).

1902   *The Valley of Decision*, historical novel set in eighteenth-century Italy, published by Scribner's in February. Wharton criticizes its design while it is being prepared. Suffers collapse (nausea, depression, fatigue) after publication. Reviews are generally enthusiastic and sales are good. Begins *Disintegration*, novel set in contemporary New York society, but does not finish it. Writes travel articles, poetry, theatrical reviews, and literary criticism, including essays on Gabriele D'Annunzio and George Eliot. Translates Hermann Sudermann's play *Es Lebe das Leben* as *The Joy of Living* (it runs briefly on Broadway and sells in book form for a number of years). Henry James writes Wharton in August that *The Valley of Decision* is "accomplished, pondered, saturated" and "brilliant and interesting from a literary point of view," but urges her to abandon historical subject matter "in favour of the American subject. There it is round you. Don't pass it by—the immediate, the real, the only, the yours, the novelist's that it waits for. Take hold of it and keep hold and let it pull you where it will . . . *Do New York!* The 1st-hand account is precious." Meets Theodore Roosevelt in Newport at christening of his godchild, son of Wharton's friends Margaret and Winthrop Chanler, beginning a long friendship. Moves into Lenox house, named "The Mount" after Long Island home of Revolutionary War ancestor Ebenezer Stevens, in September. Edward suffers first of series of nervous collapses.

1903   January, sails for Italy with ailing husband. Travels slowly north from Rome through Tuscany, the Veneto, and

Lombardy, inspecting estates for series of articles commissioned by R. W. Gilder for *Century*. Enjoys her first automobile ride. Visits Violet Paget at Villa Pomerino outside of Florence. Meets art expert Bernhard Berenson, who strongly dislikes her. Goes to Salsomaggiore, west of Parma, for treatment of her asthma. Spends summer and fall at The Mount, with interval at Newport. Sells Land's End for $122,500, June 13. Begins *The House of Mirth*. Novella *Sanctuary* published by Scribner's in October. Sails for England, early December. First conversations with Henry James, who comes up from Rye to London in mid-December.

1904   Purchases her first automobile, a Panhard-Levassor. With Edward driving, travels south to Hyères for a stay with the Bourgets, then to Cannes and Monte Carlo and back across France. In England, visits Henry James in Rye and tours Sussex with him. Returns to Lenox in late spring. Enthusiastic about motor travel, hires Charles Cook as a permanent chauffeur (he retains this position until 1921, when he suffers a stroke). *The Descent of Man*, collection of stories, published by Scribner's in April. After reading reviews, writes Brownell that "the continued cry that I am an echo of Mr. James (whose books of the last ten years I can't read, much as I delight in the man) . . . makes me feel rather hopeless." Hires Anna Bahlmann as secretary and literary assistant. Agrees with Burlingame in August to begin serialization of *The House of Mirth* in January 1905 *Scribner's*; undertakes schedule of intense work (usually writing in the morning) to meet deadline. (Finishes in March 1905; serialized Jan.–Nov.) House guests at The Mount include Brooks Adams and his wife, George Cabot Lodge (son of Senator Henry Cabot Lodge), Walter Berry, and Gaillard Lapsley, American-born don of medieval history at Trinity College, Cambridge. Henry James arrives in October with his friend Howard Sturgis, whom Wharton calls "the kindest and strangest of men." *Italian Villas and Their Gardens*, based on magazine articles, published by The Century Company in November. Returns to New York just before Christmas.

1905   Henry James visits at 884 Park Avenue for a few days in January. Whartons dine at the White House with Presi-

dent Roosevelt in March. *Italian Backgrounds*, sketches
written since 1894, published by Scribner's in March. After European trip in spring, including visit to Salsomaggiore for asthma treatment, returns to The Mount. House
guests include printer Berkeley Updike, illustrator Mon-
cure Robinson, publisher Walter Maynard, Robert Grant,
novelist and judge of the probate court in Boston, and
Henry James. Visits Sara and Charles Eliot Norton. *The
House of Mirth* published by Scribner's, October 14, in first
printing of 40,000; 140,000 copies in print by the end of
the year, "the most rapid sale of any book ever published
by Scribner," according to Brownell. Literary earnings for
year exceed $20,000. Henry James writes Wharton that
the novel is an "altogether superior thing" but "better
written than composed." Reviews generally favorable. December, undertakes collaboration on stage version with
playwright Clyde Fitch.

1906   Sails for France, March 10. Through Paul Bourget, enters
intellectual and social circles of Paris, especially those of
the Faubourg St. Germain. Among new acquaintances are
poet Comtesse Anna de Noailles, historian Gustave
Schlumberger, and his close friend, Comtesse Charlotte de
Cossé-Brissac. Goes to England at the end of April. Whartons and Henry James make short motor tour of England.
Visits Queen's Acre, Howard Sturgis's home in Windsor,
for the first time (it soon becomes the center of her English social life). Meets Percy Lubbock, young writer and
disciple of Henry James. Returns to France and takes motor tour with brother Henry, visiting cathedrals at Amiens
and Beauvais, and Nohant, home of George Sand. Returns to Lenox in June. Works on novel *Justine Brent* (later
retitled *The Fruit of the Tree*). Novella *Madame de Treymes*
appears in the August *Scribner's* (published by *Scribner's*
in February 1907). September, goes to Detroit with Edward and Walter Berry to see first performance of stage
version of *The House of Mirth*. October opening in New
York is a critical and commercial failure; Wharton calls the
experience "instructive." Edward is away from Lenox,
hunting and fishing, during much of the fall. Literary
earnings for the year total almost $32,000.

1907   Returns to Paris in January and rents the apartment of the
George Vanderbilts at 58 Rue de Varenne, in the heart of

the Faubourg St. Germain. *The Fruit of the Tree* serialized in *Scribner's*, January–November. March, takes a "motor-flight" through France with Edward and Henry James, visiting Nohant and touring southern France. Invites James to stay for another month, and takes a short automobile trip with James and Gaillard Lapsley. Engages instructor to teach her contemporary French; for a lesson exercise, writes a precursor sketch of *Ethan Frome*. April, sees much of William Morton Fullerton, forty-two-year-old Paris correspondent for the London *Times*, former student of Charles Eliot Norton, and disciple of Henry James. Spends summer at The Mount. Sales of *The Fruit of the Tree*, published by Scribner's in October, reach 60,000. Reviews are good. Fullerton arrives at The Mount in October for a visit of several days. Wharton begins a journal addressed to him. Returns to Paris in December. *The House of Mirth* appears as *Chez les Heureux du Monde* in the *Revue de Paris*, translated by Charles du Bos, a young follower of Bourget.

1908   January–February, Edward afflicted by "nervous depression." Wharton leads active social life, seeing linguist Vicomte Robert d'Humières, American ambassador Henry White, watercolorist Walter Gay and his wife, Matilda, James Van Alen, Fullerton, Comtesse Rosa de Fitz-James, Bourget, playwright Paul Hervieu, Charles du Bos, and others. February, spends time with Fullerton while Edward is away, and begins an affair with him in March. Edward, suffering from depression and pervasive pain, leaves for spa at Hot Springs, Arkansas, March 21. Wharton writes Brownell that Edward's illness has prevented her from making much progress on new novel, *The Custom of the Country*, and doubts that it will be ready for serial publication by January 1909. April, moves to brother Henry's townhouse on Place des Etats-Unis when he goes to America on business. Egerton Winthrop visits. When Henry James visits, arranges to have Jacques Emile Blanche paint portrait that she considers the best ever done of him. May, has first significant meetings with Henry Adams. Meditates in her journal on the propriety of her affair with Fullerton; writes series of love sonnets. May 22, gives Fullerton journal addressed to him; he returns it the following day as she leaves for America. On fifth day of crossing, writes story "The Choice"; resumes

work on *The Custom of the Country*. In Lenox, has difficulty breathing for six weeks. Scribner's publishes *The
Hermit and the Wild Woman*, fourth collection of stories,
in September; *A Motor-Flight Through France*, travel account, in October. Writes poetry, enjoys reading Nietz-
sche's *Jenseits von Gut und Böse* (*Beyond Good and Evil*).
Leaves for Europe, October 30. Introduced by Henry
James to aging George Meredith at Box Hill, near London; goes with James Barrie to see performance of his play
What Every Woman Knows. At Stanway, Gloucestershire
home of Lady Mary Elcho, meets two young Englishmen
who become close friends: Robert Norton, a landscape
painter, and John Hugh Smith, a banker expert in Anglo-
Russian financial affairs. Sees much of Henry James, who
soon professes exhaustion from her visits, referring to her
as "the Angel of Devastation." Crosses to France with
Howard Sturgis for Christmas. Literary earnings for year
are about $15,000.

1909   January, Edward arrives in Paris, suffering from insomnia
and inexplicable pain in his face and limbs. Work on *The
Custom of the Country* again interrupted. Edward returns
to Lenox in mid-April. *Artemis to Actaeon*, book of poetry,
published by Scribner's in late April. Continues to write
poetry, including "Ogrin the Hermit," long narrative
based on a portion of the Tristan and Iseult legend. When
lease on 58 Rue de Varenne expires, moves to large suite
in Hotel Crillon, Place de la Concorde, April. Involves
Henry James and Frederick Macmillan, Fullerton's publisher, in complicated scheme to conceal gift of money to
Fullerton to meet blackmail demands of an ex-mistress.
June, goes to London with Fullerton; they spend the
night at the Charing Cross Hotel. After Fullerton leaves
for America, writes "Terminus," fifty-two-line love poem.
Stays in England until mid-July, visiting with Sturgis,
Lapsley, and James. When Fullerton returns, they spend
night in Rye at James's Lamb House. September, Henry
Adams arranges another meeting between Wharton and
Bernhard Berenson. Friendship develops. Edward arrives
in Paris with his sister Nancy in November; soon confesses
to Wharton that during the summer he sold some of her
holdings, bought property in Boston, and lived there with
his mistress. Edward returns to Boston. Later admits to
embezzling $50,000 from Wharton's trust funds; makes

restitution by drawing upon $67,000 recently inherited from his mother.

1910   Moves into apartment at 53 Rue de Varenne, January. Writes stories "The Eyes" and "The Triumph of Night." Sells New York houses. Goes to England in March to see Henry James, who is recovering from a nervous breakdown. Edward returns to Paris, agrees to enter Swiss sanatorium for treatment of his depression. Begins short novel *Ethan Frome*. Walter Berry moves to Paris, stays in Whartons' guest suite for several months. July 3, sees Nijinsky dance in *L'Oiseau de Feu*. Affair with Fullerton ends. Visits Henry and William James at Lamb House in August. Sails in September to New York with Edward. October, Edward departs on trip around the world; Wharton returns to Paris, ill and exhausted. *Tales of Men and Ghosts* published by Scribner's in October; sells about 4,000 copies.

1911   January, confesses to Hugh Smith that "my writing tires and preoccupies me more than it used to." Tries unsuccessfully with William Dean Howells and Edmund Gosse to secure the Nobel Prize for Henry James. May, at Salsomaggiore for hay fever; resumes concerted work on *The Custom of the Country*. Returns to Lenox at end of June. Has Henry James, Hugh Smith, and Lapsley as guests. Wharton and Edward agree to formal separation in late July, then reverse decision. Returns to Europe in September after entrusting Edward with power to sell The Mount. *Ethan Frome* serialized in *Scribner's* from August through October, published by Scribner's in September. Reviewers in America and England call it one of her finest achievements. Disappointed with Scribner's reports of sales (4,200 copies by mid-November), Wharton protests lack of advertising, poor distribution, and bad typesetting. Tours central Italy and visits Berenson for the first time at his home, Villa I Tatti, near Florence, in October. Puts *The Custom of the Country* aside in November to work on novel *The Reef*.

1912   Edward arrives in February at Rue de Varenne and stays until May. Relations remain distant and strained. Visits La Verna, monastery in Tuscany mountains, with Berry; their car must be lowered by ropes for them to return. Sale of The Mount for undisclosed sum completed in June. Offers to live with Edward in United States, but he refuses. Summer, sees much of Henry James during visits to England. Arranges with Charles Scribner for $8,000 of her royalties to be given to James under the guise of an advance for his novel-in-progress, *The Ivory Tower*. (James receives $3,600 in 1913; the novel is never completed.) *The Reef* published by D. Appleton and Company, which had given her $15,000 advance. Reviews are relatively poor; sales reach 7,000. Resumes work on *The Custom of the Country*.

1913   *The Custom of the Country* appears in *Scribner's*, January–November. Receives unexpected letter from brother Henry denouncing her for coldness toward Countess Tecla, his mistress and intended wife. Sues Edward for divorce on grounds of adultery; Paris tribunal grants decree, April 16. Helps to initiate effort to raise gift of $5,000 for Henry James's seventieth birthday; effort abandoned when James discovers and angrily rejects it. Drives across Sicily with Berry in April. Friendship develops with Geoffrey Scott, author of *The Architecture of Humanism*. Favorably impressed by premiere of Igor Stravinsky's ballet *Le Sacre du Printemps* in Paris, May 29. Considers buying house outside of London, but eventually decides against it. August, finishes *The Custom of the Country*. Travels with Berenson through Luxembourg and Germany, stopping at Cologne, Dresden, and Berlin. Begins novel *Literature*, never completed. *The Custom of the Country* published by Scribner's in October; sales reach nearly 60,000. December, attends wedding of niece, landscape gardener Beatrix Jones (daughter of brother Frederic and Mary Cadwalader) and Yale historian Max Farrand, in New York. Finds New York "queer, rootless" and "overwhelming."

1914   Returns to Paris in January. Sends Henry James copy of Marcel Proust's recently published *Du Côté de chez Swann*. March, sails from Marseilles to Algiers with Percy Lubbock and Anna Bahlmann. Drives through northern Algeria and Tunisia, "an unexpurgated page of the Arabian Nights!" Frightened in Timgad, Algeria, by intruder in her room, who flees when she screams. July, tours Spain with Berry for three weeks, viewing cave paintings at

Altamira. Returns to Paris July 31, three days before outbreak of war between France and Germany. August, establishes workroom near Rue de Varenne for seamstresses and other women thrown out of work by the economic disruption of general mobilization. Collects funds, selects supervisory staff, arranges for supply of work orders, free lunches, and coal allotments. Late August, goes to Stocks, English country house rented from novelist Mrs. Humphry Ward, a trip planned before the war. Sees Henry James at Rye. After learning of battle of the Marne, makes arrangements, with difficulty, to return to Paris; succeeds by end of September. November, establishes and directs American Hostels for Refugees. Selects Elisina Tyler, friend since 1912, as administrative deputy; raises $100,000 in first twelve months. (Hostels assists 9,330 refugees by end of 1915, providing free or low-cost food, clothing, coal, housing, medical and child care, and assistance in finding work.)

1915   February, visits the front in the Argonne and at Verdun. Tours hospitals, investigating need for blankets and clothing; watches French assault on village of Vauquois. Makes five more visits to front in next six months, including tour of forward trenches in the Vosges; describes them in articles for *Scribner's* (collected in *Fighting France, from Dunkerque to Belfort*, published by Scribner's in November). April, organizes Children of Flanders Rescue Committee with Tyler, establishing six homes between Paris and the Normandy coast. Committee sets up classes in lacemaking for girls, industrial training for boys, French for Flemish speakers. Nearly 750 Flemish children, many of them tubercular, cared for in 1915. Increasingly concentrates on fund-raising and creation of sponsoring committees in France and the United States, delegating daily administration to Tyler. Arranges benefit concerts and an art exhibition. Edits *The Book of the Homeless* (published by Scribner's early in 1916), with introductions by Marshal Joffre and Theodore Roosevelt. Contributors of poetry, essays, art, fiction, and musical scores include Cocteau, Conrad, Howells, Anna de Noailles, Hardy, Yeats, Eleanora Duse, Sarah Bernhardt, Henry James, Max Beerbohm, Paul Claudel, Edmond Rostand, Monet, Leon Bakst, and Stravinsky. Wharton does most of the translations. Proceeds (approximately $8,000 from the book,

$7,000 from the sale of art and manuscripts) go to Hostels and Rescue Committee. Friendship develops with André Gide, who serves on a Hostels committee. October, makes short visit to England. Learns in December that Henry James is dying; writes Lapsley: "His friendship has been the pride & honour of my life."

1916   Henry James dies February 28. Spring, helps establish treatment program for tubercular French soldiers. Made Chevalier of the Legion of Honor, April 8. Mourns deaths of Egerton Winthrop (tells Berenson that Winthrop and Henry James "made up the sum of the best I have known in human nature") and secretary Anna Bahlmann. Informs Charles Scribner that she is working on novel *The Glimpses of the Moon* and a work "of the dimensions of *Ethan Frome*. It deals with the same kind of life in a midsummer landscape." Offers the latter for serial publication, but Charles Scribner declines, having already scheduled her 1892 "Bunner Sisters" for fall; accepts offer from Appleton for book and from *McClure's* for serial. Feels financial pressure due to expense of refugee work, reduced literary earnings, and effects of American income tax. *Xingu and Other Stories* (all except one story written before the war) published in October by Scribner's.

1917   *Summer*, companion piece to *Ethan Frome*, serialized in *McClure's* for $7,000, February–August; published by Appleton July 2. Grows fond of Ronald Simmons, young American officer and painter. After tuberculosis treatment centers are taken over by the Red Cross, establishes four convalescent homes for tubercular civilians. September, makes month-long tour of French Morocco with Walter Berry. Witnesses self-lacerative ritual dances and visits harem, noting its air of "somewhat melancholy respectability."

1918   Inspired by success of American troops, gives public lecture on American life. Summer, brother Frederic dies; Wharton, long estranged from him, writes sadly of her brother Henry's failure to contact her. Deeply grieved by death from pneumonia of Ronald Simmons, August 12. Finds Paris increasingly noisy. After long negotiation, purchases Jean-Marie, house in village of St. Brice-sous-Fôret, outside of Paris (will restore its original name, Pavillon Colombe). Novel *The Marne* published by Appleton.

1919   Rising expenses, support of financially troubled Mary Cadwalader Jones, establishment of trust fund for three Belgian children, together with changing New York real estate market and effects of American income tax, create financial pressure. Accepts offer of $18,000 from *The Pictorial Review* for serial rights to her next novel. Unable to finish *The Glimpses of the Moon*, suggests *A Son at the Front*, but both magazine and book editors feel that the public is tired of war material. Proposes novel *Old New York* (later retitled *The Age of Innocence*), set in 1875. Magazine accepts, and Appleton advances $15,000 against royalties. Leases Ste. Claire du Vieux Château in Hyères, overlooking Mediterranean. Moves into Pavillon Colombe in August. *French Ways and Their Meaning*, collection of magazine articles, published by Appleton. "Beatrice Palmato" outline and fragment, explicit treatment of father-daughter incest, probably written at this time (the story is never finished).

1920   Howard Sturgis dies in January; end of Queen's Acre gatherings. *In Morocco*, travel account, published by Scribner's in October. *The Age of Innocence*, serialized in *The Pictorial Review* July–October, published by Appleton in October, sells 66,000 copies in six months (by 1922 it earns Wharton nearly $70,000). December, moves to Hyères for several months.

1921   Resumes work on *The Glimpses of the Moon*. Writes *The Old Maid*, novella about out-of-wedlock birth (rejected by *Ladies' Home Journal* for being "a bit too vigorous for us"). Begins long friendship with Philomène de Lévis-Mirepoix (later Philomène de la Forest-Divonne, who will write journalism and novels under the name Claude Sylve). *The Age of Innocence* awarded Pulitzer Prize in May. Later learns that the jury had originally voted for Sinclair Lewis's *Main Street*, but had been overruled by the trustees of Columbia University, who thought it too controversial. Writes to Lewis in August of her "disgust" at the action and invites him to St. Brice (he makes the first of several visits in October). *The Old Maid* bought by

Red Book for $2,250 (serialized Feb.–April 1922). September, finishes *The Glimpses of the Moon*. Goes to Hyères in mid-December.

1922   At Hyères until late May; June to mid-December at St. Brice. Summer, long-time friend and correspondent Sara Norton dies. When estranged brother Henry dies in August Wharton writes Berenson that "he was the dearest of brothers to all my youth . . ." *The Glimpses of the Moon* serialized in *The Pictorial Review*; published by Appleton in August, sells more than 100,000 copies in America and Britain in six months, earning her $60,000 from various rights and royalties.

1923   Film version of *The Glimpses of the Moon*, with dialogue titles by F. Scott Fitzgerald, released in April. (Six other films were made from Wharton's works between 1918 and 1934; she had no involvement in any of the productions.) Invited by Yale University to receive honorary Doctor of Letters degree. Although reluctant to attend, decides she needs to see United States if she is to continue writing about it. Accepts degree (the first to be awarded to a woman by Yale) at commencement in New Haven, June 20. Returns to France after eleven-day visit, her first since 1913 and her last. Novel *A Son at the Front* published by Scribner's in September, fulfilling promise made a decade earlier to give Scribner's another novel after *The Custom of the Country*. Works on novel *The Mother's Recompense*.

1924   *Old New York*, collection of four novellas, published by Appleton in May in boxed sets of four volumes. Titles are *False Dawn (The 'Forties), The Old Maid (The 'Fifties), The Spark (The 'Sixties), New Year's Day (The 'Seventies)*. About 26,000 sets sold in six months, with another 3,000 volumes sold individually. Awarded Gold Medal for "distinguished service" by National Institute of Arts and Letters.

1925   *The Mother's Recompense* published by Appleton in April after serialization in *The Pictorial Review* October 1924–March 1925. Sales are good. June, receives inscribed copy of *The Great Gatsby* from F. Scott Fitzgerald. July, Fitzgerald visits St. Brice; the encounter is strained and awkward. *The Writing of Fiction*, collection of five essays, including long appreciation of Proust, published by Scribner's in the late summer.

1926   Charters 360-ton steam yacht *Osprey* for ten-week cruise with guests through the Mediterranean and Aegean, March–June. *Here and Beyond*, collection of short stories, published by Appleton in summer. *Twelve Poems* published in London by The Medici Society. Elected to the National Institute of Arts and Letters. September, travels with Berry through northern Italy. Finishes novel *Twilight Sleep* in November. Buys Ste. Claire, Hyères home, for $40,000.

1927   January, Berry suffers mild stroke; convalesces at Hyères for two months, depressed and irritable. *The Pictorial Review* pays $40,000 for serial rights to novel *The Children* after *Delineator* offers $42,000; promises *Delineator* the novel *The Keys of Heaven*. *Twilight Sleep* published by Appleton in June; sells well. Walter Berry suffers second stroke in Paris, October 2. Wharton visits him on his deathbed; he dies October 12. Writes Lapsley: "No words can tell of my desolation. He had been to me in turn all that one being can be to another, in love, in friendship, in understanding."

1928   Edward Wharton dies in New York, February 7. *The Children* is serialized in *The Pictorial Review* April–July, published by Appleton in September; earns $95,000 from sales and film rights. Begins novel *Hudson River Bracketed* after abandoning *The Keys of Heaven*. Friendship develops with Desmond MacCarthy, British writer and editor. December, *The Age of Innocence*, dramatized by Margaret Ayer Barnes, opens on Broadway, runs until June 1929, then tours for four months, earning Wharton $23,500.

1929   Severe winter storms devastate Ste. Claire gardens; describes effect as "torture." February, learns that *Delineator* began serialization of *Hudson River Bracketed* in September 1928, six months ahead of schedule. Contracts severe pneumonia in March and nearly dies. Recovers by midsummer. Saddened by death of Geoffrey Scott in August. Finishes *Hudson River Bracketed* (published by Appleton in Nov.) and begins restoration of Ste. Claire gardens.

Awarded Gold Medal for "special distinction in literature" by American Academy of Arts and Letters.

1930   Elected to the American Academy of Arts and Letters. *Certain People*, collection of short stories, published by Appleton in summer. Autumn, meets art critic and historian Kenneth Clark while traveling in Tuscany; deep friendship develops. December, meets Aldous Huxley, who introduces her to anthropologist Bronislaw Malinowski.

1931   Visits England in July and sees H. G. Wells, Harold Nicolson, and Osbert, Sacheverell, and Dame Edith Sitwell. Attends several Roman Catholic services during visit to Rome in November.

1932   January, finishes novel *The Gods Arrive*, sequel to *Hudson River Bracketed*. Rejected for serial publication by *The Saturday Evening Post*, *Liberty*, and *Collier's* because it features an unmarried couple living together. Sold to *Delineator* for $50,000 despite Wharton's anger over handling of *Hudson River Bracketed*, appearing February–August. Published by Appleton later in year, it sells poorly. Begins autobiography, *A Backward Glance*. Effects of the Depression begin to be felt in greatly diminished literary earnings; magazine offers for short stories fall drastically. Visits Rome in May. Becomes godmother to Kenneth Clark's son Colin.

1933   Catherine Gross, Wharton's companion since 1884, falls into paranoid dementia in April, dies in October. Elise Duvlenck, her personal maid since 1914, dies May 29. *Human Nature*, collection of short stories, published by Appleton. By threat of legal action, forces *Ladies' Home Journal* to honor pre-Depression agreement to pay $25,000 for her autobiography; installments appear October 1933–April 1934. June, vacations in England with Gaillard Lapsely, visits Wales for the first time; August goes to Salzburg for a week and in October visits Holland. Begins novel *The Buccaneers* (never finished, but published by Appleton-Century in 1938 with Wharton's long outline of the remainder of the story and an afterword by Gaillard Lapsley).

1934   Tours England and Scotland. Guided through National
            Gallery in London by Kenneth Clark. *A Backward Glance*
            published by Appleton-Century. Breaks with Appleton
            editor Rutger Jewett, who had acted as her agent without
            commission for over a decade, blaming him for decreased
            literary earnings; engages James Pinker as new agent.

1935   *The Old Maid*, dramatized by Zoë Akins, opens in New
            York for successful run. April, suffers mild stroke, with
            temporary loss of sight in left eye. September, Mary Cad-
            walader Jones dies.

1936   *Ethan Frome*, dramatized by Owen and Donald Davis,
            tours United States after successful New York run. Income
            from both plays is about $130,000, ending financial worry.
            Visits England in the summer. *The World Over*, collection
            of short stories, published by Appleton-Century.

1937   Sends last completed short story, "All Souls'," to her
            agent, February. Health declines; suffers stroke, June 1.
            Dies at St. Brice on the evening of August 11. Buried near
            Walter Berry in the Cimetière des Gonards, Versailles,
            August 14.

Note on the Texts

This volume, the second of a two-volume selection of the shorter fiction of Edith Wharton, presents 29 stories first published between 1911 and 1937. Twenty-six of these stories have been taken from the first editions of five of Wharton's story collections: *Xingu and Other Stories* (1916), *Here and Beyond* (1926), *Certain People* (1930), *Human Nature* (1933), and *The World Over* (1936). One longer story, "The Marne," was published by Scribner's in 1918 as a separate book and is also reprinted from the first edition. Two of the stories reprinted here were not collected by Wharton during her lifetime. The text of one, "Writing a War Story," has been taken from *Woman's Home Companion*, where it first appeared in 1919. Wharton sent the other, "All Souls'," to her agent James Pinker just over three months before her death in 1937; the text presented here has been taken from *Ghosts*, a posthumous collection published by D. Appleton-Century in 1937. The stories are arranged chronologically by date of publication of the texts chosen for reprinting here; those gathered by Wharton in book form follow the order in which they were originally presented in the collected volumes.

Wharton oversaw the publication of her stories with great care. She corrected or closely supervised the correction of typescripts, galleys, and page proofs, offered opinions on typesetting, and complained when production fell short of her standards. She tended to revise, sometimes lightly and sometimes substantially, between periodical and book publication, but she did not make revisions after book publication to any of the stories included in this volume.

Wharton arranged for the English publication of her stories, first with John Murray and later with the Macmillan Company, as they were being prepared for the press in the United States or soon afterward. The English editions were typeset directly from the American proof sheets, sometimes with Wharton's corrections, meant (as she noted in a letter of 24 July 1903 to W. C. Brownell at Scribner's) to "tally exactly with the revised American sheets."

The following list gives the sources of the stories included in this volume and details of their prior publication in periodicals.

from *Xingu and Other Stories* (New York: Scribner's, 1916). Copyright © 1916 by Charles Scribner's Sons.

    Xingu

        Scribner's Magazine 50 (December 1911): 684–96.

Coming Home
Scribner's Magazine 58 (December 1915): 702–18.
Autres Temps . . .
The Century Magazine 82 (July 1911): 344–52; 82 (August 1911): 277–78, as "Other Times, Other Manners."
Kerfol
Scribner's Magazine 59 (March 1916): 329–41.
The Long Run
Atlantic Monthly 109 (February 1912): 145–63.
The Triumph of Night
Scribner's Magazine 56 (August 1914): 149–62.
Bunner Sisters
Scribner's Magazine 60 (October 1916): 439–58; 60 (November 1916): 575–96.

Writing a War Story
Woman's Home Companion 46 (September 1919): 17–19.

The Marne (New York: D. Appleton, 1918). Copyright © 1918 by D. Appleton & Company. Copyright © 1918 by The Curtis Publishing Company.
The Marne
The Saturday Evening Post 191 (26 October 1918): 3–5, 74, 77–78, 81–82, 85–86, 89–90.

from *Here and Beyond* (New York: D. Appleton, 1926). Copyright © 1918 by Charles Scribner's Sons. Copyright © 1926 by D. Appleton & Company. Copyright renewed © 1954.
Miss Mary Pask
Pictorial Review 26 (April 1925): 8–9, 75–76.
The Young Gentlemen
Pictorial Review 27 (February 1926): 29–30, 84–91.
Bewitched
Pictorial Review 27 (February 1926): 29–30, 84–91.
The Seed of the Faith
Scribner's Magazine 65 (January 1919): 17–33.
Velvet Ear-Pads
The Red Book Magazine 45 (August 1925): 39–45, 140–48, as "Velvet Ear-Muffs."

from *Certain People* (New York: D. Appleton, 1930). Copyright © 1930 by D. Appleton & Company. Copyright renewed © 1958.
Atrophy
Ladies' Home Journal 44 (November 1927): 8–9, 220–22.

A Bottle of Perrier

The Saturday Evening Post 198 (27 March 1926): 8–10, 116, 121–22, as "A Bottle of Evian."

After Holbein

The Saturday Evening Post 200 (5 May 1928): 6–7, 179, 181–82, 185–86, 189.

Mr. Jones

Ladies' Home Journal 45 (April 1928): 3–5, 108, 111–12, 114, 116.

from *Human Nature* (New York: D. Appleton, 1933). Copyright © 1933 by the Crowell Publishing Company and D. Appleton & Company. Copyright © 1932 by Charles Scribner's Sons. Copyright renewed © 1961.

Her Son

Scribner's Magazine 91 (February 1932): 65–72, 113–28.

The Day of the Funeral

Woman's Home Companion 60 (January 1933): 7–8, 46; 60 (February 1933): 15–16, 104, 106, 118, as "In a Day."

A Glimpse

The Saturday Evening Post 205 (12 November 1932): 16–17, 64–65, 67, 70, 72.

Joy in the House

Nash's Pall Mall Magazine 90 (December 1932): 6–9, 72–75.

from *The World Over* (New York: D. Appleton-Century, 1936). Copyright © 1936 by D. Appleton-Century Company, Inc. Copyright renewed © 1954.

Charm Incorporated

Hearst's International-Cosmopolitan 96 (February 1934): 38–31, 90, 92, 94, 96, 98, as "Bread Upon the Waters."

Pomegranate Seed

The Saturday Evening Post 203 (25 April 1931): 6–7, 109, 112, 116, 119, 121, 123.

Confession

Story-Teller 58 (March 1936): 64–85, as "Unconfessed Crime."

Roman Fever

Liberty 11 (10 November 1934): 10–14.

The Looking-Glass

Hearst's International-Cosmopolitan 95 (December 1933): 32–35, 157–59.

Duration

No periodical publication.

from *Ghosts* (New York: D. Appleton-Century, 1937). Copyright ©
1937 by D. Appleton-Century, Inc.
All Souls'
No periodical publication.

This volume presents the texts of the printings chosen for inclu-
sion here but does not attempt to reproduce features of their typo-
graphic design. The texts are reproduced without change, except for
the correction of obvious typographical errors. Spelling, capitaliza-
tion, and punctuation are often expressive features and they are not
altered, even when inconsistent or irregular. The following is a list of
typographical errors, cited by page and line number: 383.1, Potter's;
560.40, Norcutt if; 681.26, hold; 766.5, statute.

Notes

In the notes below, the reference numbers denote page and line of this volume (the line count includes chapter headings). No note is made for information included in standard desk reference works such as Webster's *Collegiate*, *Biographical*, and *Geographical* dictionaries. References to Shakespeare are keyed to the Riverside edition (G. Blakemore Evans, ed., Boston: Houghton Mifflin, 1974). Biblical references are keyed to the King James version. For further information and references to other studies, see: Stephen Garrison, *Edith Wharton: A Descriptive Bibliography* (Pittsburgh: University of Pittsburgh Press, 1990); R.W.B. Lewis, *Edith Wharton: A Biography* (New York: Harper & Row, 1975); Cynthia Griffin Wolff, *A Feast of Words: The Triumph of Edith Wharton* (New York: Oxford University Press, 1977).

5.8   'Robert Elsmere.'] Novel (1888) by Mary Augusta (Mrs. Humphry) Ward.

5.12–13   Prince Rupert's *manière noire*] Mezzotint, introduced into England in the early 1660s by Ruprecht of Pfalz (1619–1682).

5.20   'The Data of Ethics.'] Philosophical work (1879) by Herbert Spencer, later collected in *Principles of Ethics* (1893).

6.26–27   *Canst thou . . . hook?*] Job 41:1.

52.30   *La joie fait peur*] Joy is terrifying.

58.21   *café complet*] Coffee, milk, rolls, and butter.

97.15   *pardon*] Pilgrimage.

152.16   *petite marmite*] Pot-au-feu; a thick stockpot soup.

166.3–4   when society . . . Academy of Music] Nilsson (1843–1921), a Swedish soprano, sang the role of Marguerite in Gounoud's *Faust* at the Academy on November 1, 1871.

185.33   'Gates Ajar'] Floral arrangement popular at funerals in the wake of Elizabeth Stuart Phelps's best-selling novel of the afterlife, *The Gates Ajar* (1869).

197.2   dielytra] *Dicentra*, Bleeding Heart.

214.22–23   Spencerian hand] A simplified method of penmanship introduced by Platt Spencer in the mid-1860s.

253.36   Mélisande lowering her braid]   Scene in Debussy's opera *Pelleas et Mélisande* (1902).

264.16–17   "Sambre-et-Meuse"]   French patriotic song (1871) composed by Jean Robert Planquette (with lyrics by Paul Cezano), later arranged as a military march.

271.18–23   a bit of Henry . . . *fought with us.*]   *Henry V*, IV.iii.64–67.

271.36   "Priez pour lui,"]   "Pray for him."

280.9   "Dulce et decorum est . . ."]   "Dulce et decorum est pro patria mori" ("It is a sweet and glorious thing to die for one's country"), Horace, *Odes*, III.ii.13.

289.27   *"Nous les tenons!"*]   "We have them!"

294.25   *postes de secours*]   Wound-dressing stations.

295.17   Avernian cave]   In Roman mythology, a fathomless passage to the underworld.

300.38–39   "Whither thou goest . . . Naomi-country]   Cf. Ruth 1:16.

308.17   *mon pauvre petit gars*]   My poor little lad.

358.20–21   'Thou shalt not . . . Exodus]   Exodus 22:18.

378.27   *"Come unto me . . . laden."*]   Matthew 3:2.

400.3–4   *"Say among . . . reigneth!"*]   Psalm 96:10.

483.26   *point de Venise*]   Venetian lace, also known as "Renaissance lace."

486.24   *piqûres*]   Hypodermic injections.

493.22   Rose Dubarry]   Chintz-patterned china.

514.16   the old Glamis experiment]   A bricked-up window visible from the grounds of Glamis Castle, northeast of Edinburgh, Scotland, indicates the location of a room in which, according to local legend, Lord Glamis was entombed by the devil for playing cards on the Sabbath.

622.23   *cabotins*]   Bad actors; hams.

630.1   *traghetto*]   Ferry.

637.21–22   *Und mein Stamm sind jene Asra*]   First line of the final couplet of "Der Asra," by Heinrich Heine (1797–1856): "And my tribe is that of Asra, / And when we love we die."

638.31–32   *"Est-ce que . . . moque de moi?"*]   "Do you mock me, Sir?"

655.28   *Heimweh*]   Nostalgia; homesickness.

672.33   the fellow in "Pagliacci"]   Canio, a jealous husband in Leoncavallo's opera (1892).

676.12   *plastik*]   Physiognomy.

714.38   *dame de compagnie*]   Lady's companion.

810.17   Mary Celeste]   Famous "ghost ship," found abandoned at sea in 1872.

Library of Congress Cataloging-in-Publication Data

Wharton, Edith, 1862–1937.
  [Short stories. Selections]
  Collected stories, 1911–1937 / Edith Wharton.
    p. cm. — (The library of America; 122)
  Includes bibliographical references.
  ISBN 1–883011–94–9 (alk. paper)
  I. Title. II. Series.

PS3545.H16 A6 2001B
813'.52—dc21

                    00–057595

THE LIBRARY OF AMERICA SERIES

The Library of America helps to preserve our nation's literary heritage by publishing, and keeping permanently in print, authoritative editions of America's best and most significant writing. An independent nonprofit organization, it was founded in 1979 with seed money from the National Endowment for the Humanities and the Ford Foundation.

1. Herman Melville, *Typee, Omoo, Mardi* (1982)
2. Nathaniel Hawthorne, *Tales and Sketches* (1982)
3. Walt Whitman, *Poetry and Prose* (1982)
4. Harriet Beecher Stowe, *Three Novels* (1982)
5. Mark Twain, *Mississippi Writings* (1982)
6. Jack London, *Novels and Stories* (1982)
7. Jack London, *Novels and Social Writings* (1982)
8. William Dean Howells, *Novels 1875–1886* (1982)
9. Herman Melville, *Redburn, White-Jacket, Moby-Dick* (1983)
10. Nathaniel Hawthorne, *Collected Novels* (1983)
11. Francis Parkman, *France and England in North America*, vol. I (1983)
12. Francis Parkman, *France and England in North America*, vol. II (1983)
13. Henry James, *Novels 1871–1880* (1983)
14. Henry Adams, *Novels, Mont Saint Michel, The Education* (1983)
15. Ralph Waldo Emerson, *Essays and Lectures* (1983)
16. Washington Irving, *History, Tales and Sketches* (1983)
17. Thomas Jefferson, *Writings* (1984)
18. Stephen Crane, *Prose and Poetry* (1984)
19. Edgar Allan Poe, *Poetry and Tales* (1984)
20. Edgar Allan Poe, *Essays and Reviews* (1984)
21. Mark Twain, *The Innocents Abroad, Roughing It* (1984)
22. Henry James, *Literary Criticism: Essays, American & English Writers* (1984)
23. Henry James, *Literary Criticism: European Writers & The Prefaces* (1984)
24. Herman Melville, *Pierre, Israel Potter, The Confidence-Man, Tales & Billy Budd* (1985)
25. William Faulkner, *Novels 1930–1935* (1985)
26. James Fenimore Cooper, *The Leatherstocking Tales*, vol. I (1985)
27. James Fenimore Cooper, *The Leatherstocking Tales*, vol. II (1985)
28. Henry David Thoreau, *A Week, Walden, The Maine Woods, Cape Cod* (1985)
29. Henry James, *Novels 1881–1886* (1985)
30. Edith Wharton, *Novels* (1986)
31. Henry Adams, *History of the U.S. during the Administrations of Jefferson* (1986)
32. Henry Adams, *History of the U.S. during the Administrations of Madison* (1986)
33. Frank Norris, *Novels and Essays* (1986)
34. W.E.B. Du Bois, *Writings* (1986)
35. Willa Cather, *Early Novels and Stories* (1987)
36. Theodore Dreiser, *Sister Carrie, Jennie Gerhardt, Twelve Men* (1987)
37. Benjamin Franklin, *Writings* (1987)
38. William James, *Writings 1902–1910* (1987)
39. Flannery O'Connor, *Collected Works* (1988)
40. Eugene O'Neill, *Complete Plays 1913–1920* (1988)
41. Eugene O'Neill, *Complete Plays 1920–1931* (1988)
42. Eugene O'Neill, *Complete Plays 1932–1943* (1988)
43. Henry James, *Novels 1886–1890* (1989)
44. William Dean Howells, *Novels 1886–1888* (1989)
45. Abraham Lincoln, *Speeches and Writings 1832–1858* (1989)
46. Abraham Lincoln, *Speeches and Writings 1859–1865* (1989)
47. Edith Wharton, *Novellas and Other Writings* (1990)
48. William Faulkner, *Novels 1936–1940* (1990)
49. Willa Cather, *Later Novels* (1990)
50. Ulysses S. Grant, *Memoirs and Selected Letters* (1990)

This book is set in 10 point Linotron Galliard,
a face designed for photocomposition by Matthew Carter
and based on the sixteenth-century face Granjon. The paper is
acid-free Ecusta Nyalite and meets the requirements for permanence
of the American National Standards Institute. The binding
material is Brillianta, a woven rayon cloth made by
Van Heek-Scholco Textielfabrieken, Holland.
The composition is by The Clarinda
Company. Printing and binding by
R.R.Donnelley & Sons Company.
Designed by Bruce Campbell.

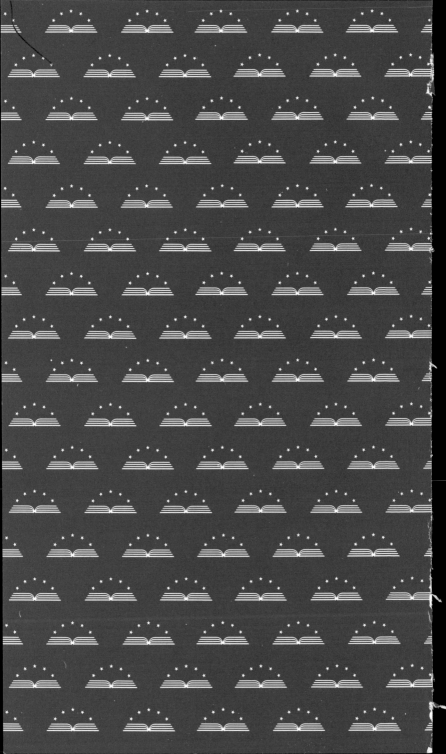